SWEET STARFIRE
AND
CRYSTAL FLAME

SWEET STARFIRE
AND
CRYSTAL FLAME

JAYNE ANN KRENTZ

WARNER BOOKS

An AOL Time Warner Company

Sweet Starfire copyright © 1986 by Jayne Krentz, Inc.
Crystal Flame copyright © 1986 by Jayne Krentz, Inc.

Warner Books, Inc., 1271 Avenue of the Americas, New York, NY 10020

Visit our Web site at www.twbookmark.com

 An AOL Time Warner Company

Printed in the United States of America

First Printing: September 2002
10 9 8 7 6 5 4 3 2 1

Library of Congress Cataloging-in-Publication Data
Krentz, Jaynne Ann.
    Sweet starfire and Crystal flame / Jayne Ann Krentz.
       p. cm.
    ISBN 0-446-53137-5
       1. Fantasy fiction, american. 2. Love stories, American. I. Title: Sweet starfire; and, Crystal flame. II. Krentz, Jayne Ann. Crystal flame. III. Title: Crystal flame. IV. Title.

PS3561 .R44 S93 2002
813'.54—dc21   2002069117

CONTENTS

SWEET STARFIRE

For Claire Zion,
an editor with enthusiasm,
good timing and that rarest of assets,
the willingness to try something different.
My thanks.

ONE

The tavern was awash with blood. Cidra Rainforest saw splashes of crimson everywhere—seeping from a gash in a man's forehead, staining the front of another's shirt, trickling from still another's mouth. Glancing down, she saw that there was even a spatter of blood on the hem of her early-evening surplice robes. To Cidra the delicate yellow-gold fabric spun of the finest crystal moss was not just soiled but frighteningly scarred.

She was surrounded by a scene she had never before experienced, never even been able to imagine, and she found herself incapable of coping with it. It wasn't just the sight of so much blood that held Cidra immobilized with shock. All around her the vicious fighting continued unabated, even though Cidra knew that by now the combatants must be experiencing unutterable pain. Yet they raged on. The violence of it horrified her.

Grunts, obscene oaths, and desperate shouts filled the long, low tavern hall. One man had been knocked unconscious by a deftly swung tankard of Renaissance Ross ale, but no one paused to help him. Rather, everyone was participating in the free-for-all with an air of what Cidra could only describe as lusty enthusiasm. No one was lying in a fetal huddle, whimpering on the edge of insanity, as Cidra would have expected, as indeed she herself would be doing had she not been using every ounce of her disciplined training to control herself. The scene around her was incredible. It was, she thought, just as the novels had described it.

A large, scarred, brutally strong hand clamped around Cidra's arm, shocking her out of her stupor.

"Come on, lady, unless you want to explain your presence to the guards. Let's get out of here."

In a daze Cidra turned to the hard face of the man she had met only moments earlier, the man she had come to this rough tavern to find. Teague Severance hadn't been quite what she had expected, and Cidra had been trying to adjust to that fact.

"The guards?" she asked, clinging to the look of strength she saw in the man's gray eyes.

"Port Valentine's safeguards enjoy breaking up this kind of thing. Thrive on it, in fact. And they'll be here any minute. Let's get going. I think we can make it out through the back."

Cidra didn't argue. The stunning violence going on around her had not only disrupted her ability to think coherently but also seemed to be playing havoc with her normally excellent sense of balance. When her escort yanked Cidra toward the door and out of the way of a falling mountain dressed in a miner's kirtle, she stumbled and fell to her knees. Teague Severance's hold on her arm was broken, and he was whisked away by two men in a fist fight who suddenly saw him as a preferable target.

But Cidra barely noticed. The huge man who had just fallen lay beside her feet, blinking groggily as he rubbed a bleeding jaw. Instinctively Cidra turned to comfort him, murmuring words of hypnotic comfort.

"Focus, my friend. Focus, focus. The pain is receding. See how it fades. Focus on it. The oblivo is being brought to you. Soon all will be serene. All will fade. All will fade. You must relax and let it flow away from you, let it flow—" Her soothing words ended abruptly as Cidra was hauled to her feet. Severance's scarred hand was once again clamped tightly around her arm; part of her had a moment to wonder how he had come by the odd lacing of scars.

"What in renegade's hell do you think you're doing? Get up off the floor, woman. We've got to get out of here. The Wolves are howling tonight, in case you hadn't noticed."

Cidra's escort pulled her unceremoniously around a writhing mass of human beings and continued to forge a path toward the tavern's kitchen.

"But that man was in such pain. . . ." she murmured, feeling more lost than ever.

"Don't worry, he won't feel a thing until morning."

A hulking figure rose in front of Cidra, all bloody grin and glazed eyes. It wore a ship suit not unlike Severance's, but the diagonally slung utility loop was of a cheap, functional synthetic, not fine rantgan leather. Cidra noticed long before two hands that, to her startled gaze, resembled grappling hooks reached for her.

"Don't run off, little lady. You and I can go somewhere peaceful for some special handling. How does that sound?"

Before Cidra could sort through her list of appropriate responses to a question she had never before encountered, her impatient escort dealt with the grisly man before her.

"Don't touch her, you renegade idiot. Are you so drunk that you can't tell she's from Clementia? What's more, she's a patron. My patron."

The glassy-eyed man blinked, frantically trying to focus his eyes. "I'm sorry, lady—I mean, Otanna. Didn't mean nothin', uh, rude. Had no idea what I was doing. No offense intended, I swear to Saints."

Cidra hurried to respond to the man's apology. She realized that he was under a misapprehension, thanks to her escort's comments. "Do not concern yourself. All is serene. And you have inflicted no real pain. I am—" But again she was not allowed to finish her sentence. With a dazed sense of surprise she realized that the hulk with the grappling-hook hands wasn't listening to her at all. He had turned to Teague Severance and was apologizing to *him*.

"Sorry about that, Severance. Never meant to interfere between you and a patron. Just a little misunderstanding. Better get her outa here, though. She'll probably go crazy any second."

"I'm working the problem. Unfortunately she's not exactly cooperating."

Cidra felt a rush of emotion that was decidedly akin to annoyance. She responded to the accusation in a tone of voice that was neither properly modulated nor serene. "I am trying to cooperate, Otan Severance. But circumstances are making it difficult."

"Just close your eyes and stop digging in your heels every time one of these Wolves gets in your way." And with that, the man called Severance once again hauled Cidra toward the tavern's back door.

Once inside the relative safety of the small kitchen, which was protected by a makeshift barricade of hastily arranged food heaters and ale dispensers, Cidra and her escort found the tavern's owner and his employees sitting around a table, playing a game of Free Market. The stacks of gleaming sardite chips in the center of the table indicated the seriousness of the stakes involved. Several bottles of ale resided at the players' elbows. The balding proprietor glanced up with a frown as Cidra and her companion burst into the room.

"Now, look here, kitchen's off-limits. You know that," the owner growled.

"We're not participating," Severance assured him, not bothering to slow down as he headed toward the rear door. "Just looking for a way out."

But by now the owner had noticed Cidra's appearance. Everything from the expensive comb of fire beryl in her carefully braided hair to the slippers embroidered with genuine emerald floss spoke of Harmonic wealth and refinement. "What do you think you're doing bringing her here? She looks like she's from Clementia."

"She is."

"Sweet Harmony, get her outa here."

"I'm trying," Severance said, his hands on the door latch. "Saints know I'm trying."

"There seems to be some misunderstanding," Cidra began hurriedly as she glanced back at the scowling tavern proprietor. "I'm from Clementia, but I'm not a . . . a Harmonic."

"Forget it. We'll straighten everything out later." Severance had her outside on the gently glowing fluoroquartz pavement. Maintaining his grip on her arm, he broke into an easy, loping stride and forced Cidra to match his pace.

In the distance the arrogant shriek of a safeguard runner sliced through the balmy night air. Cidra was suddenly very grateful that she wouldn't have to endure the indignity of being questioned. Kyrene, her mentor, would have been shocked, to say nothing of her parents' reaction.

The glowing bands of fluoroquartz supplied all the light they needed to follow the path easily in the warm darkness. The pavement was still wet from a recent rain, and drops of water, illuminated by the natural light of the fluoroquartz, glittered like jewels. Cidra wanted to stop and examine the prismatic effect. Such naturally occurring phenomena, so close to artifice in their beauty, were meant to be appreciated. But her escort clearly had no intention of slowing down, and Cidra felt it was an inauspicious moment to debate the issue.

But as she raced along beside Teague Severance, she found herself instead savoring the rich assortment of fragrances that floated on the damp, balmy breeze. Clementia was a subtly perfumed delight, it's odors carefully generated by exotic, hybrid flowers to complement the delicate noses of its inhabitants. But here in Port Valentine, Cidra's olfactory senses were bombarded by new sensations, causing her to alternately wrinkle her nose or inhale sharply. Here, Cidra had discovered the faint scent of the sea at low tide, complete with a hint of rotting vegetation, and the sour odor that could only be from some tavern's garbage bin mingling with the rich smell of the recent rain. She thought she detected a waft of fernweed smoke as Severance urged her past a dark doorway. Cidra wanted to stop and find out why anyone would actually smoke the dangerous substance when everyone knew how bad it was for the body, but Severance gave her no chance.

Two blocks later Severance finally slowed to a brisk walk. "All right, I think we're clear. The guards will be concentrating their attention on the ones inside the tavern. They won't be looking for a few who had the sense to leave. You okay?"

Cidra, her breath coming quickly even though she'd had no real trouble maintaining the pace of the last two blocks, nodded. "Yes, of course. I'm fine. Thank you for inquiring." For Cidra, such polite inquiries had always been expressed in the formal, ceremonial form, but remembering where she was, she tried to use her companion's colloquial style. "And you? Are you, er, okay?"

"Sure. Let's get off the street. There's another tavern up ahead. One that's usually quieter. We can get something to eat. I haven't had dinner yet, have you?"

"Well, no," Cidra said. "It's only two hours past the evening change, and I eat at three past."

"Is that so? Me, I'm starved. Nothing like pulling patrons out of tavern brawls to work up a postman's appetite." He gave her a roguish smile that made her strangely uncomfortable. "You can sip nectar or whatever it is you folks normally drink."

Cidra contemplated the situation. "Actually I am rather hungry. Perhaps the unplanned exercise is responsible."

Severance grinned down at her, his strong, white teeth gleaming, although the glow of the pavement lighting cast his fog-gray eyes into pools of shadow. The rest of his hard features complimented the carnivorous impression. "Perhaps."

Cidra watched as the quick, feral grin disappeared, and wondered how an expression normally intended to convey laughter and humor could be so totally devoid of either. She shivered mentally. No wonder they called them Wolves, she thought fleetingly. "As a point of general information, I'd like to inform you that we don't sip nectar in Clementia."

"Another illusion shattered."

But Severance seemed philosophical about the matter as he led his patron into a different tavern. According to the illuminated sign over the entrance, this one was called The Valentine; presumably a name coined in honor of the surrounding sprawl of Lovelady's chief port town. A heart-shaped logo enclosed the words.

Once inside, Cidra glanced around with interest. The room was gently lit with a glowing pink light and was much quieter and far more refined than the first tavern had been. Here a mixed crowd of diners and drinkers occupied booths and a dispenser bar that lined the back of the room. The atmosphere was warm and comfortable and reasonably clean. Humans, both Wolves and Harmonics, still preferred to be served by humans, and the dining room was not automated.

"I take it this meets with your approval?" Severance was watching her expression as they stood in the doorway.

Cidra flushed, sensing his sarcasm. "This will be fine. All I need is a chance to discuss my business with you."

"Wait'll I order my food. I prefer to talk business over a good steak." Severance pinned a nearby member of The Valentine's staff with a steady gaze that eventually got the woman's attention. She glanced at him and then at Cidra. As soon as she took in the sight of Cidra's formal clothing and quietly regal bearing, she moved forward in an apologetic rush.

"Sorry to keep you waiting, Otanna. I have a very pleasant booth available across the room. It's out of the way. Quite peaceful."

Cidra inclined her head in polite acknowledgment. "You are very kind." A moment later she was seated. A waiter materialized out of nowhere, bowing a little awkwardly as he set out utensils.

"I have to admit that you've got your uses," Severance said as he slid into the booth across from Cidra. "I don't usually get such good service." He glanced at the holotape menu card only briefly before coming to a quick decision. "I'm going to order the torla steak. Maybe with you here they'll make sure it's cooked the way I order it. What suits you?"

Frantically Cidra scanned the menu, looking for an item that didn't contain meat. Finally she spotted the holotape images of a familiar Lovelady tuber and something that appeared to be a pile of greens. Politely she gave her order to the waiter, who was so interested in getting it right, she finally had to ask him to listen to Severance's demands.

"I want the steak. Large size. And I want it cooked on the grill, not in a heater, understand? And when it gets to the table, I want it rare. Bloody in the middle. *Rare.*"

Cidra hid her dismay behind a serene expression. Severance went on to order two mugs of expensive Renaissance Rose ale before she could explain that she never drank it. Cidra knew that the distinctly dark and potent brew was distilled from the thorn of a flower that was lethal, and too much of the ale was also considered dangerous. She managed to maintain a look of contentment as the waiter bustled away, but once he was gone, she sighed.

"Feeling like a fraud?" Severance leaned back in the booth and stretched his booted feet out under the table.

He had been sprawling with the same rangy casualness when she had first seen him. Conscious of her own gracefully correct posture, Cidra wondered if Severance ever really sat properly in a chair. The close-fitting gray ship suit pulled taut across his shoulders, emphasizing his broad, hard chest. The suit itself was a standard pilot's outfit, cut in a severe style with functional collar and cuffs that could be worn open for comfort or neatly clipped closed for a more formal look. Severance wore both open, the cuffs pushed up on his sinewy forearms. The trousers followed his long legs neatly and disappeared into the tops of his boots. Severance was built along lean, tight lines but had a sense of solid weight that strangely disturbed yet comforted Cidra. His black hair had recently received a short no-nonsense cut, and she guessed he'd had it trimmed as soon as he'd hit port after the long trip from Renaissance. In the soft light of the fluoroquartz lamp

Cidra could see that the rantgan leather utility belt he wore had been handwrought with an eye for exquisite detail. She wondered whether Severance had carved the tough leather himself and then shook herself out of her reverie and considered his question.

"Yes, I am feeling a fraud. Everyone seems to be jumping to the conclusion that I'm a Harmonic."

"Let 'em jump. It gets action, doesn't it?"

"So it seems." Cidra studied him a moment. "You knew right away I wasn't a Harmonic, though, didn't you?"

He shrugged. "I wasn't drunk when you approached me, and I had a chance to get a good look at your eyes before that brawl broke out. I'll admit that I haven't met many, but there's something about a Saint's eyes . . . something different."

Cidra nodded. "I know." She paused. "Harmonics hate that nickname, you know."

Severance's quick, humorless grin flashed, then faded. "Saints? Impossible. Harmonics are constitutionally incapable of hating anything, least of all something as unimportant as a nick-name."

"You're right, of course. I should have said that they prefer not to be called Saints."

"Then they shouldn't be so damned perfect," Severance told her blandly. He held up a hand as Cidra started to protest. "All right, all right, I withdraw the comment. I don't want to argue with you. Not if you're from Clementia and not if you're serious about doing business." He paused then for a minute, a strange look coming into his eyes. "You are from Clementia, aren't you? Not just an actress or something?"

"I was born there," Cidra stated, and immediately regretted the show of pride. A true Harmonic was above pride. "My parents are Harmonics," she finished more quietly.

Severance eyed her with what could have been casual interest if not for the flicker of cold assessment in his gaze. "An aptitude for the Way is supposed to be hereditary."

"There are exceptions to most things, Otan Severance. I'm afraid I'm one."

"Obviously. If you weren't, you would have fainted when some drunk miner got blood on your fancy dress." Cidra cringed at the truth of his words. She had wanted to believe that she had remained relatively coherent because of her training but had to admit now that even the most rigorous discipline wouldn't have protected a true Harmonic from the violence she had seen. "So," Severance continued, "you're an exception, but you *are* from Clementia. And you want to do business."

"That is correct."

"Suits me." His glance shifted to the expensive fireberyl comb in her hair. "You look like the kind who pays her postage, and I'm always looking for patrons—" He broke off as the rich, dark Renaissance Rose ale was placed in front of them. Taking a long, obviously satisfying swallow, he met Cidra's steady gaze over the rim of the mug. "What is it you want delivered?"

Cidra cleared her throat. "Myself."

Severance put down his mug. "You'll have to try it again. A little more slowly this time. I'm just a Wolf, remember? I'm not intuitive or telepathic. I'm not even wildly good at guessing games."

"It's simple enough, Otan Severance."

"Teague."

"I beg your pardon?"

He made an impatient movement with his hand. "My birth name is Teague. Severance is my chosen name. Use either one you like, but skip the formality. No one in my line of work uses Otan."

Cidra nodded with grave politeness. "You'll have to forgive me, Teague Severance. In my world formality is everything."

Severance's mouth twisted wryly. "I know. I'm sure it works just great in Clementia. Out in the real universe it tends to be a waste of time. Why don't you finish explaining your business before we get sidetracked by a philosophical discussion on the role of the formalities."

A faint flicker of amusement touched Cidra's expression. "Are you capable of being sidetracked by such an esoteric discussion?"

"Sidetracked or bored. One of the two."

"I see." She drew a breath and went back to business. "As I said, I wish to mail myself."

He considered her intent face. "To where?"

"Wherever it is you happen to be going. I have no single destination in mind, although Renaissance is high on my list. Postmen are famous for their unorthodox schedules. According to what I have read about your profession, you'll go almost anywhere in the Stanza Nine system to pick up a package. Nor are you particular about where you deliver your cargo."

"As long as someone's willing to pay the postage," he reminded her. Severance leaned forward, planting his elbows on the table. Even the gentle light of the lamp could not soften the hard lines of his face. "But we rarely carry passengers, except in emergencies. And we never take tourists."

"I know it's not common practice."

"Do you know why?"

"I assume it has something to do with the fact that most postmen tend to be loners," Cidra ventured. "Psychologically speaking, people in your profession are often temperamentally unsuited to close social contact."

"It has to do with the fact that the ships are small and every spare centimeter has to be used as profitably as possible. Compared to packages and mail, passengers aren't a paying proposition. For one thing, passengers tend to eat. That means extra food has to be put on board. Passengers tend to sleep. That requires bunk space. Passengers also tend to want to be entertained. That's a damned nuisance. Pound for pound it's cheaper, more profitable, and infinitely less wearing to carry the mail. Go buy a ticket on one of the regular freighters if you want to tour the system."

Patiently Cidra shook her head. "The freighters only go to the main port towns on Renaissance and QED. From there I would have to find transportation to the various outposts. From what I understand that's an uncertain matter at best. It's also very expensive. And I don't have a great deal of credit to spend. I can't even afford extensive traveling here on Lovelady, let alone the other planets and their moons. Please don't be deceived by my appearance. Most of what I am wearing is a gift from my parents."

Severance stared at her. "Excuse me for being a little slow, but I seem to be missing something rather vital here. If you can't afford commercial travel, how in a renegade's hell did you expect to pay postage for the scenic route?"

Cidra smiled brilliantly as they reached the heart of her plan. "Actually, I intended to hire on as a member of the crew. I want to work my passage, Teague Severance."

Whatever he would have said in response to that was lost for the moment as the waiter appeared with the heated trays of food. A still-smoking slab of meat was thrust in front of Severance, who eyed the crosshatch grill marks with satisfaction. Cidra studiously avoided looking at the meat as she examined her own plate of vegetables. The waiter hovered anxiously until she glanced up and realized why he was hanging around.

"It's lovely. Just what I wanted. Please thank the kitchen staff."

The waiter beamed and disappeared without waiting to see how Teague Severance felt about the condition of his steak. Severance didn't mind; he was too busy slicing into the bloody heart of the meat. He was unaware that Cidra was swallowing uncomfortably as she tried to avert her eyes and struggled to control her stomach.

"Just right," he declared, chewing a chunk with the thoughtful concentration Harmonics reserved for a glass of fine ether wine. "Like I said, lady, you do have your uses. Do you know how hard it is to get a place like this to use the grill instead of the heater?"

Cidra didn't pay any attention. She was lost in her silent recitation of the chant that by Harmonic custom preceded the evening meal, a ritual that was also helping to take her mind off the bleeding carcass across the table on Teague's plate. When she was finished, she hunted unobtrusively around the table for the proper vegetable-eating prongs. Failing to find them, she settled for the all-purpose bowled fork that was lying beside a sharp-edged blade near her plate. The sight of the knife gave her a start.

The idea of a weapon at the table was unsettling. She was going to have to become familiar with the informal eating habits of Wolves.

"Are you going to finish your ale?" Severance asked.

Cidra glanced at the mug she had left untouched and shook her head. The famous brew didn't look terribly appealing.

"I'll finish it for you," Severance said, reaching across the table to help himself to her mug.

"About my passage on board your ship, Severance, I want to make it clear that I am fully prepared to work. I am not proposing that you take me along as excess baggage."

"Lady, mail ships are made to be operated by one person. They don't require any extra crew."

"But I've heard that mail pilots sometimes hire a crewmate," she protested. "Surely there must be plenty of small tasks required on board."

He stopped chewing long enough to give her a hard, steady look. "The kind of crew situations you're talking about are generally called convenience contracts. I tried it once and it was a disaster."

"Why was that?"

He stifled a muttered oath and went back to sawing on his meat. "Because the woman I contracted with nearly drove me crazy. She and I were at each other's throats by the time we reached Renaissance. I had to put her off ship at Port Try Again with enough credit to buy a commercial ticket back to Lovelady. I decided after that experience that a little loneliness was probably good for the soul and a hell of a lot cheaper than companionship."

Cidra smiled gently. "The one thing you would not have to fear is me going for your throat. I was raised in Clementia, remember?"

"Uh-huh. And what's going to keep me from going for yours?"

Cidra blinked, unsure if he was teasing her. He didn't look as if he was, but how could she really tell? Whatever sense of humor Severance had, it seemed to be on the savage side. "When I inquired into potential ships' masters, I was told you were considered a reasonably honest man. Somewhat rough around the edges and basically a loner, as are most mail pilots, but generally honest. Insofar as it is possible for Wolves to trust each other, your acquaintances appear to trust you, Severance. Among Wolves, I understand, that is not a common occurrence."

Severance drummed his fingers on the table. "Any Wolf dumb enough to completely trust another Wolf deserves what he or she gets. Just the opposite of how things work in Clementia, hmmm?"

Cidra's eyes softened. "For obvious reasons."

"Lady, you don't know what you're getting into with this plan of yours. Talk about being a Saint among Wolves!"

"Would you mind terribly calling me by my name? I would prefer it to 'lady.' " She kept her tone rigidly polite.

"Far be it from me to annoy a near-Saint. What was your name? Cidra Something? I didn't have time to catch it back in that tavern."

"Cidra Rainforest."

"Rainforest," he repeated, tasting the word. "That's your chosen name?"

"Yes."

"Have you ever seen a rain forest, Cidra?" Severance asked, his tone unexpectedly gentle. "A real rain forest?"

"No. This is my first time away from Clementia."

"How did you come to choose the word as a name?"

Cidra wanted to point out that they were not here for purposes of casual conversation, but she was too fundamentally polite to say the censuring words. "I read about rain forests on Renaissance when I was fifteen. There were holotapes and slips of them in the Archives. They seemed so beautiful, so rich and full of life. Endless blooms and endless green. I suppose the forests were very much in my mind that year, and fifteen is the age at which Harmonics traditionally choose their names. I understand that among Wolves the age of choice varies."

"You could say that. The truth is that we sometimes go through two or three names before settling on the right one. Occasionally a Wolf finds it very useful to select a new name quite frequently." When she just looked at him with a puzzled expression, Severance abandoned the subject. "Never mind. Tell me what made you decide to go planet-hopping."

"My reasons are personal, Severance."

His eyebrows climbed. "Is that so?"

She flushed a little at his tone. "In Clementia privacy is greatly respected," Cidra reminded him.

"Another good reason to abandon your idea of bunking down on a mail boat. There's very little privacy available on one of those ships."

"I am prepared to accommodate myself."

"Oh, yeah? How far?"

"I don't understand."

"Those convenience contracts we just talked about? Do you know just what that entails?"

"I assume it implies a sharing of responsibilities and tasks."

"Sweet Harmony, what an innocent. It means a sharing of bunks, Cidra. Convenience contracts are short-term sexual alliances. Contracted for purposes of sex and companionship. The six-week run to QED can be very long and lonely, Otanna Rainforest. Now do you understand?"

Her face grew very still as she contemplated his words. Then Cidra nodded thoughtfully. She should have realized that something like this was involved in the contractual situations she had heard about. Wolves were said to be prodigiously interested in sex. "Yes, now I understand. Well, I would not be interested in that sort of arrangement."

"Somehow I didn't think you would."

"Is that the only type of contract you would be willing to extend?"

"If you had been listening carefully, you would have heard me say that I'm not even interested in a convenience contract. I told you, I tried it once and it was a disaster. I'll stick to finding a little special handling in between mail hops. I'm grateful to you for getting this place to serve me a decent steak, Cidra, but I'm afraid we're not going to be able to do business together."

Cidra tried to hide her disappointment behind her mask of serene acceptance. "So it would seem. You must allow me to pay for your meal, Otan Severance. It is the least I can do under the circumstances."

He looked vaguely irritated. "Skip it. You said you were running on short credit, and I just had a fairly decent run from Renaissance. I'll get the tab."

"Oh, no, I could not allow you to do that," she protested, genuinely shocked. "It was I who approached you and took up your valuable time."

"I was sitting in a tavern about to get drunk. You didn't waste any of my time. I can always get drunk. I can't always get my steaks cooked properly." He picked up his mug and downed another healthy swallow of the potent ale. "So. What are you going to do now? Go back to Clementia?"

Cidra's eyes widened in astonishment. "Of course not. You are only the first mail pilot I have approached. There are half a dozen more here in Port Valentine at the moment, or so the Port authorities told me. I will work my way through the list. Surely there must be someone interested in a working passenger. And if not, I will wait until other postmen or postwomen arrive. They come and go constantly from what I have been told."

Severance regarded her coolly. "I don't think that's such a good idea, Cidra."

Some of her anxiety bubbled to the surface and emerged in a flash of hostility that took Cidra by surprise more than it did her companion. "Still, it is *my* idea, is it not, Severance? You needn't concern yourself with it or with me."

"Isn't there someone in Clementia who might be concerned with your notions and where they're liable to take you?"

She put down the all-purpose fork she had been using and sat very straight in the booth. "I am not a child, Severance. I reached the age of maturity four years ago and am fully responsible for my own actions. Just as you are."

"Far be it from me to give advice to someone reared among Saints," Severance growled. "Good luck, lady. Just watch out what kind of contract you end up signing. Don't forget to read the fine print." He got to his feet. "If you've finished eating, I'll see you back to wherever you're staying."

"That won't be necessary."

"It is, unless you want a scene." He slipped a credit plate into the small slot embedded in the table. When the faint glow confirmed that the meal had been paid for, he removed the plate and reached for Cidra's arm.

She hadn't argued, Severance thought later, after having dropped Cidra off at her hotel. But, then, Harmonics rarely argued, except about philosophical or mathematical problems. He remembered how his brother Jeude had always backed away from a disagreement, putting on the same mask of serene contentment he had seen on Cidra's face that evening. Emotional confrontations with other people were very uncomfortable for Saints, Severance knew. Belatedly he reminded himself that Cidra wasn't technically a Harmonic.

It was easy to forget. He could understand why others such as the restaurant personnel reacted to her as if she were indeed a full-fledged Saint. There was something very serene and innately dignified about Cidra Rainforest. Perhaps it had to do with the way she wore her long, red-brown hair in that formal coronet of braids. Or it might have been the way the elegant yellow robes flowed around a body that was as slender, graceful, and proud as that of a dancer. The clothing worn by Harmonics was naturally as dignified and graceful as those who wore and designed it. The women's high-collared gowns, with their long, wide-banded sleeves, fit closely to the waist and then flared in an elegant line from hips to ankles. The fabric was uniformly the fine, beautifully worked crystal moss. Cidra's gown was no exception. She was not a tall woman, but her robes provided an illusion of height. She was a young woman, probably about eight years younger than himself, but her eyes held more refined intelligence than a man usually saw in a woman that age. Of course, Teague reminded himself, if she'd been raised in Clementia, her education would have been thorough and sophisticated.

Severance grabbed a runner outside Cidra's hotel to take him to his ship, but his thoughts remained with the woman he had just left.

The essentially gentle quality that usually characterized Saints was a part of her, too, he mused, but in Cidra it came across differently. In true Harmonics Teague had always sensed a distant, controlled, broadly humanistic compassion. In Cidra he had seen something much more immediate, a more vivid and impulsive empathy. Severance remembered the way she had stopped to help the downed brawler in the first tavern and shook his head. It had been a long time since he'd enjoyed any special handling in the arms of a woman. Too long. Chances were that his imagination was interpreting Cidra's actions in the wrong way. He was probably just hungry for the kind of gentleness a man sometimes needed from a woman. And, for some reason, a part of him had gone ahead and decided that Cidra could give him what he needed.

A picture of her soft, slender body lying under him, her gilded nails clutching his shoulders snapped into Severance's head before he could stop it. For an instant he knew a sense of self-disgust. Surely he wasn't one of those perverts who were attracted to the cerebral and remote female Harmonics. Such men were only drawn by the sick need to despoil something they could never understand or accept.

No, Severance reassured himself, his brooding awareness of Cidra was reasonably normal. She was, after all, by her own admission a Wolf in Harmonic clothing. And while he hadn't been around many Harmonic women, he had met enough to know that they didn't project any real sense of sexuality. Cidra, on the other hand, had struck him as a very sensual creature, even though her air of serenity partially masked the raw vitality in her. He had the feeling she wasn't even aware of it herself.

A Saint among Wolves. To a certain extent Cidra would be safe because most people felt a certain instinctive protectiveness toward Harmonics. But there were all too many exceptions to that rule. Severance could think of several offhand, many of whom were fellow mail-run pilots.

At least she'd had the sense to choose a hotel in a reasonably safe section of town. Mankind's penchant for building cities around ports had changed little during the course of human development; nor had the basic characteristics of those cities changed. There were still good and bad sections, safe and unsafe areas. Cidra Rainforest had been wandering through some of the less desirable streets of Port Valentine when she had found him earlier that evening. Severance tried to ignore the fact that she'd be back on those same streets tomorrow evening, searching for a more helpful postman.

She would probably find one, he reflected as he sprawled in the back of the runner and listened to the faint shushing sound of the vehicle's twin blades on the pavement. Some renegade such as Neveril or Scates would lick his chops and produce a very neatly worded convenience contract before Cidra quite realized what was happening. She would be on her way to Renaissance, only to discover that her Harmonic trappings weren't much protection from certain kinds of Wolves.

Severance shifted restlessly as the lights of the port facilities came into view. It wasn't any of his business, he told himself angrily. By all accounts, Harmonics were quite intelligent; someone from Clementia had the ability to make her own decisions. She certainly didn't need Severance's help.

As the runner hissed to a halt Teague paid the fare with his credit plate and climbed out. He stood on the glowing sidewalk, staring at the tapering, floodlit outline of his ship out on the field. *Severance Pay* was poised for an immediate liftoff, her stubby, swept-back wings seeming to strain at the inconvenience of being planetbound. She was always ready to leave at a moment's notice. The competition for lucrative mail runs was stiff, and Severance had no intention of missing out on prime cargo simply because his ship wasn't ready to leave.

Automatically he removed one of two small remotes he carried on his utility loop and punched into *Severance Pay*'s primary onboard computer. He queried for messages and read the response on the small screen of the remote. A couple of friends had hit port and left word that they could be reached at one of the nearby bars if Severance happened to feel like a game of Free Market. There was a fuel tab that the computer had already been authorized to pay. And there was a terse message from one of the local postal agents saying that he'd had a special request from a client.

Severance knew what that meant. A patron had asked for him and his ship by name. With any luck that meant an important run. He started for the bank of comp-phones that were housed in a nearby terminal.

"Hey, Severance, you son of a renegade, where's the little Saint?"

Severance hesitated and then decided that he couldn't shake Scates by simply ignoring him. The other postman grinned and waved from the terminal doorway.

"I took her back to her hotel." Severance made to step around the man who had obviously been doing the port-strip taverns.

"Heard she was looking for a contract."

"Not the kind you mean."

"I'm not particular," Scates assured him. His broken nose twisted at an odd angle when he leered. "I take it you're not going to give her a lift?"

"No."

"You're missing a great opportunity, Severance. Me, I could think of plenty of things to teach a little Saint between here and QED."

Severance didn't bother to respond as he started through the open terminal door. But as the clear diazite panels slid shut behind him, he glanced back and saw that Scates was grinning more widely than ever. In the up-from-under pavement lighting his features seemed almost ludicrously demonic. Severance cursed his imagination again and turned away.

Even as he found a vacant comp-phone and punched in the postal agent's code, Severance knew what Scates was going to do. And as he listened to the agent tell him that there was a rush shipment of small but vital robot sensors that would pay twice the usual rates, Teague Severance was visualizing Scates offering Cidra a contract of convenience. Scates's convenience.

TWO

He shouldn't have tried to touch her.

Cidra found herself shaking uncontrollably. Perhaps, she told herself, if the man who called himself Scates had only continued to wheedle or argue, nothing would have happened. But he had reached for her, and Cidra had seen the hot lust in his eyes. She had reacted instinctively because there had been no real time to think.

All her life her body had been kept supple and strong with the ancient exercise. The training had begun before she could walk. Cidra couldn't remember a time when she didn't know the essentials of Moonlight and Mirrors. Intellectually she had known, too, that the flowing, deceptively simple movements were based on an ancient form of self-defense, records of which had arrived with the First Families of Stanza Nine nearly two hundred years ago.

But no one she knew in Clementia had ever actually used it in self-defense. She was shocked by how her body had reacted to the first genuine threat it had ever known. One moment Scates had lunged for her, and the next he was lying half conscious on the floor. The instant in between had been a shifting pattern that hadn't required any thought or preparation on Cidra's part. She had known the basics since she was a child. But she had never known herself capable of using them so effectively in this way.

The hem of Cidra's black-and-silver sleeping surplice was still swirling around her ankles and Scates had just hit the floor when the hotel room's communication panel announced another visitor. Cidra tore her stunned gaze from the man at her feet and stared at the softly lit door panel. Just then Scates stirred, groaning, and Cidra stepped quickly out of the way of his hand. The door panel hummed softly, demanding her attention. Because she could think of nothing else to do, Cidra went to the panel and switched on the screen. The fine tremors in her body seemed to grow worse when she saw who stood outside her door.

"Severance," she whispered.

On the small screen his hard, unforgiving features were etched in impatient, irritated lines, as if he didn't approve of either his surroundings or his business in the hotel. Indeed, he did look out of place in the elegant hall, his lean, dark figure a harsh contrast to the silvered carpet and the soft, waving patterns of soothing hues that decorated the walls. Behind him the subtly concealed security monitors turned politely toward his profile and then moved on, not yet alarmed.

"Cidra? Let me inside. I want to talk to you. If you don't open the door, the hall monitors are going to start recording my actions, and then we'll have to explain everything to the front desk." When she didn't respond immediately, he went on more harshly. "Come on, lady, I haven't got all night. I'm in one renegade hell of a hurry. I've got to get my ship off the ground within the hour."

"Severance, you'd better go away." Cidra's voice sounded strange to her own ears. "Something's happened. I don't think you'll want to get involved."

His eyes narrowed. "Cidra, let me in. *Now*."

The soft crack of command in his words jolted her. She was unfamiliar with such an approach to the giving of instructions. Cidra found herself releasing the computerized locks on her door without even thinking. A moment later he was striding into the room, shutting the door behind him. His gaze slid quickly over her form, assessing the apparent lack of physical damage. Then he stared at Scates, who was still out of commission. Swearing softly, Severance knelt beside the other man, feeling for a throat pulse.

"I knew it," Severance said. The words were full of morose resignation. "I knew he'd come here, and I knew you'd probably let him into your room without a second thought. Naive little fool. What did you do to him?"

Cidra locked her hands in front of her. "When he came to the door, he said he would be willing to take me with him on his mail run. I let him in and we started to discuss the matter. Then he made it clear that he was only offering one of those convenience contracts you mentioned. When I declined and asked him to leave, he . . . he touched me. Tried to grab me. His eyes were strange, Severance. Almost wild. And his hand was damp. I think he wanted to have sex with me."

Severance shot her a sidelong glance. "Yeah, I'd say that was one way of putting it. He probably thought you'd be easy game. I guess you surprised him, though."

"There was no time to think." Cidra stopped as she heard the apology in her words. Then she went on with grave honesty. "But even if there had been time to analyze the matter, I believe I would have done the same thing."

"What, exactly, did you do?"

"It's called Moonlight and Mirrors. It's a kind of dance. An exercise, really. But it's based on a very old self-defense technique. My instructors always said I had a unique style of interpretation," she added lamely.

"I can see what they meant."

Cidra watched with a frown as Severance pulled a small object from his loop and held it to Scates's temple. He pressed the small touch pad on the end of the device, and the other man's body jerked once. Then Scates went ominously still.

Deeply disturbed by her victim's new appearance, Cidra touched Severance on the shoulder. "What have you done?"

"Bought us a little time." He got to his feet, and then saw the horrified expression on her face. "Don't worry. He's not dead. I just finished what you started. He'll be out until morning, and by then we'll be long gone."

"I don't understand."

"I've changed my mind. I'm taking you with me." He began moving around the room, opening the door of the closet. "I know I'm going to regret it, but I can't seem to think of a way around having to take you along. Maybe I can dump you off in Clementia before I head out to Renaissance."

"I am not going back to Clementia, Otan Severance. I can't go back. Not yet."

He swung around, her travel pack in his hands. "We'll discuss it on the way to Lovelorn." He thrust the pack toward her. "Here, get your things together and let's get out of here. As long as Scates stays unconscious in your room, the privacy locks will protect us. Once he gets on his feet and wanders out into the hall, the security monitors will pick him up, and then the questions will start. I vote we leave him alone here to answer them. He's not likely to file any complaints against you. How could he explain that he got knocked unconscious by a lady from Clementia? His pride will be our best protection. Unfortunately it won't protect us from his friends, who will be looking for blood. So get packed, *now*."

Somehow it seemed easier to obey when he used that cold, hard tone. She was still trembling from the violence she had caused and had no desire to question Severance's decisiveness. Numbly she began to remove her formal robes from the closet and fold them in the proper manner.

"We haven't got time for you to practice the fine art of elegant garment folding. Here, I'll take care of the clothes. You get everything else together." Severance grabbed the liquid-soft garments from her hand and began stuffing them into the travel pack.

"My books," she said, trying not to watch as he treated her lovely gowns as if they were dirty ship suits. "I'll get my books."

"There's room in this pack for them," he told her.

She glanced at him in surprise as she began pulling the beautifully bound volumes from the autostorage unit beside the bed. "Oh, no, there couldn't possibly be enough room. I have a separate pack for them."

"I could get a couple hundred data slips in here," he assured her before glancing over and seeing what she was doing. "Saints in hell! Those aren't slips. They're books. Real books."

"Of course." She touched one of the handworked covers reverently. "No information storage system ever invented can compare aesthetically with a genuine book. They are such beautiful things."

It was Severance's turn to look shocked. "They must weigh as much as an exploroprobe. What do you think *Severance Pay* is, a cargo freighter? Leave 'em here. I just arranged for a crate of Rose ale to be put on board. There isn't room for your damn books."

Cidra clutched the volume she was holding to her breast. "If the books stay behind, then I stay too."

Severance lifted his eyes beseechingly. "I knew I was going to regret this. The Renaissance sinkswamps will freeze before I make a mistake like this again. All right, all right, bring the damn books. But move, will you? I've got a hot run, and it's COD."

"What's that mean?" Cidra asked, hastily placing the books in a travel pack.

"It means," Severance said as he locked the pack he had just finished stuffing with delicate clothing, "that I don't get paid unless the shipment gets delivered on time. Credit on Delivery. I don't intend to make the run to Renaissance for free, so let's get going. Here, you take the robes. They're a lot lighter. Let me have those damn books. Anything else?"

"No, that's everything." She edged around Scates's prone body. "You're sure he'll be all right?"

"Unfortunately yes. Now just act normal out in the hall, understand? Pretend you've changed your mind about staying here and have agreed to spend the night with me. You've paid for the room?"

Cidra nodded and then asked, "It's true, isn't it?"

"What's true?" Severance closed the door and set the locks.

Then he shouldered the travel pack and started down the hall, Cidra following close behind.

"Wolves think constantly about sex. It's what that man Scates wanted from me, and it is the excuse you think the hotel security system will accept for our unexpected departure."

"By now you ought to have learned for yourself that Wolves aren't nearly as elevated in their thinking as your friends back home in Clementia."

"It's not a question of refined or elevated thinking," she responded seriously as he herded her out of the hotel lobby and onto the glowing sidewalk. "It's a matter of the relative importance of the subject to an individual. Sex is obviously a great deal more important to Wolves than to Harmonics."

Severance opened the panel of a waiting runner and stuffed Cidra and her packs inside. Then he slid in beside her and punched in their destination. When he was finished, he leaned back in his characteristic lounging fashion and folded his arms across his chest. "Maybe if sex were a little more important to Harmonics, they would be able to increase their birthrate. Everyone knows they don't produce enough children to keep up their population. If it weren't for the random occurrence of natural Harmonics among the Wolves, there probably wouldn't be enough Saints to keep Clementia running."

"The system works fine the way it is," Cidra told him firmly. "It's good to have the new blood constantly being introduced into the Harmonic society."

"If everything is so great in Clementia, what are you doing here?"

She looked out the runner's diazite window, staring at the passing town, which had been founded according to a careful plan but had since grown into an eclectic and sprawling mix of architectural styles on meandering streets. The glow from the sidewalks illuminated everything from old, squat buildings fashioned by the early colonists of enduring anthrastone to the newer, gleaming structures built of obsidianite. Both materials had proven plentiful and cheap once the colonists had discovered how to pull them from the heart of the eastern mountains. One adventurous designer had done an entire hotel in the ubiquitous fluoroquartz. It was quite garish and tacky to Cidra's eyes. But, then, much of the town was. The jumble of styles and materials was visually unsettling when Cidra mentally compared it to the beautiful proportions and harmonies that dominated Clementia's graceful, simple architecture.

All this passed before Cidra's eyes fleetingly, as she gathered her spirits to answer Severance's question, since he was helping her, she felt she owned him the truth.

"You don't understand, Severance," she finally said quietly. "I can't go back to Clementia. Not as I am. I don't belong."

Raising a skeptical eyebrow, he turned to her. "A person either is or is not a natural Harmonic," he pointed out gently. "If you aren't one, there's no use fighting it, is there?"

Her head snapped around, and all the years of grim determination blazed for a moment in her vivid green eyes. "I will find a way to be one of them, Teague Severance, if it takes me to the end of the Stanza Nine star system and beyond. I will find the answer. It's out there. I know it is. I have traced the legend since childhood, and now, at last, I'm actually going after it."

He looked at her blankly. "Going after what? What legend?"

Cidra bit her lip and sank back into her corner of the seat. "It's out there, Severance. The tool with which I can become a Harmonic. The instrument that can fit my mind into the natural patterns and rhythms of everything I see or touch. Maybe it won't quite duplicate the way a Harmonic's mind vibrates in tune with whatever it chooses to focus on, but I think it can imitate the telepathic element. I think it can help me bridge the gap that my lack of natural ability has always put between me and the world I was meant to join." Her hands tightened in her lap. "I have almost all of it, Severance. I have the training, the rituals, the education. I have studied the Klinian Laws and the Rules of Serenity as the most devout of students. All I lack is the ability to achieve communion with the others and that intuitive element that makes the

Harmonic mind so unique. But I'll get it. Or something almost as good. I swear I will."

The silence in the runner seemed frozen as Severance regarded her taut features. Finally he said, "That's why you want to ship out with me? You're searching for a legend?"

She nodded once, sharply, wishing she had kept her mouth shut. "A Ghost legend."

"Ah, Cidra. There are a million Ghost legends. All of them created by humans after they reached Stanza Nine and found all that junk lying around on Lovelady and Renaissance."

"It's not junk! We're talking about the artifacts of a vanished civilization. And this legend is based on one of those artifacts. I found too many hints of it in the Archives. The tool is out there somewhere, and I'm going to find it." She shook her head wonderingly. "How can you call the artifacts junk?"

Severance's mouth curved wryly. "I'm sure that when they originally encountered the Ghost ruins, the First Families were suitably startled. But that was a couple hundred years ago, and when everyone realized how common the leftover Ghost garbage was, the novelty wore off. Even the Harmonics who are archaeologists are interested in only the most unusual finds. They don't want to be bothered anymore with every little shard or carving that turns up. If Stanza Nine ever attracts any tourists, we'll all make a fortune selling Ghost junk, but until then, it's practically worthless. The legends are even more worthless. We invented them. Every company explorer who ever had a bad dream while camped out on Renaissance has a new so-called legend. And the miners on QED are just as bad. Hell, for that matter there is still enough unexplored territory right here on Lovelady to breed tales. If you're chasing a legend, Cidra, you're chasing moonlight."

"Moonlight," she said, thinking of the dance patterns that had recently subdued Scates, "is something I have been taught how to chase."

Severance groaned. "I should have had the ship off the ground the minute I had the mail on board. I knew this was going to be a mistake."

"Then why did you change your mind and come after me?"

"When I think of a sufficiently sound answer, you'll be the first to know." And with that, the runner that had been slowing as it neared the port terminal slid to a stop.

A few minutes later, her pack of clothing in hand, Cidra followed Severance toward the small, streamlined mail ship. She watched as he punched codes into both a computer remote and the gadget he'd used on Scates. Then he led her aboard.

The interior lights came on as they stepped over the threshold. Cidra stood looking around at the compact, painfully limited cabin space and wondered for the first time if she had really given due consideration to the problems of living in such confined quarters with another human being, and a Wolf at that. She was still worrying the question when the scruffy rug beneath her feet moved abruptly. Startled, Cidra glanced down in time to see the motley piece of rug silently display three rows of tiny needle teeth.

"Watch out for Fred," Severance said as she backed hastily. "He hates being mistaken for a rug."

"Fred?" She watched the creature move in an undulating motion toward the seat in front of the command console.

"Fredalius is his full name. But I just call him Fred."

"Who named him?" she asked.

"My brother," Severance answered, his back to Cidra as he stowed away his pack.

"Does your brother fly with you occasionally?"

"Not anymore," he answered in a clipped tone. "He's dead."

"Oh." It didn't take a Harmonic's empathic abilities to realize that she had blundered onto a painfully raw topic. Automatically Cidra sought to soothe the discomfort she had caused. "I'm sorry, Severance. I had no idea. It was thoughtless of me to ask after him. I seem to be causing a great deal of unpleasantness tonight."

"Forget it." He busied himself with sealing the ship. "Stow your packs under my bunk for now. That's where I had the ale put, so you'll have to fiddle a bit to find room. We'll decide what to do with those damn books later. Right now I just want to get off the ground."

"We're leaving for Renaissance?"

"First we're hopping over to Lovelorn. I got word of another good shipment. Then we'll off-planet for Renaissance. Once we're in space we'll have two solid weeks to drive each other crazy. If we reach Renaissance without having murdered each other, we'll talk about extending the contract."

Cidra decided that this wasn't the time to argue her intention to stay aboard. It also didn't appear to be a good time to discuss the exact nature of the contract she had apparently entered into. She finished shoving her travel packs under the safety net beneath Severance's bunk. It wasn't easy. The crate of Renaissance Rose ale took up a great deal of room. Cidra wondered if Severance intended to drink all of it before reaching Renaissance. The thought was unsettling.

Then she took the single passenger seat located behind and to the left of the pilot's seat. Fascinated, she watched Severance run fluidly through the pre-liftoff procedures. It seemed to her that the computer had barely signaled that permission had been received to take *Severance Pay* into the air before they were, indeed, off the ground.

The lights of Port Valentine hung beneath them for a moment and then receded into the distance as Severance set a course that would take the ship to the mountain town of Lovelorn. Cidra knew that within the confines of the planet's atmospheric envelope *Severance Pay* was powered by standard jet engines. Only when the ship thrust into the freedom of space could they safely switch to the distance-crunching power of the STATR drive. Cidra studied Severance covertly. She admitted to herself now that he had been occupying her thoughts since the moment she had met him.

He was all business as he worked, his intent expression illuminated by the glow of the console lights. She was aware of being strangely fascinated by him in a way that was new to her, and the knowledge was disquieting. She should be viewing him simply as a man with whom she was doing business, but Cidra was honest enough and uneasy enough to admit that her reaction to him right from the start was far more jumbled and complex than such a simple arrangement warranted.

When he had first been pointed out in the tavern, she had experienced serious doubts about approaching him. It was obvious from the start that he was a hard man, a true Wolf. There was an aggressive harshness about him that made it clear he was a man who had not been softened or refined by too much contact with Harmonic values or ways. But she also sensed a quietly brooding element deep within Severance and wondered what had happened in his past to cause it. Something told Cidra it would be instinctive in Severance to avoid those ritualized behavior patterns and codes of conduct favored by people who tried to emulate Harmonics. He would have his own way of doing things, his own code of ethics and standards. And he would stick to it.

The people whom she had questioned at Port Valentine had been in agreement about one thing when it came to Teague Severance: He was a man of his word, and among Wolves that meant something. It had to mean something. It was all the general population had when it came to insuring trust. Wolves were forced to depend upon such things as reputation and experience to judge their acquaintances. They could never be completely certain of each other. They were forever denied the unique telepathic communion of minds that allowed Harmonics to establish such firm bonds between themselves. Trust was implicit in the way Harmonics lived and communicated; it was an unavoidable given, because they could know each other's minds. But when trust existed absolutely between a man and a woman, and was combined with the indefinable chemistry of shared pleasures and intellectual interests, it could lead to a lifelong commitment that was unique among mankind.

Cidra's parents shared that type of commitment. Talina Peacetree and Garn Oquist had a bond between them that Cidra had always longed to experience, herself, with the right man. Knowing that was impossible as long as she lacked true Harmonic telepathy had been the misery of her life. And her determination to overcome her own shortcomings was the driving force of her existence.

The covenant of marriage had taken on new meanings as Harmonic society had evolved. It stood now as so many Harmonic ways did, as an ideal. Wolves frequently used portions of the formal Harmonic wedding ceremony for their own nuptials.

Harmonics had always appeared at random in the human population. For countless generations many had died young. Others were driven insane by their instinctive efforts to reconcile reality with the inner harmony they saw in the world around them. A few had lived lives that appeared normal to others who never guessed at the effort it took to survive as a Harmonic among Wolves.

Special aptitudes and genius were common among Harmonics, and a few of the early ones had been strong enough to achieve a great deal before they died. Usually the achievements came in spite of a life racked with trauma and mental strife. Many others had simply perished without ever flowering.

The world of Wolves was a harsh one, and true Harmonics seldom coped well. A few hundred years ago, just prior to the unprecedented outpouring of mankind into the galaxy, it had been recognized that both Harmonics and Wolves fared better if they lived a separated, if symbiotic, existence. When the first of the beautiful, interstellar shimmer ships had left the home star system carrying colonists to new worlds, they had carried small contingents of Harmonics aboard.

No one had been egocentric enough to believe that the galaxy could be colonized into a tightly knit empire. Distances were too vast, and the demands of different worlds required too much physical and emotional adaptation, and the streak of independence in human nature was too strong. But the early planners had felt the need to insure that the best of what was human went with the colonists. Sending a small group of Harmonics along with each colony ship had not only guaranteed philosophical continuity, it had also provided a resident brain trust for each new world.

But, beyond that, each world had proved unique. Cidra knew from her work in the Archives that the Stanza Nine social structure was different in sometimes subtle, sometimes elaborate, ways from that of the home worlds. And since the ability to maintain contact with the home planets had been lost, the distinctions between Stanza Nine and other human systems no longer seemed to matter. Adaptation meant survival. And both Harmonics and Wolves believed in survival.

The crash of the colony ship that first reached the Stanza Nine system had been a complete disaster. Not only did the home planets believe there had been no survivors, but the First Families, thus isolated, had been deprived of much of the technology that should have been their heritage. The need to dig in and establish a foothold on a new planet without the aid of the machines that would have made the task relatively simple had bred a rugged sense of independence in the colonists. That sense of independence had even permeated the Harmonic contingent of the culture, where it was quietly accepted that each individual had both the privilege and the responsibility of achieving success on his own.

Technology had developed erratically from the bits and pieces of information left in the heavily damaged data banks after the crash of the colony ship. Regaining spaceflight had been of paramount importance because the human population was intent on establishing itself throughout the Stanza Nine system. After finding the remains of the Ghosts it had become even more important to determine if humans were going to have to share Stanza Nine with anyone or anything else. It had taken a hundred and fifty Lovelady years to get back into space, and the secret of the faster-than-light speeds that had brought the colonists to Lovelady had still not been found.

The majority of the population, the Wolves, respected the levels to which the Harmonics raised human virtues because the seed of those virtues lay in all humans. When a Wolf viewed a Harmonic, he saw the best of himself; he saw the most valuable essence of his own nature developed and channeled. Intelligence, integrity, honesty, serenity, and an appreciation for every element of the universe were traits to be protected and respected. Every human knew this. Not every human reacted in a positive manner to the knowledge, but none could avoid it.

Cidra drew the first deep breath she'd allowed herself since the man called Scates had lied his way into her hotel room. She was tired, but the adrenaline was still flowing through her system. Through the cabin window she could see the white disc of Lovelady's single moon, Gigolo. That small, dead world was also shining on Lovelady's southern town of Clementia. Her home was a serene, protected landscape of beauty and order. There lay everything she understood and loved. For a moment her heart yearned for another glimpse of the delicate fountains and the formal gardens that lined the white stone paths. But she had never been truly a citizen of Clementia. The magic of it had been denied her, even though she had been raised in its midst and taught its ways. Her own shortcomings had been pointed out quite graphically this evening.

Severance finished one last procedure at the command console and then swung around in his seat to face her.

"You look exhausted. Maybe you'd better grab a nap before we reach Lovelorn."

"I couldn't possibly sleep."

"Still seeing Scates coming at you?" he asked gruffly. "Don't worry. You're safe now."

"It's not that." She glanced out into the darkness and then back at Severance. "Do you realize that tonight was the first time in my life I've done violence to another human being?"

"You've led a sheltered life."

"It's not funny, Severance."

He sighed. "I know. But it's not the end of the universe, either."

"Perhaps not, but it worries me."

"Listen, Cidra, you want to worry? Worry about what would have happened if you hadn't had all that fancy Moonlight and Mirrors training. Now that's something to fret about."

"You don't understand," she snapped. "I should be begging for a shot of oblivo. I should be flat out on the floor, half catatonic."

"And instead you're just sitting there shaking like a leaf?"

"Don't laugh at me, Teague Severance." She was near tears now, and the knowledge infuriated her. Quickly she used her years of training to regain her self-control. "I want to be one of them. All my life I have been trained in the ways of the Serene path. Surely I have some Harmonic sensitivity in me. I was born to Harmonics. Yet tonight I used the ways of a beautiful dance to hurt someone else."

"Who was trying to hurt you. It's called self-defense, Cidra, and I know enough about Harmonics to know that they're not philosophically opposed to self-defense. They're just lousy at being able to act on that belief. Be damned grateful that your only problem right now is that you've got the jitters instead of a full-scale anxiety attack. I've seen what happens to a Harmonic who runs into real violence and it's not very pleasant."

She eyed him curiously. "When did you see a Harmonic deal with genuine violence?"

Severance ran a hand through his thick black hair, his face drawn, gray eyes suddenly bleak. "My brother was one of those random occurrences you mentioned earlier. A Harmonic born among Wolves."

"Why wasn't he sent to Clementia?" she asked, frowning.

"It's a long story, and I'm not in the mood to tell it right now. Take a nap, Cidra."

"I don't think I can sleep yet."

"Suit yourself. I'm going to sack out for a few minutes. It's been a long night."

Severance got to his feet and brushed past her, heading for the sleeping area at the rear of the cabin. He unlatched the upper sleeping berth so that she could climb into it if she changed her mind, and then he threw himself down onto the lower bunk. He was already half asleep when he felt Fred undulating up onto the bed to drape himself over his master's feet.

Severance awoke once during the flight and realized that

Cidra hadn't tried to nap. He peered through the gloom of the dimly lit cabin and saw her seated cross-legged on the metal deck. Her eyes were closed in silent meditation.

Probably still worrying about Scates and how she'd handled the situation, Severance reasoned in sleepy irritation. She looked very soft and gentle sitting there with her black-and-silver gown flowing around her. A little lost. But it would have taken a fair measure of strength and coordination to throw Scates. She couldn't be all sweetness and light, even if she wanted to believe she was.

Beneath the fine crystal-moss fabric of the robe she wore, he could see the rounded upsweep of her breasts. It seemed to him that the womanly curves would fit his hands perfectly. Then he recalled what she'd said about Wolves being very interested in sex. Severance turned over to face the wall and ordered himself to go back to sleep.

THREE

Cidra felt the shift in altitude and speed as *Severance Pay* automatically began its approach. The subtle changes jerked her out of the meditative trance she had been using to calm her mind and body. Opening her eyes, she saw new console lights wink on, while others changed color. For the first time she noticed there was a second computer on board. It didn't appear to be involved with the landing operation, either. A glance over her shoulder told her that the ship's master was still sound asleep.

She got to her feet, feeling delightfully rested, and went to the nearest viewing port. A few scattered lights in the distance heralded the presence of Lovelorn, a manufacturing town that had been located near the ore-rich deposits of the continent's western mountains. Beyond the mountains lay an ocean that extended most of the way around Lovelady. It was almost totally unexplored, although research indicated it would ultimately prove even richer in raw materials than the continents.

There was a lot of Lovelady waiting to be thoroughly explored and even more of Renaissance and QED. Beyond the three close-in planets lay one other, Liquid Assets, a frozen ocean of a world that lacked a breathable atmosphere. It hadn't experienced more than a few exploratory landings so far. The Stanza Nine system was still a frontier, its population centers small, even on Lovelady, which was its most heavily populated planet.

Cidra felt a glimmer of excitement rush through her. She was on her way, off in search of a legend. For the first time she acknowledged that the search, itself, was going to prove fascinating.

The ship altered course again, and this time Cidra turned around a little anxiously to see if Severance had awakened. When she saw him lying spread-eagle on his stomach, face to the cabin hull, she decided to act. She went over to the bunk and reached down to touch his shoulder, only to find she had made a terrible mistake.

There was no startled shout or sleepy, questioning groan. Severance simply exploded off the bunk at the touch of her hand. He was on the deck, feet spaced apart in a fighter's crouch, before Cidra quite realized what had happened. The small weapon he had used on Scates was in his right hand. Somehow he had gotten it out of the utility loop he'd hung beside the bunk.

Cidra froze, not daring to breathe as his eyes flickered in recognition. With a muttered oath Severance dropped the black metal object back into his loop. The poised tension went out of his body. On the bunk Fred exposed his teeth briefly, and then went back to posing as a rug.

"A few more surprises like that, Cidra, and one of us isn't going to make it as far as Renaissance."

She cleared her throat. "I just wanted to tell you that we're approaching Lovelorn. The ship seems to be altering course. I assumed that, as pilot in command, you might have some interest in the matter."

"Not much," Severance assured her. "This baby can land herself if necessary." Nevertheless he went forward to check the winking lights on the command console. "Saints know she's done it before." He yawned and massaged the back of his neck with one scarred hand as he stood staring down at the controls.

"Severance?"

"Hmmm?"

"What is that instrument you carry? The one you had in your hand a moment ago?"

"It's a remote for a Screamer." He leaned down and depressed a red-lit control, watching the screen in front of him as he did so. *Severance Pay* banked gently into a turn.

"I've never heard of a Screamer," Cidra said.

"I don't imagine you've got a lot of use for them in Clementia. They're not exactly legal."

"But what does it do?"

"It's very good at making uninvited visitors scream."

His obvious preoccupation bothered her. "That's not much of an explanation," she said reproachfully. Cidra was accustomed to an educational system that answered all questions as completely as possible. She was also trained to keep asking questions until she was satisfied with the answers.

Severance shrugged, still watching the landing setup on the screen. "It's a device that's designed to jam the frequency of human nerve impulses. That's about the only way I can explain it. I've got the main system installed here in the ship. I carry the remote with me."

"Scates didn't scream when you used it on him."

Severance glanced at her. "He was already half out. The remote just finished the job you'd started."

Cidra stiffened. She wasn't sure if she had been rebuked. But her curiosity persisted. "Does the device function automatically whenever someone comes aboard?"

"It can be set that way. I leave it on when I'm gone and switch it off with the remote when I'm ready to come back aboard. But it can also be triggered manually. See that switch there on the console?"

"Yes."

"That will trigger it. There's another one back near the head of my bunk."

"You would turn it on while you, yourself, were on board? What about your own nerves?" she asked.

"Curious little thing, aren't you?"

"I'm sorry," she apologized formally. "I don't mean to pry into your private business."

"Uh-huh." He sounded skeptical. "Well, the answer is that I can set the remote to protect me from the effects of the main system. Fred's safe because his nerves work on a different frequency than ours. Have a seat, Cidra, we're ready to hit dirt."

She realized that his patience had reached its limit, so obediently she strapped herself into the passenger seat and fixed her gaze on the lights of Lovelorn. A few moments later *Severance Pay* settled gently down into the landing field, and Severance cracked the hatch.

"I'll be gone for about an hour. No more than that. We haven't got time for you to wander outside and have a look around. You wouldn't find much of interest, anyway. This is a pretty dull town. You stay here and guard the castle. When I return, I'm going to put this ship into space as fast as possible. If you're not here, you'll get left behind. Clear?" He sealed the collar of his gray ship suit as he spoke.

Cidra nodded, and then asked impulsively, "Have you ever seen a real castle, Severance?"

He glared at her. "It was a figure of speech, not an invitation to more questions."

"I've heard that the Ghosts left behind a structure that might have been a fortress," she ventured thoughtfully. "On Renaissance."

"Why don't you take a nap, Cidra?"

Her eyes widened. "I couldn't do that. You're leaving me in charge."

Severance muttered something unintelligible and started through the hatch. "That was a figure of speech too. Forget I said it. Fred is in charge. Stay out of trouble, Cidra, if you want to see Renaissance." With that he vanished into the cool Lovelorn night. The hatch hissed shut behind him, sealing and locking itself.

Cidra felt movement near her sandaled feet and looked down.

Fred was investigating the hem of her black-and-silver robe. Even as she watched, Cidra saw his three rows of teeth appear. She yanked the fabric out of reach just in the nick of time.

"Don't you dare chew on my clothes! Just because you're the one who is officially in charge, don't get the idea you can terrorize innocent passengers." Then she smiled at the creature. Fred continued to expose his teeth, and Cidra chose to believe he was smiling back. She reached down to scoop him up into her arms and discovered it was difficult to pick up a rug. There seemed to be no stable bone structure inside Fred.

He didn't appear to mind the awkwardness of her grip, however. He simply wrapped himself around her forearm and continued to grin. Cidra looked for something resembling eyes.

"You're a Lovelady rockrug, aren't you? I've seen holotapes of your kind sunning themselves on mountain rocks. How do you like shipboard life?"

There was no answer, but the three sets of teeth disappeared into the tatty fur covering. As Fred settled down to sleep on her arm Cidra thought she saw a couple of small black eyes wink shut. It was hard to be certain because of the scraggly fur. Her arm felt pleasantly warm with the rockrug wrapped around it.

She wandered around the tiny cabin, investigating the functional, if spartan, lavatory facilities and the miniature galley with its preserver and heater. She checked the preserver to see if there were enough nonmeat food packs aboard to hold her until Renaissance. It was a limited selection, at best. Teague Severance was definitely carnivorous. Typical Wolf. Well, if he were willing to do without some of the vegetable packs, she might not starve to death. For someone who had been brought up to appreciate exquisitely prepared food, the prospect of two weeks of preserved vegetables was not a pleasant one.

But one had to make sacrifices when one set out on a quest, Cidra reminded herself as she shut the preserver. The heroes in the First Family novels always sacrificed comfort when they went adventuring. She ought to know. She was an expert on First Family novels. The only real expert in Clementia. She wandered over to the sleeping berths and fished around beneath Severance's bunk for her precious pack of books. Before she found it, she encountered a small metal chest wedged in behind the crate of ale.

She was far more intrigued by the unimposing storage container than she should have been, perhaps because she knew immediately that the box would contain something that was very personal to the enigmatic man who was taking her into space. For the first time in her life Cidra found herself wanting to explore the private side of another human being without waiting for an invitation. It took an amazing amount of fortitude to push the unopened chest back into the sticky storage net. But the ingrained rules of privacy were far too strong in her to allow Cidra to do otherwise. She pulled out the pack of books.

Her mind and body had settled down again. She would happily occupy the next hour reading. She deliberated between the elegantly worked volume of Nisco's *Serenity and Ritual* and the anonymous collection of essays and poetry known as *Passages to Appreciation*. She knew she ought to choose something from one of them, but somehow she wasn't in the mood. Cidra dug a little deeper into the pack and came up with a hidden bundle of data slips that contained her collection of novels. Novels didn't warrant much more than cursory interest on the part of Harmonics specializing in social history. She'd had no competition when she'd chosen to become an expert on them. But Cidra loved novels. She had acquired a sizable collection on slips, and when the time had come to leave Clementia, she had been unable to abandon them.

Cidra removed the reader and a slip that contained one of her favorite tales and curled up on the lower berth to read once more the adventurous story of a mythical First Family colonist. Without any hesitation at all she skipped along until she came to the love scenes. The love scenes in such stories held an interest for her that she had never stopped to analyze. But she was more exhausted than she realized. Cidra was in the middle of a torrid seduction when she fell asleep.

It was the distinct impression of wrongness that awoke her a few minutes later. For a moment she lay quietly, eyes closed, and tried to analyze the feeling. She immediately realized that Fred was no longer wrapped around her arm. She could feel the warmth of him lying on her stomach, but he didn't seem quite as boneless as he had earlier. There was a tension in him that had communicated itself to her and awakened her.

Cidra opened her eyes and looked up into the muzzle of a Garing Immobilizer. A part of her recognized the classic safeguard side arm, even while her brain sought to adjust to the shock of seeing one pointed at her. A large, gloved hand was wrapped around the grip.

"Just keep calm, lady, and nothing's going to happen to you."

At the sound of the rough voice Cidra managed to jerk her eyes from the Immobilizer to the swarthy face of the safeguard holding it. When he saw her stricken look, he smiled bleakly and used his free hand to display his certificate of authorization.

"I don't understand," Cidra murmured, confusion replacing some of the initial fright. Harmonics never had trouble with the authorities for the simple reason that Harmonics never committed crimes. Both safeguards and Harmonics knew it. She had grown up with that serene knowledge. It was built into her. Then she remembered Scates lying on the floor of her hotel room. "What's wrong? He's all right, isn't he?"

The man holding the Immobilizer appeared amused. "Who? Severance? As far as we know. Don't worry about him, he'll be back in about forty minutes. He ran into a little delay collecting his mail, you see. We arranged it that way."

They didn't seem to know about Scates. Feeling simultaneously relieved and guilty, Cidra relaxed slightly. "But what are you doing here?" She realized that a second uniformed man was standing near the command console, and her searching gaze rested briefly on him. "How did you get on board? The hatch was sealed."

The man standing over her answered. "Didn't you look at my certificate? We're port security. We have bypass plates for all registered mail ships. Now sit up very slowly. You from Clementia?"

She nodded. Fred scuttled down into her lap as she sat up crosslegged on the bunk. Her hand brushed past the small switch that could activate the Screamer, but Cidra hardly noticed. She was watching Fred bare his teeth. He didn't appear to be smiling this time.

"Good. That should make things nice and simple. We won't have any trouble with you, will we?"

Obediently Cidra shook her head. "Of course not."

"Fine." He glanced at his companion. "We won't even need to put a tangler on her, Des. She's a Harmonic. She'll stay out of trouble."

"But what do you want? If you have business aboard, I would have been happy to open the hatch. I don't understand what this is all about." Cidra turned an unwavering gaze on the armed man. "Whatever it is you're after, you should consult with the master of the ship."

"We're not quite as formal here in Lovelorn as you folks are in Clementia. We don't always have time for good manners. What we're after is in the cargo bay, and on this ship it can only be unsealed through the command console."

Cidra kept her hands carefully folded in front of her. "Then you should definitely speak to Teague Severance."

The safeguard grinned. "He's not likely to be very helpful under the circumstances. We're here to remove some cargo he picked up in Port Valentine."

"But the shipment from Port Valentine is scheduled to be taken to an outpost on Renaissance." Cidra kept her voice very clear and polite. She betrayed nothing of the uneasiness she felt, realizing that her best defense right now lay in maintaining the impression these men had of her. They couldn't have dealt with many Harmonics. In their line of work they simply weren't likely to encounter people from Clementia. Her appearance and dress had led them to mistake her for a Saint, so she would play the part.

"Don't worry yourself about it, Otanna. This isn't Harmonic business. This is a matter of port security." The man holding the weapon spoke to the silent figure by the console. "Find what we need, Des?"

"It's here. The bypass is working through possible code combinations now. We'll have the bay opened in a minute or so. What about her?"

"She's not going to give us any trouble."

The first man holstered the Immobilizer and smiled again. He smiled a lot, Cidra thought. Too much. She didn't like him, and neither, apparently, did Fred. There was a curious humming sound coming from the vicinity of the three rows of teeth. Automatically Cidra reached out to stroke the rockrug.

"We're all set," the man called Des announced with cool satisfaction. "The bay's open. Let's get the stuff and get out. I don't want to be hanging around here when Severance returns."

"I couldn't agree more." The first man started for the rear of the cabin where the inside cargo hatch was located.

The valuable shipment lay undefended. It was COD, Severance had said. He would get nothing for it if it wasn't delivered. With a kind of stark clarity Cidra realized that she had to act. In Severance's absence she was in charge of his ship. "Guard the castle," he had told her.

Yet these men were official representatives of Lovelorn law. The law was one of the few formalized institutions Wolves had. It was to be respected. Harmonics knew it often fell short of the ideal, but that was no excuse for failing to honor it. Still, she felt she had to do something.

"Wait," Cidra called urgently as the first man was about to step into the cargo bay. "I must protest this action. I insist you wait until Teague Severance returns. This is his ship and his cargo. You must discuss this with him."

"Why don't I just go ahead and put her out?" Des unholstered his weapon and calmly pointed it at Cidra.

"Forget it. She's not going to get in our way. Give me a hand, Des. I knew we should have brought a servocart. This thing's heavy."

"Please," Cidra said, "I'm asking one last time that you wait and take this up with the ship's master."

"Shut up, lady. You're beginning to annoy me. Why don't you

meditate or something?" Des started to follow his companion into the cargo bay.

Fred suddenly leapt from Cidra's lap, undulating with incredible speed across the cabin floor. Des whirled around, aiming his side arm at the small creature.

"No!" Cidra stopped debating the philosophical quandary in which she found herself. Her hand swept out, yanking at the Screamer trigger imbedded in the wall behind her.

And then she found out why the shipboard defense system was called a Screamer. She was barely aware of the strangled cries of the two safeguards. Her own mind was suddenly bursting with the screams of every nerve in her body.

She had never experienced anything approaching such pain, and after the first few seconds, it held her totally immobilized. Lights flashed in front of her eyes, her ears seemed to hear every harsh, discordant sound in the universe, and her skin was on fire with a rash that made her want to claw at herself with her own nails. But she couldn't even move her hand far enough to switch off the screamer. Cidra could only sit on the bunk and struggle to maintain some hint of sanity, for a primitive part of her was still alert enough to fear being driven insane by the cacophony. And that was the most terrifying prospect of all.

Instinctively she mentally grabbed for and clung to the intense discipline that was a fundamental part of her Harmonic training, using it to search for and find a thin sliver of consciousness and sanity to guide her through the pain. A true Harmonic would not have been able to apply her training under such fearsome circumstances. It was an ironic indication of Cidra's lack of true talent that she could use the training now in a way for which it had never been intended. But Cidra was not contemplating the right or wrong of it all; she was simply holding on for her life.

Severance was worried even before he got out of the runner. He stood for a moment on the curb, the small courier pack locked to his wrist. Then he fished the computer remote out of his utility loop. The tiny notation on the screen informed him calmly that the

Screamer had been activated. He stared at the object in his hand, unable to believe what he was seeing. He picked up the package of preserved vegetation meals he'd wasted valuable time purchasing on the way back to the ship and broke into a run.

Severance Pay sat in heavy shadow on the landing field, giving no hint that all was pain and chaos aboard. The Screamer put out no audible sound. When Severance punched the remote to open the hatch, he found that it hadn't been locked. Had Cidra left the ship after all? The knowledge infuriated him, but he found himself praying that she had. If she was still on board when the Screamer had activated, she would be limp, quivering marshjelly by now. He knew what the Screamer could do to the most hardened of Wolves. He couldn't bring himself to imagine what it would do to someone who was almost a Harmonic in so many ways.

Damning everything and everyone around him, Severance used the Screamer's remote to cancel the defense system. But he knew that if Cidra was inside, the damage had been done. He leapt aboard, his eyes sweeping the ominously still cabin.

For an instant he couldn't see his passenger. She wasn't on her bunk and she wasn't lying on the floor. He saw the prone bodies of two men near the open cargo bay before he realized that Cidra was slumped on his bunk.

"Damn it to a renegade's hell. Cidra. *Cidra.*" He crouched beside the berth, searching for her throat pulse. It beat far too rapidly beneath his fingers. The stiffness in her body alarmed him more than anything else. She should be unconscious by now. Even a minute of the Screamer's effects was sufficient to knock most people out. Yet the tension in her body indicated that on some level she was still aware, still trying to fight the nerve-jamming impulses even though they had ceased. He began stroking her, petting her as if she were a wild creature he was trying to soothe and tame. There was no quick remedy for the Screamer's damage. It took time to recover. Victims knocked unconscious generally awoke a long time later with a headache that could only be described as violent.

"Cidra, can you hear me? It's over. Listen to me. It's over. Let go, lady. Let go."

Severance caught a brief movement out of the corner of his eye. He glanced toward the cargo bay and saw Fred release the leg on which he had been gnawing. The rockrug flowed toward his master. "What the hell happened in here?" Severance asked softly, wishing the rockrug could answer.

Fred hummed a little in response and undulated up into the bunk to settle on Cidra's stomach. Then he began shifting his pliable body in a rhythm that didn't take him anywhere but seemed to emulate the stroking movements Severance's hands were making.

"It's all right, Cidra. It's all over. Can you hear me? All over. You're safe now."

Very slowly some of the unnatural tension seemed to seep from her body. Beneath his hand Severance could feel the gradual unknotting of the muscles in her arms. Her head began to move restlessly. He kept talking to her, muttering meaningless words of comfort. Even though he knew there was no instant cure for the Screamer's results, Severance decided to get Cidra to the nearest med facility. If nothing else, they could tranquilize her into unconsciousness.

Her lashes lifted just as he started to get to his feet. Instantly he knelt again beside the bunk.

"Cidra?"

She seemed to have trouble focusing on him, but at last she realized who was beside her. Her lips moved, shaping soundless words. She touched her tongue to the dry surfaces and tried again.

"Is the castle . . . safe?"

"Everything's safe, Cidra. Don't try to talk. Just try to sleep. It's the only way out of this. Try to sleep."

"I know you left Fred in command," she whispered, "but they were going to shoot him. There wasn't anybody left . . . except me."

Relief poured through Severance as he realized that she was starting to breathe normally. It didn't look as though he would need the med facility after all. Gently he continued stroking her.

"We'll talk about it when you wake up. Go to sleep, Cidra. Close your eyes and go to sleep."

He watched her relax slowly into unconsciousness, and then he got to his feet once more. He studied the two men lying near the cargo bay while he unlatched the courier pack he had just picked up from a patron. It was being sent to Renaissance, and the shipper had been most anxious that it travel under computer lock. To humor him Severance had performed the little drama of latching the pack to his wrist. It was an ancient shipping custom that could still impress customers although Severance privately thought it wasn't very practical as a security technique. But it seemed to have reassured the patron. It had also taken up precious time.

Dumping the pack carelessly into a nearby storage bin, Severance went toward the cargo bay to investigate the intrusion that had apparently caused Cidra to pull the Screamer. With the toe of his boot he nudged one of the unconscious uniformed men onto his back. Then he went down on one knee and pulled out the man's certification card.

For a long time Severance studied the port security identification. It appeared almost genuine. It would easily have fooled Cidra, who wasn't accustomed to double-checking a stranger's ID.

The second man was sprawled halfway through the cargo bay opening. His arm still lay across the shipping container bearing the red COD seal.

Suddenly it all made sense to Teague Severance.

All except one small matter.

Twenty minutes later, as *Severance Pay* lifted off for the long trip to Renaissance, Severance was still pondering the fact that Cidra Rainforest must have gone against everything she had ever been taught when she'd used the Screamer to stop two safeguards from stealing the shipment.

A postman could do worse than go into space with a woman who was willing to risk her life for the mail.

FOUR

Cidra's first thought when she awoke was that a giant torla had accidentally stepped on her head. Such a thing could only happen accidentally, as torlas were too stupid to do anything on purpose except eat. They were also too stupid to move once they had accidentally stepped on someone. So, of course, Cidra assumed, the beast was still crushing her.

Unless, of course, this was the first assault in a war of revenge against the human population of Lovelady. If it was, Cidra could hardly blame them. The big, dumb, placid torlas had become a prime source of meat shortly after the First Families arrived. Knowing torlas, it might have taken them two hundred years to wake up to the fact that they had an enemy.

"I'm a vegetarian." Cidra didn't even try to open her eyes as she squeaked her protest. The torla on her head didn't move.

"I know," came the response from somewhere to her right. "Just one more problem. Here, I've got some 'gesics. They won't knock you out like that oblivo stuff does, but they'll help the headache. Open your mouth, Cidra. They have to dissolve under your tongue."

A strong, sinewy arm slid under her shoulders, lifting her. The pain in Cidra's head changed from a steady state of heavy pressure into sharp bolts of lightning. Tears burned beneath Cidra's eyes. The humiliation washed over her, momentarily more intense than even the agony in her head.

"I apologize," she gritted.

"For what?" Severance asked, calmly shoving two small objects under Cidra's tongue. "The tears? Forget it. Most people would be screaming about now."

Cidra sensed a faint fizzing sensation as the tablets dissolved. Experimentally she lifted her lashes and found herself looking up into Teague Severance's gray eyes. He didn't appear especially pleased with her as he knelt beside the lower bunk, cradling her in one arm. There was a grimness around the edges of his mouth.

"The act of screaming would only make it worse," Cidra explained with grave logic. She managed to blink back the incipient tears.

"It can't be as bad now as it was when you cranked on the Screamer. Saints in hell, lady, that thing must have ripped you apart."

"I thought that's exactly what it was doing." Automatically she looked down at herself. The black-and-silver surplice was a mess, stained in places from her damp, perspiring body. The finely spun crystal-moss fabric looked as crumpled as she felt. But she seemed to be all in one piece. Then she realized she didn't feel quite right even though nothing appeared to be missing. "Are we in space?"

"Two hours out of Lovelady. I've got the grav on." Severance steadied her with one hand while his other went to her braided coronet.

The artificial gravity explained the faint strangeness she was feeling. "What are you doing?" Belatedly Cidra realized that Severance was freeing the fireberyl comb in her hair.

"I thought your head might feel a little better if you loosen those braids." He tossed the expensive comb down onto the bunk beside her and deftly began unpinning her hair.

The intimate touch of his hands was vaguely alarming. Cidra wasn't accustomed to much physical contact. Harmonics had a great respect for the privacy of another person's body. Instinctively she tried to draw away from Severance. His grip on her shoulders tightened in response.

"Hold still. I'll have these down in a minute."

"I'll do it." She lifted her hand to her hair, trying to take over the small task. Her fingers came in contact with his, tangling for an instant. He ignored her efforts, pushing her hand aside. She felt the roughness of his scars.

"I've almost got it. This must be harder to put together than a coalition of free miners on QED. How long does it take every morning?" Two long braids tumbled free, falling down over Cidra's breasts. As if intrigued by the intricate braiding, Severance's fingers followed the line of one braid all the way down to the tip. His hand hovered there, filling Cidra's body with a new tension.

Her concentration was abruptly torn between the pain in her head and her intense awareness of the proximity of Teague's fingers. She realized that she was holding her breath, knowing that if she inhaled, she would thrust herself against his hand.

"I work my hair during the first morning change." She couldn't think of anything else to do except answer his question. He was beginning to unwind the individual braids now, starting from the bottom and moving upward. Cidra drew a small sigh of relief as the masculine fingers moved to her shoulder. She could risk breathing again.

"Well, you'll have plenty of time on this trip to fool with your hair. How's the head?"

"Better."

"Good. With any luck no one will find those two fake guards for a whole day or two. They won't have any 'gesics to help with the headaches." There was a certain distinct satisfaction in Severance's voice.

Cidra looked up at him as her hair loosened beneath his touch. "Fake guards? They didn't represent port security at Lovelorn?"

"No more than I represent a convention of Saints. Good ID, though. I'm not surprised you bought their story. And they must have had some good connections too. It's not that easy to get hold of an official mail ship bypass."

"Why were they trying to steal your cargo?"

"Those sensors we've got on board are one of a kind gadgets. The latest designs out of ExcellEx labs. The company wants them shipped to their exploration post on Renaissance."

"I've never heard of ExcellEx."

"It's a small outfit run by a tough little guy who left one of the big exploration companies a few seasons ago to start his own firm. His name's Quench. He's shrewd, and he's willing to slit throats when necessary. I've handled a few private shipments for him lately. He seems satisfied. If he can get ExcellEx up and running within the next three or four seasons, he'll own one of the hottest exploration companies in the system."

"And you'll be one of his most trusted mailmen. He'll give you the most lucrative runs. Maybe even employ you full-time so you won't have to scrounge for shipments."

Severance showed his teeth. "Nobody ever said Harmonics aren't as fast as everyone else when it comes to figuring out a business deal."

"Harmonics have to be fast at analyzing business situations," Cidra informed him demurely. "If they weren't, they'd get eaten alive by unscrupulous Wolves."

"They seem to do all right. Where do you think the phrase 'rich as a Saint' comes from? I don't know of too many poor ones, except perhaps for the young ones who are still doing research or perfecting their art and music."

Cidra shrugged and instantly regretted it as the pain flared back to life in her head. Severance was right. The Harmonics participated in the freewheeling business practices that dominated commerce throughout the Stanza Nine system. Clementia produced and marketed the results of scientific research, as well as fine art, poetry, and music that thrilled the senses. Wolves were a ready market for the talents of Clementia. But when it came to business, Harmonics couldn't rely on the customary goodwill of the general population. Agents who were Wolves, themselves, were used for the often fierce negotiating that took place when a Harmonic product went up for sale. Her own father had made a sizable fortune selling sophisticated investment strategies. Constructing and analyzing complex economic models of the wide-ranging commerce of the worlds of Stanza Nine was a hobby for Garn Oquist. He was a mathematician by training and inclination.

Cidra considered what she had just been told. "So someone else wants those sensors?"

"Looks like it. Since they're supposed to be top secret, that presents an interesting problem." Severance finished untwisting one long braid. He drew his fingers down through it slowly. There was an oddly preoccupied expression on his face as he watched the red highlights hidden in Cidra's hair come to life in the thick stuff.

Cidra, herself, found it difficult to maintain a casual conversational tone as she asked, "If the sensors are so valuable, why weren't they shipped out on a commercial freighter under company guard?" Instead of answering right away, Severance began to work on the second braid. This time his hand seemed to be almost resting on her breast as he began unwinding the strands. And when he spoke, Cidra heard a new harshness in his voice.

"In addition to the fact that it costs three times as much to ship that way, Quench wasn't sure it would really buy him any protection. There's no method of keeping that kind of shipment secret. He was hoping that if he sent the sensors with me on a normal private mail hop, no one would notice. It was a risk, but that's how you make good credit."

"Well, someone did notice." Cidra began to breathe again as Severance's fingers moved upward. A part of her felt strangely disappointed, but another part was appalled at her own sensual curiosity. She had been so sure she had outgrown the very un-Harmonic desire for physical knowledge that had tormented her socially as a young girl. "Do you know who?"

"Who knew the shipment was traveling with me? No. I have no idea."

"Those men who came into the ship . . ."

"Were probably mercenaries. No telling who hired them."

"What did you do with them?"

"Stuffed 'em into a storage locker outside the terminal at Lovelorn." He finished his self-appointed task and sat back on his haunches to survey the effect. Cidra's soft red-brown hair flowed in a cape over her shoulders. He stared at it for a moment, and then his eyes shifted to catch her questioning gaze. "They're lucky I didn't leave them with something more permanent than a killer of a headache."

The coldness in him reached Cidra in a wave, chilling her to the bone. For the first time since she had left Clementia she allowed herself to remember that murder was not an unheard-of crime among Wolves. A movement around her ankles broke the spell. Grateful for the small interruption, she turned her head to see Fred undulating into a more comfortable position across her legs.

"Fred was quite a hero. You should have seen him go after that one guard," Cidra said with a weak smile.

Severance's attention stayed on her profile. "I saw what he did to the renegade's leg."

"I wondered earlier if Fred might bite. I guess I know now."

"He did a little more than bite the bastard. Fred's got three layers of teeth. When he starts chewing on something, he makes a real meal out of it." Severance stood up beside the bunk. "Think you'll be okay?"

Hastily Cidra nodded. "My head is much better, thank you."

Severance leaned forward, his face suddenly very intent. "It wasn't Fred who was the hero. He was only acting out of instinct. You were the one who had to go against some fairly strong conditioning to try to stop those two renegades. I know Harmonics normally don't get mixed up with safeguards. I owe you, lady."

Cidra realized that she was feeling inordinately pleased by his words. She smiled for the first time since she had awakened with the awful headache but offered the formal response to his praise. "It was as nothing. No sense of obligation is required."

Severance stared at her for an instant and then grinned. "That's a Harmonic for you: Polite to the last drop of blood." He turned from the bunk. "Feel like a cup of coffade?"

"Yes, thank you." Cidra lay back carefully on the bunk, aware that she now missed the comfort of his touch. It said a lot about her weakened condition that she would have liked to have him continue to hold her.

She watched as he dialed open the compact preserver and removed the container of green crystals. He poured the coffade into two mugs and shoved both into the heater. The machine added water and brought the mixture to a quick boil. Severance opened the heater and brought one of the mugs over to Cidra. He held the other one in his fist as he watched her cup her hands around the pleasantly warmed mug.

"When you're feeling better, we're going to have a talk."

She inhaled the fragrant steam. "I realize that. You'll probably want to outline my duties for the next two weeks. I'm really feeling much better already. We can talk now if you like."

"Your duties," he repeated, sounding as if he were repressing a groan. He dropped down onto the bunk beside her, staring at the bulkhead. Leaning forward, he rested his elbows on his thighs, the mug of coffade loosely suspended between his knees. "Yes, there is the little matter of your duties on board. We'll come to that later. There are other things that have to be resolved first. You've never been in space?"

"My parents took me on a commercial freighter once when I was younger. It was more of a sight-seeing trip than anything else. Other than that, I haven't spent any time on a ship."

"Uh-huh." He paused, apparently trying to find the exact words. "You will note that, as I mentioned over dinner, there is very little room in here."

"Don't worry, I don't think I'm claustrophobic. Of course, I haven't spent several days in a confined area before. But I'm sure I'll be able to handle this."

"Claustrophobia is not what I was worrying about." He took a long sip of the coffade. "Let's see if I can put this so that it sounds reasonably diplomatic. Harmonics, as I understand it, are accustomed to a great deal of privacy."

"Yes."

"They are also accustomed to a great deal of personal independence."

"Of course." She waited expectantly, wondering where he was leading.

"There is very little of either on board ship," Severance concluded bluntly. "Small mail ships such as this one are not exactly bastions of democracy. The only way we're going to survive without resorting to violence over the next couple of weeks is if you understand that I'm in charge. I know Harmonics are brought up to question everything. But around here, when I give an order, I am not bringing the issue up for debate. Whenever there is a choice about the way something is done, we do it my way."

Cidra told herself not to be offended, but she knew her voice sounded overly formal. "I assure you I understand the tradition of a captain being in charge of his own ship."

He looked at her in mild astonishment. "You do?"

"I read a great deal," she confided. "I'm a trained archivist. One of my areas of expertise is the fiction written about the First Families and the early explorations."

"Wonderful." His mouth crooked dryly as he took another swallow of the coffade. "I'm sure all that reading will have prepared you to slip right into shipboard life. I've had trouble with the few previous passengers I've had on board, but I can see that won't be the case with you."

Perhaps the residual pain in her head was making her more sensitive than usual. Whatever the reason, Cidra felt a touch of annoyance. "There's no reason to be flippant. If you've had trouble with previous passengers, my guess is it's because you were impolite or abrupt in your manner of giving orders."

"Orders sometimes have a way of sounding rude and abrupt. I just want it clear that the tone of voice in which they are given does not alter the fact that they're still orders. Understood?"

"I have the feeling I've just received the first command. Message clear and comprehended, Otan Severance."

"I've told you to skip the Otan."

"Would you prefer that I address you as Captain Severance?"

"Now who's being flippant?" he drawled. "Use my name. Either name. I don't think the informality will do much damage to the sense of discipline in the remainder of the crew." He glanced at Fred.

"Did Fred ever have any sense of discipline to begin with?" Cidra asked.

"Not a lot." Severance was quiet for a while. "I don't suppose you know how to play Free Market?"

"Harmonics do not gamble."

"I was afraid of that. It's going to be a long two weeks, isn't it?"

Cidra hesitated. But she did want to be as accommodating as possible. "I could learn to play the game," she offered tentatively. "It's not necessary to make wagers, is it? I expect that the game is played the same, with or without credit being exchanged."

"The stakes are what make the game interesting."

"Oh. Well, it's a moot point. I don't have anything to put forth as a wager except perhaps a few novels on data slips. I don't imagine that would interest you." She felt relieved. She had made the offer, and it was obvious that Severance wasn't too excited about it. Cidra felt off the hook.

"I could try teaching you the game first, and then we can decide whether you've got anything worth wagering," Severance said slowly.

A faint thread of wariness unfurled inside Cidra. She studied Teague's unreadable face. "I've heard that many Wolves are quite addicted to gambling."

"It's just a way of passing time. A form of recreation. Not to be taken too seriously."

"Then you are not one of the addicts?" she asked cautiously.

Severance smiled, that same grin that showed so many fine, strong teeth and so little real humor. "Of course not. I'm only a casual player."

"Oh, good." She felt vastly relieved. "Well, in that case, I suppose I could attempt to learn to play Free Market."

"We'll give it a whirl after we've had some sleep. I keep standard Lovelady days on board ship." He got to his feet. "Think you can make it up into your own bunk? Or do you want me to carry you?"

Gingerly Cidra started to sit up. Fred moved off her feet with a low, grumbling sound. Cidra ignored him, concentrating on her body's reactions to the movement. Her head still hurt, but the pain seemed distant, a dull threat but not a major disaster any longer. She massaged her temple, aware of a vague sense of weary disappointment.

"What's the matter? Still feel like your head's going to explode?" Severance slid a rough hand under her curtain of hair and began kneading the nape of her neck.

"It's not that. I feel much better. It's just that—" She broke off and moved her hand in a gesture of dismay. "I shouldn't."

"Shouldn't feel much better?"

"Never mind. It's hard to explain."

Severance continued to work on the base of her neck. "Still worrying because you don't have a Saint's catatonic reaction to pain?"

"It's just one more reminder that I have a long way to go before I become a Harmonic. You must understand. I don't want to feel pain. No one does. But every time I do, I'm aware of the fact that I don't react to it in a normal fashion."

"Normal for a Saint."

"That's what I was born to be, Severance," she said with a soft insistence. "I remember once when I was very young. I had slipped away from my parents and was trying to climb into one of the plaza fountains in Clementia. They're so beautiful with the light beads mixed into the water. I wanted to go swimming in that beautiful, shining water. That was before I realized that one didn't do that sort of thing," she added hastily.

"Naturally. Very un-Saintlike, climbing into a fountain."

"Yes, well, I slipped and fell, cutting myself. But I was so excited by having gotten into the fountain at last that I didn't pay much attention to the fact that I was bleeding into the water. When my mother found me, she nearly went into shock. Everyone nearby was horrified. Someone came rushing up with a dose of oblivo, and the next thing I knew, I woke up in a med facility. I found out several years later that small wounds such as the one I had gotten in the fountain are treated rather casually among Wolves."

"And you had automatically reacted casually at the time. Because you're a Wolf in Harmonic's clothing." Severance removed his hand from the nape of her neck. "Stop worrying about it, Cidra. We both need some sleep. You want a bath?"

She stood up a little shakily but without kick-starting the headache. "That sounds wonderful." With a sigh she examined her rumpled sleeping robe. "Have you got a fresher on board?"

"Sure. Give me the dress and I'll run it through a cleaning cycle while you hit the lav."

"Thank you." She moved toward the tiny lavatory facility, wondering how she was going to find room even to turn around inside, let alone undress. The ship's lav was nothing like the comfortable facility in her parents' home. When the privacy panel hissed shut behind her, she struggled free of the sleeping surplice with some difficulty. Every time she shifted position she came into contact with some object in the miniature room. Severance knocked on the door just as she finally freed herself of the gown.

"Ready?"

"Here. I appreciate your help." She opened the panel a tiny distance and pushed the black-and-silver robe into his outstretched hand. "How do you move around in here? It's barely big enough for me, let alone someone your size."

"I leave the panel open," he told her calmly. The robe and his hand disappeared.

Never in a million seasons would she leave the panel open, Cidra decided. Turning carefully, she activated the orange controls set in the bulkhead. A wonderfully refreshing hot spray filled the small room. Cidra closed her eyes and gave herself up to the pleasure of it.

It was a long time before she reluctantly deactivated the spray, dried herself with the warm air jets, and plaited her hair into one long braid that hung over her shoulder. Feeling infinitely better and deliciously sleepy, she cautiously cracked the panel.

"Severance? Is my robe ready?"

There was no answer. Pushing the panel open a little farther, Cidra tried again. "Teague?" Still no response. The cabin lights had been dimmed. In the faint glow of the control console she could see the black-and-silver surplice draped over the back of the command seat. There was no sign of Severance. Belatedly Cidra realized that he was in his bunk.

She waited another moment or two, the sight of her robe on the seat tantalizing her. It was obvious that Severance had gone to sleep in the same quick, uncomplicated way he had napped on the flight between Valentine and Lovelorn. The only option she had was to get the robe herself.

Taking a deep breath, she slipped out of the lav and stood poised for a few seconds in the shadows. There was no movement from the lower bunk. Cidra padded barefoot across to the command console and quickly put on the surplice. She relaxed as the garment swirled comfortably around her. Running around naked in front of a strange man and an even odder beast was not her idea of proper decorum. Gathering up the hem of the robe, she went to stand at the foot of the bunks. There was a narrow rope ladder hanging from the upper berth. Presumably that was how one climbed into it.

Experimentally Cidra took hold of the flexible side of the ladder and fit her foot into the bottom rung. After that it was easy. She was safely into her berth a few seconds later. The knowledge that she was truly at the beginning of her quest once again swept over her, making her considerably less sleepy than she had been only moments before. She sat cross-legged on the bunk, closed her eyes, and sought the calming influence of the evening meditation ritual. She was halfway through the elaborate sequence of silent logic when Severance spoke from the bottom bunk.

"Do you always spend that long in the lav?"

Cidra opened her eyes with a start. Instantly visions of herself darting naked across the cabin to retrieve her robe leapt into her mind. "I thought you were asleep," she said weakly.

"I dozed off waiting for you to emerge from your bath. Rule number one on board *Severance Pay* is that passengers don't treat the water supply as if it comes from one of those inexhaustible fountains in Clementia."

"I assumed it was a recirculating, full-recovery system." She was embarrassed and offended.

"No system is one-hundred-percent full-recovery. You lose a little every time you use the lav."

"I understand," Cidra said stiffly. "I will be more careful next time." She gave up trying to meditate and crawled under the covers.

On the bottom bunk Severance folded his arms behind his head and stared thoughtfully up at the bunk above. Chewing out a Harmonic always made a man feel guilty. He'd felt the same way whenever he'd lost his temper with Jeude.

Damn it to a renegade's hell, though—Cidra was not a real Harmonic. There would undoubtedly be ample opportunity to remind himself of that fact during the next two weeks. He allowed himself to dwell for a lingering moment on the sight of her nude body outlined in the dim console lighting as she padded quickly across the room to don her robe.

Small, sleek, with an unmistakably feminine grace. Her breasts were delicately curved, just the way he had imagined they would be earlier when he'd unbound her braids. Nicely rounded buttocks too. Lush and tantalizing. She wasn't a beauty, but she was intriguing on too many levels for his peace of mind. And she was not a Harmonic, regardless of what she thought or wished to be.

For some reason it was becoming important that he make her admit that. Severance realized he wanted Cidra to acknowledge fully that she was a real Wolf, just as he was.

It was a long while before he went to sleep.

The smell of hot coffade and a steaming prespac breakfast brought Severance awake eight hours later. He opened his eyes slowly, letting himself luxuriate in the fragrance. The little fake Saint was obviously up and about. He stretched slowly and climbed out of the bunk. Fred had vacated the premises earlier. He was draped over the back of the console seat, watching Cidra slip another prespac into the ship's heater. Severance yawned loudly, and Cidra whirled around, smiling. The smile slipped, and her eyes went momentarily quite wide as she absorbed the fact that he was naked. After a startled instant she turned hurriedly back to the heater.

"Good morning, Severance. Are you hungry? I hope you don't mind me digging out the prespacs. I was just thinking, this could be one of my shipboard duties, couldn't it? Getting the meals ready?"

The deliberate chattiness of her voice amused him. He stepped into the lav, leaving the panel open. "I've got news for you. Shoving a food prespac into a heater and pulling it back out again doesn't exactly constitute a full-time job. Now, if we had a grill on board and some fresh food, I might be willing to negotiate."

"Still," she insisted, "it is a task, however small. And we have to agree on something useful for me to do."

He leaned out of the lav, reaching into a storage bin for the trouser portion of his gray ship suit. "Afraid of getting bored?"

"No. But I definitely want to work my passage, Severance."

He didn't respond to that—didn't *dare* respond. With a grim effort, he forced the panel shut behind him. He had spent too much of the night envisioning exactly how she could make herself useful on board, and Severance knew Cidra would be repelled by the graphic pictures he had formed of her. When he stepped out of the lav a short time later wearing only worn, close-fitting trousers, he said simply, "We'll think of something."

"You keep saying that, but what will we think of?" She set the steaming prespacs on the small serving table and handed him a mug of coffade.

"So earnest and industrious," he muttered as he sat down. The coffade tasted better than usual for some reason. Maybe it was because he hadn't had to make it himself. "Give me some time, all right? I haven't had an opportunity to really contemplate the situation. Everything's happened a little fast since I met you on Lovelady."

She smiled, but he noticed she was having to make an effort to keep from staring at his bare chest. He blinked lazily, set down the mug with a small sigh of resignation, and reached into a bin for a loose, comfortable, wide-sleeved shirt he sometimes wore on board. He shrugged into it but didn't bother to fasten the front seal. Cidra looked relieved.

"Thank you," she whispered. "I'm not a prude, you understand. I have had courses in human anatomy. But Harmonics are generally quite formal in their attire. I'm accustomed to it."

"Yeah, I'm getting that impression. I warned you about the lack of privacy on board."

"Yes." She concentrated on her food. "You did."

"Things on Renaissance are even more, uh, informal."

"I'm prepared for that."

Severance studied her for a moment, taking in the determined carriage of her head. She had her hair back up in the strict coronet, and he wondered how long it had taken her to do it. Her surplice was red, embroidered at hem and cuffs and throat with a delicate purple floss. She was a note of color and restrained elegance against the general gray backdrop of the ship. Quite suddenly he was intensely curious about her.

"What's going to happen if and when you find your magic artifact, Cidra?"

She frowned. "It's not magic. When I find it, I'm sure I will also find a perfectly good scientific explanation for how it works."

He held up a hand. "Sorry. No magic, then. Your scientifically explainable artifact. What will you do with it?"

"Go back to Clementia, naturally."

"Someone waiting there?"

She glanced up, green eyes wary and quizzical. "My parents. My teachers. My friends."

"A lover?" He almost surprised himself with the question— almost but not quite. The hard edge of his words told him more than he wanted to know about his own reasons for pushing in this particular direction. The color that surged into Cidra's cheeks fascinated him.

"That's a very personal question, Severance."

"I know. I'm rude on occasion." He finished his meal and tossed the empty prespac into the disposal unit. He was disgusted with himself.

Cidra smiled tentatively. "I suppose it's just another example of a Wolf's natural interest in sex."

Severance regarded her laconically as he got to his feet and walked over to the control console. "You're a Wolf, lady, whether you like it or not. Don't you have any interest in the subject?"

She quickly cleaned up the remains of the breakfast prespacs, avoiding his half accusing stare. "You must understand that for me a relationship with a man will be much different than it would be between two Wolves."

"There is a man back in Clementia, isn't there? A Saint." He leaned against the console, irritated by the way she was sidestepping the subject.

Cidra turned to face him with quiet reproach. "There is a man," she began very carefully, "but I am not ready for him."

"He thinks he's too good for you because he's a Harmonic and you're not?"

She shook her head. "Mercer would never think such a thing. He is a brilliant, kind, intuitive man. A fine Harmonic who has been both teacher and friend to me. He is in charge of the Archive where I work. I have never told him that I would like the relationship to become more . . . more intimate. I would not burden him with that knowledge until I can come to him as a true Harmonic."

"You're just stood in the shadows, pining from afar, is that it? For how long?" Severance didn't even bother to soften the words.

"Three and a half seasons," Cidra admitted wistfully. "We have so much in common intellectually that I just know things will harmonize beautifully between us once I have overcome the barrier of my non-Harmonic mind."

"I think I may get sick."

Instantly Cidra swept forward, concern marking her features. "You're ill? Why didn't you say something sooner?" She took his arm. "Lie down while I get the med kit. Here, I'll help you to the bunk—"

"You do take things literally, don't you? Forget the med kit, Cidra. I'll survive. Come here. I want to show you something." He pushed her gently down into the seat in front of the ship's second computer. "Ever seen one of these?"

"A Consac Four-ten. I've never seen one programmed for use on board a ship, but I'm familiar with the basic model. We use a Consac Sixteen hundred in the Archives." She eyed him uncertainly. "You're not sick?"

"Not the way you mean." He nodded toward the computer control panel. "A Conny is a Conny. If I give you some introduction, you ought to be able to manipulate this one."

"Probably," she agreed with no false show of pride; the simple fact was that she could. "I learn very quickly. What do you want me to do with it?"

"You said you wanted to work your passage."

Her eyes lit up. "Definitely. There's something you want done on the computer?"

"I'd like some advice from someone who's had a good education. Presumably, since you were raised in Clementia, you've had the best."

She smiled. "The best."

FIVE

Fifteen minutes later Cidra shook off her intense concentration long enough to smile up at Severance as he hovered over her and the computer. She understood now what he wanted.

"This is your lucky day, Teague Severance. I told you I'm a trained archivist. I could just as easily have been a microgeologist or a professional poet. And then, while I might have been able to give you some general guidance or advice, I wouldn't have been qualified to really dig in and program a first-class record-keeping system for you. But as it is . . ." She let the sentence drift off as she turned back to the computer.

"As it is," Severance concluded, "this is my lucky day. I should have known. Wonder what I did to deserve having you on board?"

"There you go, being flippant again."

"I think it's more than flippancy," Severance murmured. "I think at times I'm bordering on outright sarcasm. Postmen aren't noted for their social graces." He leaned closer, peering over her shoulder at the screen. "You really think you can get up some kind of workable records and business management program for me?"

"I've been designing and applying records management programs since the day I first set foot in the Archives."

"Yeah, but the stuff you file and retrieve at Clementia is different. I'm not trying to figure out a way to handle a bunch of old slips filled with First Family diaries or middle-second-century poems. I need hard data I can call up on a second's notice, and I'll need it cross-indexed a hundred different ways. I figure that if my plan is going to work, I'll have to be able to access everything from personnel information on company presidents to meteorological details on QED."

"I thought the weather only came one way on QED: dry."

Severance glared at her. "Now who's being flippant?"

"I apologize."

He ignored the formal, self-deprecating inclination of her head. "Weather on QED can be damned tricky when you're trying to land a Class A mail ship in the mountains. In addition to that kind of stuff I'm going to need full payroll capabilities. That means I need to be able to zap credit into employee accounts from anywhere in the system."

"Only the big exploration companies have payroll systems that flexible," Cidra noted. "Just how big are you planning on becoming?"

He lifted one shoulder with seeming negligence, but Cidra saw the glittering determination in his eyes. "I want to build a real organization. Right now private mailmen like me operate on a haphazard basis. Each one of us functions independently with no set schedules. The competition can be cutthroat."

"How cutthroat?"

"Pilots can get killed in this business."

Cidra blinked. "You mean because of the dangers of landing on Renaissance or QED?"

"No, Cidra," he said with patently false patience. "I mean, they can wind up dead because of the stiff competition."

"Murdered?" She felt queasy. "I've heard of some criminal activity among the more aggressive pilots, of course, and occasionally one hears of a landing accident or some such incident, but murder?"

"I don't imagine it makes the newscasts in Clementia. Harmonics probably prefer not to pay too close attention to Wolf news. It isn't always intellectually stimulating."

"You've got a point there." She was beginning to feel mildly irked by his attitude. He was right, it did border on sarcasm. Stepped over the border, in fact. For the first time she wondered if Teague Severance didn't number among the more aggressive in his business. She had just decided not to ask any more questions about the criminal behavior of mail pilots when a thought came to her. As usual she sought an answer without even stopping to consider the consequences. "Do you think those fake safeguards who came aboard at Lovelorn were from a rival mail ship?"

Severance lifted his dark brows. "It's a possibility. It's more likely that they were working for a rival of ExcellEx, though. I'm going to collect good credit for the delivery of those sensors, but I don't think it's enough to get killed over. The shipment has great value to an exploration company in competition with ExcellEx but not to another mailman. I've carried cargo that's paid better than those sensors will."

Cidra decided that she would not ask what that cargo had been. "All right, I think I understand the scope of what you want done. You're going to go into the private post business in a big way. Hire other pilots to work for you. You want to create a computerized inventory system, a payroll system, a general information and retrieval system for business and scientific data, and a personnel file."

"Those are the basics. I want to offer a professionally operated service, one companies and individuals can count on instead of having to take their chances with the schedules and the personalities of whatever independent postman happens to be in port at the moment."

"Don't the commercial freighters already offer that alternative?"

"They're inflexible. The ships are limited to the biggest ports, and they don't offer door-to-door delivery anywhere. And they aren't willing to take risks for a single patron. The reasons the independents stay in business is because they make it a point of honor to do whatever it takes to deliver the mail. My goal is to maintain the versatility the independents offer but add the elements of reliability and dependability."

"What are you going to call this empire?"

"The same thing I call it now. Severance Pay, Ltd."

"That name doesn't allow equal billing for any partners you might decide to take on in the future," she pointed out.

He gave her a hard look. "I don't plan to take on any partners. I had one once. Once was one time too many. Severance Pay, Ltd. is all mine, and it's going to stay all mine."

Cidra smiled. "Another Wolf on the prowl."

"Anything wrong with a little ambition?"

"Of course not. Our whole economy is based on ambition, although I don't think your idea of ambition qualifies as 'little.'"

"Stanza Nine is a big system, Cidra. Lots of room to operate for a man who's willing to work hard."

"And you're willing to work as hard as it will take to build this kind of business?" She held up her hand. "No, forget I asked that. I can see the answer is yes. I do have one other question, though. Most of the systems you want designed from scratch could be purchased already set up and running. Why create your own?"

"I don't want a system anyone else uses or understands. I need something tailored to the way I operate, something unique. I realize that for things like the payroll package I can use the fundamentals of a commercial design, but I'd rather start from the bottom. I can handle changes and modifications to the programs, and anyone with a decent education can program a Conny, but the basic design of a new system is something else. It takes a special kind of ability, a special way of thinking."

"It takes someone who's been thoroughly trained to think both logically and intuitively." Cidra felt some of her earlier assurance slip away. "You'd be better off hiring a true Harmonic, Severance. This is the kind of thing they do so well."

"It's also the kind of thing for which they'd charge more credit than a miner could pull out of QED in a year. I can't afford a true Harmonic, Cidra, but I seem to have someone on board who thinks she's almost a Harmonic. Someone who says she wants to work for her passage. Give me two weeks' worth of basic design work, Cidra, and we'll call it even."

She gave him a knowing glance. "Typcial fast-talking Wolf. It will be a little more than even if I give you what you want. You said yourself that this kind of design work costs. I'm not familiar with your postal rates, but I have the feeling that what you want would cost you a great deal more on the open market than the price of a passage to Renaissance."

"Yeah, but this isn't exactly an open market, is it? You've said you want to pay your way. This is what I need. It's the only option I'm offering at the moment. Take it or leave it."

Her head came up proudly. "I'll take it, of course. I'll do the best I can for you, Severance. You have my oath on it."

"The oath of a true Harmonic is solid credit," Severance mused. "But you're not quite a true Harmonic, are you?"

Cidra fought back a rush of anger. She had spent her whole life learning to moderate her emotions. She would not let this Wolf upset the careful balance she worked so hard to maintain. "No, Otan Severance, I am not a true Harmonic. Until I am, you will have to trust me."

"That's asking a lot," he drawled. "I make it a practice not to trust anyone completely."

"I'm aware that among Wolves trust is always a grave risk."

"I suppose you trust your friend Mercer in the Archives?"

"He's a Harmonic," Cidra reminded him calmly. "I trust him absolutely."

"But you wouldn't think of trusting a Wolf that way, would you?"

Was he deliberately goading her? Cidra turned back to the computer. "No more than you would. If I am to design the fundamental approaches of the systems you want, I had better get started. Two weeks is not very long for this kind of task."

"Work hard, Cidra. I want my credit's worth."

Cidra bit back the retort that jumped into her mind. Taking firm hold of the intense concentration the Harmonic educational system had bred into her, she immersed herself in the monumental job Severance had assigned. It would take a lot more than two weeks to do it properly, but she was determined to give him as much as she could. She would not have any Wolf saying that she had tried to cheat him.

Severance worked beside her, describing his needs in detail and explaining the idiosyncracies of the Consac Four-ten system. Their conversation became businesslike and efficient, but by the time Cidra was ready to break for a meal, she had a new image of Teague Severance. He was a man with a goal, and he was willing to do whatever it took to achieve it. A part of her understood him on that level. She had her own goals. But Cidra couldn't help wondering what Severance would be like by the time he had built his dream. His ambitions were the sort that gave free license to a Wolf's most competitive, combative instincts. The worlds of Stanza Nine provided the kind of anything-goes, make-it-any-way-you-can atmosphere that encouraged people such as Severance. But an unrestrained Wolf was a dangerous creature.

Only after they had eaten what corresponded to the evening meal did Severance again bring up the idea of teaching Cidra to play Free Market. She had secretly hoped he might forget the whole thing. Games rarely interested her. But she forced herself to agree politely. Perhaps accommodating him would insure that his mood remained stable. There had been occasions during the short time she had known him that she had wondered about the reliability of his temperament.

He had been gentle with her when she was recovering from the effects of the Screamer, but he had also been inclined to goad her into responses that would have been impolite and angry. She didn't understand him all that well, which was only to be expected under the circumstances. No one raised in Clementia could always predict the behavior of a Wolf. Wolves weren't very good at explaining themselves. But Cidra sensed a restlessness in Severance that worried her. She didn't want to do anything that would make him snap.

So she reluctantly agreed to learn Free Market.

Severance first poured two full-size mugs of the Renaissance Rose ale he seemed to enjoy so much. Then he set out the markers, the sardite chips, and the three-dimensional playing field that constituted the game of Free Market. Cidra watched the process with a tinge of wary curiosity. She sensed a carefully leashed anticipation in her teacher. His was not going to be the formal, patient style of instruction to which she was accustomed.

"Think of this as broadening your education," Severance said blandly as he straddled the stool across from Cidra. He absently shook the handful of numbered cubes he was holding in his left fist. The small table they used for eating had been set up with the field and playing pieces. "Harmonics are very big on broadening their educations, aren't they?"

"Yes." She watched as he tossed the cubes onto the top level of the playing field. "But games don't generally interest us . . . them."

He smiled, again showing ominously white teeth. "That's probably because they don't believe in gambling."

"It's not a question of not believing in it. More a matter of simply not finding it very interesting or pleasant."

"Cidra, my sweet little would-be Harmonic, you've missed something along the way." He leaned forward. "Now pay attention. I'd just as soon not have to explain anything twice." He pushed half the sardite chips over to her side of the table. "The goal here is to take every last sardite your opponent has."

She picked up one of the dull green chips. "I don't see why. Sardite is neither particularly beautiful nor useful. It's also extremely common."

"Don't give me the innocent-as-a-Saint bit. In a real game each chip represents whatever your opponent is actually wagering, and you know it. Here, count the cubes and check the numbers on each."

"Why?" She removed them from the top level of the playing field and obediently counted them. Then she added up the numbers on each cube.

"Because it's one way you make certain your opponent isn't trying to cheat you."

"I imagine that's an important consideration in a game between Wolves."

Severance's hand closed over the cubes she had just counted. "A very important consideration."

"I won't cheat you, Severance," Cidra promised, offended by the way he was now making a show of counting the cubes himself.

He didn't bother looking up as he checked each cube. "You better believe you won't." He tossed the cubes back onto the field. "All right, let's get started."

He was right about one thing, Cidra decided twenty minutes later: He certainly didn't believe in explaining things twice. She was fortunate she was such an adept learner, for her new mentor was not long on patience. Too many years alone in the confines of a mail ship, together with very little grounding in the rules of etiquette and ritual, Cidra concluded.

By the time Severance had run through an explanation of the basic playing strategy of Free Market, she was still wondering why anyone bothered to play the game. The process of tossing cubes, tabulating the results, and shuffling the playing pieces down through the various levels of the playing field seemed innately dull. There appeared to be an almost endless number of rules, none of which were written down anywhere. So many rules, in fact, that it occurred to Cidra that a few could be added or deleted, and a novice player would never know the difference. No wonder Wolves had to worry about protecting themselves from being cheated. There was skill involved, but winning seemed basically dependent on a combination of luck and the ability to outguess or outbluff one's opponent.

At the end of the basic lesson Severance insisted that they start a game.

Cidra was doubtful. "I'm not sure I've memorized all the rules."

"You'll pick them up as you go along. Easiest way to learn is to play. Take the cubes." He lounged back against the bulkhead, every inch of his long body giving the appearance of a casual, relaxed player about to begin a friendly game.

Thoughtfully Cidra launched the cubes on the field, resolved to do her social duty and play. With any luck she would lose her chips quickly and the game would be over.

As it turned out, she did lose her chips in a very steady, rapid stream. A little too rapid, Cidra decided a short time later as she frowned at the pile in front of Severance.

Severance caught the frown and asked smoothly, "Want to try it again?"

"Perhaps once more. I'm still not certain I have all the rules straight. And there are certain elements of the strategy that I don't fully understand." She reached out to take back half the sardite chips.

"You did fairly well for a beginner." He watched her pile the sardite into neat little stacks. An odd smile hovered at the edge of his mouth.

At least he seemed to be in a good mood now, Cidra thought as she carefully counted the cubes. It was worth playing the game if it kept Severance in a mellow frame of mind. Fred appeared to be enjoying the spate of good temper also. He was lazily draped over his master's shoulder, proving himself to be as good at sprawling as Severance himself. There was no sign of the small button eyes or the teeth. Cidra had long since decided that both Fred and Severance were more comfortable to be around when their teeth weren't showing.

She dropped the cubes into the chute and picked up her playing pieces. Brows drawn together intently, she studied the numbers on the cubes.

The sardite chips disappeared from her side of the table a little more slowly this time, but they disappeared just the same. The ale in Severance's mug vanished relentlessly too. Cidra tried a sip of hers and found the potent brew more interesting than she had expected. She didn't try any more, aware that she needed her full attention to be on the game, but her opponent didn't appear to have any similar concerns. Severance seemed blessed with an endless capacity for Renaissance Rose ale. A very small, unexpectedly churlish part of Cidra hoped at one point that the famous backlash effect of the strong ale would go to work on Severance's playing ability. But the thorn stayed hidden, and Cidra was left feeling ashamed of her unethical thoughts. As if in punishment, she promptly lost the last of her sardite chips.

"I can see there is more to the game than I had realized," she conceded graciously as Severance scooped up the last of her chips. "You play it very well, Severance. I'm afraid I made the winning quite easy for you."

"Like taking nectar from a Saint," he agreed, laconically returning the cubes into their container. "That's enough for now." He picked up a bottle of ale and poured yet another measure into his mug.

Dubiously Cidra watched the process. "Yes," she said. "Enough for now. If you will excuse me, I think I will read for a while."

"Suit yourself." Severance picked up his mug and went forward to drape himself in the pilot's seat. He dimmed the cabin lights and leaned back, mug in hand, to stare out into the endless night that surrounded the ship. Fred clung to his shoulder perch, continuing to doze. Cidra had the feeling that the little rockrug had spent many hours in this way. The runs to Renaissance, QED, and Lovelady were long, and the supply of ale on board was extensive.

Quietly Cidra prepared for bed and climbed up into her bunk with a book in hand. With the aid of the small fluoroquartz reading chip she had brought, she bent her attention to an analysis of a chapter of Argent's *The Role of Ritual*. The familiar passages were still an intellectual challenge to the most expert philosophers of

Clementia. Deliberately Cidra lost herself in the deceptively simple writing.

A while later when she finally grew tired and put away her reading, she saw that Severance was still sitting in the command seat, mug in hand, stargazing.

The next three ship days passed in similar fashion as they settled into a routine that, while not always meeting Cidra's approval, was reasonably bearable.

She worked on Severance's computer for a good portion of each arbitrarily designated day-night cycle. Cidra also set aside a certain amount of time to devote to her Moonlight and Mirrors exercise. It was impossible to find sufficient room to develop the full patterns, but she did enough to satisfy herself that she was keeping her body in shape.

Severance's own physical routine consisted of a harsh workout on a compact exercise machine he'd had installed in the bulkhead wall near the cargo bay. It seemed to Cidra that the sweat he worked up during the hour he spent on the machine was excessive. After the workouts she was vividly aware of the rivulets of moisture that trickled down through the hair on his bare chest. His sleek shoulders gleamed wetly, and she could not seem to take her gaze away from the strong contours of his back and the flat, hard planes of his stomach. The scent of his perspiring body would be strong in her nostrils before he stepped into the lav.

After the second such workout in a one-day cycle, Cidra tentatively mentioned the scientific fact that there was a point of diminishing returns in exercise. One session a day on the sophisticated machine should be quite sufficient. Severance responded with a short, blunt splash of temper that left Cidra determined to keep her mouth shut on the subject of exercise. He continued to work out two or three times a day.

After the evening meal Cidra indulged Severance with a couple of games of Free Market. He still won every time, but her stacks of sardite chips disappeared more slowly with each new game. She was getting better, Cidra thought, and was surprised to find satisfaction in that knowledge. When the games were finished, she climbed into her bunk to read, leaving Severance to his lonely vigil in the pilot's seat. She was usually asleep before he finally dropped into his own bunk.

On the morning of the fourth day in space, Severance revealed an interest in something other than exercise and his embryonic business programs. Cidra had spent two hours experimenting with management theory designs, using the computer to do long-range projections and then carefully varying certain factors such as fuel cost and employee problems. Severance had been intently peering over her shoulder as usual most of the morning but was now gone. She hadn't noticed when he'd vanished. After running the fourth viable change in the design Cidra decided she needed a break.

She turned in her seat to find Severance sitting at the command console, a diazite globe in front of him.

"What have you got there?" Rising and stretching, Cidra wandered over to look down into the clear ball between his hands. There was a complex little panel built into the base of the globe. She recognized the object just as Severance answered her.

"A light-painting globe." He did something to the panel, and instantly the inside of the diazite ball began to shimmer.

Cidra leaned closer in pleasurable anticipation. There were many fine light-painters in Clementia. "Let's see what you've got stored."

"Not much," Severance said coolly. "I rarely record my work. I'm not that good a painter. It's just something I do to pass the time on board."

"What are you going to work on now?"

"I don't know yet. Just thought I'd take a break from watching you run variables." He hunched over the globe as he began to work the controls on the panel. A band of black light appeared inside the diazite, narrowing and changing color as Severance manipulated the controls.

Cidra watched in fascination as the black band became a thin, gray-brown sliver of light. The sliver crinkled into a jagged shape that reminded her of mountains seen from a distance. With a patience that astounded Cidra, Severance called up a new band of color, this one faintly orange, and slowly worked it into the landscape.

"Did anyone ever tell you it's hard to work with someone looking over your shoulder?" Severance asked mildly.

"You've been looking over my shoulder for four days." But he had succeeded in making her feel awkward, as well as annoyed. Cidra went back to the computer. It irritated her whenever Severance provoked a retort or an act of rudeness from her. She should be above that sort of behavior.

During the next few hours she sneaked side glances at the strange landscape forming inside the light-painting globe. She had seen master light-painters at work. The best were usually Harmonics, and the results of their creations were commonplace in Clementia. But the modern schools of light-painting tended to be abstract swirls of color and light blended with infinite care. Most professional light-painters avoided creating exact duplications of scenes from real life. They concentrated instead on prompting an intellectual or emotional response from the viewer with complex, intriguing patterns. The degree of excellence achieved was usually measured by the variety of responses elicited.

But the landscape forming inside Severance's globe was definitely representational. There was nothing abstract about it, Cidra thought as the painting drew more and more of her attention. In fact, it was almost too real.

Inside the globe a brutal landscape of a barren world was emerging. An appallingly desolate expanse of red-orange terrain swept toward distant gray mountains. It was clear that the mountains offered no hope of relief from the barren plains, no promise of vegetation or water, only more endless desolation. The land looked as if it suffered from far too much heat, yet there was a strangely chilled feeling to the scene. Harsh, dry, endless, the landscape provoked no pleasure. Yet Cidra found it harder and harder to look away from it.

"Is it a QED scene?" she asked quietly after a long time.

Severance didn't look up. "Yeah."

"It looks different in your painting than it does in the holotapes I've seen," she ventured, trying to understand herself why that should be so. On the surface Severance's painting looked to be a highly accurate representation of a landscape. But she had seen plenty of shots of QED's empty lands and un-forested mountains. None of them had made her uneasy the way this light-painting did.

"This is the way it looks to me."

Cidra slipped out of her chair and edged closer. "Have you spent a lot of time there?"

"No more than I can help." Severance straightened, staring down into his creation. He studied it for a moment, and then his hand moved briefly on the control panel. The globe shimmered and emptied.

"You didn't save it!" Involuntarily Cidra reached out to catch his fingers, but the damage was done. The painting had disap-peared but not into the memory bank of the light-painting globe. It could never be recalled now. She felt his scarred hand under her palm and hastily withdrew her own hand.

"I told you, I don't save much of my work. It's just a hobby." Severance shut down the globe and stood up to replace the paint-ing machine in a storage bin.

"It's more than a hobby. You have real talent, Severance. I've never seen anything quite like that."

He braced himself with one hand against the bin he had just closed and eyed her steadily. "You like art?"

"Well, doesn't everyone?"

He nodded thoughtfully, appearing to come to a decision. "I'll show you some real art." He paced back to his bunk and went down on one knee to reach into the storage bin underneath.

Cidra watched with interest as he withdrew the metal con-tainer she had spotted her first evening on board. A part of her sensed that she was about to see something very personal, some-thing very important to Severance. In spite of her earlier curiosity about the contents of the box, she was suddenly a little uncertain. She moved a hand instinctively, on the verge of telling Severance that she didn't need to see what was in the container. But it was too late. He had already opened it.

Cidra went toward him slowly, half afraid. Then she caught a glimpse and relaxed with a pleased smile, feeling her mood lighten instantly. Not an uncommon occurrence for viewers of the sort of objects housed in the box. The small carvings often had that effect.

"Laughing Gods! They're wonderful, aren't they? Don't tell me you collect them, Teague Severance. Not after all those disdainful comments you made about leftover Ghost junk." She grinned at him and reached down to pick up one of the exquisitely carved stones.

The object was about the size of her hand and seemed to smile up at her as it lay in her palm, inviting her to smile back. The strangely compelling expression etched into the stone was eons old. No one had yet succeeded in dating the Laughing Gods with any real accuracy. The stone from which they were made was as old as Lovelady and Renaissance. For that matter, no one knew if the creatures were even supposed to represent Ghost gods. Some theories held that the carving might represent individual Ghosts themselves. If that was the case, they had been a very beautiful people, even though they appeared intriguingly alien to human eyes.

Cidra turned the carving over in her hand, admiring the wide, slanting eyes, the vaguely feline profile with its delicate but obviously sensitive nose, lips, and ears. It was difficult to tell what the body was like, because in all the carvings she had seen the Gods wore intricately designed clothing that seemed to float around a slender frame.

It was the smile that bridged the gap between human and alien. The lingering, utterly charming, endearing smile gleamed in the eyes and shaped the full-lipped mouths. There was a subtle, warm laughter in that expression, and on some gut level humans knew that any species that had laughed like that had to be a species with whom communication would have been possible. If the Ghosts had survived and if these carvings were, indeed, representative of them, there could have been contact and perhaps understanding.

"So you don't consider all Ghost finds as garbage, hmm, Severance?" Cidra laughed, handing back the carving she held. "When did you start this collection?"

His expression was unreadable as he stayed on one knee beside the container. "I didn't start it. My brother did. I hung on to it after he died. Once in a while, when I find a good addition, I pick it up."

"I see." She sensed that she had trespassed again, but this time she didn't feel embarrassed or guilty. Severance had more or less invited the conversation. Cidra also sensed a new ambivalence in him, as if a part of him wanted to go on talking about his brother, but another, more dominant, part forbade such openness. She was trying to pick her way through the uncertain situation, wondering if she should ask about his brother, when Severance closed the container without any warning. Cidra blurted out her question.

"When did your brother die?"

"Two years ago."

Intuition made Cidra ask, "On QED?"

Severance shot her a hard look as he rose to his feet. "How did you know?"

She bit her lip. "Something about the light-painting led you to mention the Laughing Gods. Opening the container made you mention your brother."

"Is that a fact? Real Harmonic intuition at work, I imagine."

Cidra flushed, but her eyes were steady. "I'm sorry, Severance."

"Don't be. Did your brilliant Harmonic intuition tell you anything else? Like how my brother died?"

"No, of course not. Please, Severance. I meant no rudeness." She bowed her head very formally. "I'm sorry for your distress. I won't mention the subject again."

"Forget it. My temper is on a short leash these days."

Cidra blinked. "I've noticed. Perhaps you would like another game of Free Market after dinner?"

"Sweet harmony. Always trying to soothe the savage Wolf, aren't you? What I would like after dinner is another large bottle of Rose."

He fit action to words. When Cidra attempted to interest him in a game later that evening, Severance brusquely declined.

"I can't seem to work up any enthusiasm for winning another pile of worthless sardite from you tonight." He uncapped the fresh bottle of Renaissance Rose ale and headed for his familiar evening post in the dim cockpit of the cabin. "Go to bed, Cidra."

She started to say it was too early, but one look at the hard set of his shoulders warned her to keep quiet. She did as she was told, aware that for some reason Fred wasn't assuming his usual position on Severance's shoulder. The rockrug followed her into the lav, fussed around her feet while she changed into her sleeping gown, and then undulated pitifully until she picked him up and carried him into the upper bunk.

"What's the matter?" she whispered. "Don't tell me you're afraid of him tonight? He's just a little tense."

Fred did not appear wildly reassured. He flowed down to Cidra's feet and went to sleep. Cidra closed her eyes and used several rounds of meditation exercises to put herself to sleep. She was as aware of Severance's tension as Fred, and she didn't feel particularly reassured by her own words, either.

She didn't know what woke her a long time later. Nothing had changed in the quiet cabin. The rockrug was still warm and motionless on her ankle, the lights were still dimmed in the cabin, and when she drowsily opened her eyes, she could see Severance's figure still sprawled in his seat. There was a third bottle of the potent ale open beside him. As she watched she realized that he was no longer bothering with the formality of a mug. He was drinking straight from the container. She frowned across the cabin at the ship's clock. Half the sleeping period had passed, and Severance hadn't yet gone to bed.

Cidra experienced a wave of compassion. She knew she

should ignore it. She should bury herself in the bedding, go back to sleep, and forget about Teague Severance sitting in the shadows with his ale. But memories of the way he had looked this afternoon when he'd mentioned his brother filled her mind. The images wouldn't let her take the sensible approach.

Cidra slipped out of the bunk, leaving Fred behind. Severance had been increasingly tense for the past four days. She didn't want to think about what his mood would be like by the time they reached Renaissance. He needed less ale and more rest. Perhaps he needed to talk.

Barefoot, she went forward. She didn't think he had been aware of her approach. He hadn't moved. But as she came to within a pace of the seat in which he reclined, his graveled voice stopped her.

"Get back into bed, Cidra."

She hesitated. She had never heard quite that tone from him. It was laced with ale and warning. Firmly she took another step closer. "It's time you, too, were in bed, Severance."

"I'm the one who makes the decisions on board, remember?"

"Severance, please. For your own good. Go to bed."

"For your own good get back into your bunk. I've had a lot to drink, Cidra. And my mood isn't real sweet."

"It's your brother, isn't it?" she asked gently, putting a hand on his shoulder. Severance's muscles were knotted with tension. "You're sitting here thinking about him. Perhaps it would help to talk."

His hand moved, capturing her wrist before Cidra realized what he was doing. When he lifted his head, there was a fierce hunger in Severance's eyes, a hunger that was clearly visible in the shadows, a look made even more intense by the darkness. Cidra reacted to it physically, a small tremor passing through her. For a moment both of them were completely still. Cidra couldn't have moved if she'd wanted to. Her wrist was chained beneath Severance's marked hand.

"Your intuition doesn't seem to be working very well tonight, little Saint." His voice was a husky rasp along Cidra's nerves. "You should have stayed in your bunk."

"Should I?" Her mind-body connection was no longer functioning properly. Cidra knew with absolute certainty that Severance was right. But her brain seemed to be filled with a jumbled collection of thoughts and emotions, reminding her of the inside of a light-painting globe.

Severance's eyes never left her face. Then, abruptly, his fingers released her wrist. "One last chance. Go on, Cidra. Go back to your bunk."

He had released her, but she didn't feel as if she'd been set free. Cidra desperately tried to sort out the conflicting emotions leaping to life within her. There was an element that wanted to offer comfort to this man. Another part of her sought to understand him through the physical act of touching him, something that made no sense at all to her. And there was still another aspect with which to contend: a confusing flare of warmth in the pit of her stomach that seemed to be spreading into her veins.

She didn't move. "Severance?"

His scarred hand closed once more around her wrist, but somehow the strong grip was more gentle this time. "You had your chance, my sweet, false Harmonic. Come here and let me see how much Wolf blood there is in you. Wondering about it has been driving me slowly out of my mind."

He used his grip on her wrist to pull her down across his thighs. Before Cidra could analyze the situation further, Severance's mouth closed over hers.

SIX

Cidra's first instinct was to free herself. It was an automatic reflex reaction to finding herself so completely off-balance.

She twisted as Severance brought her down into his arms, pressing against his shoulders to try to uncoil herself from the unfamiliar position. But he wasn't paying any attention to her efforts. He cradled her close, his hands large and strong on her thigh and shoulder. His hold tightened as she tried to push away, and with a shock she felt the heavy strength she had sensed lay beneath his lean frame.

But it was the dark, warm, startlingly intimate feel of his mouth on hers that succeeded in stilling her small struggle. She had been kissed before but only in the ritual expressions of affection and greeting that were exchanged between family members and friends among the Harmonics. Those kisses were brief, fleeting touches of lips to cheek, the barest of intimate contact.

This was different, far different, from anything Cidra had ever experienced. She felt her lips urged apart with an aggressive sensuality. She found she couldn't help but respond. Something deep within her seemed suddenly bursting to get out. With a shock she realized that although she had never experienced this kind of thing before, she knew about it. Something that had always lain dormant within her knew everything about this. And the knowledge had nothing to do with what she had always been told about sex.

And, of course, Cidra had been told all about sex by her parents and teachers. They had explained it to her, just as the principles of poetic kinetics and programming theory had been explained. What no one had succeeded in conveying was the sense of anticipation and excitement. No one had told her how her body would grow warm and languid or that there would be a small, curling flame in the pit of her stomach. She shivered, and Severance was immediately aware of it.

"You're a woman under that Harmonic garb, aren't you? A real woman." Severance's voice was husky and textured against her mouth. "Cidra, I need a woman."

Cidra could feel that the tension in Severance was not abating. Rather, she realized that it was being channeled into the physical contact with her. His palm moved on her thigh, exploring the shape of her through the delicate fabric of her gown. She could feel the heat of Severance's body reaching out to envelop her. His fingers tightened on her shoulder as he began to probe her mouth with his tongue. She tasted the ale he had been drinking.

Cidra resisted the intrusion, needing time to adjust to the whirl of new sensations. Severance groaned deep within his chest. His hand under her shoulders shifted, moving upward to capture her head and hold her still.

"Just let me have what I need tonight. I've been going out of my mind. Should have known better. Too much thinking. Too damned much thinking. Eats a man's soul for breakfast."

The sense of compassion that made her climb out of the bunk and come to him washed over Cidra again in full force. Severance needed her. She had never really been needed by anyone in her entire life. Harmonics needed each other but not in this primitive, fundamental, physical manner. Human need in Clementia was on a higher plane, a matter of deep understanding, friendship, and intellectual communion. Cidra had never been able to offer the telepathic contact that enabled such need between two Harmonics to exist and be satisfied. But Severance was asking her to fulfill another kind of need. The concept was strange and infinitely compelling.

Cidra's hands were still braced against his shoulders. Instead of pushing away from him she began to relax. He felt the change in her and deepened the kiss. Without conscious thought her gilded nails flexed, sinking into the fabric of his shirt and then into the sleekly muscled skin underneath the shirt. When he groaned her name, she shivered again.

She felt him tasting her, sampling her as if she were a new glass of Rose ale. He was moving inside her, touching her tongue with his own, and as she became accustomed to the odd caress, she found herself compelled to explore him in return. The desire was suddenly fierce, and she lifted her palms to frame his hard face. Cidra felt him suck in his breath, and she felt his body tremble with yet more tension.

She probed cautiously, wonderingly. The unique intimacy was delicious but also vaguely alarming. His ready response was a lure she hadn't expected, and it would have been difficult to deny even if she had been thinking of resisting it. She wanted this man to react to her, wanted him to respond with greater and greater need.

His arm moved again, fingers gliding down along her side. She froze for an instant when he touched her breast.

"It's all right, Cidra. You feel so good. So soft and strong and delicate. I like the feel of you."

The pad of his thumb moved lazily over her nipple. The gossamer material of her robe offered only a slight barrier. The sensation was tantalizing, and her body reacted to it with a curious tightening. Cidra stirred, suddenly wanting to feel more of him. As if he could read her mind, Severance cupped her breast completely.

As if he could read her mind. But, of course, he couldn't. No more than she could read his. The sensation of emotion and mental closeness was an illusion. This wasn't the physical extension of an intellectual and emotional communion. This wasn't love the way it existed between Harmonics. This was Wolf sex.

The stray thought cut through Cidra's spinning mind, bringing a note of uneasiness into what had been until now a rising, focused crescendo of emotion. "No . . ."

Severance must have felt the flash of uncertainty. He held her tighter, his hand on her breast becoming possessive instead of tantalizing. He broke the contact with her mouth to mutter urgently against her throat, "Be still, Cidra. Don't panic, my sweet Harmonic. I'm not going to hurt you."

"I know." And she did. The sense of certainty came from within herself. His hand moved gently, coaxingly, on her breast, and then his fingers were sliding inside the surplice, seeking a budding nipple. She was suddenly aware of the straining manhood beneath her thighs and inhaled sharply. Slowly he withdrew his hand from under her clothing and slipped his palm down across her stomach. His fingers rested warmly on her robe, just above the gentle mound.

"I only want to hold you, touch you. It's been a long night. Too many long nights."

Too many long nights spent thinking about his brother? Cidra wondered as tenderness filled her. "I understand," she whispered, stroking her fingertips through the thickness of his hair. "It's all right, Severance. I understand. But I don't think this will buy you the peace of mind you seek," she added sadly.

His hand stopped moving on her body, and he went still. Slowly Severance raised his head to look down at her. "I'm willing to give it a try. I could use a little peace of mind."

"I know," she said gently. "I can feel the need in you. But you're going about it in the wrong way."

His eyes were narrowed and gleaming now. "Am I?"

She nodded, smiling tremulously. A part of her wanted to keep quiet and let him take what he thought he needed from her. But that was selfish and dangerous, and it wouldn't give her what she had dreamed of all these years, either. Neither of them would obtain any real serenity.

"You need to talk to a skilled therapist. Someone who has been trained to work with people who have experienced your kind of loss. There are many such doctors, both Harmonic and Wolf, who could help you. You could talk to them, discuss your feelings about your brother. Having sex with me tonight would only buy you a temporary respite."

He stared at her and then swore softly. "Sweet Harmony in hell! I don't believe this. You don't know what you're talking about. Dumb as a torla."

She stiffened under the insult. "Now I've made you angry."

"Well, you sure as a renegade's hell have managed to kill the mood. You thought I needed a little special handling tonight to help me forget Jeude?"

Cidra swallowed unhappily. "Special handling," the mail pilot's slang for quick, easy sex, was not the term she wanted to hear applied to what might have been between herself and Severance. The phrase made it sound light, virtually meaningless. And while she knew intellectually that sex for a Wolf was on a different plane than the communion between Harmonics, she didn't want to think of sex between herself and Severance as being just a little "special handling." But, apparently, that was exactly how Severance saw it.

"I assumed you were sitting here brooding. We had talked about your brother earlier, and there was that light-painting you did. And you've been drinking so much before you go to bed lately." She lifted one shoulder helplessly. "I thought perhaps sad memories were still bothering you."

He closed his eyes in obvious disgust. "I should have known better than to try to take a fake Harmonic to bed." His lashes lifted, revealing a hard, glittering gaze only slightly skewed due to the amount of Renaissance Rose ale in his system. "Let's get one thing understood here, not that it's going to do me any good to explain it. I have not been sitting here getting spaced every night since you've been on board because I'm suffering from deep depression. Jeude was killed a little more than two years ago. I learned to handle that some time back. In fact, I spent one reeting hell of a year as a bonus man on Renaissance, learning to deal with what happened to Jeude. I don't need some damned therapist. Renaissance was my therapist. I do not spend every night drinking myself into a stupor because of Jeude."

"I see." She wondered what a bonus man was.

"No, you don't, but I'm too drunk to explain it to you." He rose to his feet with her in his arms.

Cidra's sense of balance wavered unpleasantly again as Severance staggered a bit, trying to regain his own equilibrium. She clutched at him and tried to wriggle free. "Put me down, please."

"I should." He started toward the tiered bunks. "I should put you down right in the middle of my bed and make love to you until you can't think. I've decided that thinking is part of your problem, Cidra. The Harmonics taught you to think too much. Gave you too much education. Oughta be a law against teaching fake Saints to think. *Therapy.* Saints in hell! The last thing I needed tonight was therapy."

"Severance . . . ?" She realized that he wasn't going to stand her on her feet. Alarm shot through her as they neared the bunks.

"Sure as first-class postage, I'm going to regret this." He halted and lifted her high in his arms.

"Severance!"

Before she could protest further, he dropped her onto the top bunk. Physically it was something of an accomplishment, Cidra had to admit as she tumbled out of his arms and onto the bed. The act of lifting her that high required extensive use of the muscle tone he had obviously been developing on his exercise machine. Considering the fact that he'd been drinking strong ale for hours, it was an even more amazing performance.

Fred awakened with a shudder as Cidra bounced on top of him. She gasped as she felt him move under her leg. For a split second she was afraid that the rockrug might react instinctively, taking a chunk out of her ankle. But he simply slithered to one side in what probably passed for a huff among his species.

Severance glowered at Cidra over the edge of the bunk. "For a while back there you weren't thinking in therapeutic terms, lady. For a while you weren't even thinking in Harmonic terms. For just a short time you were thinking and acting like a real female Wolf. Like a woman. Wonder what the noble Mercer would have thought if he'd seen you with your fancy gold nails digging into a Wolf's neck."

Cidra followed Fred's example and slithered back a few inches. "There's no need to bring Mercer into this."

"You're right. He wouldn't have the vaguest idea what was going on, would he? He wouldn't have known what you were feeling when you were clinging to me like a sexy little snapcat. But I do know, Cidra. I felt what you were feeling."

She flushed under the words, remembering from somewhere that the snapcats found in the central plains of Lovelady's main continent were well known for their almost constant state of being in heat.

"I understand why you're trying to insult me, Severance. You're upset and you've had too much ale. If you have any sense, you'll fall into your bunk and pass out. As for me, I don't have to discuss this sort of thing with you. If you want to talk about it in the morning when you've calmed down and are no longer *spaced*, I'll be willing to sit down and talk. Until then I'm going to sleep."

He shook his head in mock admiration, hands on his hips. "Understanding, intellectual, and formal to the last. A true inspiration to the rest of us lowly mortals."

"Good night, Severance." She turned her back to him, sliding down into the bedding and pulling it up to her throat. She was trembling, but she knew she had to remain quiet and firm. Giving him anything to react to would be inviting more trouble. Severance was obviously spoiling for a fight. All the pent-up tension that he had been unable to release on her body was being funneled into a different sort of release. He was a Wolf looking for combat.

Cidra had had her share of classes in Wolf psychology.

"Cidra!"

She flinched as she felt his hand on her arm. "Please, Severance. Go to sleep. I don't think you're going to want to remember this in the morning."

"You're probably right." His hand fell away. "With any luck I won't."

A small jolt went through both bunks as Severance's full weight hit the bottom one. An unnatural quiet filled the cabin. Cidra's eyes were wide as she gazed at the bulkhead wall. Severance had warned her more than once that the cabin of a mail ship could be a very small place for two people.

"I hope," Severance muttered from the lower bunk, "that you have a lot of trouble falling asleep tonight."

Cidra was quiet for a moment, remembering the feel of his hands on her. She ought to keep her mouth shut, but the question was out before she could stop it. "Severance? How did you get those scars on your hands?"

"Don't you ever stop asking questions?" He paused for a moment, then let out a deep sigh. "I had a run-in with a killweaver once. Their webs leave marks. We can't all have soft, smooth hands like yours, Cidra."

Cidra wanted to ask more questions on the subject, but common sense finally won over to stop her. But she was awake for a very long time trying to analyze the events of the last hour. There was a great deal to assess, but a single, stark fact emerged from all the rest and would not dissolve: She had reacted to Severance's lovemaking with a dismaying intensity. Somehow she needed to deal with that because the discovery of her own desire was a threat to the future she envisioned.

Step by step she reran the scene in her mind. She had gone to Severance initially out of compassion. Very well, that was an understandable, even laudable, motivation. When he had initiated the embrace, she had sensed a raw need in him that she assumed was based on his effort to break the brooding mood caused by thoughts of his brother. Her response to his kiss had again been understandable, if not exactly within normal bounds. She had instinctively wanted to comfort him. It was an extension of the compassion she had felt.

But compassion and the desire to comfort had all too quickly metamorphosed into something else—something dangerous. Ever since she was a child she had learned to keep a tight rein on the emotional reactions that betrayed her Wolf heritage. There was no other way she could hope to fit into Harmonic society.

Severance had a way of shaking loose the grip she worked so hard to maintain, and tonight he'd succeeded in unleashing a very primitive, very Wolf side of her nature.

Bravely Cidra faced the implications. She was a Wolf. But if her quest was successful, she would be able to transcend her status. In the meantime there would be times when her actions would not be those of a true Harmonic. She had known that all her life. Nothing had changed tonight. She could deal with the problem. And in one sense her actions tonight were perfectly comprehensible. After all, she was bound to be curious about certain aspects of her nature. Every thinking human being, Harmonic or Wolf, needed to explore and understand his or her own personality. It was a sign of maturity.

Cidra began to relax as she found the handle she needed to accept her responses in Severance's arms. Like it or not, part of her was still Wolf. That part had a right to be investigated, analyzed, and understood. Someday, when she found the object of her quest, she would be leaving behind the Wolf components of her nature. It only made sense to learn something about those components while she could. No knowledge was to be disdained. And knowledge, she told herself firmly, was all she had been seeking in Severance's arms.

Her response to Severance had been in the nature of an experiment.

Severance awoke with a headache that must have rivaled the one the Screamer had given Cidra. He opened his eyes with great caution. The smell of hot coffade was wafting through the cabin. Unmoving, he stared up at the bottom of Cidra's bunk.

In a just universe any man who'd had as much Renaissance Rose ale as he'd had the night before would have suffered a convenient lapse of memory. But Severance had learned long ago that the universe was short on justice, at least in the tiny corner occupied by the worlds of Stanza Nine.

'Gesics. He needed a fistful of the fizzers. Slowly Severance sat up on the edge of the bunk, realizing that he hadn't bothered to undress before passing out. A swirl of red materialized at his elbow. Coffade was thrust into his hand. Severance decided he wasn't too proud to take it. First things first, and the noble apologies could come later.

"Thanks," he muttered. "You know where I keep the 'gesics?"

"I'll get you one." The too-cheerful red morning surplice robe moved toward the small locker where the ship's medical stores were kept.

"Several," Severance directed in a soft voice. "I'll need several tablets."

She returned with two. He didn't argue. He wasn't up to arguing. Popping them under his tongue, he waited for the analgesic to hit his system. When the tablets were dissolved, he took a long swallow of the hot coffade. A swollen Renaissance swamp-bubble occupying the place normally filled by his brain slowly began to shrink. It had been close; another few minutes and it would have burst. Severance lifted his head and saw that Cidra had slipped back to the front of the cabin.

"Smart female," he growled. "Give the beast his coffade and 'gesics, and then get out of his way. Where did an almost-Harmonic learn such a practical program of human relations?"

"I keep telling you, Severance, I'm a fast learner." But she smiled at him from the computer console where she had apparently already begun the day's work.

"Learn a lot last night?" Stupid crack. Severance regretted the words as soon as they hit the air.

"A great deal. Feel like eating?"

"No." Her smile annoyed him. "I mean, no thanks. Not yet."

"Let me know when you are. I'll put a prespac in the heater."
She turned back to the console.

Severance thought about the situation. "There's something
wrong here," he finally announced.

"You're just not feeling well, that's all."

He gritted his teeth. "I mean, there's something wrong in ad-
dition to that small problem." He shot her a suspicious glance.
"You are not, by any chance, operating under the assumption that
I don't remember what happened last night, are you?"

She didn't look at him, her attention on the screen in front of
her. "I assume your memory is as good as mine."

"Unfortunately." Severance climbed slowly to his feet. Better
to get this part over and done. He held on to the edge of the upper
bunk and glared balefully toward his companion. "Cidra?"

"Yes, Severance?" She turned her head with polite inquiry.

"I regret what happened last night," he began in an incredibly
stilted tone. "You are a passenger on board this ship. You are entitled to my protection. As the pilot in command, I have an obligation to remain, above all, in command of myself. I assure you
that what happened last night will not happen again." He felt both
martyred and heroic.

Cidra regarded him for a long moment, her gaze searching
and, he could have sworn, gentle. Then she inclined her head in
formal acceptance of his apology.

"Thank you, Severance, but there is no need for you to accept
the blame for what happened last night. I do not view the incident
as anything serious."

He stared at her. "You don't?"

"Of course not." She waved the passionate scene aside with a
graceful movement of her hand.

Severance began to feel something besides martyrdom and
heroism. He began to feel irritated. "Then you obviously don't
know what the consequences could have been."

"I realize what might have happened if matters had gone to
the extreme conclusion. I have studied the principles of human
reproduction."

Severance's hand tightened on the edge of the bunk. "I keep forgetting your extensive education."

She smiled quite brilliantly. "Precisely. And that is exactly how I view last night's events. They were quite educational. Because, while I have studied the physical interaction of male and female, I have not yet had an opportunity to examine it on a personal level. There are risks involved in such a study, of which I am well aware. But I admit I have enough Wolf in me at this point to be curious about such matters. And I realize that once I have found the object of my quest, I may never again be interested in pursuing this particular line of investigation. Harmonics in general don't seem very interested in sex, as we both know. Once I am one, I will also probably lose interest. In the meantime there is something to be learned, and last night I had a sudden, unexpected interest in learning. You mustn't blame yourself or take responsibility for the risks involved. I was a willing participant. I am, however, also cognizant of the risks, and I give you my word that I will exercise better judgment in the future."

Severance listened to the little speech with a growing desire to break something. "Let me get this straight," he finally said faintly. "You're taking responsibility for last night's little fiasco?"

She inclined her head in that formal, gracious way that was beginning to infuriate him.

"And you view the 'incident' as simply a learning experience?"

"An experiment," she amplified, smiling even more graciously.

"An experiment," he echoed. Slowly he pushed himself away from the bunk. "A scientific experiment." He paced toward her. His headache was breaking through the barrier raised by the 'gesic tablets. He realized that something of what he was feeling must have been showing on his face, because the brilliance in Cidra's smile was fading. A distinct wariness was beginning to take its place. She stood up as he glided to a halt in front of her, but she didn't back away from him.

"Uh, Severance . . ."

He ignored the uncertain tone. Deliberately he reached out,

catching her chin with his hand. "Listen to me, my sweet, false Harmonic. I am in charge around here. I told you that the first day. And I am taking full responsibility for what happened last night. You were not conducting a scientific experiment. You were being seduced. Furthermore, you will never conduct scientific experiments with me, is that understood? *I will not be used to further your education.* If we ever wind up in a bunk together, it will be for the usual Wolf reasons. It will be because we've got a hunger for each other that can't be satisfied in any other way. It will *not* happen because you're conducting experiments! Do I make myself clear, Cidra Rainforest?"

"Clear as diazite, Teague Severance."

He hesitated a moment longer, making sure that the last of the gracious brilliance had disappeared from her expression. Then, satisfied, he released her chin and stalked to the lav.

An experiment. Saints in hell! One thing was for certain, Severance decided as he stood under the spray: He was going to have to keep a lid on his consumption of ale after dinner. The feelings of martyrdom and heroism returned.

But there was another sensation too. A tantalizing, aching, hungry sensation that didn't fade as the ship day progressed. It stirred every time the memory of Cidra's response in his arms flickered through his brain. Severance was afraid he was going to have to learn to live with it, because as long as Cidra was around, his awareness of her was not going to disappear.

Cidra did her utmost to adhere to the normal ship-day routine. The morning's scene stayed fresh in her mind, and she knew that for the first few hours following it she was walking on thin crystal. One false step and everything might shatter.

There was more than one meaning of the term *Wolf.* It referred in part to an ancient, mythical creature reputed to be an extreme carnivore, an animal well adapted to violent survival. The other meaning was just as old. Wolf also meant a discordant, unharmonious chord struck in music, an instance of dissonance. Both meanings suited the general population of non-Harmonics, and Severance was a fine example. But today he seemed as determined as she was to tread lightly, and by the time of the evening meal, things seemed relatively normal.

When Cidra suggested a game of Free Market after dinner, she thought at first that Severance was going to refuse. She saw him glance at the half finished bottle of ale he had started during the meal, and then he seemed to change his mind.

"All right," he agreed, reaching for the playing field.

Anxious to please, Cidra had an idea. "I know the game isn't very interesting for you without real stakes."

He shrugged and set out the cubes. "I'll survive."

She coughed delicately, feeling quite adventurous. "I was thinking," she began cautiously, "that we might try livening up the game for you by making genuine wagers."

Severance's hand paused over the stack of sardite chips. Something gleamed in his eyes and then vanished beneath an expression of polite inquiry. "What sort of wagers?"

"Well, I haven't got much, and it would be foolish to bet anything valuable, anyway, since you're bound to win, but there is the matter of preparing the meals. We've been more or less alternating the task, but we could decide that the loser would put the prespacs into the heater for, say, a full ship day."

Severance lowered his lashes, ostensibly concentrating on counting out sardite chips. "A possibility."

"Well?"

"All right. It's a bet. Whoever loses gets stuck fixing meals for the next cycle."

Cidra felt a strange rush of excitement, an emotion she hadn't yet experienced when she played Free Market. She nodded and sat forward, determined to pay extra close attention to the game. She would probably lose—she always lost to Severance—but perhaps not as badly this time.

It came as an almost overwhelming surprise when she won. At first she couldn't believe it. Cidra stared at the blank spot in front of Severance where his sardite chips were normally stacked. All of the chips were on her side of the table. She was suddenly quite euphoric.

"I won!"

He leaned back in his seat, mouth twisted in a dry smile. "So you did. How does it feel?"

She grinned with unabashed enthusiasm. "Very pleasant. You're going to do all the meals tomorrow?"

"Looks like it."

"You don't mind?" she pressed.

"A man's got to pay his gambling debts." He leaned forward and scooped up cubes and playing pieces. "Want to try another game?"

She did, but there was a problem. "I can't think of anything else to bet."

"How about one of my Laughing Gods against that fireberyl comb you wear?" Severance suggested very casually.

Cidra was shocked. "They're both much too valuable."

"That's what will make the game interesting."

She shook her head firmly. "I couldn't."

"The way you just played, I doubt you'll have any trouble winning again. You seem to have gotten the hang of Free Market."

That much was true. She was obviously improving rapidly as a player. The strange euphoria was still bubbling in her blood. Recklessly she smiled. "All right, Severance, it's a bet."

He smiled too. That smile with all the teeth.

Then he coolly and methodically proceeded to demolish her in the next game.

When it was over, Cidra sat feeling dazed by the loss. She realized belatedly that she hadn't expected to lose. The first win had given her an unnatural confidence in her new skills. It was an unwarranted confidence, apparently. Severance said nothing, waiting for the impact of the loss to sink in. Wistfully she watched him retrieve the last sardite chip from her side of the table, and then she lifted her gaze to his.

"You won."

"Ummm." He sat waiting quietly, with an air of grave expectation.

"I suppose you want the comb."

"It's customary to pay a gambling debt immediately."

"Of course." She straightened proudly, determined to be a good loser. She fished the beautiful fireberyl comb from her coronet of hair and slowly held it out to him.

He took it from her and examined it. The trapped flames of the polished fireberyl flickered in the light. "It's very beautiful."

"My parents gave it to me when they saw me off on my quest." Memories of her mother's gentle, understanding expression as she had said good-bye to her daughter tugged at Cidra for the first time in days. Her father had been equally compassionate. Their understanding was tempered with the natural emotional distance a Harmonic instinctively maintained with a Wolf. They had both known that this farewell had been coming since the day Cidra was born. Their young Wolf cub had to find her own way. They could offer shelter, but they could not provide a true way of life for her.

Severance looked up. "So your parents know you're on your way to Renaissance?"

Surprised by the question, Cidra hesitated and then admitted, "No. I don't think so. I implied that I would begin my search on Lovelady. They would have had doubts about the wisdom of going to Renaissance."

"Especially as a passenger in a mail ship."

"They might have had doubts," Cidra said firmly, "but they would not have argued with my decision. I am an adult. They respect that status. I simply did not wish to cause them undue concern. Renaissance has a reputation for being very dangerous."

He studied her for a moment. "Your parents don't know you very well, do they?"

"They are kind, intuitive people who saw to it that I had an excellent education and proper training in the Klinian laws," Cidra informed him proudly.

"But no matter what they did, they couldn't make you into a Harmonic. You're a Wolf. So they don't really *know* you."

"You don't really know me, either, Severance, so don't make any judgments," she heard herself retort. "You can't ever get to know me the way Harmonics know each other. Wolves aren't capable of that kind of communication." She got to her feet, aware that she was trembling. Without a word she retreated into her bunk with her precious copy of Nisco's *Serenity and Ritual*.

Severance made no move to stop her. He put away the playing pieces, stashed the field, and then carefully tucked the fireberyl comb into a pouch on the utility loop that was hanging near his bunk. He decided that he, too, would read tonight. He could do without any more ale for a while.

When he finally stretched out to sleep, he had a last mental image of Cidra in his arms. In the fantasy she was wearing nothing except the fireberyl comb in her hair. The flames in the comb were dim compared to the flames in her eyes.

Cidra spent the next couple of days working diligently on her programming project. The tensions of the first week had been far more severe than she could have imagined. Occasionally she had unpleasant visions of how much worse her situation would have been if she had accepted passage with someone such as Scates, the man who had come to her hotel room in Valentine.

There was no doubt that living in close quarters with Teague Severance had its risks and that his mood could be somewhat volatile, but she was learning to manage the unstable atmosphere between them. And she had to admit that Severance was able to deal with the situation. He seemed grimly determined to get to Renaissance without losing his temper or his self-control again. She knew instinctively that he placed a high value on his own sense of control. He was the pilot in command, and the concept was important to him. His sense of responsibility ran deep.

They were four days away from Renaissance when disaster struck in the lav. Cidra had just turned on the spray and was anticipating her all-important evening shower when she realized that something had gone wrong. The spray bubbled briefly from the surrounding walls and then died. She stared at the disappearing drops of water in dismay. Keeping the length of her showers to a minimum was hard enough; to do without a spray altogether was unthinkable.

"Severance!"

He was at the panel in an instant, sounding alarmed. "What's wrong?"

Clutching the panel to shield her naked body, she peered around the edge. "The spray fixture is broken. There's no water."

His alert, concerned expression turned into one of sardonic interest. "Is that a fact?"

"Severance, this is serious! We're four days from Renaissance. What are we going to do?"

"Use a lot of deodorant?"

She glared at him. "This is not a joke."

"I know it's not for you. Anyone who spends a couple of hours a day in the lav probably finds this a full-scale catastrophe."

"I do *not* spend two hours a day in here, and it *is* a full-scale catastrophe. I have never gone one day in my life without a proper bath."

"It's all right. Fred and I aren't overly sensitive to a little sweat. We've learned to take things in stride. I'm sure that after a couple of days we'll all be accustomed to each other."

Cidra was appalled. "I can't possibly go four days without a bath. You have to do something, Severance."

"Such as?"

"Such as fix the spray! You keep telling me you're the one in charge around here. Well, here's your chance to prove it."

He leaned against the bulkhead, arms crossed, and considered the situation. "What's in it for me?"

"A clean passenger."

"I was thinking of something a little more useful."

She eyed him warily. "What do you want?"

"A kiss from my passenger."

Cidra blinked in astonishment. "That's all you want in exchange for fixing the spray?"

"Do we have a deal?"

"Maybe you can't fix it. Maybe that's why you're teasing me like this."

"A deal?" he persisted.

"Can you fix it?" she countered.

"Lady, I may not have your education, but I'm good with my hands. In a situation this critical, a few practical manual skills are a hell of a lot more important than a headful of fancy Harmonic philosophy."

She smiled winningly up at him. "I have great respect for knowledge of any kind."

"A deal?"

Cidra nodded once, very firmly. "A deal."

Severance straightened away from the wall. "Stand aside."

He had the spray working twenty minutes later. Cidra was elated. "You're a magician, Teague Severance. Where did you learn such skills?"

He activated the spray experimentally to make sure it was now functioning properly. "Here and there," he said vaguely. "I've always had a knack for keeping machinery running. Comes in useful on Renaissance."

"On Renaissance?"

"Yeah. That planet's hell on machinery. The heat and humidity are enough to cause problems on their own, but there are also a whole bunch of corrosive plants and soil materials. A good mechanic can name his own price on Renaissance. Stuff is always breaking down."

"Were you a mechanic for a while?"

"I told you. I spent a year as a bonus man." He gave her a brief, hard smile.

"A bonus man is a mechanic?" she asked.

"In a way. He does whatever he gets paid to do." He stepped back. "Your spray awaits, Otanna."

"Thank you, Severance." She hesitated and then quickly moved close to him. Balancing on her toes, she braced herself against his shoulders and brushed his mouth with her own.

Cidra had disappeared into the lav before Severance could catch hold of her and claim a more thorough kiss. He stood staring at the closed lav panel and tried to tell himself that it was just as well. No sense fueling the ache in his gut.

But a part of him didn't buy that logic for a minute.

SEVEN

Cidra's first impression of Renaissance was that it was too green. As the planet had filled the observation port during *Severance Pay*'s approach, some of that endless green had been broken up by the blue expanse of oceans. But once the ship had touched down, there was little to interfere with the sensation of endlessly lush, dark foliage, stretching forever in all directions.

Port Try Again was merely a drop of nongreen plunked down into the limitless jungle at the mouth of a major river. It would surely vanish at once if its human builders and maintainers ever departed. The jungle looked fully capable of washing over the pitifully frail-looking structures of gleaming triaton and diazite, gobbling up everything in its path and closing up the small wound. The tough triaton was an alloy formed from elemental metals wrested from the small polar regions of the planet. It had proven to be one of the few building materials capable of withstanding the corroding effects of the jungle. Its discovery had been a boon to company exploration teams, saving the firms the cost of importing heavy, expensive materials.

Try Again hardly seemed the major port city of a planet, Cidra decided as *Severance Pay* settled onto the landing strip. It was a small, shaggy boom town, the one place on Renaissance where employees of the highly competitive exploration and development companies supposedly mingled without risk of hostility or outright violence. Renaissance was a tough world, and the people imported by the companies to tame it had a reputation that matched the planet's in many respects. Port Try Again had very few written laws but several unwritten ones. Among them was the understanding that the representatives of the different companies would coexist peacefully while in town. Chief among the written laws was that the town was the one place on the planet where it was illegal to carry a pulser. Outside the gates the side arm was a familiar sight.

Everyone needed the clearing in the jungle that was Try Again. It was the point of shipping and receiving for the planet, a supply depot, a place where people could relax in safety. The town had been hacked out along the banks of the wide, silty river that offered a green-walled highway into the vast depths.

But even before Cidra had begun to take this all in, she noticed that there was something wrong with the air of Renaissance.

"You'll get used to it," Severance told her.

"It's like breathing soup!" It wasn't that bad, Cidra admonished herself as she followed Severance toward the terminal buildings. But the still, heavy muggyness was a drastic change from the clean, crisp air of Port Valentine and an even greater change from the perfumed gardens of Clementia. With a sense of dismay she realized that the fine fabric of her formal midday surplice was already damp and clinging. The light, gossamer, green material seemed suddenly to have acquired a different texture. Green had been the wrong color to wear, anyway, she decided. There was far too much of it around.

She put the condition of her clothing out of her mind in favor of concentrating on the new and strange surroundings. In spite of the thick heat and the unrelenting backdrop of jungle, she felt a rush of anticipation. Renaissance was the first stop on her journey of discovery. Her quest had begun in earnest.

"Stay in sight while I arrange to have the cargo put in time-lock storage. I'm going to be busy, and I don't want to have to waste time wondering where you are." Severance gave the order somewhat absently as he led her into the air-conditioned terminal building.

Cidra didn't bother to acknowledge the instructions. She was too occupied with observing the jumble of people and luggage surrounding her. A commercial freighter had recently arrived, and the new load of mostly company employees was a mixed lot. The majority were wearing the distinctive uniforms that identified their employers on sight. Here and there amid the spiffy, dashing uniforms was a ship suit of dull gray or brown, similar to the one Severance wore. Independent pilots or a temporarily unemployed worker looking for a job, Cidra deduced. There were plenty of high-paying jobs to be had on Renaissance if a person was willing to work.

Nowhere in the crowd were there any other formal midday surplices. Cidra felt strangely isolated. She was aware that she was attracting a certain amount of polite interest. Harmonics rarely traveled alone on the rare occasions when they left Clementia. They were almost always to be seen in the company of other Harmonics, moving through crowded passenger terminals in small, protected clusters. Her lone status no doubt seemed strange to those around her.

Cidra edged closer to Severance, who was leaning over a desk. He had both hands planted on the surface. Out of the corner of her eye she saw the grim set of his mouth and idly wondered what the young woman behind the desk had done to earn his displeasure. The woman was an attractive creature, Cidra realized. Her long blond hair was loose around her shoulders, framing an elfin profile. She was wearing the uniform of the company that had the terminal operation contract, and Cidra guessed that the outfit had been specially tailored for her full-breasted figure. Becoming interested in the interchange, Cidra turned to study the situation more closely.

"Don't give me that, Gena," Severance snapped. "You know I've got a priority claim on a time locker. Saints know I've paid your company enough for it. I want my mail off-loaded and put into storage within an hour."

"I'm sorry, Severance, but the computer doesn't show any record of your claim. You'll have to get in line behind every other pilot who wants a locker."

"The rest of those pilots can go line up at the nearest lav." He reached into a pouch on his utility loop and removed a strip of plastic. "Shove this into your computer and see if it jogs its memory banks."

"There's no need to shout, Teague."

"I'm not shouting. Not yet. You'll know it when I do. Find my locker, Gena, or I'll pile the mail here on your desk."

Cidra saw the rueful dismay in the woman's eyes. Apparently she believed Severance. Gena took the plastic record-of-contract and fed it into the port computer. There was a pause while the machine scanned the information and tried to correlate it with its records. A second or so later a lush, feminine voice responded to the waiting humans.

"Time-lock storage priority claim acknowledged. Assign locker G17."

Severance smiled faintly in triumph, taking back his strip of plastic. "Thank you, Gena. You're always so helpful. Don't know what I'd do without you."

"Teague, you know you'd get a lot more help from me if you tried a more diplomatic approach once in a while."

"No point in being diplomatic with a computer."

The blonde's eyes widened innocently. "I'm not a computer, Teague. Not a single ounce of cold metal anywhere in my body. And I can prove it." Gena inhaled deeply, filling the specially tailored uniform to perfection. She smiled.

Severance returned the smile, his mouth curving with dry, reluctant amusement. "I'll just bet you can, Gena. The only problem is, I'm not sure I'd survive the experience."

"I'd go easy on you the first time," Gena assured him softly.

"Appreciate that. I'll let you know if I ever work up enough nerve to give it a try." He turned away without waiting for a response, his smile vanishing. He caught hold of Cidra's arm. "Let's go. We've got work to do."

Cidra thought about the smiles she had just witnessed. She had felt uncomfortable during the blatantly sexy bantering. And she was very much aware of Gena's thoughtful gaze following her as she was swept through the terminal.

"What are we going to do, Severance?"

"First we take care of the mail."

Cidra nodded. "The mail always comes first."

"You're learning," he said approvingly. "You can handle the computer manifest while I supervise the unloading."

"And then?"

"Then I'm going to take you to a friend's place and stash you for the duration."

Alarmed, Cidra halted in her tracks. "Stash me for the duration? What are you talking about, Severance? I must have complete freedom to move around whenever we're in port. I'll need to consult the local Archive computer and talk to people who might be able to confirm some leads I'm following. I will not be stashed."

"Calm down, will you? All I'm saying is that you're going to have to stay someplace while we're in port. You'll be free to do what you need to."

"Why not on board *Severance Pay*?"

"Because I'll be staying on board ship," he told her grimly.

"So what's changed? We've both been sleeping on board for the past two weeks. I don't see why I have to move out for the short time we're here at Try Again."

"Take my word for it, it will do us both good to have a break from each other."

"But Severance, I—" Cidra closed her mouth abruptly as she

remembered Gena's smile. And then she remembered Severance's bouts of heavy exercise and even heavier consumption of ale. Most of all she remembered the night he had pulled her down across his thighs and told her he needed a woman. "Oh, I understand."

He shot her a sidelong glance as he propelled her toward the ship. "It's wonderful traveling with an educated woman."

Cidra smiled wryly. "As long as you're going to stash me, why not in a hotel? Why do I have to go to your friend's home?"

"You'll be more comfortable with Desma," he informed her cryptically. "Hotels in Try Again can get a little rough."

Desma Kady was something of a surprise to Cidra. The older woman was large without being fat; she was tall and commanding with pale blue eyes that held intelligence and humor in fairly equal proportions. Her face had once been beautiful and had matured into a combination of features that could best be described as striking and interesting. There was a forceful personality in that face, and Cidra liked it.

Desma met Severance and Cidra at the entrance to a long building fashioned of triton walls and diazite windows. Cidra knew the diazite had been tempered for extra strength because it had the peculiar yellow cast the process produced. She wondered why the already tough, clear material had needed to be turned into virtual armor for this building. Desma was wearing a one-piece white jumpsuit, the kind usually worn by lab workers.

"Severance! You're back. Bring me my new scope?" Desma laughed engagingly, including Cidra in the welcome.

"Have I ever failed you, Desma?" Severance held out the package he had retained when the rest of the mail had gone into temporary storage at the terminal.

"Never. It's one of the things that makes you so wonderful." She leaned forward and kissed him on the cheek in a motherly fashion, and then she smiled at Cidra. "Otanna, you are most welcome. You honor my home."

The formal greeting was a soothing balm on Cidra's ears. She hadn't realized how much she had missed the small, socially comforting rituals of Clementia. Although she was no Harmonic, this woman obviously knew the ceremonies. With a sense of gratitude Cidra inclined her head.

"You are most gracious, Otanna Kady. I thank you for your generosity, and I regret the inconvenience of my sudden arrival."

"The inconvenience is as nothing. Please do not regard it."

Severance stepped in before Cidra could follow up with the next formal statement. He must have remembered that this could go on for a long time before a ritualistic conclusion was reached. "That's enough, both of you. Desma, this is Cidra Rainforest. She's not really a Harmonic; she just looks like one because she was born and raised in Clementia. A clear-cut case of an overeducated female. Cidra, meet Desma Kady. She's another female with a lot of education. Mostly in the biological sciences."

Cidra made some quick connections in her mind and then once again inclined her head, this time adding the nuance of deep respect. "Of course. Desma Kady. A most distinguished specialist in the field of bioluminescence. I read your last monograph when I was preparing to enter it into the Archive computers. The one on the Rigor Mortis Mantis."

Desma laughed in delight, dropping the formality. "That's me. The lady who works with bugs that glow in the dark. Where did you find Severance?"

"In a tavern," Cidra said honestly.

"That doesn't surprise me. What were you doing in the sort of place he'd hang out in?"

"Looking for transportation to Renaissance." Cidra smiled proudly. "I'm a member of his crew."

Desma flashed a quick glance at Severance. "Is that right?"

"She's on a crew contract, Desma, not a convenience contract. Mind if we go inside? It's hotter than a miner's temper out here."

"You don't want to come into the lab. It's no cooler in there." Desma looked at Cidra. "Have to keep it at normal Renaissance temperature and humidity. The bugs like it that way. Let's go to the house."

She started off, leaving Severance and Cidra to follow her next door to a smaller, company-built structure that looked much like all the other standard-issue, company-built housing Cidra had seen in Port Try Again. The structure was the usual octagonal design, the rooms inside cut up like pieces of pie under a convex roof. Deliciously cool air awaited beyond the invisible electronic grid of the deflector screens used to keep out small, flying insects. The invention of the screens was one of the technological advances that had made the exploration of Renaissance possible. When they were constructed along larger, heavy duty lines, the deflectors were capable of warding off most Renaissance wildlife. Huge networks of the screens protected the perimeter of Try Again.

"How long are you going to be in Try Again this time, Severance?" Desma led her guests into a wide, wedge-shaped seating area and punched up a selection of cold drinks from a serving tray. She motioned Cidra to sit down.

"I'm figuring five or six days. Long enough to find a few good shipments to take to some of the company outposts I'll be hitting later." He shrugged, helping himself to a mug of iced Renaissance Rose ale. "Maybe I'll get lucky and pick up some mail for QED. We'll be leaving Renaissance in a couple of weeks."

"Did you want to stay with me while Severance is running around in the jungle, Cidra?" Desma leaned back in a chair and crossed her legs at the ankle as she sipped from a glass of fruit juice.

"Oh, no," Cidra assured her quickly. "I'll be going with Severance when he makes his trips to the outposts. I agreed to a crew contract with him because I want an opportunity to visit as many places as possible."

"Off to see the Stanza Nine system after all those years stuck in Clementia, hm?" Desma was amused.

"Not exactly," Severance answered in a flat voice before Cidra could respond. "She's looking for something. Something she thinks will let her go back to Clementia as a full-fledged Harmonic. Waste of time, but she'll probably learn a lot en route. Cidra's bound and determined to expand her education."

Cidra flushed under the thinly veiled derision. She was getting used to Severance's remarks regarding her quest, but she was embarrassed that he would make them when others were present. "You must forgive him, Otanna Kady. His manners appear to be very unformed at times."

"I know," Desma said easily, ignoring Severance's scowl. "I'm used to it. Don't be embarrassed for him."

Severance stood up without any warning. "I'll let the two of you dissect my character in private. I've got work to do. I've got to find the local rep for ExcellEx and get his sensors off my hands. Cidra, you're to stay with Desma until we're ready to leave Port Try Again."

"I understand, Severance."

His glare intensified at her meekness. "And stay out of trouble."

"Yes, Severance." She deliberately made her voice even gentler and more acquiescent.

Severance seemed briefly undecided about what to say next. Finally he turned to the older woman, who was watching the exchange with barely concealed amusement.

"Thanks, Desma. I appreciate this."

"Anytime, Severance. Anytime, that is, that you turn up with an intelligent, well-mannered houseguest. I'm sure it won't happen often."

"Sweet Harmony. Why is every female in sight picking on me today?"

"Probably because you make such a good target," Cidra offered far too politely. When he swung around to confront her, she smiled her most brilliant smile. "Have a good time, Severance. I'll be here when you're ready to leave."

"Yeah, that's what I'm afraid of." He stalked to the door and disappeared into the glaring heat. The deflector screens hissed faintly as he passed between them.

A long, speculative silence pervaded the cool room. Through

the window Cidra could see nothing except the row of octagonal houses and lab buildings across the dusty street. The street shouldn't have been dusty. It was paved with an impermeable membrane that was almost as tough as the triaton and diazite of the structures. But there was a general grittiness in the air that hung over the entire town.

Desma Kady took a long swallow of her fruit juice. "Well," she announced at long last, "this is all very interesting, you know. Small towns like Port Try Again tend to thrive on new gossip. And you're bound to create some. I hope you won't mind?"

"I'm rapidly becoming accustomed to Wolf ways," Cidra told her. She tried her fruit juice. She couldn't recognize the flavors but found the drink delicious. "A local product?" she asked, indicating her glass.

"Oh, yes. Like it?"

"Very much." She took another sip.

"I'm very glad to have you stay here, Cidra. My husband is away for several days doing some fieldwork on toxins. It will be nice to have company. But I have to admit, I'm slightly curious. Why aren't you staying on board ship? Severance usually does, and if you're a member of his, uh, crew . . . ?" She left the question hanging delicately.

Cidra adjusted the fold of her midday robe. "I believe Severance wants a little privacy for a few days. The cabin of a mail ship is a small place for two people to share for two weeks. He thought we should have a break from each other."

"Ah."

Cidra looked up, hoping her polite expression hid the faint wistfulness she was feeling. "I think he needs the privacy for other reasons too. There's the matter of his obtaining some, uh, special handling. Wolves are very interested in sex, you know."

"I know," Desma assured her, smiling faintly. "I've been married for some time. Four children, all grown now."

Cidra swallowed fruit juice. "I'm sure you understand the situation."

"So this really is a crew contract you've signed? Not a convenience contract?"

"Definitely."

"This gets more intriguing by the minute. You know, Severance signed a convenience contract once. No one knows for certain what happened, but the contract was terminated by mutual consent by the time *Severance Pay* hit Renaissance. I almost felt sorry for the young woman. She was absolutely enraged, according to those who saw her. Not many did. She never even left the terminal. Severance bought her a return ticket and she left on the next outbound commercial freighter. People said it was a miracle that the woman and Severance had avoided killing each other somewhere between Lovelady and Renaissance."

"He told me the story."

"Did he?" Desma seemed surprised.

"By the way of warning, I think. I informed him I wasn't interested in a convenience contract."

"And he took you on as crew? There's a registered agreement?"

"Well, at the moment it's still an informal, verbal agreement, but Severance and I both take it quite seriously."

"More and more interesting," Desma mused. Then she set down her empty glass. "Did you really read that dull piece I did on bioluminescence?"

Cidra nodded eagerly. "One of the advantages of being an archivist. One gets to explore so many different fields. Unfortunately I'm not an expert in any one area, except First Family fiction, which is not exactly on the cutting edge of research. But I can assure you that your article was far from dull. There were many requests for it from Harmonic researchers doing work in related fields."

Desma looked pleased. "Would you be interested in seeing the lab?"

"I would enjoy that very much."

The long lab structure was just as Desma had promised, hot and muggy like the outside air. In addition the heavy atmosphere was overlaid with a distinctive, unpleasant odor that caused Cidra to wrinkle her nose as she stepped inside.

"Bugs," Desma explained cheerfully. "Put a lot of them in one place and they tend to smell. We keep things as clean as possible, but you can't ever escape the odor completely. You get used to it."

"That's what Severance said about the humidity." Cidra looked around with grave interest. Long aisles of cages constructed of clear panels stretched from one end of the lab building to the other. In some cases the panels were of tempered diazite, just like the windows. Cidra contemplated what that said about the creatures housed inside. It took a great deal to cut through tempered diazite.

"Acid," Desma said, pausing beside a yellowed diazite cage to peer inside. "That's the reason for the tempered walls. Some of these critters produce an acid that can dissolve normal diazite or clear silitron."

"Severance said there were many corrosive elements on Renaissance. He said it was hard on machinery." Cidra looked into the cage. "I don't see anything in there."

"Keep looking. There, on that branch. See the eyes?"

Cidra saw the eyes, all right. She gasped and took an automatic step backward before remembering that the malevolent gaze was trapped on the other side of a strong, clear wall. "I've never seen anything quite like it," she breathed, unable to look away now. The eyes were hard, glittering, faceted structures of deep amber. They stared out at her as if the insect brain behind them longed for nothing more than to be able to suck the blood from her body. Huge, folded wings, more delicate-looking than the spun crystal moss of her gown, shimmered with an eerie phosphorescence. Long, spindly legs were bent into a springing position. The creature had been hard to detect for a moment because its general color was the same as its background. It was an uncomfortably large creature, almost a full meter in height.

"Cute little Bloodsucker, isn't he? Raised him from a pup," Desma declared.

Cidra swallowed. "Is Bloodsucker its name or what it does?"

"Both. He sucks blood when he's hungry," Desma said, "which is nearly all the time. Nothing on Renaissance passes up the chance for a meal. No guarantee about when the next one will be coming along. I'm doing some work on the phosphorescent effect produced in the wings. My husband is working on the venom it uses to kill its prey. It's the acid in the venom that can eat through most cage materials." She straightened. "Over here I've got a rather nice assortment of Stoners. Pretty tame compared to the Bloodsucker but interesting all the same. A Harmonic expert in Clementia and I have been exchanging information quite regularly for a year or so. We're going to collaborate on an article soon."

"You're working with someone at Clementia? " Cidra asked.

"Otan Greenlove. Do you know him?"

Cidra nodded. "A most respected teacher. I had a class in bio-ecological theory with him." She had also had a very un-Harmonic crush on the man that she could only hope she'd managed to conceal at the time. She had found concealing such things difficult when she was in her sixteenth year, but she'd practiced hiding her emotional responses from a very early age. She had known almost before she could walk that strong emotional responses were not viewed as normal behavior among Harmonics.

"He's been a tremendous help to me in my studies. Has access to computer simulation equipment I can't get here on Try Again." Desma leaned down to gaze affectionately at the tiny-waisted insects in the cage. "Handsome as any renegade too. Met him a few months ago. Pity. All those dark good looks wasted on a Harmonic. Ah, well, I'm a married woman." She grinned at her houseguest. "Ready for the rest of the tour?"

With eager curiosity Cidra followed Desma Kady down the long aisles, gazing with fascination at each new horror. Some of the creatures were half familiar to her from her academic work, but most were strange and marvelous. Some crawled on legless bellies, others floated in the air, waiting endlessly for prey. A few hopped around on fragile legs that could be regrown in the event one was lost. Cold, gleaming eyes of every shape and hue looked out at Cidra, assessing her status as potential food. It was an unnerving experience to be gazed upon with so much malicious intent.

Desma and her husband had combined their fields of expertise, doing a great deal of crossover work and sharing the same lab facilities. They worked for an aggressive research firm that funded the studies in exchange for full rights to anything marketable they produced.

"Our latest success was an interesting new pesticide. It's being tested right now on Lovelady. Doesn't seem to alter the environment or the agricultural product in any way but has an uncanny effect against glitterbugs."

"I read a lot about them in the First Family novels and memoirs. They were a real scourge in the early days. Destroyed countless plantings. They've been just barely under control for years, haven't they? They keep mutating, so don't new pesticides have to be found on a regular basis?"

Desma smiled at Cidra's familiarity with the subject. "With any luck our company will be producing the newest counterassault. Should make a tidy bundle for all of us." Desma moved on. "Over here I've got my current pride and joy. These two beauties were the basis for that monograph I wrote on bioluminescence."

Cidra studied the two creatures behind the tempered diazite. They were a pale, washed-out shade of green, unusually unassuming compared with their more colorful neighbors. Huge, faceted eyes followed her avidly as she moved around in front of the cage. The wings were folded over its elongated body. The back two tiers of legs were clearly designed for long, ground-covering leaps.

"They're smaller than I would have expected," Cidra said. "Considering the damage they're capable of doing." The insectoid creatures were about half a meter in height. "But they're not glowing! In your monograph you said they glowed all over, bodies as well as wings."

"The luminescent effect is selective. They can activate it at will, and they only do so when they've located prey. And they only hunt in the dark. They use the glow to momentarily paralyze the victim."

"That's right," Cidra said, recalling the rest of the monograph. "I remember now about them hunting at night. The eyes are heat-sensing as well as motion-sensing?"

"Definitely. Watch, I'll give you a free show." Desma walked across the room and touched several pads on a wall panel. The light faded, and the windows were sealed with automatic shutters. There was a general rise in the chittering, chattering, clacking sounds from the inhabitants of the cages as sudden darkness descended.

Cidra waited for her eyes to adjust to the lack of light. "They're still not glowing."

"Take a step closer to the cage and act like prey."

With a laugh Cidra stepped closer. "How do I do that?"

"Just breathe. You'll have to get fairly close because the diazite interferes with their normal ability to sense heat. If you touch the cage wall, you'll really get a reaction."

Cidra waited, breathing deeply. Blindly she put a finger on the diazite cage. And quite suddenly she had her answer. The two Rigor Mortis Mantises lit up with harsh intensity, their bodies glowing with a blue-white light that was startling and terrifying. Brilliant eyes locked with hers for an instant, projecting such an inhuman hunger that Cidra's stomach turned to ice. She saw the glowing liquid venom drip from hard mandibles. She had time enough to see the segmented, upraised front limbs poised to seize her throat, and then the mantises leapt. The terror of the moment froze her to the spot. Every nerve in her body was shouting for her to run but she couldn't move. Her mouth was open but no scream emerged. Cidra knew beyond any shadow of a doubt that she was about to become food.

There was a small clicking noise as the mantises struck the tempered diazite, but it took several seconds for Cidra to register the fact that there was a barrier between herself and death. Slowly she tried to regain her self-control, a part of her brain all too well aware that she would have been mantis food by now if there had been no diazite. She shuddered with a sense of genuine horror. The lights came on at once. The mantises went back to being an unassuming shade of pale green. It seemed to Cidra, however, that they looked irritated at having been denied their prey.

"Sorry about that," Desna said, hurrying forward. "Everything okay? It does make for a fairly graphic display, doesn't it?"

"I knew what to expect, but I was still quite stunned when they switched on that glow. I've never seen anything like it, Desma. It's terrifying." With a great effort of will Cidra forced herself to calm down. The adrenaline was still hurtling through her system. "They sensed my body heat through the diazite?"

"They are exquisitely sensitive to heat. But they rely on the prey's movements, as well, to map out the general location of the victim. Altogether a highly sophisticated sensory system, which they need, naturally, because they only attack in the dark."

"Amazing."

"My husband has found that their venom is capable of producing a temporary paralysis in a creature as big as a man. The mantis attacks, administers the venom, and then backs off to wait until the victim has been immobilized. Then the mantis sits down to a leisurely dinner. The paralysis looks a lot like rigor mortis and takes an hour or so to wear off. By then there's usually not much left of the victim."

"I can imagine," Cidra said, trying to sound appropriately academic about the whole thing. Unfortunately she could imagine the scene all too well.

Desma cast her a keen glance. "Field research tends to be a bit raw compared to the work done in Clementia's nice clean labs."

"You can say that again. The labs in Clementia focus on computer modeling and elaborate cell techniques. I've never seen live animals in a research facility."

"Wolves like me do the dirty work in the field and leave a lot of the fancy analysis and application work to Harmonics. It's a good system." Desma grinned at Cidra's pale face. "What I always need after a day in this joint is a good stiff drink," Desma Kady announced. "And I see it's getting close to a decent drinking hour. Come on, Cidra, the men are away. We might as well play."

It occurred to Cidra that she should spend the evening in the local Archives pursuing her research. But after two weeks in space with a short-tempered male and the unnerving demonstration of the local fauna, a drink sounded like an absolutely wonderful idea. For the first time she thought she understood the fundamental appeal of alcohol for Wolves.

"I'll change into my evening robe," Cidra said.

EIGHT

One hour and one large mug of Renaissance Rose ale later, Cidra realized that she was enjoying herself very much. She had discovered that one could become accustomed to the heavy, tart ale. Considering the fact that the tavern was crowded, noisy, and only inefficiently cooled, she was interested to find herself having a good time. There were other factors, too, that ought to have hindered her sense of pleasant relaxation. When she had first arrived with Desma, she had attracted a fair amount of covert interest. Initially it had made her uncomfortable.

"We don't get too many Harmonics here on Renaissance. And when they do come, they tend to keep to themselves."

"But I'm not a Harmonic," Cidra had begun to explain with painful honesty.

"You look like one at first glance. Don't worry, they'll lose interest after a while." Desma dismissed the clutter of company uniforms, ship suits, and lab-tech outfits that sat, lounged, or slouched around the smoky room. Not only was the air-conditioning machinery having trouble with the heat, it wasn't doing a particularly good job of filtering the air, either.

Still, by the time she finished the first mug of ale, Cidra didn't really care. When Desma came back from the drink dispenser with a fresh mug for herself, Cidra picked up the conversation where it had been left off.

"There's no doubt in your mind, then, that life on Renaissance shows the same evolutionary and genetic background as life on Lovelady?"

"We've still got a long way to go to be certain, but so far we've found nothing to contradict Maltan's Theory that species on Renaissance are evolved from the same genetic sources as species on Lovelady."

"Which means that the Ghosts must have evolved either here or on Lovelady and then colonized the neighboring planet, taking their flora and fauna with them."

"It makes sense," Desma explained. "We know from the few records that survived the crash of the First Families' colony ship that statistically life is an exceedingly rare event in the universe. The odds are certainly against two planets in one star system developing life independently. And the odds of them developing similar life-forms is just astronomical."

"But the creatures you showed me in the lab look so different from the common life-forms on Lovelady. Hard to believe they're related. Everything here on Renaissance seems so much more violent by nature."

"Ain't adaptation a wonderful thing?" Desma observed cheerfully. "And believe me, here on Renaissance it's a case of adapt and conquer or die. There are winners and losers here but nothing in between."

Cidra glanced around at the boisterous crowd. "Where do humans fit in, I wonder."

"Right now we're learning to adapt. In some small areas we're even doing some exploiting and conquering. But that could change overnight. We could still run into something here on Renaissance that is capable of flicking us off the planet the way a torla flicks off a scatterbug. We've barely scratched the surface."

"It seems wrong to think in terms of exploitation and conquering," Cidra said thoughtfully. "This is a lush, primeval world. It has its own intrinsic harmonies. It would seem that a more positive approach to exploration would be one that took a different philosophical basis. We should be looking for the underlying harmonic rules, trying to fit ourselves into them."

"Spoken like a true Harmonic." Desma laughed. "The problem is that nature has no qualms about changing the rules on us without much warning. Nature isn't static, and therefore I don't think it's possible to ever be completely in harmony with it. Remember the glitterbugs. No matter what we come up with, they blithely keep mutating—"

"A perfect example of what I'm trying to say," Cidra interrupted happily. She found nothing more entertaining than an intellectual debate. And it was even better, she was discovering, when conducted over a mug of ale. "The glitterbugs mutate in an effort to reestablish the basic harmony humans have destroyed with pesticides."

"Nonsense. The mutation occurs as a means of adaptation in an effort to continue exploiting and conquering. If glitterbugs had a brain and a set of vocal cords, they'd tell you they could care less about harmony. They're out to take over as much of the world as they can get. Just like everything else that's really viable."

"But philosophically that's an approach that leads to a constant state of imbalance, even warfare among various life-forms. It's a destructive theory and leads to a destructive methodology of exploration."

"Maybe that's why Harmonics don't visit Renaissance very often. They can't quite approve of the way we're attacking the planet. The principles of company exploration don't follow the principles of the Klinian Laws. The folks back in Clementia are hungry for new knowledge, but getting it sometimes conflicts with their basic beliefs."

"It can be an uncomfortable quandary," Cidra explained diffidently.

"You bet your Book of Ritual it can."

Cidra smiled. "You've studied it?"

"Had to a long time ago." Desma chuckled. "My husband, Fence, and I were married in a full-scale Harmonic High Ritual wedding ceremony. Well, almost full-scale. We did skip the two hours of meditation and telepathic communion that's supposed to take place in the middle. The guests would have been bored stiff during the meditation, and nobody present was telepathic."

"It's a very beautiful ceremony," Cidra said softly, knowing many non-Harmonics used it to lend solemnity and ritual to the nuptials.

"It's supposed to be a lucky way to start marriage, and I guess it's worked so far for us. I'm still married to the man, although he can be a pain in the rump on occasion."

"Luck? There's no luck involved in a High Ritual ceremony! It's a matter of philosophy and focusing, not luck."

Desma grinned. "Another matter of adaptation. Wolves use the ceremony because they think it's lucky, among other things."

"That's a terrible misunderstanding of the underlying philosophy of the ceremony," Cidra protested.

"Ummm." But Desma was no longer paying any attention to her companion. She was gazing with narrowed eyes at a man who was levering himself away from the bar and starting toward the table occupied by the two women. "Speaking of unharmonious principles," Desma murmured, "did Severance ever tell you he once had a partner?"

"You mean his brother?"

"No. A man named Racer."

Cidra frowned thoughtfully and turned to glance at the man in a khaki ship suit who was weaving his way through the crowd. "Severance mentioned something about a partnership that was dissolved some time back. He didn't talk much about it or about the other man."

"Hardly surprising. The two of them hate each other's guts."

Desma leaned forward conspiratorially. "Do me a favor. If Severance ever asks what you did or who you met this evening, don't mention Racer."

Cidra wrinkled her brow. "You want me to lie to him?"

"You will if you're at all interested in maintaining any semblance of harmony in the universe." Desma broke off with a superficial smile as the man halted beside the table. "Hello, Racer. I didn't know you were in port."

"Life," said Cord Racer, looking down at Cidra, "is just one renegade's surprise after another."

Severance stepped out onto the tough membrane that served as pavement on the streets of Try Again. Behind him the door panel of the building that had once housed the offices of ExcellEx snapped shut to the accompanying hiss of the antibug deflector screens. Severance wished that the local ExcellEx rep were a bug. He'd like to see him sizzled by the screen's electronic impulses. Damn Quench, and damn the whole fast-moving ExcellEx corporation.

Severance kept to the side of the street although it wasn't difficult to dodge the few runners and sleds that were zipping from one end of town to the other. Try Again was not big enough to warrant a lot of vehicular traffic. Most people walked from one point to the other.

Above him the night sky proudly displayed Renaissance's twin moons, Borgia and Medici. A record of the words had survived the colony ship's crash two hundred years ago, but the references had been lost. Some research indicated that they were linked to the term Renaissance, and so the names had been attached to its moons. There was a constant hum from the jungle on the other side of the triton walls. As he walked toward Desma's house Severance batted absently at one or two night-flying insects that somehow escaped a deflector screen. His mind was occupied with the task of telling Cidra that plans had changed.

She wasn't going to be thrilled. She had been counting on at least five days here at Try Again. Time enough to consult local archives and the tall tales of exploration men. She was going to be upset when he informed her that they were leaving the day after tomorrow.

Well, he couldn't help the inconvenience, Severance told himself. Cidra was the one who had insisted on a crew contract. She would just have to learn to accommodate herself to the unpredictable schedules of a mail ship.

He turned a corner, heading down the street that was lined with the majority of Try Again's company stores and taverns. The distant hum of the jungle was a familiar sound, and he tuned it out. After a year as a bonus man he had developed fairly good instincts for Renaissance. A man either learned when to get nervous or he died learning. Companies didn't pay huge bonus credit for ordinary manual labor. Bonus credit was paid for risks, and risks on Renaissance were usually in the life-and-death category.

"Hey, Severance." A man emerging from a nearby tavern hailed him. "You the one who just hit port with a Harmonic in tow?"

Severance halted. "Hello, Craft. As usual you're up to date. A man would think you're telepathic yourself, the way you always seem to know the latest gossip. How did you know about Cidra?"

Craft chuckled, unoffended. He'd known Teague Severance a long time. "No magic this time. Saw her with Desma Kady 'bout an hour ago. They're in the Bloodsucker." He nodded up the street.

Severance swore in disgust. "Desma took her there?"

"It's not like we got a whole lot of choice when it comes to night spots in this town," Craft reminded him. His faded, friendly eyes assessed Severance in the poor light. "Nothing to get upset about. Looked to me like they were both having a good time."

"You wouldn't think someone raised in Clementia would have developed a fascination for dives like the Bloodsucker, would you? The lady's taste seems to be degenerating." Severance sighed and moved off purposefully. "See you, Craft."

"Sure." The older man nodded, but Severance was no longer looking at him. He was heading toward the Bloodsucker. Craft chuckled again to himself and decided that he could use another drink after all. He went back into the tavern from which he had just emerged. Bound to be some folks inside who'd want to hear about Severance and the little Harmonic. And Cord Racer's presence added a nice extra fillip. Too bad he hadn't had a chance to mention Racer to Severance. No matter. They'd find each other soon enough, and word had it that Racer had already found the little Harmonic.

Desma watched Racer settle into conversation with Cidra. There wasn't much she could do to stop it, short of making a scene and hauling the younger woman out of the tavern. A woman born in Clementia, Harmonic or otherwise, would be thoroughly humiliated at being the object of the kind of attention that would garner.

Objectively speaking, there was nothing wrong with Racer. He was reasonably well mannered, especially compared to the majority of Try Again's population. He was good-looking in an open, breezy kind of way. Red-haired with blue-green eyes and a disarming sprinkling of freckles across his nose, Racer was tall and physically well proportioned. He wore the snug-fitting khaki ship suit and boots with a certain swagger that was not offensive. Women tended to find it endearing, in fact. About the same age as his former partner, Cord Racer was also doing very well for himself as a mail pilot. And he was better educated than the average pilot. Desma had already sensed that for Cidra, intelligence and a good education were vastly more alluring than physical attractiveness in a man. The result of her Harmonic upbringing, Desma supposed.

The only thing wrong with Racer was the hostility that simmered just below the surface whenever he and Severance came in contact. No one, not even that professional gossip, Georg Craft, knew what had dissolved the partnership three planet years ago, but whatever it was, it had been traumatic and probably violent. Everyone was amazed that one of them hadn't made sure the other suffered some sort of unpleasant accident over the years. Perhaps they avoided it by taking pains to avoid each other.

Cidra responded warily to Racer's cheerful conversation. She used formal politeness as a facade behind which she could hide while she analyzed the man. If Severance disliked him as intensely as Desma seemed to think, there had to be a reason. But for the life of her Cidra couldn't find anything particularly jarring or dismaying about Cord Racer. He seemed quite pleasant.

"How long will you be here on Renaissance?" she inquired politely during a short break in the conversation.

"I'll be leaving soon. Got a run for QED. Is it true you're on crew contract with Severance?"

"Quite true."

"Mind my asking exactly what you do for him? I mean, I have a ship the same size and class as *Severance Pay*, and to be honest, they're a one-man operation."

Desma spoke coolly. "The nature of her work on board is hardly any of your business, Racer."

Racer shrugged. "Just curious."

"It's all right," Cidra said quickly, sensing the tension in Desma. "I'm doing some programming work for him. In return he's providing me with free passage."

"Ah, I get it," Racer said easily. "A business arrangement."

"Exactly."

Desma made another attempt to take hold of the conversation. "Cidra, it's getting late. We should probably be heading home."

"You're staying with Desma?" Racer asked, ignoring the older woman.

Cidra nodded, smiling. "That's right. She's been most gracious. I'll be at her place for the next few days while Severance picks up some mail and arranges some delivery contracts."

"Desma, here, is a very nice lady," Racer said agreeably.

"Desma," announced Desma in tones of foreboding as she looked over Racer's shoulder, "may have just made her worst mistake of the season." She smiled weakly. "Hi, Severance. Cidra and I were just about to leave."

"I know." Severance sounded very sure of that fact. He arrived at the table and stood looking down at Cidra. He didn't even glance at Racer. "I came to escort you home. Let's go." He reached out to put his large hand under Cidra's arm and hauled her unceremoniously to her feet.

"Severance, please!" Cidra was mortified by the rudeness.

"Take it easy, Severance," Racer said coolly, climbing out of the chair he'd been straddling. "Maybe the lady isn't ready to leave yet."

Desma got uneasily out of her seat, paying the tab quickly with a credit slip.

"The lady works for me," Severance said, still not bothering to look at Racer. "And I say she's ready to leave. Aren't you, Cidra?"

"There is no need to be so impatient," Cidra hissed, aware of his fingers digging into her arm. "What are you doing here, anyway? I thought you were gong to spend the night on board the ship."

"I came to tell you that there's been a change in plans. I'll explain outside." He flicked a glance at Desma. "Are you coming?"

"I'm coming." Desma stifled a groan as she saw the embarrassment on Cidra's face. "You could be a little less heavy-handed, Teague."

"And you could use a little more judgment, Desma."

"Severance!" Cidra was more than embarrassed now. She was shocked. "This is my hostess. You will not talk to her in this way."

"Forget it," Desma advised. "I've heard worse. Let's get going."

Racer stepped closer to Cidra, his blue-green eyes concerned. "Are you sure you want to go with him, Cidra? Just because you're under contract doesn't mean you have to let him ride you this way."

"Stay out of this, Racer." Severance finally deigned to glance at Racer. His eyes were full of warning, and something else. Something that might have been contempt.

"If the lady wants my assistance, she's got it." Racer returned the contempt with a rough hostility.

Cidra realized immediately that she was not the issue. She was the catalyst both men were using to confront each other. The tension in the air was almost palpable. The two Wolves were circling each other, searching for openings and excuses for battle. She had to put a stop to it at once. She smiled tentatively. "It's all right,

Racer. I really must be going. It's been pleasant chatting with you. Perhaps some other time?"

"Any other time," Racer stressed, his eyes locked with Severance's. "Any other time you want."

"Don't hold your breath," Severance advised. He turned away, more or less dragging Cidra with him. Desma followed without further demur.

Cidra waited until the three of them were out on the street before she gave way to her feelings of humiliation and anger. Then she rounded on Severance. "I have never been so thoroughly embarrassed in my entire life, Teague Severance. You have the manners of a torla. You should be ashamed of yourself, and if you're not, it's only because you don't have the sensitivity to manage it! How can you possibly excuse such ill-mannered behavior?"

"I won't bother to find any excuses. I don't *have* to find any excuses. I'm your employer, remember? And this is a direct order: Stay clear of Racer."

"You'll have to provide a reasonable explanation for such a ridiculous order."

"As long as you're on crew contract I don't owe you any explanations. Want to terminate the contract right now? Your option."

"Easy, Severance," Desma advised softly.

Cidra threw herself back into the argument. A temper she had never dreamed existed seemed to be bubbling alive inside her. It was as if the hot, humid air of the planet had stirred the heat in her veins. "Don't you dare threaten me, Severance. I demand a full apology for the scene you created in that tavern."

"You're not going to get one. Make up your mind, Cidra. Are you under contract or not?"

"You're not going to get rid of me this easily! I won't let you use a stupid argument like this one to force me to terminate the contract."

"Fine. Then you'll follow orders."

Desma tried again, saying mildly, "Why did you come looking for us in the first place, Severance?"

He glared at Desma and then at Cidra as they arrived at the Kadys' octagonal home. Cidra thought he hesitated for an instant before dropping his bombshell. "ExcellEx has moved its main operations to a field camp upriver. They want the sensors delivered there. I've made the arrangements. We're leaving the day after tomorrow. I've contracted with a guide who's taking some other supplies to the camp."

Cidra blinked, realizing what that meant. "But my research! I haven't even started. Severance, I'm not ready to leave Try Again yet. I have so much to do."

"Then you shouldn't have wasted an entire evening in a place like the Bloodsucker, should you?"

Desma moved toward the door. "If you'll excuse me," she said dryly, "I'm going inside. I've got a squeamish stomach." The deflectors hissed behind her, leaving Severance and Cidra alone on the membrane.

"Severance, is this really necessary, or are you concocting some excuse to leave town because that man Racer is here?"

"Racer is strictly second-class postage. I wouldn't let him affect anything I do. We're leaving at dawn the day after tomorrow because I'm running a business. I've contracted to deliver the sensors, and that's what I'm going to do. As long as you choose to work for me you stay with me. Understood?"

"Oh, you're doing an excellent job of making yourself clear."

He closed his eyes in brief disgust. "I'm sorry, Cidra. This can't be helped. The potential of more work for ExcellEx is too good to pass up. There'll be other opportunities here for you to search the Try Again files."

She considered the matter. "You could leave me behind while you make the run to the field camp."

Severance's eyes were very steady. "Not a chance. I'm not leaving you alone here. As long as you work for me I'm responsible for you. I want you where I can keep an eye on you."

"It is Racer, isn't it? You don't want me left here near him. Why do you hate him so much, Severance?"

"That subject isn't open to discussion. Good night, Cidra."

"Good night, Severance." She turned stiffly, the hem of her gown swirling around her. "I hope you enjoy what's left of the night."

He caught her arm, spinning her around to face him. She sucked in her breath as she saw the glittering intensity in his eyes. Before she could say anything, he was kissing her, his mouth hard and possessive on hers. She shivered in his grasp, a soft moan echoing far back in her throat. When he lifted his head, Cidra had to put out a hand to steady herself. Wide-eyed, she stared at him.

"I won't, you know," Severance said too calmly.

"W-won't what?"

"Enjoy what's left of the night."

"What's the matter?" she flung back. "Didn't your arrangements for a little special handling work out?"

"No. Fred doesn't take to strangers on board." He released her and pushed her gently toward the door panels. "Go inside, Cidra. I'll see you in the morning."

Cidra was safely through the panels when she realized with a secret satisfaction that Fred had never seriously objected to her presence on board *Severance Pay*.

A muted but nerve-rasping whistle woke Cidra several hours later. The sound seemed to pierce right through her mind, bringing her to a sitting position in bed with a pounding heart. She was gazing at the door to her room, trying to remember where she was when it opened. Desma Kady stood there, struggling into a white lab suit.

"Don't worry, Cidra. It's just an equipment alarm from the lab. Probably means the air filtration system has gone down again. I didn't see any lights when I looked out the window, so it could be that the lighting timer has failed too. Damn. If it isn't one thing, it's another. You have no idea how hard it is to keep machinery in good repair here on Renaissance. The last time this happened we found several kilos of swarming doomlizards tangled in the filtration fans. I'll be back in a few minutes."

"Can I help?"

"Don't worry. This will only take a little while, I'm sure. Stay where you are and get some sleep." She waved absently and left.

Wide-awake now, Cidra went over to the diazite window and watched Desma hurry toward the long lab building. Nights on Renaissance were a couple of hours longer than on Lovelady. She estimated it must be about three hours from dawn. Through the gloom Cidra saw Desma disappear into the lab. She leaned on the windowsill and waited. The thought of going into that long, dark building full of bugs was not a pleasant one, but she supposed Desma was accustomed to her "pets."

Cidra didn't know when or exactly why she began to worry. When the low level of illumination she had noticed earlier that evening in the lab didn't come back on soon after Desma disappeared inside, she began to get nervous. Desma had seemed to think the problem was a minor one that could be easily solved.

Minutes ticked past and there was still no sign of her hostess returning from the lab. Perhaps she could use some assistance after all. Cidra put on her delicate emerald-floss slippers and walked down the hall and out into the night. Her black-and-silver gown made her almost invisible in the shadows. The company that had the current contract for street lighting here in Try Again didn't believe in importing too much heavy, expensive fluoroquartz. Most of the buildings on the street were shrouded in darkness, including the lab.

Visions of a long barn full of horrific insectoid creatures were very bright in Cidra's mind when she tentatively opened the door Desma had already unlocked. The fetid smell from the interior assailed her as soon as she stepped inside. It seemed somehow worse in the oppressive darkness. The small, scurrying, screeching, and clacking noises were at full volume as the creatures in the cages went about their shadowy night business.

"Desma?"

There was no response. Cidra took another step inside. Tiny pinpoints of light darted about in the cage to her left. Up ahead she could see another faint, phosphorescent flicker. The natural luminescence of some of the inhabitants wasn't nearly enough to light the aisles in front of the cages. Cidra took another cautious step, letting her eyes adjust to the deep shadows. She could barely make out the entrance to the first aisle.

"Desma? Where are you? Did you find the problem? Want me to get a quartzflash?"

Still no answer. Perhaps Desma was working on the machinery at the rear of the building. Slowly, not wanting to touch the cages she was passing, Cidra moved down the aisle. She knew that if she kept going straight, she would wind up at the back of the room where the control panels were installed. The fact that Desma was not responding was really beginning to alarm her.

When her foot caught on an object in the middle of the aisle, Cidra's first thought was that one of the caged horrors had escaped and she had just become its prey. Her startled, panicked scream was muffled as she lost her balance and sprawled facedown on the metal floor. Frantically she twisted, intent only on getting away from whatever had tripped her. Her hand lashed out to ward off the unseen attacker and came into contact with fabric. Lab-tech uniform fabric. A small object rolled free of the fabric, clattering softly on the floor. It was gone before Cidra could reach for it, disappearing into the thick darkness under the cages.

"Desma!" A new kind of fear assailed her as Cidra groped about, swearing with words she must have learned from Severance. "Desma, what's wrong?" The woman's body was limp, but when she found a throat pulse, Cidra breathed a sigh of shaky relief. Almost at once the fear returned, however. Whichever of the lab creatures had done this was still about, skulking in the shadows under the cages. She had to get herself and Desma out of the building. There was no telling what had bitten or stung Desma, and there was no telling how much time she had left.

Cidra awkwardly found the woman's wrists and was getting to her feet when she realized that there was someone else in the lab. For an instant she froze as she heard the gliding footstep.

There was no possibility of the sound belonging to someone who would offer help. If that had been the case, whoever it was would have responded to her call for Desma. Cidra knew with absolute certainty that whoever was moving down the aisle toward her was the one responsible for whatever had happened to Desma.

Instinct prompted her to release her grip on the unconscious woman. The human hunter was now intent on new prey. Cidra crouched motionlessly, wondering why he didn't simply flick on a quartzflash and pin her in the light. And then she realized what the object was that had rolled under the cages. Desma must have fought back briefly, knocking the flash free from her attacker's hand.

Cidra strained to hear the next footfall above the soft, ominous chittering and chattering. It came after several excruciating heartbeats. She had to get away. Like any wild creature seeking safety, Cidra slipped to one side on her hands and knees, searching for the dark shadows under the cages. She was able to perceive a faint movement in the aisle as she stared out from under a cage. The clicking sound grew stronger, coming from directly overhead now as the creatures above her also sensed movement. There was a flurry of scratching sounds on the diazite, and then, whoever was in the aisle moved on. The insects above settled back down to a normal hum of activity.

Cidra hugged herself, drawing the dark, concealing folds of her sleeping robe around her ankles. She tried to breathe as lightly as possible, using the skills she had learned in meditation practice. One thing was for certain. She couldn't stay here. And she mustn't risk allowing her pursuer time enough to find his lost quartzflash. No one who might be passing on the street outside would hear a scream from the heavily built lab structure. She had to find her way silently to the door.

But now the hunter was between her and the exit. Cidra contemplated that, trying to imagine what he might be thinking. He must have realized that she would try to get out the way she had entered. When she finally lost her nerve and made a dash for the door, he would be waiting. She would probably blunder straight into him. What she needed was an advantage.

In the darkness she needed light. But it had to be light she controlled. Slowly Cidra unwound and crawled out from under the cage. Instead of heading toward the door she began inching her way, still on her hands and knees, down the aisle toward the rear of the building.

Whoever waited for her heard the soft scuffling sounds. Cidra sensed him moving down the aisle, following carefully in the darkness. She stayed low, ready to dart back under the row of cages. As she moved she counted diazite structures she was passing, trying to remember exactly where she was. The tour of the lab that afternoon had been very thorough, and she had a well-trained memory. What good was an education if you didn't put it to use?

The man behind her was gaining slowly, growing more confident as he followed the soft sounds she was making on the metal floor. When he spoke for the first time, Cidra almost screamed. His voice was a rasping whisper.

"Come on out, lady. Let's get this over with. You don't want to spend the rest of the night with these bugs, do you? No telling when one of them might get free. Why, I could open a couple of these cages myself with this little can opener I brought along. I might just do it, too, if you don't cooperate." He glided closer.

Cidra's heart was hammering as the fear-induced adrenaline ricocheted through her system. Something was wrong with her insides. She felt almost sick. Steadily she moved down the aisle, forcing herself to count each cage. Three more to go . . . two more to go . . .

One more to go. One more, that is, if she had remembered exactly where she was when she had started and if she hadn't lost count. She paused and listened. There was no sound from the inhabitants of the cage overhead. Flattening herself on the cold metal floor, Cidra waited. If she wasn't beside the right cage, she was going to be trapped. She had to let the hunter get close. Too close to allow her to have a chance at escape if she had made a mistake.

She huddled into herself as the footsteps came nearer. He was making no effort to hide himself now. The confidence of the hunter was born of arrogance and the belief that he held the upper hand. Just the same sort of attitude that could get a person into trouble when he was playing Free Market.

The footsteps came to a halt. Now, in the shadows, Cidra could make out a pair of heavy boots not more than two meters away. She drew in her breath and knew he heard the sound.

"There you are, little lady. I told you there wasn't much point in hiding."

Cidra put up her hand and flattened her warm palm against the diazite of what she believed was the Rigor Mortis Mantis cage. For a heart-stopping moment nothing happened. Then the creatures inside reacted with an instantaneous flare of eerie blue-white brilliance, illuminating themselves to the man in the boots facing them on the other side of the diazite.

Cidra was not staring up into the cage. She was waiting for a glimpse of her pursuer's face. It came, the features bathed in blue-white terror as the Mantises switched on the paralyzing luminescence. She had time to note the fear, time to see the pulser grasped in one huge hand, and time to realize that the mantises were very good at their work. Their victim was literally immobilized with shock and horror. He couldn't even scream, although Cidra could see the panic in his eyes as she leapt to her feet.

The mantises had bought her only a few seconds, but that was all the time Cidra needed. She flowed into the deceptively gentle movements of Moonlight and Mirrors.

NINE

I can't let you out of my sight for a minute." Severance slouched as usual in his seat, morosely regarding Cidra. Behind him the green wall of vegetation slipped past at a quick, steady pace as the skimmer, riding just above the water, followed the river into the dark heart of the jungle.

"That's going to make things awkward, isn't it? Because, after that display in the Bloodsucker, I've learned that I can't take you anywhere." Cidra knew she was being dangerously flippant, but the truth was that she was getting tired of the never-ending lectures. They had been going on in one form or another since she had dragged Desma out of the bio lab and called for help. Help had come quickly enough, but so had Severance.

"This isn't a joke, Cidra. You could have been seriously hurt. Maybe killed. You should never have gone into that lab alone. As soon as you opened the door and realized something was wrong, you should have called a company guard. They get paid to go into places like that. You don't. Come to think of it, I probably ought to dock your salary for bad judgment."

"You're not paying me a salary, remember? Just providing transportation and scenic sidetrips such as this one." Cidra's eyes widened slightly as she had a flash of intuition. "I think you're chewing on me as if I were a bite of torla steak because I let him get away."

Severance leaned forward with an abrupt movement and lowered his voice so that it was only barely audible above the hum of the skimmer's power cells. "If you really believe that, then you're functioning on fewer brains than a novakeet."

The image was not a pleasant one. Novakeets, with their splashy orange-and-red plummage, were pretty enough creatures, but on Lovelady nature seemed to have decided that such beauty didn't need a lot of brainpower. Cidra cast a quick glance toward the front of the skimmer where the pilot was safely out of earshot inside the diazite cabin. Then she glared at Severance.

"Why are you so angry with me, Severance? You've been this way since you found out what happened."

"I'm angry because you came so damn close to getting yourself hurt, you little idiot!"

She searched his fierce gaze for a moment. "Desma was the one who got hurt."

"I'm aware of that. Just promise me that next time you're on the threshold of a situation that looks serious, you'll go get help, not try to handle things yourself."

Cidra considered the request. It seemed reasonable. "All right. I promise." She was silent for another moment. "Do you think I'm likely to run into many such situations while I'm traveling with you?"

"Not if you do as you're told." Somewhat mollified, Severance leaned back in his seat again. "Saints in hell, you gave me a scare."

"Believe me. It was nothing compared to the scare that intruder got. I've never seen anyone's face twisted in such a way. It was as if he were wearing a mask. Which is why I had so much difficulty describing him later to the company guards."

"They know he was carrying a pulser, at least. That's illegal inside the walls. Did you knock it out of his hand when you went into your Moonlight and Mirrors routine?"

Cidra closed her eyes, trying to remember those awful few moments. "I don't know if I disarmed him or if he simply dropped the thing in his terror. He was quite frozen with fear for a few seconds. And I wasn't far behind. Even though I wasn't looking at the creatures and I knew something of what to expect, that eerie brilliance they produce is very hard on the nerves. In the darkness the man couldn't see the diazite between him and the mantises. Even if he knew that logically speaking they were probably in a cage, his mind reacted first to the terror. When they leapt toward him, he saw them move. The next thing he knew, he *felt* me attacking. In his fear I think his mind mixed up the two sensations and assumed that the Rigor Mortis Mantises actually had hold of him. He didn't try to fight me as if I were merely a human being. He screamed and fled. Which is why I was not successful in detaining him. His terror gave him a great deal of strength."

"And you're just damn lucky he didn't use it against you."

"Severance, if you say another word along those lines—"

He held up his hand. "I know. It's just that I'm still recovering from shock. Thank Sweet Harmony that you and Desma are both all right."

"I just hope Desma's not in any danger now that we're gone." Cidra still felt uneasy about leaving her new friend behind in Try Again, even though Desma had displayed no such concern.

"She's hardly alone," Severance said bluntly. "Her company will be giving her and the lab full-time protection now that they know someone has his eyes on one of the products she's on the verge of producing."

"She thinks the intruder was after some record of the results of her work on a new pesticide," Cidra murmured. "Apparently it would be worth a great deal to a rival firm."

"All the more reason for her company to take care of her. She and the lab both qualify as company property." Severance's mouth lifted slightly in the first trace of amusement Cidra had seen since he'd shown up after the incident in the lab. "And you come under the heading of company property yourself. Right now you belong to the firm of Severance Pay, Ltd. It's my responsibility to keep track of you. So you will stay in sight so I can do exactly that."

Cidra withdrew into the remote, polite facade that she was learning served her well during times when she wished to halt a conversation with Severance. She was careful to maintain a serene expression so that he couldn't accuse her of sulking. There were advantages to some of the Harmonic tricks she'd learned over the years.

She turned her attention to the wide swath of river that served as a highway for the skimmer. Occasionally they passed the mouth of one of the many tributaries that fed into the main stream. The network of rivers was extensive, and many of the smaller ones still had not been fully explored. The water passing under the skimmer was a murky color, thick with the sediment it had picked up on its meandering journey. She couldn't see more than a few centimeters under the surface. The vegetation grew right to the water's edge and into it. Huge leaves of an impossible green hung over the banks. Occasionally Cidra caught a splash of movement as some river denizen leapt out of the water to snatch a tasty morsel that had made the mistake of journeying too far out on a broad leaf.

At one point she thought she had seen a set of reptilian eyes just above the water, watching the skimmer sweep past. When she had pointed them out to Severance, he had shrugged and said she had probably seen a river dracon.

"I'm not familiar with river dracons," she said. "What do they look like?"

"You don't want to know," he told her.

"Nonsense. All knowledge is good."

"Even knowledge that gives you nightmares?"

She let that pass. She hadn't slept easily the previous night. Images of huge bugs shining with unnatural light had invaded her dreams.

Tough reeds and floating flowers that were almost a meter wide battled for living space near the banks of the river. Beyond them the jungle was a wall of green that discouraged any attempts at penetration. The companies involved in exploration work had soon learned that it was easier to use the rivers as roads than to try to rip out the vegetation and pave the jungle floor. There were one or two other small settlements similar to Try Again where a mail ship or small plane could land on the continent, but for the most part, field camps and outposts were accessible only by river skimmer.

The skimmer rode a short distance above the water, sinking back down onto the water when the engines were cut. It was a lightweight boat, made to carry small amounts of cargo and passengers. The crew usually consisted of just one individual who also acted as guide. In this case the pilot's name was Overcash. He wore the uniform of the ExcellEx company. If Overcash had a birth name in addition to the one he'd chosen, he hadn't bothered to dispense it when he had been introduced to Cidra. It hadn't surprised her. She was growing accustomed to the lack of formality among Wolves. She was also getting used to the fact that outside Try Again, people were armed. Overcash and Severance both wore pulsers strapped to their thighs, the small, personal weapon the lab intruder had held. Pulsers were blunt, ugly instruments that would kill.

The skimmer had a clear, enclosed cabin in which the navigation instruments were housed. There was room inside for the pilot and one or two passengers to shelter in the event of a storm. Since they had left Try Again, however, Cidra and Severance had been sitting in the stern of the craft, which was open. That had suited Cidra just fine because she was fascinated with the scenery. The river seemed to have its own scent, a distinctive combination of vegetation and water thick with life. Unfortunately Severance had utilized the privacy afforded in the back of the skimmer to continue with his endless commentary on the events in the bio lab.

Cidra shifted slightly, vaguely uncomfortable in her new clothes. She had never before worn anything but one of the formal Harmonic surplice robes, and she felt odd. The tough fabric of the trousers and long-sleeved shirt Desma had insisted she wear were rough against skin that had only known the touch of finely spun crystal moss. The garments were designed in the manner of the functional uniforms worn by most people on Renaissance: snug trousers and a cool, loose-fitting shirt. The fabric was heavy and largely insect-proof, although it wouldn't be much help against something the size of a Bloodsucker. There was a hood that could be drawn over the head in the event of bad weather or a swarm of flying creatures such as the stinging bandini Desma had described. When she moved around, Cidra was aware of a sensation of being partially undressed. It seemed to her that the trousers and shirt defined her body too revealingly. More than once she had caught Severance eyeing her in the new clothes. He seemed especially fascinated with the shape of her buttocks.

In spite of the excitement in Desma's lab, Severance had seen to it that he and Cidra had left on time that morning. The mail must go through, Cidra thought humorously, especially when it was COD. At least she'd had a chance late yesterday afternoon to query the official Try Again Archive computer. The company in charge of maintaining it had charged a fee for access. Cidra was learning that the competitive free enterprise system that was so much a part of the worlds of Stanza Nine was especially fierce on Renaissance. Nothing was free here.

There hadn't been time to do a thorough search, and she hadn't had time to study what she had copied onto data slips, but she had the slips with her and fully intended to read them during the journey. Overcash had said that they would arrive at the ExcellEx field camp in two days' time. He would be returning as soon as he had dropped off the supplies, and Severance had promised Cidra that they would be going back with the pilot to Try Again.

"Four days of sight-seeing on this river is more than enough," he had said with a touch of grimness.

Cidra had agreed with him initially because she was so anxious to continue with her research. But now, as she watched the awesome scenery sweep past, she wasn't so sure. She was familiar with holotapes and data slip reproductions of Renaissance, but nothing could convey a true picture of the incredible, overly lush tangle of vegetation. Nor could any holotype duplicate the startling quantity of animal life. Four days wouldn't be nearly enough to drink in this amazing world, Cidra decided.

When the skimmer rounded a sweeping bend in the river and started up a long, straight stretch, Overcash locked the guide stick and came out of the cabin to join his passengers. He was a big man, taller than Severance and built along heavy, chunky lines. Cidra suspected that the chunkiness wasn't composed of much fat but was just muscle. His face was deeply tanned, made up of blunt features carved with a heavy hand. He had all the assurance of physical strength one would want in a guide in this wild land. Overcash stood with one thumb hooked into the utility loop he wore and nodded at Cidra.

"Enjoying the scenery, Otanna?"

She inclined her head, surprised by the polite title. "It's fascinating. But please call me Cidra."

Overcash nodded agreeably. "Ever been to Renaissance before?"

"Never."

"Kinda overwhelming at first. But you get used to it. There's a thousand different fortunes to be made here. Maybe ten thousand if you're willing to work for bonus credit." His narrowed gaze swept along the passing riverbank. "Assuming a man survives to make his haul."

"I understood that statistically most workers are safe now, as long as they follow the company rules and safety regulations," Cidra noted. "I thought the accident rate had declined sharply during the last few years with the invention of the deflectors."

Overcash laughed, a big booming sound that echoed along the water and caused a stir of activity in a tree on the bank. Something with a wingspan that seemed much too wide lifted into the air, its long, toothed beak outlined evilly against the sky.

"The statistics are probably accurate. Any renegade who

wants to work hard and follow the rules can make a nice salary and probably stay out of trouble. But that's not how you make real credit on this planet. The companies all have what they like to call bonus plans. Take a few risks for your firm and you're guaranteed a bonus. 'Course, you got to survive to collect the bonus. I'm not sure how many bonus men who don't come back make it into the statistics. Companies got a way of doing things to statistics."

Severance threw a glance at the pilot. "And Renaissance has a way of doing things to bonus men."

"Yeah, well, it's like Free Market. Got to take a risk now and then, or it's not worth playing the game. You know that, Severance."

Cidra's mind winced at the philosophy. Having not played Free Market since *Severance Pay* had set down at Try Again, she had deliberately forgotten some of her odd, increasing enthusiasm for it. Severance obviously hadn't forgotten, however. He grinned wickedly.

At least he was smiling at her, even if he was showing his teeth. It was far more pleasant than being chewed on. Cidra looked down over the side of the skimmer. The thick water was ruffled on the surface from the effects of the skimmer's lift thrust. As the skimmer swept past she thought she saw another set of cold, wide-set eyes hovering a few centimeters under water. In that brief moment Cidra glimpsed the outline of a frighteningly long body. Perhaps Severance was right; getting a close-up view of a dracon might not be very pleasant. The eyes she had seen reminded her of some of Desma's lab creatures.

"Everything here on Renaissance seems to be out to eat everything else," she remarked.

"Just don't decide to trail your fingers in the water when we stop for the evening," Severance advised.

"I won't." She glanced at Overcash. "Do we stay on board the skimmer tonight?"

"No. Some dracon or a skater might decide to get playful. Skimmers are safest when they're in motion. We'll stay on shore."

"Is that any safer?"

Overcash chuckled. "Sure. We've got the heavy-duty deflectors and the armor tents. No problem. If something does decide to come looking for a midnight snack, we'll have plenty of warning. Not much can get through a deflector. Severance, here, wouldn't have brought you along if there was any real danger."

"On the contrary," Severance informed him. "I *had* to bring her along because she digs up the worst trouble when she's on her own."

They turned off the main river later that afternoon, swinging into a tributary that wasn't quite as thick with sediment as the first waterway had been. This river was also narrower than the first, and the walls of vegetation on either side seemed to loom higher and closer. But that might be just a trick of the waning light, Cidra told herself. She realized that she wasn't looking forward to camping out this evening.

As if he sensed her uneasiness, Severance became more talkative. He gave her a dissertation on how effective the big deflector screens were and how they had revolutionized field maps on Renaissance. The invisible grids they produced were based on the same principle as the Screamer. They were set to repel any creature with nerve impulses different than those of human beings.

"I get the feeling that some things out there haven't even got nerves." But Cidra made the observation with a smile to show Severance that she wasn't really worried. Wonderful what Harmonic training could do when it came to covering up one's true feelings. Or perhaps she was so adept at it because she had been covering up the Wolf side of herself for so many years.

Overcash chose the campsite just as the shadows along the river became uncomfortably long. With the instinct of a good guide he managed to find a rare break in the undergrowth. Carefully he slowed the skimmer, letting it sink down onto the water. The craft rocked slightly in the lethargic current while the pilot made it fast. A flexible landing plank emerged when Overcash activated a control panel.

"I don't see enough room here to erect a couple of tents," Cidra observed, eyeing the bank. The vegetation was thinner along this stretch of bank, but it was still fairly spectacular to her eyes. She watched as a small, wriggly creature flashed on the bank and slid into the water. Cidra had a mental picture of it sliding just as easily into a tent.

"Don't worry, we'll make a little space for ourselves." Overcash went into the cabin and came back with a long-barreled machine that had a squat base.

"What's that?" Cidra asked.

"A crisper." Overcash switched on the machine, and a narrow band of white flame jumped out, searing the vegetation it touched. With a few sweeping movements the guide cleared a relatively large area along the bank. The undergrowth that had fallen into the path of the crisper smoked for a moment, wilted, and then disintegrated.

"I guess that's one way of dealing with too many weeds." Cidra was a little appalled by the small devastation.

"Too bad this thing hasn't got a longer range," Overcash remarked, stowing the machine. "It would make a useful weapon."

The deflector screens were hauled out next. They were charged on the skimmer's power cells and then carried ashore. Severance helped the pilot set them up so that they produced a grid that completely encircled the campsite. Occasional tiny hissing noises gave notice that the screens were working. Inside the protected area the light metal tents were erected—two of them, Cidra noticed. Severance moved his and Cidra's small travel packs into one. Neither he nor Overcash seemed to have any interest in how Cidra felt about the sleeping situation. It was apparently a foregone conclusion that she belonged in Severance's tent. She shouldn't have been surprised. Among Wolves it was clear that when a man and a woman spent time together, it was assumed that they had a sexual relationship.

Well, she thought bracingly, she'd already lived with him for two weeks in the confines of a mail ship. This wasn't much more intimate, all things considered. She just wished she had a proper sleeping robe. It occurred to her that she might be expected to undress before she climbed into the air-cushioned sleepers. The thought of sleeping naked was more unnerving than most of her other recent experiences. She couldn't do it.

The background clamor of the jungle changed perceptibly as the night shift took possession of the premises. The deflectors had no effect on the sounds that permeated the shadows, and Cidra found the clickings, clackings, screams, and cries disturbing. Severance had had the forethought to insure that some vegetarian prespacs were on board the skimmer, and she flashed him a look of gratitude when hers came out of the portable food heater. He had also made sure a few containers of his beloved ale were on board.

It was going to be a long night.

Hours later, Severance lay awake in his sleeper, aware of the tension in the woman lying next to him. Her body was insulated from his by the plastic fabric of the sleepers, but Cidra was lying so still, she was clearly wide-awake.

He had said nothing when she had crawled into the sleeper wearing her clothing. She clearly had not felt comfortable in the trousers and shirt all day, so he had resisted the urge to tell her what a sweet, sassy little rear she had. Harmonic males undoubtedly did not say things like that to their women. Harmonic males didn't even think in terms of "their women."

But Wolves did think in such primitive terms, Severance was discovering. Like it or not, he was starting to think of Cidra that way. "Company property" he had called her, but she hadn't seemed to realize just what he was saying. His feelings of possessiveness were stronger than ever, yet he hadn't even had her in his bed. He wondered how he would ever get as far as QED without trying to seduce her. The only option he had—terminating her crew contract—was not one he wanted to consider. She would fall into the path of some piece of second-class mail like Racer.

Severance turned onto his side, watching Cidra's too-tense outline. The movement made him aware of the second pulser he had stowed under his sleeper. The Screamer was in the utility loop that hung within reach, and he could put out his hand and touch the first pulser, the one he had worn strapped to his thigh during the day. He'd had the second one in his travel pack and, as a general precaution, had decided to sleep on top of it. Renaissance was a dangerous planet, and not all the hazards were from its natural flora and fauna. Some of them were man-made.

Seeing Racer two nights ago had made Severance remember just how dangerous the human species could be. A part of him still burned with a frozen flame of anger as he recalled the emotion that had shot through him when he'd entered the Bloodsucker and seen Racer sitting with Cidra. There was no way he could have left Cidra behind on this trip. She might have been reasonably safe from the perils of Port Try Again, but she wouldn't have been safe from Racer. Every gut-level instinct had warned Severance that Racer would have found a way to use Cidra.

"Severance?"

The quiet whisper of her voice made him jump. "What is it, Cidra?"

"Are you awake?"

"No, I'm just making conversation in my sleep." He smiled to himself as she wriggled around in the sleeper to face him.

"Do you hear those weird clanking sounds?"

He could barely see her face in the shadows, but he sensed the genuine tension in her voice. "I hear them. Probably zalons. They've got shells as hard as armor. And they like to fight a lot. Sometimes you can hear the clanking for several kilometers. They're huge, but they eat only plants."

"Why do they fight?"

"Male zalons fight over female zalons. Mating rituals. They mate frequently."

"Everything on Lovelady and Renaissance seems to mate frequently," she said, almost to herself. "Desma told me she has four children."

"That's a small family by Wolf standards. Last I heard, the average number of children was over five per family."

"I can't even imagine having brothers and sisters. When I was growing up, there were hardly any other children in Clementia."

Her voice trailed off but not before Severance picked up the unspoken inference. He knew without being told that those other children hadn't provided much in the way of companionship for the little Wolf born among Harmonics.

"My family was smaller than average too. I only had one brother," he heard himself say.

"The one who was a Harmonic?"

"Yes." He was quiet for a while. "Jeude was a late bloomer in a sense. We didn't realize he was a Harmonic until he was in his late teens. Just thought he was a little different—quiet and thoughtful. A bit eccentric in some ways. My parents had just begun to acknowledge that he might be Harmonic when they were killed."

"Oh, Severance," she said gently, "what happened?"

"They were geologists with a big mining company on QED. There was an accident. An explosion." He sensed her movement, and the next thing he knew, she was stretching out her hand to touch his. "Jeude took it hard. Very hard. And he refused to be separated from me after that. He wouldn't hear of being sent to Clementia."

"So you let him run mail with you?"

"He was good at it. Very determined. Once in a while I let him take a ship out alone while I made deliveries and arranged contracts here on Renaissance or on Lovelady. He liked going to QED by himself with just Fred along for company. Said it gave him a lot of time to think. I knew I should have insisted he go to Clementia for training, but he kept resisting the idea and I just didn't have the heart to force him. He got killed because of my lousy judgment."

"Was he killed on that red plain? The one you light-painted on board ship?"

She might not be a Harmonic, but there were times when the lady was too damn intuitive. "He went straight into the ground answering a distress signal in a QED sandstorm. Nothing that flies can survive one of those storms. The only thing a pilot can do is run from them. But Jeude didn't run." Severance felt his hand clench into a fist under the sleeper cover. Very deliberately he forced himself to flatten out his palm. "Fred survived. The rescue crew found him wrapped around Jeude's leg when they arrived. The ship was destroyed, pieces of it scattered over a wide area. They never did find all the cargo."

"I'm so sorry, Severance."

"I know." He didn't doubt it for a moment. Cidra's compassion was as real as her ability with Moonlight and Mirrors. Sweetness and light were her inner core of strength. He shook off the brooding feeling as he thought about the conflicting image. "It's in the past, Cidra. I wish I hadn't mentioned it." Severance rubbed his eyes wearily, thinking that he hadn't talked about Jeude to anyone for a long time.

She didn't press him. Her hand slipped back into her sleeper, and she turned on her back to stare at the low ceiling of the tent. Another distant clanking sound echoed in the night, and a small scream split the air close to the camp.

"Overcash is right. Renaissance is somewhat overwhelming," Cidra said quietly.

"Frightened?"

"No, of course not. I understand about the security systems and the deflectors and all. There's nothing to worry about."

"Cidra . . ."

"Too bad they haven't come up with some way of blocking out some of the night noises, though. It's very hard to sleep with so much jungle racket."

Severance said again, "Cidra."

She ignored him again. "I hope Fred is enjoying his stay with Desma. He certainly seems to like her. He'll be in for a shock if he wanders into the lab, though, won't he?"

Severance unfastened the opening of his sleeper. "Cidra, come in here with me. There's room for two."

Her head snapped around. "Severance, no, I don't think that would be a very good idea."

On one level he agreed with her. But he couldn't spend the rest of the night listening to her tension. "Then relax. I'm not about to fight my way through those trousers you're wearing. I'm just offering a little human comfort."

"I'm not a child."

"Did anyone ever hold you until you fell asleep when you were a child?"

There was a long silence. "Harmonics don't touch each other except when they're in full telepathic communion. My parents were never able to experience that kind of bond with me."

He heard the careful explanation and then reached across to unfasten her sleeper. "Come here, Cidra. I'll hold you until you fall asleep."

"Really, Severance, that isn't necessary. I'm just fine the way I am."

He sat up and pried her gently out of the sleeper. She resisted slightly at first, and then, with a warm, scrambling rush she was inside his sleeper, curved against his body. She lay still for a moment, and then he felt her begin to relax. The distant clank of zalon armor sounded again, but this time she didn't flinch. The lumbering warriors continued to fight their battle in the darkness while Cidra gradually ceased to be an unwilling audience.

Some time later, when he was absolutely sure that she was asleep, Severance allowed himself to cradle Cidra more intimately. His hand drifted to her breast and rested there as he yawned deeply. She felt good nestled into him this way, her firm buttocks tucked against his thighs. He liked the relaxed way she was finally sleeping. It made him feel good to have her trust him, even on an unconscious level. She was so concerned with trust, so convinced that she could never establish it completely with a man until she was a Harmonic.

Cidra wasn't born to be a Harmonic. Severance knew that with a certainty that burned deep. He wondered how long she would pursue her fruitless quest. It wasn't in her to acknowledge defeat. The only thing that would deflect her from her goal was if she, herself, changed her mind. And from what he knew of her that wasn't likely. She was a stubborn woman.

He allowed himself the luxury of resting his hand on her breast and decided that he could be just as stubborn as any false Harmonic. With that, Severance finally slipped into sleep himself.

It wasn't the clanking of zalons or the screams of another jungle denizen, but the sound of human voices and the hum of a river skimmer that awakened him the next morning. For a moment Severance lay still, considering the coincidence of another skimmer having chosen this tributary to travel. It wasn't very likely an accidental event. According to what Severance had been told, only the ExcellEx field camp lay along this tributary, and Overcash was the only skimmer pilot supplying that base. He yanked on his trousers.

Overcash's greeting boomed out over the water. "Hey, come ashore for some hot coffade. We're just about to eat."

"Sounds good," came the response. "I'm coming in."

Severance heard the answering voice and reached for his pulser holster.

"Severance?" Sleepily Cidra blinked and looked up at him. "What's wrong?"

"Nothing yet." He finished strapping on the pulser and slid out of the sleeper.

"Then why are you . . . ?"

"Racer's here."

"Racer!"

She sat up, startled. Her face was flushed and her braid half undone as she stared at him in astonishment. Severance wished he had the freedom to get back into the sleeper with her and conduct an intimate discussion on the merits of human comfort. But that option wasn't open to him.

"It's one renegade hell of a coincidence that he's running the same river with us. I don't trust him any farther than I can ship him without postage."

Severance stepped out into the dawn to find Racer was already on shore, his skimmer bobbing lightly behind him on the water. The man's blue-green eyes followed Severance as he emerged from the tent.

"Spend a pleasant night teaching new tricks to the Harmonic, Severance?" Racer smiled and lifted the pulser in his hand until it was pointed at Severance's bare chest. "Maybe before this is all over I'll take the opportunity to add to her education. But for now, drop the pulser, Severance. I'm here to do a little business. Bonus business."

TEN

Whats the matter, Overcash? ExcellEx bonus money not good enough for you? Think Racer's going to pay more? You're in for a surprise. Racer's not all that reliable. Take my word for it. I've had firsthand experience."

Inside the tent Cidra listened in shock to Severance's cool, contemptuous voice. She shoved aside the feathery light sleeper. As she struggled with the awkward boots that went with her new outfit, she could hear the three men very clearly. Their rough, tense tones sounded infinitely more lethal than the noises of the jungle morning.

"Shut up, Severance," Racer said. "We're just going to conduct some business. After which we'll leave you in peace. Where are the sensors, Overcash?"

"In the skimmer's cargo hold."

"Get 'em out. Load them onto the skimmer I brought."

"But why?" Overcash sounded honestly confused. "I thought we were going to take both skimmers back with us."

"I've changed the plans slightly."

Severance interrupted mildly. "He does that a lot, Overcash. Racer's changes of plans have a way of leaving a man holding a lockmouth by the wrong end."

"I've told you to shut up, Severance. Call the little Saint out of the tent. You can't hide her in there forever."

Cidra was already stepping through the iris diaphragm opening. She spoke very softly. "I'm here, Racer. There's no need to shout."

"Stay where you are, Cidra," Severance ordered without turning to look at her. "Don't come any closer."

Obediently Cidra halted, taking in the scene with a quick glance. Overcash was transferring the carton of ExcellEx sensors from his skimmer to a second craft that had been made fast alongside. While he labored Cord Racer kept a pulser trained on Severance. The pulser Severance had been wearing was missing from its holster. Racer had taken it.

Severance stood with his customary ease. If there had been a chair nearby, he probably would have sprawled in it as usual. Nothing except the contempt in his expression gave any indication of his tension. But Cidra sensed the leashed fury in him so clearly, she thought for an instant that she had almost read his mind. The sensation was disconcerting.

Racer showed his tension much more visibly. It radiated through his body as he faced Severance. His eyes were narrowed, and the hold he had on the pulser seemed far too tight. When his gaze flicked briefly to Cidra, she knew he had already dismissed her as a source of trouble. She knew that in his mind she occupied the status of a "harmless Harmonic." And at the moment she did feel harmless. The frustration was enough to push aside some of her fear and allow anger to take its place. But as she stood silently beside the tent Cidra kept all of her emotions sheltered behind a serene facade.

"We'll make this short and sweet, Severance," Racer said. "Wouldn't want to take up too much of your valuable time. You're going to need it to try to walk out of this jungle by sunset."

Overcash finished loading the cargo and jumped to the bank.

"There's no way he can walk out by sunset. I made sure we came far enough yesterday to make that impossible for anything but a zalon. Want me to collapse the tents?"

"No need," Racer replied. "They won't do him any good. That lightweight armor isn't enough to do any more than keep the bandini off him. And I don't want to waste time. We've already wasted too much as it is."

Severance looked at him with idle interest. "Those were your men at Lovelorn? The ones who posed as port security?"

Racer shrugged. "A couple of incompetents. But I didn't have time to be too choosy. Quench moved unexpectedly when he commissioned you to make the run with the sensors. I'd been expecting him to delay for another few days. As it was, I barely got word of it in time to make any kind of try at all. I'd like to know what you did to those guys, Severance. They were almost incoherent when I finally found them."

"You should have told them that coming aboard *Severance Pay* without an invitation wasn't going to be a simple slide-in, slide-out job."

"I figured two of them could handle it. Especially with you running around Lovelorn trying to pick up some extra credit from one more patron. A good postman like you couldn't resist just one more commission, could you?"

Severance nodded. "I wondered about that deal at Lovelorn. Especially yesterday, when I couldn't find the man who was supposed to be waiting so eagerly for the case."

"Good help is hard to find," Racer drawled. "And getting harder all the time. Didn't have much luck with the renegade I hired to pick up Cidra the other night, either. After I met her at the Bloodsucker it occurred to me that she might be a handy sardite chip. Thought if I had her, you might be more amenable to a little bargaining."

For an instant Cidra felt her outward control slip. "That was your man in the lab? The one who hurt Desma?"

Racer gave her a short, wry glance. "He wasn't after Desma. But he figured she would head for the lab when she got the malfunction alarm. The idea was that you would be alone in the house. Easy pickings."

"But she followed Desma to the lab instead," Severance said.

Racer shrugged. "It still would have worked if one of those bugs Desma keeps as pets hadn't gotten loose. The way Payne told it, he was lucky to escape alive. This time I decided I'd better handle things myself. My clients are getting impatient."

"I'll just bet they are," Severance murmured. "You've missed twice so far. What makes you think you're going to have any more luck this time around?"

"In case you haven't noticed, Severance, my luck is running very high today. Thanks to some advance planning." Racer spoke over his shoulder to Overcash. "Is the skimmer I brought ready?"

"All set. I'll take the deflectors."

"No, we'll leave those behind along with the tents. The screens have already been used all night, haven't they?"

"Sure, but . . ."

"Then they haven't got more than a few hours' charge left. Without the skimmer's fuel cells there's no way to recharge them."

"What are you going to do with the skimmer I brought?" Overcash demanded.

"It's going to be in a severe accident. And that's what this whole scene will look like in a couple of days. An unfortunate, but not untypical, Renaissance river accident. Skimmer sinks and the crew is left on shore with failing equipment. By the time another skimmer heads up this far, there won't be much left. Renaissance will see to that for us."

"You're a fool, Racer," Severance said wearily.

Overcash moved uneasily, his hard face knotting into a frown. "I don't know, Racer. Might be better to make sure of 'em before we leave."

Racer shook his head. "Too much chance another skimmer will be along in a couple of days. If we use the pulser, there'll be evidence. I've heard too much lately about that renegade named Quench who runs ExcellEx. He's trying to build a reputation as a company owner who looks after his own. If he hears that his handpicked mail pilot got shot trying to deliver the sensors, he'll demand an investigation. And he's getting big enough to force one. Hell, he'll pay for it out of his own pocket if he gets really mad. No, this has to look like an accident." A terrifying screech sounded from the jungle followed by a bitten-off scream. Racer smiled. "Come on, Overcash. We're not leaving anything to chance. No one spends a night in a Renaissance jungle without equipment and lives to tell about it. Everything will be over by morning."

Overcash looked unconvinced, but he obviously wasn't going to argue. He turned and jumped on board the second skimmer and made ready to loosen the moorings. Twin dracon eyes emerged briefly in the river as if curious. They disappeared again with barely a ripple.

Severance studied Racer as if he were looking at the man through a microscope and didn't like what he saw. "Think it will work this time?"

"It'll work," Racer said roughly.

"Maybe. Maybe not." Severance gave every appearance of being only mildly interested.

"Tell you what," Racer said, glancing at Cidra, who was still standing motionless in front of the tent. "I'll do you a favor. I'll take Cidra with me."

Cidra started, growing cold inside. "No."

Severance was watching Racer. "And do what? Throw her in the river when you've finished with her? She might as well stay with me."

Racer grinned, sensing that for the first time he had a handle on the situation. He seized it, motioning Cidra with the pulser. "Get on board the skimmer, Cidra. You don't want to stay behind. Something in this jungle is going to have your shipmaster for dinner tonight, and you'll be dessert if you're hanging around."

"No," Cidra said again. She looked to Severance for some support, but he was quiet, almost thoughtful. "I'm staying here."

"She's a Harmonic, Racer. If the right people find out you've hurt her, there'll be a reckoning. You know that."

"I might not have to get rid of her," Racer temporized, "if she has the sense to keep her mouth shut. Do you, Otanna?" He made the formal title a mockery.

"I don't understand." Cidra's tone was aloof, but her heart was beating much too quickly, and the palms of her hands, folded serenely in front of her, were damp. This was as bad as facing the intruder in the lab had been.

"Sure, you understand. Harmonics are real good at understanding, aren't they? They're also real good at keeping their promises. I'm going to take you with me. At the end of the trip you'll have a choice. Give me your word as a Harmonic that you'll keep quiet about what happened here this morning and I'll put you on the next freighter to Clementia. Refuse and I'll feed you to a dracon."

"Why don't you simply leave me here with Severance?"

"Because knowing you're going to be warming my bunk for a couple of nights will eat him up inside. I want to give him something to think about while he's waiting for the deflector screens to fail."

Cidra understood. Racer thought that she and Severance were lovers. He thought he could use her to twist the blade in Severance. She knew in that moment that there was far more between the two men than was obvious. This kind of hatred went back a long way. She shivered and unconsciously stepped closer to Severance.

"Go with him, Cidra."

She was stunned at Severance's soft order. "I will not go with him. I work for you. I'm staying here."

"Cidra, with him you've got a chance. Take it."

"No."

Overcash snarled. "How long are we going to stand here and chat, Racer?"

"No longer." Racer lifted the pulser slightly. "Get on board the skimmer, Cidra, or I'll kill Severance and be done with the whole thing."

He would do it. Cidra looked into Racer's face and knew he

had been pushed far enough. Any farther and Severance would die. He wouldn't even have the hours until nightfall that the deflectors could provide. She was trained to analyze a situation and react logically. Without a word she stepped past Severance and walked toward the skimmer.

Racer visibly relaxed, a satisfied expression in his eyes. "They always say Harmonics are bright. Be interesting to see how good one is in bed. The next couple of nights are going to be amusing. Think about them while you're waiting for the deflectors to run out of power, Severance."

"You know what'll happen if I make it out of here, don't you, Racer?" Severance asked very softly.

"We both know you'll never make it out, so there's no need to worry about it. If I were you, Severance, I'd stop wasting breath on threats and start thinking about how long those deflectors will last without a recharge." Racer backed to the boat, keeping the pulser trained on Severance.

When he was on board, Overcash slipped the last tethers holding the skimmer in place and moved into the cabin. Cidra stood in the stern, her eyes on Severance as the skimmer's fuel cells hummed to life. The power packs glowed green beside her in the rear of the boat. She was cold and sick inside. When Severance met her gaze and smiled faintly, she felt an unfamiliar stinging sensation behind her eyes. Her hands tightened in front of her.

"I'll take the wheel," Racer said as the skimmer moved away from the shore. "This next little surprise has got to be timed properly." He holstered the pulser as Overcash stepped out of the cabin.

Cidra tensed as the skimmer drifted farther from the bank. Severance was walking back toward the tent. He seemed in no hurry, but Overcash frowned and palmed his own pulser. The base of the weapon glowed red. "What's he doing?"

"There's nothing he can do," Racer told him from inside the cabin.

"I don't like it."

"You don't have to like it. In another couple of minutes the skimmer will go to the bottom and, with it, any chance he's got of getting out of this in one piece."

Cidra listened to the exchange, aware that in typical Wolf fashion both men had assumed that she was incapable of being a threat. They were right. She could not hope to use her Moonlight and Mirrors on both of them at the same time. Not when each man was armed with a pulser. But their attention was not on her, and this was the only opportunity she was going to get. She edged toward the high gunwale of the skimmer. It would be better if she could take off the boots, but that was not possible.

"He's disappeared!" Overcash yelled. "I think he's inside the tent. I can't see what he's doing."

"This will bring him out in one renegade hell of a hurry." Racer activated the control of the small instrument he was holding in one hand. "Watch. I rigged your boat for you, Overcash, before you left Try Again."

There was a muffled roar. The skimmer left floating near the bank seemed to shudder, and then it imploded with a sickening crunch of diazite and metal. Slowly but inevitably the boat crumpled in on itself and sank into the river. Cidra waited no longer. This was the best chance she was going to get.

Overcash was staring in fascination at the disintegrating skimmer when Cidra went over the side. She launched herself in a smooth, flat arc, aiming for the shallowest possible dive. The last thing she wanted to do was go any deeper into the river than was absolutely necessary. Behind her she caught part of Overcash's outraged yell.

"She's gone over!"

"Forget her," Racer yelled back. "She's dead meat."

"The renegade bitch!" Overcash raised the pulser.

Cidra was on the surface, stroking strongly toward the bank. Her main concern was trying to keep from getting any of the muddy, brakish river water in her mouth. It was Severance's order that stilled her movements in the water.

"Cidra, stop swimming! Float, damn it. Just float. Don't splash. Don't make a sound. Keep yourself on the surface."

She obeyed, glad that the awkward boots seemed buoyant in the water. With practiced ease she floated while she turned toward the shoreline to spot Severance. She didn't notice if he was there or not; instead she found her gaze locked with a pair of malevolent eyes between her and the bank. A dracon was cruising toward her.

Cidra had never known this kind of terror. Only instinct kept her moving her hands in smooth, gentle sweeps around her midsection. The small movements were sufficient to keep her afloat. But compared to the fear that engulfed her as the dracon approached, drowning seemed a pleasant alternative. She could not yet see anything other than the eyes, but she sensed the vastness of the creature moving toward her. More terrifying, she sensed its relentless, endless hunger. It wasn't certain yet whether she constituted a potential meal, and dimly Cidra realized that it was probably because she was floating on the surface like a log rather than behaving like normal prey.

Another set of eyes surfaced to Cidra's right. She wanted to give in to the panic and have done with it. Anything was better than waiting for the dracons to leisurely start sampling her arms and legs. Perhaps they wouldn't even bother with a sample. Perhaps one of them would simply swallow her with a single gulp. Still she floated, vaguely aware of Overcash's agitation in the skimmer. Racer hadn't thrown the boat into motion yet. He kept it hovering behind Cidra, and she knew that he and Overcash were waiting to see how long it would take the dracons to move in on her.

"I'm going to draw some blood," Overcash announced. "It'll get things over with a lot sooner." Standing in the stern of the skimmer, he raised the pulser and aimed it at the floating Cidra.

Everyone's attention was on Cidra and the dracons. No one noticed Severance when he stepped around the tent, the pulser he'd slept on during the night now in his hand. He aimed the weapon at Overcash and gently squeezed the trigger.

Behind her Cidra heard a man's scream. A second later there was a loud splash and then, with blinding speed, the dracons were in motion. She closed her eyes, waiting for the horror to engulf her. A pair of eyes passed within inches, and she felt the brush of a huge, scaled body against her leg. But there was no tearing sensation. Another set of eyes flowed past, also ignoring her. Cidra didn't stop to question fate. Using all her strength to keep her body as much as possible on the surface, she stroked again for the bank.

There was another scream behind her, but Cidra didn't pause to glance back. She heard the thrashing sounds in the river and, slightly louder, the hum of the skimmer as it was shoved urgently into high speed. The bank seemed very far away.

Then Severance was there, wading into the river and reaching for her. He caught her wrist and dragged her the rest of the way to shore. Cidra wanted to scream as he pulled her up beside him. She automatically turned to see what was happening in the river. There was a flash of a huge, obscene shape that seemed to be made entirely of teeth. And there was something between its jaws, something that had once been human.

"Don't look." Severance forced her head against his shoulder. "It'll all be over in a minute. Just don't watch."

Cidra stood shuddering in the circle of his arm, trying not to think of what she had seen and trying even harder not to think of how it might have been her own torn and mutilated body held fast in those fearsome jaws. In the distance she heard the skimmer's hum fade.

"Racer's gone," she gasped, more for something to say than anything else.

"Racer's good at leaving a friend in an awkward situation. Not that he could have done much for Overcash. Once the dracons sensed blood, nothing on this planet could have stopped them."

"He was going to shoot me. I heard him say a little blood would get things over more quickly."

"He was right."

"You killed him to stop him from shooting me," she said into his damp shirt. She wasn't certain which stunned her more, Severance's killing Overcash or Overcash's willingness to kill her. Cidra felt dazed.

Severance hesitated. "I would have shot him even if he hadn't been trying to wound you. I needed something to feed the dracons. In another minute or two they would have decided you were prey, after all."

"Oh." She couldn't think of anything else to say.

"I would have preferred feeding Racer to the river, but I couldn't get a clear shot at him. Overcash was in the way."

The awful thrashing sounds died away. Slowly, still afraid to turn and look toward the river, Cidra lifted her head. She realized that she was leaning heavily on Severance, seeking strength in him. "It's over," she whispered.

"No," he answered, gently freeing her to look down into her stricken face, "it's just beginning. Why did you jump overboard, Cidra?"

"I had no choice. I couldn't go with him."

"There was a chance he would have believed you really are a Harmonic, and a chance he would have let you go eventually if you'd given him your promise to keep quiet."

"Which I would never have done, so there's no point discussing it, is there?"

"Cidra . . ."

"Stop it, Severance." She pushed away from him, still looking anywhere but at the river. "I could not go with him, and that's all there is to it."

He touched her cheek, his finger rough on her wet skin. "You would have survived rape, Cidra. I'm not so sure about the jungle."

A sudden, fierce rage welled up in her. "I would not have survived rape. He would have had to kill me before he succeeded in raping me. Haven't you heard of death before dishonor?"

Severance looked at her. "Not lately."

"It would have been utterly degrading for me to have submitted to that man in exchange for my life after he'd left you to die. And it would have been equally dishonorable to have given him my promise not to tell the company authorities what had happened."

"That's a little extreme under the circumstances."

"I work for you, Teague Severance. Have you forgotten our contract? I have sworn my loyalty to the firm of Severance Pay, Ltd. It would have been a breach of that act to have let Racer use me. He only wanted to add to your suffering, you know," Cidra explained, lowering her voice. "And it would have bothered you greatly. Not because I was your lover but because you feel responsible for me. Racer didn't seem to understand that I am merely your employee."

"Lately I've had trouble understanding that myself." Severance reached out and wrapped his palms around the nape of Cidra's neck. He pulled her close and kissed her with a quick roughness that betrayed the tension he had hidden so well all morning. "Sweet Harmony in hell, Cidra Rainforest. I've never been so scared in my life as I was when I saw the dracon eyeing you. Don't ever, ever do that to me again."

She smiled mistily as he freed her. "I'll make a note not to go swimming in the near future."

He stared down at her for another long moment, as if he wanted to say more. Instead he released her and turned toward the tent. "I guess I'd better get moving."

Surprised, she stepped after him. "What are we going to do?" A sloshing sound reminded her of her wet boots. Gingerly Cidra sat down on the charred ground and removed them, shaking out the river water.

"I'm going after Racer." He spoke from inside the tent.

"Going after him? But, Severance, he's got a skimmer. He's long gone."

"He's got a skimmer that's in trouble, although he may not realize it yet. It's going to take a while for the fuel cells to start losing power." Severance reappeared outside the tent carrying his travel pack. He put it down on the ground, crouched beside it, and began going through the contents.

Cidra watched him. "Why should the fuel cells fail on his skimmer?"

"After I shot Overcash, Racer ducked into the cabin. I had a clear view of the engine section of the skimmer. And I got in a couple more shots. One cell was glowing yellow when the skimmer took off up the river. Yellow means that the charge was already starting to diminish. Racer will realize what's happening when he calms down and has a chance to check his controls."

"Then what will he do?"

"Panic, I hope. He tends to lose his nerve when the sardite's down. I'm counting on him losing it this time too."

"You speak from past experience with the man?" Cidra asked carefully.

"This isn't the first time we've tangled."

"You said he was once your partner."

Severance removed a thin blade from the travel pack and slipped it into his utility loop. "The partnership dissolved the day he left me to fight my way out of a sinkswamp here on Renaissance."

Cidra sucked in her breath. "He's tried to kill you before?"

"Not exactly. We had a mail run into a field camp that was doing some work in the swamps up north. There was trouble with the sled. Always something going wrong with machinery on this damned planet. The sled started to slip into a sinkswamp with both of us on board. When we realized what was happening, we managed to attach a wire line to a tree. The plan was to use it to climb to safety. Racer went first. When he reached the tree, the line broke. He was getting set to toss me another one when he saw the killweaver. The things live in the swamps, and this one apparently decided to investigate the activity going on over its nest. It surfaced beside the sled. Big ugly thing with very unappealing pincers. Racer took one look and fled."

"Leaving you behind?"

"Guess he figured I didn't have much chance, anyway. He made it to the company's field camp a couple hours later and somehow neglected to mention that he had left me behind in the sled sitting on top of a killweaver's web. I think he was busy realizing just how convenient the whole setup was. In one fell swoop he was now sole owner of the ship and all our equipment. It was somewhat disconcerting for him when I wandered into camp an hour behind him. We've made a practice of avoiding each other ever since."

"How did you get away from the . . . the killweaver?" Cidra struggled with the dim recollection of a holotype she had once seen of a huge spider shape. Another typical Renaissance horror. Even the wild parts of Lovelady seemed tame in comparison to this planet.

"It's a short story. The trick with dracons and killweavers is to distract them with a convenient meal."

Cidra shuddered. "What did you find to feed the killweaver?"

"Something equally mean and ugly." Severance got to his feet, having removed several small objects from his travel pack.

"But you didn't find this, uh, distraction until after the web had burned your hands?"

"It never pays to be slow on Renaissance." He dropped the travel pack and checked the contents of his loop.

"Are we leaving already?" Cidra asked.

"I'm leaving. You're staying here."

She shot to her feet. "Severance, no!"

His face softened. "You'll be all right. There's enough charge left on the deflectors to last until nightfall. I'll be back by then. Just stay inside the screens and don't wander outside for any reason. Understood?"

"I refuse to stay here alone while you take off into that jungle!"

"I'll be staying close to the riverbank. Don't worry, Racer won't get far. When he realizes that the fuel cells are faltering, he'll bring the skimmer into shore, set up the deflector screens, and call for help. I intend to arrive long before help does."

"I don't like this," Cidra began earnestly.

"I'm not especially thrilled with the mess we're in, either. But since I'm the one who got us into it, I'd better start fixing things.

Once the fuel cells start to go, the skimmer won't have enough power to stay afloat, but there'll still be enough of a charge left in them to keep the deflectors and a comm unit going for quite a while. I can float the skimmer back down the river if necessary. Relax, I'm supposed to be the one who's good with his hands, remember?" He walked toward her, coming to a halt a short distance away. "Don't look at me like that, Cidra. It's going to be all right. This is my fault and I'll take care of it."

"It's hardly your fault!"

"I'm the pilot in command. The head of Severance Pay, Ltd. That makes it my job to clean up the situation. Besides, even if I wanted to delegate the responsibility, this is a very small firm. I don't see any convenient vice-president standing around to send after Racer."

"There's me."

"You've already done more than your share to defend the mail and the firm. It's my turn. I'll be back before the screens fail. Believe me? I spent the year after Jeude's death getting to know this jungle very well."

She chewed helplessly on her lower lip and then nodded once. "I believe you, Severance." And she did. If he didn't come back before the screens failed, it would be because he couldn't come back. She didn't want to think about that possibility.

"I'll see you before nightfall, then."

"And then what?" she challenged. But she knew even as she spoke that she had accepted the inevitable. There was no choice but for him to leave. Taking her with him would slow him down far too much.

"When I come back, I'll bring the skimmer and a fresh set of screens. If we can't repair the skimmer, we can still use the communications equipment to call for aid."

She drew a deep breath. "What about Racer?"

Severance didn't look up as he adjusted the utility loop. "What about him?"

She searched his face. "You're going to kill him, aren't you?"

"Don't think about it, Cidra. Racer is my problem." He leaned down to brush his mouth over hers. When he lifted his head, he was smiling again. "I've got to stop doing that."

She touched her lips with her fingertips, realizing how accustomed she was becoming to his brief, intimate gestures. She remembered how she had felt when she'd stood in the stern of Racer's skimmer and watched as she was dragged farther and farther away from Severance. Then, in a wordless rush, she threw her arms around his neck.

"Be careful, Severance. Please be careful."

"I'll be back for you before nightfall." He held her, his arms closing with bruising fierceness around her slender body. Then he released her and moved through the screens without glancing back.

Cidra watched until he was out of sight. It didn't take long. The undergrowth closed behind him, and it was as if he had never been standing there with her at all. Out on the river all was once again placid, giving no hint of the living hell that cruised just below the surface.

Cidra was staring at the spot where the skimmer had floated when she caught sight of something shiny out of the corner of her eye. It was a container of Renaissance Rose ale that had apparently survived the explosion of the skimmer. It was caught in the reeds near shore. Cidra risked a quick trip through the deflectors to rescue the container. Severance would appreciate the ale when he returned.

Holding the Renaissance Rose as if it were a talisman that could somehow guarantee Severance's safe return, Cidra slipped back into the safety of the deflectors.

ELEVEN

He had to get the deflectors and the skimmer's communication equipment. And he would probably have to kill Racer to do it.

Severance didn't try to fool himself. There was an outside chance that Racer would allow himself to be dragged back to Try Again and turned over to the company authorities, but it wasn't likely. He had too much to lose. He was far more likely to force Severance's hand, counting on what he knew of his ex-partner to keep him from getting killed. Deep down Racer was probably convinced that Severance wouldn't have the guts to kill him.

Severance moved through the undergrowth along the river-bank, trying to make as little noise as possible. There was no chance that Racer would hear him, but there was every chance something else might come to investigate the strange movement. Without the deflector screens a man with a pulser and a utility knife was among the more poorly armed of Renaissance's inhabitants.

Severance knew that all of his senses were on full alert. He had reached that unpleasantly acute state of awareness he had come to

know well during the year after Jeude's death. It didn't take much
to translate awareness into panic. There were a lot of things that
could kill on Renaissance, but panic was one of the surest methods. Severance let his eyes and ears and the hairs on the back of
his neck do their job while he thought about Racer.

Racer, who had once been his friend. Racer, who in some ways
he knew better than any other living man in the universe. Racer,
who had tried to take Cidra as a battle prize while he left his former partner to die.

A band of dark green slithered through the light green river
grass ahead of Severance. Automatically he brought the pulser up
and trained it on the wedge-shaped head. But the green slicer apparently had better things to do than sample a jungle boot. It
moved out of the way, shivering iridescently in the morning light.
Behind him Severance heard a startled squawk that ended with
telling abruptness. The green slicer had found another meal.

Severance kept moving, using the utility knife when the tangled vines became too thick to push aside. He tried to calculate
how far Racer could get with a failing set of fuel cells. The second
and third pulser shots this morning had done real damage; Severance was sure of it. But it was difficult to tell how far the craft
would go before it started sinking toward the water line. As long
as Racer ran the skimmer at top speed, the end was bound to
come quickly. And he was certain Racer would force the craft as
far as he could at the highest possible speed. Racer was the nervous type under pressure. He tended to panic.

That tendency was a side of the man few people would ever
know. Only when you had worked with a man in a high-pressure
situation did you learn his real weaknesses, the ones that could
get you killed. Severance had learned them the hard way. Finding
yourself facing a killweaver alone had a way of making a lasting
impression.

So he'd learned his lesson. Never trust anyone—except perhaps a Harmonic—completely. Severance's partnership with Racer
had dissolved. Life went on, and Severance saw to it that he and
Racer rarely came into contact. Racer had been cooperative in that

respect. Severance also avoided any more attempts at forming a partnership. Severance Pay, Ltd., he'd decided, would take a slightly slower route to success.

There was a flurry of black wings up ahead. Severance paused and gave the flying reptile the chance to get off the ground with its prey impaled in its toothed beak. Then he started moving again, circling a stand of suspicious-looking flowers. Anything as beautiful as those flowers had to be deadly on this planet.

A pair of eyes watched him from the river. Severance didn't look at them. For the rest of his life, whenever he saw dracon eyes, he would think of those sickening moments when Cidra had been the center of dracon attention. The memory made his hand tighten on the grip of the pulser. Deliberately he forced himself to relax. A too-solid grip made the weapon more difficult to aim properly.

Cidra had floated. The image of her hovering quietly in the water as the dracons moved closer was still a source of amazement to Severance. Doing so had been her only chance, of course. She had bought him the time he needed to find the monsters another meal. But the terror would have overcome most people, *should* have overcome a gently raised lady from Clementia. Most people would have panicked. But Cidra had heard his desperate instructions and she had obeyed them.

Racer had put her to that savage test and nearly gotten her killed. And it was Racer who had tried to carry her off, knowing with a man's sure instinct that Severance's helpless rage would be a worse torment than the knowledge that the deflector screens were going to fail by nightfall.

Severance had half convinced himself that Cidra might be better off with her captor than left behind to face the Renaissance night, but that belief had been his rational, thinking side speaking. His emotional side hadn't come close to seeing that logic. His guts had been twisted with fury at the thought of Racer trying to rape Cidra. And it would have been rape. Cidra would never willingly submit to Racer. She would have seen it as a betrayal of herself and of Severance.

"Death before dishonor." He wondered where she'd picked up that phrase. Probably from those First Family tales she was so fond of reading. No telling where the First Family writers had picked up the concept. Must have been a part of the folklore they had brought with them to their new world.

Even though he had feared for her life when she had dived from the skimmer, Severance acknowledged that a part of him had been exultant. Cidra belonged to him, and on some level she had acknowledged that. He didn't know any other woman who would have chosen to stay behind with him in a Renaissance jungle when the alternative was some hope of survival.

He swore silently. He was getting as primitive in his reactions as everything else on this planet.

The time slipped past. Severance heard no distant hum from the skimmer. But he did perceive a change in the atmosphere, a lengthening shadow from the heavy, bloated clouds building high overhead. Just what he needed, Severance thought—a storm. Renaissance did thunderstorms the way it did everything else—on a grand scale.

Heavy rain would have no effect on the deflector screens surrounding Cidra, and she could stay reasonably dry in the tent, but the storm was bound to be unnerving for her. And it could slow him down. With common sense, a certain amount of knowledge, luck, and a pulser, a man might survive Renaissance during the day. Night was another story. The only consolation was that the storm would also slow the failing skimmer. Maybe Racer would start to panic sooner than he might otherwise.

The cloud shadows had nearly blocked out the sunlight entirely when Severance detoured around a broad-leafed tree that was as thick in the trunk as a small building. Suddenly he realized that he could hear metallic sounds. Not the hum of a skimmer— for an instant he thought he might have had the unbelievably good luck of happening across someone else camped on the riverbank.

He slowed, using the thick foliage for concealment, and edged toward the sounds. Severance saw the skimmer first. It had been pulled into shore and made fast. Racer had apparently used the crisper to carve out a small clearing on the bank. He wouldn't want anything sneaking up on him while he was occupied with the skimmer, and from the hot, sweaty look of him, he had already been working on the machinery for quite a while. He had left the engine panel in the stern open and was bent over the controls inside.

Seeing Racer, Severance felt a wave of seething fury sweep through him. He grimly waited for it to pass. It would only cause his hand to shake and his brain to function on partial power. It wasn't the way for a predator to confront prey. And, this time around, Racer was the prey.

Severance gave himself another moment or two to control the anger, and then, pulser raised, he stepped out into the open.

"Don't waste your time on it, Racer. You won't be needing transportation."

Racer's head came up with a hard jerk that betrayed his nervous state. For a second he simply stared at Severance from the stern of the skimmer. There was desperation in his face, something Severance had never seen in him before. He stepped closer.

Racer threw himself down onto the deck of the skimmer. Severance fired the pulser, not at the empty stern but at the diazite cabin wall. The wall crackled and exploded, sending a shower of jagged shards down onto the man hiding behind the gunwale.

There were several startled screams and a brief scurrying in the vegetation behind Severance as a few of the local inhabitants opted to vacate the area. He knew that while some fled, others would be big enough and hungry enough to indulge their curiosity. They would come closer to investigate.

But the diazite shower had had the desired effect. Only something as powerful as a pulser could break up diazite, but when it did fracture, the shards were like jagged blades. Racer didn't wait for the next wall of the cabin to be splintered. Pulser in hand, he leapt over the side, using the craft as cover while he waded the short distance to shore. He risked a shot over the bow, driving

Severance behind the house-sized tree, and then ran for shelter at the edge of the small clearing he had made with the crisper.

"It's all over, you renegade bastard," Severance called. "Did you really think I'd let you get away with it?"

"You don't stand a chance without the skimmer and screens, Severance. Throw down the pulser and I'll consider a deal."

"You don't have anything to bargain with. I'm claiming the skimmer."

"You'll never get close to it. From here I can cut you down before you get aboard." Racer wasted a pulser shot demonstrating his line of sight. A small vine that had been missed earlier by the hurried crisping job fizzled, smoked, and died. "Won't do you any good, anyway. You really did a job on those fuel cells. The only thing working on that damn boat is the communication equipment. I was just about to put in a call. We're both stuck here, Severance, until I make that call."

Severance listened as Racer moved uneasily on the other side of the clearing. "I was always better with equipment than you were, Racer. Remember?"

A pulser shot was the answer. Overhead several huge leaves crumpled. The angle of the shot was different. Racer was trying to edge around the clearing. Severance slipped away from the shelter of the tree trunk, paused to let a small creature with oversize antenna scurry out of the way, and then padded quietly to a different position.

"Be careful, Racer. You never know whose mouth you'll step into out here. Maybe something like a killweaver. Something that takes its time sucking a man dry."

There was a silence from the other side of the clearing. Too much silence. Severance could guess what Racer's imagination must be doing to him. He knew damn well that his own imagination was operating in high gear. Grimly he clamped down on it, refusing to let himself see fangs in every trailing vine. That kind of thinking wasn't going to get him far. Slowly he worked deeper into the vegetation. Racer would stay close to the clearing's edge while he tried to find Severance.

There was a flash of movement at Severance's right shoulder. He froze. A long, forked tongue emerged from between jaws that could grind rocks. The tongue tasted the air and then delicately extended to taste Severance's sleeve.

There was no way he could lift the pulser and fire it before the scaled head struck. Severance didn't move, hoping the fabric of his sleeve wouldn't taste very good. Beyond the tongue, two small eyes that looked like bottomless pits stared at him. The tongue touched the sleeve and flicked about in confusion. Severance didn't move.

"I'm willing to talk, Severance. We can deal. We were partners once. For old time's sake I'm willing to make a deal."

Racer's voice came from somewhere behind Severance. He didn't dare turn around. He would have to rely on the vegetation to conceal him while he waited for the tongue to finish sampling his sleeve. The death that lurked in the creature's eyes was closer and more certain than the death in Racer's weapon.

At the sound of the voice from another location the tongue darted about in more agitated confusion. Finally it disappeared back into the rock-crunching jaws. With another flash of movement the baleful eyes vanished too. Severance began to breathe again. Turning slowly, he listened to Racer. The other man was only a few meters away now, but he couldn't yet be seen.

"You'll need my help to get back to camp. You left your little Harmonic there, didn't you? If you don't get back by dusk, she'll be food. Come on, Severance. You don't want that. The longer you play this hunt-and-stalk game, the weaker those deflectors are getting."

Severance said nothing. He was too close. He caught a glimpse of clothing as Racer edged forward in the undergrowth. The other man slipped past within arm's reach.

"I'm going to call for help, Severance. Another skimmer can get here by midday tomorrow. You want that distress call put in as much as I do."

Severance waited a few more seconds and then glided forward

until he was directly behind the other man. "Drop the pulser or I'll end this now."

Racer went still, but he didn't drop the weapon. "You won't kill me, Severance. You need my help. And I'm willing to give it."

"I need you about as much as I need a visit from a dracon. Drop the pulser."

"Bastard!" Racer broke, diving into the tangled vines and leaves to his right.

Severance raised the pulser but held his fire as he listened to the other man charging wildly through the undergrowth. Racer was in full flight, and he was in a panic.

The scream that echoed through the jungle a moment later was almost anticlimactic. Severance tensed, waiting for it to be cut off with the usual deadly abruptness. He didn't want to think about what had gotten Racer.

But the scream didn't die. It kept reverberating, chilling Severance's nerves. He would have given a great deal of credit to have it cease. But there was no escape from it. Racer kept screaming.

There was no walking away from that kind of human fear and despair. No man deserved to die that slowly. Severance worked his way toward the terrified cries. He kept the pulser in front of him, dreading what he might see. The sound wasn't shifting direction. Whatever held Racer was confident enough not to bother carrying its prey back to its lair.

Severance edged around a leaf wider than he was tall and stared at the predator that held the screaming man. It was a flower. The most spectacularly beautiful flower he had ever seen. Huge, lacy petals shimmered gold and purple and red, the colors flowing into each other. The whole thing was twice as big as Racer.

He had blundered into the very heart of the flower and was now held fast by a sticky center. The huge, lacy petals were just beginning to fold shut, enclosing their prey. Racer's pulser lay on the soft, musty ground.

"Severance! Severance, save me! Stop it. You can't let this happen. You know you can't. You'd never be able to live with yourself.

You were always so big on doing things by your own damned code. Let me die like this and your reeting honor won't mean a thing. And you'll know it. You'll know it, even if no one else does. For the rest of your life you'll know it. You'll have to live with it the way I've lived with it. Waiting. Always waiting for someone to find out."

Severance looked at the flower, fascinated by the lethal beauty. The edges of a couple of the lacy leaves had just begun to cradle Racer as if he were a lover. Racer screamed again as he felt their touch. He tried to pull one hand free from the sticky substance and failed. His face was a mask of growing terror.

"Severance, it's starting to eat me. I can feel it. Stop it. You've got to stop it!"

"I'm trying to think of one good reason." Severance waited. "Come on, Racer. Give me one good reason. After what you've done . . ."

"It was an accident," Racer screamed. He was almost incoherent now. "I never meant to kill him. He wasn't supposed to die. How did I know he'd follow that signal into the ground? Do you hear me, Severance? I didn't intend to kill Jeude."

Severance felt as if a giant shock wave had caught him and hurled him to the ground. He was still standing, but there was something wrong. He wanted to scream too. Not in fear but in rage. Slowly he raised the pulser and took aim at the base of the flower. He squeezed the trigger. It took three shots to eat through the tough fibers of the deceptively graceful stem.

The flower, severed from its base, fell limply to the jungle floor. Racer was still trapped inside. He was weeping uncontrollably when Severance reached him. Carefully Severance pried open the lacy leaves, using the pulser once or twice. Then, avoiding any contact with the sticky, hairy heart, he reached down and pulled Racer free.

It was hard work. The flower, even dead, did not willingly give up its prey. When Racer at last rolled free, Severance saw that his clothing had already been dissolved in places and that there were bright red marks on the skin that showed through the holes.

"Get up."

Racer crouched at Severance's feet, still weeping.

"I said, get up."

Racer shook his head, brushing his eyes against his sleeve. "You'll kill me. I knew you would. I figured you'd rather do it than let that . . . that *thing* do it once I told you about Jeude. A pulser's better than being eaten alive."

"Why, Racer? Why couldn't you just stay the hell out of my way? Why did you have to kill Jeude? Why did you try to take Cidra? You should have just come after me, Racer. You should never have gone after them."

"This time I figured I had you too," the kneeling man whimpered. His voice broke into a hoarse whisper. "I couldn't stand it anymore."

"Couldn't stand what?"

"The way you look through me as if I weren't worth a single credit. I knew what you were thinking. I kept wondering when you'd decide to have a laugh and tell someone else what really happened that day in the sinkswamp. You knew what it was doing to me. Never knowing when you'd decide the game had gone on long enough. You were just biding your time, waiting for a really good moment to tell everyone how I'd left you to face that kill-weaver. And after you'd made your announcement I'd never have worked as a mail pilot again. No one would have trusted me. I couldn't let you hold that weapon over me forever, Severance."

"Why did you go after Jeude?" Severance realized that his hand was trembling. He ached to pull the trigger.

"It was supposed to be you," Racer said bleakly, staring at the spongy ground. "It was supposed to be you in that ship. I didn't know you'd stayed behind until afterward. All I wanted was the cargo. I wanted to make it look like you'd sold the cargo to a higher bidder. But the sandstorm came up so quickly. Jeude didn't stop following the distress beacon. He just kept riding it."

"Right into the storm and then into the ground. I should have left you in the flower, Racer."

"You wouldn't," Racer said. "You couldn't. That's the thing

about you, Severance. You're soft in some ways. Too soft." He climbed slowly to his feet, more assured now. "I don't think you're going to use the pulser, either. You'd have done it by now if you were capable of killing me in cold blood. You'll take me back for a nice, neat legal trial, won't you?"

"Sorry, Racer. I've got better things to do than see you get that kind of justice. Besides, a good trial costs credit." Lowering the pulser, Severance walked around the man, heading back the way he had come.

"Severance!"

Severance ignored him. He didn't trust himself to turn. It would be so easy to use the pulser. The memory of Jeude and the image of Cidra filled his head. The pulser grip was warm in his hand. Too easy. Racer didn't deserve it that easy.

"Severance, you can't leave me!"

There was a scrambling sound behind him. Severance heard it and knew instinctively that Racer wouldn't risk tackling him, which left only one other explanation for the frantic, scuffling movements. Racer was going to the weapon he had dropped when the flower had caught him. Severance swung around and fired just as Racer, kneeling, raised the pulser he had found. He gave only one short, chopped-off cry. The familiar, horribly abrupt scream of one more Renaissance victim.

Severance lowered the pulser. Too easy. Jeude's killer should have died more slowly. He had wanted Renaissance to execute the sentence in its own inevitable, fearsome manner. The fact that neither Jeude nor Cidra would have wanted that kind of end for Racer was immaterial. They had nothing to say about it. Severance was the judge, the jury, and the executioner.

The rain broke out in a torrent. Severance holstered the pulser and raced for the skimmer. Water would be filling the engine housing already. Racer had left the panel open when he had been surprised. Renaissance was so good at destroying equipment.

The rain caught Cidra by surprise. She had watched the clouds build up all afternoon, but the sudden, drenching downpour had begun without any warning drops. The skies of Renaissance simply opened. She dashed for the tent and was thankful to find it dry inside. Huddled on a sleeper, she went back to doing what she had been doing since Severance had left: she waited and thought.

A great deal went through her mind as she sat in a position of meditation. Thoughts of Clementia's tranquil gardens, memories of the games of Free Market she had played with Severance, and a desperate curiosity to know what was happening between Severance and Racer all crowded her head. The one thing she didn't allow herself to think about was the amount of time left on the deflector screens. She had checked the controls before escaping into the tent, and she knew the charge was already beginning to weaken.

The rain was a steady roar on the curved shell of the tent. At least the drumming was a change from listening to the screams, clickings and occasional thrashing noises that were a part of normal jungle life. Cidra tried meditating and found it impossible to concentrate. She consoled herself with the thought that even a true Harmonic would have had trouble meditating under such circumstances.

That thought only led her to the next, inevitable bit of logic. She was farther than ever now from being a true Harmonic. Everything from her interest in gambling to her growing hunger for Severance's brief, possessive kisses was ample evidence that she had too much Wolf in her. She had to face the possibility that even if she found the relic for which she searched, she might never be entirely free of her Wolf heritage.

And if Severance did not succeed in finding Racer, neither of them would be free of this damned jungle. Surprisingly she wasn't as worried about that as she ought to have been. She discovered that she had a great deal of faith in Teague Severance's abilities. She also knew that when he found Racer and secured the skimmer, he would be back for her. She knew it with the same certainty as she knew the deflectors were going to fail by nightfall.

Cidra was not at all so sure of what would happen to Racer

when Severance found him. Or perhaps she simply didn't want to think about it. What would it do to Severance if he killed a man? Perhaps he had killed in the past. She had no way of knowing. She had seen so much violence already during her short visit to Renaissance. The planet seemed to inspire it. Only a true Wolf could survive here. Cidra didn't want to imagine what would happen if a group of Harmonics was abandoned on Renaissance.

The steady roar of the rain became hypnotic. Gradually Cidra stopped thinking about what might be happening to Severance. She sat quietly and just listened to the rain, which sounded as if it would come down forever. On and on it poured, the sound driving out all other thought. Cidra drifted in her mind, staring at the curving wall of the tent.

The first, gentle call passed by her almost unnoticed. Cidra became vaguely aware of a feeling of curiosity. For some reason she was suddenly interested in exploring the world outside the tent. She shook off the odd thought. It was utterly impossible. There was no point in getting soaking wet again today. Drying off after the swim in the river had taken long enough. She dismissed the strange curiosity and went back to drifting in her mind. The rain continued to beat down on the metal tent. Outside, the charge on the deflector control panels went down two more levels.

Another soft tendril of thought curled in her head, beckoning pleasantly. Not all of Renaissance was violence and death. This was a beautiful world that had once been under control.

Cidra lifted her chin from where it had been resting on her folded arms and stared, puzzled, at the tent wall. Under control? She wondered where that thought had sprung from. She shifted position, wishing there was something constructive she could do. This business of waiting, knowing nothing of what was happening to Severance, seemed to be affecting her brain. She wondered if he could even move in the skimmer in this rain.

There seemed to be a slight altering in the steady beat of the water. Cidra waited until she was reasonably sure of the change in intensity and then unsealed the iris opening. It did appear that the rain was lessening. The knowledge brought a measure of relief. One less obstacle for Severance to surmount.

The rain passed slowly but surely, leaving in its wake a jungle smelling fresher than usual. Cidra was surprised at the almost pleasant fragrance. Also, the squeaks and screams seemed to have faded as everything took shelter. There were a few calls from the creatures living high in the trees but no close screams. Cidra unsealed the iris closure completely and stepped outside.

The ground was muddy, but in general, the water had drained off quickly into the river. Overhead, the clouds were already breaking up. Unfortunately the sunlight was not returning with reassuring warmth. Stanza Nine was already sinking slowly over the green horizon. Cidra listened to the occasional hiss of the deflectors and shivered. She didn't want to examine the control panel again.

She was standing near the edge of the bank, staring out over the river when she caught sight of the skimmer. Incredible relief swept through her, even as she realized that there was no accompanying hum of the craft's engine.

"Severance!" Belatedly she realized that he was poling the floating skimmer, using a long, thick limb to keep the craft away from the bank. In complete silence the skimmer glided toward her. Cidra saw that two of the cabin walls were shattered. Frantically she scanned Severance's body as he jumped into the shallows and pulled the craft into shore. Diazite tinkled on the deck of the boat. Cidra knew what it must have taken to shatter the tough material.

"It's all right, Cidra. I've got the screens." Wearily he made fast the boat and turned to face her.

Cidra took one look at him and knew what had happened to Racer. "Oh, Severance." She ran forward, throwing her arms around him. He was hot and sweaty, and there was a feeling emanating from him that she could only describe as hard and bleak. It made her want to cry. Instead she hugged him even more fiercely. "I've been so frightened for you."

His arms went around her. "It's all right. It's over."

She didn't ask about Racer. Instead she helped him finish securing the boat, and then she carried the screens ashore as he handed them to her from the cargo hold. The deflectors were the first concern. The old ones were stored in the skimmer as the new ones took over.

"There's not enough power left in the fuel cells to get the skimmer off the water, but there is enough to keep the deflectors charged. I've stopped the fuel leak. Be careful of the diazite," Severance added as Cidra stepped into the craft.

"I wanted to see if there are any prespacs on board." She walked carefully forward and opened the galley bin. There were several prespacs containing meat and two containing vegetables. Gratefully she pulled out two packages—one for her and one for Severance—and shoved them into the tiny skimmer heater. Food was what Severance needed.

When she brought his heated prespac into the tent, she found him sitting on a sleeper. He looked up without much interest as she handed him the food.

"Thanks."

Cidra reached down and found the container of Renaissance Rose ale she had rescued and held it out to him with a tentative smile. He raised an eyebrow in surprise, and then his hand wrapped around it. Without a word he downed a good portion of the brew.

"You know how to welcome a man home," he said. Then he slipped back into his bleak silence.

They ate without talking for several minutes. Cidra was aching to ask questions but afraid to interrupt whatever thoughts were going through Severance's head. He seemed very remote this evening. More distant than she had ever seen him. When he finally spoke, it was to give her a few facts.

"The communication equipment has to have a chance to dry out completely. It's housed in the engine compartment, and that got flooded. We won't be able to make any calls until morning." He went back to chewing methodically.

Cidra hesitated and then asked, "What if the comm equipment doesn't work when it's dried out?"

"The worst possible case is that we have to pole the skimmer down the river the way I did this afternoon. It's slow going and there are some risks, but it works. We'll do it that way if necessary." Severance lapsed back into silence.

Cidra could think of nothing to say, no way to break through the barrier that existed between them. In silence they prepared for bed, crawling into separate sleepers. For a long time Cidra lay awake, aware that Severance was staring into the darkness.

"Severance?"

"What is it, Cidra?"

"You had to kill him, didn't you?"

"I killed him." The words were flat, final.

Cidra lay in silence, wondering what to say next. Severance needed comfort, and she knew he would never ask for it. She wasn't even sure how to go about offering it to him. But then she felt that trying was pointless. He would reject it.

But after another long silence Cidra shifted in the darkness. She unfastened her sleeper. And then she reached out to unfasten Severance's sleeper.

"Are you scared again tonight, Cidra?" He didn't move as she slipped in beside him. She could feel the tight tension in him.

"Yes," she whispered. But not of the jungle outside, she added silently. She was frightened by the remoteness in him, terrified by the memories he must be rerunning in his head. He cradled her against him, and she felt the taut muscles in his arm. He hadn't even begun to relax, but she knew he must be thoroughly exhausted.

"Go to sleep, Cidra."

"I won't be able to sleep until you do."

He turned his head to look down at her as she lay in the circle of his arm. "Then you're going to be awake a long time."

"I know." She put her palm on his bare chest.

"Cidra, I think you'd better go back to your own sleeper. I'm not feeling normal. I'm not feeling in control."

"It's all right, Severance." She nestled closer.

"I want you."

"I know."

"You don't understand," he said roughly.

"I understand." She waited.

Severance shuddered, then turned suddenly and pinned her beneath him. His mouth came down on hers with the urgency of a man who is running toward the promise of safety in a wild and uncontrolled land.

TWELVE

Cidra was startled by the sudden intensity of hunger she felt in him. Severance overwhelmed her. She had thought him exhausted, in need of comfort and human warmth; she had wanted to offer him gentleness and relaxation. But he was gathering her to him as if what she had to offer was life itself. As though he would feed on her in some manner.

"Sweet Harmony in hell, Cidra. I need you."

His urgent mouth tasted her, following the line of her jaw to the curve of her throat. She flinched in surprise when she felt the edge of his teeth and then shuddered from the excitement of the sensation. Her gilded fingertips sank into his sleek shoulders, and she turned her head into his throat. He groaned when she touched him first with her lips and then tried out her own sharp little teeth. The shudder that sent through him was reward enough to tempt her further. Cidra's arms slipped higher, curving around his neck.

"Yes. Tighter. Hold me as tight as you can, Cidra."

She obeyed, her uncertainty fading as a new wave of feeling

took its place. His mouth locked on hers, in an intimate contact that enthralled her. She parted her lips at his urging, allowing him inside. Severance didn't hesitate. In his hunger he would take everything she gave. His tongue tangled with hers. Cidra moaned softly as the wealth of sensation poured through her. She closed her eyes and let herself edge closer to a whirlwind she could not yet name.

Severance's hand had been cupping her face, holding her still for his heavy kisses. Now his palms slipped down, seeking the fastening of the shirt Cidra wore. He raised himself a little bit away from her, and she shivered when his fingers parted the material. Then he pushed aside the fabric and lowered himself back down on top of her. Cidra's soft breasts were gently crushed beneath the unyielding hardness of his chest. It was a strangely satisfying kind of pressure, and she instinctively moved beneath him.

"Cidra, my sweet, strong Cidra. You're so soft." The words were a dark murmur against her skin as Severance shifted his weight.

Cidra felt his hands gliding over her shoulders and down to her breasts. When his fingers found one budding nipple and began to stroke it, she whispered his name far back in her throat.

The small cry seemed to please him. It also fed the physical urgency in Severance. He lowered his head, taking the taut nipple between his teeth. Cidra shivered as excitement unfurled deep in her body. Her leg moved languidly, sliding over his. The fabric of their trousers was an unnatural barrier, one she no longer wanted.

Severance took instant advantage of her small, unconsciously enticing movement. He pushed his leg between hers, letting her feel for the first time the waiting heat in his lower body. Even through the clothing Cidra was made fully aware of the straining male power in him. She wanted time to grow accustomed to the physical changes going on in herself as well as in him. But Severance seemed driven now. He went to work on the unfastening of her trousers.

"Lift up, Cidra. Hurry, sweetheart. I can't wait much longer for you." His hand was under her buttocks, raising her slightly so that he could force the pants down her legs.

His hand followed the clothing as she pushed aside the trousers. She felt his fingers curling into her hips, her thigh, and her calf. Then the trousers were gone and she lay nude beneath him. Her lashes lifted, and she found herself looking deeply into his shadowed gaze.

There was a drawn harshness in his face that brought back some of her earlier uncertainty. This wasn't how she expected a Wolf to look when he made love. She had always imagined that there would be more gentleness, a kind of lingering tenderness.

She felt very vulnerable. At the same time there was a heated excitement flowing through her that even the uncertainty couldn't quell. This was Severance. Everything was all right with him. Tentatively Cidra drew her palms down his back, feeling the strong, muscled contours.

His hand flattened on her stomach, and he stroked her as he whispered rough words of desire against her throat. She responded to the words as much as to the touch, trembling a little as his hand moved lower. When his fingers tangled in the dark nest of hair about her thighs, she gasped.

"It's all right, sweetheart. It's all right. It's going to be so good. I swear, it's going to be good. I need you so much. Let me touch you. Just relax and let me touch you."

Under the soothing onslaught of his words she parted her legs, allowing him an intimacy that left her feeling dazed. His hand slid lower, fingertips drawing strange, curling patterns over a part of her that had become unbearably sensitized.

"Severance?"

"You're so hot and damp." He seemed awed by the response he was evoking. "So welcoming and ready. I want everything, Cidra." He rested his head on her breasts. "I know I should take this more slowly. But I can't. . . . You don't know how it's been for me. I want you so damned much."

She laced her fingers into the depths of his hair. "I want you, too, Severance." The whispered confession startled her. But as soon as the words were out, she realized that they were nothing less than the truth. All thought of dispensing comfort or human warmth had vanished. She ached for something else now. There was a growing need to have him closer. His hand moved again between her thighs, and this time she knew she wanted more. She lifted herself, pleading silently for even more intimacy.

He pulled away from her with a muffled groan, fumbling with the trousers he still wore. In the shadows she saw the strong shape of his thighs, the flat planes of his hips and stomach. There was an alluring strength in him that made the blood sing in her veins. Cidra felt at once light-headed and heavy. Then Severance came back down beside her, gathering her close again, she was aware of the strong, hard thrust of his manhood pressing against her.

"Open yourself for me, my love." His hand was on her inner thigh, gently but firmly pushing apart her legs. She clung to him as he slid into the warm place he had made for himself.

"Severance, it feels good. So strange, but good."

"I know. Sweet Harmony in hell, I know."

She felt him move closer, felt the blunt probing shaft at the gate of her femininity. He was moistening himself with the dampness he had brought forth there. She moved, savoring the promise of even more intense sensations.

"Now, Severance?"

"It has to be now. I'll go crazy if I wait any longer. Look at me, Cidra." She opened her eyes and saw the barely controlled desire in his narrowed gaze. "I want to see your eyes when I take you. I want to see if you really understand this."

"I understand."

"I'm not talking about the kind of knowledge you've known before from books. I want to know you understand what this *means*." He groaned deep in his chest. "Ah, hell, I can't explain it and I can't wait. Hold on to me, Cidra. Just hold on and whatever happens, don't let go."

She obeyed, her hands on his shoulders as she felt him surge against her. The short, sharp pain took her by surprise, and she opened her mouth to cry out. But he covered her lips with his own, drinking the small, startled sound as he continued to push forward in a single, strong thrust. Only when he was embedded in her did he stop and give her a chance to adjust. She felt a shudder go through him as he fought to control himself.

But Cidra wasn't at all sure she could adjust. Her body had tensed instinctively at the moment he had entered her, and now, instead of the deliciously satisfying feeling she had been anticipating, she was aware only of feeling invaded.

"Easy, sweetheart. Don't fight it. Trust me. Can you trust me, Cidra? Give me a chance to show you what it's supposed to be like."

Her tongue touched the edge of her parted lips. Her breath was coming in quick little gasps as she met his eyes. "I trust you."

He muttered something she couldn't quite catch, nestling his head beside hers as he slowly, carefully, began to move within her.

Cidra waited, unsure of what to expect next. But the too-tight sensation faded beneath a compelling rhythm that gradually became far more important than the initial discomfort. Slowly she began to echo the pattern Severance was establishing, lifting to meet his heavy thrusts. One of his hands slid down to cup her buttock.

"That's it, sweetheart. You feel so right. So perfect."

She tightened her arms around him as her body began to eagerly seek each new surging thrust. Each time he withdrew slightly, she sank her nails into his skin, pulling him back with a fierceness that seemed to deepen his desire. The driving strokes filled her until she thought she would burst.

"Ah, Cidra, I can't stop. I can't wait."

She wasn't certain what he meant, but she tried to reassure him, anyway. "Severance, it's all right. It's all right," she whispered, unconsciously using the same words he had used earlier.

"*Cidra!*" He drove deeply into her one last time, and his body shuddered heavily. There was an exultant shout caught somewhere in his throat, and then slowly he collapsed along the length of her.

For a long time Cidra lay still beneath him, her palms tenderly stroking the damp skin of his back. She felt him recover his breath, felt his heartbeat return to normal, and then he slowly lifted his head to look down at her. In the shadows his gray eyes were dark and unreadable. He touched her mouth with his fingertip. She smiled tremulously. He didn't respond. Instead he searched her face.

"Are you all right?" he finally asked.

"I think so." Her smile widened. "What about you?"

He bent his head and brushed her lips with his own. "I'm much better than all right. I feel normal again. Better than normal. I feel good. Very tired and very good. Because of you, Cidra." He cradled her head in the curve of his arm. "Go to sleep, sweetheart. Next time I promise it will be better for you."

She stretched a little and nestled against him, inhaling the musky scent of his body. "I can't imagine it being any better. I felt so close to you, Severance. I've never felt that close to another human being in my life. Maybe that's why Wolves are so interested in sex."

He chuckled sleepily. "Maybe. I wish I could show you how really good it can be for you. Next time. I promise you that next time I won't be so damned exhausted and so out of control."

"Go to sleep, Severance. It's been a long day."

"You can say that again," he said, the words fading as he closed his eyes and slipped into deep sleep almost at once.

Cidra stayed curled in his arm, wondering why she wasn't equally sleepy. For a long time she lay still, thinking of the jumble of emotions and physical sensations she had experienced during the day. They had all culminated tonight in Severance's arms. His lovemaking had left her feeling dazzled and dazed. She wasn't quite certain what to make of the experience. It had been, as she had anticipated, a very physical act, and yet there had been so much more. The feeling of oneness, the sense of closeness, had been totally unexpected, and it added a whole new dimension.

Dreamily she listened to the usual cacophony of night sounds from the jungle. A curious lethargy stole over her, but she was no nearer sleep than she had been earlier. It wasn't Severance who was keeping her awake now. In the darkness she could make out the hard lines of his face. They didn't appear any softer in repose than they did when he was awake. Cidra wondered what he would say to her in the morning. And then she occupied several long minutes wondering what she would say to him.

The first words after a night like this ought to be significant, she thought. But she wasn't sure in what way. The knowledge that their relationship had been fundamentally altered was vaguely disturbing. It had been easier when she had been able to consider herself simply a temporary member of his crew. Now she wasn't sure what category she fit into.

The night sounds didn't seem as harsh tonight. After a while Cidra realized that she wasn't hearing very many of the usual chopped-off screams. That was a relief. It made one think of what this planet might have been like if it hadn't evolved along such violent lines. It might have had some truly beautiful places in it, places that offered a green and welcoming tranquillity. Places where even a Harmonic might feel at home.

There were such places here, Cidra thought with sudden certainty. And they weren't far away. The jungle outside wasn't as dangerous as it seemed. A person simply had to understand it. Humans were always struggling to subdue it, and, of course, the jungle had to fight back. But if a woman simply walked into it looking for the tranquil places, she would find them. They were so close.

Slowly Cidra slipped away from the shelter of Severance's arm. He didn't stir. She sat up, listening. The night noises were definitely quieter and less threatening this evening. The twin moons would be shining, illuminating a path through the thick foliage. It would be an easy matter to follow that path to the gentle, tranquil spaces hidden in the jungle.

Her compulsion to follow the moonlit path grew. Moonlight and Mirrors. She knew how to chase moonlight in mirrors. The jungles of Renaissance were open to her. All she had to do was walk into them.

Cidra got up and pulled on her trousers. Then she reached for her shirt. She found her boots near the tent entrance. When she had them on, she opened the iris closure and stepped out into the night.

She had been right. The twin moons were shining very brilliantly tonight, revealing a path through the jungle. Borgia and Medici weren't their true names, she decided. They had once been called by other names, names that she couldn't quite say. The words were strange in her head. Without any hesitation Cidra turned toward the path.

Severance came awake with the startling certainty that something was wrong. He turned on his side and realized that Cidra's warm weight was no longer pinning his arm.

"Cidra?"

When there was no response, a flare of panic reared up within him. He got to his feet. She was not in her own sleeper.

"Cidra!" Memories of her in his arms flooded his mind. And along with those memories came others. She wanted to be a Harmonic more than she wanted anything else. After tonight she would feel farther than ever from her goal. How would she react to that? He felt slightly sick as he reached for his boots. Surely she wouldn't do anything rash just because she had been forced to face the fact that she was a true Wolf. It had hardly been rape, for Harmony's sake. He'd seen the passion in her eyes, felt the throbbing, moist warmth between her legs. She had clung to him with a woman's stirring need.

But what if she hadn't been able to accept her own desires afterward? Severance thought wildly. He ignored the rest of his clothes and activated the tent opening with a savage twist of his hand. An instant later he was outside.

He saw her almost at once and breathed a sigh of relief. Then he realized that she was on the other side of the deflector screens, heading into the wall of vegetation.

"Cidra! Come back here. What in a renegade's hell do you think you're doing?" Severance raced through the screens reaching for Cidra as she started into the mass of night-darkened greenery surrounding the campsite. He caught her shoulder and spun her around.

"Severance?" She smiled, but she didn't seem to be quite focusing on him. She waved her hand gracefully at the jungle. "Isn't it beautiful tonight? I never realized how beautiful it was."

"What's the matter with you? Are you out of your mind? If you think I'm going to let you walk into that green hell just because you finally discovered sex, you're dumber than a novakeet." He yanked her back toward the safety of the screens.

"But, Severance, it's not a green hell. That's what I'm trying to tell you."

"You're dreaming on your feet. Why didn't you ever tell me you walk in your sleep?"

"I don't walk in my sleep. Severance, there's no need to hide behind the screens anymore."

He ignored that, pulling her through the invisible safety net. There he turned to confront her. The moonlight seemed to shine in her eyes as she looked up at him. Something was wrong, and he couldn't figure out what it was. He tried shaking her gently. She blinked and some of the moonlight seemed to fade from her gaze. He got the impression that she was starting to really see him. He clasped her shoulders firmly and tried another small shake.

"Cidra, listen to me. I don't know what you think you're doing, but I'll be damned if I'm going to let you do anything stupid because of what happened tonight. You're coming back into that tent with me. In the morning everything will be all right. You'll see."

She frowned slightly, almost thoughtfully. "I'd rather not go back into the tent with you, Severance."

"You haven't got any choice, damn it!" He picked her up and carried her back to the opening. He stepped through and set her down on his sleeper. Methodically, he began stripping off her clothing.

"Severance, listen to me."

"Why? So that you can give me some illogical reason for trying to commit suicide?"

She seemed genuinely shocked. "I wasn't trying to commit suicide."

"You're upset because of what happened between us." He tugged off her boots. "I can understand that. First time around, sex is a little upsetting. Like everything else, it improves with practice. I know I wasn't the greatest lover between here and QED tonight, but I'd had a tough day. That's no excuse for you to start thinking in terms of death before dishonor. I didn't rape you, Cidra."

"I know that," she said gently.

He sat on the edge of the sleeper and yanked off his own boots. "Furthermore, you liked it. Or at least you liked most of it." He bore her back down onto the sleeper, sprawling across her so that her legs were pinned beneath him. "This time around I'll see to it that you like all of it. I swear it."

Before she could protest, he sealed her mouth with his own. Beneath him he felt her stir, and the movement of her naked body began the chain reaction that led to the hardening in his groin. Severance forced himself to stay under control. He was going to make it right for her. If he satisfied her completely, maybe she would be able to accept her normal passions. She had to accept them. Damned if he would let her kill herself because he'd made love to her.

Clamping down on his rioting reactions, Severance deliberately began to stroke and coax the response he wanted from Cidra. After a brief struggle that seemed to stem more from her surprise and confusion than any real desire to fight him, she stopped resisting. Her arms went around his neck, and he knew a vast sense of relief. It was going to be all right this time. He could make her want him.

"Say it, Cidra. Say you want me." He probed between her legs, finding the nubbin of exquisitely sensitive female flesh. He flicked lightly with his fingers and felt her react almost at once. "Say it, sweetheart."

"I want you," she whispered, arching against his hand.

He kept up the light teasing between her thighs while he lowered his head to draw first one nipple and then the other into his mouth. She shivered in his hold, and another wave of satisfaction went through him. Relentlessly he kept up the tender assault, even after she was trembling under his hands. She responded to him the way a flower responded to sunlight, opening herself and welcoming him.

"Severance. Please. I can't stand any more." Her eyes were squeezed tightly shut, her head arched back over his arm.

But he didn't stop, and he didn't move to cover her. This time he would make sure everything went right. Slowly he began working his way down her body, tasting her with his tongue, nibbling at her until she cried out for more. All the while he kept his fingers moving on her and in her. She twisted and writhed in his hands, and he gloried in it.

When he dropped an intimate kiss into the triangle of hair at the apex of her thighs, she cried out again and clutched at his shoulders.

"That's it, sweetheart. That's it."

The scent of her was dark and spicy, the essence of her femininity. Severance thought it would surely drive him over the edge. Still he maintained his self-control. He touched the nubbin with his tongue and felt Cidra's whole body tighten convulsively.

Deliberately he deepened the passionate caress. The little cries in her throat were the most beautiful songs he had ever heard. He felt her nails digging into his shoulders and knew another lightning jolt of satisfaction.

"Severance!"

"Let go, Cidra, just let go!" He parted the pliant opening with his fingers, and she whispered his name again. He loved the tight, husky, aching way she said it. He slid two fingers gently into her, his tongue still curling around the bud of throbbing flesh.

She tensed again, breathed his name again, and this time a thousand tiny shivers flooded her body.

"Severance. Sweet Harmony, *Severance!*"

"That's the way I want to hear my name." Intoxicated with the knowledge that he'd brought her complete satisfaction, half

spaced with his own anticipation, he flowed back up along her
body and slipped between her legs. He drove into her before the
tiny convulsions had ceased. The last of them pulled him deeply
into her. A moment later it was Cidra's name that was filling the
tent and his body that was shuddering in completion. And then
he went still on top of her.

When he finally came back to his senses, he was aware of
Cidra's fingers moving languidly in his hair. Severance decided he
liked it. He moved his head a little closer.

"I wasn't trying to kill myself, Severance."

"You were upset. Scared, maybe."

"Scared of what?" she asked.

"Scared of what's happening to you. To us."

She appeared to give that some thought. "It's confusing, but I
don't feel really frightened."

"Good. We'll talk about it in the morning."

"I'm wide-awake," she told him. "I wouldn't mind discussing
it now."

He opened his eyes and found that his line of focus took in the
peaks of her breasts. It was a pleasant view. "You need the sleep,
Cidra. And so do I. We've got a long day ahead of us tomorrow."

"I feel strange, Severance."

"You'll feel better in the morning."

"I don't feel bad," she emphasized. "Just strange."

"I'm sure it's a normal reaction."

"I don't know." She sounded genuinely puzzled. "I also feel a
little sore."

He winced guiltily. "I'm sorry, sweetheart. You'll feel better in
the morning. And next time you won't feel sore afterward."

She yawned. "You sound very sure of everything."

"I'm the pilot in command, remember? I'm supposed to sound
sure of everything." He lifted himself up on one elbow and looked
down at her. "Cidra?"

"Hmmm?"

"You swear you weren't thinking of doing anything rash because of what happened tonight?"

"Why would I want to kill myself after enjoying such plea-sure?"

He smiled and kissed her. "That's the true Wolf outlook."

"You know what the best part is, Severance?"

"What?"

"Feeing so close to you. It's very nice."

"Very," he agreed.

As he drifted back into sleep Severance decided that Renais-sance wasn't such a bad place to stake his claim on Cidra. He hadn't intended to rush things. He had wanted the right time and the right background. During those two weeks on board *Sever-ance Pay* he had fantasized more than once about the perfect set-ting. In his mind he had constructed a picture that included good ether wine, Harmonic music in the background, a wide, lush bed, and all the time in the world.

Here in the middle of a Renaissance jungle he'd had none of those props, but it didn't seem to matter. There was something primitive and new about the jungle, and it fit in well with the way he felt about Cidra. The more he thought about it, the more ap-propriate the setting became. She had been right earlier when she had tried to tell him that the jungle wasn't really a green hell. It was an exotic, exciting, primitive world, not a hell.

A man could survive in the jungle without deflector screens and crispers, Severance decided. Hadn't he survived today? There were places in the jungle that were soft, green refuges. In such places he could make love to Cidra beneath twin moons with strange names all night long. It would be good to see her soft, slender body bathed in moonlight. He fell asleep with that last image in his mind.

When he awoke again, he knew it was nearly dawn. Lazily he turned, feeling for Cidra. Then he sat up with a jerk. She was gone again. This time Severance didn't feel the rush of fear he had felt the last time he had awakened and found her gone. She hadn't had time to get far, he thought as he pulled on his clothing. And she would be safe enough. The jungle was safe for her. And for him.

He stepped out of the tent, fastening his shirt, and glanced

around. There was no sign of Cidra, but he was curiously unconcerned. He sensed the direction in which she had gone, and he set
out to follow. He was just about to step through the deflector
screens when a niggling sense of unease stopped him. For a moment he couldn't figure out what the problem was. Then he
thought about the pulser and utility loop he had left behind in the
tent. It wasn't like him to go anywhere on this planet without either. He felt undressed without them. Habit was hard to break.

Shrugging, Severance walked back toward the tent. He
wouldn't need a weapon, but since he seemed uncomfortable
without it, he might as well get it. Inside the tent he strapped on
the holstered pulser and reached for the utility loop.

With the familiar weight of the pulser and the utility loop in
place, he walked back outside and through the deflectors. A
strange impatience was beginning to eat at him now. He wanted
to catch up with Cidra. She might be quite a way ahead of him by
now. He pushed his way through the underbrush, deciding not to
worry about what sort of creatures might be hiding in the vicinity. Hadn't he already realized that the jungle was not really a hell?
It was a good place, a natural place, one where a man could feel
in harmony with nature. Perhaps this was how Harmonics had always felt. If so, he could understand Cidra wanting to become
one. Poor Jeude. He'd never had his chance to become a trained
Harmonic.

Severance frowned and then relaxed, pushing thoughts of his
brother aside. Jeude had been avenged. His memory could be put
to rest. Renaissance was a good place to do that too. It was a
planet of rest. Gentle, green rest.

He kept walking, not bothering to question his absolute certainty of direction. After all, he'd always had a good sense of direction. The jungle didn't fight him. Why should it? It was
expecting him.

He stepped through a wall of trailing vines and saw Cidra. She
was only a short distance ahead of him, right where he had known
she would be. Severance smiled, quite pleased with himself. But

he didn't call out to her. That seemed unnecessary. Instead he simply moved a little more quickly.

She glanced at him when he caught up with her. Her eyes had that slightly unfocused expression again, but that was all right. He knew what she was thinking of now. There was no need to communicate. He was thinking of exactly the same things she was. The shared knowledge was pleasant.

Green hell.

No. Green shelter. Peace. Tranquillity. Rest.

It all waited up ahead. Not far now. Severance was sure of it.

So was Cidra. She moved unerringly in the right direction, following the gentle, guiding call. It wouldn't be long now. The safehold was very near. All the answers were very near.

She and Severance stepped through the last wall of tangled vines and leaves and into the clearing. Cidra halted, drinking in the sight of the safehold bathed in the last of the night's moonlight. Severance stopped beside her, equally enchanted.

It was a graceful, airy thing. The Ghosts had had a light, perfectly balanced touch when it came to architecture. And the safehold had been designed with special care, for it housed important secrets.

Even as Cidra and Severance watched, walls of translucent stone caught the first light of the morning dawn and glowed with it. The vaulted doorway was open wide, an invitation that could not be denied. The structure seemed lighter than air, circular in shape, and yet it rested firmly on the green velvet of the clearing. It was not a large building, not much bigger than Desma Kady's octagonal living quarters. It appeared to have been carved out of a single huge block of stone. The roof was arched, revealing delicate veins in the material. Through the vaulted entrance nothing could be seen, but it was obvious that light was passing through the stone to gently illuminate the interior.

Cidra stepped forward eagerly, and Severance followed more slowly. For a moment just before she entered the safehold, Cidra had time to realize that it was unusual to find anyplace on Renaissance where nature was not in a constant state of combat. Yet here the green velvet underfoot was obviously not having to compete with other foliage. No stray shoots of vines had encroached from the surrounding jungle. There was no sign of any wildlife within the protected circle. Not even insects. In the clearing all was tranquil and serene. A small brook emerged from the jungle on the far side of the protected clearing, bubbled through it, and disappeared into the foliage on the opposite side.

"Just like a garden in Clementia," Cidra breathed as she came to a halt in front of the entrance. "Smell the air, Severance. It's so soft and fragrant."

"I know," he said, glancing around curiously. Some of the feeling of quiet sureness was receding in him. "Maybe too soft and fragrant, Cidra."

"Nonsense. This is how the Ghosts lived. I know it. When they were here, the jungle was a place of harmony. Just like this clearing. Come on, Severance. Let's go inside."

He hesitated, struggling now with something in his mind. Severance's eyes were vaguely troubled as he looked down at her. "Cidra, I'm not sure . . ."

"I'm going inside." She stepped through the entrance.

Severance shook his head, trying to clear it. Then he realized that there was no need to clear it. All was in order. All was serenely in order. He followed Cidra through the open gate.

THIRTEEN

The first thing Cidra noticed was the silence.

"Like the inside of a grave on QED," Severance said.

"No. Like the Hall of Archives in Clementia." Cidra stood just inside the entrance and glanced around. The curving walls allowed sufficient light into the room to see a floor that was made of the same white stone. The far end of the circular room was in soft shadow. There were no lines of joining between walls and roof or walls and floor. "It's that kind of quiet, Severance. A place where something has been stored for the ages."

"But there's nothing here." He reached out to touch the translucent stone wall. "Perhaps long ago it was a . . ." He hesitated, struggling for the right word. "A safehold."

"Yes."

"Cidra. What's a safehold? We don't have any facilities called safeholds. Where in hell did I get the word?"

"From whatever led us here."

"I don't like it."

She was surprised by the underlying resistance in his voice. "You don't like what?"

"Having words put in my head. I don't like being led through the jungle by something I can't see. Something in my mind."

"Why did you come, then?" Cidra asked.

"I don't know. Seemed like a good idea at the time."

"Severance . . ."

He turned to her, anger and growing concern in his face. "I said it seemed like a good idea at the time. But it wasn't *my* idea."

She put out her hand, touching him lightly. Cidra smiled wistfully. "Calm down, Severance. This place is good. It's safe. It's in control of the jungle, can't you tell? The Ghosts could deal with the jungle. And that feeling of having something or someone communicate with you mentally?"

"What about it?"

"That must be what it's like to be a true Harmonic, Severance. It may be as close as I'll ever come to knowing that feeling."

He shook his head. "That wasn't communication, Cidra. That was an act of control. We didn't consciously decide to come here. We were pulled here. We could have been killed at any point along the way by anything from a green slicer to a lockmouth."

"No. I think that whatever led us to this place of safety had the strength to make the path here safe too."

"I wonder if it will bother to make the path back safe or if it only works one way." Severance took a few more paces into the dimly lit room. "All right. We're here. Now what?"

"This may be all that's left." Cidra began moving along the wall, following the curving surface to the far end of the room. As she walked she trailed a hand along the warm stone surface. It was pleasant to the touch. "But once there was something more here."

"How do you know so much about this safehold?" he demanded. He was moving behind her, unwilling to let her get too far out of reach, even though he could see nothing that looked dangerous.

"I'm learning about this because I'm willing to *listen*. I'm open to it. You must be able to listen, too, Severance. After all, you were able to follow the call. Stop being so wary of it. Be still a moment and let yourself absorb it. Do you really feel anything wrong here?"

"Yes and no."

She swung around, her eyes full of amusement. "Yes and no? Come now, Severance, you're not usually so ambivalent."

He shrugged, scowling. His hand was resting on the butt of the pulser. "I can't explain it. I didn't feel anything wrong on the way here, although I should have, and part of what I feel now is acceptable, I guess you'd say. Strange but not dangerous. But there's something else that I don't like. It's just a feeling."

"Perhaps just a sensation of alienness. After all, this is the first complete Ghost structure ever found as far as I know. There are records of hundreds of fragments of their buildings but nothing complete and in good condition like this."

"Have any of those records of the fragments mentioned this kind of building material?" Severance eyed the gently glowing stone.

"None that I"ve come across," Cidra admitted. "This is truly unique. Perhaps it's newer than the others. If so, then it might help us date the Ghost civilization. Severance, this is such an important find. We're so lucky to have discovered it."

"We didn't discover it," he said flatly. "It discovered us. There's a difference, Cidra."

She decided to ignore him. He was obviously going to be difficult. Cidra started walking again, curious to see the far end of the hall that lay in shadow. She was aware of Severance reluctantly following. "I think there's something back there." Excited by the possibility, Cidra hurried forward.

"Cidra, wait. Hell, the floor is changing color!" Severance stared down as the white stone began to shade into a pearlescent pink. "We're getting out of here." He grabbed Cidra's arm, jerking her to halt.

"I want to see what's at the back of the room." She tried to pull free, but his hand was clamped around her arm like a manacle.

"Severance, please. This is what I've been looking for. Don't you understand? What's here could be the source of the legends I'm following. This place might hold the key I need to go home."

"I don't care if this place holds a lifetime supply of Rose ale. We're not hanging around any longer." Roughly he hauled her toward the entrance.

But the floor was changing color quickly now, shimmering from pink to red and then to violet. Other colors were filtering to the surface, and even as Severance watched, the shifting colors bled upward into the walls and ceiling. Then, without any warning, there was something more than colors. There were shapes. Shapes that weren't restricted to the two-dimensional surface of the walls. They seemed to be stepping out into the room.

"The Laughing Gods, Severance. Look at them. They were real. Just look at them."

Stunned, Severance came to a halt in the middle of the room, still holding Cidra with one hand. His other hand hovered above the holstered pulser. He heard the wonder and excitement in Cidra's voice and knew that he felt the same sense of awed anticipation. The feeling of alienness was gone. What filled him now was a magnificently amplified version of the serenity and quiet pleasure he got when he handled his collection of stone carvings. The Laughing Gods were everywhere in the safehold. They surrounded Cidra and Severance, but it was clear that they had no substance. They were an illusion, something like a holotype projection but far more perfectly reproduced. It was like being in the midst of Ghosts.

Mesmerized by the reality of what he was seeing, Severance continued to stand still. Cidra didn't move beside him. There was no sound, only the shifting images on the ceiling and walls and in midair.

"It's a record," Cidra whispered. "I was right. This place is an Archive. These are the Ghosts."

"They look different than they do in the carvings."

"I don't think so. It's only their clothing that's different. That would make sense if these are images of them at a later period of their development."

The drive to get out of the safehold was gone. Severance felt relaxed again. Cidra stopped struggling to free herself when she realized that she wasn't going to be hauled forcibly out of the room. They stood quietly, watching the shifting images that filled the room. The Ghosts had been a handsome people. The vaguely feline features expressed a deep intelligence and an awareness that was obvious even to people whose ancestors had come from another solar system. They moved with a lithe grace, walking on two legs. Their clothing was more simply styled in these images than the clothing worn by the statues. The portions of the body not shielded by the simple robes were furred.

As Cidra watched, the crowded figures began to fade. Unhappily she watched the swirling images disappear. "Severance, they're going."

"The picture is just fading. They were never really here to begin with."

"But I need answers!"

"There's no reason to expect any," he said gently.

He was right. She knew that, but a part of her wanted to cry out in protest. There was so much to learn, so many questions she wanted to ask. Above all there was the mystery of how she and Severance had been led here in the first place. "Damn it. I wanted to know."

"We've already seen more than any Harmonic archaeologist has ever seen."

"I realize that, but it's not enough. I need to find the key." She stopped talking as she realized that not all the graceful images had disappeared. Five Ghosts remained, shimmering between her and the doorway. "Look, Severance. There's more."

He said nothing, watching as the five robed figures coalesced in midair. In addition to the simple white garments, these Ghosts appeared to have a golden band around their furred wrists. Long, delicate fingers tipped with curving nails reached out.

For a wild moment Cidra thought that the creatures were gesturing toward her, and then she realized that the gentle, slanting eyes were not really seeing her. This was still only a projected image. But there seemed to be a purpose to the gestures. When all five Ghosts pointed toward the wall to their right, she automatically followed the tapering hands.

A new series of pictures sprang into existence on the curving wall and began flowing out from it. More Ghosts appeared, moving through a wild jungle setting that could only have been Renaissance. But the hands of these Ghosts were tipped with long, dangerous-looking claws, not well-trimmed nails. There were crude weapons worn on leather belts. Very little clothing was evident, but there were quite a few pieces of primitively ornate decorative items on furred throats, wrists, and ankles.

"The Ghosts' ancestors?" Cidra asked.

"Could be. I get the feeling there's a lot of distance between those cats with the claws and the five guys standing in the middle of the room."

Even as Severance spoke, it became obvious that the scene evolving around them was a hunt. The handful of ghosts were prowling. There was no doubt about it. They moved with a menacing care, and it wasn't long before the object of the hunt came into sight. A horned animal stood on six legs nibbling leaves off a tree. Severance thought the creature resembled a modern-day Renaissance mannator.

Cidra swallowed as the Ghosts attacked. The six-legged animal went down amid a flurry of thrown knives and scrabbling claws. As it struggled, its throat was ripped out. The fine quality of the illusion made the blood look very real. She was sure that what was happening was a simple and necessary hunting operation, but the violence of it was sickening. It brought back memories of feeding dracons. When she glanced briefly at her companion, she saw that he wasn't particularly affected by the gory scene.

The lifelike mural continued, showing the Ghosts engaged in other activities besides the hunt. Cidra became interested in what was apparently a religious ceremony. Five Ghosts conducted the proceedings from behind an altar made of stone. The observers were seated cross-legged on the ground, swaying to an unheard beat. The fact that there were five leaders was interesting because that was how many Ghosts had appeared a few minutes ago in the room. Cidra tried to see if there were gold bands on their wrists but got distracted when a large, scaled animal was thrown down onto the altar. Too late she realized what was about to happen. She didn't manage to look away in time to avoid seeing the knife dragged across the belly of the sacrifice. Again she felt nausea welling up, threatening to choke her for a moment.

Averting her eyes from the bloody scene, Cidra glanced back toward the middle of the room. The five Ghosts in white robes continued to stand pointing toward the moving illusion. Reluctantly she looked back.

"This is getting awfully gory, Severance. I don't understand. It isn't how I imagined the Ghosts would be."

"You don't think it was easy surviving on Renaissance, do you? Nothing that becomes dominant on this planet is going to be sweet-natured."

"But the carvings show a gentler nature. And those five standing over there, they couldn't have been like this."

"Wait and see."

The images continued to shift, fading in and out of the walls. They moved more swiftly now, slowing only to show the details of a scene of weaving, the preparation of a meal or the carving of stone. It became clear that there was an element of time and progress involved. Clothing changed, becoming more elaborate. The design of structures altered. The early images showed the Ghosts sheltering in huge, wide-limbed trees. As the scenes progressed, however, shelters were created out of rocks and vines.

"It's moving too quickly." Cidra wanted to slow the images and savor each nuance of information contained in them. "There's too much to see."

"Maybe the Ghosts weren't sure how long a visitor's attention span was going to be."

"How can you make a joke out of it? This is the most important find of the century. Perhaps the most significant discovery since the First Families arrived and found the first Ghost relics."

Severance thought for a moment. "There's another possible reason why the scenes are moving too swiftly."

"What reason?"

"It could be because there's a great deal of history to be conveyed. We could be dealing with several thousand years, here. Or a million, for all we know."

"The rise and fall of a whole species?" Cidra watched as a scene of a village being built between the jungle and the sea took shape. "It looks like an alien version of Port Try Again. Right down to the walls built to hold out the jungle."

It was clear that every inch of progress was a struggle. The Ghosts of Renaissance paid a high price for their growing civilization. Images of Ghosts being attacked by huge, fanged snakes and other horrendous forms of wildlife flickered on and off the walls. Pictures of tiny villages being trampled by lumbering, armor-plated animals were common.

"Zalons," Severance told her. "Or at least an earlier version of them. The horns look slightly different, and the ears are smaller."

"You said they were vegetarians."

"They are. But that doesn't make much different to something smaller than they are that happens to get in their way. Zalons are a little clumsy."

There were other kinds of difficulties. Volcanic eruptions, flooding rivers, intense storms. Then came the even more unsettling pictures of warring tribes. Cidra couldn't watch the battle scenes. Such violence between Ghosts didn't fit the mental image she'd always had. Severance watched with intent interest.

Regardless of the setbacks, natural disasters, and war, the Ghosts continued to expand as a species. They grew in numbers. In fact, Cidra noticed at one point that there were a great many images of children in the mural. Scenes of them playing, practicing with weapons, and going about their daily lives were frequent.

It was clear that the Ghosts were holding their own and beginning to thrive in the jungles of Renaissance. Small mechanical devices appeared. Technology began on a small scale. After that the little villages grew into towns. Gradually the jungle was tamed. It was never wiped out, but in the regions where Ghosts lived, it was under control.

Scenes shifted more and more rapidly, showing towns growing into cities. And then came the leap into space. The colonization of Lovelady was easy for a people who had tamed a jungle world. QED and Frozen Assets were also featured briefly, although it was obvious that they had never been fully colonized. The spaceships never left the Stanza Nine system as far as Cidra and Severance could tell. It was as if the explorers ran out of interest or energy.

Eons passed. How much time, Cidra had no way of knowing. But gradually things began changing again. The technological trappings of civilization began to fade in the scenes. They were replaced with pictures of translucent structures such as the one in which Cidra stood. The jungle was controlled now without obvious technology. Quiet, serene clearings were common, and in them, quiet, serene Ghosts went about their daily business. These people no longer had the undeniably aggressive element that had been so common in their ancestors.

"They're changing," Severance said.

"Evolving. They're developing mentally now instead of technologically." Cidra was sure of her analysis.

"There's something different about these pictures."

She frowned. "What do you mean?"

"Where are all the kids that were always running around in the earlier scenes?"

He was right. Cidra searched the new pictures, looking for some sign of the laughing, playing, practicing young Ghosts. Once or twice a youngster appeared, but it was becoming increasingly rare. As rare as a child in Clementia. She did see more of the gold wristbands, though. They were becoming a common form of jewelry. Almost all the Ghosts wore them.

The interaction between the Ghosts had changed too. There

was no longer evidence of hostility or rivalry, no more open warfare. A sense of peace and gentleness pervaded the mural.

"It's beautiful, Severance. They became a people of harmony and grace."

"Two worlds full of Harmonics. Must have been kind of dull."

"Damn it, Severance! Why do you have to be so cynical?"

"It's in the blood. I'd still like to know what happened to all the children."

"Maybe they developed a very long lifespan and had to control their population."

"Or maybe, like Harmonics, the Ghosts simply lost interest in sex and the results thereof."

Cidra shifted uneasily, the memory of her own recent interest in that field plaguing her for a moment. Severance was studying the graceful illusions closely.

"I think there's more than just a few kids missing here," he finally said. "The whole population seems to be declining. There aren't as many Ghosts as there were earlier. No sense of huge cities or bustling economies. Just more and more of these quiet little parks."

Cidra felt a sharp pang of regret. "What's happening, Severance? Do you think we're coming to the end?"

He nodded slowly. "The population level is falling. No evidence of children being born to replace their parents. Fewer and fewer towns."

"Maybe species just get old and die the way individuals do," Cidra suggested. Her pang of regret was turning into a pervasive sadness.

"Or maybe this particular species took a bad evolutionary road."

"At what point?" For some reason she felt defensive.

"When they stopped spreading outward and started turning inward. When they stopped having children. When they became more interested in mental and spiritual development and stopped worrying about keeping the species alive physically."

"You don't know what you're talking about, Severance. We're

only looking at pictures. We can't know what really happened. We can only draw inferences." Even as she argued, the images were fading. It was obvious that the civilization they depicted was fading too. The last picture was of a circular building carved from a single block of translucent stone. In it five Ghosts sealed the history of a species and then clasped hands. The golden bands they wore on their wrists glowed in unison for a moment. Serenely, effortlessly, without any sign of struggle or regret, the five died. When the image on the wall vanished, so did the five figures who had been projected into the room earlier. Cidra wanted to weep.

"That last structure was this place," Severance observed as the image flickered and faded into the wall. "You were right. This is an Archive. Saints in hell. We're going to be rich."

Cidra was astounded. She brushed the moisture from her eyes to glare at him. "Rich? What are you saying?"

"We can sell the location of this place to any number of research companies or to the Harmonics. There's enough in here to keep investigators happy for fifty years." He swung around to face her. "Don't look so shocked, Cidra. What did you plan to do with the information we've found here?"

She hesitated. "I suppose it will have to be turned over to some company to analyze. But it seems wrong to sell it. This is a precious discovery."

"Damned right. We'll find out just how precious when we put it up for sale." He glanced at the chronometer on his utility loop. "Sweet Harmony. We've been in here for hours. It's already the middle of the afternoon. We've got to get going."

"Wait, Severance. I want to see what's at the back of the room."

"Later. I don't know how I lost track of time so completely. Hours. *Hours*. We should have called for help early this morning. As it is, it might be another full day before a skimmer can reach us. That means we'll probably be spending another night here in the jungle. Damn it to a renegade's hell. How could I have let this happen?" As he berated himself he was hustling Cidra toward the door.

"Still playing pilot in command, Severance? Why can't you just calm down and admit that we've found something absolutely extraordinary. We're safe enough for the moment. We've got time to explore further. If we have to spend another night in the jungle, we might as well spend it here. It's obvious that nothing violent from outside ever enters. This is one of the last refuges. A safehold."

"We have no way of knowing just how safe it really is."

They were almost at the entrance. Cidra resigned herself to being force-marched back to the campsite. "All right, stop dragging me along like a sack of mail. I'm coming with you."

He shot her an assessing glance and decided that she was going to be cooperative. Severance unholstered the pulser.

"What's that for?" Cidra asked.

"Just in case we don't get the same guided tour out that we had coming in. Stay close to me and don't touch anything you pass if you can avoid it."

"I'm sure we'll have no trouble. Whatever protected us on the way here will probably protect us as we leave."

"Uh-huh." Severance checked the charge in the pulser. He obviously didn't believe in the lingering protection of the Ghosts. "All set?"

Cidra reluctantly started through the door and then screamed at the sight of the huge Bloodsucker blocking the entrance. She stumbled backward, frantically trying to put distance between herself and the facet-eyed monster. It was far bigger than the Bloodsuckers she had seen in Desma's lab.

"Severance!"

His hand closed on her shoulder, spinning her out of the way. The pulser came up, and he fired twice. Nothing happened. The Bloodsucker moved forward on its long spindly legs. The mandibles clicked together. Severance fired again, backing slowly. None of the shots were registering. It was as if they passed right through the creature.

"Get back, Cidra. Move toward the back of the room." Slowly Severance edged backward himself, covering Cidra's escape.

"They're not supposed to be that big," Cidra gasped.

"Maybe you'd better remind it." He raised the pulser again and aimed carefully at the braincase. Once more the charge passed straight through without doing any damage. "Either this thing is absorbing the charge with no effort or it's an image, just like the ones we've been watching."

"Nice theory. How are we going to test it?"

The Bloodsucker was still approaching. Cidra and Severance kept backing toward the far wall. Cidra glanced behind her.

"There are some stones back here."

"Toss one toward this Sucker and see what happens."

Cidra quickly examined the large triangular-shaped pile composed of five perfectly round stones. Each was slightly bigger than a human head. Experimentally she lifted the top one. It was pleasantly warm to the touch.

"It's heavy," she gasped, struggling with the weight of it. "But it'll roll." She dropped the stone to the floor and shoved with all her might.

The stone rolled right through two Bloodsucker limbs with no sign of any resistance. The creature didn't appear to notice, either. It raised its forelegs and reached for Severance.

Cidra shouted, trying to yank him out of the way. Severance swung his arm out in a reflexive movement. The hand holding the pulser passed through the lowering head of the Bloodsucker as if it weren't there.

"It *is* just an image, Cidra. Let's go." He reached around to catch her wrist with his free hand.

Cidra wanted to scream and claw free of that hold. The Bloodsucker was too terrifyingly lifelike. She had known that the moving mural of the Ghosts was an illusion from the start. But this thing seemed far more real. Its forelimbs were waving around in the air now, seeking the prey in front of it. But she followed Severance as he warily circled the image, tugging Cidra with him. The creature lunged at them, and Cidra shut her eyes, convinced that in another instant she was going to find herself just another victim of Renaissance.

Nothing happened. When she opened her eyes again, Severance had pulled her halfway back toward the entrance. The Bloodsucker had winked out of existence. They were almost at the door when an unnatural light filled the formerly dim room. This was no pale, translucent, filtered sunlight but a searing blaze. Instinctively Cidra closed her eyes, wondering if she'd been blinded. She felt Severance stop and knew it had affected him the same way.

"I can't see," Cidra whispered.

"Neither can I. It's probably another illusion, but I can't see the door. Let's find the wall. We can follow it around to the entrance."

Cidra hooked her fingers into his utility loop, and together they groped blindly for the solid wall. The chamber was still filled with the searing light. Whenever Cidra risked a glance through slitted lashes, the unnatural brilliance overwhelmed her. She felt Severance pull up short and mutter a short, expressive oath.

"The wall," he said grimly. "Now we'll try following it."

A rush of screaming noise crashed into existence around them. Cidra reeled, feeling Severance stagger under the impact of the wild sounds. She let go of his utility loop to clutch at her ears, but it did no good. Once before she had tried to block out such noise. Frantically Cidra tried to remember when, but she couldn't concentrate on anything but the agony in her head.

"Don't open your eyes, Cidra!" She heard Severance's voice without realizing how she could over the strange cacophony.

"The light?"

"It's still there, but it's full of things."

"I can't stand it, Severance. I can't stand this!"

He didn't answer, and Cidra knew with a terrifying certainty that he wasn't faring any better than she was. They were both helpless under the bombardment of sensations.

And then the crawling began on her skin. She sensed it first on her legs. Something had gotten under the fabric of her trousers. Something with white hot pincers and venomous fangs. Screaming, she slapped at her legs. She could feel nothing under the fabric, but that knowledge didn't lessen the pain. Suddenly she remembered when and where she had faced this kind of assault.

"The Screamer," she choked, stumbling against Severance. "It's like the Screamer."

"Something's playing on our nerve endings. All of them," he agreed.

He fumbled with his utility belt. Cidra didn't risk opening her eyes, but she could feel him trembling as he fought to master himself. "What are you doing?"

"I'm going to see if the Screamer can jam whatever is jamming us."

Another burst of white-hot noise cascaded through the room, and Cidra groaned under the weight of it. The force of it drove her to her knees, and she was aware of Severance hunched down beside her. She sensed that he had the small Screamer remote in his hand. He leaned against her, assuring her that their bodies were touching, and activated the remote.

The riot of sensation altered suddenly. For a few seconds everything disappeared—the noise, the light, the physical sensations, even the chamber itself. Cidra found herself in a gray limbo. She drifted mindlessly in the wonderful silence, drinking in the pain-free void, and then it was over.

A new kind of whirling terror shot through her. This time she recognized it. This was what the Screamer had done to her on board *Severance Pay*. She clamped her hands over her ears in agony, and then chaos faded back into grayness again.

There were a few seconds of peace before the white light and noise started to build again.

"We'll have to move during the short periods when the Screamer wipes out the other stuff," Severance said tensely. "I can only buy us a few seconds at a time. If I keep it up too long, the Screamer goes into effect."

"I understand. The wall?"

There was a burst of blinding noise as the seconds of grayness faded back into a violent sensation. She waited agonizingly for the next burst of grayness.

"The wall," Severance agreed. He was already up and moving, keeping a hold on Cidra so that the Screamer's effects worked on both of them.

It was a painful tightrope of a journey. Between bursts of staggering sensation Cidra and Severance found the curving wall and doggedly followed it to the entrance of the chamber. Cidra lost all track of time, just as she had when the murals had been in motion. But when she tumbled through the vaulted opening, all of the mind-numbing noise and light disappeared. The relief was awesome. Almost frightening.

She lay on the soft, green velvet ground cover of the protected circle and tried to regain her breath. Severance sank down beside her and dropped the Screamer back into the utility loop. They huddled together, knees drawn up, heads cradled on folded arms, and waited to regain some sense of normality. For long moments neither of them spoke. They stayed close, seeking silent comfort from each other while their nerves adjusted to the standard range of stimulation on Renaissance.

"I never thought Renaissance would look 'normal,'" Cidra finally said.

"After what's inside that chamber, anything would seem normal. At least we're not suffering too many aftereffects. It could have knocked us out the way the Screamer usually does when it's used for more than a few seconds."

"Mostly I just feel exhausted, as if I've been running for hours."

Severance glanced at the sky and then at his chronometer. "We've lost more time. We've spent nearly a whole day in that damned place."

"I'm aware of that. My body is starting to remind me that the facilities don't include a lav." Wearily Cidra got to her feet. " I'll politely turn my back if you'll turn yours."

Severance managed a brief, amused grin. "It's a deal."

"I hope the Ghosts don't mind us using their magic circle as a lav."

"As far as I'm concerned, they deserve it." Severance turned his back to her.

Cidra felt on the defensive again. "I can't believe the Ghosts were responsible for all those awful illusions and that wall of noise and light."

"Any other bright suggestions?"

"No," Cidra admitted. "It just doesn't fit, that's all. By the time they built this place they were a peaceful, gentle people. It doesn't seem in their nature to build such traps."

"There's a lot we don't know about their nature, Cidra, and don't forget it." Severance turned around. "Ready?"

She nodded. "Uh, I've just thought of something."

"What?" He was checking the pulser.

"A minor point. Do you know how to find our way back?"

"You should have worried about that last night when you went for your joy walk." Then he saw the look on her face. "Stop worrying, I can find the way back." He pulled a small instrument out of his loop. "We didn't come that far according to this."

"What's that?"

"A directional system. Everyone who works on Renaissance carries one. It'll home in on deflector screens, a skimmer's comm unit, or anything else that puts out a man-made signal." He walked to the edge of the protected area and peered ahead. Then he glanced at the small instrument in his hand. "Okay, let's try this one more time, shall we? Remember what I said. Stick close and don't touch anything."

They got no more than two meters outside the Ghosts' serene, sheltered circle before the lockmouth attacked.

FOURTEEN

If he'd ever been given a written guarantee that the universe played fair, Severance would have sued now. It was all too much. He was too exhausted, too slow, and too anxious to get back to the safety of the deflectors. And the lockmouth was too hungry and too fast.

The clawed feet ripped downward as the scaled head that was twice as large as a man's opened its cavernous mouth. A reserve of sheer, blind instinct, not nimble, clever resourcefulness, threw Severance backward at the last possible instant. The claws, each as long as his fingers, slashed across his chest and shoulder instead of his throat.

He heard Cidra shout something as she struggled to pull him out of the way. He thought about telling her that it was too late to run. But there wasn't time to explain just how fast and vindictive a cheated lockmouth could be. Severance shoved at her, sending her sprawling.

The long, evilly shaped creature with the oversized head was already plunging down out of the nest of vines where it had been waiting for unwary prey. The mouth opened wide. Lockmouths could swallow a human being whole. They did it slowly. Once the locking mechanisms in the powerful jaws were closed, the only way to free whatever was trapped inside was to cut off the huge head. By then, there wasn't much point.

The lockmouth crouched briefly, preparing the final spring. This time it wouldn't miss. Severance decided he'd better not miss, either. On Renaissance there were very few second chances, and he'd already used up his quota for a year. He was sorely tempted to fire the pulser straight into the creature's gaping mouth but resisted and aimed for the eyes. Behind them resided whatever the creature had that passed for a brain.

The pulser withered one huge, glassy eye, and the lockmouth jerked spasmodically. Severance used the second's grace to edge backward. He heard Cidra breathing quickly into the sudden, hushed silence, but she said nothing.

That was the thing about Cidra, Severance decided as he fired again. She knew when to keep her mouth shut.

The lockmouth jerked once more and then crumpled heavily to the jungle floor. The jaws slammed shut, locked for the last time in death.

"Severance, you're bleeding."

"I know. It's one of the dumber things a man can do on Renaissance." The pain was lancing through him now as the short-term anesthetic effects of adrenaline and fear wore thin. He looked down at where the lockmouth's claws had ripped through the tough fabric of his shirt as though it were made of spun crystal moss. There were three savage scrapes across the tough hide of the rantgan leather utility loop. The loop had kept the lockmouth from ripping up his chest as well as his shoulder. Warm blood of an interesting shade of crimson had already dampened too much of the shirt. It was running down his arm and dripping on the ground. A small, innocent-looking flower suddenly spread its petals to absorb the moisture.

"The Ghost circle." Cidra stepped forward, clamping a hand solidly over Severance's bleeding wound. Blood seeped between her fingers but began to slow as she applied pressure. "We'll be safe there while we bandage your shoulder."

Severance didn't argue. He was feeling strangely dizzy already and was alarmed. He couldn't afford the luxury of any picturesque wounds. He had to get Cidra back to the safety of the deflectors; had to put in the call for help. Damn it, he should have been faster back there when the lockmouth attacked. Being exhausted and a little slower than usual were not acceptable excuses on Renaissance.

"I guess this answers the question of whether we're going to get the same escorted tour back to the campsite that we got coming here." He tried to seat himself calmly on the rich green ground cover inside the perimeter of the magic circle and wound up collapsing, instead. Not a good image for the crew, he chided himself. The one in charge was supposed to look as if he really were in charge. He hadn't done too well in that area recently.

"I don't understand," Cidra said. She studied Severance's shoulder with a grim intensity while she kept up the steady, blood-slowing pressure with her hand. "Why doesn't the protection work both ways?"

"Who in a renegade's hell knows? Maybe we got here through pure luck the first time. Or maybe the signal, whatever it is, has grown too weak to work well. Or maybe it never was designed to work both ways." He flinched and gritted his teeth.

"You've been badly hurt, Severance."

"Yeah, well, I wasn't going to call it just a small flesh wound." He groaned, more in frustration than from pain. "No wound on Renaissance qualifies as a minor flesh wound, unfortunately. Any amount of blood draws too much interest." At the edge of the circle there was a flash of movement. Fangs gleamed for a moment and then vanished. "See what I mean? Thank Sweet Harmony this circle seems to be holding." He fumbled with the utility loop. "There's some emergency stuff in here somewhere. The antiseptic is the most important thing."

He cursed, a soft, sibilant sound, as he withdrew the small

spray vial. Cidra took it from him, maintaining her pressure hold on his shoulder.

"I think the bleeding is slowing," she said.

He scanned her steady face. "It doesn't seem to be making you sick to your stomach."

She glared at him. "Nothing has made me sick to my stomach so far. Why should this?"

"Getting cocky, are you, little Wolf?"

She saw the affectionate amusement that briefly replaced the pain and frustration in his eyes. "It isn't blood that bothers Harmonics. It's knowing someone else is in pain that bothers them. I don't have to worry about that, though, do I? You're doing an excellent job of playing the stoic hero."

"Fool, not hero." He closed his eyes as she peeled away the torn fabric of the shirt. Wordlessly he handed her the small utility knife. Cidra looked at him in horror. "Don't worry. I'm already ripped up enough as it is. You don't have to do any cutting except on the shirt."

"Oh. For a minute there I thought I was going to have to perform minor surgery."

"Just spray the area with the antiseptic, and then we'll try bandaging it."

"Perhaps I should wash the wound first."

"Get some water from that stream. I've got a bag you can use to collect it. And there are some standard-issue purification drops somewhere on this damned loop."

"But I'm sure any water flowing through this circle would be clean and pure," she protested.

"You've got a hell of a lot more faith in the Ghosts than I do. Have you forgotten that last set of illusions inside that safehold?"

"No, but I'm sure there's an explanation for them."

"I'm sure there is too. Just like there's an explanation for everything on this planet. The trouble is, it may not be one we want to hear."

Cidra said nothing, collecting water in the clear plastic bag from the cheerful little stream. She added the chemical drops and waited while the water turned a strange shade of purple. Then she carefully bathed the wound, relieved to see that the bleeding was under control. When she was done, she reached for the antiseptic.

"Ouch!"

She stopped spraying antiseptic and glanced worriedly at Severance's face. "Does that hurt?"

He set his teeth. "No. Not a bit. What makes you ask?"

"Severance . . ."

"Finish spraying. I'll work harder at playing the stoic hero."

She hurried, aware of his growing pain. When she was finished, she dropped the spray back into his loop. "What do we use for bandages?"

"A mailman is always prepared. Try the small pouch near my shoulder. I've got some plastic adhesive in there."

She applied the liquid adhesive with quick strokes and watched as it hardened into a strong bandage. "I think that stopped the last of the bleeding. How do you feel?"

"I still feel like a fool." He looked down at her handiwork. There was a lot of blood and gore on his arm, but the adhesive seemed to be holding.

"This was hardly your fault, Severance." Cidra leaned back on her folded knees. "The responsibility for getting us into this mess is mine."

"I'm the one who set off on a midnight garden walk through the jungle with you instead of dragging you back to the tent, remember?"

"Yes, but . . ."

"But, nothing. I'm the one who screwed up." He held up a hand to keep her from arguing further. "The subject is closed for discussion. We'll reopen it later when I feel more like fighting with you. Right now I haven't got the energy."

She subsided, not liking the pallor on his tanned face. "If you're not up to fighting with me, Severance, then you probably aren't up to trying to make it back to the deflectors."

"Trust a Harmonic to grasp a difficult situation the first time out."

"I'm not a Harmonic."

"Hush, Cidra." He paused for a moment, eyes closed. "It looks like we're stuck here for the night. I'd say we had to try for the deflectors if this weird circle didn't seem to be working, but it does, so I guess our odds are better staying here than trying to hike back. It's going to be dark soon." He swung an assessing glance around the perimeter of the circle. "Let's move over to the wall of the safehold. That should protect our backs just in case."

Cidra tried to help him as he staggered to his feet. He was shakier than he wanted to admit. He looked down at her supporting hands.

"You're stronger than you look, aren't you, Cidra?"

She ignored that. "At least we'll be warm enough."

"Food," he announced succinctly, "will be our next problem."

She glanced at him as she eased him down with his back to the translucent wall. "Any ideas? Can we eat any of the vegetation around this circle?"

Severance leaned his head back, taking a few seconds to gather his strength. Cidra crouched beside him. When he opened his eyes again, she breathed a small sigh of relief. His gaze was steady, not showing any signs of disorientation. He gazed at the jungle growth that ringed their shelter. "I'm no botanist. Any of this stuff could be deadly or simply inedible. The safest thing to eat on Renaissance is what most everything else eats: Meat. If you can kill it before it kills you."

Cidra felt her stomach lurch for the first time. She cleared her throat. "Actually, there shouldn't be more than a few hunger pangs if we simply wait until we get back to the campsite tomorrow. No harm in going a day without eating."

He looked up at her through slitted eyes. "Personally I'm starved. Neither of us has had anything since yesterday, and we've gone through a lot of our stored energy since then. Renaissance has a way of doing that to a body. By tomorrow we could be light-

headed. That's not a good condition to be in when we make another try for the campsite."

"I understand." She said no more. This was a matter of survival. There was no obligation to follow the Kinian dietary restrictions under such circumstances. Vegetarianism was a luxury
she could not afford tonight. "What do we do?"

He unholstered the pulser. "We sit here very quietly and wait
for the crowd to arrive."

"What crowd?"

"The guests who will be sitting down to dine on the late, un-
lamented lockmouth. Sooner or later something will pass by on
the way to the meal. I'll try to get it before it realizes we're a
threat."

Cidra nodded, quelling her stomach with a stern effort of will.
She sat huddled in silence beside Severance as the darkness descended. Before long, the dinner guests began arriving. The first
indications were eyes. Far too many eyes. They flickered and
flared in the shadows.

Next came the sounds of scufflings and one or two piercing
screams. This was not a well-mannered crowd, Cidra decided.
And some of the guests had just become entrées themselves. She
shuddered at the thought and stayed very still.

The unwary, overanxious diner who passed too close to the
circle was a small four-footed hopping creature that had fur instead of scales. Cidra had been rather hoping for something with
scales. It was easier to dislike scaled things. A totally irrational,
even primitive reaction, but one she couldn't shake. She shut her
eyes when Severance brought up the pulser and fired in a smooth,
sure movement.

"Get it," he snapped, "before something else does."

Cidra leapt to her feet and dashed to the edge of the circle.
The little hopper lay dead less than a meter away. It looked very
cuddly and pathetic until she saw the fangs in its mouth. She
reached out, grabbed it by the fluffy tail, and hauled it into the
safe area. Her heart was pounding, and her insides again moved
uncomfortably. Huge, dead eyes gazed up at her in mute reproach.

"I'd better clean it on the edge of the circle." Severance made his way painfully to the perimeter and pulled out the utility knife. He removed the miniature quartzflash he carried and set it on the ground to light the hopper. "Ever do any dissection work in those biology classes you're always mentioning?"

She swallowed. "No. Everything was demonstrated with holotapes. I wasn't going to be a biologist, so there was no need to actually do dissections."

"This isn't going to look like any neat, clean holotape. Why don't you start the flamer while I take care of this?" He handed her the tiny can of instant fire he had removed from his loop and turned back to the hopper.

Cidra looked away, busying herself with igniting the emergency flamer. She had it going quickly and adjusted the wide flame to a reasonable level. The fire was very comforting here in the middle of the jungle, she discovered.

Severance was tiring very rapidly. Cidra kept a wary eye on him as he washed his bloodied hands in the bubbling stream. But she said nothing as he doggedly roasted sections of meat on the narrow point of the utility knife.

Cidra listened to the hissing of animal fat and tried to close her nostrils to the smell of roasting meat. When Severance handed her a portion, she took it without a word.

"Careful, it's hot." He bit hungrily into the hindquarter he was holding.

Cidra stopped breathing as she took a tiny bite. She'd never eaten meat in her life. Closing her eyes, she chewed woodenly, trying not to taste. On the other side of the small flamer Severance chewed vigorously and watched her. Under his steady gaze she forced herself to swallow the first bite, trying to think of it as medicine.

"We're very lucky you remembered to bring the utility loop and the pulser with you," she remarked, trying for light dinner-table conversation. In the shadows the other diners weren't being nearly so fussy. Their conversations consisted of squeals, growls, hisses, and shrieks. She hoped they would finish quickly.

"It was probably instinct more than luck. It certainly wasn't careful, foresighted planning. I wasn't thinking clearly at the time. I just remember feeling undressed. Wearing the loop is second-nature to me. And carrying a pulser on Renaissance has gotten to be an unconscious action." He finished gnawing on a leg. "How are you doing?"

"Fine," she said tightly, and forced down another bite.

"You look a little green." He scrutinized her in the flickering light. "Sure you're okay?"

"Yes."

His expression softened. "Poor Cidra. Just one new experience after another these days, isn't it?"

"This trip has turned out slightly different than I had anticipated."

"What an understatement."

She felt obliged to hold her own. "But thanks to your unorthodox way of doing things, I might have discovered a shortcut to my goal." She glanced behind her into the darkened entrance to the circular chamber.

"You think whatever drew us here is the source of the legend you're chasing?" His eyes were unreadable now in the firelight.

"It's possible. There was definitely a telepathic sensation involved, don't you think? I felt the first trickle of it yesterday afternoon while I waited for you. I wonder if the failing deflector screens allowed the call to get through. Maybe deflectors normally block it."

"But last night the screens were working at full strength."

"True," Cidra mused. "But by then the mechanism responsible for projecting the call might have had a fix, so to speak, on our location. Maybe it can't compete against other distractions, but in the quiet of the night it was able to touch us."

Severance shrugged and said nothing as he spitted another chunk of hopper and held it over the flame.

Cidra continued, trying to reason out the logic of the situation. "If one or two others in the past have felt the call, they might have told the tale to their friends. Over the years the stories would have grown more involved and complex."

"Until they reached the point where they made it into the Archives? It's possible. But if others have heard that call and followed it, why hasn't anyone discovered this safehold?" Severance asked in a reasonable tone.

"I don't know."

"Perhaps they heard the call but didn't follow."

Cidra frowned. "Why wouldn't they follow? We did."

"We were camped in the vicinity for two nights. The others might have merely caught traces of the call as they went by on a skimmer. The odds are no one's ever camped in that particular spot before. It might take a while for the call to focus in on a mind and become strong enough to draw someone to this place. If it's a mechanical device, it might have to tune itself."

She nodded. "That makes sense."

"There's another possibility. Someone may have found this place before but not lived to tell about it. If a man thought that he'd get the same protection going out as he got coming in, he'd be in for a rude surprise. I wasn't expecting protection, and I was still rudely surprised. Your Ghosts have a nasty sense of humor."

"I don't think they would have set a trap to lure intelligent beings here, show them their history, and then leave them unprotected. Perhaps they assumed that whoever found this place would be smart enough to protect themselves on the way back."

He groaned. "Never make assumptions. Case in point sitting right here in front of you."

She was shocked at her own words. "Oh, Severance, I never meant to imply that you . . ."

"That I'm not very bright? Don't worry. You don't need to imply it. Facts speak for themselves."

"Are you always so hard on yourself when things go wrong?"

"Only when they go wrong badly enough to get someone killed."

"Neither of us has been killed, Severance."

"I'll cling to that thought."

He stood up again and walked back to the stream to wash the grease from his hands. He needed rest very badly, Cidra thought as she unobtrusively put down the uneaten section of her meat. She didn't think she could swallow any more. Something was very wrong in the region of her stomach.

"Let's try to get some sleep. Since we don't know for certain just how reliable this circle is, we'll take turns keeping watch."

"I'll take the first watch," she volunteered.

He shook his head. "I'm liable to feel worse later on tonight. I'll need the rest then. I'll take the first watch while I've still got some energy left." Severance sank down onto the ground with his back to the curving wall. "Turn off the flamer. Don't want to waste fuel. We'll use the quartzflash for light."

"I think the circle is very safe. Nothing has even tried to cross the boundary." Cidra was only absently aware of what she was saying. Her attention was on the growing nausea that was simmering in her stomach. She was swallowing rapidly now, and her forehead felt damp from something other than the local humidity.

"Cidra?"

"It's all right, Severance. Just give me a minute." She kept her back to him and walked slowly to the edge of the circle, just beyond the range of the quartzflash.

"Cidra, come back here. What do you think you're doing?"

At that moment she lost the battle with her stomach. Her first meal of meat exited the way it had entered, leaving Cidra shuddering with unpleasant convulsions. She felt Severance's good arm around her even before she was finished.

"I'm sorry," she whispered. "I guess eating meat takes a little practice."

"I'll admit you don't seem to be taking to it as readily as you do to other Wolf ways." Gently he led her over to the stream, purified some water for her, and started to bathe her face.

"I'll do it." Embarrassed, she took the bag of water from him and knelt to finish washing her face and rinsing her mouth. "I'm all right, Severance, honestly. You must be careful not to start that shoulder bleeding again."

"Yes, Otanna."

She shot him an uncertain glance and realized that he was smiling laconically. Hastily she finished washing herself. Then she joined him at the wall where he was trying to settle into a reasonably comfortable position with the pulser resting on his drawn-up knee. His other leg was stretched out in front of him. Slowly she sank down beside him.

"You'll call me when it's my turn?" she asked.

"I'll wake you. Try to get some sleep, Cidra. Put your head down on my leg."

Carefully she obeyed, intensely conscious of the long, smooth muscles of his thigh as she used it as a pillow. She couldn't think of anything appropriate to say under the circumstances, so she lay very still, listening to the sounds of the darkness and trying not to think of the previous night's lovemaking. After all, she lectured herself, this was neither the time nor the place to dwell on the emotional and physical intimacy she had found in Severance's arms.

His arm moved, draping across her shoulder and breasts with casual possessiveness. Cidra flinched and then relaxed. His touch was comforting, she decided, not sensual. She went back to trying not to think of what she had experienced with him.

But she was very much afraid she would never forget that time of pleasure and passion. There had been a raw, primitive response coursing through her last night that had nothing to do with serenity and calm ritual. It was an emotion totally pegged to the man who had held her, and Cidra knew that a lifetime would not be long enough to dim the memories. Severance kept telling her she was a Wolf, like it or not, and last night he had proved it.

"Go to sleep, Cidra. Stop thinking about it." His hand stroked her arm with reassuring gentleness.

She knew for a fact that he couldn't read her mind. "Stop thinking about what?"

"Last night."

She grimaced. "How did you know that's what I was thinking about?"

He chuckled softly. "It was either that or else you were think-ing of what you had for dinner. Since you weren't showing any signs of getting nauseated, I decided it was probably sex that was keeping you awake."

"Your ego at work, no doubt."

"No. Actually it was a lucky guess based on the fact that I was thinking about the same thing."

"Oh."

There was a pause before Severance said gently, "It changes everything, you know."

"I don't see why it should." But she was lying and she knew it. He was right. Everything had changed.

"Sweet liar." He bent his head and brushed her cheek with his lips. "You're picking up all sorts of new habits, aren't you? I'll bet you never told a single lie all the time you lived in Clementia."

The truth of that observation was disturbing. "I didn't make this journey to become a Wolf, Severance."

"I know." The brief amusement faded from his voice. "I know. Go to sleep."

She closed her eyes and was surprised to find that she could obey.

When Severance awakened her a few hours later, Cidra stirred stiffly, sitting up slowly and yawning as she shoved the butt of the pulser into her palm. She blinked sleepily, realizing vaguely that in the light of the flash his face looked more drawn and exhausted than it had earlier. She didn't think his eyes appeared quite as clear, either.

"How are you feeling?"

"Lousy. But I'll live till morning. Know how to use the pulser?"

"I know the theory, yes." She was surprised by how cold and heavy it felt in her hand.

"Shoot first if something crosses the edge of the circle. Believe me, I'll be awake shortly thereafter." He stretched out along the side of the wall, pillowing his head on her lap as if it were the way he bedded down every night. His eyes closed immediately.

Tentatively Cidra rested her arm on his chest. It seemed to her that he felt very warm. Too warm. She hoped the antiseptic spray she had used earlier was doing its job.

Staying awake with a pulser in one hand proved to be a formidable task. Cidra decided that she had never given enough credit to the heroes in the First Family novels who spent so much time standing guard. The problem was boredom.

Behind her back, the wall of the safehold continued to radiate the warmth it had collected during the day. Rather than being uncomfortable, it was rather pleasant, although by rights the balmy air should have been sufficiently warm. Beyond the edge of the circle, night things moved about their deadly business. Cidra occasionally got disconcerting glimpses of prowling eyes. Fortunately, for her peace of mind, very little else was visible. The circle was holding. The knowledge made her wonder again why the mind call had not provided a safe path back to the campsite.

That thought led to another. She realized that she was totally unaware of any lingering call in her mind. Having served the purpose of drawing the visitors to the safehold, the telepathic lure had dissolved. And with it, perhaps, had dissolved her chances of discovering the truth behind the legend.

If this safehold was the source of those small hints and uncertain promises she had set out to track down, she might be at the end of her quest before it had even properly begun. Furthermore the results of that quest showed every sign of being useless. A faded mind call left by a people who had long since passed into the shadows held little hope of being converted into the magic elixir that would make her a true Harmonic.

There was always the possibility that the mind call was not what had prompted the legends, however. If this safehold had survived the centuries intact, who knew what else might be hidden on Renaissance? She let her mind drift back to the history she had seen in the safehold. The ending bothered her. It wasn't just a sense of sadness she felt for the passing of a great civilization. Cidra realized that she also felt anger. Deep inside she hadn't wanted the Ghosts to fade away without a struggle of any kind.

Unconsciously she had wanted them to fight back against their fate, not bow serenely to it.

Severance shifted slightly, not waking. She touched his forehead and found it dry and hot. Anxiously she examined the wound. As far as she could tell, no blood was leaking through the plastic adhesive. The flesh around it was swollen and red, but that probably wasn't unusual under the circumstances. Cidra rested her head against the safehold wall again and stared out into the darkness. Renaissance had a way of forcing a person to view things in fundamental terms. She found maintaining a belief in wispy tales and legends difficult when she was constantly being faced with so many real-life monsters and challenges.

Sooner or later she was going to be forced to decide how far to follow her personal dream. Every step with Teague Severance had an odd way of moving her goal farther from her grasp. Yet she could think of no other method of pursuing her quest. The thought of dropping the search altogether left her feeling shaken. She had dreamed for too many years.

Memories of the twinkling fountains and perfumed air of Clementia drifted up to tease her, reminding her of what she sought. But the delicate fragments of her visions kept getting demolished by the more powerful memories she was accumulating with Severance.

Even as she said his name in her mind he stirred again on her lap. She touched his forehead again and began to worry in earnest. He was far too warm. The wound must be infected. That thought left her feeling helpless. There was no way she could guide a wounded, sick man through the jungle. They would be easy prey.

Perhaps Severance carried other medicine in his utility loop. Trying not to disturb him, she began going through the pouches one by one. The contents were varied and curious, covering everything from the utility knife to a spare set of Free Market cubes. Sometime she would make a point of asking him why he carried the extra cubes. The explanation, Cidra was sure, would prove interesting.

She found a packet of tablets that had long since lost its label. No point speculating on what they might be. But other than the antiseptic and the adhesive bandages, there was nothing else that appeared medicinal.

Severance turned on his side, clearly fretful and uncomfortable in his sleep. Cidra hesitated and then decided to get some water from the stream. She could soak his shirt in it and use it to cool him down somewhat. Gently she lifted his head off her lap and pillowed him on the ground cover. She opened the lightweight bag and hurried to kneel beside the stream. The water felt cool against her hands, and she hoped it would have the same effect on her patient.

She was getting to her feet when she realized that Severance was trying to stagger erect. Alarmed, she went back to him. In the moonlight she could see that he wasn't focusing on her. His eyes were fevered and restless.

"Lie down, Severance. I'm going to cool you off." She tugged coaxingly on his arm.

He reacted as if he weren't even aware of her. Pulling free of her grasp, he leaned against the wall of the safehold and began making his way along it toward the entrance. Cidra suddenly realized where he was going.

"Severance, no!" She raced forward and caught his arm again, this time much more firmly. "You can't go in there. Lie down. You'll feel better when I bathe your face. Lie down, Severance."

Again he shook free of her and started toward the entrance. Cidra became frantic. If he got inside and activated the illusion trap, she would never get him back out, not in his present condition. There was no telling what the terrifying images would do to him while he was burning up with fever. They were hard enough to deal with when one was feeling normal.

He was almost at the entrance when Cidra acted out of desperation. Smoothly, swiftly, she moved against him with the dancing patterns of Moonlight and Mirrors. Given his current condition, the motions should have folded him gently to the ground.

But when he felt her touch, Severance reacted as if he were under attack. He swung around, blocking her with a swift, violent throw that caught Cidra totally off-guard. She was flat on her back before she even realized what had happened.

"Severance, wait!"

It was too late. He had vanished inside the safehold.

FIFTEEN

Severance was out of his head with fever. But even as she reached that conclusion, Cidra had to wonder where he had gotten the strength to toss her aside so easily. The next question was what had made him, even in a delirium, want to go back into the safehold?

She scrambled to her feet and raced to the vaulted entrance. There she braced one hand on the wall beside her. Touching something solid as she leaned into the chamber gave her a small sense of security. Inside, she could see nothing at all. The walls that allowed light to pass through them during the day produced no illumination during the night. There wasn't any sign of either the Ghost narrative or the illusion trap.

"Severance? Come back, Teague. Please. You don't want to be in there. Turn around and walk back toward me."

When there was no answer, Cidra darted over to where the quartzflash had been left. She picked it up, flicked on full power, and swung the beam around inside the safehold entrance. The light fell on Severance almost at once. He was crouched beside the heavy stone Cidra had tried to use against the apparition of the bloodsucker. His large hands were curved around the smooth surface.

"What is it?" Cidra asked, cautiously taking a step into the safehold. She had to talk him out of here if she could. If both of them got trapped inside by the illusions, she wasn't sure she would have the strength to lead him out. "Tell me what you've found, Severance."

He was totally oblivious to her. His whole attention was on the stone. Cidra took another step inside, wondering at what point the illusions would be activated. Perhaps not until she tried to turn around and walk out. She studied Severance's crouching form in the light of the quartzflash and knew she wasn't going to be able to talk him out of the safehold. She was going to have to lead him forcibly back to safety.

Counting her steps in the hope that she could retrace them even through a hail of illusion, Cidra advanced slowly into the darkened safehold. Her cautious movement didn't trigger any images. When she reached Severance, she touched his shoulder. This time he looked up at her. Cidra was shocked to see the raging fever in his eyes. She put her arm around him, and her voice instinctively slipped into the gentling, hypnotic cadence Harmonics used when they sought to soothe one of their own.

"Come with me, Severance. All is safe with me. Let me lead you to safety. Outside, the air is cool and calm. You'll feel better outside. Come with me and be safe. Outside, all is serene."

She felt him tremble and sensed that somewhere in his fevered mind he was trying to understand. Cidra also had the impression that he was torn between conflicting needs. She saw the way his hands rested on the stone.

"Is it the stone you want? Bring it with you, Severance. Pick up the stone and bring it with you. Let's go outside where it's cool and clear."

His shoulder muscles flexed beneath her arm, and he picked up the stone. Cidra straightened, relieved when he stood up beside her. When she tugged on his arm, he followed her docilely.

Warily she guided him toward the doorway, fully expecting to find their exit impeded by anything from a giant bloodsucker to a wall of light.

Nothing happened. Using the quartzflash, Cidra made it back outside with her patient in tow. Breathing a sigh of relief, she guided Severance to the wall and eased him down onto the ground. He was still astonishingly docile, willing to go where she led as long as he had the stone.

"What is it about the rock, Severance? Why do you want it?"

He clutched it protectively. "Warm. Feels good. Feels warm. I'm so cold."

"You're already burning up," she whispered, knowing that he didn't really hear her. "Lie down and I'll see if I can break that fever." She pushed him down onto the ground. He curled around the stone and closed his eyes.

He did seem calmer, Cidra decided as she began bathing him. Perhaps the stone was having some beneficial effect. She couldn't imagine what it could be, though. When she touched it, the hard, smooth sphere felt faintly warm. Perhaps it carried a residue of the heat it had collected during the day.

The hours dragged on toward dawn. With one eye on the small movements that occasionally occurred around the edge of the circle, and another on Severance, Cidra kept watch and worried about the fever. The pulser was never far from her hand, although she no longer had any fear of something crossing the unseen boundary of the circle. She kept the pulser close primarily because Severance's last, clear instructions had been to do so. He was still the pilot in command, she thought as she filled the water bag for the fifth time. And she was still the one and only member of his crew.

As dawn filtered slowly through the tangle of overhead leaves and vines, Cidra decided that the stone wasn't doing Severance much good. He still clung to it, but she didn't like the way he seemed to have become dependent on it. The fever wasn't abating, and the added warmth of the stone might easily be doing harm. Kneeling beside him, Cidra tried to remove it from his grasp.

"No." He reacted sharply, protecting the sphere with both arms. For a moment his eyes opened, staring at her with fierce resistance. "Don't touch it," he said very clearly.

They were the first clear words he had spoken all night. Cidra tried to reason with him. "It's warm, Severance. You need to be cool. Give me the stone. You can have it back later."

"Don't touch it." His eyes closed again, but his grip on the stone didn't loosen.

Cidra gave up on the task and went back to trying to cool him down with stream water. Around the perimeter of the circle the shift from night to day was taking place. A few choked shrieks marked the efforts of a few lingering hunters. She was getting used to the sounds of the jungle, Cidra realized dispassionately. She was amazed at how many things she was becoming accustomed to seeing, hearing, and doing these days.

As the day began to warm, Cidra became aware of a slight dizzy sensation. The light-headedness Severance had warned her about, she assumed. She wasn't sure what to do about it. She didn't dare risk eating any of the plant life. Severance had been convinced that there was too much possibility of being poisoned. Without the proper equipment she couldn't test for toxins.

For a while she tried to convince herself that she could go another day without eating. After all, she had fasted more than once for a day or two in a secret effort to open her stubborn mind. It had been a long time ago, back when she had still believed she might be able to catapult herself into Harmonichood by sheer willpower. The exercise hadn't worked, although it had produced a light-headed feeling that for a while convinced her she might be onto some useful technique.

The problem today was that she simply couldn't afford to be light-headed. Not with Harmony-knew-what prowling around outside the circle and a sick man on her hands. She had to maintain her strength, both physically and mentally. And that meant she was going to have to find something to eat.

She glanced toward the perimeter of the protected ground, looking for the remains of the hopper Severance had skinned and cleaned the previous evening. He had pushed the entrails outside the circle. There was no sign of anything, not even the head. Renaissance had taken care of the garbage in its own sure fashion.

Not that she wanted to eat whatever was left of the poor hopper. Cidra's stomach grew queasy again just at the thought. She went back to the endless task of bathing Severance and tried to put food out of her mind.

But when she stumbled a little on a trip to the stream, she began to worry. She had no idea how long she was going to be trapped inside this circle with Severance. Common sense dictated that she not let herself grow weak. She was going to have to eat. Just existing on this planet seemed to take a lot of inner energy. Cidra eyed the pulser and wondered how hard it would be to hit something such as the hopper.

Surely the principles of aiming and firing a weapon couldn't be fundamentally different than the task of collecting and focusing a mind for deep, concentrated study. Harmonic philosophy taught that all things could be assessed and comprehended. In addition to focusing and concentration, she would need a certain amount of coordination, Cidra supposed. She had that from her training in Moonlight and Mirrors.

Picking up the pulser, she went to the edge of the circle and sat cross-legged. It could be a long wait until something edible wandered close enough to assure her a clear shot. She took the time to slowly clear her mind of extraneous thought. If she was going to do this, she would do it quickly and cleanly. Using the techniques of meditation, she willed herself to an outer and inner stillness. She would become one with the weapon, not a fake Harmonic holding a foreign instrument of destruction. She must make the pulser an extension of herself.

Deliberately she fused herself and the pulser into a single entity. It wasn't particularly difficult once she had cleared her mind of the ramifications of what she was about to do. In some ways she was merely applying the methods she used for programming a computer or writing a poem. The underlying philosophical harmony of all tasks was the same.

Time passed, bringing nothing into range except a slithering green snake that didn't look very edible to Cidra. She waited. Behind her Severance was quiet, still wrapped around his precious rock.

When the small hopper flitted into view, Cidra's hand came up and her finger squeezed the trigger without any hesitation. It was what she had been waiting for, and her body responded accordingly. The hopper flipped over, quivered for a second, and then went limp. Cidra lowered the pulser.

Slowly she got to her feet and shook herself out of the trance. As she stared at the dead creature all of her natural revulsion to eating meat returned in a sickening wave. This time she kept her stomach under control. She stepped cautiously out of the circle, caught the hopper by the ears, and yanked it back to safety.

For a moment she simply looked at her catch, wondering how she was going to find the nerve to cut into it. She had almost talked herself out of making the effort when she experienced another wave of unsteadiness. There was no point in waiting any longer. Resolutely she went over to where Severance lay and reached into the utility loop for the knife.

The job was, as Severance had said, not neat and tidy like a holotape of a dissection. Twice Cidra had to stop long enough to let the racking heaves pass. Both times she recovered and went back to the task. She knew the theory of what needed to be done. She'd had a very thorough education. When she was finished, she pushed the entrails and the head outside the circle.

She washed the hopper's blood from her hands and let her stomach have its way one more time. Then she switched on the flamer and spitted a hindquarter on the point of the knife. Ignoring the hissing of crackling fat, she roasted her kill. She stilled her mind and her body before she took the first bite by repeating the familiar words that preceded a Harmonic meal.

This time the food stayed down. It took an effort of will, and there were a few seconds when Cidra wasn't sure she was going to win the contest with her stomach, but in the end she did. Slowly and methodically she ate the entire hindquarter. Then she roasted the second hindquarter and carried it over to Severance.

"Try to eat," she coaxed, letting him have a whiff of the meat. He didn't respond. When she tried to insert a bite between his lips, he spit it out. With a sigh Cidra sat back on her heels and wondered what to do next.

An hour later she happened to glance across the circle and saw that the remains of the hopper were gone. Another Renaissance meal was concluded, bones and all. Nothing went to waste on this planet.

The day progressed with painful slowness. Twice Cidra dozed, snapping uneasily awake each time. Perhaps it would be better if she slept during the daylight. If she didn't, she was bound to drift off to sleep tonight. The circle seemed so safe. The third time her eyes closed, Cidra allowed herself to drift into sleep.

A faint cracking sound woke her some time later. She opened her eyes slowly and realized that dusk was setting on the jungle. She and Severance had spent another whole day here. The thought of her companion made her glance automatically in his direction. He was still sleeping soundly, curled around the stone.

She heard the cracking noise again and roused herself fully, reaching for the pulser in her lap. She climbed to her feet and peered around the circle. Nothing stirred near the edge as far as she could see. When the sound came a third time, she suddenly realized where it was coming from and whirled around toward Severance. She saw the rock he was holding shiver in his grasp.

"Sweet Harmony!" Cidra edged closer, trying to see what was happening. Severance was still huddled around his possession, but the stone seemed to be quivering in his arms. Even as she watched, a distinct crack appeared in the black surface. Unaware of what she was doing, Cidra brought up the nose of the pulser and stepped forward. This time she would take the stone away from Severance by force. Surely, after all these hours of fever, he was no longer strong enough to stop her.

There was a sharp splintering sound from the rock just as Cidra reached for it. Severance groaned and hugged it closer. She succeeded in pushing one of his hands out of the way and had just gotten a grip on the sphere when it cracked completely open.

She heard the savage hissing before she saw the damp reptilian head emerge from the broken stone. Frantically Cidra struggled to pull the rock away from Severance before whatever was inside escaped. Fragments of the shell came free in her hand. The head whipped out, snapping at her hand with a mouthful of tiny sharp teeth.

Cidra yelped and yanked her fingers out of the way. The creature turned immediately toward Severance's midsection, its blue, leathery body uncurling from the remains on the shell. With a sudden shock of logic Cidra realized what was going to happen. Severance was intended as the hatchling's first meal.

She didn't dare fire the pulser at this range. She would surely kill Severance as well as whatever was trying to eat him. Furiously she banged the nose of her weapon against the creature's snout. The blow managed to get its attention away from Severance. The creature hissed again and struck at the offending pulser. Its teeth closed around the metal and then released it as it apparently realized that the pulser couldn't be eaten.

Frantically Cidra slammed the weapon against the leathery blue head once more. Again she got the creature to snap at the muzzle of the pulser. This time she jerked upward and out. With its mouth still locked around the metal mouth of the pulser, the blue reptile was carried with it. The creature released its hold in midair and fell to the ground in a hissing coil. It struck at Cidra as if realizing that she was the source of the problem.

Cidra raised the pulser and fired with the same unthinking sureness she had used to bring down the hopper. The reptile jerked twice. It writhed horribly on the ground, attempting even in its death throes to get back to its intended meal. Cidra fired again, and at last it went still.

Behind Cidra Severance groaned sharply, still not waking. He moved restlessly and spoke in a slurred, hot tone. "Cidra, *Cidra.*"

She ignored him, her attention still on the dead stone creature. She wanted it out of the circle. It was wrong here. Dead or alive, it had no business in this place. She kicked at the body with the toe of her boot. It flipped over, revealing four appendages on the iridescent light blue belly. The front pair terminated in projections that looked too much like human fingers for Cidra's peace of mind. She kicked at the dead body again, intent on getting it out of the circle. The sense of wrongness was almost overpowering now. She knew for certain that she didn't want to touch it with her hands.

Three more kicks brought the stone creature's body to the edge of the circle. Cidra swung the toe of her boot one more time and pitched the remains into the thick greenery on the other side of the magic perimeter. There was a stir of activity almost at once. She got a glimpse of a furred tail as something pounced and then heard the crunch of jaws on a blue, leathery body. Renaissance would take care of the problem. Cidra hurried back to Severance.

He was more restless than ever. The front of his shirt was ripped where the creature had taken a bite out of it, but there were no marks on his skin. Cidra breathed a sigh of relief and knelt beside him. His stirred under her hand.

"So hot. It's so reeting hot. I can't stand it." He tore at his shirt with his hands.

"Stop it, Severance." Firmly she pulled his fingers free of the shirt. "I'll cool you down. I promise." She reached for the bag and poured water over his head, throat, and chest, dampening the shirt. He shivered and quieted. Lapsing back into an unintelligible mumble, he curled up again and appeared to be about to go back to sleep. Cidra wetted him again and waited. The delirious mumbling halted finally, and Cidra decided that he was asleep. She sat back and tried to think.

The first thing that came to mind was the memory of the four black stones that were piled in the safehold. She had to destroy them. There was no telling when Severance might decide to make another trip inside and carry one out. Furthermore, there was no telling when one of those awful eggs might hatch of its own accord. The thought of four of the dark blue reptiles wandering out

of the safehold seeking food was more than Cidra wanted to contemplate.

Wearily she got to her feet again and went to stand at the entrance of the safehold. From the walls came a faint glow, illuminating the interior now. At the far end of the room the four stones
rested in shadow. Cidra tried to decide what she would do if she
went into the room and accidentally triggered the illusions. She
would need the Screamer. She went back to Severance and removed it from his loop. Then she tightened her grip around the
pulser and stepped inside the chamber.

Nothing happened, just as nothing had happened the first
time she had entered. Staying close to the wall in case she needed
to use its surface as a point of reference, she walked slowly around
the room. She reached the small group of eggs at the back without having touched off either the Ghost history or the horrific illusions. Facing the eggs, Cidra took aim and systematically shot
each.

At first nothing happened. The tough stone casing around the
creatures seemed to absorb the energy of the pulser. She stepped
closer and fired again. This time one of the shells cracked. When
it fell apart, Cidra could see that the reptile inside was dead. She
used the pulser to break open the rest of the shells so that she
could assure herself that all the creatures were destroyed.

A part of her wanted to clear the remains out of the safehold,
but she didn't feel up to the task. She would have to content herself with knowing that the eggs were no longer a menace. Cidra
turned back toward the entrance, one palm still flattened on the
curving wall, and trotted quickly toward the sunshine.

Expecting a wave of illusions to block her path, she didn't realize she was holding her breath until she stepped outside without incident. It occurred to her that perhaps the illusions were
somehow tied to the eggs. Perhaps a protective device. With the
eggs destroyed the trap might not work any longer. As for the
Ghosts' history projection, perhaps it was simply so old that it had
faded into oblivion after one last showing.

There was no point speculating on either possibility. She had her hands full, tending Severance. For the next two hours she kept up the cooling baths. He slipped in and out of a troubled sleep, muttering occasionally and once in a while knocking her hands away in restless irritation.

At the end of the two hours of bathing his fevered body, Cidra thought she detected some improvement. He seemed to be cooling down at last. She peeled off the bandage and examined the wounds. They were red and swollen but not alarmingly so. She sprayed more antiseptic on them and then covered them again with the plastic adhesive. Severance opened his eyes just as she was finishing the task. His gaze was clearer than it had been for hours.

"Did I hurt you?" Cidra smiled, relieved to see something besides fever in his eyes. He still looked dazed and uncomprehending, but she could see him struggling to identify her.

"How could you hurt me? You're from Clementia."

Cidra shook her head at his logic and touched his temple. "You're on the mend, Severance. Your fever is breaking."

"I didn't take care of you. I almost got you killed."

"No, Severance. You saved my life. More than once."

He moved his head in restless denial. "Just like Jeude. Almost got you killed, just like Jeude."

"Hush," she soothed. "You didn't kill your brother."

"Should never have let him go to QED alone. He was too soft. Too gentle. Followed a distress signal right into the ground. Never realized he'd been tricked."

Cidra frowned. "Be easy, Severance."

"Had to kill Racer. Racer set up the signal. Racer tried to take you from me. He would have hurt you, Cidra. He wanted to hurt you to hurt me."

"I know," she whispered, wondering about what he had said earlier. "Racer drew your brother to his death with a fake distress signal?"

"Racer murdered Jeude. Said he hadn't meant to, but he did. And I never even knew until . . . until—" He broke off, clearly groping for some sense of time.

"It's all right, Severance. It's all over. Everything's over. Racer is dead."

"All my fault," he muttered again. "I put you in danger. Just like I put Jeude in danger."

"Severance, listen to me. It is not your fault. You've taken care of everything. Racer is dead."

But he wasn't listening. The gray eyes looked up at her with unnatural intensity. "I let Jeude get killed, and I almost let you get killed. You're like him. I'm supposed to protect you. You and he both belong in Clementia." His voice faded as his eyes began to close. "You're like him."

Cidra stared down at his hard face as he drifted back into sleep. "No, Severance. You're wrong. I'm not like Jeude." Her eyes fell on the pulser that lay close at hand on the ground. "I'm not at all like Jeude."

She bathed him once more, but now she was certain that he had turned the corner. The fever was definitely subsiding. A damp, healing sweat filmed his skin. Cidra concentrated on getting Severance to drink plenty of water. Toward nightfall she stationed herself near the edge of the circle, slipped into the trance that made the pulser a part of her, and waited for another unwary hopper. Now she was amazed that anything as stupid as a hopper survived on Renaissance. The food chain was a complex thing. Right now she was sitting on the top of that chain: a reasonably well-adapted predator.

For someone who had never before eaten meat, doing so was a major change. But, then, everything else in her life was changing, so her eating habits might as well also. A flicker of ears caught her attention. The hopper made a dash through a relatively open area of vegetation, and Cidra killed it in mid-leap.

This time she didn't throw up when she cleaned the carcass. Cidra wasn't sure if that was an improvement or not. It seemed to her that part of her should still be fastidious enough to get sick at the thought of killing and butchering food. On the other hand, a steady stomach was proving much more convenient than an unsteady one.

When Severance awoke long enough to eat some of the roasted meat and drink more water, Cidra stopped worrying about her weakening vegetarian ethics. She was too busy being grateful that she had managed to get her patient to eat.

After dinner she settled herself against the wall of the safehold and cradled Severance's head in her lap. Fingers wrapped around the grip of the pulser, she leaned back against the wall and wondered if she would be able to stay awake all night. Probably not. She was exhausted. She could only hope that the ring of safety would protect both herself and Severance during the times she was unable to keep her eyes open.

She slept off and on during the long night. Every time she awoke she could tell by the chronometer on Severance's loop that she had only been napping for fifteen or twenty minutes. The usual screams and cries of the jungle went on all around the edge of the circle, but nothing encroached.

Severance slept soundly, pillowed in her lap. Cidra could tell that the fever had left his body. With any luck he would be feeling much better in the morning. She still wasn't sure how long he would need to recover enough to risk the trip back to the campsite, but at least he was on the mend. If need be, they could spend another couple of days here in the circle.

Once or twice Cidra awakened during the night to discover Severance burrowing closer to her, his face turned into her midsection as if he sought comfort from her warmth. She wrinkled her nose as she caught her own unbathed scent. In the morning she would clean herself at the stream. Never in her life had she gone so long without a bath. She fantasized for quite a while about having unlimited access to one of Clementia's elegant bathing rooms.

The night passed without incident. When dawn filtered once more through the green canopy, Cidra yawned and gently eased Severance's head out of her lap. She left him sleeping while she undressed and knelt beside the sparkling stream. The water looked clear and pure, and she could no longer resist it.

The liquid felt wonderfully cool and bracing in the morning

air. She even undid her frazzled braids and washed her hair in the bubbling stream. She arranged it loosely around her shoulders to dry in the sun. By the time she was finished, Cidra decided that she felt like a new woman. She put her trousers back on but decided to rinse out her shirt. Leaving it to dry on the green carpet, she picked up the pulser and walked to the edge of the circle to look for breakfast. Carefully she put herself into the trance that enabled her to become a hunter.

Severance yawned and stretched, distantly aware of an ache in his shoulder. He flexed it irritably and felt the pull of bandages. Slowly memory returned. He was stiff, and his head no longer felt nearly as comfortable as it had when he'd been sleeping in Cidra's lap.

Cidra's lap.

The thought opened his eyes. He saw the curving translucent wall rising above him, felt the green cushion under his back, and wondered how in a renegade's hell he'd been so stupid as to let himself get used for target practice by a lockmouth.

Reluctantly he rolled onto his side, looking for Cidra. He saw her rise from the edge of the stream, her slender body nude from the waist up. Her sweetly curved breasts looked perfect in the primitive morning light. The dark brown fire of her hair gleamed damply in the sun. Severance stared at her in silence, absorbing the sight of her, and then he winced at the direction of his thoughts. He was definitely feeling better, Severance decided.

He was about to speak when he saw Cidra bend down, scoop up the pulser, and walk to the edge of the circle. At first he thought she had seen something to alarm her, and then he saw her sink down into a cross-legged position. She went very still, her slender back elegantly straight. Before long, there was a flash of movement in the bushes. As calmly and coolly as a lifelong huntress she squeezed the trigger. A hopper flopped to the ground within easy reach.

Severance stared at the scene with a sense of shock that quickly changed to admiration. He sat up as she reached out of the circle to catch hold of the hopper by its ears.

"Is this the same lady who can't look a torla steak in the eye?"

"Severance!" She whirled around, the hopper in one fist, and gazed at him in delight. For an instant, relief and happiness lit her whole face, and then she remembered that she wasn't wearing her shirt. A tide of pink flowed into her cheeks and throat. She dropped the hopper and made a dash for the damp garment she had left beside the stream. "How are you feeling?" she asked as she turned away from him to put on the wet shirt.

"Like I've been hit with a freight sled."

She turned around as she finished fastening the shirt and peered at him. "You look much better. I've been very worried, Severance. You were quite feverish from the wound."

He shrugged his injured shoulder, assessing the pain critically. "I think I'm going to live. How much time have we lost?"

"We've spent two nights here in the circle." She came forward slowly. "Do you remember any of it?"

He smiled. "Some. You have a very nice lap." He started to get to his feet. Something sharp on the ground dug into his leg. He reached down and picked up a small, jagged object. "Where did this come from?"

Cidra glanced at the scrap of shell. "Now that," she said, "is a very interesting story."

"You can tell it to me while I clean the hopper."

Her eyes brightened. "Do you feel up to cleaning it? I can't say I like the job."

He grimaced. "How many have you cleaned?"

"Two."

Severance shook his head wonderingly. "Incredible. You've become a real carnivore."

She made a face. "I prefer not to think about it."

He held out his hand. "I can handle the pulser again too. Maybe not quite as well as you seem to be doing, but it would make me feel useful."

She glanced down at the weapon in her fingers. "I've grown used to having it around."

Severance realized that her reluctance to give him the pulser was real. Gently he took it from her and examined the charge window. "How many shots did it take to get the first hopper? The charge is way down."

"Oh," she said easily, "I've been shooting a lot of things besides hoppers."

Her words sent a distinct jolt through him. A fleeting glimpse of a nightmare cropped up from out of nowhere. There had been something evil and dangerous in his fevered dreams, something that had demanded his help. The image flickered and died, leaving behind an unpleasant taste.

"I think you'd better tell me what I've missed," Severance said.

SIXTEEN

Eggs, Severance. Those stones were some creature's eggs. Really nasty little renegades too. The one you were clinging to tried to eat you alive the second it hatched. Don't you remember anything at all about going back into the safehold to bring out one of the stones?"

Severance concentrated on the task of butchering the hopper. "No." Then he hesitated, his jaw tightening. "There were some dreams, though."

"Dreams?" Cidra waited, aware that he was struggling with himself. She couldn't decide if he was trying to remember or trying to forget.

Severance paused with the knife in his hand and stared unseeingly into the jungle. "I remember having to do something. It was important. No, it was *imperative*. Something's life depended on it. And if I obeyed, I would stop freezing. I was so damned cold. That's all I remember."

Cidra wasn't sure she believed him, but she did believe that was all he wanted to remember. "You insisted on going back into the safehold. I tried to stop you with my Moonlight and Mirrors routine. I might as well have been trying to dance with you."

His head came around quickly, eyes alarmed. "Did I hurt you?"

"Knocked me flat," she assured him cheerfully. Seeing the expression on his face, she relented. "Don't worry about it. I'm fine. You weren't out to hurt me, you just wanted to be left alone. The interesting part about all this is that when you went inside the safehold to get the egg, you didn't trigger the illusions."

"How do you know? Perhaps I was too far gone to know what I was seeing."

"I know because I went in after you, and I didn't see a thing."

"You went in after me?" He sighed as if in resignation, but he didn't launch into a lecture. "Go on."

She told him about the hatching of the egg and her decision to destroy the rest of them. "The illusions didn't stop me when I tried to leave the safehold after finishing off those eggs, either. I think they were tied to them somehow. A protective device. I wouldn't be surprised if the idea was that the illusions trapped the prey close to the eggs."

"Food for the hatchlings?"

"And perhaps a source of warmth for them. No telling how long those eggs have been in there. It wasn't until you curled around one that it hatched. What kind of creature could it have been, Severance? From everything we've seen nothing else on this planet except us has crossed the boundary of this circle or gone into the safehold."

"Except the Ghosts themselves," he pointed out.

"I refuse to believe that those blue things are related to the Ghosts in any way."

"You're the well-educated member of the crew, Cidra. You should know by now that refusing to believe in something doesn't mean it doesn't exist."

"Those egg creatures are something out of a nightmare," she insisted. "The Ghosts were a gentle, civilized people."

Who at one time conquered this very ungentle, uncivilized

planet. They might have become soft at the end, but they sure as hell weren't at the beginning."

"I'm not going to argue with you about it. I just know that those blue things aren't related to the Ghosts."

"Maybe they were watchdogs for the Ghosts," Severance suggested thoughtfully. "Guardians for the safehold?"

"I don't think so. There's something wrong about those eggs and the creatures inside them. They don't fit in here on Renaissance."

At that comment Severance laughed shortly. "Anything that can kill its own food and eat it raw fits in just fine here on Renaissance."

Cidra folded her arms across her chest, pacing restlessly around the circle. "It wasn't just that they were vicious and ugly. Lots of things here seem to be vicious and ugly. But even the worst of them, that lockmouth for instance, seem to belong in some way I can't explain. Those eggs don't. Or didn't. Remember when we first went into the safehold, you said there was a feeling of alienness?"

"Yeah. You didn't agree, though. You were too wrapped up with Ghost stories."

"It wasn't the Ghosts who felt alien. But the presence of the eggs might have bothered your instincts on some level."

"My instincts are fairly basic, Cidra. Chiefly focused on staying alive, eating, sleeping, and, uh, one or two other fundamental matters. They're not the elevated, intuitive instincts of a Harmonic. I don't see why I would have sensed the eggs in some special manner."

She stopped pacing at the edge of the circle. "Well, whatever they were, they're gone now."

He stood up, leaving the skinned hopper on the ground near the edge of the circle. Coming up behind Cidra, Severance said softly, "Thanks to you. I'm not sure I'm paying you enough. I've never had a crew member quite like you, Cidra Rainforest. Loyalty and resourcefulness above and beyond the call."

She turned, aware of a deep feeling of pleasure. She dipped her head formally. "It is as nothing, Teague Severance. Do not concern yourself. All is serene."

He grinned, a brief flash of teeth that disappeared quickly as his eyes grew serious. "Still a few remnants of Harmonic ways left, hm? Amazing. How are you handling the transformation, Cidra?"

Her flush of pleasure faded. She thought about killing hoppers and little blue monsters. Memories of trying to stay awake with a sick man lying in her lap and a pulser in her hand flooded her mind. "There has not been a great deal of choice in the matter."

He looked at her oddly. "No, there hasn't, has there? I haven't given you much choice." Abruptly he turned away to set up the flamer.

Sensing his inner withdrawal, Cidra stood quietly, watching his efficient manners. "Your arm seems much better this morning."

"Yes."

"Severance, while you were delirious you said I was like Jeude. But I'm not, am I?"

He studied the flame he had started before answering slowly. "Jeude had great courage. He would have done what had to be done. But it would have torn him apart."

"It hasn't torn me apart." She made the observation almost to herself.

"You shouldn't have had to face what you've faced since you shipped out with me. You weren't raised to confront murderers and monsters. I should have followed my instincts that first night and packed you off to Clementia."

"You didn't have that choice, Teague Severance. I make my own decisions."

"Let's argue about it after we get back to Try Again."

She wanted to argue now. Cidra lifted her head proudly, prepared to defend herself and her rights. But she stopped cold as her eye caught a flash of movement at the edge of the circle.

"Severance!"

He was on his feet at once, the pulser in his fist. "What is it?"

"The hopper. The one you just finished cleaning. It's gone."

He swore, striding toward the spot where the carcass had lain on the ground. "I left it inside the circle."

Cidra's eyes widened. "I know. Something with a long orange tail just reached into the circle and grabbed it. Severance, in all the time we've been here nothing has come inside that circle."

"Either there's something else besides us that's immune or . . ." He dug the toe of his boot into the invisible line of protection. A small worm slithered to the surface and disappeared again. Until now there hadn't even been any worms inside the protected area. "Or the circle is shrinking."

"Why would it start shrinking now?"

"How should I know? It might have been a lot bigger once than it is now. It might have been gradually shrinking all along but at such a slow rate that you haven't noticed."

"Or perhaps it started fading when the mind call was activated one last time. It's probably all connected." Unhappily she stared at the edge of the circle. "I hope everything we've found isn't going to disappear. There's so much to learn here, Severance. So much to be explored."

"We can worry about that later. Right now we've got another problem."

"What problem?"

He absently massaged his shoulder. "I was thinking of spending one more night here and leaving in the morning. But if this circle is shrinking, I don't want to risk it. The whole reeting thing could disintegrate in the middle of the night, and we'd be left in what would definitely qualify as an awkward situation. We'll have to start back to the campsite today."

"Do you feel up to making the journey?" Cidra asked anxiously.

"My shoulder's stiff, but I feel fairly normal."

"I would have thought that fever would have left you feeling exhausted."

"I know. But maybe the fever wasn't caused by the wound," Severance said thoughtfully. "Maybe it had something to do with what happened in the safehold. If I've been as sick as you've said,

I shouldn't be feeling this good so soon. But my shoulder feels the way it should after two days of that antiseptic. And I'm not weak the way I should be after spending several hours in a delirium."

"You think the eggs caused the fever? I wonder. What if they were capable of sensing your weakness after the lockmouth clawed your shoulder? Perhaps they sensed the blood and somehow focused on you. Something drew you back into that safehold. And when you came out, you wouldn't let go of that stone."

His mouth tightened. "I think our luck here is running out. We'll be better off making a try for the campsite than sitting here waiting for the circle to collapse. This time around I'll make it a point to stay alert on the trip out. Let's get our stuff together."

Cidra obeyed, collecting the water bag and the knife as Severance repacked the utility loop. She paused when she spotted the stone shard on the ground. "I think I'll take this back to Desma. She'll find it interesting." She dropped it into her pocket.

"All set?"

Cidra nodded, glancing back at the safehold. "I hope it lasts until someone gets here with a holotape set to record the history stored inside."

"Even if the circle doesn't hold much longer, it will take quite a while for that safehold to be reduced to rubble, even here on Renaissance. Let's go."

"Does it strike you, Severance, that you're always asking if I'm ready to go?"

"You'll get used to it." The pulser was gripped in his right fist as he started back into the jungle. The utility knife was in his left hand.

Cidra smiled to herself and followed.

One hour and two dead green slicers later, Severance called a halt. He tapped the face of the directional indicator and sighed. "We've got a problem."

Cidra battled at a small buzzing creature intent on landing on her cheek. "You're thinking we didn't walk for much more than an hour that first night?"

"I see that the thought has crossed your mind too."

"We might have been totally unaware of the time," she offered.

"It was dawn when we reached the safehold. I think we left the campsite just shortly before dawn. No more than an hour before."

"What does the directional gadget show?"

"That we're within a few meters of the skimmer."

Cidra looked around at the heavy vegetation surrounding them on all sides. "I don't see a river."

"Neither do I."

"Perhaps we're just a few meters away." Tentatively Cidra shoved at a hanging vine. "This stuff is so thick, we could be a short distance from the river and not be able to see it."

"We should be able to smell it."

She remembered the unique scent of the muddy water. "You've got a point. Okay, fearless and respected leader, what next?"

"We'll give the beacon another ten minutes. If it hasn't led us to anything familiar by then, we'll backtrack."

"Is that why you took a whack out of a tree with your knife every couple of meters? So we'd have a trail to follow back to the circle?"

He lifted one shoulder negligently. "You can't be too careful on Renaissance."

"So I've noticed. How are you feeling?"

"Fine. The shoulder's stiff, but it's not getting in my way."

"Want me to wear the utility loop for a while? I imagine it gets a little heavy. You've got so many interesting things packed inside." She stepped close, reaching for the closure of the rantgan leather loop. "I was going to ask you a couple of questions about what you carry around with you, Severance." As she moved, the edge of her skirt brushed against Severance's arm.

"Forget the loop. I said I'm fine. I'll feel naked without it." He was staring at the directional device as she stepped back. "Do that again, Cidra."

"Do what?"

"Come close."

She saw the direction of his attention. "Something wrong?"

"Just brush up against my arm again."

Uneasily she did as she was told. When she started to move back, Severance caught her wrist and held her close. "What is it?" she asked.

"Look at the signal," he muttered. "It's going crazy."

"You mean, I'm causing it to go crazy?" Cidra's mouth felt very dry.

"Or something you've got on you. I don't understand. These things are virtually fail-proof."

"Desma says mechanical stuff is always breaking down on Renaissance."

"Empty your pockets. Hurry!"

She reached inside her shirt, and the first thing her hand touched was the stone shard. Slowly, with a feeling of doom, she brought it out and held it toward the directional device.

"Sweet reeting hell." Severance jerked the shard from her hand and waved it back and forth across the surface of the device.

"I'm sorry, Severance." Cidra stood in dismay, bearing the full weight of a heavy guilt. "I didn't realize it would cause trouble."

He tossed the shard as far as he could into the undergrowth. "Neither did I, although I suppose we should have made an educated guess on the subject. I wonder what it was about that slice of eggshell that could screw up the signal on this thing."

"How does it read now?"

"It says the skimmer is west of us and not very close. We've got a long walk ahead." He looked up and started to say something else.

Cidra held up her palm. "Don't say it. I'll say it. Let's get going."

A reluctant smile edged Severance's mouth. "You're learning." He started forward with Cidra close behind.

They hadn't gone more than a few paces when Cidra saw the

glint of black stone. "Severance, there's the shard. But I thought you threw it much farther."

He turned to glance back. "I did. And I threw it in a different direction. That's not the shard." Cautiously he used the knife to push aside the heavy mass of creeping vines. A black, curving surface glinted in the dappled light.

"Sweet Harmony in hell. It looks like a giant version of one of the stones."

"Severance, we've got to get out of here!" Cidra tugged at him frantically, but he shook off her hands. "If it's another egg, it's a huge one. Anything that hatches from that thing isn't going to be stopped very easily. You saw how much of the pulser charge it took to destroy the little eggs."

"If it's an egg, it's already cracked."

"What?" She peered around his shoulder to see what he was looking at. The huge sphere was crumpled and jagged on one side, revealing a gaping hole. Inside there was only darkness. Cidra edged back, trying to pull Severance with her. Everything within her that had felt wrong about the eggs was reacting violently to this discovery.

"It's not made of the same material as the egg, although it's the same color." Severance touched the black surface. "It's a metal of some kind. Like nothing I've ever seen." He dug out the quartzflash and shined it into the dark hole. He sucked in his breath. "It's a ship, Cidra. Some kind of vehicle. It's got to be!"

She stared at the array of mechanisms revealed in the light of the flash. The shapes were oddly distorted to her eyes, unfamiliar and strange. "Not a human ship."

"You can say that again." Severance stepped closer, clearly fascinated. "Not a Ghost ship, either. At least nothing in here appears designed to fit one of the creatures we saw in that history lesson we got in the safehold. Their hands were similar to ours, and anything mechanical they built would have had similar gripping surfaces. The height of everything is wrong too. Some of it's too high and some of it's too low. Everything's made out of this same black metal."

"Severance, it looks too much like one of those eggs. The same color, the same shape, and it was that shard in my pocket that drew us here. I told you those blue things were alien to this planet. Let's get out of here."

But he was already moving closer to the gaping black hole. It occurred to Cidra that any man with Severance's natural aptitude for keeping machines in working order was probably going to be overcome with a fascination for this alien gadget.

"Whatever was once in this thing is long gone, Cidra. If it survived the crash, it probably stepped outside and became a meal for one of the natives."

"No," she said with quiet certainty. "First it carried its eggs into the safehold. Maybe it was following the same mind call we followed. Maybe the call draws anything above a certain level of intelligence to it. Perhaps that's how it screens out the rest of the jungle life. It was meant as a record for another intelligent species to find. Whatever was in this ship must have found it. The safehold probably looked like a good place to leave the eggs."

"You're assuming that the ship and whatever was inside was alien to Stanza Nine."

"I know it was," Cidra said stubbornly. "There's something wrong about it, I keep telling you."

"It will take a full-scale scientific investigation to find out the truth. Perhaps another intelligent species developed on this planet."

"No."

He waved the quartzflash around inside the ship. "You can't be sure of that, Cidra."

"Severance, please come away from there. After what I saw of those eggs, we've got to assume that the ship is dangerous. Maybe it's protected the way the eggs were."

"Just a minute. I want to get a closer look at this stuff. Doesn't look like this metal has had the corrosion damage most metal gets on Renaissance." He whistled soundlessly between his teeth, his eyes gleaming with barely suppressed excitement. "We've got to be able to find this ship again." Severance punched a code into the directional indicator. "Between this thing and the safehold, I'm going to make enough credit to launch Severance Pay, Ltd. in a big way."

"Is that all you can think about? Selling this information? You've got a one-track mind, Teague Severance! This is the find of the century, ultimately maybe far more significant than the safehold. And all you can talk about is how much you'll get when you sell the location."

"Yeah, well, a man has to keep his eye on the main chance." He edged closer, shining the flash around the edge of the jagged metal. Suddenly they heard a sharp hiss, and something with a long tail and four short legs leapt from the darkness. Severance ducked, and the disturbed inhabitant of the ship disappeared into the trees.

"What was that?" Cidra took a deep breath.

"A roacher. They like caves. That one must have thought he'd found a really nifty home when he came across this thing." He wrinkled his nose as he leaned forward again. "What a stench. The roacher's been living here awhile."

Cidra stepped closer, caught a whiff of the rancid odor, and nearly choked. "Are you going inside that ship?"

"I just want to take a quick look around."

"I don't think that's a good idea, Severance."

"I'll be just a minute." He stepped over the jagged edge. "Stay here in the opening where I can keep an eye on you."

Reluctantly she moved closer, aware of a deep curiosity that was at war with her instinct to put as much distance as possible between herself and the ship. The ramifications of the discovery were endless. She could certainly understand Severance's fascination with it. But Cidra didn't like the feel of the whole thing any more than she had liked the feel she'd gotten from the eggs.

The quartzflash moved around inside the ship, falling on banks of alien machinery that stood silent and blank. There was a lounge that might have been a seat or a bed for a body the size of a man, but it was shaped oddly. Cidra had a passing mental image of one of the blue monsters, grown to the size of a man, lying on that lounge, and she shuddered. The creatures from the eggs were bad enough when they were hatchlings; she didn't want to imagine what the adult version looked like.

"Look at this, Cidra." Severance shone the light along the surface of a long, sealed case. It was made of the same black metal as the hull of the ship, but the top was fashioned of a clear material, perhaps a hard plastic. There were scratch marks on the clear portion, as if something hungry had tried to get inside. Whatever it was had not succeeded in prying open the case.

"What do you think it is?" Cidra asked.

"Some kind of storage facility probably. I can't see what's inside. The cover looks clear, but it's not when I shine the light down through it. Too much dirt and grit caked on it. Maybe I can get it open."

"Don't, Severance. It looks too much like a coffin. Let's leave it for an exploration company that's got equipment and time. We don't have either right now."

He paused as if a part of him realized the truth of what she was saying, but Cidra saw his eyes drift back to the long case. She realized that getting him out of the ship wasn't going to be easy. She remembered all too clearly how stubbornly he had insisted on fetching the egg from the safehold. Cidra decided to try a drastic approach to breaking the spell the ship seemed to have on him.

"I'll just be another minute or so, Cidra." He ran his hand along the line on the metal case where the clear section joined the black portion.

"Fine." She swung around determinedly. "I'm leaving."

"Cidra! Don't be a fool. You can't leave without me."

"Want to bet?" She was sure of herself, absolutely convinced that she had to get him out of the ship. The same sense of wrongness was permeating her senses as she had experienced when she had kicked the blue reptilian carcass out of the protected circle.

"Damn it, Cidra, come back here. That's a direct order."

"No. You'll have to come with me if you don't want me to leave alone." She paused, about to shoulder her way through a wall of vines, and glanced back. "Severance, I mean this. I'm leaving and I—*Severance!*"

His name was a scream on her lips as she looked back and saw him silhouetted in the doorway. Behind him a deathly black light flashed inside the ship. But light couldn't be black, Cidra thought in horror. For a timeless instant everything seemed frozen. Energy crackled from the depths of the round ship, flickering around Severance's body as he stood poised with the pulser in his hand. For a few seconds he stood staring out at her, his face a mask of agony, and then he collapsed backward, out of sight. The black glare flashed again and then died out.

Cidra caught her breath in fear and raced forward, slamming to a halt at the opening in the ship. "Severance, where are you?" She could see nothing. The quartzflash no longer shone in the darkness. He was dead, Cidra thought in a flash of hysteria. No, it wasn't possible. She refused to believe it. Frantically she started to scramble over the torn hull. She had one leg swung over the edge when she heard the heavy scrape of claws on metal.

Cidra froze. She knew with sure instinct that the long coffin-like case had opened. The shock of that knowledge was enough to make her feel dizzy. Clutching at every ounce of willpower she possessed, she started to edge back out of the ship. Slowly, her eyes never leaving the jagged opening, she backed away from the horror that lurked within. But her body seemed to be moving in slow motion. It was like a dream in which she was trapped, knowing that she should flee but finding herself unable to make her body respond.

The blue, leathery body appeared in the opening of the ship. Cidra was mesmerized by the shock of its size. As tall as a man but far heavier. Standing erect, its pale, iridescent blue belly looked obscenely shiny. The head was massive, built to hold the teeth of a predator. Red eyes gleamed with the flat, lethal, un-emotional expression of a true reptile. The little appendages she had seen on the hatchling were indeed sickeningly handlike. One of them held Severance's pulser.

The jungle was safer than what waited in the alien ship. Cidra whirled to run.

"Racer!"

Stunned to hear Severance's voice, Cidra glanced over her shoulder. There was no sign of him. The alien lifted one massive clawed foot over the edge of the jagged metal. It was coming after her. Frantically Cidra tried to peer around it.

"Severance, where are you?"

"Damn you to hell, Racer. You're dead. This time you'll stay dead." The blue reptile raised the pulser it was holding, aiming it at Cidra.

The voice was coming from the mouth of the alien. Disoriented, Cidra reached out to grab a tree limb to steady herself. The creature moved closer. "Severance, if you have any control over that thing, make it stop. Don't let it come any closer."

"Stop talking with Cidra's voice, damn you. Where is she? What have you done with her? You're already dead meat, Racer. Tell me what you've done with her or I'll make it slow this time."

"No!" With a staggering sense of disorientation Cidra began to realize what must be happening. "Severance, listen to me. Can you hear me?"

"Cidra, where are you?" The six-foot reptile swung its scaled neck, searching the vegetation. The pulser didn't wave.

"Severance, is that you holding the pulser?" She was trembling with the force of will it took to stay where she was, instead of fleeing into the jungle.

"Of course it's me. Where are you?" The huge mouth moved as if having trouble shaping the words, but the voice was definitely Severance's. "Come out, Cidra. It's all right."

"I'm standing right in front of you, Severance, it's another illusion trap. I must look like Racer to you, and you look like a monster to me. Please put down the pulser." She took another step backward and found herself with her back to a thick tree.

"An illusion? It can't be. It's too damn real."

But he was staring at her, the hideously unemotional gaze full of a deep, savage hunger. In spite of her analysis of the situation,

Cidra was terrified. Even if she was right and the creature facing her was Severance, she might not be able to convince him of who she was before he pulled the trigger of the pulser. "It's me, Severance. Please believe me. It's only another illusion. Saints know we've seen enough of them lately."

The creature took another ponderous step closer. "An illusion? Prove it. Take my hand, Cidra." One of the clawed palms was extended toward her. The pulser was still aimed at her breast.

"Don't touch me!" She was certain that what she was seeing was only a bad dream, but her instinct for self-preservation was stronger than her logic. She pressed herself tightly against the tree.

The creature that claimed to be Severance took another step forward, holding out the handlike appendage that wasn't gripping the pulser. "Cidra, if it's really you, prove it. Take my hand. Don't look at me like that."

"Stay away from me until I figure out what's going on. We've got to break the illusion."

"I'll know it's you if I touch you. Nothing on this planet could feel quite like you feel."

"Please stay away from me." She was trapped against the tree, and the creature took another pace closer. The eyes raked her. If she was wrong, she was already dead.

The reptile halted. The hand holding the pulser came up with a swift, sure movement, aiming at her head. Cidra closed her eyes. There was no time to run. It would be better to go like this than to have her head snapped off between those fierce jaws. "Severance," she whispered.

The creature triggered the pulser. Cidra waited for the withering shock, wondering what it would feel like, hoping it would be quick. There was a sharp movement in the tree beside her. She opened her eyes to see a mouthful of fangs fall past her head and land at her feet. The fangs were connected to a sinuous, mud-colored body. She stared at it in dazed astonishment. Whatever it was, it was dead. Hesitantly, she raised her eyes. The blue reptile still held the pulser, but it was no longer aimed at her.

"Come away from the tree, Cidra. You never know what's hiding behind trees around here." Once more a blue, handlike appendage was held out to her.

Slowly Cidra moved away from the tree, her eyes never leaving the awful mouth that spoke with Severance's voice. "Are you sure it's you, Severance?"

"From the way you look at me I admit that I've got my doubts. But I know Racer is dead. He has to be dead. A little trust is all we've got to work with, so we'll take it from here." He continued to hold out the appendage.

He was right. A little trust and some common sense was all they had to work with at the moment. Uneasily Cidra touched the leathered palm. The inhuman fingers closed around hers. She closed her eyes, waiting for disaster. Then, slowly, the universe seemed to right itself. The hand holding hers felt warm and familiar. She relaxed slightly.

"You're right," Severance said, sounding wearily relieved. "Whatever it is, it's just an illusion."

"Yes," she agreed shakily. "But it's so real. I'm afraid to open my eyes."

"Try it. As long as you're holding my hand, you can keep telling yourself who I am. Believe me, you don't look like Racer any longer."

Slowly she risked a glance through slitted lashes. When she saw Severance's familiar face watching her with narrow-eyed concern, she breathed a sigh of relief. "You're back to normal," she told him.

"Says who?" But he grinned briefly.

"What happened to you in there? I saw a strange flash behind you, and you fell backward. When I got close to see what had happened, you came toward me looking very blue and very hungry."

"I don't know. I felt a sort of shock that knocked me down. I lost the quartzflash. When I got up again, you were screaming but you looked like Cord Racer. I feel all right. Do I still look okay to you?"

She nodded, afraid to let go of his hand for fear that he would turn back into a monster. "I've about had it with things messing around with my head."

"I thought you were the one who was so convinced that mind link was the ultimate form of orgasm."

She was outraged. "I never said any such thing!"

"I beg your pardon. My misunderstanding."

"Harmonic mind link is a beautiful, creative, sensitive experience. It is not an . . . an orgasm, and it is not made up of horrible illusions."

"How do you know? You've never experienced it, remember?"

"One doesn't have to have experienced something to have an understanding of it."

"I keep forgetting about your educational accomplishments." Severance headed back to the gaping hole in the ship. "Yell if I start turning into a blue monster again."

"I'm going to start yelling right now. Severance, I think we ought to get out of here."

"I agree. I just want to see if I can find the quartzflash first, though." He used the flame for illumination as he leaned back inside the ship and scanned the interior. "There it is. We'll need it tonight. Stay here while I get it."

"The last time you went inside, you came out wearing an ugly blue suit. I'm not sure I could stand it a second time around."

He was already inside, scooping up the flash. He flicked it on one last time. "Look, Cidra. If I hold the light just right, I think I can see into that case." He used his fist to scrub off some of the dirt. "Sweet Harmony, I think it's a skeleton."

Leaning through the opening of the ship, Cidra caught a glimpse of a huge skeleton mouth through the murky case cover. She shuddered. "Look at those teeth."

Severance grinned briefly. "Definitely a carnivore."

Cidra glanced at his own rather feral smile. "His teeth remind me of yours. Damn it, Severance, if you don't come out of there, so help me, I'll—" A flash of black light at the end of the case interrupted her words. Once more energy sizzled, although it seemed weaker this time. "The light! Severance, that's what happened before!"

Severance felt the same tingling shock he had experienced earlier. Energy clawed him, not as strong this time, but enough to force him to his knees. With both hands he gripped the pulser and aimed for the source of the eerie light. He squeezed off one shot and then another before a small explosion rocked the shattered ship. He heard Cidra call his name, and then everything went still.

Slowly he got back to his feet, watching as the light flickered and died at the end of the long case. "Cidra?"

"I'm all right, Severance. So are you. What happened?"

He examined the charred metal fixture that had produced the crackling energy and the light. "Whatever it is, it's useless now. Tough to keep machinery working on Renaissance."

SEVENTEEN

The hike through the jungle to the river's edge was without further incident. Cidra was exceedingly grateful. When the campsite came into view, looking very much as it had when they left, she smiled with relief and headed for the tent.

"I can't wait to change these clothes. This habit Wolves have of wearing one set of clothes all day long is bad enough, but to be stuck in the same set for three days is very annoying." She plucked at the fastening of the oversize shirt as she walked through the silent deflector screens.

"Wait a minute, Cidra. Let me make sure nothing has decided to take up residence in the tent. The deflectors have been off for at least a full day." Severance caught her arm.

She stopped short. "Yes, of course. Details."

"Paying attention to details is supposed to be one way of staying alive on this planet." He stepped around her and cautiously opened the tent, pulser in hand.

"If you ask me, sheer luck has a fair amount to do with staying alive around here."

Satisfied with the tent search, Severance turned to give Cidra a laconic glance. "I didn't know you believed in luck."

"I've learned a lot lately." She sauntered past him as he waved her into the tent. "What I'd really like is another bath."

"I don't know how you survived without your usual two hours a day in a lav."

"'A clean body aids in the development of a harmoniously tuned mind,'" she quoted from inside the tent.

"One of your Kinian Laws?"

"A minor but important one." She stuck her head outside the tent and smiled winningly. "Feel like fetching some water for me?"

His mouth kicked up at the corner as he took in the blatantly coaxing expression. "You're not the only one who could use a bath. I smell like the inside of that egg-laying spaceship. I'll rig up something."

"You always manage to rig up something." She ducked back inside the tent.

There were more important things to worry about first, however. Severance stepped into the skimmer and critically scanned the instruments and the innards of the powerhouse. There was still sufficient power to recharge the deflectors. He snapped the power pack out of the pulser, replaced it, and then got the deflectors operating at full strength. When he was satisfied with the security of the campsite, he put in the call to Port Try Again. The comm set worked after a bit of relatively minor tinkering.

"Where in a renegade's hell have you been, Severance? I've had ExcellEx reps yelling at me for two days. Seems they're expecting some sensors. Where's Overcash?" The security official sounded short-tempered and inclined to be abusive.

"Overcash became a meal. So did Racer."

"Racer? He was on a run upriver to the Masterson field camp. How did you connect with him?"

"It's a long story. I'm requesting a skimmer and pilot to pick us up."

"Who's us? Oh, you've still got the little Harmonic with you?

If Overcash and Racer wound up feeding the local wildlife, how did she make it?"

"She's tougher than she looks. How about the skimmer?"

"Give me your coordinates. I'll get someone out to you as soon as possible. Can you make it through another night?"

"Yeah, the deflectors are working, and we've got a pulser."

"I'll have a skimmer out to you by midday tomorrow."

"Thanks," Severance said, and waited for the inevitable final question. Nothing came for free on Renaissance. Or anywhere else in the Stanza Nine system for that matter.

"Who's picking up the tab for the rescue run? ExcellEx?"

"No. Charge it to my account," Severance said.

There was a short wait while his account was pulled up from the computer. "Good enough," the security officer said. "Your credit is still first-class. Looks like you always pay your bills."

"Always," Severance murmured, and switched off the comm set. He sat for a moment in the gently rocking skimmer and idly watched a pair of dracon eyes that were watching him.

Nothing came for free. There was a price on everything. How much of a price had he forced Cidra to pay in order to survive? He'd had no right to subject her to the events of the past few days. He should have taken better care of her. His job was to protect her.

Instead she had taken care of him. He remembered the comfort she had given him when he had been swimming in and out of his fever. In addition to the hazy nightmares he saw fleeting images of her gentle touch, the cooling baths, and the soft warmth of her lap as she cradled his head. She had come aboard *Severance Pay* as a delicate, cultivated creature accustomed to the finest manners and the most elevated of lifestyles. This morning he had awakened to find a young huntress rising from the edge of a stream to bring in the day's meat. Because of him she had been forced to become a carnivore. That seemed unpleasantly symbolic to Severance.

She had learned other things from him too. He'd had no right to teach her about passion. But even as he berated himself, Severance knew deep in his gut that, given the chance, he would have repeated the lesson. The woman pulled too strongly at his senses and his mind. The two weeks on board *Severance Pay* alone with her had been sweet hell at times. He had known then that if she stayed with him on the run to QED, she would end up in his bunk. As long as he was anywhere near her, he would have no peace unless he knew he could possess her. He could not allow her a choice. She affected him too fiercely, made him ache with need, filled him with the desire to put a claim on her. At the same time he was aware of a violent desire to protect her. The possessiveness and the protectiveness went hand in hand, seeming natural and inevitable until the twin goals foundered on the ultimate dilemma. How could he protect her from himself?

Everything he did for her and to her took Cidra farther and farther from the one thing she wanted most in life. Because of him her goal of becoming a true Harmonic was more distant than it had ever been. He had forced the Wolf in her to the surface after she had spent years struggling to suppress that part of her nature.

As he watched, the dracon eyes disappeared under the water. Severance continued staring unseeingly at the point where the creature had vanished. It seemed to him that Cidra had given him more than he'd had any right to take. She had welcomed him in her arms, drawn him into her with an honest, sweet passion that had taken away his breath. She had given him an intense loyalty, the kind he had learned not to expect from anyone since Jeude had been killed. Severance could not imagine any female of his acquaintance who would have thrown herself into a river full of dracons rather than have allowed herself to be carried off and used against him. But Cidra offered more than loyalty and passion. She radiated a sense of rightness, a quiet certainty that he didn't fully understand.

"Severance? Where's the water?"

He shook off the bittersweet mood and got to his feet. She was standing on the bank, gazing curiously into the shattered wall of the skimmer's cabin. He grinned. "I'll have something ready in a few minutes." He opened the skimmer's cargo hold. As she had said, he was good at rigging things. Fixing a bathing apparatus for a fastidious lady from Clementia shouldn't be an impossible assignment.

In reality the job wasn't difficult, given the contents of the skimmer's cargo hold. He was cutting a length of plastic tubing when he noticed the carton of sensors. The bright red COD seal was still in place. Mail still waiting to be delivered. He looked at it for a long moment and then went back to work on the bathing arrangements.

When he was finished, he handed the bucketful of water and the plastic tubing to Cidra. "Try this. When you're done, I'll use it."

She eyed him critically. "Do you have any depilatory cream left in your travel pack?"

"Don't worry, Cidra. You'll look just as cute with hairy legs."

"My legs are fine," she informed him. "The cream I use lasts for a month. It's your beard that needs work."

Severance touched the side of his face, felt the stubble, and grimaced. "Oh." For some reason he was oddly embarrassed. The knowledge annoyed him, and he frowned. "There'll be a skimmer out from Try Again at about midday tomorrow."

She nodded, seemingly content as she examined the bucket and hose she was holding. "What about your ExcellEx delivery?"

"Funny you should mention it. I was just thinking about that myself. As late as it is, I'll be lucky to collect for it."

She looked up, alarmed. "If ExcellEx doesn't pay for it, don't give it to them."

"It's better for Severance Pay, Ltd.'s reputation if I deliver late rather than not at all. Besides, I'm getting tired of people trying to steal those reeting sensors. Let ExcellEx worry about them."

"Severance," she said sternly, "you are not going to simply hand them over without getting paid for them. Not after all we've been through to protect them."

His gaze narrowed in faint amusement. "You're beginning to sound like a real member of a mail ship crew."

Her chin lifted proudly. "I *am* a real member of the crew. I don't know why you insist on forgetting that fact when it suits you. You certainly had no trouble remembering it the night you came into the Bloodsucker and announced that we were leaving on this little joy run up the river."

She was right. "I should have left you behind after all."

"Nonsense. Racer would have gotten hold of me one way or another and used me as a hostage or something. He was a very determined man, wasn't he?"

"Yes," Severance said, thinking about it. "He was."

"As long as you were alive, you were a constant reminder to him. He couldn't forget his actions that day in the sink-swamp, and he never knew when you might tell someone else about them. On top of that he was the one who got your brother killed. He must have known that if you ever figured it out, you wouldn't rest until you'd settled the score. It must have eaten at him for ages before he finally decided to take care of the problem permanently."

"You're a very perceptive woman at times, Cidra Rainforest."

She smiled. "I've been trained to be perceptive. Now turn around, Severance. I want to take my bath."

He hesitated, wanting to ask her how she really felt deep inside about the fact that he had killed a man. Then, deciding it might be better not to know the answer, he turned his back and went to work foraging in the skimmer's cargo hold for other useful items.

"I've been thinking about that skeleton back in the alien ship," Cidra said later as she finished eating her vegetables. She had been tremendously relieved to find a prespac that contained something besides meat. She didn't think she would ever grow to actually enjoy the taste of meat. Severance had no such qualms, naturally. He was into his second full prespac meal. Wolfing it down, as it were.

"Don't think about it. It'll give you nightmares," he advised.

"I wonder if that creature was the pilot of the ship," she persisted, ignoring his advice.

"That sphere didn't look big enough to house two monsters that size. Whatever it was must have been traveling alone."

"Except for the eggs."

Severance paused, chewing thoughtfully. "Yes, the eggs. That's going to give several biologists a lot to think about. I wonder if the ship was a small colony vessel."

"Maybe we humans aren't the only ones who have started settling other worlds." Cidra had a sudden thought. "What if that ship was just one of many, Severance?"

"If there were others, we have to assume that they didn't fare much better than that one did. No one has recorded a sighting of anything like that blue monster. At least, I'm not aware of any such sightings."

"It's a big planet."

"True. But an aggressive, intelligent species would have probably made its presence known by now. We've been here for several decades."

"They did appear aggressive, all right." Cidra shuddered. "Didn't do them much good, though. They didn't survive."

"Thanks to you."

Cidra allowed herself to absorb the shock of his simple observation. All by herself she had destroyed the only known members of an intelligent, space-faring race. She was unnerved by the thought.

Severance saw the look on her face and hastily changed the subject. "I wonder how old those eggs were. The skeleton in the case wasn't exactly fresh. It could have been lying in the ship for hundreds of years. But the eggs were ready to hatch."

"They might have been capable of staying viable for years in the shell until the right conditions occurred for them to hatch," Cidra pointed out. "Perhaps the pilot of the ship was wounded in the crash. He followed the mind call and left the eggs in what appeared to be a safe location. Apparently that telepathic call works on any sort of intelligent mind. He set up his own protective device to insure that eventually something would wander into the safehold and become food for the eggs. Then he went back to die in the ship. The case in which we found the skeleton might have been some sort of medical facility."

"Which failed."

"As people keep observing, it's hard to keep machinery working on Renaissance." She smiled. "You seem to do a fairly good job of it, though."

He shrugged. "I told you, I've always been good with my hands."

"We make a good team, don't we? My brains and your brawn."

He gave her a sardonic glance. "I may not be a near genius like your friend Mercer, but once in a while I manage to think my way through things. I can still take every piece of sardite you have in a game of Free Market."

At the mention of Mercer, Cidra flinched. She hadn't thought about him or about Clementia for quite a while. The humor faded from her eyes as she grew pensive. "Yes, you're still better at Free Market than I am."

Severance swore somewhat viciously and asked himself what in a renegade's hell had made him mention her idol, Mercer. Cidra was right. He might be good with his hands, but he wasn't always the fastest thinker in the universe. Severance slowly finished the last of his prespac, aware that Cidra had slipped off into her own thoughts.

She was thinking of Clementia. He knew it, and the realization hit him in the gut: Clementia and a lofty relationship unsoiled by a Wolf's passion and need. Severance asked himself bluntly what he had to offer compared to the wise and distant Mercer. The cabin of *Severance Pay* was a far cry from the formal gardens and glowing fountains of Clementia. Hardly the sort of place in which a gently bred woman would want to set up housekeeping with a man who occasionally drank too much ale and who would frequently reach for her with a hunger he couldn't disguise as platonic love.

"Are you going to give up your search, Cidra?"

She blinked herself back to an awareness of him and smiled wanly. "I think I've had enough of alien mind-tapping. Perhaps one has to be born a Harmonic to feel comfortable with the idea of someone or something else inside one's head."

"It doesn't seem right somehow," he agreed. "I didn't like being manipulated by either the good guys or the bad guys during the past couple of days."

"We learned to control the manipulation to a certain extent," she reminded him.

"I still don't feel comfortable with the whole idea of mind communication." Severance set down the prespac and leaned back on his elbow, gazing into the flamer. "I never will."

She followed his gaze. "As I said, perhaps one has to be born a Harmonic to have mind-touch feel natural and right. I wasn't born a true Harmonic."

"But you were raised as one."

"Yes."

"Cidra," he began with a rough edge in his voice that he couldn't control, "you can go back to Clementia, can't you?"

She raised her eyebrows in surprise. "Of course. No one kicked me out. I left of my own accord. It's my home. I can go back whenever I wish."

"And work in the Archives?"

"I'm a good archivist, even if I'm not a Harmonic," she said firmly. "Besides, I'm the only archivist they've got who's bothered to make a speciality out of First Family tales. I have virtually a whole field to myself."

"What would they do without you?" He tried to make it a joke but didn't think he pulled it off. She took the question seriously.

"They'd relegate First Family tales to the bottom of the pile of acceptable literature. No big deal. It's already on the bottom of the pile. I did get Mercer to admit once that the sociological implications of some of the first traditions were interesting, but that was about all."

Severance stared at her grimly. She could and would go back. He had nothing to offer her to induce her to stay. Nothing to put up against all that Clementia could offer. She would go home and take with her all the tenderness, companionship, loyalty, and passion she had brought into his life. Severance's hand tightened into a frustrated knot on his thigh. Coolly he forced himself to relax. He would take her back to Port Try Again, put her on a freighter, and never see her again. Something knotted up again, this time inside. *Never see her again.* The years stretched out ahead of him, as empty as the farthest reaches of the galaxy.

"We'd better go to bed. We've had a long day." He got to his feet and began the small ritual of checking the deflectors. Out of the corner of his eye he saw Cidra obediently pick up the remains of dinner and dispose of them. A few minutes later she disappeared into the tent. He kept himself busy for as long as possible, thinking of her crawling into her own sleeper and fastening the closure. When he could delay things no longer, he went into the tent.

She had blanked the light, and it took a while for his eyes to adjust. Severance peeled off his shirt and yanked off the boots. Unconsciously he put the pulser and utility loop within easy reach and fumbled for the opening of his own sleeper. Deliberately he kept his eyes off the other portable bunk. If he allowed himself to look at Cidra in bed, he knew he would crawl in with her, regardless of whether or not she invited him. He was selfish enough to take what memories he could. Hell, he was *Wolf* enough to take what he could.

He took a deep breath and a savage grip on himself and turned to slide into his sleeper. His hand touched a bare female shoulder before he realized that the bed was already occupied.

"Cidra! What are you doing in here?"

She smiled up at him in the shadows. "Waiting for you. What took you so long?"

"You shouldn't be here."

"Going to throw me out?"

"Sweet Harmony, I haven't got the strength." He unfastened his trousers and stepped out of them, leaving them lying on the floor of the tent. With a heavy groan he crawled into the sleeper and found Cidra naked and waiting. He buried his face against her breasts, aware that his body was hardening already with a fierce desire. "I doubt that I'd ever have the strength to throw you out of my bed."

"I'm glad." Her fingers laced through his hair as her body stirred against his.

He felt her soft leg moving along his thigh, and the tight ache in his loins became a fire almost instantly. She had such a powerful effect on him that he would have been alarmed if he hadn't been so excited. Severance stroked her, savoring the curve of her hip and the smoothness of her belly. At this moment he easily convinced himself he had a right to this night. She would be gone all too soon from his life.

Hungrily he sought and found her lips, drinking the taste of her into his veins. He would never forget the sensation of probing the sweet warmth of her mouth. Her small tongue darted around his a little anxiously at first and then with greater boldness. Her body arched, opening to his touch. When he drew a palm across one breast, he could feel the nipple tighten. The response sent a wave of excitement through him.

She was his. The need and the longing roared through him swamping the knowledge that soon he would have to send Cidra back to Clementia. The primitive certainty that she belonged to him and no one or no place else was too strong in that moment. Severance forgot about the morning and what it must bring in the way of reality. Tonight was his, and he was going to take all he could get.

"Cidra, you feel so good. Do you know what you're doing to me?"

"I'm learning."

He moved one hand lower, threading his fingers through the wonderfully soft tangle of hair below her stomach, and then he could feel the gathering moistness between her legs. The sensual dampness dazed him, almost overwhelming him with a sense of anticipation. He probed gently, and when she gasped, he probed again. He could never get enough of her soft cries of excitement. "Touch me, Cidra. I want to feel your hands on me."

He caught her hand and guided it down to his throbbing manhood. When her fingers closed tenderly around him, he shut his eyes and forced himself to take a calming breath.

"What's wrong?" She sounded anxious.

"Nothing," he told her, his voice tight. "You have the damnedest effect on me, little Saint. Touch me again. I'm a glutton for punishment."

"Like this?"

He nipped her shoulder as she obeyed. "Yes," he muttered as she gently used her nails on him. "Yes, sweetheart. That's exactly right."

He gloried in the feel of her, moving his hand beneath her lushly rounded buttocks and finding the dark cleft between them. She flinched in the unfamiliar caress, and he held her more tightly until she relaxed again and let herself respond. When he had her straining urgently beneath him, he let his hand rove elsewhere. He teased the parting folds of flesh that guarded the entrance to her warm, fragrant core. She moved pleadingly under the touch, closing her thighs around his hand as if she would draw him further into her.

"Do you want me?" he asked, his voice harsh with his own need.

"I want you. I want you, Severance."

"Not half as much as I want you." He lifted himself, sliding her into position under his heaviness, and then lowered himself along the length of her. "Wrap your legs around me, love."

She did. He had been poised on the threshold, and when she lifted her legs to clasp his thighs, the movement forced him into her. He heard his name on her lips and felt her shiver as he thrust forward, taking her completely.

Then she was clinging to him, her breasts soft beneath his chest, her body strong and supple as she held on to him with all her might. He would never be able to get enough of her, Severance thought fleetingly. Not even if he had her all to himself for the rest of his life.

She accepted the rhythm he established, augmenting it with her own inner muscles. The resulting harmony sent both of them

spiraling upward to an inevitable conclusion. Severance lifted his
head to watch her face as he felt the beginning of her joyous release. He wanted to watch her expression forever, but already the
sight and feel of her satisfaction were driving him over the edge of
his own. He sucked in his breath and surged forward one last time,
sinking himself into her until all sense of separateness was gone.
The two of them felt like a single entity. And then he just held on,
clutching her more tightly than he would hold on to a pulser in the
middle of the jungle.

"*Cidra.*"

It was a long time before either of them surfaced in the darkness of the tent. In mutual silence they lay listening to each other's
breathing and to the sounds of the night beyond the deflectors. At
long last Cidra stirred, stretching luxuriously in a movement that
brushed her breast along Severance's rib cage.

"Good night, Severance." Her voice was soft and sleepy as she
curled into him.

"Good night, Cidra." He felt her drift off to sleep, a bundle of
feminine contentment in his arms. Then he lay awake for a long
time and thought about the future.

Cidra awoke the next morning feeling decidedly stiff. The
sleeper could accommodate two people in a pinch, but it wasn't really designed for the extra crowd. Tentatively she moved her leg
and felt Severance turn in response. His arm, which was lying
across her breasts, tightened. He yawned in her ear.

"Do you think your bunk on the ship is going to be big enough
for both of us, or will you rig up something to connect the upper
and lower berths?" she asked drowsily.

"My bunk? Do you mean on the ship?"

"Uh-huh."

"I hadn't thought about it."

"Well," she announced grandly, "you'd better, hadn't you?
You're the one who's always worrying about little details."

He stilled for a moment and then slowly levered himself up on one elbow to gaze down at her searchingly. She smiled smugly, wondering why he was looking so serious.

"You're talking about staying on *Severance Pay* with me?"

"I'm a full-fledged member of the crew, remember?" She reached up and toyed with his tousled hair. He ignored her.

"You're going back to Clementia."

"Nope. I'm going to QED to help deliver the mail." She tugged at a lock experimentally. He didn't seem to notice. The first faint trickle of alarm passed through her. "Severance?"

"You have to go back to Clementia, Cidra." His voice sounded raw.

"Why?"

"Because that's where you want to go."

She shook her head with grave certainty. "No. Not anymore. I want to be with you."

"But you belong in Clementia. It's your home. Your work is there. The people you care about . . ."

"I care about you now."

He drew a deep breath as if preparing himself for an unpleasant task. "You have to go back."

His dogged stubbornness began to make an impression. "Why do I have to go back? Just because you say so?"

"Yes, damn it!" He sat up abruptly, pushing aside the cover of the sleeper. In the muted morning light that passed through the tent screen, the muscles of his shoulders and back were set and rigid. "You have to go back to Clementia because you've been saying all along that you belong there. Your life's ambition is to be a Harmonic."

"I'm not a Harmonic. I never was one and I never will be one. I know that now."

He looked at her. "But you can live like one. You can change your fancy gown four times a day, practice all the rituals, study the philosophy and the laws. Part of you is Harmonic, Cidra. Hell, Harmonics aren't an alien race living among humans. Some part of every human being is Harmonic. You can indulge that part of yourself. All you'll lack is the telepathic ability. You were born into that world, and you can't possibly know for certain that you want to leave it permanently."

"I do know for certain," she said calmly. "I'm ready to leave it permanently."

"Get one thing straight, Cidra. If you do leave it to come with me, you can never go back. I wouldn't let you go back. Do you understand what I'm saying?"

"Do you want me to come with you?" she countered.

He closed his eyes for an anguished instant. When he opened them, his gaze was very hard. In that moment he was all Wolf. "Sweet Harmony, yes. Yes, damn it, I want you to come with me. But not unless you're absolutely sure it's what you want too."

"I'm sure."

"Cidra, you can't possibly know that. It's too soon."

She tilted her head as understanding dawned. "You don't trust me, do you?"

He was startled. "What do you mean, I don't trust you?"

"It's true. You don't trust me. You're afraid I don't know my own mind. Well, that's one thing about being a Wolf, Severance. You have to learn to trust the hard way. You have to take a chance."

"I'm not going to take a chance on this. It's too important. And don't give me any lectures on what it means to be a Wolf. I'm the Wolf here."

"So am I."

"Only because I made you into one!"

Cidra began to get angry. "Don't go taking all the credit for everything, Teague Severance. You're always so anxious to assume responsibility, to be the pilot in command, that you tend to forget I'm capable of free will and clear thinking too. I've got news for you, this is a decision I'm making all by myself."

"Be reasonable, Cidra. You've only been away from Clementia for about three weeks. So much has happened to you in that time that you can't possibly be thinking clearly."

"I was trained to think clearly under all circumstances!"

He eyed her. "You're starting to lose your temper."

"Astute observation. I'm getting very angry, Severance."

"Cidra, all I'm asking is that you consider this in a calm, rational manner. You've been under a great deal of strain lately."

"Strain? I've been seduced, assaulted by wild beasts, attacked by alien illusions, obliged to eat meat, and taught to gamble. Yes, I've been under a strain. But that doesn't mean I can't think straight. It's Wolves such as you who get muddle-headed in emotional circumstances. And the fact that you are presently in just such a circumstance is the only reason I'm making allowances for your behavior at the moment. I'm the best crew mate you ever had, Teague Severance. I'm loyal, trustworthy, and intelligent. If you had any sense, you'd realize just how lucky you are and get down on your knees in gratitude!"

He stared at her as she sat up in the sleeper, her long hair spilling around her shoulders and dancing across the tips of her breasts. Her eyes were full of fire and daunting determination. He felt himself wavering in the face of it. Summoning all his fortitude, he stood firm. "Cidra, I know you think you mean what you say."

"I do mean what I say!"

"But this decision is too important."

"To whom?"

"To me, you little idiot. Will you listen to me? I'm trying to do what's best for both of us."

"You're just trying to protect yourself," she retorted.

He started to argue and then halted abruptly. "Maybe I am." He looked away from her. "I couldn't bear it if I took you with me and you changed your mind a season or two from now. I couldn't bear to watch you pining for the gardens of Clementia and the love of a man who will never want to make love to you. It would destroy me, Cidra."

She heard the gritty truth in his words and knew her first sense of genuine uncertainty. She didn't doubt her own feelings for a moment, but she had to acknowledge that Severance had a right to be unsure of her. From the moment he had met her she had talked mainly of finding a way to go back to Clementia. She couldn't blame him for doubting her change of heart and mind.

"What about a compromise?" she asked softly.

He swung around to face her. "What kind of compromise? I'm not going to be a visiting lover for you. I won't agree to just drop in and sleep with you occasionally when I happen to be near Clementia."

Her head came up proudly. "I'm not interested in such a . . . a thin relationship, either. For the record I won't be a convenient resource for a little special handling when you're between mail runs."

"I know that."

"Very well, then, why don't we try a more or less platonic association for a while."

"The way we did for two weeks on the hop from Lovelady to Renaissance? You're out of your tuned mind. I'd never survive. Talk about strain!"

"Then you suggest something," she shot back.

His face hardened. "All right, I will. Go back to Clementia. . . ."

"But, Severance . . ."

"Go back to Clementia while I finish the run to QED. When I get back, I'll come to Clementia. If you're still sure you want to come away with me, I'll take you."

She drew a breath. "It's six weeks from here to QED and then eight more to get back to Lovelady. That's a long time, Severance."

"Long enough for you to be sure of what you're doing."

Cidra felt her stomach tighten as she saw the determination in him. "You really don't trust me to know what I'm doing, do you?"

"I think you need time."

"What if you don't come back for me, Severance?" she asked softly.

"You'll have to trust me to come back, just as I'll have to trust you to be waiting."

"Wolves have a very hard time with trust, don't they?" she whispered sadly.

"Yes."

EIGHTEEN

"It's amazing how sophisticated and cosmopolitan Port Try Again looks after a few days in the jungle." Cidra grinned across the table at Desma Kady, who was halfway through a meat stew. "Renaissance has a way of giving one a new perspective on things."

Desma chuckled. "I know what you mean. But cosmopolitan as we may be, you're still drawing a few stares. Most of these renegades wouldn't blink at a charging zalon, but they've blinked several times at that beautiful dress." She inclined her head to indicate the other diners in the restaurant.

Cidra glanced down at her yellow-gold early evening gown. "I didn't mean to cause a scene. It's just that it felt so good to get back into my own clothes." She added quickly, "Not that I didn't appreciate your advice on the practical clothing for the jungle. I don't know what I would have done without the trousers and shirt."

"I doubt Severance would have allowed you to go trekking off without the right gear. He's usually very conscious of details such as that. I wonder where he is."

"Attending to more details." Cidra grimaced. "He's negotiating a deal with two of the biggest scientific firms who have representatives here at Try Again. He's been at it ever since we got back last night."

"When it comes to business, that man has the tenacity of a lockmouth," Desma observed. "He deserves a break like this. He's worked hard to build Severance Pay, Ltd. into one of the most reliable of the small mail runners. The stake he gets from selling the information you two discovered will go a long way toward helping him set up a major business operation." Desma's eyes glowed. "Sweet Harmony, what a find. Absolutely fantastic. I just hope my firm makes the high bid. With any luck I'll get a piece of the project."

"I'm sure Severance will sell to your company," Cidra said politely. "He knows you'd like to be involved."

"He'll sell to the highest bidder. Period. When it comes to something this big, Severance isn't going to let sentiment interfere. How are the veggies?" Desma peered at the pile of greens and tubers on Cidra's plate.

"Wonderful. To be quite honest, I don't care if I never have occasion to eat meat again."

"Poor Cidra. This whole thing has been quite an adventure for you, hasn't it? Starting with that night in my lab when you drove off the intruder."

"I take it he hasn't turned up?"

Desma shook her head. "No, damn it. I'd give my last research report to get my hands on him. The company guards have circulated the description, but I'm afraid it wasn't very useful."

"I know." Cidra's mouth curved wryly. "The one look at his features that I got wasn't very good. He had such an expression of horror and fear on his face and the light from those bugs was so bizarre that I doubt I'd recognize him again myself."

"Well, if he knows what's good for him, he won't come near enough to you to let you have a good look. Severance would feed him to a dracon." Desma stopped short at the look on Cidra's face.

"What's the matter? Did I say something wrong? It's just an expression."

"I know," Cidra assured her hurriedly. "I'm still getting accustomed to Renaissance colloquialisms." She blanked out her mental image of the last meal Severance had fed to the dracons and grimly went back to work on her greens.

"You'd better get used to the local slang," Desma said cheerfully. "Severance spends a fair amount of time on Renaissance." Her friendly eyes narrowed. "I take it you will be traveling with him for a while?"

"I'll be traveling with him. As soon as he gets through behaving in his current stubborn, authoritarian, dictatorial manner." Cidra's smile thinned. "He's insisting that I return to Clementia until he gets back from the run to QED."

"Interesting," Desma murmured. "Is that connected to the reason why he spent last night in the ship and you're rooming with me again? Somehow, when I saw the two of you yesterday, I got the feeling that certain matters in your, uh, partnership had been resolved."

"We don't have a partnership. I'm just a member of his crew." Cidra stabbed at a golden-skinned tuber. She was getting better at using a knife on food. "What do you make of the alien ship, Desma?"

"From what you've told me it could be almost anything from a long scouting foray that went astray to a colony ship. Assuming it is an alien vessel. There's still the possibility that the point of origin is somewhere in the Stanza Nine system. We may never know."

"There were only five eggs. Hardly enough to colonize a new planet."

"Perhaps there were several small ships headed somewhere else, and this one went off course."

Cidra chewed her lower lip. "I hope this was just a lone ship. I would hate to think of facing a large number of those blue monsters."

"The hatchling's behavior when it emerged from the egg seemed entirely instinctive?"

"Oh, yes. All it wanted to do was eat. I think there was some kind of homing device built into the shell. Probably designed to lead it back to the ship eventually. Who knows what's stored in that ship? Perhaps the equivalent of an Archive. Perhaps once led back to the ship, the young would discover their heritage. I imagine Renaissance looked like paradise to whatever piloted them here."

"Well, it didn't prove to be a paradise," Desma observed coolly. "The machinery broke down and the hatchlings fell victim to the first intelligent predators who found them."

Cidra swallowed uncomfortably. "Don't remind me. Do you have any idea what it's like to know you've wiped out the five surviving members of an intelligent race?"

"Don't start feeling guilty. From what you've told me the first hatchling was going to eat Severance for lunch. Probably would have turned on you next."

Cidra nodded gloomily. "You know, it was strange, Desma. There's no sense of alienness about the Ghosts. They're different from us and we're fascinated by them, but we're more or less comfortable with the idea that they belonged in this system. It wasn't the same with the blue creatures. They felt wrong, somehow. I hated that hatchling on sight."

"Small wonder. You've still got your primitive human instincts, Cidra, even if you have been reared in Clementia. I'm sure those instincts were working at full strength when you saw the egg crack. Your primary reaction was to protect Severance."

"And a brilliant reaction it was too," declared a new voice.

Cidra glanced up in surprise as Severance grabbed a vacant chair, shoved it near hers, and sank down onto it in his usual sprawl. He looked extraordinarily pleased with himself. He signaled for a mug of Renaissance Rose ale and leaned back to smile smugly at the two women.

"I take it," Desma said, "that you have concluded a successful negotiating session?"

"Right. And you'll be happy to know that your firm coughed up the necessary credit to get first crack at the ship."

Desma's eyes gleamed. "Fantastic. Who got the safehold?"

"Viton Archaeology."

Desma nodded. "They'll do a first-class job. When do you show them their new finds?"

"We leave at dawn tomorrow. It's a big event. Four skimmers and two research crews. After I've helped them locate the safehold and the ship, I'm going to take one of the skimmers on up the river to the ExcellEx camp. I've still got those reeting sensors to deliver. You don't mind if Cidra stays with you for a few days?"

"Of course not."

"She'll be returning to Lovelady on the next commercial freighter. But it doesn't leave until the end of the week."

Cidra cut savagely into another tuber. "How much, Severance?"

He gave her a sidelong glance. "How much what?"

"Credit. How much did you get in exchange for the locations of the safehold and the ship?" She didn't look at him. Her whole attention was on her meal.

"Five hundred thousand."

Cidra nearly dropped her knife. "Five hundred thousand? Sweet Harmony, that's a fortune."

"I know." The ale arrived, and Severance took a healthy swallow. His eyes were glittering over the rim. "A very nice stake."

"Five hundred thousand." Desma's tone was awed. "Congratulations, Severance."

"I'll want a recorded contract for my share, naturally," Cidra said. "Two hundred and fifty thousand."

Severance set down his mug with great care. "I beg your pardon?"

"You heard me." She continued eating the remains of the tuber. "I'll want a contract. Properly sealed and recorded. And I'll want it before you leave tomorrow morning. We'd better find a contract office tonight."

Severance's gray eyes slitted. "Why do you want a recorded contract?"

"You know the answer to that. Remember all those games of Free Market, Severance? The one lesson you drilled into me was that you can't trust a Wolf. Always count the cubes before you start to play. In the case of a two-way split of five hundred thousand, I'll want to get it on tape and get it recorded."

The frozen silence at the table was broken only by the sound of Cidra continuing to eat the tuber. Desma stayed very still, watching the other two from under her lashes. Severance just stared at Cidra, his gaze brooding and malevolent.

"You don't need a contract and you know it," he finally said.

"How do I know it? You're taking off for QED as soon as you get back from this little jaunt up the river. After QED, who knows where you'll go and what you'll do? I may never see you again." She smiled grimly. "I have to protect my share of the profits."

Severance continued to glare at her for another moment, and then he turned to Desma. "Did you put this idea in her head?"

Hastily Desma put up a hand. "Not me. I had nothing to do with it."

"I," said Cidra calmly, "thought of it all on my own."

"This is ridiculous." Severance's voice was tight. He took another large swallow of ale.

"A woman alone can't be too careful."

"This is a form of retaliation, isn't it? You're madder than hell because I'm sending you back to Clementia."

Cidra waved her fingers in a graceful, airy gesture. "I'm merely putting into practice all the things I've been learning recently."

"Yeah?" He leaned closer. "And what else that you've learned recently are you planning to put into practice?"

Cidra smiled gamely even though she was fully aware of the newly erratic nature of her pulse. She had to struggle to control her breathing. Severance could be very intimidating when he chose. "You needn't concern yourself with anything except the details of splitting the credit."

"Why, you little . . ." He made an obvious effort at regaining control of his own temper. Then he slammed the half empty mug down on the table and got to his feet. "You want a recorded contract? All right, you'll get one. We'll take care of the details right now."

"But I haven't finished my dinner."

"We do it now or not at all." He turned to Desma. "You," he informed her, "can act as a witness."

Desma struggled to hide her amusement. "I'll be happy to do so." Quickly she paid for her meal and stood. "Ready when you are."

The deed was done in almost total silence. By the time her signature had been recorded and her voiceprint used to verify it, Cidra was almost shaking. Severance was furious. He scrawled his name beside hers, barked into the voiceprint recorder, and escorted her out of the contracts office in a chilled silence. He didn't speak until he had deposited the women at Desma's door. Severance stood in front of Cidra, feet braced slightly apart, one thumb hooked on his utility belt. He was the very picture of a man scorned.

"I'll see you when I get back." His words sounded more like a threat than a promise.

"Fine." Cidra hung on to her poise with sheer willpower, wrapping it around herself like an early evening gown. "I trust you will have a swift, safe trip."

"Thank you for the kind wishes." The heavy irony in Severance's tone was enough to dampen any further gestures of reconciliation. "Just one more thing."

"Yes, Severance?"

"You are now officially a very rich young woman. As long as my name was the only one on the credit account, no one would have bothered you. But as of tonight, you've become a prize."

"A prize?"

"Any reeting renegade who thinks he can talk you into bed and out of your credit will probably try."

"I'm not that naive, Severance."

"You'd better exercise some common sense while I'm gone. If I get back and find out you've done something foolish, I'll—"

"You'll what?" she challenged.

"I'll feed whoever succeeded in seducing you to the river. And when I'm finished with him, I'll tear several long and painful strips off your soft hide."

Uneasily Cidra tried to outglare him. "You have no rights over me."

"Don't bet on it. Officially you're still a member of my crew. And I'm still the pilot in command." He stepped closer and seized her by the shoulders, pulling her against his hard body. "Goodbye, Cidra. Behave yourself while I'm gone or there'll be hell to pay when I get back. I promise you." His mouth came down on hers, quick and hard. Then he turned on his booted heel and started down the street.

"Severance!"

He halted and glanced back, his face set in forbidding lines. "What?"

"Don't you dare give away those sensors. You make sure you get paid for delivering them, do you hear me?"

"I can hear you just fine. So can everyone else in the vicinity." He vanished into the night.

Cidra awoke the next morning to find Fred collapsed across her ankle. She opened one eye and tentatively wriggled her foot. "Up and at 'em, Fred. You can't sleep all day."

The rockrug wriggled into a more comfortable position. He had been as happy as a rockrug could be to see both Severance and herself when they had returned, although Desma claimed that he had made himself at home in her household. So much at home, in fact, that he had munched two of her valued exhibits before someone discovered he'd wriggled into a cage. The huge flutter moths inside hadn't stood a chance. Fred had been discovered with a wingtip still draped rakishly from one corner of his mouth.

Cidra worked free of the rockrug's light weight and headed for the large, comfortable lav. It was a joy to spend as long as she wanted under the invigorating spray without worrying about Severance reading her a lecture on conservation.

The thought of Severance sent Cidra into a reverie that lasted for nearly half an hour. The spray pummeled her as she considered her parting argument with the self-proclaimed pilot in command. He hadn't been pleased by her lack of trust.

"Well what did he expect?" she demanded at Desma at breakfast. "Sometimes he makes me very angry. He's being so arbitrary about packing me off to Clementia."

"So arbitrary that you felt compelled to get even?" Desma poured coffade and savored the aroma.

Cidra winced. "I don't know what came over me. I hadn't planned to insist on a contract for my share of the credit. Severance would never have cheated me. But when he came into the restaurant looking so smug and in charge last night, I couldn't stand it."

"There's nothing wrong with insuring your half of the deal."

"Except that I insulted Severance in the process. I think he sees himself as having some obligation to protect me. He's got a very overdeveloped sense of responsibility, Desma. That's the real reason I'm being shipped back to Clementia. Severance feels obligated to give me a chance to make up my own mind about the future. He feels guilty for having pushed me into everything that happened here on Renaissance."

"The decision to come to Renaissance was yours, wasn't it?" Desma looked at her searchingly.

"Oh, definitely. But that doesn't seem to keep Severance from assuming the responsibility."

"Maybe it's because you remind him of Jeude. He's always felt responsible for what happened to his brother."

"Well, I'm not Jeude. What's more, I've learned that I never will be a Harmonic. The truth is," Cidra added slowly, "I wouldn't want to be one now, even if someone could wave a wand and turn my mind into a harmonically tuned brain."

"Because of Severance?"

"Because of a lot of things. Severance is the main reason, but there are others." Cidra paused, remembering the scenes in the safehold. "Wait until you see the tapes of the Ghosts' history, Desma. It's very sad. From what I can tell they were once a strong, aggressive race that managed to control Renaissance. Then they moved on to populate Lovelady and QED. But they never went any farther. Something happened. It's hard to tell from the visual record, but it looks as though they simply stopped expanding and started turning inward. For a while toward the end of the history, everything appears idyllic. The architecture is beautiful, the faces are serene, the life-style looks gentle and harmonious. But it doesn't last long. There are no children in the later images, just fewer and fewer Ghosts, gradually fading away until the jungle swamps them. I realized later that it made me angry to see them just give up and die out. I wanted them to go on living, to fight back, to expand. Instead they became so serene and so passive, they lost the will to survive as a species. It made me think of what might happen if all humans suddenly became Harmonics."

"You don't think they'd survive?"

"I think they'd go the way of the Ghosts," Cidra said bluntly. "The truth is, Harmonics are not really constitutionally built to survive under adverse circumstances. Do you know that my mother had to be totally unconscious for hours before I was born? The trauma of childbirth is enough to kill a Harmonic female, even if there are no complications. That's one of the reasons why it's such a major decision when a Harmonic couple decides to have a child. Desma, I don't want to be that weak. I've learned a great deal about myself during the past few days. Given a choice, I'll fight. I think, under the right circumstances, I could actually kill another human being. And I've already proven that I can kill other creatures."

"Does the knowledge scare you?"

"A little. But I've accepted it. I don't want to retreat to Clementia. Harmonics are a luxury for the human race. They are valuable and to some extent they are our conscience. But I'd rather be a survivor than a luxury." Cidra's mouth curved. "And I'd rather fight with Severance than go back to Clementia and worship Mercer from afar."

"Who's Mercer?"

Cidra grinned. "Another Harmonic on whom nature wasted a pair of gorgeous shoulders and the darkest eyes you've ever seen. For ages I told myself I loved him for his mind. I lied."

Desma burst out laughing. "Does Severance know about him?"

"Ummm. Irritates the hell out of him. But I think Mercer worries him too. Severance is afraid I'll start dreaming of the perfect platonic relationship somewhere between Renaissance and QED."

"I never could imagine Severance being very good at a platonic relationship with you," Desma mused.

"He's not. Oh, he tried hard for a while. Inspired by his noble sense of responsibility, no doubt. But it didn't last. Now I'm the one who's worried. He's shipping me out on a commercial freighter, the same way he shipped out that woman with whom he once signed a convenience contract. What if he doesn't come back for me, Desma?"

Desma smiled reassuringly. "You've got a contract with him to split the credit from this trip, remember? Nothing like a business agreement to tie two people together."

Cidra brightened a bit. "That's true."

Severance had been right about one thing. During the next two days Cidra was aware that she was attracting more than merely curious attention. "Friends" of Severance materialized out of nowhere, professing eager interest in Cidra's health and welfare. Most were concerned that she enjoy herself in Port Try Again while Severance was gone. Cidra was frequently stopped on the street, and Desma was prevailed upon to make introductions. Cidra handled the new attention with classic Harmonic politeness.

"It would be humorous if it wasn't for the fact that all this interest in me merely proves Severance was right one more time," she told Desma at one point. "I've had three invitations for dinner this evening, four for tomorrow night, and half a dozen offers to buy me a drink. One very nice man asked if I was interested in playing Free Market. I got the feeling that I was going to be encouraged to put up my contract as a bet."

"Severance would explode if he found out."

Cidra smiled a little savagely. "Yes, he would, wouldn't he? What's happening to me, Desma? I never used to be vindictive or . . . or irrational and emotional."

"You're scared," Desma said gently.

"I'm afraid so. I have no real hold on Severance. A couple of nights in his bed and a shared adventure. That's all. It's pleasant to think that the contract ties us together, but it won't. Not really. Not the way I want it to hold us."

"He's said he'll come back for you."

"I know. But he's a Wolf."

Desma frowned. "You're afraid he won't keep his word?"

"I'm afraid he'll change his mind; that perhaps when he made the statement, he didn't really know his own mind."

"You're a Wolf too. You might change your mind or fail to keep your word. You might not be waiting for him several weeks from now when he returns from QED. Perhaps the gardens of Clementia will hold more appeal than you remember."

"No." Cidra spoke with conviction, aware of her inner decision. "I won't change my mind. If he comes back for me, I'll be waiting."

"He has no way of knowing that for sure."

"He shouldn't put us to the test."

"Severance is looking for reassurance, if you ask me."

"It's odd, isn't it, Desma? We've trusted each other with our lives more than once during the past few days. Yet we're afraid to trust each other's feelings."

"I imagine things are much simpler in Clementia."

"Yes," said Cidra. "They are."

Severance silently sent up a word of thanks when the holotape crew managed to trigger the Ghosts' presentation inside the safehold. He had been mentally holding his breath, afraid that the showing he and Cidra had seen had been the final one. If that had been the case, he would have had to take a penalty cut on the contract he'd signed with the company. The safehold, itself, was still valuable but not nearly so valuable as the contents. The mind call itself was no longer functioning. Either that or the conditions weren't right for activating it. When Severance and the exploration crew had finally located the safehold by a process of quartering all the terrain within an hour's walk from the river, he had seen at once that the protected circle had shrunk. It was obviously fading, and that meant the valuable scenes inside were probably about to disappear also.

"I'm not sure we'll get it to trigger again," the crew chief announced, "but we've got it down on holotape." He looked pleased. "A hell of a find, Severance. When you stumbled across this, it was really your lucky day. Enough history in here to keep half of Clementia busy for years."

Severance stood in the vaulted entrance of the safehold, gazing at the bubbling stream where Cidra had been bathing the morning he'd awakened from the delirium. The stream was still barely inside the protected area. "My lucky day," he agreed softly. He forced himself out of the reveries as a crew of technicians bustled past. "Any sign of a mechanism to explain how all this operates? We could use the secret of keeping the terrain clear. Whatever the Ghosts used, it's more efficient than the deflectors."

"Nothing so far. We've picked up no energy readings and no indications of any hardware hidden in the safehold walls. We may never find the answer. Might not be able to comprehend it if we do find it. This is damn sophisticated stuff, Severance."

He nodded thoughtfully. "They had the ability to survive. But in the end they just gave up."

"Never even made a try for space travel beyond the local system," the crew chief said. "Doesn't make any sense. So much technical expertise gone to waste. Other things became more important, I guess."

Severance looked at him. "What could have been more important than the survival of the species?"

"I don't know. What's more, I don't think I want to know. When are you taking the Vinton crew to the home of the big blue monsters?"

"Now. Shouldn't be as hard to find as this was. I got a fix on it with a directional indicator." He also wanted to try another shard of one of the shells to see if it still had a homing effect.

The Vinton crew was elated with their find. The shard worked as a directional device but not because of mechanical reasons.

"The shells are naturally attracted to the metal of the ship," one technician announced. "Like magnets that work over long distances. No wonder you had trouble with your signal." He ducked into the floodlit hole in the ship where uniformed men scurried around with great caution. "What the hell happened to that gadget on top of the long case? The damage looks fresh."

Severance ambled in after him and scrutinized the results of the pulser on the device that had activated the illusions. "Had a little trouble with that." He looked into the case. "Going to open it?"

"No. Not here. It'll have to be done under controlled atmospheric conditions. Don't want the skeleton dissolving into dust."

"Do you think it's that old?"

The technician shook his head. "No. But we don't know how it will react to the atmosphere once the case is opened."

Severance hung around the rest of the day, assuring that his clients were satisfied. When the teams headed back toward the river to spend the night, he made his decision to leave for the ExcellEx camp in the morning. The sensors were long overdue.

"Hey, Severance, stop worrying about the mail," Rand Bantforth said during dinner. "You're making enough off these discoveries to let you forget whatever ExcellEx was going to pay for the COD delivery."

"It's the principle of the thing," Severance growled.

"Yeah, well five hundred thousand is a lot of consolation for a principle."

Another man spoke up as he helped himself to ale. "Severance isn't making five hundred thou off of this. He's only getting two hundred fifty. His lady gets the other half. That's one interesting female you left behind in Try Again, Severance. She's got enough credit to her name to buy a man his own mail ship. If I were you, I wouldn't wait too long to get back to her, or somebody else will take on the job of keeping her amused."

"Cidra's not naive enough to fall for some fast-talking rene-gade's line of torla manure." Severance swallowed his ale and hoped to hell he was right.

"I don't know," the other man offered. "It's hard to figure women."

Severance thought about that. He had figured Cidra out al-most completely. But he needed her to be sure of herself and she hadn't had the time and the distance to do that. She had been through too much, too quickly, thanks to him. He owed it to her to give her time and the peacefulness of Clementia in which to make her decision.

"Hey," said one of the holotape technicians, "I brought along a Free Market playing field. Anyone interested?"

Severance smiled. "I just happen to have a set of cubes on me."

As he crawled into a lonely sleeper that night Severance was aware of the same sense of heroic martyrdom he had experienced on board ship when he'd managed to refrain from seducing Cidra. He had discovered then that the feeling wasn't much compensa-tion for denying himself her warm, sweetly willing body. Tonight he decided that heroic martyrdom didn't improve with practice.

Fear gnawed at him as he lay staring at the curved ceiling of the tent. What if she was drawn back into the safe, serene world of Clementia? He was taking such a stupid risk by sending her back home.

But he had to be sure of her.

NINETEEN

I'm scared, Desma. That's what the problem is. I'm just plain scared." Cidra gazed morosely into her half empty mug of ale. Around her the patrons of the Bloodsucker went about the business of enjoying themselves amid a canopy of smoke and the occasional clatter of Free Market cubes. A big commercial freighter had arrived in port today, and the normal tavern crowd was augmented by the shipload of newcomers. The freighter was due to leave the following afternoon, and Cidra was scheduled to be on it.

Desma eyed her friend with affection. Cidra was wearing her early evening gown, and her hair was done in its traditional, neat coil of braids. Cidra was her old, elegant self this evening, except for one thing: she was on her third mug of Renaissance Rose ale. Desma found the process of watching Cidra drink interesting. Desma kept waiting for the effects to show. Surely the fine manners and the gentle grace would start disintegrating at any moment. The fact that neither had faded so far only went to show how strong a force good breeding could be. Desma was fascinated.

"If you're really scared, Cidra, you're certainly using a traditional means of overcoming the fear."

Cidra gazed at her mug. "Severance likes this stuff."

"I know."

"He should have been back yesterday, Desma. He said he'd be back in three days. This is the fourth day."

Desma sighed. "I realize that. Renaissance has a way of making folks change their plans in the field. You know he's all right. He checked in with Security this morning. He's not in trouble, Cidra."

"He's deliberately delaying his return so he can avoid having to see me again before I leave."

"You're getting paranoid."

Cidra considered that. "Do you think so? Harmonics never get paranoid. Everybody likes Harmonics. No reason to be paranoid. But I'm not a Harmonic. So it's okay for me to be paranoid."

"That's a wonderful string of logic. Have some more ale."

"Thank you," Cidra said with grave politeness. "I will." She sipped reflectively and then said with an air of great insight, "He's a loner. That's the real problem. I think he likes me, but he's basically a loner. He doesn't want to allow anyone, especially a woman, into his life on a permanent basis. The cabin of a mail ship is very small, you know."

"I know. But the two of you got here from Lovelady without murdering each other."

"And now he's sending me away."

"He's the one who's scared, Cidra. He knows he can't offer you the things you'll have if you go back to Clementia."

"Hah. Severance could have used that excuse before he negotiated five hundred thousand in credit for the safehold and the alien ship. It won't wash now. He's rich."

Desma's mouth curved wryly. "Don't forget he's only got two hundred and fifty thousand."

Cidra flushed guiltily. "He annoyed me. That's the only reason I made him give me a separate contract. I was very irritated."

"The fact is, even if he had all five hundred thousand, he'd spend every last credit on Severance Pay, Ltd. This time he's determined to make his plans a success. He's seen everything fall apart on him at least twice already."

Cidra frowned. "What are you talking about?"

Desma shrugged. "He went into partnership with Racer because Racer had some capital and wanted to be a wheeler and dealer. Racer had the credit but not enough business sense to make it work."

"Severance had the business sense?"

Desma nodded. "Severance had the ideas and the ambition. But he partnership didn't work out."

"It's a little difficult to continue in a partnership with someone who's willing to leave you in a sinkswamp with a kill-weaver," Cidra said.

Desma arched one brow. "Is that what happened? Interesting. Everyone knew something catastrophic had happened, but no one knew exactly what."

"Don't tell him I told you," Cidra said urgently. "I think I might have had a bit too much ale. I seem to be babbling."

"Don't worry, Cidra. I won't say a word. As I said, after the partnership was dissolved, Severance was left with only his ship and virtually no capital. He and his brother started building things up again, and just as they were beginning to see some progress, Jeude went down on QED."

"I know." Cidra swallowed a wave of sadness. "It was very hard for Severance to handle."

"The emotional trauma was only part of it. The other half of the story is that the loss of the ship sent Severance Pay, Ltd. back to circle one. For a year Severance took some awful risks as a bonus man here on Renaissance for some exploration companies. ExcellEx was one of the firms he worked for during that period."

"Do you think he took the risks because he just didn't care anymore?"

"I don't know. People take risks for different reasons. I know he was a bitter, angry man for a long time. He spent more time in the jungle than he did in Try Again. But when the year was over, he seemed to have pulled himself together. In the meantime he had accumulated enough bonus money to finance *Severance Pay*. He's been working his way back for a third try at the big time ever since."

"And now he's got another crack at it." Cidra sighed. "I suppose I shouldn't get in his way."

"But are you going to get in his way?" Desma asked perceptively.

"I prefer to think of myself as a useful and extremely valuable member of his crew." Cidra took another sip of ale. "Now all I have to do is make him see me that way."

"Hey, Severance, how much will you take for the little lady?" Craft grinned cheerfully as he helped make the skimmer fast to the dock. He examined Severance's dusty boots and sweat-stained shirt, which were revealed under the marina's bright lights. It was obvious that the past four days had been hard and long. But, then, most days on the river and in the jungle were.

The balmy night air was thicker than usual, heralding the approach of a storm. Borgia and Medici were quickly being veiled by clouds. Severance and the skimmer's pilot had made it back barely in time. Skimmer avoided travel by night if at all possible, especially when a storm was in the offing. But Severance had pushed for the unorthodox travel that afternoon because they were so close to Try Again and Cidra was due to ship out the next day. The thought of not seeing her before she left had led him to give the skimmer pilot an extra fifty in credit for traveling after dark. Folks were always on the lookout for easy bonus money on Renaissance.

"You haven't got enough credit to buy her, Craft, and you know it." Severance jumped onto the dock, his stained travel pack slung over one shoulder. "Even if I decided to sell, you'd have one renegade devil of a time trying to collect. The lady's got a mind of her own."

"She's also got two hundred and fifty thousand of her own from what I hear." Craft chuckled as he reached down into the skimmer to take a container the pilot was handing him. "A lady like her draws a considerable amount of attention in a place like this."

Severance, about to walk down the dock toward shore, glanced back. "Anyone been making too much of a nuisance of himself?"

"Why? You going to feed him to the river if he has?"

"After I separate his head from his neck. Let's have it, Craft. What's been happening?"

"Calm down, Severance. She and Desma haven't been seen apart since you left. Saints know a few hopeful types tried to get Cidra interested in a nice steak dinner or something, but no one had any luck."

"She doesn't like meat." Severance readjusted the travel pack and stalked off toward the bank.

"Maybe that's why she's drinking ale at the Bloodsucker tonight," Craft called after him. "A lot of protein but not much meat in a glass of Rose ale."

"One of these days, Craft, someone's going to accidentally push you into the river." But Severance didn't pause this time. He headed away from the dock facilities and up the dusty street, driven by a sense of urgency. He had so little time left with Cidra.

She must have gotten very bored to have gone to the Bloodsucker for a drink. Maybe Desma had talked her into it. Cidra never did more than sip elegantly at a glass of wine or ale. At this late hour she was probably tired of killing time in a tavern. She wasn't really cut out for spending her evenings that way. At least there was no Cord Racer around to cause trouble that night. Severance decided he wouldn't chew Cidra out for spending a couple of hours in a tavern. After all, there wasn't much to do in a place like Try Again. Besides, from what Craft had said, it sounded as if Desma was doing a good job of playing chaperon. He paced more quickly along the street, anticipating the pleasure in Cidra's eyes when she saw him again.

It was Desma who saw Severance come through the door. She glanced up, took in his dusty, stained appearance and the intensity of his eyes as he scanned the room, and then she smiled at Cidra. "He's back."

Cidra blinked. She had just finished the last of her third mug of ale. "Who's back?"

"The love of your life."

"Oh, him." Eyes narrowed to help her concentrate, Cidra looked around and saw Severance starting toward her down an aisle of tables. She smiled wistfully. "Isn't he wonderful, Desma?"

"He's interesting, I'll say that for him."

Cidra's smiled congealed into a frown as Severance reached the table. She glared up at him. "You're late," she announced.

Severance tilted his head to one side, studying her as he let the pack slide to the floor. "You're drunk."

"I have been drowning my sorrows. Ask Desma."

Severance slid a grim glance at Desma. "How the hell did she get into this condition?"

"I did it all by myself," Cidra answered.

"I can see that. Why is it that every time I leave you on your own you get into trouble?"

"I'm not in any trouble. You're the one in trouble. Did you give those sensors away to ExcellEx?"

Severance leaned down, planting his hands on the table, to confront her. His eyes were glittering with a mixture of masculine irritation, desire, and possessiveness. "No, I did not give the sensors to ExcellEx."

"Did you get full credit on delivery?" she demanded.

"Yes, Otanna Rainforest, I did. Satisfied?"

"No. You should have gotten hazardous duty credit on top of the agreed-upon fee."

"I got a contract for another shipment instead. Does that please you?"

Cidra's severe expression changed back into a warm, approving smile. "Oh, Severance, that's wonderful."

"Thank you." He looked at Desma, who was smiling. "How much has she had?"

"Three mugs. Holding it very well, I might add."

"She's spaced out of her little mind."

"She's been waiting for you," Desma said simply. "Today she started worrying that you wouldn't return until after she left."

"She should have known better. That's no excuse—"

"I," Cidra interrupted grandly, "don't need any excuses. I am a financially independent woman who can do as she likes."

"Too much education and too much money. It's a bad combination in a woman." Severance straightened. "Are you ready to leave, Cidra?"

"Yes, please. Where are we going?"

"Someplace where there's a bed." He reached down to take her arm.

"You need more than a bed, Severance. You need a shower." Desma grinned up at him. "Why don't you take her back to my place? I won't be home for a while yet. You're welcome to spend the night. Fred's waiting there too."

"I appreciate the offer, Desma. I'll take you up on it." He started to tug Cidra out of her chair.

"Now wait just one spaced second." Cidra lifted her chin. "I have decided that this relationship of ours is based entirely too much on bed. It's too physically oriented. We need to talk. We need to explore the intellectual side of this whole thing. Then we need to discuss the business aspects of it. You'd better sit down, Teague Severance. We have a lot to discuss."

Severance regarded her politely. "The thing is, Cidra, you're not in any condition to carry on an intellectual analysis of our relationship. You're spaced, Otanna Rainforest. Drunk as a renegade on a bonus spree."

"Oh. How interesting. I hadn't realized."

"It's all right," he assured her, hauling her to her feet. "Just leave everything to me. I'll handle it." He scooped her up and slung her easily over one shoulder. Cidra's yellow-gold gown swirled around his stained shirt.

Cidra examined the floor from her upside-down position. Then she steadied herself by grasping his utility loop. She smiled reassuringly at Desma. "It's all right. He always handles things. Pilot in command, you know."

"I understand," Desma said gently. "Good night, Cidra."

"Good night, Desma."

Desma spoke to Severance. "The door's keyed to Cidra's voiceprint."

"All I have to worry about is getting her to say something coherent when we get to your place. See you in the morning, Desma. And thanks."

Severance clamped one hand firmly around Cidra's thighs, plucked the travel pack off the floor, and started toward the door. He ignored the interested attention of the tavern crowd. He was out on the street, striding toward Desma's before he realized that Cidra was humming contentedly.

"I didn't know you were musical," he growled.

"I can do a great many things. Excellent education."

"I'm going to put you in a bed and let you show me what you do best."

"You don't think we're placing too much emphasis on the physical side of this relationship?" Cidra asked with both whimsy and worry.

"I think," Severance told her, "that memories of you wrapped around me are all I'm going to have to keep me warm for a long time."

Cidra sighed. "You shouldn't send me away, Severance."

"I have to send you away."

"I know. I've thought it all out. I know you have to do it. But I'm scared, Severance."

"So am I."

Cidra lapsed into silence for the remainder of the trip. When Severance stopped at Desma's door, she obediently said her name into the voicelock and then felt herself being carried into the house. Severance walked into the bedroom she had been using and stood Cidra carefully on her feet. She circled his neck with her arms and smiled wistfully up at him.

"I've missed you."

"Not half as much as I've missed you." He pulled her close, feeling her gown whip lightly around his legs as he did so. She lifted her face for his kiss, and he took her mouth with a hunger he knew he would be feeling frequently during the days and nights to come. For a long moment he simply helped himself to the promise of her, drinking deeply of the nectar that was waiting. She melted against him the way he had remembered, and Severance wondered how he would last without her during the long time ahead. The thought that she might not be waiting when the ordeal was over filled him with a dangerous tension. He realized abruptly that his kiss was growing rough and heavy. She was such a soft little creature.

"I don't want to hurt you."

"You're not hurting me." She framed his face between her hands.

"I should get cleaned up first."

"Later," she murmured. "We have so little time."

"Cidra, do you know what it does to me when you look at me like that?"

"Like what?"

"As if you want me so much, you'll dissolve if you don't get me."

"I might."

His fingers were trembling as he undid the delicate fastenings of the yellow-gold robe. It slid to the floor, a heap of treasure around her feet. Severance decided it was nothing compared to the treasure it had concealed. He unhooked the utility belt and draped it on the table beside the bed. Impatiently he tugged off the rest of his clothing. When he was finished, he reached out to touch Cidra. It occurred to him again that he should get under a hot spray before he claimed such a sweet-smelling woman, but he couldn't seem to stop himself. Already he was pushing her backward onto the bed.

"Watch out for Fred," Cidra said.

"Where is he?"

"I don't know. He's usually in here somewhere."

Severance looked up and saw three rows of teeth grinning at him from the window ledge above the bed. "Hello, Fred. Go back to sleep."

The three rows of teeth winked out of sight. Severance gathered Cidra into his arms. He heard her soft sigh, felt the warm, eager welcome in her arms, and wondered how he could let her go in the morning. Then he stopped thinking of the future entirely. All that existed for him was the present with its promise of passion and satisfaction. On Renaissance a man took what he could get.

He made love to Cidra with the burning need of a man who knows he's going to go hungry for a long time.

Severance didn't know what brought him up out of sleep later that night. He came awake the way he usually did on Renaissance with a sudden alertness that kicked his system into full gear. He lay listening to the shadows, unmoving. One arm was wrapped securely around Cidra as if even in his sleep he was afraid of losing her. Her rounded rear was nestled intimately into his thighs, and he could feel the curves of her breasts under his palm.

But it hadn't been Cidra who had awakened him. She was sound asleep. He listened intently, and then he heard a faint movement on the window ledge. Fred was awake too. Perhaps he had only heard the sound of his movement. The rain had begun, pouring down outside with enough force and noise to mask any sounds from the street. Severance wondered if it had been Desma's return to the house that had brought him up out of sleep. But he could hear nothing from the hall.

Then he heard another sound, and this time he recognized it: the hiss of a deflector screen as a man moved through it. The faint noise was coming from the deflector that guarded the window across the room, Severance slitted his eyes and turned his head a few fractions of a centimeter. A shadow moved on the other side of the diazite pane. On the window ledge over the bed Fred shifted again.

Severance reached up and touched the rockrug. Fred went

still, his body still and alert. Satisfied that the creature was going to obey the silent command, Severance reached for the knife in his utility belt. Logically, whoever was outside the window shouldn't be able to open it. The diazite was locked. But there were ways around locks. Too many ways.

Severance wasn't very surprised when the diazite pane swung inward without a sound. The figure coming through the window was holding a pulser. He got no more than one leg hooked over the windowsill. Severance came to a sitting position in a smooth rush of movement, launching the knife in his hand with the full power of his shoulder and upper arm.

The heavy-duty utility knife caught the intruder in the right side of his chest. The pulser dropped to the floor as the victim yelled in pain and rage. The force of the blow sent him spinning backward, out of the window and onto the ground.

"Severance!" Cidra came awake with a startled gasp, clutching at the sheet. Rain was pouring through the open window. "What happened? What's wrong?"

But he was already out of bed and leaning out of the window. An instant later he was through it and crouching on the ground outside. Cidra heard Fred moving agitatedly on the ledge above her, and then she felt him undulating down onto her shoulder and along the bed. He was moving almost as fast as Severance had moved. The rockrug crossed the room and wriggled onto the other window ledge. Cidra wasn't far behind both of them.

"Severance? What are you . . . Sweet Harmony, it's him!" She stared at the man lying flat on the ground in the pouring rain. Severance was hunkered down beside him, his nude body gleaming sleekly from the steady downpour. "It's him," she said again, dazed. "The man who attacked Desma and me in the lab."

Then she saw the blood mingling with the rainwater that was running down the man's chest. The hilt of the utility knife protruded from his rumpled clothing. She caught her breath. "Is he . . . is he dead?"

"No. My aim was a little off. It's hard to get an accurate shot from a sitting position. Especially when you're in a hurry." Severance was examining his victim. "You're sure it's the same rene-gade?"

She stared at the stricken man, whose face was twisted in a grimace of pain. It was an expression that wasn't all that different from the one of fear she had last seen him wearing. "It's him. What's he doing here? Everyone assumed he'd disappeared."

"Since he's still alive, we'll be able to ask him a whole lot of in-teresting questions. See if Desma is home yet. If not, use her comp-phone to get company Security out here."

Cidra hesitated, deeply aware of the pain the intruder must be feeling. "We've got to stop the bleeding, Severance."

He looked up at her as she stood framed in the window. For the first time Cidra saw the expression on his face. Rain washed over his hard features, revealing a grim, hollow stare that shook her to the core.

"I'm almost sure he came through that window to kill you," Severance said much too softly. "I don't give a damn if he dies right here and now. Go wake Desma."

She still had far to go yet before she became completely ac-customed to Wolf ways, Cidra thought as she went in search of Desma. There was no sense fooling herself. In some respects she would never become a true Wolf. She wondered if it was that weakness in her nature that made Severance wary of taking her with him.

Severance watched the window as Cidra disappeared and wondered if she could ever accept the part of him that was capa-ble of this kind of violence. Then he looked down at the man on the ground and felt like slitting the renegade's throat. The temp-tation to finish the job he'd begun with the utility knife was strong. Not only had the intruder represented a threat to Cidra, he had given her one more glimpse of Severance as a man who was about as far from being a Harmonic as it was possible to get.

Cidra stood in the departure lounge the next day waiting for Severance to confirm her reservation. She was wearing her em-broidered green midday robe, and her hair was in its usual coronet. Her hands were clasped in front of her in the formal position of patience. Around her the hustle of passengers and crew flowed unheeded, not touching her either physically or emotionally. She felt isolated and intensely alone, her eyes following Severance as he verified her flight. As he turned to make his way back through the crowd she searched his face, hoping for some sign of a reprieve.

There was none. Severance had made up his mind, and she knew better than to expect to change it at this late hour. Cidra felt a rush of anger and resentment at the midnight intruder, not because he had come through the window with the intention of killing her so that she couldn't identify him, but because he had succeeded in ruining what was left of her last night with Severance. The man had been questioned by company Security immediately after he had received medical aid for the knife wound. Then Severance and Cidra had both been obligated to give statements. It was all cut-and-dried as far as the legal aspects went. Violence within Try Again was dealt with severely. Renaissance couldn't afford to encourage it inside the one safe zone on the planet. Bad for business. The intruder was under computer lock, but no one could give Cidra back the rest of the night with Severance. Morning had arrived all too quickly.

"You're all set. I upgraded your cabin. This way you'll have more room."

She inclined her head in formal thanks.

"Bigger lav too," he added in a deadpan tone. "You can bathe to your heart's content. You'll be able to spend the whole trip under a spray if you feel like it."

"It was very thoughtful of you. I am in your debt."

Severance winced. "Could you cut out the ritualistic good manners? Sometimes lately I've had the feeling that you use them when you want to be sarcastic. I'm never sure how to take them."

"I'm sorry, Severance," she whispered unhappily. Nothing was going right. Severance had been short-tempered with her since he had used his knife against the man who had tried to kill her. Time was running out, and they seemed to have less and less to say to each other. Cidra was aware of a sensation of panic waiting to swamp her.

Severance ignored her soft apology, took her arm, and guided her over to a quieter section of the lounge. "I've got something I want you to do for me."

Cidra's heart lifted for the first time that morning. "Of course," she said simply, but her eyes were shining.

He handed her a credit plate. "Take it."

She stared at it in dismay. "But it's for your account."

"I've had it opened for you. You can use that card to access it."

"But, Severance, I don't need any credit. I have plenty of my own, remember? What is this all about? I don't understand. If this is some gesture of warped responsibility on your part, you can just forget it. I don't want your share of the stake!"

"Cidra, try not to get hysterical on me over a little thing like this. I am not exactly giving you the entire contents of my credit account."

"Then what are you giving me?"

"Access to it. I'm going to be stuck on board *Severance Pay* for the next several weeks. On board, communications are limited. You know that. I don't have the facilities to do research or make investments from the deck of a mail ship. On the other hand, you're going to be running around Clementia with access to the best information sources on three planets. I don't want my two hundred and fifty thousand sitting still in a credit account. I want it working."

"You want me to invest it for you?"

"Something short-term and highly profitable," he said bluntly. "You're the one with all the education. Do something useful with it and with my stake. Take good care of it, Cidra. Lose my capital for me and I'll—"

"I know," she said. "You'll take it out of my hide." She was gazing up at him with a palpable glow as she clutched the credit slip tightly in her palm. "I'll take care of your stake for you, Severance. I swear it."

He smiled crookedly. "I know you will. I trust you."

Not with his heart and not yet with his future, but he trusted her with his credit. It was a hopeful sign, and Cidra clung to it. She dropped the credit slip carefully into the concealed pocket of her robe. It was a bond between herself and Severance, one that would surely draw him back for no other reason than to find out what she had done with his capital. Any kind of trust at all from a Wolf like Severance was a small miracle.

"You will be very careful, Severance?"

"I'll be careful." He touched the tip of her ear. "You'll go straight home to Clementia and stay out of second-class taverns and dives?"

"I promise."

"Cidra—" He broke off as if uncertain about what to say next.

Cidra touched his hand. "It's all right, Severance. I understand. It has to be this way. This is the only way you can be sure of yourself and of me." She stood on tiptoe and kissed him lightly. Then she stepped back. "I'll be waiting for you." She turned and was gone.

Severance felt his gut twist as she walked into the crowd of departing passengers. Her slender, green-robed figure was lost amid the hulking uniforms and standard-issue Renaissance jungle garb. For an instant he almost gave into the sense of panic that was clawing at his insides. She was out of reach already. The panel doors of the boarding gate were sealing shut, cutting her off from him, perhaps forever.

He had been a fool. He should have taken his chances, should have risked the odds and kept her with him. He'd taken so many risks in his life; why hadn't he been able to take this one?

But he had no right to try to make up her mind for her. She needed time and the peace of Clementia. Only then could she be sure of what she was doing.

Severance reached into a small pouch on his utility belt and let his fingers close around the fireberyl comb. The feel of it seemed to soothe the gnawing uncertainty that he knew was going to be a close companion during the long weeks ahead.

TWENTY

QED looked different on this trip, Severance realized as he oversaw the unloading of the mail. The endless vistas of orange and red dust were as barren and forbidding as ever, but the sight of them no longer made his stomach tighten or caused his mind to beat at him in angry frustration.

Revenge was exactly what he had always suspected it would be: calming and satisfying. It hadn't taken away the old pain or allowed him to forget his own sense of responsibility for what had happened to Jeude, but it had quieted him inside. The pain and the feeling of being partially responsible were things he had already learned to live with during the past two years. Time diluted the self-recriminations and would continue to do so. But exacting a measure of justice had eased him inside in a way that time would never have succeeded in doing. Racer's death had paid not only for the threats to Cidra but also for Jeude's death, and it had balanced some internal scale.

QED was never going to be his idea of the ideal vacation spot of the Stanza Nine system. The planet would always hold memories of the death of his parents and his brother. But Severance could view the raw, boomtown of Proof and the outlying orange hills with a sense of perspective now. It occurred to him that it wasn't simply revenge that had enabled him to gain perspective. He had learned something from Cidra too. Her gentleness had also eased something inside him.

This was an ore- and mineral-rich land. Companies and individuals were wresting fortunes out of the ground with the assistance of the ubiquitous spidersleds. Severance was obliged to step out of the way of one of the mobile metal monsters as he crossed the landing field to the port office. Its long, insectlike legs, so useful for covering rough terrain, narrowly missed his boot.

"Hey, up there," he yelled to the man in the driver's seat, "if you can't operate that thing properly, someone's going to show you how it's done the hard way."

"Don't need any advice on how to do it the hard way," the middle-aged ex-miner rasped. "I do it that way all the time. Back again, huh, Severance? Miss the local fun spots?"

"The only thing I've missed is taking your loose credit in a game of Free Market, Tanner." Severance stopped beside the spidersled as the man halted it. "You interested in trying to take back some of what you lost last time I was in Port?"

"Sure, if we can use my cubes." Tanner grinned hugely, his weathered face crinkling into a hundred creases.

"The day I let you use your cubes is the day I'll be too spaced to play."

"Don't trust anyone, do you, Severance?" Tanner observed with mock admiration.

Severance thought about it. At one time his answer would have been a ready no. "Maybe one woman I know."

"Severance, you're a damn fool if the one person you decide to trust is female. I do believe you've got a problem."

"I'm coping. See you this evening. And I'll bring the cubes." He moved away from the spidersled as it lurched into motion.

One night was all he would be spending on QED this trip. Severance no loner cared if he missed a few mail contracts by rushing back off-planet. He didn't care that he would be turning around to face another six weeks of empty space without more than a one night's break. All he cared about was starting the journey back to Lovelady.

The six weeks from Renaissance had been the longest and loneliest of his life, even worse than the dark season after Jeude's death. At least during that period he'd had his own bitterness and self-reproach to keep him company. But for the past six weeks the only company he'd had aside from Fred had been memories of Cidra.

The ship had seemed deserted without her. It had amazed Severance at first. He was accustomed to being alone on board with only Fred as a companion. He shouldn't have been so shocked to find himself alone again, but he was. He would wake up in the morning longing for the smell of hot coffade and someone to share it with. He would stand under the spray in the lav, and his mind would be filled with images of Cidra's charming tendency to waste water. She was so scrupulously clean and sweet-smelling.

He missed other things too. She'd had the ability to share time with him without demanding that he entertain her. Cidra was a woman with whom he could be quiet. For hours at a time she had retreated to her bunk to read or become absorbed in her programming while he worked out on the exercise machine or fiddled with a gadget. But he had always been pleasantly conscious of her presence, a satisfying sensation. She had become a companion, not just a passenger.

She had withstood his temper too. Severance knew he had been abrupt with her on more than one occasion. But she'd handled it without sulking or crying.

Most of all he missed having her in his arms. The memories of her sweet, hot warmth had plagued him every league of the way from Renaissance, and Severance knew he would be goaded by them every league of the trip back. There had been other thoughts that had eaten at him too. He'd found himself picturing her at home in Clementia, surrounded by the serenity and ritual in which she had been raised.

But a part of him had begun to insist that his Cidra could never be truly happy in Clementia. When all was said and done, she was no Harmonic. Her passion, her spirit, and her strength would forever bar her from her world just as surely as her lack of telepathy.

If Cidra wasn't fated to be happy in Clementia, then he had a right to take her with him. That knowledge had been growing steadily since he had put her on the freighter back to Lovelady. He had a right to take her, Severance decided, because she belonged to him now. She would always belong to him. If she didn't yet realize that, then he would have to make her understand.

The restless desire to be on his way back to claim his woman made Severance lengthen his stride toward the port offices. The sooner he completed his business on QED, the better. The most important thing in his life was waiting.

"You'll go with him when he comes for you, won't you, Cidra?" Talina Peacetree smiled gently at her daughter, who sat across from her on a white stone bench. The bench had been handcarved by an expert craftsman who had worked the hard substance into a light and balanced piece of sculpture. It had cost a great deal of credit, but Talina and her husband, Garn, could afford it. The garden in which the stone bench resided was even more expensive. It was shaded with a unique variety of graceful pala trees that had been cultivated to order. Formal swirls of flowering plants added color and scent to the perfectly designed scene. All was serene.

"If he comes for me, I'll go with him." Cidra finished the last step of the highly ritualized ceremony that proceeded the serving of ether wine and handed her mother a crystal goblet full of the golden liquid. Her green eyes met those of her mother. "I will be going away even if he doesn't come for me."

Talina nodded with an air of quiet acceptance. "I know. I have always known that one day you would leave. But remember that Clementia will always be here for you when you wish to return for a while."

"I would never cut myself off from my home. Even though I am not a true Harmonic, the Way is a part of me."

"It is a part of all humans," Talina said.

Cidra's mouth curved in amusement. "That's what Severance once said."

"Your Severance sounds perceptive."

"He's also occasionally rude, arrogant, and obnoxious."

"He's a Wolf." Talina's hand moved gracefully in her lap. She was wearing one of her exquisite early-afternoon gowns, a cream-colored robe embroidered with silver floss. Her silvered hair was bound in the same regal coronet that Cidra wore. She had bequeathed many of her features to her daughter, but in Talina those features were overlaid with an internal serenity that Cidra could only approximate.

"I am also a Wolf."

Talina watched her daughter as she made the quiet declaration. "It is not difficult for you to accept that now?"

"No."

"Then your adventures on Renaissance have indeed been worthwhile. You have learned much."

"I have learned to accept myself for what I am. But the most interesting part is that even if I were offered a clear choice now, I would not choose to become a Harmonic. I don't think I could bear to give up what I have found waiting inside myself."

"Then you will be content with your future. I am glad for you, my daughter. Most glad." She sipped the wine and then turned her elegant head as her husband stepped into the garden from his study. "Ah, Garn. Will you join us for a glass of wine?"

"With pleasure." Garn came forward to sit beside his wife. His clear blue eyes were full of intelligence as he regarded Cidra. Garn Oquist wore the shorter, masculine version of the early-afternoon surplice, a deep brown robe belted with a knotted thong of multicolored braided floss. His handsome face with its strong nose and high forehead held the same air of inner serenity that his wife's wore.

When Garn took his seat beside his wife, Cidra sensed the

brief, silent mental communion that took place between her parents. It was a quiet touching of minds that Cidra had once envied with all her heart. Once that subtle communication had made her feel left out and deprived. But today she found she was accepting it for what it was: a Harmonic way that she could not follow. She had other methods of communication open to her. They might be less certain, more vulnerable to risk, but when they worked, they worked well. She was satisfied with them now. They held their own rewards.

"What are the two of you discussing?" her father asked.

"My future," Cidra said with a smile. "But the truth is that I've got something far more immediate and important to discuss with you, Father. I need advice in one of your areas of expertise."

"Which one?" Garn sampled his wine with judicious care. He had many areas of expertise, some of which had made him rich.

"The theoretical aspects of the credit system."

"I never realized you had an interest in the financial system."

"I never had enough credit to make it worth worrying about." Cidra's smile broadened into a small grin.

"But now you do."

"Yes," she said. "Now I do. I want to invest, Father—the full five hundred thousand."

Her father had been considering his daughter's fortune ever since he learned of it. Now he spoke his mind. "Whoever negotiated the sale of your discoveries did an excellent job."

"I know. But now it's my turn. I'm in charge of investing the credit. Something high-yield and relatively short-term."

Garn reflected seriously for a long moment and then nodded. "There are some young and aggressive exploration firms that offer excellent prospects. According to my information they are presently seeking capital investment. One in particular, a firm called ExcellEx, has intrigued me lately. We can query your computer about it this afternoon if you would care to do so."

"That sounds perfect." Of course, it would be perfect, thought Cidra. Most things were perfect in Clementia. For the first time she understood one of the reasons why she had never really felt at home here. Great quantities of perfection and serenity could be a little boring.

Severance paused inside the gates of Clementia and gazed at the vista of gardens and beautifully proportioned architecture. Here there were no ugly or jarring structures that had been hastily erected or incompletely thought out prior to construction. Around him people garbed in simple, elegant robes nodded politely as they passed him on the wide stone paths that wound through the gardens. There was no shushing sound of a passing runner or sled. As far as Severance could see, there were no vehicles at all.

Behind the small, walled city rose the majestic coastal mountains. In front of the gates stretched a quiet, sheltered bay that rarely knew the turbulence of sea storms. Jeude would have been at peace here.

Severance took a deep, steadying breath and reminded himself that while this would have been the ideal environment for his brother, it was not for Cidra. He made his way toward the Archives, a structure that had been pointed out for him by the Wolf who guarded the gate.

"You can't miss it. Big domed building in the center of the campus." The Wolf had regarded Severance quizzically. "You here to attend classes?"

"No," Severance had answered. "I'm here to find someone."

"Who?"

"Cidra Rainforest. She works in the Archives." He had waited impatiently while the Wolf had contacted Cidra's home.

"I talked to her mother. Seems Otanna Rainforest is expecting you." The guard had waved him through the gates.

There were other non-Harmonics in the vicinity, probably students who attended the university, but the majority of the people wore the formal gowns and serene expressions of true Harmonics. Among them Severance felt large, awkward, and out of place. Rather like a torla in a garden. Not for the first time that day doubts rose to undermine his determination. Cidra wasn't a torla in this garden. With her grace and poise she could blend in beautifully.

But the weeks of gathering uncertainty had done their work well. He had to find her and take her with him. She might be able to mingle with Harmonics, but under the surface she was his passionate, loving woman, and if she had forgotten that in the time she had been back in Clementia, he would remind her. He needed her with him.

Severance found the Archives without further instructions. The curved structure seemed to rest almost unsupported on the ground, its diazite walls protecting the array of computers, study areas, and treasured bound volumes within. The bits and pieces of knowledge that had survived the crash of the colony ship had formed the heart of Clementia's Archives. In the intervening years a great deal of new information had been added. It was the center of learning for the Stanza Nine system.

Only when he was inside the building did Severance realize just how large it was. He would need help in locating Cidra.

"Try History. She works with First Family files a lot," an attendant at the front desk told him. "Straight ahead and to your left."

Severance followed the directions to a room that had been designated as the repository of First Family diaries and written records. He saw Cidra almost at once. She was wearing a morning robe, her neat head bent attentively toward a computer screen. She didn't notice him. For a long moment Severance simply stood staring at her, waiting for the sudden, aching surge of hunger to fade back to more manageable proportions. Sweet Harmony, but he had missed her! What in a renegade's hell was he going to do if she hadn't missed him?

She looked up at that moment and saw him.

"Severance!" Then she was on her feet, flying toward him with a lover's welcome in her eyes.

He caught her up fiercely and swung her around as she threw herself into his arms. The exhilaration washing over him was almost shattering in its intensity. He realized he was shaking. "I've come to steal you out of Paradise."

"It's about time you got here."

"I know." He captured her face between his hands and kissed her. "I know."

It was a long time later before Severance had Cidra to himself. Her parents had been gracious and hospitable, accepting him immediately. He had been grateful for that. One niggling concern he'd had to face on the long trip back to Lovelady was the issue of how he would deal with a set of Harmonic in-laws. But with Harmonic civility Talina and Garn had taken all obstacles out of his path. They were content with their daughter's decision. And with Garn, at least, Severance had found some common ground. He had spent two hours going over the investment program Cidra's father had mapped out.

After dinner, during which Severance had worried excessively about his table manners, Cidra had invited him out into the gardens. He had welcomed the escape, pulling her into his arms beneath the shelter of a flowering tree. In the moonlight her eyes were luminous. Severance knew that he could get lost in them.

"I was afraid from time to time during the past few weeks, but deep inside I think I knew you'd be waiting," he said.

"I know. I had a few anxious moments myself. But somehow I knew you'd come for me." She leaned her head on his shoulder and smiled. "We belong together. When are we leaving?"

"As soon as possible. But there are one or two things we have to take care of first."

She lifted her head and wrapped her arms around his neck. "Such as?"

"Such as getting married." He brushed a stray strand of her hair behind her ear. "I love you, Cidra. I want this done right. I want the bonds in place for life."

"I love you, Severance."

"I know." He smiled. "I saw it in your eyes today when you came running into my arms."

"It must have been in my eyes when you put me on the freighter back to Lovelady because I knew I loved you then too."

"I couldn't see things as clearly then," he admitted.

"And now you can? You're sure of your decision, Severance? I couldn't bear it if you changed your mind."

"Cidra, it was never my own mind I was unsure of. I only wanted the time so that you could be certain of what you were doing."

"We could argue about who didn't trust whom all evening, but it doesn't matter any longer. You're here now and I'm going with you."

"Yes." He stroked his hands down to her hips and smiled slightly. "Absolutely. Sometimes we Wolves sort of blunder along until we get things right, but when we finally do get them right, we stick to them. I'll never let you go, Cidra."

Her mouth curved teasingly as her eyes mirrored her love. "Wait until you hear my marriage terms before you make any rash promises."

"I'm listening," he drawled.

"I should warn you that by leaving me alone for the past few weeks you've given me plenty of time to work out these terms."

"Obviously a mistake on my part."

"Yes, well, first, I am no longer satisfied to sign on as a mere member of *Severance Pay*'s crew. I am demanding full partnership status."

"Ah."

She nodded vigorously. "Ah, indeed. Next I must insist on a full High Ritual wedding ceremony."

He groaned. "Why?"

"For luck. We can skip the two hours of telepathic meditation in the middle of the ceremony if you like."

"Given the fact that the bride and groom can't communicate telepathically and would be bored to their toes, I think that would be wise," he agreed.

"And last but not least, I want some more opportunities to learn the fine points of Free Market without having to wager every fireberyl hair comb or emerald-floss slipper I happen to own. And don't even think of suggesting I bet genuine credit. It's all invested along with yours."

"You know the game's no fun unless the stakes make it worthwhile."

"Until I get to the point where I've got half a chance at winning occasionally, we're going to have to settle for wagers that won't bankrupt me."

Severance pulled her close. "I'm sure," he said, his mouth hovering just above hers, "that we can find something for you to bet that has nothing to do with credit or fireberyl combs. Don't worry. I'll think of something."

"You're so resourceful."

"Ummm. Good with my hands too."

"Does this mean," Cidra asked as she lifted her face for his kiss, "that you're accepting my marriage terms?"

He grinned in the moonlight, all male and all Wolf. "Your terms are nothing compared to mine. Wait until you hear them. I intend to go over them in great detail with you."

"It's all right," she assured him. "Whatever they are, I accept."

"Just like that?"

"Of course. I trust you, Severance."

His silent laughter faded to reveal the intensity of the love in his eyes. "And I trust you, sweet Cidra, to the ends of the universe." He sealed the vow with a kiss.

CRYSTAL
FLAME

ONE

It was understood throughout the great Northern Continent of Zantalia that assassins were invariably male.

Clutching the marriage contract in one hand, Kalena stood on the wide threshold of the Traders' Guild Hall and considered what it meant to be an exception to that rule. She had been waiting since the summer of her twelfth year to carry out the lethal task that would set her free. Now she was finally on the brink of a future she had only been able to dream of in hazy images; a future as a freewoman with obligations to no one but herself.

She gazed in wonder at the noisy, bustling activity going on inside the wide hall. She had arrived in the thriving town of Crosspurposes only a day earlier, but already her life back home in the farming town of Interlock seemed very distant. That was fine with Kalena. She had no intention of ever going back to the rich, fertile fields of the Interlock valley with its prim, conservative farmers and villagers. Nor did she have any desire to return ever to the harsh, bitter company of her aunt. The marriage contract she held in her hand was her ticket out of bucolic boredom and the stifling demands of her aunt. But for Kalena, the contract was more important as her first step toward freedom.

Still, Kalena wasn't yet completely free of the past. There was a price on all things, and she still had to pay for her ticket to a new life. The packet of poison she carried sewn into her journey bag was the means by which she would fulfill her final duty to the House of the Ice Harvest.

Kalena, the last daughter of the Great House of the Ice Harvest, had been sent to Crosspurposes to avenge her devastated clan. The mandate had been handed down from the last Lady of the House, her father's sister, Olara. Olara knew as well as anyone that entrusting a mission of vengeance to a woman was a risky thing to do, but there was no choice. Olara and Kalena were the only members of the House of the Ice Harvest left. Kalena's mother had died shortly after learning of the deaths of her husband and her son. Olara herself was a Healer, and so could not kill. That left only Kalena.

Kalena had known for some time that Olara wasn't particularly satisfied with her niece as a potential assassin, but neither she nor her aunt had any choice. Someone had to carry out the task of assassinating the man responsible for the deaths of men of the House of the Ice Harvest. More than murder had been done. An entire Great House had been terminated with the deaths of the men of the clan. Such an act required the most extreme form of vengeance, and if there was only a woman left to mete out justice then so be it. Olara had made her plans accordingly. What Olara didn't know was that Kalena had a plan of her own.

Kalena gazed at the colorful scene before her and tasted the first, heady essence of freedom. She would do her duty as honor demanded. There was no question of that. Kalena had been taught the importance of one's responsibility to one's honor before she could walk. But she hoped to buy more than vengeance with her victim's death. She intended to use his death to buy a new future for herself, the kind of unlimited future most women on the Northern Continent never knew.

She had been working on her plan to accomplish these two

goals since the summer of her twelfth year. Never for a moment had Aunt Olara allowed her to forget her destiny. But once she had recovered from the shock of the death of her family and accepted her dangerous task, Kalena had begun to dream her own dreams.

So be it. Life was Spectrum. For every action there was another, opposing action that would ensure an ultimate balance. Kalena understood that fundamental philosophical principle. She might have been raised in a farming town since the fall of her House, but she'd had an excellent education. Aunt Olara had seen to it that the last daughter of the House had been brought up in accordance with the high standards that befitted her heritage. The works of Zantalia's most influential polarity philosophers had been available for her to read. Kalena had studied well.

Now she looked up at the second tier of offices that ringed the large Guild hall. She couldn't help being impressed by the elaborate architecture. There was nothing quite like this back home in Interlock Valley. The building was two stories high with massive, arched windows lining the ground floor, and flooding the open central hall with light. The second floor was lined with small rooms on all four sides. Every facet of construction, from the elaborately inlaid floor to the heavily carved pillars of expensive moonwood, served to emphasize the wealth that the business of trade brought to Crosspurposes.

Overhead several people were lounging against the upper railing watching the crowds down on the main floor. Kalena wondered which, if any, of those strange faces belonged to the man whose name was on the marriage contract alongside her own.

A trio of laughing, joking men arrived in the open doorway behind Kalena. Their lanti skin boots were caked with dried mud and their trousers and wide-sleeved shirts were dusty from travel. Kalena guessed that they were traders returning from a venture and she stepped out of their way. As they went past two of them hailed a friend they spotted in the crowd. The third man turned his head and saw Kalena standing in the shadow of the arched doorway. He grinned wickedly and started to say something to her. But before he could speak another group of males sauntered through the door, providing a shield for Kalena. She used the small distraction to slip into the crowd.

Moving through the busy hall, she searched for someone who looked as if he or she would be willing to take a minute to help her. Most of the people she passed seemed noisily intent on business and boisterous conversation.

As Kalena made her way through the large, two-tiered hall she surreptitiously observed the clothing of the few women present in the crowd. The first thing she noticed was that the colorful tunics they wore over their narrow trousers were much shorter, almost knee length, and slit far higher up the side than her own. Earlier, she had noted the same type of clothing on women she had passed in the street.

Town fashion was obviously a great deal more daring than the styles favored in the Interlock valley. Kalena made a mental note to make some changes in her own wardrobe as soon as possible. She would have to do something about her hair, too. The women here in town all seemed to wear theirs quite short in back, with chin-length ringlets of curls framing their faces. Kalena felt distinctly old-fashioned with her own thick mass of golden red curls held back from her face by a wide, embroidered band.

One of the women she was studying turned suddenly and Kalena's eyes collided with the stranger's. Embarrassed for having been caught staring, she started to turn aside and then changed her mind. It would be easier to ask another woman for directions than to try to get the attention of one of the rough and burly male traders. Tentatively, Kalena smiled.

"Could you help me, please? I'm trying to find someone. I was told he would probably be here in the Guild hall at this time of day."

The other woman eyed her intently for a moment, taking in her obviously provincial appearance. She apparently decided to take pity on the young woman, and asked in a kind voice, "Who is it you're trying to find?" She stepped closer to Kalena so they would be able to converse above the din.

"A man named Ridge. I don't know the name of his House. He works for the Trade Baron Quintel of the House of the Gliding Fallon."

The woman's eyebrows rose and she pursed her lips for a few seconds. "You have business with the Fire Whip?"

Kalena shook her head. "No, Ridge is his name. I'm quite sure of it. It's written here on the contract."

Curiously, the woman glanced at the folded document in Kalena's hand. "Contract? What sort of contract do you have with Quintel's Fire Whip?"

"A trade marriage agreement." Kalena felt quite daring as she said the words aloud. Trade marriages might be legal, but they were hardly respectable. She had a hunch the woman in front of her knew all about trade marriages. "And I've explained, it's not with someone called Whip. It's with a man named Ridge."

"The Ridge who works for Quintel is known as the Fire Whip," the woman explained impatiently. "Here, let me see that contract. I can't believe you've really got a trade marriage arrangement with him. He's not a regular trader. He's Quintel's private weapon. Quintel uses him the way another man uses a sintar."

"I see," Kalena said, although she didn't. "Is . . . is Fire Whip the House name of this man, Ridge?"

The other woman laughed as if Kalena's question was genuinely funny. "Hardly. Ridge has no House. He's a bastard. In more ways than one, some people say. Has a temper that can make—" She broke off at the sight of Kalena's chagrined expression. "Never mind. Let's just say that wise folks do not go out of their way to provoke him."

"If he works for Quintel, then he's the man I seek," Kalena said quietly. The other woman didn't understand, Kalena realized. She wasn't upset because her future husband had a reputedly fiery temper; Kalena didn't expect to be around this Ridge person long enough to provoke him. Rather, she was startled to learn that she was signing a marriage contract—even something as straightforward as a *trade marriage* contract—with a man who could claim no House at all, not even a small one. Olara hadn't warned her about that aspect of the situation.

Kalena hesitated, then handed over the trade marriage agreement, watching closely as her new acquaintance scanned the legal document. She was fascinated by her first encounter with what appeared to be a freewoman who made her own living and her own decisions. With a little luck and a little successful vengeance, Kalena herself might be joining the ranks of such free females.

The woman in front of her was a few years older than Kalena. She had a strong, full-figured body and carried herself with an almost aggressive air. Her hair was dark and done in the town fashion, the long side curls framing a handsome face and challenging eyes. She wore no House band on her wrist, which was not surprising. Only members of the Great Houses wore such symbols of rank and recognition. The families that comprised the vast majority of less important Houses were not entitled to wear them.

Under most circumstances, no female member of a Great House would have been allowed to involve herself in trade or any other similar business. Kalena's ability to do so was only one of the many exceptional circumstances of her life. Her own House band was hidden away in her travel bag along with her father's jeweled sintar and the packet of poison. She had not been allowed to use her real House name since the summer of her twelfth year. Olara had forbidden it in an effort to hide her niece's identity. Kalena had grown accustomed to introducing herself as a daughter of a small House called the Summer Wind. But in her heart she was always conscious of her rightful name and heritage.

But what fascinated Kalena about her new friend was not so much her lack of a Great House band as it was her lack of a man's lock and key around her throat. In Kalena's experience, females who had reached this woman's age were invariably married. At least that was the case in the Interlock valley. Kalena was somewhat taken aback by this first tangible proof of the kind of freedom that was really possible. Until now Kalena's imagination had been able to conjure up only vague, uncertain images of what it meant to be a freewoman; she was quickly realizing a whole new way of life truly did wait for her. Her dreams could more than come true. She couldn't wait.

The woman looked up abruptly, her eyes mirroring a kind of wry amazement. "By the Stones, you're telling the truth, aren't you? You truly do have a trade marriage contract with Quintel's Fire Whip. And your name is Kalena of the House of the Summer Wind?"

Kalena inclined her head, embarrassed that she hadn't properly introduced herself. "I'm from the Interlock valley." The contract contained no hint of her connection with the House of the Ice Harvest, of course. Kalena and Olara wore their false names like a cloak.

"Welcome to Crosspurposes, Kalena," the woman said in a now friendly voice. "I'm Arrisa." She paused and then added carelessly, "House of the Wet Fields." Obviously she didn't use her House name very often. The words sounded rusty. "I'll be glad to take you to meet Ridge."

"You are very kind."

"Not at all." Arrisa grinned, leading her charge toward the far end of the teeming hall. "I'm just in the mood for a good joke."

Kalena's chin lifted with a faint touch of Great House arrogance. "You think I'm going to be a source of amusement for you?"

"We'll see, won't we? Ridge is probably up there on the second level. That's where the trade offices are."

Arrisa led the way up a wide, curving staircase that opened onto the second level gallery of offices. Kalena followed, still holding tightly to her precious contract. Olara had made it clear that it was absolutely necessary to contract the less-than-acceptable trade marriage in order to get close to the intended assassination victim. He was far too well protected to be reached otherwise.

Yes, she realized, it was still precious to her, even if it was a contract with a houseless man. No matter how much below her the groom-to-be was, this marriage was still her ticket to freedom. Once she had accomplished the assassination, Aunt Olara had assured Kalena there would be no need to go on the trail as a trade wife. If all went well, Kalena would carry out her task on her wedding night. After all, in the depths of a Far Seeing trance, Olara had caught a glimpse of Kalena's intended victim dying amidst the boisterous confusion of a large wedding party. Olara's trances had a way of proving very accurate.

When Olara had come out of that particular trance, she had assured her niece that the chaos that would be caused in the household after the victim's death by an apparent heart attack would serve to protect Kalena. The death would appear to be of natural causes and the resulting confusion should insure that immediate, short-term business arrangements such as a trade marriage would be terminated with any members or associate of her victim's House. But Kalena was especially glad of Olara's reassurances now that she knew her intended husband was a man without a House name of any kind. Honor and duty could demand many sacrifices from a woman in Kalena's position, but carrying out the responsibilities of a wife, even a trade wife, to a bastard would have been asking a great deal. The prospect of becoming a murderess was bad enough.

"Quintel's business is handled on this side of the gallery," Arrisa explained, leading Kalena past a row of small rooms in which industrious looking clerks were working. The clerks were all males, naturally. Quintel might use women in some areas of his trading business, but not in any role as prestigious as that of clerk.

Kalena wondered what type of man she was about to meet. Perhaps this Ridge would be shy and unassuming like one of these clerks. Things would certainly be easier if he were, she decided. She could see herself having no trouble at all manipulating someone like that. More probably he would prove to be a rough and uncouth trader who had risen through the ranks. Even if that were true, Kalena told herself, she was confident she could handle the situation. It should be simple to intimidate such a man with her Great House manners and accomplishments. Her spirits rose cheerfully at the thought.

"If I'm right, we'll find Ridge in this last office," Arrisa said with an air of gleeful expectation. "I hope you don't mind if I stick around to watch?"

"Watch what? This is a business arrangement, Arrisa. I don't understand why you think it's going to be amusing." Kalena halted behind her guide as the other woman stopped in front of an arched, open door. As Arrisa slapped her hand against the side of the wall to get the attention of the two men inside, Kalena tried to peer around her shoulder.

"Excuse me, Traders," Arrisa said with a formality that sounded almost mocking. "I have a visitor here who says she has business with Trade Master Ridge."

The man sitting at the desk facing Kalena looked up with an annoyed frown. He was plump and balding and he had a strip of reading glass dangling from a cord around his neck. He was older than Kalena had expected, but other than that she saw no problem. Pure clerk mentality, she told herself. The daughter of a Great House could handle him. She smiled winningly, ignoring the other man who still sat with his back to her, booted feet resting casually on the desk as he studied a document in his hand. Kalena waited for Arrisa to make the introductions.

"What is this all about, Arrisa?" the balding man asked irritably. "I am extremely busy at the moment."

"Don't fret yourself, Hotch," Arrisa said soothingly. "I told you, my companion is here to see Ridge, not you."

"Damn it to the far end of the Spectrum," the man called Hotch muttered, snatching up a pen. "How am I expected to accomplish anything even remotely connected with business when I'm faced with continuing interruptions? Kindly take care of this matter, Ridge, and then return so that we may finish Quintel's report. I do have a job to do, you know."

So it's not the clerk, Kalena thought in mild dismay. Her attention swung to the second man in the room as he slowly put down the document he had been studying and turned his head. His golden gaze flicked disinterestedly across Arrisa's features and settled with jolting intensity on Kalena's face.

Definitely not the shy, unassuming type, Kalena decided. It

occurred to Kalena in that moment that matters might not be fated to proceed as easily as Olara had led her to expect.

Ridge removed his boots from the desk and got slowly to his feet with a lazy grace that implied he knew his manners but didn't always choose to use them. His eyes never left Kalena. She found his curious, golden gaze unexpectedly riveting. She had seen the brown-gold eye color that some labeled tawny before, but Ridge's eyes did not fit that description. When she met his gaze, Kalena found herself looking into the golden flames of a fire. The title Arrisa had used for him floated through Kalena's mind: *Fire Whip*.

He looked somewhat older than herself, by perhaps eight or nine years. Ridge was a grim-featured man, his face carved with a harsh elegance that held no room for conventional handsomeness. His hair was a shade of brown that was almost black, and he wore it slightly longer than the other townsmen Kalena had seen, letting it brush the edge of his collarless shirt in back. He had apparently thrust it behind his ears with a careless hand, but if it fell forward it would undoubtedly reach the lobes of his ears.

Ridge wore the wide-sleeved shirt favored by many of the traders on the floor below. His was undyed, still the natural light shade of the lanti wool from which it had been woven. It was round at the neck, slit halfway down the front and laced together with a thin leather tie. Ridge had left the top two lace openings undone and Kalena could see a hint of the dark hair that apparently covered his chest. The shirt's cuffs were deep and narrow, holding the fullness of the material out of the way in a practical fashion. The hands that emerged from the wide cuffs seemed rather large to Kalena. They also looked quite strong, capable of controlling a mount, a weapon and, perhaps, a woman. A flicker of amusement went through Kalena as she found herself hoping he didn't attempt all three tasks simultaneously.

The trousers Ridge had on were belted with a heavy strip of zorcan leather. The garment fit him closely from waist to thigh, revealing the taut, hard planes of his body before disappearing into the knee-high lanti skin boots. A plain, unadorned sintar sheath hung from his leather belt together with a simple money pouch.

He was a strongly built man with wide shoulders and a lean quality that was almost feline from the chest down. No, Kalena thought, not feline, but whiplike. For a moment her imagination saw in him the same promise of lethal danger that lay in a sheathed weapon.

She glanced at the sintar on his belt. For some reason the stark, undecorated blade seemed to summarize the entire man. The sintar was a weapon that had long since evolved into a fashionable, frequently gaudy dress accessory among the males of the Great Houses. The one Kalena carried in her travel bag was a perfect example. It had belonged to her father and had been chased with gold and studded with gems. It was a showpiece, and had never been used as anything but an adornment. But this blade of Ridge's was of a far different nature. There was no doubt in her mind that the steel of this sintar had been forged with one object in mind: to taste blood. Something tightened within her at the thought.

"I'm Ridge. What can I do for you?" He spoke quietly, ignoring Arrisa, who watched with glinting amusement. His voice was as dark and shadowed as the rest of him, and it seemed to touch Kalena's nerve endings.

Kalena held out the document she had brought with her from the Interlock valley and forced herself to remember that, intimidating though he might be at first glance, Ridge wore no Great House band on his wrist. He couldn't even claim a small House name. That made her more than his equal. It might be a petty consideration, especially given the fact that she was the last of her devastated House, but in that moment Kalena decided she needed a slight edge. She was going to have her hands full with this man. Olara should have warned her, she found herself thinking.

"I am Kalena, from the Interlock valley," she said with grave formality. "My aunt Olara negotiated this contract with Trade Baron Quintel. It is an agreement for a trade marriage between you and I. My aunt said that everything had been arranged and that you would be expecting me."

Ridge took the paper from her fingers, his eyes still on her face. Kalena could read nothing in the banked fire of his gaze, but she was suddenly, vividly aware again of the size and strength of his hands as his fingers brushed hers.

Ridge scanned the contract for a long, silent moment. Kalena was conscious of the curiosity in the clerk's eyes and of the humorous expectation in Arrisa's manner. Kalena found herself growing rather anxious. For the first time, she realized that, should Ridge claim no knowledge of the marriage contract, she would feel horribly embarrassed in front of Hotch and Arrisa. She realized such a concern was stupid—some would say quite *feminine*—when her main objective was of such a bloody nature, but Kalena couldn't help it. She hoped Ridge would not make a scene in front of the others, even if he was surprised. Pride was a definite burden at times, and Kalena knew she had her full measure of it.

Ridge looked up as if sensing the anxiety she was experiencing and Kalena held her breath. Abruptly, he nodded once and refolded the contract.

"It's about time you got here," he said calmly. "Let's go someplace where we can discuss our business in private."

Kalena let go of the breath she had been holding and smiled brilliantly, aware of Arrisa's startled surprise and Hotch's thunderstruck expression. The older man practically sputtered in his haste to speak.

"Now just one minute, Fire Whip. I don't know what this is all about, but you can't just go racing off. I must have the information I need to finish this report for Quintel."

"I'll give you the information later." Ridge glanced at Kalena. "This, too, is Quintel's business, and I promise you it's more important than the report on the bandits operating in the Talon Pass. Besides, as of five days ago the bandits have ceased their raiding activities. Quintel knows that. I told him as soon as I got back from the pass. Your report is old news."

"But, Ridge . . ."

Ridge ignored the clerk and Arrisa as he moved toward Kalena with a sleek stride that was deceptively balanced. Kalena knew instinctively it was a fighter's stride. Before she could say farewell to Arrisa, Kalena found herself being steered toward the wide staircase at the end of the hall.

"Well, Kalena," Ridge growled softly as they started down the stairs, "you aren't quite what I expected, but I guess you'll have to do. Quintel always knows what he's doing, and if he's decided you're what I need on this trip, then he's probably right. Have you ever contracted out as a trade wife in the past?"

"No," she admitted, hitching her tunic up higher so that she could descend the stairs at his swift pace. She really was going to have to get some new clothes. "My aunt doesn't approve of trade marriages."

"Hardly surprising," he commented wryly. "Most properly brought up people don't approve of such arrangements. Your aunt must be desperate for the Sand."

Kalena remembered her cover story. "My aunt is a fine Healer, Ridge, but she is almost out of the Sands of Eurythmia. All the Healers in the Interlock valley are running low. There is no more to be had anywhere at home or even here in Crosspurposes. Since Quintel's traders have not been successful in bringing back fresh stores for many months, the Healers of the Interlock valley will have to stand in line behind the Healers of the large towns for a portion once a shipment does get through. You know that."

"But your aunt has cleverly decided that if she sends you along as a trade wife, she'll at least be guaranteed a portion of the cargo. I'll have to admit she's pretty sharp."

"My aunt is a highly intelligent woman, Ridge. She also has the talents of a natural Healer." Kalena spoke a little sharply, somewhat affronted by what she sensed was criticism. She had no great love for Aunt Olara, but Kalena was far too proud to allow others to criticize her only remaining relative. Whatever else could be said about Olara, she was the Lady of the House of the

Ice Harvest. As such she was entitled to a certain show of deference from a mere bastard.

"I don't doubt your aunt's intelligence one bit. After all, she was smart enough to convince Quintel to sign that contract. You do understand the terms of the agreement, don't you? You will be my wife for the duration of the journey. When we return to Crosspurposes, you get a ten percent share of the total cargo." Ridge smiled humorlessly. "That should be enough to make you a rich woman in the Interlock valley."

"Thirty percent," Kalena said quietly.

Ridge looked down at her, his eyes narrowed. "What?"

"I am to receive thirty percent of the total cargo," she pointed out politely, thinking it hardly mattered as she had absolutely no intention of going on the dangerous journey to the Heights of Variance. Her goal was far more immediate, and when it was accomplished the trade marriage for which she had been contracted would be automatically terminated. Aunt Olara had negotiated for the higher percentage merely to ensure that Quintel believed Kalena's cover story.

"I've never heard of Quintel negotiating away thirty percent of any cargo, let alone a shipment of Sand. Your aunt must be a remarkable woman."

"Oh, she is," Kalena said quite truthfully. "Where are we going?"

"To the trade baron's home. I stay with him when I'm going to be in town for a short while," Ridge explained casually. "This time I'll only be here long enough to make preparations for the trip to the Variance Mountains. Where's your luggage?"

"At the inn where I stayed last night."

"I'll send one of Quintel's servants to pick it up."

Kalena took a deep breath, astounded by how easy it was going to be. Olara had interpreted the auspicious omens correctly when she had gone into her Far Seeing trance two months ago. A strange excitement gripped Kalena as she and Ridge stepped out into the warm sunlight, but she tried to keep her voice calm as she said, "I was afraid you might be taken by surprise by the contract.

I knew it had been negotiated by Trade Baron Quintel in your absence."

Ridge shrugged. "I've been away for the past two months. There was some business in the Talon Pass that had to be handled. I knew Quintel was getting worried about the Sand trade, and it was hardly a surprise to find out he wanted me to check out the situation as soon as I returned. There would have been no time for me to find a suitable trade wife on my own, so it made sense for him to handle the matter for me."

"Yes," Kalena agreed in a distant voice, "quite sensible." Well, at least she didn't have any persuading to do. Ridge seemed quite content with the arrangement his employer had made, both for the trade marriage and for herself as the trade wife.

Kalena gazed at the sights around her with great interest. She had only been in Crosspurposes for a short time, and most of the sprawling, bustling town was still new to her. The distinctive pink stone that had been used in most of the buildings seemed to give everything a warm glow. In the warm end of the summer weather, the windows overlooking the streets were open to catch whatever breeze happened past. Few of the buildings were more than two stories, although a couple went as high as four levels.

Crosspurposes had sprung up at the juncture of several important trading routes. Precious gems from the Talon Pass, medicinal herbs and the Sands of Eurythmia from the Heights of Variance, and lanti hides and wool as well as grain from the plains of Antinomy all flowed through Crosspurposes and on to their final destinations. The town had become wealthy as a result of its fortunate location, and that wealth showed in the fine buildings, busy shops and well-dressed citizens.

The streets were active. Several carts pulled by the huge, flightless creetbirds rattled past with loads of produce and market goods. People thronged the stone walkways, the women in colorful, short tunics and trousers, the men in the more subdued shirts, pants and boots. Children bounced around or clung to their parents. A few stray cotlies darted across the streets and disappeared into alleys in search of food. The sight of the animals' long ears

and wagging tails made Kalena smile wistfully. Her pet cotly had
died the year before, and Olara had refused to allow her to replace
the small, furry beast. Perhaps her aunt had sensed how attached
Kalena had become to the animal. In Olara's mind, nothing must
be allowed to come between Kalena and her ultimate goal, least of
all any sort of emotional attachment.

The thing was, Kalena thought, Olara had never realized just
what Kalena's ultimate goal really was. It wasn't the assassination
Olara had planned for so many years. It was the new life she
would gain for herself afterward that kept Kalena so firmly fixed
on her course of action. True, before now she had had difficulty
trying to imagine that new life in detail. Her own lack of knowledge about the lives of the almost legendary freewomen she had
heard rumors about kept Kalena's vision for her own future hidden in a misty cloud, but she never doubted that it awaited her.
She sensed instinctively that after she had performed her duty to
her House, her own future would become clear and vivid.

"Do you think Trade Baron Quintel will object to my staying
in his house?" Kalena asked in a soft voice as Ridge stopped in
front of a massive, arched moonwood door. In another moment
she would enter the house of the man she had come to assassinate.

"He'd better not," Ridge said flatly. "He's the one responsible
for your being here, isn't he? He can damn well put a roof over
your head while we make the trip preparations." He reached up to
rattle a heavy metal doorknocker to the house of the man Kalena
had been sent to kill.

As Ridge waited for one of Quintel's servants to open the door,
he threw a sidelong glance to his companion. What had Quintel
done? he wondered. Finding out that he was expected to journey
to the Heights of Variance to discover what had happened to the
lucrative Sand trade had not surprised him. Learning that Quintel
had negotiated a trade marriage for his Whip while he had been
gone these last two months did not surprise Ridge. But discover-

ing that his short-term saddle wife was an innocent young woman straight off some farm in the Interlock valley *did* surprise him.

Trade wives, by nature, tended to be tough, shrewd creatures who were inured to the social criticism that was often their lot. Trade marriages were legal associations, but hardly socially acceptable among the middle or upper classes. Even a farmer's daughter would normally be above this kind of arrangement.

The regrettable fact of business was that the Healers of the Variance Mountains would not deal with a man. Healing was a skill that came from the Light end of the Spectrum, and as such it was the province of women. Trading was the province of men. When Quintel had opened up the Sand routes he had been forced to find a compromise; his answer was the concept of a trade marriage. With a little political pull, Quintel had gotten the arrangements recognized in law. As an additional incentive for women to contract such marriages, he gave trade wives on the Sand route a small percentage of the profits.

Women were involved in other trade activities, sometimes accompanying the traders as cooks and sleeping pallet companions, but that sort of arrangement was not satisfactory to the Healers of the Heights of Variance. They demanded that the women with whom they dealt be properly married, although no one was sure why. The High Healers of the Variance Valley were, after all, unmarried women themselves.

Ridge could see why Quintel had jumped at the chance of having a recognized Healer's niece along on this trip. Surely the niece of a Healer would have a certain tendency toward the Talent herself. It ran in families. Quintel was hoping that the High Healers of the Variance Valley, who had been refusing all trade lately, might look favorably on dealing with a woman who could be presumed to have a touch of the Talent. They certainly hadn't been favorably disposed toward any of the other women who had been sent along on the trade caravans to deal with them in the past few months. Quintel's profits had been suffering badly.

But even so, knowing what he did about the situation, Ridge had nevertheless found himself taken by surprise when he had turned around in Hotch's office and looked at Kalena for the first time.

His first thought was that she had eyes the color of the precious green crystals that miners wrested from the mountains near the Talon Pass. Cool, ice green eyes that waited to be ignited into green flames by the heat of a man. Ridge sucked in his breath as he realized that, with the aid of a trade marriage contract, he was going to be the man who awakened Kalena. This situation was going to prove interesting.

Her eyes were not the only thing that had caught his attention. There was a sunset in her hair. A mass of small, red-gold curls had been pulled back from her face and fell in a rich waterfall down her back to a point well below her shoulders. Ridge found himself wanting to thread his fingers through those curls. He wondered how they would look spread out on a pallet pillow.

Her face was not beautiful, but her clear, delicate features intrigued him. There was something striking about her faintly slanting eyes, high cheekbones and firm, straight nose. She was of average height for a woman. The top of her head would have just touched his jaw if she had been standing close enough to do so. He could bend his own head and kiss her easily in such a position.

The long-sleeved, purple tunic she wore over yellow trousers was belted to reveal a small waist and gently flaring, very feminine hips. Her breasts were full but delicate and sweetly curved. Ridge decided that they would fill his hand pleasantly. He also sensed that, were she to realize just what he was thinking, she would be shocked to the toes of her little velvet boots.

Ridge wondered just how much Aunt Olara had explained to her niece about a trade marriage. Kalena seemed to be treating the whole thing as a purely business matter. For an unsophisticated farmer's daughter who had probably never been out of the staid, conservative Interlock valley before in her life, that was a little odd.

Perhaps she didn't realize just how long and lonely the nights could get on the long trail to the Heights of Variance. Ah, well, there would be plenty of time to introduce his trade wife to the realities of business. For the first time since he had learned of his next assignment, Ridge began to look forward to it with a sense of anticipation. He was playing with that thought when the moonwood door to Quintel's mansion swung silently open. He stepped aside politely to allow Kalena to enter.

Ridge watched her walk across the threshold, his golden eyes filled with cool appraisal. She might be a farm girl, but she held herself with the dignity and grace of a Great House lady. He was a bastard, an unclaimed son of a Great House that chose to ignore his existence. But it occurred to Ridge as he followed Kalena through the door into the large hall that a man like himself, who was intent on founding his own House, could do worse than ally himself with a farm girl who knew how to walk like a lady.

There would be plenty of time on the journey to the Heights of Variance to decide if Kalena might turn out to be the woman who was destined to fit into the long-range future plans he had for himself.

The man they called the Fire Whip discovered he was looking forward to the journey.

TWO

By the stones, man," Quintel said, "at least admit a portion of the truth. I thought I did a fairly good job playing matchmaker. You would have done a lot worse on your own and you know it."

Ridge glanced at him from the other side of the room, aware of the faint humor edging his employer's slight smile. Quintel lounged in the round-backed chair, his black Risha cloth shirt and black trousers a sharp contrast to the snowy white cushions.

It was no accident that Quintel had dressed in black this evening and proceeded to entertain his guests in the Snow Room. The man had an eye for contrasts and opposites. He indulged his appreciation of them at every opportunity.

Quintel came naturally by his personal tastes. His hair was an unusual shade of silver gray that began at a peak above his high, intelligent forehead and was brushed straight back. The silvery shade was a strong counterpoint to the near blackness of his eyes which was, in turn, a contrast to the fairness of his skin. When he dressed in black, as he frequently did, he dominated any gathering. He most certainly dominated the white chamber in which he now sat.

Of course, Ridge decided objectively, even without such adornments, Quintel of the House of the Gliding Fallon would dominate any crowd. The wealthy descendant of an old, established Great House, he wore his inherited power and authority with unconscious masculine grace. He could be utterly charming, as he had been earlier that evening in Kalena's presence, or he could be quite ruthless, especially in business. Ridge knew better than most just how ruthless his employer could be.

According to town gossip, Quintel was no longer satisfied with operating some of the most lucrative trade routes in the Northern Continent. Some said he had his eye on a seat in the new Hall of Balance, the fledgling legislative assembly that represented the scattered towns and communities of the continent. The new central governing body was still feeling its way and the local communities were not about to surrender too many of their precious rights to it, but there was no doubt that the town of Concinnity, home of the Hall of Balance, was becoming a center of power. One of the more important prerogatives the Hall of Balance had recently assumed was the right to recognize and legitimize newly established Great Houses.

Physically, Quintel resembled the symbol of his proud House. His features were sharply aquiline, not unlike the bird of prey called a fallon. His body was lean and oddly slender. Ridge was aware that women often found Quintel fascinating, although everyone within his small circle of trusted employees knew he was not interested in females. He wasn't interested in men, either. In the years Ridge had worked for Quintel he had never known the House lord to demonstrate any real sensuality. Quintel's passions were reserved for his studies.

Quintel was the most learned man Ridge had ever met. His intellectual curiosity was wide ranging. He had developed a private library that was the envy of the University of the Spectrum and had, on several occasions, entertained masters who taught various subjects at the university. Such invitations were always eagerly accepted.

Quintel's personal interests might be centered on intellectual matters, but he also had a business empire to run. The company of other learned men might interest him, but he had a practical need for a man who could be trusted to handle the dirty side of things. Operating trade routes demanded a certain amount of muscle. Ridge could not even remember when people had begun calling him Quintel's Fire Whip.

Ridge walked across the room to a carved stone table and helped himself to another glass of warm red ale he was sharing with his employer. "All right, so you have hitherto unsuspected talents in the field of matchmaking. She isn't what I expected when you told me about her two days ago."

"You thought I would arrange for one of the professional trade wives to accompany you to the mountains?"

"It seemed logical."

Quintel shook his silvered head. "No, Ridge. Not logical at all. I want nothing to go wrong on this investigative journey of yours, and that includes the actual trade for the Sand. Your main task is to find out what has kept the last three trade masters and their parties from getting into the Healers' valley, but I also want a fresh supply of Sand. For that you need a woman, and my instincts tell me that this time you will need a woman with some share of the Healing Talent, someone the Healers are likely to accept. Even before the trade masters and their caravans began returning empty-handed, the High Healers of Variance were becoming increasingly difficult. Women, no matter how talented, have a way of making unnecessary difficulties." Quintel grimaced wryly. "The Healers had begun cutting back on the routine orders from their various medicinal concoctions and they were refusing to trade the usual amounts of Sand. The trade masters in charge told me it was because the Healers weren't getting along with the trade wives who had been contracted for the journeys. They claimed they didn't find them *acceptable*." Quintel's fine mouth curved downward in another disgusted grimace. "The Healers of Variance said the wives in question were neither real wives nor women with any share of the Healing Talent. They didn't want to deal with them. Then I started getting reports of some sort of barrier across the pass. After that no one who set out for the Heights of Variance was able to get through."

"Even if I am successful, I won't be able to bring back much Sand, let alone any of the Healers' potions. I'll only have room for what I and the woman can carry in our saddlebags. I can't take any pack creets with me, Quintel. It would slow me down too much."

Quintel nodded, taking a sip of his ale from the elegantly chased goblet he was holding in one hand. "I only need a single shipment, just enough to prove that I can still supply the damn stuff. When you return with the problems resolved, I will dispatch a major trade party."

Ridge walked to the window to gaze out into the garden. As did most private homes in Crosspurposes, Quintel's large house was focused inward around its many exotic gardens. On the street side, windows were few and narrow, designed to keep out the dust and noise of the town while allowing some cross ventilation. But inside, all rooms opened onto lush greenery and flower scented air. There was a red sheen of light on the exquisitely designed garden outside the Snow Room's window tonight. Symmetra, the red moon of Zantalia, was at full strength. Ridge studied the beautiful scene with absent interest as he thought about Quintel's words.

"Has someone questioned your ability to bring back Sand?" Ridge asked softly.

Quintel hesitated and then admitted, "The subject arose in the last meeting of the Town Council. I assured the members that the problems were temporary and that normal trade levels would resume soon."

"They would not dare take the route from you and give it to another." Ridge spoke with absolute certainty.

"No one is above the power of the council, Ridge. The Sand is considered a crucial trade item here in Crosspurposes. It's one of the things that gives the town its wealth and a lot of its power. If the town is threatened with a loss of that route because the trade baron in charge can't control it, then the council will act to preserve the route. We both know that."

Ridge turned away from the window. "You'll have your Sand when I return," he promised evenly.

Quintel smiled. "I know." There was a slight pause. "I should mention one other detail. While the caravans have returned empty-handed, my last investigator did not return at all."

"Who did you send?"

"Trantel."

Ridge considered that. "He's good."

"I have reason to believe he's dead."

Ridge frowned. "The Healers might become stubborn or difficult, but they would never kill. Healers *can't* kill. Everyone knows that."

Quintel shrugged. "I don't know what's going on, Fire Whip. That's why I'm sending you to find out."

The two men silently regarded each other across the width of the white room. They had no need to discuss the mission further. Ridge had been given his assignment; he would complete it. Both accepted that as a fact.

"About the woman," Quintel finally said slowly.

"What about her? You picked her, I assume you knew what you were doing, even if you are new at the matchmaking business," Ridge said casually.

Quintel waved aside the mocking comment. "She's our best bet as far as dealing with the Healers of Variance. True, she's not a professional Healer herself, but her aunt is, and presumably Talent is in the family's female line. It usually is. Kalena might not have enough of the Talent to enter training as a Healer, but even a touch of it would increase our chances of getting the High Healers in the mountains to deal with her."

"No chance of getting a proven Healer?"

"Unfortunately, no. Healers are proud. Most would consider themselves far above the level of a trade wife. By the Stones, the most talented and dedicated among them become High Healers, move to the Heights of Variance and shun the company of men altogether." Quintel's disparaging tone made it clear that he, in common with other men, failed to comprehend such stubborn independence. "Regular Healers and women with a touch of the Talent are almost always married. They are considered excellent wife material. A Healer adds prestige to any House, large or small. No true Healer need settle for the role of trade wife. And what man would allow his woman to travel as a trade wife, even for the sake of a share of the Sand?"

Ridge's mouth curved faintly. "By the Dark end of the Spectrum, I certainly wouldn't."

"No," Quintel agreed with a knowing look, "you least of all. You have as much pride as any Great House lord, don't you?"

"Even though I'm only a bastard?" Ridge concluded bitterly. "Why not say it, Quintel? We both know it's true."

"Your birth status will only be a temporary handicap for you, Ridge. I am as certain of that as I am of Symmetra's full status each month," Quintel said evenly. "The time will come when you will found your own House and it will be a Great one. I may have picked you up off the streets of Countervail and taught you your manners, but the fires of the man you are today have always burned within you. They will take you far."

"Soon," Ridge said almost to himself. "Very soon."

"Possibly at the end of this venture," Quintel drawled gently. "If you prove as good at seducing a woman as you are at handling a sintar."

Ridge's head came around with a swift, inquiring movement. "What are you talking about?"

"I am talking about giving you the full profits of your journey." Quintel took another swallow of ale while he waited for his words to sink in. "Less the thirty percent that goes to the woman and her aunt, naturally. In addition, I intend to turn a percentage of the route itself over to you. I was thinking of somewhere around twenty percent. In exchange, you will operate that route for me in the future."

Ridge waited tensely. "I don't understand."

"Yes, you do." Quintel leaned forward, his dark eyes suddenly intent. "It is vital to me that the trade route be reopened and that a certain amount of Sand be brought back to prove that I can still manage the route. But beyond that, I am not interested in a profit on this venture. Whatever the Sand brings when you return to Crosspurposes is yours. As for the future arrangement, I will admit that I'm growing tired of devoting so much of my time and attention to managing the trade routes I own. I wish to turn some of the burden over to others without losing complete control of the routes. Who else can I trust as much as I trust you, Fire Whip? Think of it, Ridge. The more Sand you bring back, the richer you will be. If you bring back a sufficient quantity and deal it shrewdly, you might make enough to begin establishing your House. Add to that financial basis a slice of all future income from the Sand route and you have what I hope will be a very attractive incentive. Money is the root from which power springs. It takes both money and power to found a Great House."

Ridge felt the adrenaline flood his bloodstream as if he were facing an armed attacker. But instead of deadly anger, he felt a fierce elation. Only after taking a deep, slow breath could he say, "You are very generous, Quintel."

"No. I am practical. You have served me long and well, Ridge. I owe you a great deal. Sooner or later you will found your House. Nothing short of death would stop you. I understand that the goal is the most important thing in your life. Very well. I can repay the years of service and loyalty you have given me with the chance to make your fortune in one single venture."

Ridge met the other man's gaze. "I don't know what to say."

Quintel smiled. "Say nothing to me. But you might spend a little time talking to Kalena. Actually, it's going to take more than a little conversation, I'm afraid. You will need her willing cooperation on this trip, Ridge."

Ridge narrowed his gaze. "She's willing enough. Her share of the profits are quite an incentive."

"That's not what I mean. You're going to have to seduce her, Trade Master. Quite thoroughly. You're going to have to make a real wife out of her. Ridge, when the last two trade masters who got through to the Healers' valley returned, they said the High Healers had begun complaining because the trade women weren't 'true' wives."

"Surely by that point in the journey the trade masters were sleeping with the women they had brought along," Ridge observed wryly. "There was a marriage document to make it all legal. What more was needed?"

"The Healers of the valley understood this, but they still refused to accept the relationships."

"Why not?"

"For some reason known only to them, they did not consider the marriages valid, even though they accepted such marriages in the past. They had no adequate explanation, but as near as the trade masters could tell, it had something to do with a lack of bonding between the wives and the traders. The existence of a sexual relationship and a piece of paper declaring the marriages legal are no longer enough for the Healers of Variance, it seems. They want more."

"How much more is there?" Ridge asked blankly.

Quintel sighed. "I'm not sure. A link, perhaps. An emotional bond between the man and the woman involved. Something understood by the woman, at least, to be more than a business arrangement. You know how women are," he added. "So emotional. Apparently, previous trade wives have been quite open with the High Healers concerning the temporary nature of the trade marriage. It would seem the Healers have begun to object. Who can fully comprehend the Healers of Variance or women in general? The impression I received was that they wished to deal with a woman who was not in the marriage strictly as a business partner. I think, Ridge, that by the time you reach the mountains, you had better have your trade wife bound to you with more than just a formal marriage contract. That, Trade Master, is where your talents in the art of seduction will be put to the test."

Ridge stared at him. "I still don't understand."

"All I'm saying, Ridge, is that you'd better try wooing the lady.

By the time you reach the Heights of Variance, make certain she is committed to you and to the relationship. The Healers will be able to tell, and if they don't find her truly *married* on an emotional level, they won't deal, even if you find a way past this barrier they have erected across the pass."

Ridge swore softly. "By the Stones, you're determined to make this venture as difficult as possible, aren't you?"

"It's not me who's making life difficult for you. Blame those illogical, female Healers."

"I'm supposed to make certain Kalena feels committed to me by the time we reach the mountains even though the relationship ends when we return to Crosspurposes?"

Quintel nodded. "Yes. Even though it will end then. The process by which a woman is convinced to trust her emotions rather than her intellect is called seduction. You'd better be prepared to practice that particular art."

Ridge laughed mirthlessly. "You may have picked the wrong man for this job, Quintel. I might be reasonably good at cutting throats for you, but seducing a woman takes real skill. I've never been especially good at it."

"I have great confidence in you, Fire Whip. Especially with the incentive I have provided you."

Ridge thought about the chance at the future he had always dreamed of that Quintel was offering him. "It should prove to be an interesting journey."

"I'm sure it will be," Quintel agreed.

Ridge contemplated the task that lay before him; then he smiled faintly as a stray thought crossed his mind. "She showed excellent manners at dinner this evening, didn't she?" He was aware of an odd sense of pride in the fact. "You'd never know she was raised on an Interlock farm."

"Whatever her heritage, there are Healers in her family. They are a cut above the average farm House woman and they know it. Kalena has undoubtedly been given a fairly decent education and some training in manners and deportment. She did, indeed, behave herself very well this evening. A most charming guest."

If one overlooked the fact that she seemed particularly fascinated with Quintel, Ridge thought, remembering the times he had caught Kalena covertly studying her host as they dined. Kalena's curiosity about Quintel had annoyed Ridge on some level. He would have to explain to her that even if Quintel did have a weakness for women, which he did not, he was not an option for Kalena. She was contracted to marry Ridge, and he would see to it that she abided by the terms of that contract in thought as well as deed. Nothing was going to stop him from returning from the Heights of Variance with a shipment of Sand. Ridge got to his feet with a sudden sense of decisiveness. No better time than the present to begin making certain of Kalena's sense of commitment. He smiled rather grimly at his lord.

"You have not set me a simple task, Quintel. You realize, of course, that even though she's only a farmer's daughter, she can still claim a better heritage than I can."

Quintel gave him an odd, understanding look. "You have spent most of your life proving to me and everyone else that the fact you were born a bastard wasn't going to keep you from taking what you wanted in this world. Surely you're not going to let a mere country girl intimidate you. Besides, once she's been a trade wife, she can hardly claim more respectability than you can."

Ridge shrugged. "Perhaps. I wonder if she knows."

"Knows what? That you have no House name? I'm sure she does by now. There won't be any lack of people willing to inform her that you grew up on the streets of Countervail without the benefit of a father's name. I wouldn't let it worry you."

Ridge's jaw tightened as he pushed old memories aside. There was no point thinking of those early days. He had escaped from the poverty and the brutality of that world and the life that had killed his mother. She had been worn out before Ridge was even eight. She had died of some respiratory disease that could easily have been cured by a Healer, if his mother could have afforded one. No, his mother hadn't survived the grinding life of the streets, but Ridge had. Quintel was right. Ridge wasn't going to let his past concern him now. His goals were within reach, and if seizing his destiny meant first having to seduce and control his new trade wife, then so be it.

"If you will excuse me, I think I will go to my chamber. It's late and I've had a full day." Ridge started for the door.

Quintel set down his goblet. "It's time for me to retire also. I still have my studies to attend to this evening."

Ridge smiled. "Has anything ever kept you from your appointed hours of study?"

"Nothing," Quintel said simply. He rose, his black-clad body looking ascetically thin. "Iwis will be at my study door any minute now with my evening glass of Encana wine."

Ridge nodded and turned to leave the room. "I wish you good evening, then, my lord."

"Ah, Ridge, there is just one other thing."

Ridge halted and turned to confront his employer warily. "Yes?"

"This marriage of yours . . . I think we should celebrate it properly."

Ridge eyed the other man. "It's a business arrangement. It needs no celebration."

"For the woman's sake, Ridge. It will make the arrangement seem more of a real marriage to her. More romantic, more emotionally binding. Besides," Quintel said, allowing himself one of his rare grins, "I have a mind to see you properly wedded, my boy. You have always escaped the necessity of taking a trade wife in the past. Who knows? First time out may prove lucky for you. This contract you have with Kalena might become permanent. I think we should give you both a proper send-off."

"You've decided to indulge your odd sense of humor at my expense, haven't you, Quintel?" Ridge said with a stifled groan.

Quintel's grin disappeared. "My instincts tell me the wedding would be a good first step for this venture. I want all the luck on the Spectrum I can get for this trip."

"Putting me through the paces of a formal wedding ceremony strikes you as lucky?"

"Don't complain. I'll be paying for it."

"Somehow," Ridge said as he turned again to leave, "I have a feeling I'll be the one who winds up paying. One way or another."

He opened the curved moonwood door, the only point of color in the all-white room, and walked down the hall with a feeling of deep irritation. He would kill for Quintel if the necessity arose, and had done it more than once in the past. But being forced to endure a full-scale wedding ceremony when the bride was merely destined to be a short-term trade wife was almost too much. He wondered how Kalena would take the news.

Ridge left the softly lit hall and stepped out into the oblong moonlit garden that divided Quintel's side of the house from the servants' quarters and the guestrooms. Quintel was a gracious host, but he insisted on his own privacy, regardless of how many people he chose to entertain under his expansive roof. No one violated Quintel's private sphere without permission.

Ridge could have walked all the way around the garden under the shelter of the colonnaded portico that surrounded it. But tonight the garden paths of gleaming, iridescent rainstone were far too inviting to ignore. The rainstone was bathed in the red glow of Symmetra, reflecting the moonlight with almost unbelievable brilliance. Ridge glanced up at the red orb and decided Quintel probably knew what he was doing. He usually did. The time of the month when Symmetra was at its fullest was an auspicious time to begin a major venture. A full moon was traditionally a trader's moon, and although he was not strictly a trader, Ridge had his share of belief in trading luck. In his view there was always room for the random appearance of luck at any point along the Spectrum, even if a man had to create that luck for himself.

He was halfway across the garden, almost to the black and white onyxite fountain with its shimmering black and white spray of water, when Ridge realized his quarry was not waiting conveniently in her chamber. He stopped, unconsciously using the shadow of the perfectly proportioned fountain to shield himself as he watched Kalena make her way through the garden. Perhaps the light of the red moon on the rainstones had lured her from her room. Or perhaps she was simply restless. Ridge wished he knew more about women in general. He sometimes found it very difficult to tell what they were thinking, even more difficult to tell what motivated them. But could a man be expected to understand that which sprang from the Light end of the Spectrum? He could only do his best to control it.

He watched Kalena for a moment, aware that he found her pleasing to look at in the moonlight. Her hair was a tumbled mass of red tinted curls, her light colored tunic an odd shade of gold beneath Symmetra's glare. She moved with the grace he had noted earlier and it made him wonder how she would move beneath him in bed. Something within him suddenly ached to find out. He was considering his unexpectedly fierce physical reaction when he realized she was heading for the portico that ran along Quintel's side of the large house.

Kalena didn't realize anyone else was in the garden until Ridge spoke quietly from directly behind her. At the sound of his voice, she whirled around, startled.

"Those are the trade baron's apartments," Ridge said quietly, his eyes unreadable in the red moonlight. "No one goes into that portion of the house without an invitation from Quintel himself."

Kalena struggled to regain her poise. "I'm sorry. I did not realize I was on the verge of intruding. This house is so large, it's easy to become confused." That last bit was true. The house, with its two stories of spacious rooms and its endless gardens, was far larger than any home she had ever seen, even the half-remembered Great House of her early childhood. The mansion was made up of a sequence of rooms and gardens perfectly designed to present contrast after contrast. Circles and ovals were separated by squares, rectangles and oblongs, each room carefully proportioned to compliment the adjoining chambers and gardens.

But Kalena's reference to the elaborateness of the house was only a ruse, and she hoped Ridge would not realize that she wasn't as lost as she claimed to be. She had known very well that she was nearing Quintel's apartments, having casually asked a servant to explain the layout of the house. An assassin needed to make plans, and to do that she needed to know Quintel's evening routine. Olara's instructions were certainly detailed, but Kalena knew she would feel more confident of herself if she checked matters out firsthand. She had been attempting to discover more about Quintel's evening habits just when Ridge startled her.

In the red moonlight Ridge's expression was austere, almost cruel. Standing in the shadows, he seemed very large and intimidating. She was far too conscious of his size and strength—and of something else. With a shock, Kalena suddenly realized that something in this man compelled her on a deep, primitive level. The realization frightened her for an instant, because she knew this man was not for her. There would doubtless be men in her free future, but she didn't see how Ridge could be among them. He was tied to Quintel, and when her mission was over, Kalena would start down a new and different path. Her very safety would depend on her never seeing Ridge again. Quintel would appear to have died of natural causes, but Kalena wouldn't want to stick around to take chances on anyone getting suspicious. More importantly, Olara had forbidden her niece to explore the most dangerous of temptations: sexual freedom. Kalena knew Olara's injunction did not stem from her aunt's notions of proper female behavior, but from a firm belief that the discovery of her own sensuality would spell disaster for Kalena's mission.

"Never mind," Ridge said, taking firm hold of her arm.

"I'll guide you back to your quarters. I wish to speak to you, anyway."

Kalena glanced at him uneasily. "Of course, Trade Master."

"I think you had better drop the title and start calling me Ridge."

"Very well. As you wish."

He said nothing for a moment, walking in silence while he gathered his thoughts. Kalena waited anxiously, wondering what he was finding so difficult to discuss.

"Quintel has decided he would like to give us a proper wedding," Ridge finally stated somewhat aggressively, as if he expected an argument.

Kalena relaxed, relieved that she wasn't about to be interrogated about her activities in the garden. "That's very generous of him." A large wedding, Kalena thought, just as Olara had predicted.

"Quintel has decided a proper wedding ceremony would be a good way to start our journey," Ridge continued, his voice still heavy with the weight of authority. "He is not a man to ignore omens and he has what I suppose you could call a feeling for situations that is sometimes amazing."

"He sounds a good deal like my aunt," Kalena observed tartly. "Does he go into trances, too?"

Ridge muttered something crude under his breath. "Of course not. That's a female thing. No man would pretend he was capable of going into a Far Seeing trance."

Kalena smiled impishly. "You mean a man would be too embarrassed to admit he had been endowed with such a female talent?"

Ridge made an obvious bid for patience. "I only meant to imply that my employer has excellent instincts—trader's instincts. Furthermore, he is nothing short of brilliant. I never argue with him when he makes a firm decision." Ridge broke off and then added reluctantly, "Or at least I don't argue with him very much. He's almost always right."

"And because he has decided you and I are to go through this farce of a wedding, you have decided it's a good idea?" She couldn't resist teasing him when he was so obviously ambivalent about having a full-scale wedding ceremony.

Ridge hesitated. "He's convinced it will contribute toward the successful completion of this venture," he finally said very formally.

"Hmm. Which, translated, means he thinks the High Healers of Variance might be more disposed to deal with me if I seem more like a real wife to them. He's hoping a proper wedding might make me appear more truly married, isn't he?"

Ridge halted abruptly and turned to look down at her. His golden eyes gleamed with a reluctant admiration. "It would seem you have your own fair share of female intuition."

"I prefer to think of it as an ability to reason with masculine logic," she murmured, knowing that the comment would irritate him. Men did not like to admit that women were capable of great feats of logic. Logic was considered a masculine talent, a gift that had its origins at the Dark end of the Spectrum. To her surprise, Ridge did not rise to the bait.

"I won't argue fine points with you this evening, Kalena. The final verdict is that you and I will be going through a formal ceremony in three day's time. I suppose you had better buy a wedding cloak," he added vaguely. "Get whatever you need and tell the shopkeepers to send the bill to me. You better purchase a few things for the trail, too. I'll make a list. While you're at it you can pick up a couple of new shirts for me."

Kalena raised her eyebrows mockingly. "You are beginning to sound like a husband already."

To her surprise, Ridge took the comment seriously. "Yes, I am, aren't I? Do you feel like a bride, Kalena?"

"No," she said bluntly. "As far as I am concerned, this is all playacting." And her role in the play would end when she had completed her duty. "What we have between us is nothing more than a business arrangement."

Ridge eyed her narrowly, then settled his hands on her shoulders. Kalena felt the weight and strength of him and drew a deep breath. She saw in his eyes that Ridge had just come to some inner decision. In that moment she did not know whether to regret he had found her in the garden or be glad. She was not accustomed to the company of men in general, and never had she stood alone in the moonlight with a man's hard hands on her shoulders. For an instant she was afraid, and then she reminded herself that soon she would be starting a whole new life, one that was certain to include men. Surely allowing herself a small taste of what the future might hold would do no real harm to her mission.

"Perhaps," Ridge drawled, his voice dangerously soft, "I

should take my duties as a husband-to-be seriously. If I am going to be made to feel like a husband, Kalena, then I think you should be made to feel more like a wife."

Kalena stood very still, excitement shafting through her as she realized he was going to kiss her. For an instant a vision of her aunt's outraged face rose to haunt her. Olara would be horrified. In truth, Kalena was slightly horrified herself. She had been telling herself for days that someday soon she would learn what it was like to be held by a man. Indeed, she had been looking forward to it with a nervous anticipation. But quite suddenly the moment was upon her, and she wasn't as certain as she had been about what she wanted. It wasn't that she feared the embrace, Kalena realized abruptly; it was that she wasn't at all sure Ridge was the right man with whom to experiment. So much was at stake.

She stirred belatedly as he lowered his head, but by then it was much too late. His hands tightened on her shoulders, pulling her closer to his waiting strength, and his mouth was on hers.

Kalena felt curiously suspended in the red moonlight, as if she was no longer completely herself but was somehow on the verge of becoming joined with another—her born opposite. The sensation was disorienting, unlike anything she had experienced before. Very distantly, Olara's warnings rang in her ears: *You must not surrender to a man's embrace until you have done your duty and avenged the honor of your House. Such an act would be extremely dangerous for you.* But surely Olara had meant the complete act of making love, Kalena told herself. What harm could there be in a kiss?

Ridge's mouth moved on her lips, slowly, inevitably taking control, and then demanding a response. Kalena briefly felt his teeth in a tiny nip that took her by surprise. She parted her lips in astonishment. Before she could utter a protest he was there, inside her mouth, his tongue exploring and tasting her with a boldness that left her breathless.

Kalena moaned faintly and felt Ridge's hands slip from her shoulders down her spine and to the small of her back. Her arms went around his neck and she heard him inhale deeply. She had a fleeting impression that Ridge, too, was feeling unexpectedly disoriented, as if the kiss wasn't turning out quite as he had anticipated. She could have sworn the large, strong hands that held her had trembled slightly. But almost immediately he seemed to regain control of both himself and the situation. His palms curved around her full hips as he urged her forcefully against the hardness of his lower body. She did not sense a calculated sensual expertise in Ridge's embrace, but rather a determined hunger that seemed to have taken Ridge as much by surprise as it did her.

Kalena's mind was suddenly spinning with the excitement of sensually clashing opposites. Her gently curving breasts were crushed against his tautly muscled chest. Ridge spread his booted feet and her soft thighs were trapped between the hard lines of his legs. She felt his strong, blunt fingers luxuriating in the lush shape of her buttocks and heard him groan. The heat of his mouth was colliding with the coolness of her own, bringing alive sensations that she had never experienced.

No wonder the sexual act was considered an example of a perfect union of opposing forces, Kalena thought. If a mere kiss brought such incredibly sweet devastation to her senses, she could only imagine what sharing a pallet with Ridge would do to her.

She opened her eyes bemusedly when Ridge finally released her mouth. In the red moon's light she looked up at him, her lips still parted, her eyes half-veiled behind her lashes. Ridge studied her face for a long moment, his own expression shadowed and brooding. Then he lifted his hand to touch her hair.

"The color of a sunset," he muttered, twisting his fingers through her thick curls. "The time of day when light and dark meet and embrace."

Kalena said nothing, aware that she was waiting for something and not sure how to ask for it. Ridge's finger dropped from her hair to the line of her jaw. He ran his thumb along it with a touch that was all the more sensual by virtue of its obvious restraint. His eyes never left hers as he moved his hand lower, slipping it down the column of her throat until his palm settled on her breast.

Through the fabric of her tunic Kalena was vividly aware of his touch. His palm glided across her nipple and she felt her own response. An unfamiliar warmth flooded through her body and she knew Ridge was aware of it because he let his hand trail farther down and slide over the small curve of her stomach until his palm rested on the focus of the strange, heady heat that was filling her veins.

Kalena continued to stand very still, not daring to move. Their eyes were locked together and she knew only an outside force could break the contact. From a far corner of her mind, one of Olara's teachings emerged to taunt and warn her: *When perfectly opposing points on the Spectrum are brought into close proximity, the power they generate can be devastating.* Kalena knew then that for better or worse, the luck of the Spectrum had ordained that she meet her perfect opposite when she encountered the man they called the Fire Whip.

And that thought was the jarring interruption Kalena needed to break the dangerous contact. Drawing a deep breath, she gathered her senses and stepped back a pace, aware that she was trembling. Her arms fell from around Ridge's neck. He made no move to stop her, merely watching her with an intentness that was almost alarming.

"I wish you good evening, Ridge." As if pulling free of a delicate but sticky web, she took another step back. Instinct told her she should run, not walk from Ridge's presence. She turned away.

"Kalena." His voice was strangely harsh, deeper and more husky than usual. "There is one other thing we should discuss this evening."

She didn't turn around, but she did pause on the rainstone path. "What is that?"

"I am the man you are contracted to marry."

"I'm aware of that."

"Quintel is not for you. Not for any woman, for that matter.

But females are often foolishly fascinated by him. Don't let your curiosity lead you to try anything reckless or stupid."

If anything was needed to break the passionate spell of the red moonlight, that was it. Kalena's chin lifted with cool arrogance. Did this Houseless bastard think he could give lectures on behavior to a daughter of a Great House? Even if she were only the farmer's daughter she pretended to be, he was still out of line.

"Remember that you are merely going to be playing the role of husband, Ridge. Don't let your sense of duty go to your head."

"The marriage might be contracted for only a short period of time," Ridge said evenly, "but it is very real while it lasts. Do not forget that, Kalena."

She ignored him, forcing herself to walk sedately along the rainstone path until she reached the shelter of the portico. There, hidden by the shadows of the graceful colonnade, she picked up the hem of her tunic and dashed for the safety of her apartment.

THREE

Ripples of brilliantly hued sarsilk floated through Kalena's fingers. She stared in delighted wonder at the array of fabrics spread before her. The collection of expensive sarsilk brought all the way from Antipodes was only a portion of what was available here on Weavers Street.

Today she had seen velvets in every color of the Spectrum, from fine lanti wool for winter cloaks and tunics to beautifully woven Risha cloth, a fabric made locally in town. Kalena had never had such an array and she was almost overwhelmed by the prospect of choosing her selection. But even more amazing to her was the knowledge that she wouldn't have to sew these garments herself. For the first time since she had been a child, someone else could be paid to make clothes for her. Kalena wanted to laugh at the small sense of freedom that fact gave her. Not that she minded sewing, but having someone else do it was so much more pleasant. Standing on the threshold of real freedom was a giddy experience.

"The tunics are no problem," remarked the shopkeeper, a

strong-featured woman of middle years and extensive bargaining skill. "I can have those ready this afternoon. The riding clothes will be ready by tomorrow. The trousers should be properly fitted for comfort, you understand."

Kalena nodded. She wanted the stylish new tunics as quickly as possible, but there was no great urgency about the riding outfit. After all, she had no intention of leaving on the contracted journey with Ridge. She had only ordered the riding clothes because Ridge was sure to ask if she had. Kalena had given much consideration to the matter of who should pay for the riding garments and the wedding cloak. Ridge expected to do so and she had finally convinced herself that there was nothing dishonorable in allowing him to pay the bills.

After all, once Quintel was dead, a journey to the Heights of Variance would be impossible until another trade baron had been approved by the Town Council. With its reason for existing in the first place gone, the marriage contract would, no doubt, by mutual agreement be cancelled. But Kalena could hardly explain to Ridge why the equipment and clothes for the journey were unnecessary, so she really had no choice but to let him pay for them.

Kalena was relieved by her decision. The issue might involve a fine point of honor, but for the daughter of a Great House, even the finest points were important. Nodding with satisfaction, she turned to the shopkeeper and said, "I will also need a wedding cloak."

The woman's eyes lit up with mercantile enthusiasm. This farmer's daughter did not appear to be wealthy, but even a woman from a farm town would want to spend as much as possible on a wedding cloak. With a little ingenuity it might be possible to coax this client into spending more than she had originally planned. "But of course. I have several suitable fabrics in stock. The sarsilk is considered appropriate. Have you decided upon a color?"

It was the bride's right to choose the color in which she would be married. The matter was important because the groom was obliged by convention to wear a man's cloak in a properly contrasting color. Traditionally, brides chose pale colors from the

Light end of the Spectrum, making it easy for their grooms to find a suitable counterpoint. But Kalena thought this was as good a time as any to begin her permanent break with tradition.

"Something in red," Kalena said smoothly, a perverse sense of humor making her finger a piece of scarlet sarsilk. Red was an assertive choice. There was little that could counter it. Kalena looked forward to seeing how Ridge met the challenge.

The shopkeeper raised one eyebrow but said nothing. The scarlet sarsilk was very expensive and she was not about to kill a good sale by reminding the bride that she was flying in the face of convention. "I have no cloak available in this fabric, but I can have it made up by tomorrow afternoon. When is the wedding?"

"The day after tomorrow," Kalena said, moving along the counter to examine a bolt of green Risha cloth. "Have the cloak sent to the House of the Gliding Fallon. And send the bill for it and the riding clothes to the man named Ridge who works for the lord of that House. I will pay for everything else."

"The House of the Gliding Fallon?" The interest in the shopkeeper's eyes quickened. "You are to be married to an employee of Trade Baron Quintel?"

Before Kalena could respond, the wooden door of the shop swung open and a familiar voice answered the question. "I saw the contract, myself, Melita. This farmer's daughter is indeed going to marry a man who works for Lord Quintel, and her groom is no mere servant of the House, believe me. Ridge is almost a son of the House." Arrisa turned, a brilliant smile of greeting on her face. "Hello, Kalena."

Kalena returned the other woman's smile tentatively. "I wish you good morning, Arrisa. Are you shopping on Weavers Street today?"

"Umm," Arrisa murmured offhandedly. "I need a new pair of boots but I thought I saw you come in here and I decided to see how things went yesterday. What do you think of your future trade husband?"

Kalena hesitated briefly, remembering the scene in the moonlit garden. "I found him formidable in some respects," she admitted dryly.

Good-natured laughter burst from Arrisa as she sauntered over to the counter. "Formidable. I like that. What a pretty way of putting it. It would be most amusing to discuss the matter with you on the morning after your wedding night when you are serving your husband his yant tea."

Kalena smiled politely, hiding her embarrassment. It seemed that almost any subject was acceptable on the streets of Crosspurposes. She was aware of the old custom of a wife rising in the morning to brew and serve yant tea to her husband before he left the pallet. Kalena had vague memories of her mother performing the small ritual for her father. No matter how rich a House or how many servants it employed, the wife alone made her husband's morning tea. The standard joke among married men was that they judged the mood of their wives by the bitterness or sweetness of the drought that was served.

"Has anyone told you yet why Ridge is called Fire Whip?" Arrisa asked conversationally.

"You told me yesterday that he is called Quintel's whip because the trade baron uses him to clear up trading difficulties on the routes," Kalena answered carefully.

Arrisa waved that aside. "I am referring to the fire part of his name, not the whip. Has no one told you the rumors?"

Kalena's mouth curved downward. "I get the impression gossip is not encouraged in the House of the Gliding Fallon. The servants are a very silent lot."

Arrisa grinned. "That doesn't surprise me. Quintel can afford anything, even silence from his servants. Well, Kalena, since you are going to be sharing a sleeping pallet with Ridge, perhaps you should be told why there is fire in his name. I feel a sisterly obligation to warn you. Women have to stick together, don't we?" Her voice lowered and automatically both Kalena and the shopkeeper leaned closer. "It is said that he is one of those rare men who can make the steel of Countervail glow red with the force of his anger."

For an instant hushed silence filled the shop. Even the woman behind the counter was taken aback. She stared at Arrisa while Kalena frowned, trying to remember the tales. "The stories of such men are just that for the most part," she finally protested. "Mere yarns woven by the story spinners. It is said there are such men in every generation, but they are very few and far between. The odds of encountering one are unbelievably high."

Arrisa shrugged. "The stories surrounding Ridge are strong enough to have given him a name. There must be some element of truth to them."

"It takes little to hang a name on a man," the shopkeeper pointed out.

"True, but why this name on this particular man?" Arrisa countered.

"Perhaps because the trade master is possessed of a quick temper," Kalena said placatingly, not wishing to argue over the matter. "Legend has it that the ability to heat the steel of Countervail goes hand-in-hand with a savage temper."

"Most men have bad tempers," the shopkeeper pointed out philosophically. "It has always seemed to me that it takes very little to anger a man. Since my husband died I have not been in any hurry to remarry because of that fact. The calm at home has been a relief. And the profits from this shop are all mine to spend as I see fit."

"The kind of fury it takes to make the steel of Countervail glow with the heat of fire is only distantly related to your average dose of masculine temper," Arrisa announced. "Personally, if I were you I would be cautious, Kalena. You have contracted a dangerous marriage."

"It is merely a business arrangement," Kalena insisted mildly. She turned to the shopkeeper. "Please have the cloak made up in the red sarsilk. I'll pick up the tunics later this afternoon."

"And the riding outfit?" the shopkeeper asked quickly, making notes with an ink-filled quill.

Kalena thought about it for a moment, wondering if she

would ever wear the garment. "Have it made up in the dark green."

"Excellent." The shopkeeper smiled in satisfaction. "I have your measurements. I will set the seamstress to work immediately. Now, the bill for the cloak and the riding clothes go to this Ridge at the House of the Gliding Fallon, but the other garments you will be paying for yourself?"

Kalena caught the not-so-subtle hint. She removed the small wallet from the belt she wore at her waist and began counting out grans. The heavy coins clinked on the countertop under the shopkeeper's watchful eye. When a suitable stack of them had been set out the woman smiled again and scooped them into a drawer.

Arrisa watched the transaction with interest before falling into step beside Kalena, who made to leave the shop. "What's next? Boots, perhaps?"

"Yes," Kalena admitted, "and a couple of shirts for Ridge."

"Aha. Has you buying his shirts already, does he? The man means to take full advantage of the convenience of a wife. The next thing you know he'll have you embroidering his initials on his garments." Arrisa laughed, then turned to Kalena with narrowed eyes. "That business with a cloak . . ."

"For some reason Trade Baron Quintel wishes to have a formal ceremony to seal the contract," Kalena explained as they stepped out onto the stone path.

"And Ridge will humor him, of course. Ridge will do just about anything for the trade baron. Remember that, Kalena," Arrisa said with unexpected seriousness. "Ridge's first loyalty will always be to Quintel. It's said that Quintel rescued him from a life on the streets of Countervail and since the day they met, Ridge has repaid him with absolute loyalty." Then, almost instantly, her mood lightened again. "But if you are to sacrifice yourself on the altar of a contract wedding, you should have a proper trade wife send-off," she announced with sudden enthusiasm. "Don't you agree?"

"A proper send-off?" Kalena gave her companion a curious, questioning glance.

"A last night of freedom before you hit the trail. My friends and I will come for you shortly before the evening meal tomorrow night," Arrisa said decisively. "I have several friends who will be glad to join us. We'll make certain you enjoy the night, Kalena."

"The night? We will spend an evening in the taverns?" Astounded excitement lit Kalena's eyes as she considered the prospect. Such an evening would have been unheard of back home. No respectable woman went out at night to a tavern, alone or even in the company of other women. But apparently it was not looked down on here in the town; another small taste of what lay ahead in her free future.

"The prospect interests you?" Arrisa asked with a grin.

"Very much," Kalena said enthusiastically. "I'll wear one of my new tunics. I ordered some short ones, just like yours. You are very gracious to invite me to join your friends, Arrisa."

Arrisa chuckled. "It's going to be an amusing evening."

The formal dining chamber of Quintel's magnificent house was done in subtly contrasting shades of tan and pale blue. Kalena had become accustomed to the strongly balanced hues used throughout the house. She was grateful for the softer shade of sand and sea used in this room. Normally she was fond of vivid colors, but these middle Spectrum tones were more soothing to her nerves tonight.

To say the least, she found it somewhat stressful to sit down to dine with the man she had come to kill and the man to whom she was contracted in marriage.

It had all seemed so distant and abstract back home in Interlock. The man called Quintel had been only a name, part of her aunt's endlessly repeated tales. Marriage to a stranger named Ridge had been only a means to an end. But for two nights she had shared a meal with both of these men, and her aunt's bitter stories had taken on the substance of reality. Kalena found herself abnormally quiet during the evening meal.

The low, round table in the center of the softly colored chamber was inlaid with tiny, exotically colored tiles that formed a swirling, undefined pattern. Kalena had spent some time trying to analyze the meaning of the design and had failed. The restless chaos in the tilework would have been disconcerting but for the pale tones used. Kalena, Ridge and Quintel were seated on low cushions, their fingerspears resting on small carved stands in front of them. The men sat with traditional masculine casualness, their attire making it easy for them to change position when the mood took them.

Although Kalena was wearing one of her new, shorter tunics, she found herself too self-conscious to sit in any position other than the formal, kneeling, feminine style. Her trousered legs were gracefully curled beneath her and her back was elegantly straight. From this position she was expected to handle any service at the table that was not taken care of by the silent servant who brought in the various dishes. Pouring extra wine or dishing out second helpings was considered a female occupation. Good-naturedly, Kalena accepted the inevitable role of a woman at the evening table, telling herself it was only temporary. She wondered privately what Quintel and Ridge did when they had no female present. She would bet her last gran they were quite capable of serving themselves.

Kalena was in the act of pouring Ridge another goblet of the golden Encana wine when he turned from his conversation with Quintel and spoke to her directly. "You made your purchases today?"

"Yes," she responded politely, setting down the crystal wine bottle. "I bought everything you told me to get, including your shirts. I'll send them to your apartments later this evening."

For some reason she decided not to mention that she had been overcome by an unexpected attack of a traditional sense of duty toward her future husband late this afternoon. Or perhaps it had been guilt. Kalena wasn't sure. She still didn't know why she had purchased the embroidery silk and needles when she had bought Ridge's shirts. Later, as she had sat sewing a small, discreet initial R onto the shirts before dinner, she had chastised herself

for succumbing to such an old-fashioned gesture of feminine respect.

But some aspects of one's early training ran deep, she had discovered with a small sense of amused resignation. Besides, she
had seen enough of Ridge's clothing to know that no woman
bothered to personalize his shirts with his initial. Considering the
fact that he was a Houseless bastard, that was hardly surprising.
Kalena told herself that Ridge was more or less an innocent pawn
in the whole scheme of vengeance in which she was involved. The
least she could do was embroider one or two of his shirts for him.

Modestly, she lowered her eyes to the dish of hot, whipped
columa berries in front of her. She had no wish to actively participate in the table conversation. But Ridge seemed determined to
push her into the discussion.

"What about the wedding cloak? Did you find one?"

Her mouth started to lift in a private smile. Firmly Kalena stifled it. "Yes, Ridge. I found one."

Casually, Quintel asked the next question. "What did you select, Kalena?"

She looked up, meeting Ridge's gaze. "Red," she stated boldly.
"A most interesting shade of scarlet."

Quintel laughed in genuine amusement, raising his goblet in
mock salute to Ridge whose expression was wry. "Very good. The
lady has issued a challenge, Fire Whip. It would seem she has decided not to be a boring sort of bride. Tell me, what will you wear
to counter the challenge?"

Ridge picked up his wine and swallowed. "She's chosen the
color of red Symmetra. Therefore Kalena leaves me little choice. I
will have to wear black, won't I? The black of the night that en-
folds the moon, the way a man embraces his woman."

Kalena felt the heat surge into her face, knowing her small act
of assertiveness had just been well and truly squashed. "The entire matter of the wedding would seem quite pointless under the
circumstances."

"No," Quintel said gently, "it is not pointless. Not in this instance. You must trust my judgment in this matter. I have made

all the preparations. The wedding will be at the customary hour of sunset and it will be followed by a proper feast."

"You have invited a lot of people?" Kalena asked anxiously. A good-sized crowd would make her task easier. Olara had foreseen a large crowd.

"A number of traders and their associates. Men Ridge knows. Forgive me for not asking if there was anyone you would wish to invite, Kalena. I assumed that since you are alone in town there would be no one you would wish present."

"I'll let you know tomorrow evening," Kalena said firmly.

Ridge immediately picked up on that remark. He shot her a quick, speculative glance. "What happens tomorrow evening?"

"It is then I hope to meet some new friends. Perhaps I will ask them to the wedding. The bride is entitled to bring her own witnesses, is she not? She is entitled to have women friends to attend her and make certain she has her time of privacy after the ceremony before the groom comes to her room." She had to have that traditional hour of privacy. It was essential to her task.

"Of course you may invite whom you wish," Quintel murmured.

Ridge scowled thoughtfully. "What friends will you be meeting? You know no one in town."

"Except Arrisa. You remember her?" Some of Kalena's earlier enthusiasm returned. Her eyes sparkled. "She has arranged to give me what she calls a trade wife send-off. She and her associates will be calling for me tomorrow evening. Oh, that reminds me, my lord," she added, turning to Quintel. "Please do not expect me for the evening meal tomorrow."

Ridge shifted slightly, one arm looped around an upraised knee, his wine goblet grasped in his fingers. His golden gaze was narrow and suspicious. "You plan to spend the evening with Arrisa and her friends?"

"Arrisa was kind enough to invite me when I ran into her on Weavers Street this morning."

"I don't think you realize exactly what sort of evening you might be letting yourself in for," Ridge began with the familiar arrogance of a male who is about to straighten out a sadly naive female. "Arrisa and her friends are not the sort of acquaintances you would wish to encourage."

"Why not?"

"Well, several of them have been trade wives in the past or have accompanied the caravans in, uh, certain capacities. All of them have a reputation for rather loose behavior."

Kalena smiled brightly. "But I am going to be a trade wife myself. These are the sort of women whom I shall be associating with in the future. I should get to know their ways; be accepted among them."

Ridge's mouth tightened. "Your aunt is a respectable Healer. I am sure she would not approve of your plans for tomorrow evening."

Kalena managed to resist pointing out that her aunt was the one who had contracted for the trade marriage in the first place. "I expect you're right. My aunt has extremely restrictive notions," Kalena allowed diplomatically.

"Not half as restrictive as a husband's notions." Ridge clattered his goblet warningly as he set it down on the table.

Kalena chose to ignore the gesture. "I haven't got a husband. Not yet," she said softly.

"Two nights from now that particular detail will be corrected," Ridge informed her meaningfully. "In the meantime you will behave yourself in a proper manner."

"I will behave myself in a proper *trade wife* manner," Kalena agreed politely. "But since I don't yet know exactly how trade wives behave, I shall first have to learn something about the subject, won't I?"

"Not from Arrisa and her friends," Ridge said coldly.

Aware of Quintel's amused attention, Kalena decided to drop her end of the argument. She had no need to quarrel over the matter. She fully intended to join Arrisa and her friends the following evening and nothing Ridge could do would change that. She would gain nothing by making a spectacle of herself at the trade baron's table. Meekly, Kalena went back to her columa berries.

They weren't quite as good as the ones she was accustomed to getting back in Interlock, she decided.

Ridge watched her broodingly for a short time and then apparently decided he had successfully handled the situation. He appeared relieved, and proud of his first attempt at exercising husbandly responsibility. "Did you remember to buy riding clothes?"

"Yes, Ridge. I remembered the riding garments. The shopkeeper said they would be ready tomorrow afternoon."

"Boots?"

"I ordered boots. They'll be delivered tomorrow also."

He nodded, satisfied. "I'll take care of everything else."

"I assumed you would."

He ignored that, turning to Quintel. "We'll leave at dawn the morning after the wedding. There's no reason to delay any longer."

"I quite agree," Quintel said. He took a small bite of the meat and vegetable mixture on his plate. Quintel ate sparingly at all meals. "Tell me, Kalena, did your aunt encourage you to train as a Healer?"

Kalena shook her head, knowing that the art of Healer was the last path down which Olara would have sent her. Such a calling would have made the goal for which Kalena had been raised impossible. Healers found it impossible to kill except in self-defense. Furthermore, Olara had always told Kalena in no uncertain terms that she saw no evidence of the Talent in her niece, anyway. That fact had always made Kalena strangely sad. She would have liked very much to have been born with the Talent. But it was unlikely Olara was wrong in her opinion on Kalena's lack of ability. Olara was a very gifted Healer. Some said she could have been a High Healer if she had chosen to join the women of the Variance valley. She was almost never wrong. "No. My aunt had other ambitions for me."

"I see. Does your aunt think you might have inherited some of her Talent?"

Kalena looked at him, sensing a question behind the question.

"Don't worry, my lord, my aunt is certain I can accomplish my role in this venture."

"Then I must be satisfied with her certainty. You say your aunt handled your education. Did she teach you about the Stones?"

"I know the legend of the Stones of Contrast as well as the tales of the Keys to the Stones," Kalena said carefully. "I have also been instructed in the Philosophy of Contrast."

"But you do believe the tales?"

"My aunt believes in the Keys," Kalena said thoughtfully. "It would be difficult to find a true Healer who did not believe in them. The Light Key is said to be the source of the power of the Sands of Eurythmia and therefore an asset to all Healing. My aunt is a very wise woman and if she chooses to believe in the Keys, then I'm inclined to think there may be some substance to the tales."

"Very cautiously spoken," Quintel said with a small smile. "I myself am careful when asked such questions. But I keep an open mind."

"It would seem that any intelligent person would keep an open mind on such a subject. Zantalia is very large, and the portion of it that we occupy here on the Northern Continent is so small in comparison to the unknown regions on the other side of the world. Who knows what mysteries will be uncovered when all the world is explored?"

"A very wise frame of mind," Quintel said approvingly.

He meant considering the fact that she was a woman, Kalena thought, aware that Ridge was listening closely. "Thank you, my lord," she said politely. "If even a portion of the legends about the Stones of Contrast are discovered to be true, we shall have a very interesting problem to unravel, won't we? There is the whole matter of who or what the Dawn Lords really were and whether they truly commanded the incredible power of the Stones, let alone the power of the Keys."

"It is only in large towns such as Crosspurposes and relatively progressive areas such as the Interlock valley that anyone even questions the legends, Kalena," Quintel pointed out. "When you travel with Ridge to the Heights of Variance you will learn that in other places the tales of the Dawn Lords and their Stones of Contrast are assumed to be fact."

"And," Ridge put in deliberately, "you will not bring up philosophical questions on the matter to the people we meet on our journey, understand? In some villages such comments could get us mobbed or hounded out of the community."

"I shall be guided by your actions," Kalena murmured with suitable meekness.

Ridge looked pleased with her wifely response. "I'll take care of you, Kalena, and see that you don't come to harm."

Two hours after the close of the lengthy meal, Kalena put the last embroidered stitch in Ridge's shirt. Putting down the needle and thread, she held the garment up to the soft light of a firegel lamp and examined her handiwork with a critical eye. She was never going to be able to make her living as a professional seamstress, but the job was passable, she decided. If Ridge complained he could rip out the embroidery himself.

Kalena uncurled from her stool, stood up and stretched. She still wasn't certain whether she had been motivated by guilt or an unreasonable notion of duty, but it hardly mattered. The deed was done. She folded the two shirts and went to the bell to summon a servant. Hand on the bell rope, she paused. Ridge's apartments were only a few doors down from her own. She could deliver the shirts herself. His reaction would be interesting to see, Kalena decided. She picked up the folded shirts and headed down the corridor.

But by the time she reached Ridge's moonwood door, she was experiencing a severe attack of second thoughts. Maybe this wasn't such a good idea after all. She should have sent the shirts along with a servant. Kalena chewed her lip thoughtfully, her hand raised to knock.

Before she could make up her mind, the door swung open and she found herself staring at Ridge. He returned her gaze with a somewhat suspicious expression.

"What is it, Kalena?" he asked. "Is something wrong?"

Impulsively, she shoved the shirts into his hands. "These are the items you asked me to purchase today. Knowing the way shopkeepers work, the bill for them will probably be arriving bright and early in the morning. I didn't want you wondering where the shirts were."

He glanced down at the soft lanti wool garments he was holding, his eyes thoughtful. "They're embroidered."

"I'm not very good at that sort of thing," Kalena explained hurriedly. "So I didn't make the Rs very large."

Ridge continued to stare down at the embroidery. Kalena had used a dark brown thread to contrast the neutral color of the wool. Wonderingly, he stroked one of the letters with the tip of his thumb. "I've never worn an embroidered shirt."

Kalena cleared her throat, feeling ridiculously nervous. "Yes, well, after you examine my workmanship under a good light, you might not want to wear these. I wish you good evening, Ridge." She took a step backward.

"Wait." His head came up quickly, a small frown darkening his eyes.

"Yes, Ridge?"

"Thank you, Kalena. Your work is beautiful. I shall wear the shirts with pride."

She grinned at that. "No need to exaggerate."

His expression relaxed into one tinged with humor. "I take it needlework is not your favorite pastime?"

Kalena wrinkled her nose. "Weren't there any tasks you had to master while growing up that you would just as soon never have learned?"

The amusement faded from his eyes. "There are definitely some things I wish I had never had to learn, Kalena. Sometimes we have no choice, do we?"

"No," she whispered. "Sometimes we have no choice in what we must master." She took another step away from him, summoning a smile of polite farewell.

He studied her shadowed face for a moment. "Are you afraid of our coming venture together, Kalena?"

Surprised at the question, she just looked at him for a moment. Oh, yes, she thought silently, she was afraid. She was now beginning to realize just how afraid of her task she really was. Her whole future hinged on committing an act of horrible violence. How could she not be afraid? Failure meant being forever disgraced; success meant she would be a murderess. But she had no choice. She must claim her own future.

"Have I reason to fear, Ridge?" she countered aloud.

"It would be only natural for a young woman in your position to be a little nervous, I think," Ridge said earnestly. "But I promise to take good care of you on the journey."

Kalena was touched by the sincerity she saw behind his words. She could hardly tell him he wouldn't have to worry about being burdened with her on the trip, so she just smiled again. "Thank you, Ridge. I trust the journey will go well."

He coughed slightly as she once more made to leave. "Uh, Kalena, I didn't mean I would just take care of you on the journey, itself."

"Yes, Ridge?" she prompted, a little confused by his obvious awkwardness. Ridge was not normally a hesitant man by any stretch of the imagination.

"I meant," he plowed on stolidly, "that I will be a good trade husband to you."

"Oh." She didn't know what else to say. Kalena was painfully aware of the warmth rising on her cheeks and was grateful for the shadows. He was having a difficult time and she almost felt sorry for him. "Thank you for the reassurance," she managed to say dryly.

"Dammit, Kalena, I'm making a poor job of this. What I'm trying to say is, you won't have cause to regret signing the trade marriage agreement with me instead of some other man." His big hands tightened on the folded shirts. "And thank you for the fine needlework," he concluded gruffly.

"You're welcome, Ridge." This time Kalena made good her es-

cape, although she was conscious of Ridge standing in the doorway of his room watching her until she slipped safely into her
own apartment. When she glanced back one last time she thought
he was looking down at his shirts, his expression oddly pleased.

The Fire Whip was not looking at all pleased as evening fell
the following day. He encountered Kalena as she waited in the
wide, tiled entry hall of the house for the arrival of Arrisa and her
friends. In honor of the occasion, Kalena was wearing her most
vividly hued tunic, a daringly short affair of yellow and red Risha
cloth over blue-green trousers. She had high-heeled velvet boots
on her feet and her best combs in her hair. Her one indulgence in
the area of jewelry yesterday had been to purchase a set of ear
clips fashioned of tinted glass gems that were supposed to imitate
the fabulously expensive green crystal mined near the Talon Pass.
The sparkling glass stones were mounted on narrow, flexible
strips that encircled the entire outer curve of her ear. Kalena had
never worn anything like them before in her life. All in all, she
was feeling quite adventurous about the coming evening.

Ridge came around the corner of the hall, apparently on his
way to Quintel's apartment. He was wearing one of his new shirts
with a small R worked on the left shoulder. He took one look at
Kalena and his golden eyes came alive with angry heat. "So.
You've decided to join Arrisa and her friends, after all."

"I had intended to join them all along," Kalena answered
pleasantly. "I simply didn't choose to argue about it over dinner
last night."

The flames in his golden eyes burned higher. "I forbid it."

She sighed. "We both know you haven't that right, Ridge."

"By tomorrow night I will have every right," he snapped. "By
the Stones, Kalena, I will not tolerate such behavior. Do you think
I am forbidding tonight's little jaunt just because I enjoy exercising my authority?"

"Umm. Yes. That seems to be the general reason men forbid
women to do things."

He took a long angry step toward her. "I have made this decision for your own good, you contrary little wench. The same way I will be making other decisions during the course of our marriage. I expect you to have the sense to obey me. Last night I got the impression you had some measure of common sense. I assumed—"

The heavy knocker sounded outside and a soft-footed servant slipped into the hall to open the door. Kalena heard Arrisa's voice, and she smiled up at Ridge. "Have a pleasant evening, Ridge. This is your last night of freedom, also. You should celebrate. I'd invite you to join us, but I'm afraid the other women would object."

"Dammit, Kalena, listen to me. This is not the sort of crowd you should be joining."

She swept eagerly toward the door. "You're wrong, Ridge. This is precisely my sort of crowd. I have waited a good many years to be a freewoman."

"After tomorrow night, you won't be free," he vowed, taking one more dangerous step toward her. "And the moment you are officially put into my keeping, I'm going to take measures to start correcting your stubborn ways."

"I can see that you are going to make a very dull sort of husband." Kalena threw him a last, laughing glance and hurried outside into the balmy evening. The door closed behind her, blocking out the sight of Ridge's glowering face. "Arrisa, I'm ready."

Arrisa stood on the stone path along with three other women. All were dressed in a dazzling array of bright tunics and flashing jewelry. They greeted Kalena with wide, infectious grins as Arrisa made introductions and Kalena knew the evening that lay ahead of her would be unlike any other she had ever experienced.

"Let's be off," Arrisa commanded, taking charge of the small crowd. "I have ordered an evening meal at the Sign of the Dark Key. After all, we'll let the night take us where it will. Don't worry, Kalena, we'll have you back here in time for your wedding."

Helpless to stop Kalena and thoroughly disgusted by that fact, Ridge opened the great hall doors and watched the brightly dressed flock of women disappear down the street. Their cheerful laughter floated back to him on the soft evening air. Tomorrow night, he promised himself, things would be different. Kalena would learn what it was to have a husband. She was tasting the heady air of freedom tonight, probably for the first time in her life, but she would only have one night of it. Enough to satisfy her curiosity, Ridge told himself, but not enough to corrupt her.

Ridge further calmed his temper by telling himself that Arrisa knew better than to go too far when it came to showing Kalena the life of the freewomen of the town. She knew she would answer to Ridge if she got Kalena into real trouble. Arrisa was a little wild, but she was not stupid, he decided. She would exercise some discretion this evening. In addition, Kalena would undoubtedly discover that the fast nightlife offered by Crosspurposes was more than a little shocking to her country bred sensibilities. Her good upbringing should afford some protection and caution.

Consoling himself with that thought, Ridge slammed the heavy moonwood door and continued down the hall toward Quintel's apartments. Tomorrow night, he vowed silently once again, tomorrow night everything would be different. Unconsciously, he reached up to touch the silken embroidered R on his shoulder.

The dark hour of midnight came and went without causing a single, disturbing ripple in the boisterous party. Kalena noticed the time when she happened to glance at a water clock as they entered the fourth tavern of the evening. She and her new friends then sat at a low plank table in the smoky room and ordered another round of red ale to share. Almost everyone else in the tavern was male, although a few other bold women were scattered here and there. Kalena and her friends were drawing stares, just as they had done in the last three taverns, not just because they were women, but because their laughter and the jests were becoming increasingly loud. Kalena's voice was already quite hoarse from the effort of projecting above the general din.

"A toast to the new trade wife!" the blonde woman named Vertina announced for perhaps the tenth time. Each toast had been a bit bawdier than the last. "May she finally learn the truth about the Fire Whip."

"What truth?" Arrisa demanded, lifting her tankard.

"Why, the truth about his ability to make the steel of Countervail glow red hot," Vertina said with a wicked grin. "I figured if it's ever going to glow, it will do so in bed. Pay attention tomorrow night, Kalena. The steel between your husband's legs is from Countervail, you know. Ridge was born there, I was told. I, for one, have always been curious to know just how hot it can get."

Kalena flushed at the crudeness of the joke, torn between laughter and shock. Even after spending the evening with this crowd, she was still finding herself startled by some of their ribald remarks. "I'll, uh, try to pay attention," she mumbled into her tankard.

"That reminds me," another woman interrupted, pulling a small lanti skin pouch out of her pocket. "I have the bride's present. Surely it's time we gave it to her?"

Amid more loud laughter, everyone agreed. Kalena smiled expectantly. She had never received many gifts from Aunt Olara. "That's very kind of you," she said, meaning it. Eagerly she accepted the pouch, untying the leather thong. Inside, she saw a powder. Cautiously Kalena sniffed. For a moment she couldn't identify it, and then she remembered Olara preparing a certain concoction at the request of neighboring farm women. The pungent odor of the selite leaves identified the powder. Kalena's cheeks turned red again.

"Thank you," she murmured. "It's very thoughtful of all of you."

"You should probably start taking it now," Vertina said. "Just a pinch. Use the ale to wash it down."

"But, I, uh, won't need it until tomorrow night," Kalena protested gently.

"Ha," Arrisa said laughingly. "You don't know that for certain. No telling what the rest of the night holds. Take the powder and be safe, Kalena."

It would do no harm, Kalena decided. Good-naturedly, she

took a pinch of the powder women took to prevent conception and washed it down with a swallow of ale. When she was finished a cheer went up around the table.

A loud male voice from across the room shouted for the tavern keeper. "Can't you keep those women quiet?"

Arrisa smiled broadly, then responded, "Why don't you take a trip to the Dark end of the Spectrum?"

Another man from the opposite corner of the smoky room seconded the opinion of the first male. The woman with him jumped to her feet and announced her disagreement with her partner's attitude by dumping ale over his head.

"Close your mouth, Bleen, they're not bothering you."

Bleen's roar of rage was followed by a desperate bid for peace by the tavern keeper. That proved unsuccessful, however, as several other males joined with the first in protesting the presence of Kalena's group. It proved too much for Arrisa and the others. Kalena was startled to see her new friends jump to their feet and grab for full tankards of ale to hurl across the room at the offending males.

Pandemonium ensued with the inevitability of night following day. Before she quite realized what was happening, Kalena found herself in the midst of a tavern brawl. There was, she discovered, only one rule: you stuck by your friends. She grabbed her own tankard and sent it flying across the room.

Somebody called the Town Patrol almost immediately. The officers arrived shortly afterward.

The patrol runner presented himself at Quintel's door half an hour after the brawl had been quelled.

"Tell Quintel's Whip that we have a woman claiming to be his future wife in custody," the runner said gravely to the sleepy servant who opened the door. "Ask Ridge if he wants her to spend a night in jail or if he'd prefer to come claim her."

FOUR

Kalena heard the ring of Ridge's boots on the stone floor of the patrol office a few seconds before she saw him. She was grateful for the brief warning, which gave her a chance to paste what she hoped was a winning smile on her face. She was sitting on a hard bench, Arrisa and the others arranged beside her. Kalena was aware of the other women's uneasiness.

"I think I would have been better off spending the rest of the night in jail," Arrisa muttered gloomily.

"She's right." Vertina groaned, holding her head in both hands. "If you would just let the patrol take us downstairs, Kalena, things might be a great deal easier in the long run."

"That's ridiculous," Kalena declared with sweeping confidence. "Ridge will get us all out of here."

The other women looked at her as if she wasn't quite right in the head. But before Kalena could speak, the Fire Whip was striding into the room, filling it up with the force of his barely leashed fury. Kalena finally realized why his temper was legendary. The gold of his eyes was molten with the force of his anger. He pinned

Kalena for an instant with that scorching gaze, ignoring the other women. Then he spoke to one of the patrol officers. His voice was far too soft for Kalena's comfort.

"That's her. Release her. I'll wait for her outside." He turned to stalk back into the outer office without another word.

Frantically, Kalena took hold of her unsettled nerves and sprang to her feet. "Ridge, wait! What about my friends?"

"Uh, Kalena, maybe you should just shut up and go with him," Arrisa advised in a low tone.

But it was too late. Ridge had already swung around in the doorway, his hand resting a little too casually on the handle of his sintar. His face was a frighteningly expressionless mask. "Your *friends*?" he repeated in a gentle voice laced with liquid fire.

Kalena realized her pulse was racing. She was stunned to find herself quelled by the temper of a man who couldn't even claim a decent House name. For the sake of the Spectrum, where was her own pride? Kalena rallied herself, keeping her head high and her voice as serene as possible. "Perhaps I should have said my wedding guests, Ridge. I have invited my *friends* to the wedding. I cannot allow them to spend the rest of the night in jail."

There was a moment of frozen silence while Ridge looked at her across the width of the room. The patrol captain waited warily for the explosion, obviously a little uncertain about what to do when it occurred.

Kalena licked her lower lip and decided to ride out the storm by making an effort to placate the man she had contracted to marry. If she were honest with herself, she had to admit that the situation was largely her own fault. The man had a right to be angry. Quietly she said, "Ridge, please. As a wedding gift to me, will you arrange for their release?"

A strange light flashed in his eyes. "Come here," he said evenly.

Kalena hesitated, every nerve in her body aware of the challenge in him. Ridge had obviously had more than enough of her bravado this evening. He didn't repeat the command; he simply waited. Kalena counted a few more seconds, then walked slowly across the room to stand in front of him. Everyone else held their tongues and their breath.

"You're asking for a wedding gift?" Ridge didn't move in the doorway.

"Yes, please." Kalena kept her hands tightly clasped in front of her. She looked up at him with earnest, hopeful eyes and waited with what she trusted was a wifely humility. The thing was, it wasn't an act. At this moment she felt very much like an errant wife pleading for a bit of mercy from her husband. For the first time she was confronted with the fact that Ridge held real power over her in this situation. He could choose to grant the favor or withhold it. Nothing she had done so far this evening had predisposed him to grant any favors.

"If you would claim a gift, Kalena, then you must be prepared to give one in return."

Kalena took a deep breath, aware that in the matter of gift giving, as in everything else in life, a balance must be maintained. "Claim your gift, Ridge."

"Yes," he said, as if to himself, "I think it's time I did." He took her arm and glanced at the captain. "Release them. I will see to it that damages are paid."

Relief flowed through Kalena, washing out the tension and uncertainty. The crisis was past. She began to wonder why she had been so nervous. Of course Ridge would never have left her to sit in jail or denied her the boon of freeing her friends. He might have a temper that originated in the Dark end of the Spectrum, but he was a decent man. "My thanks, Ridge!" Impulsively she stood on tiptoe, threw her arms around his neck and hugged him gratefully. "I can't tell you how much I appreciate your generosity."

He looked down into her face. The fire had faded from his eyes, and was replaced by something else, something she couldn't quite identify. "You can tell me how grateful you are later when we reach Quintel's house." Disengaging himself from her arms, he guided her firmly out of the room.

Kalena turned to glance over her shoulder as she was led from the room. She grinned happily at her relieved friends. "I had a wonderful evening. Thank you very much, and I hope to see you at the wedding. You will be sure to come, won't you?"

"Are you kidding?" Arrisa asked with a laugh. "Wouldn't miss it for all the crystal in Talon Pass."

The walk back to Quintel's house was conducted in absolute silence on Ridge's part. But he had no real need to speak. Kalena occupied the entire time with a bubbling account of her evening on the town. Ridge listened without comment as they followed the light of the firegel lamps down the main avenue to their destination.

Kalena's tale didn't begin to wind down until the doors of Quintel's house swung open to admit Ridge and herself. She had a brief moment of anxiety at the thought of explaining the evening's events to the Master of the House. But that fear was put to rest as Ridge steered her forcefully in the direction of the guest quarters.

"I must admit, you were very generous back there in the patrol office, Ridge," Kalena concluded magnanimously as they approached her room. "I know Arrisa and the others appreciated your actions as much as I did. I realize you probably don't wholeheartedly approve of everything that happened this evening, and under the circumstances I think you behaved very nobly."

Ridge spoke for the first time since they had left the patrol office. "You, on the other hand, behaved like an ill-mannered, ill-bred, ill-governed female who needs to be introduced to the business end of a creet whip."

Kalena gasped at the unexpected threat. "Ridge, what a terrible thing to say! No one but a Houseless bastard would use a creet whip on a woman."

"I am a Houseless bastard, or hasn't anyone bothered to inform you of that fact?" He didn't pause at her door, but continued down the colonnaded path toward his own apartments.

"Oh, for Spectrum's sake, I didn't mean that," Kalena said, shocked as much by her own bad manners as his. "It was just an expression. Ridge, please try to understand. I have never in my life had such an evening as I had tonight. It was so exciting. I felt so free . . ."

He threw her a faintly mocking glance. "You felt free sitting there on a bench in the headquarters of the Town Patrol waiting for me to bail you out? You've got an odd notion of freedom, woman."

"Not then," she said, waving the culmination of the evening's events aside with a careless hand. "I meant earlier. We went where we wished, sat drinking in the taverns just like the men do, and when the fight broke out we held our own."

His mouth quirked wryly. "You held your own, did you? How many poor males did you brain with an ale tankard tonight, Kalena? Or weren't you keeping score?"

She laughed up at him. "I tried to keep score but it got complicated. Do you keep score when you get into tavern brawls, Ridge?"

"Don't look at me so innocently. I haven't been in a tavern brawl in years, but the last time I was I sure as hell wasn't keeping score. There's no point. The only thing that counts is coming out in one piece. Do you realize you could have been injured tonight? Some idiot might have pulled a sintar or broken your nose with his fist."

"I would have looked very interesting at the wedding with a broken nose."

"It's not funny, Kalena. It was a stupid and dangerous thing to do."

"I'll bet you've done lots of things that were much more stupid and much more dangerous."

He groaned. "I'm beginning to think we have a basic problem here."

She smiled questioningly. "What problem is that?"

"A proper wife is supposed to display a certain degree of, well, *alarm,* or at least some reasonable apprehension when her lord is forced to bail her out of jail after an evening such as you spent tonight."

"I'm not a proper wife," Kalena declared with gleeful satisfaction. "I'm going to be a *trade* wife. And technically, I'm not even that, not yet."

"You will be soon enough," he stated brusquely. "Why do I have to keep reminding you that even though this is meant to be a short-term marriage it's still a legal marriage? During the course of it you are still subject to your husband."

She tilted her head thoughtfully. "Surely you don't expect me to cower in fear whenever I'm in your presence?"

He looked briefly irritated. "There's a difference between going in fear of me and behaving with some discretion. I told you not to get involved with Arrisa and her crowd."

"Do you pay a lot of attention to people who advise you not to do what you want to do?" she asked with great interest.

He glared at her. "We're not discussing my behavior. It's your actions we're dealing with here."

"The thing is, Ridge," she said quite seriously, "I had a great time. Freedom is a wonderful thing, isn't it?"

"I wouldn't know," he said quietly. "I've never had a lot of it."

Startled, she came to a halt and swung around to stare searchingly up at him. "What are you talking about? You've been free all of your life."

"That's a matter of interpretation. I've been living with a single goal all my life. The only freedom I've had was in picking and choosing the various means I could use to reach that goal. Sometimes the choices aren't pleasant."

Fascinated, she continued to study his intent face. "What goal is that, Ridge?"

"I'm going to found my own House. A Great House." He challenged her silently, as if expecting her to mock his dream.

But Kalena felt no amusement. "Such a goal will require much from you, Trade Master. It might even get you killed."

"With any luck, it will get me rich instead." He caught her arm and pulled her forward. "But in the meantime I remain a bastard. Just ask anyone," he added with a grim smile.

Kalena came back to her senses as he tugged her after him. "Where are we going? My rooms are back there. Surely you're not thinking of actually . . . actually . . ." Her voice trailed off as he stopped in front of his room and shoved open the arched door. He wouldn't really beat her as he had half-threatened earlier, she told herself. He *couldn't* do such a thing. Even if he had no claim to any House, he would not embarrass the Great House by which he was employed by abusing a woman.

"Relax. I didn't bring you here to beat you, Kalena," he told her mildly, pulling her into the chamber and shutting the door.

"Then why are we here?" she demanded, realizing he was making no move to turn on the firegel lamps. In the deep shadows Ridge seemed very large and threatening. At times he was indeed a creature of darkness; something dangerous and forbidding.

"We're here," he said bluntly, "so that I can claim my gift. You aren't going to tell me I have no right to it, are you?" He began unlacing the leather that fastened the front of his shirt. His movements were deliberate.

In the red-tinted moonlight drifting through the window, Kalena saw the lambent flames in Ridge's eyes. The fire in him was still evident, but it had taken on a different kind of heat. She caught her breath as full realization flooded over her. In the wake of that womanly knowledge came another emotion, a blossoming excitement of the kind she had first encountered in the garden the night before. Perhaps her rising euphoria also had a few roots in the surging physical excitement she had experienced during the tavern brawl. Kalena wasn't sure and she didn't feel much like analyzing the matter. Not now. She didn't move as myriad thoughts half-formed and then faded in her head. One remained, prodding her to ask the single question that needed to be asked.

"Are you doing this to punish me for what I did tonight?" Her voice was a husky whisper.

Ridge finished the last of the laces and stood with his shirt open. He studied her, lifting one hand to catch her chin. "No, Kalena, I'm not going to make love to you in order to punish you."

"Then why?"

"It's our wedding day," he pointed out quietly.

She shook her head. "But not our wedding night."

His mouth curved faintly in the moonlight. "We'll make it our wedding night."

"Will we?" The excitement was flickering through her, as undeniable as it was dangerous. Aunt Olara would be furious if she knew what was happening. Olara's fierce objections to this moment of feminine discovery sounded once more in Kalena's head: *You must not allow a man to embrace you until you have accomplished your mission. The honor of your House is at stake. You must not allow yourself to be deflected from the path that has been ordained for you. Passion is dangerous. It can cloud the mind and blind it to what must be done. Nothing and no one must stand between you and your destiny as the last daughter of the House of the Ice Harvest.*

But she was on the brink of that destiny tonight, Kalena told herself. Surely it was too late for a man's passion to deflect her from her goal. She would do what had to be done. The honor of her House would be avenged, Kalena promised herself. But tonight belonged to her. She was filled with a wild, reckless energy that convinced her she could handle both her mission and this passionate encounter.

Tonight she could have still another taste of the heady freedom that would be hers when she had killed Quintel. She was strong enough to risk it. Olara was wrong. She was not so weak as to be seduced from her task by temptations, Kalena told herself. She could sample the temptation and still do her duty.

She felt the rough edge of Ridge's hand on the line of her jaw. If something went wrong, if she failed in her task, or even if she succeeded but managed to bungle somehow, she could easily be dead by this time tomorrow. The thought of dying without ever having known the end result of this flaring exhilaration was infinitely depressing. Surely she could ignore Olara's warnings tonight. It was too late for any damage to be done. A few hours of passionate discovery in this man's arms would not cloud her mind or turn her aside from the task that awaited.

"Do you swear on your honor that you have no intention of punishing me for disobeying you tonight? That only desire guides you now?" she asked softly. If she was going to defy Olara's teachings and take the risk of giving herself to the Fire Whip, she had to be certain that his motives were as simple and honest as her own. She would take the risk of surrendering to passion and freedom, but she would not submit to some warped notion of retribution. She might be the last daughter of a Great House, but she was, nevertheless, a member of that House. She would act as such.

Ridge cradled her face between his large hands, his fingers strong and sure and curiously gentle on her skin. "I think, sweet farm girl, that you have been breathing the intoxicating air of freedom for the past couple of days. You like it, don't you?"

"Very much," she agreed with a tremulous smile.

"Tonight you think you have discovered just how exciting it is to be on your own, calling no man lord, husband, or master." His eyes gleamed. "You've had quite an adventure, haven't you? Was it fun running a little wild?"

Kalena sensed the new element of indulgence in him. "Yes," she admitted breathlessly, "it was fun." More fun than she had ever known in the years spent under Olara's bitter, vengeful, eye.

"I don't intend to punish you for the fun you had tonight, Kalena," Ridge assured her in a low voice made almost lazy with sensuality. "I plan to show you that there is more excitement to be found on my pallet than you'll ever discover in a tavern brawl."

Kalena lightly touched one of his hands as he held her face. Her fingers were trembling, she realized vaguely. In fact, her whole body was shivering ever so slightly. She felt light-headed as the reckless elation that had guided her all evening surged to a new strength, a thousand times more powerful than it had been even in the midst of the brawl. Freedom beckoned and could no longer be denied.

"Ridge . . ." She put her palms on his shoulders, fascinated with the heat of his skin that penetrated the sturdy fabric of his shirt.

"Come with me, farmer's daughter, and let me show you how exciting town life really is." Ridge shifted, one arm sweeping under her knees, the other behind her shoulders.

The moon-tinted chamber swung dizzyingly for an instant as Kalena was lifted high against Ridge's chest. She closed her eyes and clung to him, aware that he was striding toward the low, curtained pallet at the far end of the room. She would not think of the past or her future, she promised herself. What was happening now had nothing to do with her duty or her heritage. This moment existed only for her.

The wide sleeping pallet was on a low, raised dais of richly carved wood. Ridge lowered Kalena to her feet, letting her body slide along his own until she was standing in front of him.

"I'm glad Arrisa and the others didn't get around to cutting your hair," he muttered thickly, burying his fists in the mass of curls. He used his hold to tilt her head back for his kiss.

Kalena trembled again as she sensed the full force of his barely leashed desire. Her nails sank urgently into his shirt, seeking his hard, muscled shoulders under the fabric. Ridge groaned and deepened the kiss. His tongue surged into her mouth and Kalena got a sample of the fire in him. She whispered his name, her voice hoarse with pleasure.

Eyes closed, her mouth flowering under his, Kalena was only dimly aware of Ridge's hands on the fastening of her tunic. A moment later she felt the beautiful material slip to the floor, forming a pool of soft color at her feet. She was left wearing only thin, narrow trousers and soft velvet boots. Kalena was bared to his touch from the waist and the knowledge made her insides tighten with anticipation and desire.

"You have a dancer's back," Ridge murmured wonderingly, letting his fingers knead the sensitive curve above her lush buttocks. "Very proud, very elegant. How did a farmer's daughter absorb such pride and elegance into her very bones?"

But he wasn't waiting for an answer. He urged Kalena closer until her nipples touched his chest through the opening of his shirt. Crisp, masculine hair teased the sensitive tips of her breasts until she couldn't tell if the sensation was exquisitely exciting or exquisitely painful. She sucked in her breath and pulled back slightly.

"Don't be afraid of me, Kalena. I'm going to be your husband. It will be my duty and my pleasure to take care of you. Relax and learn to trust me, sweet wife-to-be. You must learn to trust me."

Ridge lowered her down onto the pallet and knelt on the rug in front of her. Steadying herself once more with her hands on his shoulders, Kalena watched through heavy-lidded eyes as he carefully removed her boots.

"Are you very sure, Ridge?" She wasn't certain of the exact nature of her question, but knew that she needed some kind of assurance from him.

"I'm very sure." He eased her back against the pillows and flattened his hand on her soft stomach. When she looked up at him with a wordless longing, he murmured something under his breath and stroked the delicate trousers down to her ankles in one easy, sweeping motion.

For a moment he simply gazed at her, and then, sitting on the pallet, he impatiently yanked off his own boots. He got to his feet, golden eyes gleaming down at her in the shadows. He discarded his shirt and unbuckled his belt. The sheathed sintar clattered lightly as it struck the floor beside the pallet. With one last, swift movement, he was naked.

Kalena looked at Ridge, fascinated by the hard, male shape of him. She had lived all of her life in the country and had been raised by a professional Healer, but she had never seen an unclothed man before. She was absorbed by the sight of Ridge, and put the image of him into the only context she knew.

He was a fine male animal in his prime, smoothly muscled and boldly, aggressively formed. The taut planes of his chest gave way to the flat, hard surface of his stomach. Below that the powerful outline of his manhood was enlarged and heavy with the unmistakable evidence of his desire.

"Do you like looking at me, country girl?"

"Yes," she whispered, vividly aware of his strong hands on her waist as he came down beside her.

"Then we're in luck. Because I like looking at you. Very much."

He moved his hand to her breast, cupping her gently as he bent his head to taste the skin of her throat. Kalena stirred beneath him as he used his thumb to tease and tantalize a nipple. Her hands went around him instinctively.

"Go ahead and touch me." Ridge groaned heavily as she obeyed. "You're so soft, so beautifully soft and round and warm," he muttered against the curve of her breast. Then he was taking the erect nipple into his mouth, tugging gently until Kalena cried out softly. "That's it, my love. Those are the words I want to hear tonight."

His hand slid lower, shaping the small curve of her waist and finding the gentle roundness below. Kalena's breath came more quickly as the sensual heat was stoked higher in her body. The fire in Ridge was reaching out to consume her. She let her own hands slip down the length of him, delighting in the hard contours of his shoulders, experimenting with the feminine magic she was discovering within herself.

When Ridge's questing hand reached the soft nest of hair at the juncture of her thighs, he lifted his head to look down at her. "Part your legs for me, Kalena. Open yourself. I want to touch all of you. I *have* to touch you."

She hesitated, more out of a lingering uncertainty than any real fear. But when he coaxed her ankles apart with his foot, she forgot about the vague unsureness she had been feeling and buried her face against his shoulder. She opened herself to him, lifting her hips against the heat of his hand.

"Ah, Kalena, you are as ready for me as the lock is ready for its key. And we are going to fit together just as perfectly."

Kalena shuddered as Ridge touched her with deep intimacy. His fingers explored her gently, finding the center of her excitement and teasing her there until her hands were clenched into his shoulders, her nails like tiny sintars. Then he stroked inside the dampening channel that seemed to be the core of her body.

"Ridge!"

"Soon, my sweet farm lady. Very soon. When I have made you

so hot you think you are going to burst into flames, that's when I'll take you."

"I'll go out of my head," she gasped, reaching down to capture his hand and press it more tightly against herself.

"That's exactly how I want you," he told her, his voice huskier than she had yet heard it. "Exactly how I want you."

"Please, Ridge." She knew this building excitement had to have a release, and she was beginning to long for it as she had never longed for anything in her life.

Ridge said nothing, but bent his head to drop a lingering kiss on her stomach, just above the damp nest he was teasing with his fingers.

"Please, Ridge, *now.*"

His answering laugh was thick with his own passion. "I think you're right. Even if you could last a little longer, I couldn't. Part your legs a little more, Kalena. Show me you want me."

She did as he instructed, making a place for him between her thighs. He came down along the length of her, covering her slowly and completely, resting his weight on his elbows as he looked down at her. Kalena lifted her lashes to find herself looking into a golden fire in his eyes that was not quenched even by the shadows in the room. She wanted to say something in that tension filled moment and could find no words. Her hands gripped his upper arms.

"Wrap your legs around me, Kalena. I'll take care of everything else."

She obeyed, aware of the heavy shaft poised at her opening. Tentatively, and then more urgently, she clung to him. She felt infinitely vulnerable, fully aware of her own inability to control what would happen next. A belated fear that was very primitive and very feminine suddenly coursed through her. Ridge felt it at once.

"It's all right, Kalena," he soothed. "I told you I would take care of you, didn't I?"

"Yes."

"You must learn to trust the man you're marrying today." His thumbs stroked the line of her cheek, gentling her until some of the uncertainty receded. Then he reached down between their bodies, fitting himself to her until she could feel the blunt, hard heaviness of him beginning to stretch her in a way that she had never known. He burned at the entrance to her body.

The sensation was exotic, exciting. Kalena forgot the last of her short-lived fear and clutched Ridge more tightly to her.

"I knew I could set you on fire. The first moment I saw you, I knew. Like holding a match to kindling. Like making the steel glow." His fingers moved tantalizingly over the small nub of pleasure he had discovered earlier and Kalena moaned helplessly. "Close your eyes," he whispered deeply, "and follow me."

She did as he said, squeezing her eyes shut against the tight, thrilling sensations that were overwhelming her. Then there was a relentless, building pressure between her legs as Ridge pushed himself against her. In that instant Olara's warnings crowded back into Kalena's mind, shrieking at her, somehow mingling with the physical shock of Ridge's sensual invasion. Kalena's senses whirled and she cried out, her whole body tensing.

Ridge halted abruptly while Kalena gasped in response to the friction that threatened to turn into pain. She made no protest, but her nails bit deeply into his shoulder as if she would brace herself against what was coming.

"Relax, Kalena."

"I can't—" But she broke off in bewildered astonishment as Ridge bent his head without warning and took her earlobe between his teeth. He bit down quite sharply.

The totally unexpected assault on her ear brought a small yelp from Kalena, and in that instant Ridge surged fully into her. Her mind was still responding to the nip on her ear when the small flash of pain occurred between her legs. She was barely aware of it. When Ridge was buried fully within her he stopped, his whole frame taut with sexual tension.

Kalena blinked in astonishment as her body adjusted to the reality of the completed invasion. The last of Olara's warnings faded from her mind. It was too late to heed them now. "That," she finally managed to declare breathlessly, "was very sneaky."

"Did I hurt you?"

"My ear may never recover."

His smile evolved into a short, sexy, savage grin. "It isn't your ear I'm worrying about. How is the rest of you?"

"I'm not sure," she said honestly.

"Let's find out."

He began to move in her, slowly at first, until she began to respond. When Kalena closed her eyes and murmured his name Ridge increased the rhythm. He began to breathe in heavy gasps as he pushed himself to the limits of his self-control. Kalena could feel his muscles tense as he reigned himself in almost violently. She knew the promise he had made her: tonight was hers. He would not give into the flames beginning to consume him until she found the excitement he had promised.

The small cries she made were a soft, utterly feminine counterpoint to Ridge's guttural groans. Her passion was a total surprise to her. Kalena had never expected to feel like this. Ridge was shuddering with the force of his own response. She would never forget tonight, Kalena realized. No matter how long she lived or what the future held, she would never forget tonight.

Just as the realization flared in her mind, Kalena felt a new level of tension seize her. She tightened around Ridge, her whole body beginning to shiver with tiny convulsions of ecstasy. Unaware of what she was doing, Kalena sank her sharp little teeth into Ridge's strong shoulder as she cried out his name in final surrender.

Ridge groaned, holding himself back so that he could drink in the sensation of Kalena's satisfaction but his own pounding need washed over him, overcoming the iron control he had been exerting. A stifled shout was ripped from him as he surged heavily into Kalena one last time and gave himself up to the mindless release.

He was fire and she was the only one who could quench the flames and bring him peace. The flashing thought crystalized for an instant in Kalena's mind and then it was gone.

Long moments passed before Kalena felt Ridge stir in her arms. Languidly, she became aware of the drying film of perspiration that formed a fine sheen between her breasts. Ridge's chest was damp with moisture, too.

Ridge smiled slightly as he watched her reorient herself to the shadowed room. He made no attempt to change his position, continuing to lie along the length of her, although he gently eased himself out of her body. Kalena was aware of the lingering dampness between her legs and the pungent scent of their lovemaking. In that moment she couldn't begin to define her emotions, but she was aware of being in the grip of a strange state of suspension. It was an odd sensation, as if something important that had been in the back of her mind all along was suddenly trying to free itself and the constraints that had been imposed on it were weakening rapidly.

"I would keep you here if I could," Ridge said. "But I think I had better take you back to your own chamber. I won't have the servants gossiping about you." He glanced out the window into the garden. "Not that much remains of the night." He sat up reluctantly, his hand skimming over the curve of her hip with remembered pleasure. "You must sleep late this morning. You'll need your rest for our wedding night. And the following morning we must be up early to start the journey."

"I can tell you are going to prove to be a harsh husband," Kalena murmured. The truth was, she had no intention of arguing with him. She wanted to be alone to analyze this strange thing that was hovering at the edge of her awareness. She needed to understand it before she released whatever it was from its cage. There was a danger here, one she didn't want to fully acknowledge.

Ridge was laughing softly as he quickly pulled on his shirt and trousers. He emanated masculine satisfaction. "I think you are already discovering ways to handle me." He gave her the thin trousers she wore under the tunic and tugged on his boots while she dressed. When she was ready he took her arm and led her toward the door. Kalena stumbled slightly as she moved away from the pallet. "Are you all right?" Ridge asked with concern.

"Yes, just a little shaky."

Amused, he shook his head as if in commiseration. "Poor Kalena, this has turned out to be quite a night for you, hasn't it? Your first taste of freedom and your first taste of marriage."

"Every woman knows the two are contradictory," Kalena couldn't resist pointing out.

"True, but I'm hoping that now you won't have too many regrets about giving up the one for the other."

Kalena found his total male self-confidence both amusing and exasperating. She couldn't think of anything to say as they walked along the colonnade to her room. At the door Ridge took her once more in his arms, his expression intent.

"I told you earlier that we would make tonight our wedding night. It's done, Kalena. This evening at sunset we will set the formal seal on our marriage, but as far as you and I are concerned, Quintel's ceremony and the feast that follows are only trappings. You are in my charge from this moment, and I swear by the Stones that I will take good care of you. I wish you good night, Kalena."

He kissed her in a manner that was strangely formal, considering what had just happened between them in his chamber.

"I wish you good night, Ridge."

He waited until she had closed her door behind her. Kalena stood listening for the sound of his footsteps to fade, then sank down wearily onto the round, cushioned chair by the window.

Her body felt strained and a little stiff. A few unfamiliar portions of her anatomy would ache in the morning, of that she was certain. The thought of spending the day after her wedding in a creet saddle was enough to make her wince in advance. Thank both ends of the Spectrum she would be spared that, at least.

But none of those thoughts touched the real reason for her new sense of nervous unease. Deliberately, Kalena probed her own mind, seeking the source of her strange, disjointed mood. True, she had been through a great deal that night. Perhaps she was only being plagued by the aftereffects of all the excitement.

No, it was something else, something infinitely more danger-ous. It had begun to break free the moment she had surrendered to Ridge, and now it was busily clanking its loosened chains in her mind.

With sudden, blinding intuition, she realized that Olara had been right. Kalena knew now she should never have given herself to Ridge.

With a soft, despairing cry she hugged herself and tried to shake off the new knowledge that had forced itself upon her. The emotional confrontation and its ultimate result had ripped the veil from that which had been hidden in her mind for years. Tonight that self-knowledge had been freed. Kalena found herself facing the shattering truth: the thought of killing was totally alien to her. She could not do it.

Yet she must.

She did not wish to carry out her duty to her House. Everything within her rebelled against the task. She did not want to be the agent of revenge and murder. Not now, when she was just begin-ning to learn about passion and freedom.

Kalena blinked back the hot tears that were burning her eyes. She had no choice in the matter. Her destiny had been ordained in the summer of her twelfth year when her House had been de-stroyed. There was no turning back; to do so would disgrace her-self and her House past redemption.

Slowly, Kalena got up and walked across the room to her pal-let, Olara's words still vivid in her mind: *You must not succumb to the embraces of this man you will name husband. Not until after your duty is done, and by then there will be no need to give yourself to him. Remember, Kalena, that this man you will be marrying is dangerous in ways you cannot dream. I have seen it in my trance. He is danger-ous.*

Kalena's last thought before she fell into an exhausted sleep was that her aunt had been right about the danger awaiting her niece in the arms of the man called the Fire Whip.

FIVE

The Polarity Advisor chosen by Quintel to conduct the wedding ceremony was dressed in the traditional black and white robes of his office. If he found it odd to be asked to officiate at what was, after all, merely a trade marriage, he was too diplomatic to say so. He could content himself and his curiosity with the fat fee Trade Baron Quintel was paying.

But a few other details about this wedding bothered the advisor. The bride, for example, appeared particularly tense. The hood of her wedding cloak was pulled low over her face, partially concealing her features, but not altogether hiding the strain in her green eyes. In the past the Polarity Advisor had been asked to officiate at ceremonies in which the bride wasn't always a totally willing party, although forcing any woman into marriage against her will was technically illegal. The advisor knew enough about reality to know that great pressure could be brought to bear on a woman when it came to marriage. Still, that could hardly be the case here, he told himself as he uncurled the lanti skin parchment that contained the formal words. After all, this was a trade mar-

riage. Supposedly, that implied that not only was the bride willing, but she had probably negotiated the contract herself. Few decent families would want their daughters involved in such an
arrangement.

In addition to the bride's obvious tension, the austere grimness that hung about the groom disturbed the advisor. Not that
the Fire Whip appeared unwilling; on the contrary, he seemed unusually determined. Ridge stood before the advisor wearing a
mantle of unrelieved black. The hood of his cloak was thrown
back. The night dark garment made a striking and unmistakably
dominant contrast to the scarlet, hooded cloak worn by the bride.
The stark colors of this wedding were enough to make any right
thinking Polarity Advisor cringe. Surely such dramatic tones pre-
saged conflict and strife.

The Master of the House watched from his seat in the center
of the long hall in which the wedding was to take place. Quintel
wore black like the groom. But then, the Polarity Advisor recalled,
the trade baron almost always wore black. Perhaps he had even
loaned the groom his mantle.

Around Quintel were ranged an assortment of vividly dressed
guests, most of whom appeared to have come straight off the floor
of the Traders' Guild hall. Even the women had the stamp of
lower class females. Their tunics were too short, their hair too extreme, their eyes far too bold. There was no sign of any guests
from a more distinguished stratum of society. But given the nature
of the marriage, that was hardly surprising.

Behind the guests musicians waited with counterpoint harps
and flutes to play for the feast that was to follow. And feast it
would be, the Polarity Advisor thought with some satisfaction.
The long, low banquet table was already brimming with an array
of food. Roasted haunches of grain fed zorcan, full bowls of rich
whipped columa berries, platters of harten liver patés, iced serin-
fish, and trays of expensive tanga fruit were just a sampling of the
offerings. A seemingly endless quantity of good red ale and fine
Encana wine was arranged nearby. More of everything would be

brought out when the party really got under way. The advisor looked forward to that part. He was, of course, invited to the feast.

But first there was a ceremony to perform. Clearing his throat, the advisor hesitated three more seconds, waiting for the last wink of sunlight outside the windows. As the fading rays lit up the sky, the crystal water clock in the great hall announced that twilight had arrived. The wedding could begin.

"The sun has given herself into the embrace of the night even as woman gives herself to man," the Polarity Advisor intoned. "It is fitting that at this moment we gather to witness another such joining of light and dark, day and night, male and female. For in this union between a man and a woman is inherent all the strength, all the power and all the energy created by the meeting of opposite points on the Spectrum. The power of this union is so great that new life may be born of it. Yet no such joining can exist without the force of resistance.

"It is the nature of the union to contain within it the seeds of its own destruction. Ultimately, one point of power and contrast must be stronger than the other or devastation and disaster will result. The union would be torn asunder. Therefore it has been ordained that as darkness swallows light and night envelops day, so must man enfold and protect woman. His strength is that of the darkness that is the universe. Hers is the flickering sources of light that dwell therein."

Kalena listened to the ancient words of the ceremony, aware of the complete attention her groom was giving the Polarity Advisor. Trade marriage or not, Quintel's Whip seemed to be taking this ceremony far too seriously. The intent and determination she sensed in Ridge panicked her. But, then, she had been on the verge of panic all day, she thought gloomily.

Kalena had seen Ridge only a few times during the day, and then only briefly. He had been occupied with the final preparations for the journey to the Heights of Variance. His preoccupation was just as well. Kalena had stayed out of sight in her chamber for the most part, pretending to be suffering normal bridal jitters. In reality, she spent the time struggling with horror of the duty that lay ahead of her. She had been grateful when Arrisa and the other freewomen had arrived early and had gleefully begun to dress the bride. Vertina had asked if she had remembered the day's pinch of crushed selite leaves and made one or two cracks about the steel of Countervail. From that point on there had been little chance to brood.

But the ceremony was almost over, and she would soon have to face the role Olara and the luck of the Spectrum had assigned her. Kalena was only half listening as the Polarity Advisor continued the ceremony. Her mind on her problem, she caught only scattered words and phrases.

"A man who accepts his wife must also accept the duty he assumes toward her. She has left the protection of her family, trusting in the protection of her husband. She is now his responsibility. Her honor is forever entwined with his own. He must protect it as he would his own."

Kalena thought she could feel Quintel's dark gaze on her and she wondered what he was thinking. As far as she was concerned, his insistence on the formal ceremony had never been satisfactorily explained. Aunt Olara had predicted the large wedding, but her Far Seeing trance had not explained why Quintel would provide such excellent cover for his own murder. Kalena clearly recalled her aunt stating that the time to strike would be on the night of the marriage, when feasting and celebration occupied the members of the household. Kalena had been told she was to use the privacy provided by the traditional hour allowed the bride after the feast.

If only she had not succumbed to the temptation the night before, Kalena thought in despair. All day long she had been paying the penalty. Her mind was in turmoil and her resolve was almost in shreds. The thought of the act which lay ahead was enough to make her tremble with nausea. She had no doubt that the time she had spent in Ridge's arms had weakened her catastrophically. A barrier in her mind had been breached and the waters of resistance and uncertainty were flooding her senses.

"A woman who accepts a husband accepts his authority. She

must remember this even though there be times when the natural reaction of opposites causes her to think of rebelling against that authority. She must trust in his guidance and strength, knowing he is the guardian of her honor as well as his own."

Kalena's attention was caught by the small, carved onyxite box that was being handed to the Polarity Advisor.

"Let this symbol of union be worn around the bride's throat. Placed there by her husband as a sign of his protection and authority, it is not to be removed by any other hand."

Kalena watched with a numb feeling of inevitability as the onyxite box was opened and held out to Ridge. Her new husband reached into the sarsilk lined interior and removed the thin, shimmering chain. One end of the chain ended in a lock of white amber. The other ended in a key of black amber. When it was in place around her throat, Kalena would be well and truly wed—at least for the length of time stipulated in the contract.

Ridge turned to her for the first time in the ceremony, the symbol of his possession in his hand. Kalena caught her breath. For an instant everything around her seemed to stand still as the panic that had been simmering just under the surface suddenly possessed her completely. She looked up into the banked golden flames in his eyes and every instinct warned her to flee. She knew she would have done exactly that if there had been any way of overcoming her body's paralysis.

Instead, she found herself standing unmoving as Ridge carefully pushed the hood of the scarlet cloak back so he could have access to her throat. She closed her eyes, felt his hands on her as he looped the chain around her neck, and then there was a slight pause as he held the key to the opening of the lock. The guests were as still as Kalena. Ridge inserted the key into the lock, thus joining the ends of the beautiful chain.

There was a faint but audible click as the key turned in the lock and a great cheer exploded in the hall. Even Quintel smiled briefly, the expression fleeting and curiously satisfied. He got to his feet and came forward to greet the bride and groom.

For the next three hours, Kalena existed in a haze of exuberant, noisy chatter, endlessly flowing wine and a table full of food that was forever being replenished by scurrying servants. The selection of guests had practically guaranteed a loud, raucous crowd. Fortunately, Kalena was not expected to participate to any great extent. Her duty consisted primarily of sitting at one end of the table, sampling bits of food and tasting from a goblet of wine. Considering what lay ahead of her that evening, she decided, it was as much as she was capable of doing anyway. Tonight, at least, she was not expected to serve. Good thing, she decided. Her fingers were shaking too much to allow her to risk holding a crystal decanter.

Ridge sat at the opposite end of the long table. He lounged at ease on the cushions, his gaze flicking frequently to Kalena's tense face. The guests plied him with bawdy jokes and an endless assortment of sexual advice. Quintel sat halfway down the table, indulgently tolerating the noise and good cheer.

"A toast to Quintel's Whip," declared one man, staggering to his feet after several others had already led such drinking bouts.

"A toast!" the others agreed, waiting expectantly.

"I give you the man they say can turn cold steel into glowing fire . . ."

Kalena was aware of Ridge's abrupt scowl. Apparently, the legend behind the label he wore was not to his liking.

"May he succeed in doing exactly that tonight in such a way that his bride will always remember her wedding night!" the trader leading the toast concluded with a leering grin.

Loud guffaws and several ribald comments concerning Ridge's alleged affinity with fire and steel and the possible uses of that ability in a sleeping pallet swamped the room in laughter. But no grin broke out on Ridge's face, Kalena noticed.

Vaguely alarmed by her new husband's silence, she looked up in time to see him lean forward across the table, his hand thrust under his cloak to rest on the sintar he wore. As the guests became aware of the fact that the joke had not gone over well, a ragged hush fell on the crowd. Ridge spoke into that uneasy silence, his voice low and harsh as he addressed the trader who had made the unfortunate jest.

"A man who doesn't know his manners would do well to keep his mouth shut on the occasions when he has been fortunate enough to be invited into civilized company. But perhaps it's not too late to teach you a few of the social graces, Laris."

Uneasy glances passed along the table. Automatically, Kalena looked to Quintel, expecting him to interrupt the proceedings before Ridge got into a fight with the man named Laris. But Quintel merely lounged on his cushions, watching his Fire Whip as if Ridge were some species of pet fangcat who was about to give a performance.

"Ah, Ridge," Laris said with an attempt at a shaky chuckle. "It was only a jest."

Ridge fingered the handle of the sintar, although he did not remove it from its sheath. "Only a jest? Perhaps you would like to apologize to everyone present for your unfortunate sense of humor? You have embarrassed my wife."

"Now, Ridge, there's no call to get upset about this," Laris said uneasily.

"Maybe not, but I'm upset anyway. What are you going to do about it?"

After one last, frantic glance at Quintel's disinterested expression, Kalena rose to her feet in a swift movement that brought all eyes—including Ridge's—to her end of the table. There was silence again as she reached down to pluck up the wine decanter. Forcing herself to smile with a demure sweetness she was far from feeling, Kalena started around the table toward Ridge. Her scarlet cloak swirled gracefully around her ankles.

"I see your wine glass is nearly empty, my husband. Perhaps that is the real cause of your ill temper. I would not have you in a bad mood tonight of all nights. Allow me to perform my first duty as your wife and refill your glass."

Ridge eyed her balefully as she knelt to pour the wine into his glass. Everyone watched in fascination as Kalena set down the decanter and picked up the goblet she had just filled. If Ridge accepted the goblet from her, he would have to take his hand from the handle of the sintar.

Kalena did not attempt to hand him the goblet straight off. Instead, she sipped delicately at the wine herself; then she offered him the delicately chased cup.

The incipient blaze in Ridge's eyes died out, to be replaced by rueful amusement. "It would seem you have a talent for the wifely arts, Kalena." He released his grip on the sintar and took the goblet from her hand. A small sigh of relief circled the table as he took a healthy swallow.

Kalena said nothing, sensing the immediate problem was solved. She got to her feet and walked back to her end of the table. The feasting and the laughter resumed, unabated.

It was when Kalena knelt again on her cushion that she happened to glance down the row of faces at the table and notice that Quintel was gone.

She looked toward the back of the room and saw his dark figure disappear in the direction of his private apartments. No one else seemed to notice. When she glanced at the crystal water clock she saw that it was the hour when Quintel always retired to pursue his studies. She had learned his habits well during the past three days.

It was time for her to carry out the task for which Olara had raised and trained her.

Kalena felt a twisting nausea in the pit of her stomach. A suitable sensation for a woman who was about to commit murder with the aid of poison, she told herself grimly. She waited for a few minutes longer and then slowly rose to her feet. The next moment would be tricky, as the bride could hardly slip away unnoticed from her own wedding celebration.

All eyes turned to her almost at once.

"Kalena, are you tired already?" Arrisa called laughingly.

"Your bride grows impatient, Ridge," one of the men hooted.

There were several other remarks made that were guaranteed to make any bride blush. Kalena merely lowered her eyes. She was beyond the blushing stage. The knowledge of what lay ahead of her had made her pale, not pink.

"If you will excuse me, I claim my hour of privacy in which to make the proper preparations," she told the guests, keeping her eyes lowered in what she hoped passed for modest confusion. "I have no wish to break up the celebration. You must all continue without me."

"Don't worry, Kalena, we'll send your groom along in a while," Vertina assured her with a grin. "You have your hour. Use it well."

One of the men added, "It will give her enough time to grow bored and fall asleep."

"Never mind, Kalena, we'll keep the men under control here," Arrisa said. "Every bride deserves her time of privacy. Be on your way."

Ridge got to his feet, facing Kalena from the far end of the table. His face was strangely expressionless, and when he spoke his voice was gravely formal.

"I wish you a good evening, wife."

She inclined her head politely. "I wish you good evening also, husband." Kalena turned, the scarlet sarsilk cloak flowing around her as she walked out of the hall. She was very conscious of the black and white amber necklace around her neck.

When she was out of sight and could hear the noise level growing once again in the feasting hall, Kalena picked up the hem of her cloak and began to run. She raced across the moonlit garden and into the safety of her apartments. Breathing far more heavily than the slight exercise warranted, she closed the door behind her and leaned back against it.

It was now or never. This was the moment Olara had predicted, the moment in time on which the honor of the House of the Ice Harvest depended. The vial of poison waited in its hiding place in the travel bag. Kalena knew she must act or forever endure the shame of failure.

Her fingers were trembling more than ever. Nightmarish images of a man writhing in his death throes, his black eyes full of accusation and fear, threatened to swamp her mind.

She wanted nothing to do with death, Kalena raged silently. It all happened so long ago. Why must she be called upon to settle the account?

No wonder the task of avenging House honor was traditionally a male responsibility. Just look at how she was weakening now that the moment was upon her. A man would be stronger, Kalena told herself derisively. Olara had been right to fear the weakness in her niece.

Perhaps, Kalena thought, if she had seen Quintel murder her father and her brother, she would not be having such qualms.

But there was only Olara's assurance that Quintel had been the cause of their death. Olara claimed to have discovered the truth in a trance shortly after the death of the men of the House. The older woman had emerged from that trance in a daze of embittered rage. The shock of learning of the double murder had hit Kalena's mother very hard. She had sunk into a deep, despairing depression from which none of Olara's remedies could rouse her. Olara had taken over what was left of the House, sweeping Kalena and her mother to safety. From that moment on Kalena's destiny had been clear. No amount of internal arguing could change the truth or her own destiny, Kalena told herself.

Her body stiff with tension, she moved away from the door and walked slowly to where her travel bag rested near the sleeping pallet. Reaching inside, she ripped at the stitching in the lining. The small leather packet of poison and her father's jeweled sintar fell into her hands.

Kalena sat on the pallet's edge, staring at the blade, wondering not for the first time just what sort of man her father had been. She hadn't known him well. He was a distant figure from her childhood, strong and aristocratic, but remote. He had been gone a lot, frequently taking her older brother with him on his travels. Kalena had been left behind in the care of her mother and her aunt. And then one day the Lord of the House of the Ice Harvest and his heir had failed to return. After that there had been only Kalena's mother and Olara. Finally, there had been only Olara.

Poison was a dishonorable weapon, Kalena thought, holding

up the packet of evil powder. A coward's weapon. A *woman's* weapon, some would say. But while Olara had disdained the method, she had seen no option. There was no way a mere woman could kill Trade Baron Quintel in honorable hand-to-hand combat. Nor was there any way, Olara had learned in a trance, that Kalena could be introduced into her victim's bed. Quintel was not the type to be seduced by a woman.

That left only poison.

Nausea roiled again in Kalena's stomach. She had to act. Soon the servant would be going down the hall in Quintel's wing of the house. He would be carrying the nightly potion of Encana wine that Quintel enjoyed with his studies. The poison must be put into the wine. Kalena had spent many hours deciding just how that could be done.

Time had run out. She must be about the business for which she had been trained.

Still wearing her cloak, she dropped the poison into a pocket in her tunic, secreted the sintar beneath the cloak and went back out into the garden. She stepped onto the rainstone paving and followed the bloodred path toward Quintel's apartments.

Back in the feasting hall, Ridge was aware of a new kind of restlessness within himself. He had been on edge all day, filled with a painful sense of awareness, the unwelcome, vivid kind that so often preceded violence. He had known it more than once in his life, the most recent time being out on the treacherous road that went through the Talon Pass. But he couldn't imagine why he felt it tonight.

He had told himself that once the wedding was complete the strange restlessness in him would be stilled, but that hadn't happened. If anything, the mood was stronger than ever. Something was very wrong, and he knew with a deep certainty that the wrongness was connected with his new bride.

She had been tense each time he had seen her during the day. Bridal nerves, Ridge had told himself. After last night she must be finally realizing just how real the marriage was to be. He had tried to quiet his own uneasiness by reminding himself of the previous night's lovemaking. By the Stones, it had been good. Unlike anything he had ever known.

It wasn't simply that the sex had been satisfying. Ridge knew on some level that a bond had been forged between himself and Kalena last night. She was his. In some indefinable manner he had known the moment he had taken her that this woman was his destiny.

Off and on during the day, stray thoughts of the future had floated in and out of his mind. With Kalena by his side and the profit from the shipment of Sand he intended to bring back from Variance, Ridge knew he could at last take steps to found his House.

Kalena was the woman he had been waiting for, the one who fit him as the lock fit the key. He had discovered that for certain the night before, but he thought he had known it all along from the moment he had met her. The knowledge had burned within him all day. He had been equally aware that he might have to force Kalena to accept that her destiny lay in his hands. But he had a good start on that goal. After all, he was now her husband.

"Another round of ale, my friend. You have a full night's work ahead of you," one of the men called from halfway down the table. "We must get you in shape to perform it, eh?"

Ridge came to a decision. He didn't bother to question it. He had learned long ago not to question his hunches. With a deceptively lazy movement he got to his feet. Knowing laughter burst out along the length of the table. He regarded his guests with a host's polite expression, unaware that his hand was resting absently on the handle of his sintar.

"The servants have instructions to keep you fed and entertained until dawn if you last that long. You must, however, excuse me. I have other plans for the night."

"Don't let us delay you, Ridge," someone called. More laughter greeted the comment.

"I won't," Ridge said calmly. "I wish you all good night."

"Wait, Ridge," Arrisa called. "Your bride has not had her hour."

"She can spend what's left of it with me." With an arrogant inclination of his head that he had unconsciously picked up from watching Quintel over the years, Ridge bid his guests farewell and strode from the hall.

When he was alone at last he came to a halt. The restless unease in him was stronger than ever. The sense of wrongness was growing. Frowning, Ridge stepped out into the long colonnaded walkway, intending to follow it around to Kalena's apartment. The thought of his bride waiting for him did not bring the pleasant anticipation it should have.

Red moonlight reflected from the rainstone paths out in the garden. Ridge watched it from the deep shadows of the colonnade as he moved silently over the stone. For no reason that he could explain, he found himself walking like a hunting fangcat.

He was halfway toward his goal when he saw the dark shape of Kalena's wedding cloak drifting across the garden. Ridge went utterly still, his hand tightening around the handle of the sintar. For an instant he couldn't believe what he was seeing.

Not after last night, he told himself savagely. She could not possibly long for the unattainable Quintel after the way she had responded to Ridge last night. She would not dare to seek out Quintel now.

But her direction was clear. The only chambers that lay on that side of the house were those that were occupied by Quintel.

Hot rage washed over Ridge in a boiling wave as he stood watching his new bride make her way to another man's chambers. He had never known anything like the blistering fury that gripped him now. He knew that if he touched the sintar, it would glow red. It took an instant of iron willpower to control the anger to the point where he could function. And then Ridge stepped out into the garden, moving along behind Kalena in lethal silence.

Kalena reached the far side of the garden and stepped, shaking, into the shadows of the colonnade. Desperately she tried to breathe through the growing tightness in her chest. The night whirled in a dark haze around her, disorienting her and increasing her sense of inner sickness. She clung to a pillar to steady herself as her fingers tightened frantically around the packet in her hand.

Suddenly, she was transfixed by the thought that she very well might not survive the night. The way her body was reacting, she began to wonder if the act of murder would actually result in her own death. Never had she felt so ill. Everything within her was resisting the task that lay ahead. Her body and mind were at total war with her destiny. Olara must have known it would be this way if the strange barrier in her mind was broken. Her aunt had tried to protect her from this weakness, Kalena thought as she took another step toward her goal. Olara had warned her.

Moving forward required more effort than wading through a cauldron of mud. The entire world narrowed down to the few steps that would take her to her goal. Kalena knew she was losing not only her nerve but her will. She wanted to give up, to surrender to the powerful forces that were trying to halt her. In that moment she wished for the coming together of the Keys, the return of the legendary Dawn Lords or even the final cataclysmic reaction that was said to be the result of the Dark and Light Stones being brought into proximity with each other. Any suitable catastrophe would be welcome tonight, anything that would give her the excuse she needed to turn aside from her duty.

No one guarded the entrance to Quintel's private rooms. Kalena had her explanations ready in case she was challenged, but as she had guessed, no one confronted her. Quintel was secure in his own household. The packet of poison was like ice beneath her fingers, or perhaps it was her fingers that were like ice.

It is your duty, Kalena. You are the last of the House. You have no choice.

Olara's words pounded in Kalena's mind as she strove to reach the door that would open onto Quintel's private wing.

Your duty.

Her hand was on the heavy, wrought metal handle. She desperately searched for the strength to twist it. Kalena shuddered with the effort, and in that moment suddenly knew that the task before her was impossible.

She had failed.

Even as she tried to come to grips with that bitter knowledge, hard fingers closed over her mouth from behind. Kalena's instinctive scream was locked in her throat. A man's arm circled her waist, trapping her. She knew even before he spoke who held her so fiercely.

"Damn you to the far end of the Spectrum," Ridge snarled softly in her ear. "*He is not for you.* I told you that. How do you dare try to betray me this way? Do you long so much to feel the touch of a creet whip? How do you dare go to him on the very night I put my lock and key around your throat?"

Kalena's eyes were wide in disbelief and fear; she made no move to struggle. She couldn't move, both because her will was totally depleted and because Ridge held her in bonds of steel. *The steel of Countervail.*

"Say nothing. Make no noise, do you understand? Or I will beat you where you stand. If you want the servants to hear your cries, so be it."

Kalena tried to nod her head to show that she had no intention of making any noise. She was beyond such action. Ridge freed her mouth, yanking her around so hard that she stumbled and would have fallen if he hadn't caught hold of her arm. His fingers dug into the fabric of her cloak, biting into her skin. Kalena could barely breathe beneath the glittering fury in his eyes.

He pulled her after him along the rainstone path. Kalena felt dizzy. She was vaguely aware that some of her physical strength was returning as she was dragged farther and farther from Quintel's door. But she couldn't think clearly. The only thing her disoriented mind could focus on was that the catastrophe for which she had wished had struck. Unlike the coming together of the Stones, it had not brought the end of Zantalia, but it would surely change her private world forever. Ridge had caught her in the act of trying to kill Quintel.

A few moments later she was being shoved inside her chamber. The door closed with awful care and Ridge turned to face her. Kalena stood her ground, concentrating on trying to steady her breathing.

"Before I give you what you deserve, tell me why," Ridge ground out softly. "Tell me why you are so fascinated with Quintel? Is it because he has no interest in women and you were challenged? Was it curiosity after last night to find out what it feels like to have another man possess you? *Why?*"

"I . . . I can't explain," Kalena managed, her throat tight with the effort of speaking. She began to realize the source of Ridge's fury. He was jealous. Well, he would be far more angry if he understood the real reason she had sought Quintel tonight. A dull sense of fatalistic apathy began to replace the sick tension that had been swamping her senses. It was over. Everything was over, including her future. No wonder she had always had trouble envisioning exactly what form her freedom would take; there was no freedom awaiting her. "But I swear on the honor of my House that I did not go to the trade baron's rooms tonight with the intention of sharing his sleeping pallet. *I swear it!*"

"The honor of your House? That's a joke. You come from some small farm in the Interlock valley. Your family might once have been respectable, but that's about all you can say for it. What you have done tonight has destroyed even that much."

Kalena's pride came to her aid. The oath had slipped out under the stress of the moment, but she had meant every word of it. It would seem that when all else was gone, several generations of House pride still remained. She drew herself up, her eyes ice cold in the light of the firegel lamps. "You are a Houseless bastard. Don't lecture me on honor and respectability. I am the daughter of a Great House and you are nothing but a rich man's tool. His whip."

Ridge took a menacing step forward. "Don't lie to me on top of everything else, woman. I will punish you as harshly for that as I will for trying to betray me in another man's arms."

"I did not betray you! At least, not in the way you mean."

"Words!" he said between set teeth. "If you had any sense you would be on your knees pleading with me and instead you stand there throwing words at me. You went to Quintel's apartments tonight. You cannot deny that."

"Yes, but I swear I did not go there to sleep with him. *Ridge!*" Kalena stepped back hurriedly as he reached for her, but she was not quick enough. He caught hold of her shoulders.

"Tell me the truth. Admit it or so help me, I will . . ."

Kalena's chin lifted, a gesture that contained all those internalized generations of arrogant breeding and House pride. "I give you my oath, on the honor of my House, that I did not intend to share Quintel's pallet tonight."

"Then why did you seek him out?" Ridge's eyes were golden pools of fury in the softly lit room.

Kalena refused to cower. Nothing he could do to her was as bad as what she had done to herself. She had dishonored both herself and her House tonight. There was nothing left to fear. "I cannot tell you."

"By the Stones, you will tell me," he bit out. His hands went to the fastening of the scarlet cloak.

Kalena closed her eyes as the garment was flung aside. She heard the faint clicking sound as the fabric-muffled sintar struck the floor. It was too much to hope that Ridge would not hear it, too. He stared at her for an instant and then silently released her to pick up the cloak. His hand moved through the garment and a moment later he withdrew the jeweled sintar.

"Where did you steal this?" he asked bluntly.

Enraged by the accusation, Kalena whirled to face him. "I did not steal it. It was my father's sintar and he is dead. I am the last daughter of the House, and by right that blade is mine!" She reached down to the open travel bag and scrabbled around inside, tearing more of the lining, until she came up with the House band she had hidden inside. Hurling the bracelet at his feet, Kalena waited for him to pick it up. "Take a good look, Ridge. That band carries the mark of my House. The House of the Ice Harvest."

Without taking his eyes off her, Ridge bent down to scoop up the band. He glanced at it once and then tossed it aside. "Did you steal it when you stole the sintar?"

"Damn you, bastard, you are as thickheaded and stubborn as any bull zorcan, aren't you?"

His hand moved so swiftly that Kalena wasn't sure of the action until she realized Ridge was holding his own sintar in his fist. It occurred to her then that he might go so far as to kill her for what he deemed his betrayal at her hands. A healthy dose of fear at last began to seep back into her bloodstream. If he was going to kill her, he might as well do it for the right reason.

She stepped backward automatically as Ridge came toward her. He did not hold the blade as if he would strike her, but kept it at his side. Kalena couldn't take her gaze off the stark, unadorned sintar. It was a blade meant for drinking blood.

And the steel blade was glowing fire red in Ridge's hands.

"Now," he said in a voice that was totally devoid of emotion. "You will answer my questions. I will have the truth from you."

Six

Any way she looked at it, she was facing death, Kalena decided. It was fitting punishment for failure. She sank down on the edge of the pallet, trying not to look at the glowing blade in Ridge's hand. What did the truth matter now? She had failed in her duty. But somehow, if she was meant to die at this moment, she would prefer to meet that death for the proper reason. That reason was her failure.

"I went to Quintel's apartment tonight to kill him. Since the summer of my twelfth year, it has been my duty, my destiny. It is the single task for which I have been raised."

Ridge's eyes narrowed in disbelief. "You what?"

Kalena held out the packet of poison she had been clutching. "I intended to put some of that into his evening wine. He would have died shortly after drinking it, of what would have looked like a heart attack. The House of the Ice Harvest would have been avenged. But I failed. The truth is, I would have failed even had you not stopped me, Ridge. You see, I lost my nerve. I was too

weak to do that which was required of me. Olara wasted all her
efforts. My whole life has been a pointless exercise in failure."

Ridge came forward slowly and took the packet from her
hand. Kalena thought she could feel some of the heat emanating
from the strange sintar he held. He kept the blade at his side while
he cautiously sniffed the contents of the packet.

"Be careful," Kalena warned in a dull voice. "Even a pinch or
two would be enough to kill you. My aunt concocted it."

"Your aunt sent you to kill Quintel?" Ridge's voice was still almost completely empty of inflection.

"She could not undertake the task herself. She is too old and
lately she has been ill. Besides, she is a Healer, a fine one. Everyone knows it is impossible for a Healer to kill. The years since our
House was brought to an end by Quintel have been hard on her.
The strain of my father's and brother's death is too much for my
mother. She never was very strong. She died shortly after they did.
I was the only one left who could avenge the House." Kalena held
out her hand in a helpless gesture and then let her fingers drop
back into her lap. "Now you will kill me and it will all be over."

Ridge stared at her. "You're saying you believe Quintel was responsible for the deaths of your father and brother?"

"Yes."

"That makes no sense," he declared harshly. "It's an insane notion."

"It's the truth. Olara saw it all in a trance. My House was a
small but wealthy one. We controlled the trading traffic on the
great Interlock River and its tributaries. My father apparently
clashed with Quintel on several occasions, although I was too
young to be aware of such matters. Finally, Quintel decided to ensure that a more cooperative House was given control of the river.
He saw to it that the men of my House suffered 'accidents' in the
mountains."

"You don't know what you're talking about."

"Perhaps not. But my aunt does. It was she who realized the
accidents were acts of murder. With my father and his heir dead,
the House of the Ice Harvest was officially ended. Control of the

river trade was immediately given over to another House. My aunt took my mother and myself to a small farm town where we were unknown. She insisted we no longer use our House name and invented another for us instead. She said she wanted to protect us."

"From what?" Ridge asked roughly. "If the men of your House were all dead, surely the women posed no threat to whoever might have killed them."

"My aunt had her reasons. She did not want Quintel to know about me. Olara was right. Quintel would never have negotiated a trade marriage agreement with the daughter of an old enemy."

Ridge realized with a kind of stunned shock that Kalena believed everything she was saying, including her own feeling of failure. There was too much self-accusation and weary resignation in her voice, too much pride in her bearing, even though she knew she faced defeat. And the packet of poison was damning evidence of the truth. She had gone to Quintel's rooms with the intention of killing him, not sleeping with him. For some reason that knowledge drained some of the heat from his veins. He felt like an idiot for being relieved, but he couldn't deny that he was.

She hadn't been about to betray him with another man.

Slowly, the heat faded from the sintar as the steel reacted to the cooling of his fury.

Only a handful of times in his entire life had the violence of his emotions spilled over into the steel of his blade. The first time it had happened he had been a barefoot kid fighting off a group of toughs at the back of a filthy alley in Countervail. Ridge had bought the sintar only a few days earlier with the profit he had made from helping a creet owner round up a flock of panicked birds that had gotten loose in the street. It had been one of his few legitimate jobs.

The gang of boys had cornered him in the alley, intending to take the sintar, Ridge's clothes and anything else he might have been lucky enough to have on him. To their astonishment, Ridge had fought back. To his astonishment, the steel of the sintar had begun to grow hot in the first few minutes of battle. The fierce glow of the blade had sent the young attackers running in terror.

Ridge had been left alone in the alley, staring at the weapon in his hand.

Two eightdays later he had met Quintel while attempting to help himself to the contents of the rich trade baron's money pouch. Quintel had caught Ridge's arm, smiled curiously and politely introduced himself. He had then asked if the young thief would like a legitimate job. Awed by the man and the offer, Ridge hadn't hesitated. After saying yes, he had never looked back.

Over the years Ridge had learned to control his emotions, especially his rage, to a large extent. Violent rage was a distinct handicap in his business. Any fierce emotion was. Self-control was the key to staying alive when he was working. When he did Quintel's work, Ridge was all business. Nevertheless, his temper had become a legend in Crosspurposes. It took a lot now to make the steel glow with internal fire, but it didn't take a lot to arouse a quick burst of his less dangerous, if scalding, masculine temper. Tonight Kalena had proven she had the power to push him far enough to heat the steel. Slowly he eased the sintar back into his sheath and eyed the woman in front of him.

"You did not intend to invite yourself into Quintel's pallet?" he asked at last.

"No!" Her voice was a muffled, choked denial, as if the idea revolted her. "Never. The man murdered my father and brother. In so doing he destroyed my House. How could I even consider letting him touch me the way . . . the way . . ."

"What way, Kalena?"

"The way you touched me," she said at last. Her eyes were focused on the opposite wall. Now that he had put away the sintar she wouldn't look at him.

"So," Ridge said slowly, "you are an assassin, not a seductress."

"A failed assassin."

"Yes," he agreed. "A failed assassin. What else did you expect?" he added almost gently. "You're a woman."

Kalena shot him a bitter look.

Ridge ignored the glance. "Tell me, Kalena of the House of the

Ice Harvest, did your aunt have any proof of her accusations? Do you know for certain that Quintel had anything to do with the death of the men in your family?"

"Stop it," she cried. "It's the truth. It has to be the truth. For years I have lived with that truth. It has dominated my life."

"The truth as told to you by your aunt?" he persisted.

"She would not lie about such a thing. She's a Healer, devoted to life and the future. She has the Far Seeing gift as well as the healing talent. Such a one does not commit herself to murder unless there is no alternative."

"She didn't commit herself to it," Ridge snapped, "she committed you to it."

"Only because she knew she could not carry out the deed herself."

"She set all this up, didn't she? She negotiated the contract with Quintel in order to get you close to him. This business with trouble on the Sand route was made to order for her. She's been keeping you stashed away on some farm in the Interlock valley until just the right moment. She thought she saw her chance and without a qualm she sent you to do her dirty work."

"It is not her dirty work," Kalena blazed. "It was my duty. If you were a member of a Great House, you would understand my position. You would know the price that such kinship demands. It is a matter of honor!"

"Don't give me that nonsense. I know the meaning of honor, woman. I also know the meaning of duty and loyalty. Perhaps I have even a better understanding of it than you do because I didn't inherit any House honor. I've fashioned my own. And I know where my responsibility lies."

She nodded. "You will kill me now because your duty is toward your employer."

Ridge felt rage begin to build again in him. Firmly he tamped it down. He'd be damned if he would let this slip of a female make him lose control. She was his, by the Spectrum. He could and would control her.

"Unfortunately, things aren't that simple any longer. You're my wife, Kalena. As of sunset this evening I have been responsible for your actions. Weren't you listening to the words of the ceremony? Your honor and my own are tied together now. Do you have any conception of the mess you have created? Do you understand what you have done? You tried to kill the man to whom I have vowed my loyalty. Quintel trusts me as he trusts no one else in this world."

"Blame him for the situation, then. He was, after all, the one who negotiated the contract of marriage with my aunt. He was the one who introduced me into his own household. He's the reason I'm here. You're entirely blameless, as far as I can tell. This does not concern you, Fire Whip. This matter is between the House of the Ice Harvest and the House of the Gliding Fallon. A bastard such as you has no business in such matters."

Ridge slammed his hand flat against the wall in a gesture of frustrated anger. "By the Stones, woman, you don't even have the sense to keep your mouth shut when you should."

"Why shouldn't I say what I wish? You're going to kill me, regardless."

That was too much. He'd had it with listening to her predict her death at his hands. Ridge stalked over to the pallet and stood towering over his new wife. "No, Kalena of the House of the Ice Harvest. I am not going to kill you, although by the time I am through with you, you may wish I had."

"You're going to beat me and then turn me over to Quintel or the Town Patrol?" she asked warily.

"There isn't time for either action, in spite of the fact that one or both might have been intensely satisfying. No, Kalena, I am not going to beat you tonight."

She looked at him distrustingly. "Why not?"

"Because if I did you wouldn't be able to sit a creet saddle for a full day tomorrow, that's why not!" he stormed. "The way I feel now you probably wouldn't be able to move for an eightday if I beat you the way you deserve. We still have a journey to make, you and I. I'm not going to let you keep me from my assigned task. I have my own duty to perform and destiny to meet." He leaned down and hauled her up to stand in front of him. "I am not going to let you keep me from getting my hands on a fortune in Sand. You may have been a fine House lady once, Kalena, but you are married to me now. You are the wife of a Houseless bastard and you will fulfill your duty to your new husband. I may not be a Great House lord, but by law and custom I am your master, Kalena. You signed the papers yourself. Your loyalty is to me now. Your sole duty is to obey your husband. And I have decided that you will be sitting in a creet saddle heading toward Variance before dawn tomorrow morning. Don't deceive yourself that I can't control you. You belong to me now. Regardless of how either of us feel about it, our destinies are tied together."

Kalena looked at him wordlessly, considering her limited set of alternatives. On the whole, a long ride in a creet saddle sounded better than the more honorable death she knew she should be seeking. The raw truth was that she was apparently not cut out to be an instrument of vengeance. Life was far too appealing to her, even life as the wife of a man who had no legitimate House name and every reason to hate her.

In the end, it didn't matter how she felt about it. She knew she didn't have the strength or will to resist Ridge. With the knowledge of her own failure had come a numbing death to her own sense of will and direction. She had no choice but to put herself in the Fire Whip's hands.

Kalena had heard that long ago, in the days of the mythical Dawn Lords, creets could actually fly. She wasn't sure she believed the story, but by the third day on the trail she would willingly have sold the Secrets of the Stones if it were true. The thought of flying was startling, even terrifying in some respects, but she was so bone weary after three days in the saddle that any change in the manner of travel would have been welcome.

She had ridden very little in her life. The longest trip she had ever undertaken had been the one from Interlock to Crosspurposes, and then she traveled by public coach drawn by creets. Creets were expensive and of little use other than for transportation. Olara and Kalena had had no need of the birds while living in Interlock.

Fortunately, staying atop one of the good-natured birds was not difficult. Kalena's saddle was deep and quite safe, even when the creets were pounding along the ground with their swift, pacing stride. But being safe did not mean the seat was comfortable, especially if one wasn't accustomed to it.

Kalena paid no attention to the passing countryside. She was vaguely aware that they were crossing the rich grain fields of the Plains of Antinomy, but the gently rolling landscape held little interest for her. Her normal sense of curiosity was completely dulled by her personal misery and the relentless stride of the yellow and white creet she rode.

She stared down at the feathered neck in front of her and wondered if it was true that the bird's small, useless wings had once been capable of lifting its large body into the sky.

Creets were strong creatures, having apparently long since given up the light, vulnerable bones that would have enabled them to fly. The long toes of each foot still sported curving, birdlike claws. Those claws could be dangerous, Kalena knew, if the birds were enraged. Some flock managers had the claws removed. A lot of people preferred to ride animals that had been so treated. But Trade Master Ridge had ordered clawed birds for the trip to the Heights of Variance. Kalena knew it was because such birds were more sure-footed. They were also better able to defend themselves if they were attacked by something as large as a fangcat or a pack of sinkworms. In any event, unlike her husband, it took a great deal to enrage a creet. They were by nature placid, willing beasts, content to preen their beautiful feathers and squabble playfully with each other when they weren't called upon to work.

Kalena lifted her head and gazed resentfully at the creet in front of her own. It was the mate of the female she rode. Creets bonded for life and were usually worked in pairs. Ridge sat astride the male, the leather reins looped carelessly through one hand. He looked as strong and grim as he had the morning they left Crosspurposes. Kalena knew he had deliberately set a punishing pace. She thought about telling him that the punishment was quite effective, but she suspected he was well aware of it. Every muscle in her body ached. For the past three days she had bitten back the complaints and willed herself to endure. By the Stones, she would not give the bastard the satisfaction of knowing how much she ached.

She felt she had done nothing but *endure* since the trauma of her wedding day. Ridge had spent the night in her bed chamber, although he had made no move to touch her. Kalena supposed the very thought of making love to a woman who had tried to assassinate his employer was repulsive to him.

Kalena had lain awake all night, clinging to the far side of the pallet so that her husband would have as much room as possible. She thought Ridge had stayed awake for a long while, too, but eventually he had slept. The next morning he had ordered her out of bed well before dawn. The household had still been asleep when he had tossed her lightly up into the creet saddle, handed her the reins and ordered her to follow him.

That first day Kalena had thought she would fall out of the saddle by the end of the day. The thought hadn't particularly bothered her. It was just something she had noted vaguely in passing. Nothing had had the power to upset or worry her for the past three days. She had been drifting in a gray emotional landscape that had no secure points of reference and from which there seemed no escape. If she thought of anything specific at all for any length of time it was her failure to her House. But even that bitter knowledge no longer had the power to hurt her as it had on the night she had come to terms with it. She had failed her House. Technically, Olara could—and probably would—disown her for that failure.

Kalena could barely stand when she finally dismounted in front of the village inn where she and Ridge had stayed that first night. She hadn't bothered with dinner downstairs in the dining hall that adjoined the tavern. Without a word she had gone directly upstairs, bathed and fallen into bed. She hadn't awakened when Ridge had come upstairs some time later. She hadn't even moved until he had shaken her into some semblance of awareness at dawn the next morning. Kalena had never been so stiff and sore in her life, but pride had kept her from saying one single word. It was odd how pride remained when all else had vanished.

The next night had been a repeat of the first. The one small, insignificant bit of retaliation Kalena had been able to effect was to totally ignore the wifely tradition of bringing her husband yant tea in his pallet. If Ridge expected tea at dawn he could damn well make it himself. It had quickly become apparent that Ridge was too smart to expect any such thing. Now, as the third day drew to a close, Kalena began to wonder if the entire trip to Variance was to be carried out in silence and unending soreness.

The fact that she was becoming aware of her own resentment was mildly interesting, Kalena supposed. During the previous two days she had been moving through a kind of emotional shock. Nothing had really fazed her except the aching exhaustion, although for some reason she had managed to remember to take the selite powder. But today her mood was starting to restabilize. She wasn't sure if that was a good sign or not. Surely one shouldn't begin to recover so quickly from the trauma of failure.

Nevertheless, when the small jumble of timbered structures that comprised a village came into view over a grassy rise, Kalena actually found herself considering the prospect of dinner. Ridge had more or less forced her to eat a small morning and lunch meal during the past few days, but he hadn't bothered her when she had neglected dinner in favor of a bath and sleep in the evenings.

The sun was setting behind the distant mountains and smoke rose from the hearths of the homes that were scattered about the dusty main street of the town. The night would be cool, cooler than in Crosspurposes, and much cooler than it would be farther east in the Interlock valley. Kalena vaguely remembered that Ridge had discussed the distance to a place called Adverse that morning with the innkeeper in the last village. This must be their destination for tonight. The creet she was riding lifted its head expectantly and gave a hopeful chirp as it sensed the end of the day's ride. Creets considered a good supply of food and a warm stable adequate reward for their efforts.

Kalena cleared her dry throat with the intention of calling to Ridge to ask him if this was where they would stay the night. At the last moment she changed her mind about speaking. He was the one who had imposed the silence between them. She'd be damned if she would be the one to break it. Kalena thought about that reaction and decided that she must, indeed, be returning to normal. It seemed strange to be feeling any real emotion, even simple resentment.

Half an hour later, Ridge halted his bird in front of an inn that carried the sign of a jeweled sintar. Kalena waited obediently while her husband went inside to arrange accommodations. From her perch in the saddle she examined the small village with the first curiosity she had felt in days.

The collection of timbered buildings was obviously the center of a local farming community. The market square in the middle of the village was silent at this time of day, but was undoubtedly the hub of activity from morning until late afternoon. This village was a great deal more rural and unsophisticated in many ways than the ones of the Interlock valley. The windows were protected by wooden shutters rather than glass panes, and the buildings had been constructed with only utility in mind, not architectural interest.

People passing through the inn yard stared at her covertly, making Kalena aware of how few strangers probably came through Adverse. Her wide-legged riding pants and short, fitted tunic jacket probably appeared quite outrageous to the women in their long, conservatively styled tunics. The men stared, too. Kalena ignored them all and waited stoically for Ridge to reappear. Before long, she grew cold as the evening chill descended.

"All right," Ridge announced brusquely as he strode back outside. "We have a room upstairs. Go on up. I'll bring the bags and see to the creets."

Kalena nodded. Such orders had been the limit of his conversation for the past three days. She slid from the saddle, clinging to the leather as her booted feet touched the ground. For a moment she held on to the saddle to steady herself while her trembling thigh muscles decided if they could support her. She knew Ridge was watching her out of the corner of his eye as he collected the reins. Refusing to give him the satisfaction of seeing her hanging onto the leather, she forced herself to step back. The wide legs of her riding pants fell together to form a reasonably modest skirt as she moved toward the inn entrance. Kalena didn't look back as Ridge led the creets to the stables.

Inside the inn people turned to stare as Kalena moved to the front desk where the innkeeper handed her a key. "I wish you good evening, innkeeper," she murmured politely. He nodded and indicated the stairs.

"I'll want a bath," she informed him.

"There is a facility for women at the end of the hall," he explained proudly. "We have installed the latest heating technique for the water. Just pull the cord in the bathing room and the water will be sent through the pipes into the pool."

Kalena smiled gratefully. "That sounds wonderful." Hurrying upstairs, she opened the door of the small sleeping chamber and examined the one pallet that awaited. Another night of pretending an invisible wall ran down the center of the pallet lay ahead of her. She would cling to her side until she fell asleep and when Ridge joined her after an hour or two downstairs in the tavern he would help himself to the largest portion of the pallet. Wondering how long such a situation could continue without some sort of explosion, Kalena prepared for her bath. Tonight, she decided, she would eat dinner downstairs.

Although a more normal sense of awareness had returned and the dull apathy had faded, Kalena knew that nothing had changed for her. She was stuck with Ridge for the duration of the journey unless he chose to terminate the marriage contract. She had, after all, signed that agreement herself. She was honor bound to fulfill the terms of the contract. She might have been a failure as an assassin, but pride demanded she not fail her other obligations as well.

*   *   *

An hour later, Ridge lounged across from Kalena as they sat at a low, wooden dining table. He was amazed that she could kneel in such a polite, feminine fashion after three brutal days in the saddle. He had shown no surprise when she had followed him downstairs for dinner, but inwardly he was relieved that she was beginning to eat properly again. He had told himself that a couple of missed meals wouldn't hurt her, but this morning he had begun to wonder if he should let her continue to skip the evening meal. She needed her strength, especially with the way he had been driving her and the creets for the past three days.

There had been no need to set such a rough pace on the trail. Ridge knew he had done so solely to work off his own anger and frustration, and to punish Kalena. He was certain she had been suffering, but she had neither complained nor pleaded. After the first day her proud refusal to do either had had the effect of angering him further. He had seen to it that the second day was no easier on her than the first. Still she had said nothing. She seemed to accept the punishment as if she believed it were her due after failing to kill Quintel.

Her bleak acceptance of this penalty of failure finally convinced Ridge his wife had taken her role of assassin very seriously. He still found the notion of a woman committing ritual vengeance totally outlandish, but he couldn't doubt Kalena's emotional reaction. She had meant to kill Quintel and considered herself a disgrace to her House because she hadn't been able to complete the act.

She had the pride of a true born House lady, Ridge acknowledged. He was forced to admire it even as he told himself he would subdue it. He no longer doubted for a moment that she was who she claimed to be.

He had wed the daughter of a Great House and she undoubtedly despised him. Ridge's mouth thinned as he took a long swallow of red ale. That was her problem, he told himself. She had contracted the marriage willingly enough and now she was stuck with it. So was he, for that matter.

One thing was for certain. The present situation had continued long enough. They faced a long trip together and Ridge decided he was not going to spend the rest of the venture with a silent, sulking woman. The time to restore a more normal harmony between them had come. They were, after all, husband and wife. Ridge reminded himself that a husband's duty was to ensure his wife's obedient and proper behavior.

He watched Kalena finish off the last of her meal and marveled silently at her perfect manners. She used a fingerspear with a grace that verified her tale of being a daughter of a Great House. He should have realized several days ago just what her excellent manners really implied. Instead of considering the matter logically, he had taken egotistical pride in the fact that he was to marry a well mannered female. A man's ego could blind him on occasion, Ridge thought grimly.

"If you're finished, go upstairs to bed. I'll join you in a little while," he told her roughly. He instantly regretted the tone of his voice. He didn't have to order her about as if she were a servant. She was his wife and deserved a measure of respect. He tried to smooth over the gruff command by adding an explanation of his plans for the evening. "I want to talk to the innkeeper and some of the men in the tavern. We're getting into more isolated, rural areas now, and it's time I started asking a few questions. One of Quintel's other trade masters disappeared near here. I'd like to avoid the same fate."

Kalena raised her eyebrows in subtle mockery of his belated graciousness but said nothing. She got to her feet, inclined her head a little too subserviently, and turned to make her way up the stairs to the second level.

Ridge watched her go, his eyes narrowed. The woman had a way of taunting him without even opening her mouth. Ah, well, her silent resentment was better than the dull, apathetic resignation she had been wallowing in for the past couple of days. At least he thought it was. Ridge picked up his ale tankard again and considered how little he knew about handling a highborn lady who laid claim to the heritage of a Great House.

But one single fact was clear. Lady or not, she was his wife.

Ridge finished his ale, got to his feet and sauntered into the smoky tavern that connected to the dining area. The place was half full of local men who might or might not be willing to gossip about the last few Sand caravans that had passed through the village, and especially about Quintel's last investigator, Trantel.

He had a job to do, Ridge reminded himself. He would deal with his proud, sulking bride later.

Kalena fell asleep the moment her head touched the pillow of her pallet. Even the lingering ache in her thighs was not enough to keep her awake. She never heard Ridge enter the room, but when he slid naked under the lanti wool blankets and put his big hand on her arm, Kalena blinked sleepily. He had not touched her in bed since the trip had begun, and even through the drowsy haze that enveloped her Kalena sensed the significance of the action.

"There will be no more sulks or silence, Kalena," Ridge announced huskily as he turned her onto her back. "You've brooded long enough. It's time you started acting like a wife. *My* wife."

In the shadows she opened sleepy eyes to find him leaning over her, harsh intent etched in every line of his face. Kalena immediately understood that Ridge had come to some inner decision. One way or another he had gotten himself a wife and he had decided to avail himself of the convenience. Resentment warred with the feminine intuition that told Kalena things might be a good deal easier if she played the role of dutiful, if not necessarily loving, bride. It was, after all, more than a role. Nothing could change the fact that she was this man's legal wife. Ridge had not dissolved the contract, and unless both of them agreed to do so, before the completion of their trade venture, it stood as a legal document.

She had been a failure in the role of assassin. Perhaps she could manage this duty better. The days of silence had been hard on both of them.

On the other end of the Spectrum, there was her pride to be

considered. Enduring Ridge's idea of punishment was one thing; submitting to his demand that she carry out the duties of a wife was another. In her sleepy daze, Kalena tried to reason out what honor demanded of her. The duties of a wife were very clear. In a sense honor demanded that she perform them. She had, after all, signed that damned contract. Normally pride was bound up with honor, but tonight it all seemed very confusing.

She found analyzing the whole thing at this hour of the night too difficult. Better to put it off until morning, Kalena decided. She needed to work on the matter of figuring out just what her honor demanded in this bizarre situation.

"Go to sleep, Ridge. You've been drinking." She turned onto her side, her back to him.

His hand tightened on her shoulder and a split second later Kalena found herself flat on her back once more. She blinked up at him, startled by the fierceness of his grip. In the shadows his eyes were gleaming.

"Spoken like a true, nagging wife," he taunted, throwing one bare leg over her thigh. He moved his leg slightly and the hem of Kalena's nightdress was abruptly pushed up above her knees. "Don't worry about the ale I've consumed. I'll still be able to perform my husbandly duty." He bent his head to cut off her protest with his mouth.

Kalena awakened in a hurry as she realized Ridge meant business tonight. Automatically, she started to struggle and found her wrists pinned to the bed as Ridge moved more completely to cover her. The hard weight of his body crushed her deeply into the pallet, and when he moved his hips against her she could feel the fierceness of his arousal through the soft fabric of her nightdress.

His lips moved on hers, not to seek a response but to ensure her submission. Kalena felt the heat of his mouth and sensed the urgent, compelling hunger that was driving him. She was torn between her natural tendency to resist his arrogant demands and the knowledge that he had every right to make those demands. He had been right; he might be a Houseless bastard, but he was her husband. She had wed him willingly enough and now she was forced to accept that fact. Things might not have turned out as she had expected, but for the duration of this venture she was Ridge's wife. And she already knew that he was capable of pleasing his woman in a very fundamental way.

Pride, honesty and the promise of passion swirled together in Kalena's mind, creating a chaos from which there was no logical escape. While she struggled to sort it all out, Ridge pushed his hand up under the hem of her nightdress and boldly claimed the treasure he sought.

Kalena, who had not yet made up her mind to choose pride or wifely humility, reacted angrily as his fingers stroked the soft petaled flower between her legs. "Damn you to the Dark end of the Spectrum, Ridge! We have much to talk about before you act the heavy-handed husband."

"We'll talk later. When you've shown me you know your duty," he growled against her throat. He used his foot to separate her legs and then his stroking finger plunged deliberately inside her, making Kalena gasp.

She lifted her single free hand with the intention of slapping at him. But in that moment he withdrew his probing finger just far enough to make her ache with sudden wanting. Her fingers clutched into the thickness of his hair instead of striking his shoulder.

"Open your eyes and look at me, wife." Ridge had meant to utter the words as a command, but they emerged sounding more like a plea.

She obeyed reluctantly, aware of the way she was dampening his hand.

"Call me by my new title, Kalena," he muttered. "Call me *husband*."

"Ridge, stop it. You've had one too many tankards of ale tonight and you have no business forcing yourself on me."

"Call me husband, Kalena. Let me hear you acknowledge your new lord." He continued to move his fingers inside her, but now his thumb was playing with the small nub that was so responsive to his touch. Kalena tightened convulsively and Ridge felt it. "Say it, Kalena."

He only asked to hear the truth, Kalena told herself as the quivering excitement rippled through her body. Surely she need not let her pride or her sense of honor stand in the way of admitting what was merely the truth.

"I know you are my husband, Ridge. I don't deny it," she whispered breathlessly.

"Show me," he growled, shoving the hem of her nightdress up around her waist and moving to settle himself between her soft thighs. "Show me you know your duty, wife."

Kalena was aware of the blunt hardness of him pressing closer. Her wrist was freed as he released it to grip her shoulders and bear down on her with his full weight. Kalena's hands twisted in Ridge's hair. Her eyes closed as he entered her with shocking abruptness, and she moaned softly as the keenly remembered sensual vortex overwhelmed her again.

Time hung suspended in the sleeping chamber as Kalena gave herself up to her husband's passion. She sensed the force of his urgent need and found that it fed her own desires. Above all she knew in some deep, secret part of her awareness that she was bound to Ridge in a way that went far beyond a marriage contract. She had known that since the first time he had possessed her. And then that knowledge fled, along with everything else, before the shimmering excitement that enveloped them both.

Afterward, Ridge rolled off of her slowly and lay on his back. He was silent for a long while, until his breathing steadied, and then he said far too calmly, "She sent you to your death, you know."

Kalena stirred, not understanding. "What are you talking about?"

"Your dear aunt Olara. She sent you to your death without a qualm."

Kalena felt dazed by the certainty of his voice. "No! That's not true. Quintel's death was to look like heart failure, not an assassination."

"It wouldn't have worked. I would have seen to it that there was a full investigation, including an analysis by a good Healer. The Healer would have found evidence of the poison in his blood. Your aunt must have known that. Therefore, she knew you would be caught and most likely killed. She raised you to die avenging your House, Kalena. You were not meant to survive once your duty was done."

"She did not send me to die," Kalena protested. "She is a brilliant Healer. The poison she prepared would have been undetectable to any other Healer."

"So she claimed."

"It's true! It must be true." Kalena had never allowed herself to question Olara's plan, or her promise that it would work.

Ridge slowly shook his head in the darkness. "I've been giving the matter a great deal of thought. It's only logical to assume that your aunt didn't care if you survived. Her only goal was to use you to kill Quintel. You mocked me once for being a rich man's tool, but at least I know my role and accept it for what it is. You were the unwitting tool of someone you were raised to trust and respect. That's a far worse fate, Kalena. You were used."

Kalena said nothing, absorbing the implications, unwilling to believe her aunt had let the need for revenge drive her to such an extreme. But Olara considered the House of the Ice Harvest at an end anyway. What did it matter if the last living female died carrying out her duty? Ridge sounded so certain of what he had deduced. Kalena shuddered, thinking of her own dreams of freedom. Perhaps she had never stood a chance of obtaining the life of a freewoman.

Ridge felt the tremor in her fingers. His mouth twisted wryly as Kalena remained stubbornly silent, refusing to argue or agree with his statement. Her pride and sense of honor were formidable indeed. Almost as formidable as her femininity and passion. He turned to gather her against him.

"I'm sorry to upset you by forcing you to confront the truth about your aunt, but there's no alternative. It's always better to know the truth."

"Better?" she questioned bitterly.

"Safer," he ammended softly. He stroked the tangled curls of her hair, wanting to soothe her. "Go to sleep, Kalena. And when you wake in the morning, remember that you owe your life to your husband. Perhaps the knowledge will make you a little more cooperative and dutiful toward him." He yawned, physically satisfied and replete. "Then again, perhaps it won't. I wish you good night, wife."

Kalena felt him go to sleep almost instantly. She lay awake for a long time, his words echoing in her head.

SEVEN

Kalena awoke with an unfamiliar sense of alertness, a keen awareness that something important had jarred her from her sleep.

She lay still for a moment, trying to figure out what had awakened her. Whatever it was had not bothered Ridge. He slept on beside her, one heavy arm wrapped possessively around her waist.

Slowly she realized there was a half familiar odor in the sleeping chamber, a scent she associated vaguely with home and with her aunt. It was an odor associated with the Healing craft.

Kalena inhaled deeply, trying to identify the smell. Her mind spun mistily for a second and then she had it: Keefer leaves. Olara burned them to anesthetize her most badly injured patients. Kalena sat upright with a jerk that brought Ridge instantly awake.

"Stones! What's going on? Kalena, what's the matter?"

Kalena glanced at him, worry etched on her face. Ridge was sitting up beside her and somehow the sintar was in his hand. He must sleep with it, she thought.

"I'm not sure. That odor. Can you smell it?"

He took a breath. "Yes, but I don't recognize it."

"It's the smell a certain herb creates when it's burned. Keefer. A little is irritating. Enough of the smoke will put you to sleep. My aunt uses it occasionally in her Healing work."

Ridge swore softly. He was already on his feet, yanking on his trousers. "Get something on, Kalena. We've got to get out of here."

She didn't argue. She was already off the pallet and reaching for her riding skirt. Before she had finished fastening the tunic jacket, Ridge was at the door. He jerked the handle once and then again.

"Somebody's locked it from the other side. The smoke is coming from underneath. We'll have to go out through the window."

Kalena nodded and turned to pull open the shutters. Already she felt dizzy from the effects of the smoke. The shutters didn't budge. "Ridge! They're locked shut."

He came forward quickly, setting one booted foot to the wooden slats. The first kick was strong enough to make the shutter sag outward. The second wasn't necessary because the shutter was shoved open from the outside. An instant later two cloaked figures came over the windowsill from the balcony and hurtled into the room.

Kalena had no chance to so much as scream. Ridge slammed her aside so hard she hit the floor. She glanced up in time to see him step forward to meet one of the attackers. The sintar glinted in the pale moonlight and then a scream of rage and pain pierced the night as the blade disappeared into the depths of the assailant's cloak.

The other dark figure had been making for Kalena, but he spun around when he heard his companion scream. His arm came up, revealing something in his fist that might have been a dart sling; he aimed it at Ridge's back.

Kalena didn't take time to think. She grabbed the heavy travel bag that sat open at the foot of the pallet and hurled it at the second attacker. He yelped, staggering as the weight of the bag hit him. Before he could recover, Ridge was upon him. There was a flurry of violent thrashing, and then the second figure went ominously still.

Kalena waited, shivering with tension as Ridge got slowly to his feet. The fragrance of the keefer smoke was being diluted by the open window. She stared at the two men on the floor, one of whom stirred and groaned. They were both dressed in black from head to foot. The dart sling carried by the second man lay next to his body. Ridge reached down to recover it.

"Ridge, who are they?"

"This one isn't going to tell us," he said coolly. He turned away from the very still figure on the floor and started toward the other man. "But I think we can probably get this one to talk."

The cloaked man raised his head. The hood fell back, revealing a gaze of pure hatred. "Never," he said in a voice hoarse from pain. He fumbled for something in his cloak and had it in his mouth before Ridge could stop him. An instant later the cloaked man gasped and fell backward into the same endless stillness that gripped his companion.

"Well, dammit to the end of the Spectrum," Ridge said with disgust as he stood glowering over his victim. "Now they're both dead."

Kalena swallowed heavily. "Dead?"

"Just my luck." He went down on one knee and tugged aside the first man's cloak. "Put some cloth under the door to stop that smoke and turn on one of the lamps. Hurry, Kalena, we haven't got much time. I want both of us out of here as soon as possible."

She tore her eyes from the dead men and hurried into the small privacy chamber to soak a strip of bedding in the water basin. The innkeeper's modernization attempts had not extended to the sleeping chambers. The sleeping chambers had only a jug of water and a basin, not the new, fancy piping systems that were becoming so popular back in Crosspurposes and in the Interlock valley.

The soaked cloth cut off the flow of smoke and the room cleared rapidly of the smell of burning keefer as Kalena switched on the firegel lamp. The volatile gelatin began to glow at once as the catalyst was introduced through the small tube opened by the switch. In the lamplight Kalena saw the blood that was staining the wooden floors beneath the two cloaked figures. She went forward slowly.

In the past there had been occasions when Olara had called upon her niece to assist her. Those times had been rare because Olara had only demanded help in absolute emergencies. In general she tried to keep Kalena well clear of the Healer's chamber. But at moments Olara had needed another pair of hands and Kalena had been the only person available. Kalena had seen death before, but never such violent death. She had never witnessed one man being killed by another. She was amazed to think she had at one time considered herself capable of murder.

"What are you doing, Ridge?" she asked softly, watching him systematically go through the cloak the first man was wearing. In her experience the dead were to be treated carefully and with respect. Ridge was handling the body like so much limp laundry.

"Looking for something." Ridge felt the lining of a pocket.

"What?"

"Anything that might tell us who they are."

"I understand," she said simply and forced herself to go down beside the second still figure. She steeled herself for the task and then cautiously parted the cloak.

The blood that had soaked the man's chest almost made her lose control of her stomach.

"I'll do that, Kalena. Get away from him." Ridge's voice was curiously urgent.

"I am not such a weakling that I cannot deal with a dead man," she said, her throat tight as she put her fingers into the pocket of the cloak.

"Kalena, there's no need for you to do that."

She was about to respond when she caught sight of the pendant that lay soaking in blood. She froze. "Ridge," she whispered softly, "is that one wearing a chain around his neck? A chain with a piece of black glass hanging from it?"

"Yes."

"Don't touch it," she ordered tightly.

"Kalena—"

"By the Keys, *don't touch it.*"

"Kalena, calm yourself," Ridge said gently as he got to his feet.

She looked up at him, her eyes wide with a fear she could not yet name. "Ridge, you must listen to me."

He held out his hand. The black glass pendant dangled from his fingers, glinting evilly in the lamplight. "Kalena, I've already touched it. There is no harm in it. It's only a piece of black glass on a chain."

Her eyes went from his face to the pendant and back again as a memory slowly coalesced in her mind. She rose to her feet, taking a step backward. Ridge's expression darkened.

"What's the matter with you, woman? We don't have time for you to have a case of hysterics."

The roughness in his voice pulled her quickly back to reality. "You needn't concern yourself. I do not intend to have hysterics."

"Then let's get going. We've wasted enough time." He dropped the pendant into his travel bag and glanced around the room. "Have you got everything?"

Kalena nodded, hoisting her heavy bag. "What about these two?"

"Let the innkeeper worry about them. I have a feeling he gave them some assistance tonight. He can deal with the results."

"The innkeeper helped them?" Kalena was shocked. She followed Ridge to the open window.

"Somebody bolted our door from the outside and managed to overlook two cloaked men burning a bunch of those damn keefer leaves in the hallway. Either the innkeeper is a very heavy sleeper or he has been well paid to feign the art of deep sleep." Ridge stepped out onto the balcony that wrapped the second level of the inn. He reached back to help Kalena. "Not a word until we're clear of the stables."

She nodded her understanding and went after him as he moved silently along the balcony. They passed several shuttered windows and a door, but no one questioned them. The timbered steps at the far end of the building led down to the inn yard. No one was stirring in the predawn darkness.

The creet stables were warm and thick with the characteristic odor that marks such places. It wasn't a bad smell, just an earthy, honest one that reminded Kalena a little of the Interlock valley farms. There were half a dozen birds and they all stirred and chirped inquiringly as the two humans entered the darkened stable. Ridge whistled faintly in the particular signal his creets had been taught to recognize. The other four birds went back to dozing. The two Kalena and Ridge had been riding for three days poked their beaked heads over the stall doors.

Ridge spoke quietly to the creatures as he began saddling the nearest. Kalena set down her travel bag and hoisted the second saddle. Ridge started to say something. He had been doing all the saddling and unsaddling on the journey so far, but when he saw the no-nonsense way Kalena swung the leather over the bird's shoulders he kept his mouth shut. Time was of the essence this morning.

Within minutes Kalena and Ridge were mounted and out of the yard. The birds were urged into their ground-eating stride and it wasn't long before the village of Adverse was out of sight. Ahead, the distant peaks of the Heights of Variance began to show purple beneath a dawning sun.

For the remainder of the morning Ridge set the same kind of brutal pace he had maintained for the past few days, but Kalena knew that today his objective wasn't to make life unpleasant for her. His only goal was to put as much distance as possible between them and the two bodies at the inn. The aches in her legs and lower back seemed marginally less this morning, and Kalena wondered if perhaps she was finally becoming accustomed to a day's hard riding. Her mouth curved wryly. If last night was anything to go by, she would have to become accustomed to nights of hard riding, too. Ridge had obviously decided to start claiming his rights as a husband.

She watched him as he rode a short distance in front of her, following the landmarks that led through the Plains of Antinomy toward the distant mountains. Occasionally, he consulted the folded maps he carried in his saddle pack. Once in a while he spoke to her or glanced back to see that she was still where she was supposed to be. On the whole, conversation today wasn't any more plentiful than it had been for the past three days. Ridge rode with a concentration and determination that left little time for idle chatter.

Kalena remembered the black glass pendant in his travel bag and frowned to herself as she recalled the vague tales she had once heard.

When the sun was overhead, Ridge finally called a halt near a stream. Kalena slid gratefully from the saddle and watched the creets amble happily toward the water. It didn't take much to make a creet happy.

"Last night I had the innkeeper's wife prepare us some food." Ridge spoke as he removed a small package from his saddle. "I think we've put enough ground behind us. These birds are fast. Faster than anything they've got back in Adverse."

"Do you think anyone is following us?"

He shrugged, unwrapping the food. "I don't know. Those two last night might have been simple thieves who work in conjunction with the innkeeper. Or they might have been something more."

Kalena accepted a wedge of white cheese and sat down on a rock to eat it. "I think they were something more than mere thieves, Ridge," she finally said.

"Because of the pendants? What are they, Kalena? What is it about them that makes you afraid? Have you ever seen one before?"

She shook her head. "No. But Olara described something like them once." Kalena hesitated, remembering the incident. "She had just come out of a trance. She was very agitated. She kept talking about the creatures who used black glass to focus."

"To focus what?"

"That's just it. I don't know. She was upset and I gather she hadn't had a clear Far Seeing trance. There were only impressions that left her disturbed. But she implied that the glass is a thing from the Dark end of the Spectrum." Kalena met Ridge's gaze and emphasized her words carefully. "The farthest, darkest end of the Spectrum. It is a thing wholly and completely masculine in the most final sense of the word. It accepts nothing from the other end of the Spectrum. According to Olara, the glass is associated with that which would destroy anything that is from the Light end of the Spectrum. Do you understand, Ridge?"

He studied her intent features as he sat on a rock across from her, one knee bent so that he could rest an arm on it. "Your aunt thought the glass was connected to something that wished to destroy anything that had its origins in the Light end of the Spectrum?"

"I think so."

"That's insane, Kalena." Ridge picked up another wedge of cheese. "Anyone with an ounce of sense knows that one end of the Spectrum can't exist without the other. Dark must always be balanced by light and male must always be balanced by female. For either to exist alone would be meaningless. How could there be any concept of night if day didn't exist?" He quoted the accepted logic of the philosophy that guided nearly everyone who lived in the Northern Continent.

"Olara did not say that those who used the black glass were sane," Kalena said calmly, finishing her cheese. "In fact, I got the distinct impression she thought them quite insane."

He was silent for a few seconds before saying, "It's fortunate for both of us that you came awake at the scent of the keefer smoke. And you were very quick with that travel bag you hurled at the second man. You kept your head in a difficult situation and you probably saved both our lives."

Kalena felt unaccountably warmed and slightly amused. "Such praise from a man of your particular talents, Trade Master, is enough to make a mere female quite giddy."

He had the grace to look faintly chagrined. His eyes slid from her face to the creets and back again as he searched for words. "I meant what I said. I could not have wished for a better companion beside me in such circumstances."

"Even though I'm only a female and not really designed for such masculine labor?"

His mouth twisted slightly. "You speak as if you resent being born female."

Kalena thought about that. "No, not really. I cannot imagine being other than I am, but there are times when every woman has cause to grow exasperated with the prejudices and misconceptions of men. You label us weak and then become resentful when we prove ourselves strong."

"No man denies that a woman has her own kind of strength."

"Such strength being acceptable so long as she confines it to the spheres of childbearing, running a house and providing a warm pallet for her husband?" Kalena asked with a hidden smile.

"Do you enjoy provoking me, Kalena?" he asked with a sigh.

"Sometimes," she admitted quite freely.

His eyes gleamed as he took another bite of cheese. "You don't consider it slightly risky?"

"You've said on more than one occasion that I might lack a certain measure of common sense," she retorted airily. "Maybe I'm just too fluff-brained to have enough sense to restrain myself from provoking you."

"Or maybe you take a certain perverse pleasure from doing so."

"Umm, a distinct possibility," she agreed, nodding.

"Some people think it's dangerous to provoke me," Ridge remarked, eyeing her narrowly.

"Yes, well, I'll admit that trick with the sintar is a little intimidating." Kalena leaned forward, trying to see the handle of the blade where it rested just under his elbow. "It's true what they say, isn't it? You really can make the steel glow. I could hardly believe it that night in my chamber when I thought you were going to kill me with the steel."

He frowned. "If you have any sense you won't mention that night again, Kalena."

"But the blade—"

"Yes, I can make it glow," he muttered, polishing off the last of the cheese. "It makes me feel like some kind of freak, but if you get me sufficiently angry, the steel will grow hot in my hands. It's not something I'm particularly proud of. In fact, it can be a damned nuisance."

"It's a very rare talent. The stories say there are few men in any generation who have such an affinity for fire. And it is only the steel of Countervail that will respond to the talent."

"It's not exactly a talent," Ridge exploded. "It's a useless trick, good for nothing more than show. The steel glows only when I've truly lost control of my temper, Kalena, and that's a very dangerous thing for me. It's a talent that might someday get me killed."

"Get you killed!" She was startled.

"No man fights well when he's enraged. I've survived doing Quintel's work precisely because I've learned to control the extremes of my temper, at least for the most part."

She looked at him wonderingly. "I see."

He lifted one brow. "I doubt it. Let's change the subject, shall we?"

"What would you prefer to discuss?"

"Something infinitely more practical. Namely, why did those two men with the black glass come after us?"

"I don't know. This is your mission. I'm merely along for the ride and thirty percent of the Sand, remember?"

His eyes gleamed. "It would seem that you are rapidly returning to normal, at least as far as your tongue is concerned. It must have been hard to maintain nearly three full days of silence."

"You were as silent as I."

"I spent the time thinking."

"As only a man would think," she retorted. "This morning's hard ride was out of necessity. But the pace you set for the past three days was deliberately designed to make me aware of your displeasure."

"Displeasure is a mild word for what I felt."

"Yes, I know."

"Tell me," Ridge said somewhat gruffly, "what did you think you would do if you'd been successful in murdering Quintel? What did you think your future would be like?"

Kalena looked toward the distant mountains. "I thought," she said eventually, "that afterward I would finally be free. The image of my future has always been vague in my mind, but I believed that something important and wonderful lay ahead of me once I had fulfilled my task. I was wrong."

"What did you think you would be free to do?" he scoffed. "Even if no one knew you were the murderess, you would already be known as a trade wife. The marriage took place before you attempted murder. Nothing would have changed your status after you signed that contract and went through that ceremony. A fine ending for the daughter of a Great House. You would have found yourself on the same level as Arrisa and the others."

Kalena smiled. "Yes, I know. I couldn't wait to find myself on that level."

Ridge was startled. "With your heritage? Your pride and family background? You *wanted* to be a trade wife?"

"I wanted to be free. Arrisa and her friends are the only truly freewomen I have ever met. They come and go as they please, with no House lord to order them about. They are not required to remember the honor of their families in everything they do. They call no man permanent husband. They spend their grans any way they choose. They do not serve the males at the table when they dine. They are free to go out in the evenings to taverns and not worry that when they return some man will threaten to beat them for their behavior. They go adventuring on the trade routes and return with money that belongs only to them."

Ridge cut off the glowing description of Arrisa and her friends with a short, rather crude oath. "You know nothing of that world. It's simply a case of the forbidden being more exciting than what you have. I must admit that probably anything would look more exciting than life on a farm in the Interlock valley. But to think of sacrificing your heritage for the sake of being able to get yourself arrested in a tavern brawl is disgraceful. There is a streak of wild-ness in you, Kalena. You need a husband to control it."

"And there is a definite streak of old-fashioned, hide-bound, straitlaced prudishness in you, Ridge, that would do justice to any Great House lord," she returned easily. "Where did you come by such conservative notions, I wonder."

"Probably from having spent too many years growing up with the kind of 'freedom' that comes from not belonging to any House, even a small one."

"Ah, then we are truly opposite points on a Spectrum, aren't we?" she mused.

"Remember that, Kalena," he said in mocking threat. "It prob-ably means we're well matched."

"That's not what you thought the night you discovered you had married a failed assassin."

To her surprise, he didn't rise to the bait. Instead, Ridge took the comment seriously. "I've had time to think about matters since that night."

She eyed him with a new wariness. "Come to any brilliant conclusions?"

"A few." He shifted his position slightly, considering her in-tently. "I understand why you tried to kill Quintel."

That truly did surprise her. "You do?"

He sighed. "If you have spent the past several years having it drilled into your brain that Quintel was the cause of your father's and brother's death, then yes, I understand. Someone had to exact vengeance on behalf of your House. Seen from that perspective, I suppose you had no choice."

"That's very generous of you, Ridge," Kalena said in astonish-ment.

"But that line of logic has a major flaw in it," he continued bluntly.

"What flaw?"

"You have no proof that Quintel had anything to do with the end of your House. Nothing except the word of an embittered old woman who is given to trances and tale spinning, from what I gather."

"She is a fine Healer and a respected woman!"

"She raised you with every intention of sending you to your death while allowing you to believe you would be free when your task was done."

"I would have been free!"

"No, Kalena," he told her implacably. "In the end you would have died. There would have been no escape. No freedom."

Stung, Kalena got to her feet and paced toward the stream. "You don't know that for certain. You're only saying that to salvage some of your own pride. You don't want to admit that you nearly failed to protect your employer. Your sense of honor is as great as any House lord's. Your pride is above your station." She glanced back at him derisively. To her surprise, Ridge was smiling ruefully, acknowledging the accusation.

"So Quintel has informed me," he said.

"You admit it?"

"Why not? It's the truth. There will come a day, Kalena, when my sense of honor and my pride will suit my station in life."

She swung around to face him fully. "I don't understand."

"It takes money and power and raw nerve to establish a fine House. More of all three to found a Great House and have it accepted. I'll have the money when I return from this trip with a shipment of Sand. I'll also have a guarantee of a permanent slice of the Sand route profits. And I have learned the ways of power from watching Quintel over the years. He has taught me much."

"I expect you were born with the necessary raw nerve," Kalena snapped.

"Perhaps I inherited it from my father," Ridge said casually.

"You said you don't know who your father was."

"I know he was the heir of a Great House in Countervail. He seduced a young woman who had no House to protect her, got her pregnant and than abandoned her to the streets. She died when I was in my eighth year, refusing to name my father to me. She wouldn't even tell me which House he represented."

"Why not?" Kalena asked softly.

"Because she knew I would try to kill him and probably get myself killed in the attempt."

"So you were born with your pride as well as your nerve. She must have recognized as much and tried to protect you," Kalena said, her voice gentle now.

"Perhaps." Ridge seemed no longer interested in the discussion of his childhood. He got up off the rock and walked toward the waiting creets, who were helping themselves to a patch of red and yellow wildflowers. "It no longer matters. One of these days I will be the lord of my own Great House and then none of the past will matter. Are you ready?"

"Yes." She walked toward her creet. Kalena had one foot in the high stirrup when she felt Ridge's hands around her waist. He tossed her up into the saddle and stood looking up at her for a moment, one hand resting on her thigh with casual possessiveness. His golden eyes flared for a moment in the warm sunlight. The fire in his gaze was not gentle or sensual or persuasive. It was a little savage and utterly determined.

"I must have a suitable wife when I return to Crosspurposes. A woman who can conduct herself like a fine lady when the occasion demands. A woman who has strength and nerve and who is willing to work hard. One whose loyalty to me is absolute and who also knows the meaning of honor."

Kalena lifted her chin. "I wish you luck in finding such a paragon. Do you want some advice?"

His gaze narrowed. "What advice would you give?"

"If you do find a suitable candidate for the post, you would do well to treat her carefully. She will be accustomed to good manners and the behavior of gentlemen. If you are wise, you will not threaten her, even occasionally, with a creet whip. Nor will you give her orders as if she were a servant. Furthermore, you will not force your way into her pallet when you have ale on your breath and a desire to copulate with any convenient female. You will wait for an invitation."

Ridge grinned in response to her short lecture. "Such a

woman, if indeed I find one, sounds very dull. It's fortunate that I have you instead of this paragon on this trip." He smiled at her wickedly. "The one thing you never are, Kalena, is boring."

He turned away to mount his own creet, ignoring a muttered comment about having a head as thick as a zorcan's. Ridge swung up into the saddle, aware that he was feeling unexpectedly good in spite of the morning's hard ride and the two dead bodies that lay behind him in Adverse.

He had been right to reestablish the sexual bond between himself and Kalena. Ridge acknowledged privately that the one place he felt he had some genuine control over Kalena was in a sleeping pallet. Last night had reassured him that her response to him still ran as deep in her veins as it had that first night, as deep and irresistible as his own response to her was. She was a proud, highborn lady, but last night she had called him husband and accepted him as much.

Ridge was congratulating himself on that fact when he started thinking, not for the first time, about Kalena's pride. Some of his masculine satisfaction slipped. It was true he had a right to demand her obedient surrender in the sleeping pallet, but he, of all people, knew how sharp a lash pride and honor could be. His actions last night must have stung her fiercely.

He didn't want to coerce her into doing her wifely duty, Ridge admitted to himself. He wanted Kalena to give herself willingly and eagerly. Morosely, he came to the conclusion that forcing her to surrender to him probably wasn't a reliable means of inducing her warm and willing cooperation. His mouth tightened, as did his grip on the reins as he came to a grim decision. He would not force Kalena again. He was a man of honor and he understood the fierceness of her own pride. She had a right to that pride. He would give her some time to come to terms with her new responsibilities as his wife before he again claimed her. He had a lot of time, Ridge reminded himself. The rest of the journey lay ahead.

Kalena's sense of honor was as strong as his own, even if it had been deliberately warped by the aunt, Ridge reflected. One of the things he had to do before they returned to Crosspurposes was to ensure that Kalena understood Quintel was not guilty of murdering her father and brother.

And Ridge had no doubt about that fact. Quintel might be capable of hiring men to act as his private weapons in order to deal with lawless bandits on the trade routes, but to murder the lord and heir of a Great House was quite another thing. Quintel was scrupulous about staying within the confines of the law. It was unthinkable that he would step so far outside it. Quintel's own sense of honor was as rigid as any other lord's.

No, Kalena must be convinced that her House obligation had been sadly misdirected by an embittered, perhaps crazy old woman. After Kalena understood that, she must be shown that the free life she sought as a lower class trade woman was not all she had imagined. She needed a husband who would ensure she didn't forget her heritage. A husband who could, perhaps, even replace the heritage she had lost with one that was just as proud.

Ridge frowned thoughtfully as he considered the long-term future. Clearly, his trade wife had plans of her own that she intended to implement when they returned to Crosspurposes. Her desire for freedom was going to be a problem. But several eight-days lay ahead of them, and much could happen to change a woman's mind in that length of time.

EIGHT

The creets were in a playful mood that evening. They had plenty of extra energy because they hadn't been pushed as hard as usual during the afternoon, but they also seemed to delight in the bubbling spring near the campsite Ridge had chosen. Not long after they camped, the creets were happily bathing in the fresh water.

As the late afternoon sunlight faded behind the distant mountains, Kalena sat curled on a rock overlooking the small stream. She watched the birds while Ridge finished the preparations for camping out on the trail.

"The problem with putting all that extra distance behind us and Adverse this morning is that it threw off the travel schedule," Ridge complained as he laid the fire. "My original plan was to be near a town every evening."

"You surprise me, Ridge. I would have thought you'd be accustomed to roughing it on the trail."

He threw her a rare grin. "Being accustomed to it doesn't mean I like it. In fact, it has a tendency to make me appreciate the comforts of an inn even more than I might otherwise."

Kalena wrapped her arms around her knees and watched him with sincere curiosity. "I'm astonished to hear a man such as yourself admit to liking the little luxuries of life."

"You have a distorted view of my nature."

"If that's true it's probably because our time together has been a little tense," she pointed out dryly. "We haven't really had much of an opportunity to get to know each other."

He paused in his work and glanced at her. "I thought we were getting to know a great deal about each other in a hurry."

Kalena made a wry face. "I think we're going about it the hard way."

He shrugged and tossed down a load of kindling. "Possibly. But it doesn't make such difference. The end result is the same. You are my wife."

"*Trade* wife," she emphasized quietly.

He gave her a slightly challenging smile. "The distinction is meaningless until the end of our journey."

Before Kalena could respond to that her attention was distracted by her creet's wild chirps. She glanced around in time to see the bird racing madly along the edge of the stream. The creet was flapping her little yellow wings in a useless effort to propel herself as fast as possible. The large male was in hot pursuit.

"Ridge, the creets!"

Ridge strode over to where Kalena was sitting, his eyes filled with lazy interest. "They're just playing."

"It looks like more than playfulness to me." Kalena got to her feet, prepared to defend her bird. "Your animal is attacking mine."

"Not exactly."

"What do you mean, not exactly? He's trying to assault her. Just look at the way he's chasing her. Stop him, Ridge."

"I doubt if I could, even if I wanted to. Don't you know it's dangerous to come between a male and his female?"

Kalena glared at him, outraged. "Are you saying your creet is trying to rape my little bird?"

Ridge cleared his throat. "They're a mated pair, Kalena," he reminded her. "Such behavior is natural."

"Is that right? Then why is she trying to escape?"

He regarded her thoughtfully. "I don't know. You tell me. Perhaps she has some wild notions of female freedom."

Kalena gasped as her bird gave a particularly loud and protesting squawk. She spun around in time to see the smaller yellow creet being tumbled to the ground by the larger bird. The female landed in a crouching position and the male quickly jumped on top of her.

Kalena groaned, finally realizing exactly what was happening. "This is embarrassing."

"Then don't watch. I thought you were raised in farm country." Ridge was already walking back toward his half finished fire.

"I was, but we didn't actually raise animals. My aunt provided for us by practicing her Healer's talents. I've never seen two creets in quite this sort of situation." Kalena hurriedly turned her back on the mating pair of birds. "It's a little on the violent side."

"Is that so strange?" Ridge asked quietly. "Sometimes things have been a little violent between us, too. The emotions between male and female can be powerful."

"We're hardly a pair of birds, Ridge!"

"I"m not sure we're all that different from other animals. They're on the Spectrum with us, aren't they? Our emotions and reactions might be more complex than theirs, but not totally unrelated."

"There are times when you surprise me with the level of your philosophical training, Fire Whip," Kalena said a bit grimly as she closed her ears to the triumphant chirps of the male creet.

"Quintel saw to it that I got a decent education." Ridge sounded offhand.

Kalena wondered about that. "He raised you like a son, didn't he?"

"Almost. He taught me manners, the ways of trading and the essentials of Great House politics. But this business of being a husband I'm having to learn on my own."

"On-the-job training, Ridge?" Kalena made no attempt to keep the smile out of her voice.

"Practice and experience make excellent teachers," he informed her blandly. "And I learn quickly. Are the birds finished yet?"

Kalena glanced over her shoulder. "Yes, thank the Spectrum. Mine doesn't even look mildly annoyed at yours."

"Why should she? She knows her role in life. And on the rare occasions when she's tempted to forget, the male reminds her."

Kalena spun around, thoroughly annoyed. She opened her mouth to tell Ridge what she thought of him, and then halted as she realized he was laughing at her. His expression hadn't changed, but there was genuine humor in his golden eyes. She sighed. "Now who's trying to provoke whom, Ridge?"

He held up one hand as though to ward off her irritation. "I'll admit there are times when I can see the lure of the sport."

Hearing a loud splash, Kalena turned once more to find the creets blundering happily into the stream. "My female is trying to duck your male."

"He'll probably let her get away with it."

"Because he's already had what he wants from her?" Kalena sniffed.

"There's nothing like a pleasant tumble with the female of one's choice to put a male in a good mood and make him feel indulgent."

"You males are definitely a simpleminded lot, aren't you?" Kalena asked as she stalked over to a saddlebag and began removing some of the trail rations Ridge had packed for emergencies.

"It's not that we're simpleminded, wife. It's just that we tend to think in a clear, straightforward fashion. We're not like women, who chase their emotions in a hundred illogical circles before coming to terms with them."

"Did you come up with that bit of wisdom on your own or learn it from some male Polarity Advisor?"

"I could hardly have learned it from a female Polarity Advisor. There aren't any." Ridge got to his feet in a lithe, easy movement. "In any event, it doesn't matter where I learned it. Lately I seem to be getting firsthand demonstrations of the truths of the old sayings."

"The problem with a man's interpretation of ancient axioms is that because he tends to think in such a marvelously straightforward manner, he misses all the subtle meaning hidden in them," Kalena explained sweetly. "In other words, he usually misses the main point altogether."

Ridge gave a shout of laughter and launched himself forward without any warning. "You never give up, do you?" he marveled.

Kalena was so startled by hearing him laugh outright for the first time that she didn't think to move quickly enough to escape him. Before she realized what he was about, he had scooped her up in his arms and was striding toward the stream. The creets lifted their heads curiously to watch the humans at play.

"Ridge, you wouldn't dare."

"I'm not sure," he retorted with mocking seriousness as he came to a halt at the edge of the stream. "We straightforward thinking types tend to do what we set out to do. It's hard to distract us. But you can try."

Kalena clung to him, strangely fascinated by her discovery of this playful side of his nature. She had the distinct impression Ridge wasn't very familiar with this element in himself, either. It was as if he were experimenting with it as he went along. *Learning to be a husband.* "How could I distract you?" she demanded.

"You could try pleading with me," he suggested helpfully.

"Surely a woman's pleas wouldn't deflect a strong, straightforward thinker such as yourself."

"You never know." He waited, grinning down at her, his eyes alight with anticipation.

"I'm not very good at pleading, but I'm willing to bargain," Kalena told him.

"Ah, this is getting more and more interesting. With what would you bargain, wife?"

"Don't leer at me like that. I was going to offer to wash your shirts for you." She wrinkled her nose. "It's about time I did so, don't you think?"

"The smell of the trail offends you?" he asked politely.

"I wouldn't dream of implying that you smell like a male creet. I was simply offering to bargain for my freedom in exchange for washing your shirts. To tell you the truth, I'm out of clean tunics myself."

"Hmm." He pretended to consider the matter deeply. "I suppose it might be a wise idea for both of us to bathe. No reason you can't wash our clothes at the same time." He opened his arms.

Kalena yelped as she fell into the stream. The creets scampered out of the way. Closing her eyes, Kalena waited for the shock of the icy water to hit her. To her complete astonishment it was like falling into a lukewarm bath. Splashing to the surface, she flung wet hair out of her eyes and glared at Ridge. The skirts of her riding trousers floated around her legs.

"Lucky for you," she snapped, "that this stream isn't ice cold. Otherwise I might never have forgiven you."

"I may be a simpleminded male, but I'm not completely stupid." He crouched on the shore, undoing the laces of his shirt. His golden eyes were still lit with laughter. Ridge was obviously enjoying himself. Although it was equally obvious that he wasn't accustomed to this kind of play.

"You knew the water was almost warm?"

He nodded, removing his shirt. "We're not that far from Hot And Cold. We'll be there two nights from now. It's a town full of hot springs. Some of the water that flows from there retains it's warmth even this far away." He wadded the shirt into a small ball and tossed it to her. "Here. Show me some of your wifely skills, Kalena."

She reached out to catch the shirt, aware that Ridge was continuing to undress so that he could join her in the stream. A warm flush rose to her cheeks and she quickly lowered her eyes to the shirt. The small embroidered R was very plain on the left shoulder. It occurred to her that Ridge was going to quickly wear out the two shirts she had initialed for him. He rarely wore anything else.

Ridge waded into the stream and over to where she stood

waist deep in the water. "I have taken much pleasure in wearing the shirts you gave me," he said gently. "But every time I put one on I am reminded that I never gave you a wedding gift."

"Yes, you did. You rescued Arrisa and my other friends the night of the tavern brawl," she reminded him quickly. Studiously, she ignored the gleam of his strong flanks just under the surface of the water.

"Ah, but you restored the balance later that night, remember?" He smiled crookedly.

Kalena kept her eyes on the shirt in her hand. "Well, yes, but—"

He put a blunt, calloused finger on her lips to silence her. "But nothing. I owe you a gift in exchange for the embroidery work you did on my shirts. Someday I shall even the balance."

Kalena looked up into his intent gaze and saw the lambent warmth that waited for her there. She blinked and made an effort to shake off the curling tendrils of emotion that were beginning to swirl in the air around her. Deliberately, she summoned a lighthearted smile. "I've got news for you, husband. Throwing me into this stream has only put you much deeper into debt. You won't be able to buy your way back into my good graces very easily."

"A man can only try," Ridge said with a philosophical shrug.

"This particular man had better try very hard," Kalena informed him. "Or he'll be eating a cold meal tonight." She began to rinse out the shirt, very conscious of Ridge's nakedness. Her own clothing was a limp, soggy weight on her body. Soon she would have to remove it.

"You have me completely intimidated now, woman." With a sigh of pleasure Ridge let himself sink under the surface of the water.

Kalena was glad that night had almost fallen. The darkness would allow her to undress in the water without revealing too much of herself. She slipped out of her clothes and gave herself up to the pleasure of the bath. She half expected to find herself having to fend off Ridge's playful antics, or perhaps something more serious, but he seemed oblivious of her nudity.

Totally oblivious.

When he climbed out of the stream a few minutes later, turned his back on her and went to fetch a towel from the saddlebags, Kalena realized she actually felt rather disappointed. The female creet chirped from the shore and Kalena glanced at the bird. "At least you got assaulted by your mate. All I got was dunked by mine," she muttered.

The bird chirped again as if in commiseration.

At first he thought the dream had awakened him. When Ridge opened his eyes several hours later, highly charged erotic images were still swirling through his brain. His body was taut with the aftereffects. The dream had been a very vivid one. In it, he had given in to the urge to make passionate love to Kalena that he had denied earlier in the evening when he had left the stream. In the dream he had carried Kalena out of the water, laid her down on the sand and covered her soft, yielding body with his own aroused one. She had responded to him with a desire that matched his own, welcoming him into her sweet, intoxicating embrace.

She was the one who could quench the flames.

Ridge shook himself free of the seductive images and sat up slowly in his pallet. Something was wrong out there in the darkness and it had nothing to do with erotic dreams.

He looked across the short expanse of distance to where Kalena lay asleep in her trail pallet and saw nothing alarming or out of the ordinary. He heard the faint rustling movement from where the creets were crouched together in sleep and realized it was just such a soft sound that had been responsible for waking him. Even as he recognized that fact, he heard the unmistakable chirp of alarm from the male.

Ridge was on his feet almost as quickly as the bird.

"Ridge?" Kalena's sleepy question floated through the shadows. "What's wrong?"

"I'm not sure yet. Stay close to the fire, Kalena."

She didn't argue. He heard her push back the pallet cover, but Ridge didn't turn to glance at her. His full attention was on the male creet who was chirping angrily. The female squeaked once or twice in alarm. With the sintar in his hand, Ridge stepped into his boots and moved towards the birds. He had worn his trousers to bed, having had the unsettling experience of more than once being dragged out of sleep on the trail to face danger stark naked. He went forward to face whatever was disturbing the creets.

The only thing he felt confident about was that whatever was out there wasn't human. The creets had no real fear of humans. From the way they were reacting it had to be one of their few natural enemies.

Fangcat, Ridge thought. Or, if his luck had really turned sour, a sinkworm. Let it be a fangcat, he decided as he headed toward the creets. He had enough on his hands without having to deal with a sinkworm.

The male creet screeched in fury and challenge just as Ridge cast his silent vote in favor of one of the big-toothed cats. In the shadows he saw the larger bird thrust the female behind itself with a rough movement of it's beak and then whirl back around to face the enemy.

A full-throated hissing sound slashed through the darkness. In the pale red moonlight Ridge saw a dark reptilian shape the size of a male creet leap to the top of the jumble of rocks near the stream. Its tail was a barbed hook that curved up and over its scaled back. The head was all faceted eyes and gleaming fangs. It crouched on four scaled legs, its broad feet heavily clawed.

Ridge stared at the creature in startled astonishment. So much for trying to choose between fangcats and sinkworms. His luck wasn't that good tonight. This was neither of those familiar denizens of the dark. The animal crouched on the rocks prepared to attack the creet was something out of a nightmare. Ridge recognized it from a description he had once been given by an old trader. It had to be the almost legendary hook viper.

But that was impossible. Hook vipers were creatures of the deepest mountain caves. Humans rarely saw them.

But the reality of the situation was something Ridge didn't have time to debate. What appeared to be a hook viper was poised for attack only a few feet from him, and he remembered hearing that the skull of the viper was as solid as a rock. The only truly vulnerable part on the head was the eye, but the odds of sinking the sintar into it at this range were minimal. There wasn't time to dig the bow or the dart sling out of the saddlebags. He would have to wait for the leap.

The male creet was screeching, its piercing challenge as deafening as the viper's hiss. The female waited in the shadows behind her mate, her head darting frantically about in anxiety. If forced to do so, she too would fight, but her instinct was to rely primarily on the male's greater strength and ability.

Ridge worked his way closer, trying to narrow the gap between himself and the viper as much as possible before the creature made its killing leap.

With another savage hiss, the hook viper sprang toward its prey. For an instant its vulnerable underside was exposed. Ridge hurled the sintar and hoped for a scrap of trader's luck.

At first he couldn't be sure the sintar had struck its target. Then the great reptile snarled in fury and pain and jerked violently in midair. It landed in an awkward sprawl in front of the male creet, who promptly ripped at the already bleeding belly with one clawed foot. With its beak it went for the dying viper's throat. The creet was more than happy to finish what Ridge had started.

"By the Stones," Kalena whispered in shock as she moved quickly up behind Ridge. "He's tearing that thing apart. I had no idea creets were carnivores."

"They're not. But that doesn't mean they can't draw blood." Ridge put his arm around Kalena's shoulders and pulled her back toward the fire. "Let's get out of the way. The last thing any sane man does is approach a creet while the bloodlust is riding it. I'll retrieve the sintar later."

Kalena was willing enough to be turned away from the sickening sight of the creet taking its vengeance. "They always seemed like such gentle creatures."

"They weren't given claws just for decoration."

"No, I suppose not. But when I think about how much they love to eat flowers . . . You're all right?"

"I'm fine. We'll just stay discreetly out of the way over here by the fire and wait until all the commotion dies down."

"What about my creet?" Kalena tried to glance back over her shoulder. "I don't see her."

"She's staying out of sight, too," Ridge explained with a flicker of amusement. "She knows better than to show herself until her mate has calmed down."

"I hope you're not going to draw any more parallels between human and creet female behavior."

"Why not?" Ridge asked lightly as he settled her down beside him on a rock near the glowing coals of the fire. From the shadows came the unpleasant sounds of shredding muscle and skin. The creet was making a thorough job of its vengeance. Ridge hoped the sintar didn't get lost in the process. "It seems to me you could learn a few lessons from your creet." He was rewarded with an elbow in the ribs for his observation. "Ouch!"

"You deserved that. I'm not in the mood for such jokes."

Ridge rubbed his bare ribs and said with sudden seriousness, "I wasn't joking. The male creet's job is to take care of the female and they both know it. Didn't you see how he stood between her and the viper? He would have died protecting her. In return for that kind of commitment, the female is willing to defer to her mate's occasional idiosyncracies." He looked down at Kalena. "It's the way of the Spectrum," he added gently. "All things must be balanced, including the roles of men and women."

She cast a sidelong glance and said blandly, "Could we skip the nature lesson?"

"Why? Because you don't want to admit the truth about the way things are between men and women?"

"I don't want you feeling obligated to put yourself between me and a . . . a thing such as that, Fire Whip. I wouldn't ask that of you or anyone."

"If the occasion arose, it would not be your place to ask or give permission," he tried to explain patiently. "I would do it because I have both the right and the duty to protect you. I'm your husband, Kalena."

"So you keep reminding me."

He stifled a long-suffering groan. "I find myself constantly having to remind you because you seem to forget the fact quite easily."

She looked down into the embers of the fire and a strange smile touched her mouth. "You're wrong, Fire Whip. Never for one moment do I forget the fact that you are my husband."

Ridge fell silent for a moment, watching her face in the faint glow of the fire and wondering exactly what she meant by those cryptic words. The thoughts of a woman could so often be completely unfathomable to a man. No wonder men had been given the strength and forcefulness of the Dark end of the Spectrum. Only such power could counter the greatest mystery of the Light end—a woman's mind.

"Ridge?"

"What is it, Kalena?"

"What was that thing you killed? I've never seen anything like it."

"Neither have I," he admitted, "although it looks like something a trader once described to me. He called it a hook viper. But I don't understand what it's doing this far from the mountains. They're very rarely seen, even by the traders who work the mountain towns. They're creatures who prefer the darkness of caves. They are said to be very shy of men."

"That one didn't seem particularly shy."

"It was probably starving. This far from the mountain caves it was undoubtedly having a hard time finding familiar food. It must have been desperate to come this close to fire and the smell of humans."

"I wonder what drove it from the mountains?"

"That, Kalena, is a very good question."

Ridge made certain they found an inn the following night. The village was the smallest they had yet encountered and the facilities were minimal, but it beat another night on the trail. The undeclared truce that seemed to have gone into effect between him and Kalena held throughout the day, right up to the moment Ridge unwittingly ruffled it by sending Kalena upstairs to the bedchamber after the evening meal.

He hadn't meant to sound arrogant, domineering or selfish, he told himself later when he found himself paying dearly for the act. He had only been exercising his sound judgment as an experienced trade master and a husband. The truth was, he had been quite shocked when Kalena had declared she would like to go into the tavern with him following the meal. He had stared at her from across the low table as if she had just announced she intended to strip herself naked and dance through the dining hall.

"That's impossible," he had finally stated flatly. "What in the name of the Stones put such an idea into your head? It might be possible to take you into a tavern in Crosspurposes, but it's out of the question in a small village like this. Everyone from the tavern keeper to the boy who sweeps the floors would be outraged. I warned you things were old-fashioned and conservative in these little towns on the trail. We have to abide by local customs, Kalena."

"But Ridge, there's nothing to do upstairs and I'm not ready to go to bed."

"I'm sorry about that, Kalena," he had told her a little helplessly. "But I can't keep you company. The journey isn't a pleasure trip. I'm supposed to be working."

"You call sitting around in a tavern drinking all night *work?*"

The woman had a way of putting him on the defensive. Ridge didn't like it. "I learn things in the taverns, Kalena."

"Such as?"

"I pick up rumors, bits of gossip. For example, I'll mention the hook viper tonight to see if anyone else says he's seen one. And there have been a few strange tales I would like to verify."

"What sort of tales?" she demanded.

He sighed, feeling driven into a corner. Apparently, he still had much to learn about handling a wife—or at least about handling

Kalena. He picked up his ale. "There have been one or two odd stories about men disappearing in the mountains. I would like to know more about those stories, especially after what happened to us in Adverse."

"I still think you could accomplish your job without lounging around a tavern," Kalena announced.

He thought about pointing out quite bluntly that if she was willing to provide a good reason for him to accompany her up the stairs, he might consider the matter. But wisely he bit back the words. They would only have infuriated her. "That's enough, Kalena. When you've finished your meal, go on up to the chamber. I'll join you later. I give you my word I won't be late. I just want to ask a few questions."

Her chin lifted. "Take your time. Don't hurry upstairs on my account," she told him with an awful politeness. She then swung with great dignity around to exit the dining hall.

Ridge watched her leave and groaned inwardly. Things had been going so well all day. He had begun to hope that perhaps tonight he would receive the invitation he wanted so badly. But Kalena obviously wasn't going to be in any mood to invite his lovemaking. Disgusted with himself and fate in general, he tossed down his fingerspears and stalked out of the dining area into the tavern. He needed a full tankard of ale.

Upstairs in the small cubicle that passed for a sleeping chamber, Kalena paced to and fro in front of the tiny window. She was feeling restless and irritated, and the tiny room with its stark furnishings felt like a cage.

In an effort to create a semblance of greater space, she stopped her pacing long enough to shove her travel bag into the little privacy chamber. It gave her a bit more room in which to pace like a tethered cotly.

The image further annoyed her. She was no tame pet to be kept on a lead.

In a burst of defiance Kalena opened the door of the room and stepped out into the corridor. If nothing else she could kill some time by going down to the stables to talk to the creets.

She was halfway down the corridor, passing the closed door of another guest chamber, when she heard the low moan. Startled, Kalena halted in her tracks and listened. The soft, pain-filled sound came again from behind the door.

Kalena hesitated, but when the moans continued she went over to the door and knocked.

"Hello?" she called softly. "Are you all right inside there?" All she heard was silence. Kalena tried again. "Do you need help?"

This time she heard a movement from behind the door, but it didn't open. A woman's voice reached her through the wood.

"Please."

Alarmed by the fear and pain in a single word, Kalena tried the door handle. It turned easily in her hand, and after a second's hesitation she stepped into the small chamber. A woman lay huddled on the pallet. She was very young and very pregnant. It didn't take an experienced Healer to realize the occupant of the room was in labor. Kalena went forward instantly.

"By the Stones, madam, don't tell me you decided to go through this all by yourself," she said, summoning up a cheerful, encouraging smile. "Has a Healer been called?"

The young woman looked up at her with a strained, frightened expression. "I don't know any Healer in this village. My husband . . ."

"Yes, where is your husband?" Kalena asked briskly as she straightened the bedding and reassuringly gripped the woman's hand.

"I'm not sure. He said he had business in town. Perhaps he stopped at a tavern."

"Exactly where one would expect a man to be at a time like this."

The stranger managed a fleeting smile that ended abruptly as a contraction gripped her body. "He doesn't know. The pains started so suddenly. I couldn't get downstairs to summon him."

"What you need is a Healer, not a helpless man. I'll be right back." Kalena got to her feet and raced out of the room.

She could hear the noise from the tavern as she swept past it on her way to the innkeeper's desk. Fortunately, the innkeeper's wife answered Kalena's summons immediately.

"I'll fetch the village Healer at once," the older woman promised. "Go back upstairs to the poor girl. I saw her earlier. She's so young. This is probably her first and she'll be scared to death."

Kalena nodded and ran back up the stairs. For the second time she ignored the shouts of laughter and the smoke that emanated from the tavern doorway.

Her breath was coming quickly by the time Kalena had finished her dash back up the stairs. She paused to collect herself before she reentered the young woman's chamber. A good Healer always presented a calm and soothing image, she reminded herself.

A good Healer. That was a joke. She was no Healer and never would be. The thought brought a wave of unhappiness that was all too familiar. Kalena would have given a great deal to have been born with the Talent. She had certainly been cursed with a longing desire to learn the arts of healing. It had always seemed so unfair to have the wish and not the ability.

Quickly, she produced a comforting smile and pushed open the door. "There is no need to worry," she assured the patient on the pallet. "The village Healer will be along very soon. We might as well get ready for her."

"You're very kind."

"Don't be silly. Women must stick together at times such as this. What woman would turn her back on another about to give birth?" Remembering the occasional glimpses she'd had of Olara at work, Kalena lit a fire on the tiny hearth and put water on to boil. She dampened a cloth to cool the mother-to-be's brow and generally tried to make the young woman as comfortable as possible. Mostly she just held her hand and felt the woman's nails dig into her palm as each new wave of pain arrived. Kalena would have given anything not to feel so helpless.

If she were a Healer she would be able to do so much more.

She had seen Olara use certain herbs to blunt the pain and stop excessive bleeding. Certainly, she knew Olara's skills could make the whole process so much easier and safer. But Kalena knew so little of them. Only a trained Healer with the Talent could really help.

The woman cried out and Kalena began to fret that the village Healer would not make it in time.

"You're doing just fine," she said soothingly as she began to push aside the bedding. If no one came she would have to deliver the babe herself. She could only hope the birth would be normal.

"Breathe deeply and don't fight the pain. It will soon be over. Just breathe deeply."

Olara always used an almost hypnotic monologue to quiet her patient's fears. Over the years Kalena had heard bits and pieces of it. She tried to remember the soft, soothing sounds.

"That's it. Everything's going to be just fine. Don't be afraid to yell if you want. You've got every right."

If only she knew more, Kalena thought in a mixture of anger and despair. She should know more. It wasn't fair that such knowledge had been kept from her. *She should know what to do.* Something within her insisted she had a right to know.

There was a quick, perfunctory knock, and then the door swung open. Kalena looked around gratefully to see a woman in her middle years step confidently into the room. The innkeeper's wife was right behind her.

"No need to ask which of you is my patient," the Healer said cheerfully. "How are we doing here?" She was removing a packet of herbs from her bag and handing them to Kalena. "Looks like everything's under control. Here, mix these in some warm water and let the little mother have a few sips. The drink will ease the pain."

Humbly, Kalena took the herb packet and did as she was instructed. The Healer took charge and the whole process of birth was soon moving along its inevitable path under the watchful eye of a trained expert with the Talent.

Kalena watched in fascination, holding the young mother's hand and letting her sip from the mug of herb tea as needed. There was something about all this that reinforced Kalena's deep sense of longing. She wanted to know exactly what to do. She wanted to be able to offer comfort and skill. The desire to be doing what the Healer was doing was so deep and so painful that for a moment Kalena felt her eyes burn with frustrated tears.

And then the baby arrived and everyone, including Kalena, was much too busy to think of anything but the present.

Downstairs in the tavern, Ridge lounged at a table, a tankard of ale in front of him, moodily considering his past, present and future.

For some reason they all seemed tied to Kalena. The past because he was just beginning to realize how empty it had been without her. The present because he didn't know how to deal with her now that he had her. And the future because he had a deep fear that he might not be able to hold on to her.

At times, he felt he was making progress with her. But inevitably such moments disintegrated all too rapidly, usually because of something he said or did. He gripped the tankard of red ale and wondered broodingly if he would ever receive the welcome he wanted from Kalena.

He was a fool to wait for it, he decided after another swallow of ale. A man's obligation was to insist on his marital rights. He had been crazy to think he should wait until Kalena came to him. At this rate he would wait forever.

By the Stones, he didn't have forever. No one did.

Surging to his feet, Ridge threw a few grans down on the table and stalked out of the tavern. He had been taking the wrong approach with Kalena. If he let her establish the rules of this game he would find himself sleeping alone for the rest of the journey. He had to ensure the bonds between them. He couldn't afford to waste any more time.

Ridge was still telling himself that when he reached the top of the stairs and shoved open the chamber door. His mouth opened to tell Kalena that things were going to be different henceforth. The words were clear in his head and his body was taut with an assertive determination.

But he blinked and floundered to a halt when he realized the room was empty. Bewildered, he glanced around and saw that Kalena's travel pack was gone.

For an instant he simply stood staring into the empty chamber, trying to adjust to the obvious fact that Kalena had left him.

Somehow he hadn't expected her to run from him. He was at a loss to comprehend the depths of his own stupidity. Of course she would run at the first opportunity. And tonight had provided that opportunity.

A wave of fury washed over Ridge. "Damn you, Kalena. *You can't leave me.*"

But of course she could. All she had to do was slip out while he was downing ale in a tavern. She knew how to saddle a creet. What else did she need to know to make good her escape?

He had been a fool to indulge her. He must have been out of his mind to be so gentle and restrained with her. What had he been thinking of when he had assumed she had accepted her fate as his wife?

Whirling around, Ridge went back to the door. She couldn't have gotten far. He would find her and bring her back, and this time he would make certain she understood her place. She was his wife, and by the Stones she would learn what that meant.

A heavy, bewildering sense of frustration that bordered on pain rose inside him to counter the explosion of anger. Ridge stormed through the door and out into the corridor just as an anxious look-ing young man reached the top of the stairs and pounded on one of the chamber doors.

"Betha?" the young man called, sounding frantic. "Betha? Are you all right?"

Ridge ignored the other man's obvious state of distress, his at-tention turned inward as he made for the stairs. He would have walked right past the other chamber without a single glance if the door hadn't swung open in that moment to reveal his flame-haired wife.

"I suppose you are the husband?" Kalena demanded of the young man in front of her.

"Please," the man said helplessly. "My wife. Is she all right?" A cry sounded from the chamber and he looked stunned. "The babe!"

"Congratulations," Kalena said disdainfully. "You have a fine son. Your wife and child are doing well, no thanks to you."

Ridge heard the chastisement in her voice and winced on behalf of the hapless young man. Kalena didn't pause in her lecture.

"What sort of husband are you to take your lady traveling when she was in this condition? She should have been safely at home with her village Healer who knows her and is familiar with her background. She should have had her women friends around her at such a time. Instead, poor Betha finds herself in some strange inn with only strangers to help her. And where is her husband? Downstairs drinking in the tavern while his son is brought into the world. I'll wager you were willing enough to participate at the conception of your babe, weren't you?"

"Please, lady. I would go to my wife," the man pleaded.

"But you took little enough responsibility for the havoc you caused," Kalena continued, undaunted. "It is a man's duty to protect his wife. She is in his care and it is his business to look after her. Where were you when you should have been honoring your obligations to your wife?"

Ridge let out a long sigh of relief and lounged against the wall, his arms crossed on his chest, to listen to the rest of Kalena's speech. Never had he been so glad to hear a sharp-tongued female tearing into a defenseless male. He simply gave thanks that he wasn't the man she was ripping apart. Safely out of range, he watched his wife with a mixture of amusement and admiration and overpowering relief.

She hadn't run from him after all.

NINE

I thought you'd left." Ridge stood at the tiny window and stared down into the inn yard below.

Kalena closed the door of the small chamber and leaned back against the wood. She had been surprised to see Ridge in the corridor outside Betha's room. He hadn't said a word as she had lectured the young father, but as soon as she had released the poor man to go to his wife, Ridge had stepped forward to take her arm. He asked her quietly if she was ready to go back to their chamber and she had nodded her agreement. His first words once inside the room startled her.

"I don't understand," she said calmly.

He didn't turn around. Instead, he braced one arm against the windowsill and continued to stare out into the darkness. "You heard me. I came up here a short time ago and couldn't find either you or your travel bag. I assumed you'd taken your leave."

Slowly, Kalena moved away from the door. "That wouldn't be possible, Ridge."

He glanced back over his shoulder, searching her calm face.

"Why wouldn't it be possible? You could have taken a creet and ridden until you found some farmhouse where you could have paid for shelter for the rest of the night. You're not frightened of the darkness and you don't lack intelligence. It would have been easy enough for you to escape me."

Her mouth curved faintly. "I can't escape you, Ridge. I'm bound by a trade marriage contract, remember? I signed the document."

"It's nothing but a piece of paper."

Kalena began to grow indignant. "It's a legal document. By signing it, I bound myself to the provisions of that contract. It would shred what's left of my pride and honor to walk away from you before the journey is finished."

Something suspiciously akin to admiration gleamed in the depths of his eyes. "You speak as if you have very little left of your pride and honor. But I can vouch for the fact that you have more than enough of both for any one woman. More than enough for any one man, come to think of it."

"Is it so hard for you to understand that a woman's sense of honor can be as great as a man's?"

"Before I met you, it would have been hard for me to believe such a thing," he admitted softly. "But you have taught me differently. There have been times, my lady, when your notions of pride and honor have made life very difficult for me. But tonight I am grateful for them."

She realized he meant every word he was saying. Kalena's brief flare of anger faded quickly. "You can be a thickheaded man, but you're an honest one." She smiled faintly. "Honesty is a good trait in a husband."

"I'm glad that on one point, at least, I'm proving satisfactory."

She blushed at the direct look in his eyes and turned away to busy herself retrieving her travel bag from the privacy chamber. "You were virtually tricked into this marriage by my aunt's manipulations. You've had every right to be annoyed with me from time to time."

"Kalena."

She paused and looked back at him. "Yes, Ridge?"

"I am satisfied with the conditions of our marriage."

She had the feeling he wanted to say a great deal more but couldn't find the words. Poor Ridge. He was far more adept with a sintar than he was with words. Quickly, she sought for some way to lighten the tense atmosphere.

"Well, as to that, I'm reasonably satisfied myself," she said easily.

"Are you?"

"Why shouldn't I be? When I return from the Heights of Variance, I will have a sizable quantity of Sand to sell, won't I? Freedom will be much more enjoyable if I have the financial resources to afford it." The lightness left her voice as a sense of bitterness returned. "It's true that under Olara's original plans I was never meant to get the Sand, but the Spectrum has balanced itself differently than Olara expected. I have disgraced myself and my House, but I may find myself rewarded for failure in a way no one could have predicted."

Ridge's gaze hardened abruptly. "Are you saying you're staying with me not because of your honor, after all, but because of the chance at the Sand?"

"What do you think, Ridge?" she asked coolly.

"There are times, lady, when you have me so confused I don't know what to think," he muttered and turned to pull down the cover of the sleeping pallet with an angry gesture. "If you've finished playing Healer for the evening, let's go to bed. We have a long ride ahead of us tomorrow."

"We always seem to have a long ride ahead of us."

"You didn't expect to get your hands on the Sand easily, did you?" he shot back as he sat down to yank off his boots.

"Does it anger you that I might be thinking in a practical fashion now about this journey, Ridge? You're hardly one to complain. You've made it quite clear that your main goal on this trip is to return with access to enough Sand to found your House. Why should it bother you that I might also be looking forward to what the Sand can buy for me?"

He wrenched off his shirt and tossed it aside. "The freedom you seek isn't going to satisfy you, Kalena."

"How do you know?"

He slid under the pallet cover and folded his arms behind his head. He watched her as she turned out the firegel lamp and began to undress in the darkness with her back to him. "Because I've held you in my arms," he said deliberately. "And I know you for the woman you are. You're a creature of passion. You won't be happy unless you accept that aspect of your nature. You will need a man to share your dreams."

"Men are always so sure of themselves when they make pro-nouncements about a woman's needs," she whispered. She pulled her sleeping shift over her head and crawled into the pallet beside him.

"I said you will need a man, Kalena, and it's true," Ridge in-sisted stubbornly.

"If that's so, then I will just have to find myself one, won't I?" she countered lightly.

"You've already found yourself one. Me." He turned his back to her with an abrupt movement. "One of these days you'll admit it."

Kalena could think of nothing sufficient to say in response. She lay on her side of the pallet, vividly conscious of the heat of his body, and wondered at the complexity of the luck of the Spec-trum. Kalena lay in the dark for a long time and was certain Ridge was asleep when he startled her by saying half humorously, "I'm glad it wasn't me you were yelling at out there in the corridor. You have a formidable tongue, woman."

"Sometimes a sharp tongue is a woman's only weapon."

"Ha. Your end of the Spectrum has armed you well. Ask any man. To tell you the truth, though, I found your lecture somewhat amusing. After all those arguments we had about the role of the male as protector of the female, you had a lot of nerve to use my side of things against that young man."

"He deserved to be scolded," Kalena declared firmly. "Right or wrong, he took the vows to protect and care for his wife when he married her. He should have honored those vows. He had no business being downstairs drinking the night away while his wife went into labor alone."

"He's just a kid."

"He's old enough to father a child, isn't he?" Kalena muttered.

Ridge mumbled something to himself, in response, then said to Kalena, "Just the same, I'm glad he was your target tonight instead of me."

"It would never have been you. Not under such circumstances as existed tonight," Kalena said simply.

Ridge was silent for a moment, then asked, "Why do you say that?"

"There would have been no need to remind you of your responsibility and commitment to your wife. You would never forget such matters. You would have made certain she was safe and protected when her time came."

"Thank you for your faith in me, wife. And now I'll tell you something I have decided about you."

"What's that?"

"I don't think you're honoring your marriage contract just because you've decided to get your hands on some Sand. It isn't greed that keeps you by my side." He sounded absolutely sure of himself.

Kalena wasn't sure just what he meant, but she didn't dare ask.

Kalena greeted the sight of the little town of Hot And Cold with more enthusiasm than she had felt for any of the other villages where they had chosen to stop. They were at the end of eight days of hard riding. The inns along the way had ranged from primitive to minimal, and the villages had run the gamut from small to very small.

But Hot And Cold promised an intriguing change of pace. Kalena urged her mount closer to Ridge's creet as he drew to a halt at the top of a hill and looked down at the tiny village.

"Is it true they have natural hot springs here?" Kalena demanded.

Ridge glanced at her. "It's true. The caravans always try to stop here. The pools are much appreciated after two eightdays on the trail."

"Two eightdays? But we've only been on the trail for one," Kalena said in surprise.

"We've been moving a great deal faster than a normal trade caravan with all its baggage and pack creets. The caravans make other trade stops along the way, too. It generally takes at least three eightday periods to reach the mountains that guard the valley of the High Healers. If all goes well, we'll start into the mountains tomorrow. We should arrive at the valley soon after that."

"If we can get into the valley," Kalena reminded him.

"We'll get in. That's what I'm here to do."

Such confidence was undoubtedly based on a lifetime of success in similar situations, Kalena thought with a sigh. She examined the tiny village below, which sat in a wooded valley nestled in the mountain's foothills. This was strange country. There was little gradual incline as the plains gave way to valleys and the valleys gave way to mountains. Everything seemed to happen abruptly. The plains simply stopped. After only a short range of low valleys and hills, the mountains took over.

"Are you disappointed that you haven't yet encountered an explanation for the failure of the other caravans?" Kalena asked. She knew Ridge had had little luck in his conversations in the inn taverns.

"No, I'm relieved," Ridge assured her dryly. "I'm paid to handle Quintel's problems, but that doesn't mean I don't prefer the quiet trips."

"This hasn't exactly been a quiet trip. What about those two men who attacked us back in Adverse?" Kalena mused slowly. "You don't think they had any connection with the problems that have plagued the route?"

"If they did, the trouble has been easily resolved, hasn't it?" He tugged lightly on the reins of his mount and started down the hill into the valley.

Kalena thought of the two dead men and their black glass

pendants and she shivered. She hoped Ridge was right in thinking there was nothing more to worry about from that direction. She urged her creet after him.

"I have heard of natural hot water pools such as the ones you say are in this village," she remarked. "Olara told me they can be very useful for certain types of healing. She has sent more than one old person from our village to a town that had hot pools. Once she sent a small child who was crippled from a fall."

"All traders love the way the pools feel after a long day's ride. They're much better than a normal bath. Apparently, there's something in the water that's unique."

"It's hardly surprising, is it?" Kalena noted. "We're very close to the Heights of Variance. It's possible hot waters that feed the pools have their origin somewhere in the mountains. It's said that the Light Key is sealed somewhere in the Heights of Variance and that its influence pervades the mountains. That's why the High Healers live and work there. The presence of the Key supposedly lends power to their medicines."

"I thought you didn't believe in myths," Ridge mocked.

"Well, I don't, but one wonders sometimes. After all, no one else has been successful in creating a version of the Sands. And we all owe much to the medical knowledge that has come to us from the High Healers. It's obvious they have some extraordinary abilities."

"The High Healers are very clever, very wealthy women who have been smart enough to build a powerful reputation based on one very marketable product, namely the Sands of Eurythmia." Ridge's voice was mildly scornful. "They shroud themselves in mystery primarily to keep everyone in awe of them. There is no good reason why they should not be willing to deal directly with men. Their insistence on trading only with married women has been a nuisance from the start. Quintel has had his hands full over the years working around their various demands and restrictions."

Kalena grinned at Ridge's display of typical male irritation. "Working around those demands and restrictions has brought a great deal of wealth and power to the House of the Gliding Fallon. You yourself are planning to make a sizable profit off this venture. Just think, Ridge. If you do return to Crosspurposes to found your House, you will owe it all to a bunch of uppity, unpredictable, difficult females."

"You have a way of viewing things from a strangely skewed perspective, Kalena." She saw the reluctant amusement in his golden eyes when he glanced back over his shoulder.

"A woman's perspective," she confirmed with some satisfaction.

More and more she found herself enjoying these moments when he gave in to his sense of humor and shared some small joke with her. Kalena knew she often deliberately provoked him just to see if she could tap into that indulgent side of his nature. The risk in such provocation, of course, lay in never being certain she wouldn't hit a vein of temper instead of good humor. But every time they were able to share this closeness, she knew the risk was worth taking. When she won an outright laugh from him, Kalena felt as though she had uncovered a cache of buried treasure.

There were times, Kalena knew, when she walked on thin crystal. Ridge's legendary temper was never far from the surface, and she had been scalded more than once by a burst of it. On such occasions she immediately ceased her provoking ways and set about placating him. It wasn't difficult. She was learning rapidly that dealing with Ridge's fiery nature was a relatively simple matter. Arrisa and the others would have been startled to hear her say so, but Kalena was beginning to feel she had a distinct and unique talent for it. It was an odd sort of talent, and probably wouldn't be of much use in the long-term, but while she was around Ridge, it came in awfully handy.

On one point, Kalena was very careful not to provoke Ridge. That was the subject of his own honor. At times, Ridge would grow quiet for long periods on the trail and she would wonder if he was thinking of how close she had once brought him to dishonor. He had absolutely no sense of humor about that, and she could hardly blame him. She realized now that that was how Ridge viewed the entire beginning of their relationship: As a near disaster for his honor. It wasn't just Quintel's life that had been at stake, but Ridge's keen sense of personal honor.

He took his role as Kalena's husband seriously; if it had been discovered that his wife was Quintel's assassin, his honor would have been savaged. Ridge owed his loyalty first and foremost to the austere man who had been his employer and his benefactor. As far as Ridge was concerned, his wife owed her loyalty to her husband. One way or another, Ridge's fierce sense of pride made him feel totally responsible for the actions of his wife.

He would make a good lord for a Great House, Kalena decided grimly. Ridge had the convoluted, overly fierce notion of responsibility necessary for the job. Any woman who committed herself to be his wife on a permanent basis would find herself trying to manage a very difficult husband. Managing him for only eight days on the trail had been hard enough.

Kalena wasn't absolutely certain she had done well by her own honor since Adverse. She had reluctantly come to that conclusion that her duty was clear. She couldn't deny that by the terms of the contract she had signed she owed Ridge the respect and loyalty of a wife. The fact that she had never intended to carry out that contract was a side issue, one that was no longer important. Ridge had a right to share her pallet. But she had come to that decision only to discover that Ridge no longer seemed interested in doing so. Even last night, when she had tried to explain that she felt obliged to honor the terms of the marriage contract, he had made no move to touch her.

The way he had ignored her presence in the sleeping pallet since Adverse confused and alarmed her. She had kept her uncertainty to herself, of course. Honor might demand that she accept her husband's claim on her, but it did not demand that she throw herself at him. Ridge was not yet getting his morning yant tea served to him in his pallet.

When all was said and done, Kalena knew only that her emotional reaction to Ridge wasn't clear, even to herself. Almost against her will she found herself respecting his authority, his ability, and even, in some ways, his outsized sense of pride. He was a tough, honest, capable, *honorable* man. The core of self-confidence and determination about him commanded respect.

But a very feminine part of her was extremely wary of Ridge, and not only because of what had happened the night of her wedding. He was a Houseless bastard, a paid employee of a Great House. Furthermore, he had a temper that surely originated at the Dark end of the Spectrum. Kalena knew she would never forget the sight of the sintar glowing in his hand. Nevertheless, she couldn't escape the fact that he was her husband. For the duration of this journey, this bastard son of a Great House had full authority over her. She wondered why he hadn't used that authority since Adverse.

They found the village inn at the north end of the dusty street that ran the length of Hot And Cold. Kalena dismounted with her usual sense of relief and examined the sign over the inn door. The design was a crude rendition of a mountain cave with what appeared to be a steaming pool. Her spirits picked up quickly.

"I want to try the hot pools, Ridge," she said. She had made it a point to ask very few favors from him during the past eightday, but Kalena had no intention of missing out on something as interesting as an underground hot spring.

Ridge frowned slightly as he started into the inn. "Perhaps. It's a little late."

Kalena's mouth firmed, but she said nothing. As far as she was concerned, there was no "perhaps" about it. She was very curious about the natural hot waters and this difficult husband of hers was not going to stop her from exploring them. She followed him into the small lobby.

The fire blazing in the huge stone hearth warmed the rustic room adjoining the tavern where several locals were lounging. They eyed the newcomers through the open doors between the two rooms. A woman, probably the innkeeper's wife, came to the front desk and Kalena greeted her with a smile. The woman hesitated and then smiled back.

"My wife and I need a room for the night and stable space for two creets," Ridge said.

The woman behind the desk nodded briskly. "We can accommodate you." She glanced suspiciously at Kalena, who sighed and causally loosened the opening of her traveling cloak so that the innkeeper's wife could see the lock and key around her throat. They proved her respectability.

"Very good," the woman said, handing Ridge a key. "Perhaps your wife would like to sample the waters? There is a section of pools set aside for women. The villagers use them frequently in the evenings." She glanced at Kalena. "It's all quite respectable," she assured her. "Many Healers have sent people here, and occasionally even a High Healer will come out of the mountains to take the waters."

"I would love to try the waters," Kalena said before Ridge could think of a reason to forbid it. "Where do I go to find them?"

"The women's pools are located in the southern caverns, just north of the inn. It's only a short walk. There will be others there this evening and the route is well lighted."

"Thank you," Kalena said before turning to smile challengingly at Ridge. "I shall go after the evening meal, while you're in the tavern."

Ridge arched one brow. "You will?"

"Yes," Kalena declared, starting past him to fetch her bag. "I will." Sometimes, she was discovering, you had to be quite firm with a husband.

Two hours later, Kalena was submerged to her neck in a rocky pool of deliciously hot water, lazily contemplating the various and assorted techniques required for managing males.

The room in which she was relaxing was a huge cavern lit by numerous firegel lamps. The cavern arched high over the many hot pools, its ceiling studded with oddly shaped mineral formations that threw strange shadows. Several uninviting dark tunnels opened up on the main pool room, but only one of these was lit.

That was the tunnel that led back to the hillside entrance of the extensive cave system.

The setting would have been unnervingly eerie if the cavern hadn't been so populated with local women who were obviously enjoying their evening relaxation. The bubbling pools were clearly an entrenched female social institution in the community.

Three other women were sharing Kalena's hot spring. They lounged naked on the natural seats formed by the craggy interior of the pool, eyeing Kalena with shy curiosity. Elsewhere in the huge cave other pools contained similar little groups. The women had been polite to Kalena, but only as they relaxed around her did they grow increasingly chatty.

"My name is Tana. I've heard you and your husband are on your way into the mountains," the woman across from Kalena said politely. She was a plump blonde about Kalena's age. Like all the other women in the cavern, she wore a lock and key around her throat. It was all any of them wore as they sat nude in the bubbling water.

Kalena nodded pleasantly, glad of the opportunity to socialize again with her own sex. "My husband wishes to trade with the High Healers."

The blonde tilted her head. "But you're not with a trading caravan."

"No."

"Lately, all of the caravans have been turned back by the veil of white mists," a second woman volunteered. "No one has gotten through the pass."

Kalena shrugged. "My husband is a very stubborn man. It will take a great deal to turn him back."

The other women nodded their understanding of stubborn males. "Perhaps the two of you will be able to get through. Who knows? The High Healers can be very unpredictable," said one.

"Have there been times in the past when so many trading caravans have been turned back?" Kalena asked.

"Not in the years I have lived in Hot And Cold," Tana said thoughtfully. "My husband says something is very wrong up in the mountains. The Healers have been unpredictable, and have occasionally done strange things in the past, but they have never cut off all communication for such a long period of time. Everyone knows the mountains have always been a little strange. It makes sense that the people who live in them are rather odd, also."

"I've heard the waters in these pools come from the heart of the Heights," Kalena ventured. She glanced down into the depths of the pool in which she was sitting. The water was so clear that she could see to the bottom of the hot pool, which was a little deeper than she was tall.

"So it's said," Tana agreed. "There's no doubt that people find the waters refreshing. Some claim they have certain healing properties."

Another woman said knowingly, "It's because of the Light Key. My grandmother once told me it's buried somewhere in the mountains."

"Do you really believe that?" Kalena asked.

"Who knows? Anything is possible," the woman said. "My grandmother had a touch of the healing Talent, although it wasn't enough to enable her to take the training. She was usually right about such matters."

Tana grinned. "Your grandmother should have been a story spinner. Her true talent was in the telling of tales." She turned to Kalena. "I saw the tunic you wore here tonight. Is that the style they're wearing in Crosspurposes?"

Kalena nodded. "The shorter length is very comfortable."

Tana sighed. "My husband would probably throw me out of the house if I shortened my tunics."

The other women laughed and turned to Kalena with more questions about the latest styles in Crosspurposes. The conversation became increasingly animated for a time. The hot pools were filled with women exchanging gossip, recipes and advice. Gradually, however, the noise level in the huge cave began to diminish as one by one the bathers dressed and made their way home for the night.

Kalena closed her eyes for a while, luxuriating in the wonderful water as she listened to the voices of her companions gradually fade into the distance. She knew the bathers were leaving the waters, knew they were toweling dry, dressing and disappearing down the lit tunnel that led outside. But somehow it seemed too much of an effort to open her eyes and climb out of the water herself.

In a little while, Kalena thought. She'd go back to the inn shortly. There was no rush. After all, Ridge would still be in the tavern, hoisting his tankard along with the rest of the local males. And never had bathing felt so good. All the aches and pains of the past eight days of riding were soaking away, leaving behind a lovely, languid, totally relaxed sensation.

It was a long time later before Kalena realized just how silent the cave had become. With an effort she finally opened her eyes and discovered she was the last bather. All the other women had left. Kalena sat up abruptly in the water, glancing around with a new sense of uncertainty. Sharing the lit caverns with a group of cheerful, friendly women was one thing; finding herself alone in the underground cavern was another matter entirely. The water seemed much less inviting now.

Kalena's sense of relaxation evaporated. She turned to climb out of the pool, reaching for the huge towel she had brought with her from the inn. Her clothes were folded on a bench near the edge of the pool and she slipped into them quickly after she had dried herself. A sense of urgency was beginning to awaken in her.

When she had entered the huge cavern earlier, Kalena had found the array of bubbling pools an interesting natural phenomenon. Now, shrouded in silence and lamplight, the pools seemed strange and vaguely alien, the creations of a story spinner. The stream that rose from the surface of the hottest of the springs seemed to have thickened, clouding the air. The steam also seemed to be causing the firegel lamps to look dimmer, Kalena thought as she hurriedly slipped into her soft boots.

Her imagination was getting the best of her, Kalena decided irritably. Still, as soon as she was dressed, she scooped up her towel and started toward the passage that led out of the cavern. En route she passed two other darkened tunnels and discovered that they

seemed more sinister than they had earlier. She stayed well clear of
the shadowed entrances of the unused tunnels and moved swiftly
toward the main one. She wished she had left when the other
women had gone back to their homes.

The lamplight definitely seemed to have faded, especially the
light in the main passageway. Kalena paused at the entrance and
gazed warily down the wide, curving tunnel that had seemed so
brightly lit when she had used it to enter the cavern. The lamps
farthest away from her were almost completely dark. Kalena shivered involuntarily and thought about what it would be like to get
halfway into the tunnel and find herself in total darkness. Smaller
passages led off the large one, and if she couldn't see she might accidentally turn into one of them. If she did that she would be in
great danger of getting lost in the endless corridors that branched
off of the main cave.

Kalena took a deep breath and started determinedly into the
tunnel. But she had taken no more than a few steps when another
distant row of lamps flickered and died. Instinctively, Kalena
stopped. The darkness that filled the far end of the tunnel seemed
unnaturally thick.

She had to go forward, Kalena told herself. She had no choice.
It was obvious, however, that she would have to provide her own
light. She backed out of the tunnel and went over to one of the
firegel lamps that circled the inside of the pool room. Lifting it
down from its hook, she held it out and started once more down
the main passageway. Very few of the lamps strung along the tunnel were still alight.

Kalena was several feet into the tunnel when the lamp she was
carrying began to falter. At first she thought she had only imagined
the gradual dimming of the glowing firegel, but three or four steps
later she knew for certain she was going to lose her light. The tunnel ahead lay in utter blackness now. There was no way she could
take the risk of continuing without a lamp. Even as that thought
crossed her mind, Kalena's firegel lamp faded and winked out. The
thick darkness reached out to engulf her.

Fear swept through her. She dropped the lamp, whirled, and

ran back toward the lights of the pool room. But the tunnel darkness seemed to be pursuing her. The last of the lamps that had lit the exit tunnel died just as she reached the pool room.

Kalena swung around, one hand raised instinctively as if she could ward off the blackness that roiled in the tunnel. She stared in horror at the ominous darkness that was encroaching into the pool cavern. All the passageways were filled with thick shadows. It was as if a black mist was making its way through all the corridors, seeking to fill the main chamber. A lamp or two on the cavern wall faded. The shadows crept farther into the room.

Kalena grabbed another lamp off the stony wall and forced herself to start toward the tunnel. She must not become disoriented and forget which tunnel was the exit. She thought she might be able to use the lamps along the walls of the tunnel to guide herself out, even though they were now dark. Only the exit tunnel had been strung with lamps, and the lampholders had been hung at about shoulder height. If she crept through the darkness finding one lamp after another by touch, she should be reasonably protected from taking a wrong turn somewhere in the tunnel.

She would not take more than three paces unless her groping fingers could find the reassuring presence of a firegel holder, Kalena decided as she advanced once again toward the tunnel opening.

It took a tremendous amount of willpower to walk forward into the thick darkness. Already the lamp she held was fading. It wouldn't last more than another few steps. Only the knowledge that she couldn't stay behind to be trapped in the pool cavern as all light gradually faded kept Kalena going. Her lamp grew dimmer as she edged toward the tunnel wall and put her hand on the first of the darkened lamps. Her fingers had barely touched the metal holder when the lamp she was holding in front of her glowed briefly and died. Darkness flowed over her.

Kalena screamed. She knew now that her imagination had not been playing tricks on her. This was no natural darkness. It was a tangible thing that writhed around her, seeking to trap her in its coils. She could not go any farther into the tunnel. She was not facing mere shadow, but a total absence of light. Kalena knew beyond any doubt that this was a sample of the darkness that filled the void at the farthest, darkest end of the Spectrum. There was no promise of dawn beyond these palpable depths. If she stepped into them she would be swallowed up forever.

Tendrils of the thick darkness coiled around her. She could feel an absolute cold touching her arm and she jerked back in an attempt to avoid it. The darkened lamp she had been holding fell to the rocky floor, the clanging sound jarring her senses.

The pools! She had to get back to the pools. The bubbling waters in the main cave were said to be under the influence of the Light Key. They were her only hope against this darkness.

Whirling, Kalena stumbled back toward the pool cavern. She could barely make out the light that still ringed the bubbling waters, but any light, no matter how dim, was a fierce beacon compared to the endless, swirling blackness that threatened her in the tunnel. Quickly, she groped her way toward the faint glow.

Kalena felt another tendril of fathomless cold touching her leg just as she reached the main cavern. It pulled at her as if it would stop her from reaching the relative safety of the pools. She tripped and sprawled painfully on the hard stone floor of the main cave. Terrified of being yanked back into the darkness by the writhing tendril, she rolled frantically onto her stomach, lurched to her feet and reached the edge of the nearest pool. When she looked back, she saw no sign of any curling tendril of chilled darkness, but the shadows seemed to have crept farther into the main room. Two more lamps along the walls went out.

Kalena edged closer to the water in the pool behind her. Shaking, she knelt and dipped her hand into the hot liquid. As soon as her fingers touched the water she knew she was right. These pools were her only protection from the cold darkness that was radiating toward her down the tunnels. She didn't understand how she could be so certain, but she wasn't about to ask questions.

She got to her feet, took yet another lamp from the wall, and threaded her way between the assortment of small and large pools until she was at the central and largest of the springs. She could only hope that the smaller pools circling it would act as a barrier against the darkness that approached. Her last resort would be to get into the deepest pool and immerse herself in the protection of the water. She didn't want to think about what she would do if even that failed, but a part of her knew she would choose to drown in this clean, warm water before she would surrender to the cold blackness.

Kalena crouched beside her chosen pool, her hand on the lamp, and battled the fear that threatened to swamp her. One by one, the remaining firegel lamps flickered and died. Within moments she could see no farther than the short distance illuminated by the lamp she held. Absolute silence filled the cavern along with the absolute darkness. Only the tiny ring of light around Kalena remained. She waited.

She had no idea how long the wait lasted. Time ceased to have any meaning within the circle of the black mists. But during the endless wait, the impact of fear began to fade. Perhaps maintaining a constant state of anxiety for a long period of time was physically impossible, Kalena decided wretchedly. She only knew that anger and another emotion were driving out the burst of terror that had threatened to overtake her consciousness. She couldn't name the second emotion, but it was a strengthening feeling. Kalena clung to it.

Half expecting the lamp under her hand to die as had all the others, Kalena was mildly astonished that it continued to burn steadily in the face of the overwhelming darkness. The large pool bubbled strongly behind her as Kalena crouched with her back to it. She didn't understand what was happening, but she knew she had been right to seek the shelter of the central spring.

More time passed and Kalena waited. Crouching beside the lamp, she huddled in on herself and endured.

Eons seemed to have passed when she first became aware of a faint lightening in the oppressive darkness surrounding her. At first Kalena refused to believe anything had changed. She would not allow hope to spin false fantasies in her numbed mind. And then she saw the faint flare of light in the depths of the enveloping darkness. Slowly, she got to her feet, holding tightly to the lamp.

"Kalena!"

Ridge's voice, distant but urgent, sounded from the depths of the exit tunnel. Kalena was so stricken with relief that he called out twice more before she was able to respond.

"Ridge, I'm here in the main room! Be careful, the place is filled with pools."

In another few moments, he emerged from the tunnel. "In the names of the Stones, woman, what have you been doing in here?" The firegel lamp he carried glowed at full power, just as though the darkness through which he had come was a perfectly normal sort of darkness. The lamplight illuminated his features in a golden glare that seemed to emphasize all the harsh planes and angles of his face.

The truth was that even as he emerged from the darkness, Ridge appeared to be at home in it. He carried the lamp casually, as if he had no fear of it going out. Walking out of the tunnel, he spotted Kalena standing beside her pool, the lamp burning at her feet. He came to a halt.

Kalena stared at him for a moment. He appeared fierce and grim and dangerous. To her desperate gaze, he also looked absolutely wonderful. She ran toward him, skirting the frothing pools, aware that the darkness no longer seemed so thick or fearsome.

"Ridge," she breathed as she threw herself into his arms, "I knew you would come for me. I knew it."

Now she realized it had been Ridge she had waited for in the endless darkness. Without even forming the thought consciously, she had known he would save her from the endless night.

TEN

Ridge had suffered a gamut of emotions in the short time since he had discovered Kalena had not returned from the underground spa. A few of them, the ones that bordered on panic, were completely new to him.

For the second night in a row, he found himself wondering if she had simply fled. But even as the thought entered his mind, he didn't believe it. He knew Kalena too well now. If she decided to leave, she would announce her intentions in a loud, clear voice—a *very* loud, clear voice. She would not sneak off in the middle of the night. That certainty gave way to a strong dose of annoyance over the fact that she hadn't displayed more common sense. She had stayed out much too late. This was a strange village and she had no business loitering with strangers until all hours.

Women. Put a bunch of them together and they lost all sense of time and propriety.

But after the annoyance, Ridge suddenly found himself suffering from a nagging sense of uncertainty. It had evolved quickly into genuine urgency which, in turn, soon bordered on the savage edge of fear. No one knew where Kalena was. He had forced the innkeeper's wife to summon some of her friends. They remembered Kalena having been in the pool cave, but only when Ridge talked to a rounded little blonde named Tana did he realize that Kalena might have gotten lost in the huge caverns.

"She was still there when I left," Tana admitted. She was nervous in the presence of this stranger whose temper was clearly on a very short leash. "I think she might have been the last to leave."

"If she left at all," Ridge had snapped, glaring at Tana's wary-eyed husband as he sought someone to blame for the situation.

"She couldn't have gotten lost," Tana assured him quickly. "The cave is well lighted and so is the exit passage. Perhaps she's fallen asleep in the warm waters or lost track of time."

"I'll get you a lamp if you want to take a look for yourself," Tana's husband had volunteered, anxious to placate the grim-faced stranger.

A few minutes later, Ridge had been on his way alone to the cavern entrance. As soon as he stepped inside he had realized that the lamps meant to light the passage weren't functioning. Not one of them. The thought of Kalena trapped somewhere in the vast darkness had sent another jolt of fear through Ridge.

Following the string of non-glowing firegel lamps to the main pool cavern had been easy. Using his own lamp as a guide, he made his way quickly through the passage. As soon as he rounded the last bend in the tunnel, he had seen the faint flare of Kalena's lamp. The sight of her crouched in the small pool of light had enraged him anew. He wanted to lash out at someone or something for having left his woman in such a frightening situation. He knew his own sense of guilt was riding him hard. He should never have allowed her to go to the cavern alone.

When Kalena answered his call and raced toward him, Ridge had trouble finding words for a few minutes. He set his lamp down at his feet and crushed her to him.

"Do you have any idea what I've been through for the past hour?" he muttered into her hair.

"It couldn't have been anything compared to what I've been

through. Ridge, it was the most horrifying experience. The lamps kept going out and all the while this cold, endless darkness was snaking down the tunnels into the pool room. I've never seen anything like it in my life."

"It's all right," he said thickly, stroking her back in an effort to reassure himself as much as her. "It's all right. It's all over now. Let's get out of here."

"Yes," she agreed wholeheartedly. "Let's do that, by all means." Her eyes widened as she pulled back to look at him. "But I wonder why your lamp is still functioning. None of the ones in the tunnel worked, and when I tried taking one from this room into the tunnel, it went out, too."

Ridge glanced around the darkened cavern as he reached down to retrieve his lamp. "I don't understand either. There must have been something faulty in the last batch of firegel put into the lamps. But this one works fine. Let's get moving."

"I think it was more than a bad firegel mixture," Kalena murmured as she took the hand he extended and moved quickly beside him out of the cavern. "The shadows weren't normal. I could feel it, Ridge. When I looked into this tunnel earlier it was like looking into the farthest, darkest end of the Spectrum."

"You've had a terrifying experience," he said gently. "Being trapped in this place would loose anyone's imagination. But it's all right now."

She fell silent beside him, and Ridge knew she didn't appreciate being told that she had been a victim of her own imagination as well as the very real darkness that had surrounded her. The truth was, he didn't believe it himself. But none of the other possibilities offered much comfort. He thought it would be easier on both of them if he could convince her that the coincidence of all the lamps fading simultaneously had probably been a natural accident.

Ridge was relieved when Kalena didn't argue. Her fingers gripped his with an intensity that made him feel keenly protective. The thought of Kalena actually seeking his protection was deeply satisfying. It was the way things were supposed to be. He kept a tight hold on her hand as they made their way out of the tunnel.

Anger simmered in him at the thought of what she had been through. He would make damn certain the Village Council was aware that Trade Baron Quintel would learn of tonight's incident. Ridge's chief regret at the moment was that there wasn't any one person he could blame for what had happened. He would have enjoyed taking someone apart for this night's work. Soon, he promised himself, before this journey was finished, he would learn the truth of what had happened. And then he would take his revenge.

Kalena didn't release her grip on his hand until they were inside the inn. The innkeeper and his wife inquired anxiously about what had happened, and Ridge responded with a controlled ferocity that cowed everyone within hearing distance.

"My wife," he began in a voice that was far too soft, "is all right, no thanks to whoever is in charge of maintaining those cavern lights. In the morning I want to know just who is responsible for those lamps."

"Ridge . . ." Kalena tugged at his hand, trying to urge him toward the stairway.

Ignoring her, Ridge took a step toward the innkeeper, who backed hastily out of reach. "Furthermore, I want to talk to someone on the Village Council. Someone who cares about maintaining the trade route contract with Trade Baron Quintel. Lord Quintel is not going to like hearing about what happened tonight."

Kalena tugged again on his hand. "Please, Ridge. Don't yell at them. They had nothing to do with what happened. It was no one's fault. I don't want to hear any more about it. Let's go upstairs."

He hesitated, torn between his desire to please Kalena and an equally strong wish to make someone pay for what had happened to her. In the end Ridge found himself surrendering to the pleading look in his wife's eyes. Reluctantly, he allowed himself to be led toward the staircase. The sigh of relief from the innkeeper and the other villagers was audible.

With one booted foot on the bottom step, Ridge paused to glance back at the innkeeper, reluctant to let his only available prey escape completely unscathed. Pinning the hapless man with his gaze, Ridge said again, "Remember. I want to talk to someone in charge tomorrow morning."

"Yes, Trade Master. I will contact a member of the council," the innkeeper assured him, grateful not to have to bear the brunt of Ridge's attack.

Kalena was still pulling on his arm, Ridge realized. He finally gave in to the gentle tug. When they reached the landing, Kalena turned down the hall to their room. She stood waiting silently while Ridge thrust the key into the lock.

As soon as he had the door open Kalena slipped past him, moving across the room to sink wearily onto the stool beside the hearth. She sat looking forlorn and withdrawn, her hands resting in her lap as she stared blankly at the wall on the other side of the room. Ridge started to close the door.

Kalena's head came up quickly. "The light," she whispered as the glow from the hallway started to fade behind the closing door, leaving the sleeping chamber in shadow.

He realized what she was trying to say. "I'll turn on the lamps." He did so before he closed the door and then he knelt to start a fire on the stone hearth. It was going to be cold this evening.

He took his time with the fire, aware of Kalena's too-silent figure huddled on the stool. It occurred to Ridge that he didn't know what to do next. He had gotten her out of the cave and she was safe. There was nothing more he could do to solve the mystery tonight. He was good at dealing with a crisis that demanded action, but he had very little experience offering comfort to a woman who had suffered what must have been a terrifying experience.

Kneeling on the hearth as the blaze caught and flared, Ridge covertly studied Kalena's withdrawn expression. She was very quiet. Perhaps she was in shock. He knew some of the Healers' tricks for dealing with physical shock, but he knew nothing about soothing a woman after an emotional trauma.

The nagging sense of masculine helplessness began to irritate Ridge. He sought to counter it the only way he knew; he got angry again. He had a general rule on the trail: When someone screwed up, you made damn sure he or she didn't do it twice.

Getting to his feet, he ran a blunt-fingered hand through his dark hair and frowned at Kalena. "You should never have gone to the pools tonight. I should never have let you talk me into it. The local people know their way around in that damn cave, but outsiders don't. You could have panicked and run down any one of those side caverns that feed into the main pool chamber. I would never have found you. This is what comes of indulging females. Every time I give you your head, you get into trouble. As your husband it's my responsibility to keep you out of mischief, so from now on I'm going to keep a tight rein on you."

Her brooding eyes swung to his. "Responsibility, duty, obligation. Is that the only way you know how to define a relationship, even a marriage?"

"Those are the fundamental elements of any relationship, especially a marriage," he shot back, gratified to have finally gotten some response from her. Any reaction was better than the silence that had gripped her while he was preparing the fire.

"I have lived most of my life with an embittered woman who felt obliged to instruct me in my duties and House responsibilities. As soon as I'm free of her, I turn around and find myself married to a man who devotes himself to the same kind of lectures. One of these days I shall be free of both you and Olara. When that day arrives, I'm never going to look back."

Ridge's back teeth clenched with sudden tension. "Perhaps if you didn't spend so much time dreaming of freedom, you wouldn't get yourself into trouble so frequently. And don't compare my lectures on duty and responsibility to those of that crazy aunt who raised you. She brought you up with the sole purpose of using you."

Kalena smiled thinly. "Didn't you marry me with the sole purpose of using me?"

Ridge felt the fragile hold on his temper slackening. "Our marriage was equally undertaken as a business arrangement."

"It was never that."

"No, because you signed the contract merely as a way of getting yourself into Quintel's house. Talk about using someone. You fully intended to use me, didn't you? You were more than willing to drag my honor and reputation through the mud while you got yourself arrested for murder."

"I think we've already had this discussion. Let's skip it and go to bed. I'm very tired, Ridge." She got to her feet and picked up her travel bag.

Frustrated at finding the argument terminated before he could release his pent-up anger, Ridge watched her disappear into the small privacy chamber off the main room. When she closed the door he swore softly and went to check the locks on the shutters.

He had handled her all wrong. He knew that now. Back in the cavern she had been overjoyed to see him. She had clung to his hand so trustingly . . . For a while she had turned to him the way a wife was supposed to turn to her husband when she needed his strength and protection. But he had managed to sever the delicate bond with the sharp edge of his temper. He had never meant to start yelling at her, Ridge told himself bleakly. He had wanted— no, needed—to yell at someone for what had happened this evening, and she had deprived him of any other likely target.

If he were honest with himself, he would admit that he should be blaming no one but himself. He should never have allowed her to go off alone to the cavern pools.

Ridge sat down on the edge of the pallet and yanked off his boots as he listened for small sounds of movement from the little chamber. She was too quiet in there, he decided. Probably brooding. He finished undressing and dimmed the lamps until only the glow from the fireplace lit the room. Still he heard no sound from the small room. He slid under the covers, his arms crooked behind his head and stared up at the shadowed ceiling. He had definitely handled her badly this evening. The trouble was, he didn't know how to go about rectifying the situation.

A long time later, the door to the small privacy chamber finally opened with a faint creak and Kalena stepped back into the main room. She was wearing her demure, high-collared sleeping shift, and as she made her way over to the pallet, Ridge decided she looked very lost and alone. She managed to crawl into the pallet beside him without touching him.

She had perfected the technique, Ridge told himself grimly. Kalena rarely touched him of her own initiative. He could pull her into his arms and coax a passionate response from her, but never had she initiated the passion.

He lay for a long while thinking of the few times Kalena had touched him spontaneously. There had been the time when he had fetched her and her so-called friends from the arms of the Crosspurposes Town Patrol. And then tonight when she had run to him in the dark cavern. In both instances she had been grateful to him. Neither case constituted what might be called a passionate plea from a woman who longed for her lover's touch. Ridge wondered what it would be like to just once have Kalena beg him to hold her.

"You don't believe me, do you, Ridge?"

Her question took him by surprise. "Believe you about what?"

"About that dark mist that filled the cavern tonight."

"I think you had a good reason to be terrified, Kalena. Anyone would have been panicked at the thought of being trapped in an underground cavern."

"Do you really think it was just a freak accident that all the lamps went out at once?" she challenged softly.

He hesitated and then admitted, "No. But I don't have any other convenient explanation for what happened in those caves tonight, Kalena. Not yet."

"It could be connected with the Sand trade trouble, couldn't it?" she pressed.

"That's a possibility. But none of it makes any sense. The Healers have cut off the trade, but they wouldn't pull a stunt like this. Why should they do such a thing in the first place?"

"There were those two men who attacked us back in Adverse," she reminded him.

"I know."

"Those black glass pendants . . ."

"I *know*," he repeated. "But I don't have any answers."

"You don't believe that there was something strange about the darkness, do you?" She sounded sadly resigned. "I don't blame you. It must have been gone when you came through the passage. If I hadn't seen it myself, I wouldn't have believed it either."

"Kalena . . ."

"I wish you good night, Ridge," she said very formally. "Thank you for coming after me this evening."

Her cool, distant words made Ridge groan silently. He turned on his side and found himself confronted with Kalena's slender back. Tentatively, he put his hand on her shoulder and felt the stiff tension that gripped her.

"You're still frightened, aren't you?" he asked with concern. "It's all right, Kalena. You're safe now. You're here with me and I won't let anything or anyone hurt you." When she didn't respond, Ridge edged closer, stroking his hand a little awkwardly over her shoulder. Making love to a woman was one thing; comforting her was another. He didn't know what to do. But he thought she relaxed slightly as he ran his palm back and forth along her arm.

For several minutes, they were both silent. Kalena didn't move, but the tight muscles of her shoulders began to loosen as Ridge continued his stroking.

Then, without any warning, Kalena turned to face him, burrowing into his arms as she sought the warmth and strength of his body. Startled, Ridge hesitated momentarily, and then resumed his slow, massaging touch.

There was nothing overtly sexual about the way she was cuddling with him, Ridge realized. Kalena wanted to be comforted and she had turned to him for that comfort. It was only right, he told himself. He was her husband. He fell asleep with that thought.

Ridge awoke shortly before dawn the next morning to find the pallet beside him empty. A small clattering sound in the corner of the chamber near the hearth made him open his eyes. Kalena was dressed to travel and she had a steaming mug of yant tea in her hand. Apparently, she had just finished making it on the small fire she had built. When she realized he was awake, she brought the mug toward the bed, holding it out to Ridge with grave politeness.

"I thought you might like to drink your tea while you dressed." She didn't quite meet his eyes.

She was embarrassed, Ridge thought with sudden perception. She had never before performed the traditional wifely duty of bringing him the morning tea in bed. For that matter, the moment was a little awkward for him, too. Ridge had never had any woman bring him tea in bed. Of course, he had never been married before. There was a first time for everything. He could get to like this small ritual, he decided as he took the mug from Kalena's hand.

"Thank you," he murmured as he took a sip of the invigorating brew.

She hesitated by the pallet. "You were kind to me last night," Kalena finally said very earnestly.

"You implied I was a short-tempered, abusive trade husband," he said dryly.

She waved the night's argument aside as if it were an entirely separate matter. "I meant later, in bed. You held me and soothed me. I was very tense because of what had happened. I appreciate your concern and care."

Ridge felt a warmth that had nothing to do with the hot tea he was drinking. He wanted to tell her she had a right to such treatment from him because she was his wife, but he was afraid she would misinterpret his words and think he was talking about duty and obligation again. So he merely nodded his head as casually as possible and said, "I appreciate the tea."

They looked at each other for a long moment. Then Kalena smiled tentatively and turned to finish her packing.

A short while later, Ridge finished fastening the travel bags to the creet saddles, double-checked the saddle buckles, and handed one set of reins to Kalena. She took them with gloved hands. The morning air was chill with the promise of mountain snow. In addition to her gloves she wore a fur-lined travel cloak over her riding clothes, the hood pulled up over her head. Ridge too wore a lined cloak and warm, flexible lanti skin gloves. The creets fluffed out their feathers to insulate themselves against the cold and pranced forward with their usual willingness.

Kalena glanced back at the quiet inn as Ridge led the way out of the yard. "I'm glad you changed your mind about yelling at the entire Village Council," she said.

"I didn't change my mind," he informed her arrogantly. "I just didn't want to waste any more time."

"Yes, of course," she murmured, hiding a tiny smile. "We wouldn't want to waste any more time. All the same, thank you for restraining yourself."

He glanced back. "You would have been embarrassed, wouldn't you?"

"Yes," she admitted. "I'm quite sure the Village Council had absolutely nothing to do with the failure of those lamps last night. Furthermore, I met some nice women in the spa and I would have felt awkward if you had turned around this morning and humiliated them by using your clout against their husbands."

Ridge shook his head. "Women," he muttered, but he sounded oddly indulgent.

Kalena breathed a sigh of relief and reached down to stroke her creet's neck feathers. Diplomacy, she was discovering, was another useful skill for a wife. It occurred to her that last night was not the first time she had managed to douse the Fire Whip's temper. She really was getting quite proficient at the task.

The wind that swept through the mountains had a definite bite to it now. The creets climbed higher and higher into the pass, following the old trail that had been carved out by the first High Healers when they had decided to move into the mountain reaches. Even during the height of summer, this trail could be chilly. The snow on the peaks of the Heights of Variance never completely disappeared.

When Ridge called a halt for lunch he took the time to build a small fire so that Kalena could prepare a warming mug of tea. He stood watching as she carefully boiled the water and added the yant leaves.

"We should reach the wall of white mist the caravans complained about by tomorrow evening if we continue at this pace," he remarked thoughtfully.

"Where do we camp tonight?"

"There are some shelters along the trail built by the early traders. Creet rations are kept stocked in them along with emergency supplies. We'll stop at one this evening."

Kalena nodded and finished the meal preparations. "I'm glad we won't have to spend the night out in the open. It's so cold here."

Ridge smiled faintly. "You don't have to worry, Kalena. I wouldn't force my wife to sleep in the snow."

"Very reassuring."

The shelter they located just before the early mountain dusk descended was reasonably cozy once the lamps had been lit and Ridge had built a fire on the hearth. Stable space for the creets adjoined the main room, enabling the animals to share the warmth of the fire. The proximity of the animals didn't bother Kalena. For one thing, she had spent too much time in a farming community to be offended by the idea of sharing space with animals. For another, she was simply too tired to think much about it. If Ridge chose to claim his marital rights tonight, he would have to find some method of keeping her awake first. She was sound asleep before he returned from checking the creets.

Kalena had expected nightmares after the previous evening's horrors, but she had suffered none so far. The mountains around them were cold, but the temperature was the natural chill of approaching snow. Kalena shifted slightly when Ridge got into bed beside her. She felt his arms go around her waist before she drifted back into sleep.

They reached the wall of white mist the following day, just as the last of the sun's rays slipped behind a high peak. Kalena knew immediately that the mist was no ordinary cloud caught among the mountains. She reined in her creet behind Ridge and stared at the veil of glistening whiteness that stretched completely across the pass.

On either side of the trail the mountains rose in stark, snow-capped peaks that were impossible to ascend. Nor was there any way around the ridges into the valley on the other side. The High Healers had chosen a well protected location and they had sealed the only entrance with a wall of snow colored mist.

"So this is what the traders meant," Ridge said softly as he swung himself out of the saddle and went forward to examine the barrier. "I thought they must have been talking about snow or clouds that had somehow blocked the pass. But this is no natural mist." He put out a hand to touch the shimmering wall and instantly yanked it back, swearing quietly.

"What's wrong?" Kalena asked. She dismounted and went to stand beside him. "Is your hand all right?"

"Damn Healers," Ridge muttered, shaking his hand as if to rid it of something that still clung. "Yeah, it's all right. What in the name of the Stones have those women done?"

"They've sealed themselves off from Quintel's traders."

"Obviously, but why? And how? What is this white stuff?" Ridge paced across the width of the pass peering closely at the curtain of white. He pulled his sintar out of its sheath and probed cautiously at the veil.

The reaction was immediate. The sintar glowed in his hand, just as if he had somehow activated it in the heat of fury. Ridge stared at the blade in amazement, knowing that for the first time the steel had responded to something other than his rage. Slowly, the glow died and he resheathed the weapon.

"This could get tricky," he finally announced.

"Let me try," Kalena said impulsively.

"No, wait, Kalena, I don't want you—"

But it was too late. Kalena had already reached out to touch the white mist. Her hand went into it easily with no obvious effect, disappearing up to her wrist. "It's like touching fog," she said wonderingly. Slowly, she withdrew her fingers. They felt fine. "I don't think this is going to be any problem at all, Ridge."

"Kalena, several trading caravans led by experienced traders have been turned back by this stuff. One trade master didn't return at all. Don't be too sure of yourself."

She glanced back at him, confidence flowing through her. "But I *am* sure of myself, Ridge. Very sure. You brought me along to get you through this veil, didn't you?"

"You're here to deal with the Healers," he stated. "Not to take chances. I'm the one who's paid to take the chances."

"But to deal with the High Healers, I have to go through this." She turned back to the white mist and stepped into it before Ridge realized exactly what she was doing.

"Kalena!"

His anxious shout faded almost instantly as Kalena moved into the mist. It closed gently around her, cutting off all sound and all sensation. She no longer felt the mountain chill. She felt nothing except a sense of peace. She felt as if she were suspended in a universe of shimmering white. There was no feeling of impending danger as there had been with the black mist in the caverns. Just the opposite, in fact. Here lay safety and serenity and warmth.

Opposites. Natural opposites. When one existed, so must the other. All things on the Spectrum seek their natural states of balance.

The words drifted through Kalena's mind as she floated in the strange cloud. This glistening white veil was the opposite of what she had encountered last night. The exact counterpoint to that dark, endless cold.

Kalena moved her hands and looked down at them. She could see her gloved fingers clearly, so she wasn't completely devoid of sensation. Carefully, she took a pace forward, unable to see the rocky path on which she must be standing. She stretched out her hand, wondering how thick the veil was. Her fingers disappeared. She moved forward again, following them. At least she thought she was moving forward. There was no true sense of direction in the mist.

Two more paces brought her through to the other side. She emerged from the shimmering white barrier and found herself looking down into the greenest valley she had ever seen. It was a small valley, with steep canyon walls embracing it and its cluster of cottages. Fields of flowers, herbs and vegetables were laid out from one side of the valley to the other. The cottages were dotted about in a pleasantly random arrangement, smoke wafting invitingly from the chimneys. The path on which Kalena was standing descended easily into the heart of the valley. This was the chosen home of the High Healers. She would have known that without being told. Some part of her recognized this place—recognized it and responded to it. For a moment Kalena simply stood and stared in wonder, and then she remembered Ridge.

Without any hesitation, Kalena stepped back into the mist. It swirled around her as before, but this time she kept moving. A moment later she stepped out on the other side and found herself in front of Ridge.

"What happened in there?" he asked tightly. The tension on his face was obvious.

"Nothing. I just walked through to the other side. It's a little disorienting, but not too difficult to move through the mist. Let me see if I can lead you through." She reached for his hand.

"I don't know, Kalena. I couldn't even touch the stuff a few minutes ago. It may be something only a woman can pass through. You may have to go contact the Healers yourself and see if they'll let me through."

"I'll try taking a creet first," Kalena suggested, reaching for a set of reins.

The creet stopped at the wall of mist, opened its beak and stuck out its tongue as if to taste the shimmering barrier. Kalena waited until it had satisfied itself that there was no danger and then she stepped through, tugging on the reins. The creet followed obediently. On the far side she tied the reins around a small rock and went back for Ridge and his animal.

"The creet went right through with no trouble. Come on, Ridge. Try it."

His mouth hardened but he didn't argue further. He put his hand in hers and allowed Kalena to lead him right up to the wall of white. She stepped in, but when she tried to pull him after her there was a sudden, fierce resistance. He snatched his hand from her grasp and Kalena turned to find herself alone in the mist. She walked back out and stood staring at him. Ridge was cradling his hand, his jaw rigid with pain.

"It's not going to work" he said grimly. "You'll have to go on by yourself and see if you can talk the Healers into letting me through."

"Something's wrong." Kalena frowned thoughtfully.

"You can say that again."

She shook her head. "No, something's wrong with you. There's something that's keeping you from following me into the mist."

"I'm a man. The Healers have probably rigged this thing to keep out males. Typical piece of female idiocy."

Kalena ignored that, her mind concentrating on the problem. She knew instinctively that she should be able to lead Ridge through the mist. There was something on him that was interfering. "Have you still got that black glass pendant with you? The one you took off that man who attacked us?"

His eyes narrowed. "Yes."

"Get rid of it."

"Kalena, that's ridiculous. It's just a piece of glass. It can't possibly have anything to do with this nonsense. This is women's trickery."

"And that glass is male trickery. *Get rid of it, Ridge.*" She was absolutely certain now. "You must throw it away before you can go through the mist."

"Dammit to both ends of the Spectrum," he sighed as he

reached into his cloak. He removed the black glass pendant and let it dangle from his fingers. "I don't see why you're so upset about this thing, but if it makes you happy, I'll get rid of it." He turned and flung the pendant far behind him. It landed several meters away on the trail. There was a tinkling sound as the glass broke.

"Now," Kalena stated with conviction. "You can pass through the mist now." She reached for his hand.

"Let's just hope I don't lose my hand completely this time," Ridge muttered as he made to follow her once more. "I have plans for this hand, you know."

But this time nothing stopped him. Leading his creet, Ridge followed Kalena into the shimmering veil and out onto the other side.

"Well, I'll be damned." Ridge stood gazing down at the green valley below.

"Remember this when it comes time to hand over my share of the Sand," Kalena said loftily. "I want it clear that I earned it."

ELEVEN

Kalena and Ridge were halfway down the trail that led into the green gem of a valley when they became aware of the change in temperature. The closer they got to the valley floor, the warmer the atmosphere became. Clearly, the valley of the High Healers was a warm oasis protected by a natural fortress of mountains and snow.

"The people of Hot And Cold are right," Kalena decided aloud. "Somewhere in this valley lies the source of the hot springs back in the caverns. I can feel it."

"Woman's intuition?" There was a faint mockery in Ridge's voice.

"Perhaps." Kalena shrugged. Ridge had been very silent since she had led him through the wall of white mist. She had the distinct impression that the closer they got to the village of the High Healers, the more uneasy he became. For her it was just the opposite. She knew her reaction was meant to counter his. "Look, Ridge, there are people in the fields."

He reined in his creet and studied the gentle scene that lay before them. Women moved among the rows of beautiful plants and flowers, tending the rich gardens. "I think," Ridge said finally, "that you had better go first. I get the feeling it's expected around here." He shifted a bit in the saddle. "This is a female place."

"Yes," Kalena agreed with confidence. "It is." She urged her creet forward without any hesitation, aware of a deep eagerness.

A few minutes later, they reached a narrow path that led between a row of perfectly plotted gardens. A woman dressed in a full, flowing pastel tunic looked up and lifted her hand in welcome. She wore the Healer's traditional tiny brazier and pouch of Sand on her belt. She was much older than Kalena, her silvered hair caught in a white mesh snood. She moved with vigor and strength as she started toward Kalena.

Kalena drew the creet to a halt and dismounted as the woman approached. Inclining her head respectfully, she introduced herself. "I am Kalena and this is my husband, Ridge. We have come a long way to talk to you and your people."

The woman's smile was warm as she touched Kalena on the shoulder. "Welcome, Kalena, daughter of the House of the Ice Harvest. We have waited a long time for you."

Kalena's hands tightened around the reins she was holding. "You know who I am?"

"We know. I am Valica of the High Healers. It is my honor to welcome you to our village." She turned to Ridge. "And this is the man you have chosen?"

Ridge nodded, distantly polite as he swung down from the saddle. "I'm Kalena's husband. I'm here on behalf of Trade Baron Quintel."

"Of course. So Lord Quintel finally grew impatient enough to act, hmm? He should have known that only a very special woman and her chosen mate could make it through the barrier. We certainly gave him enough hints. But men can be very stubborn." Valica turned, motioning with her hand. "Come with me. I will show you to your cottage. You have had a long trip and you must rest. There will be time later to talk."

Valica led them down the path toward one of the many little cottages that were scattered about the valley. The small house was square and constructed of a warm colored stone. There were windows, instead of wooden shutters, and a charming, flowering garden.

"There are stables for the creets. When you have unsaddled, I will take the birds and feed them for you."

Ridge's eyes narrowed faintly. "I'll see to the creets."

"It is not necessary, Trade Master Ridge. I will take care of them."

"I do not wish to be rude, Healer, but I make it a practice to take care of my own creets on a trip." Ridge unbuckled the travel bags as he spoke.

"As you wish," Valica said politely. "The stables are over there." She pointed to a small structure behind the cottage. "There is food and water for the birds. By the time the two of you have bathed and rested it will be the hour of the evening meal. You are invited to join us. We meet in the large hall near the herb gardens."

"Thank you, Valica," Kalena said quickly, before Ridge could find something else to argue about. "We will see you at the evening meal."

Valica nodded and left. Kalena turned on Ridge, who was unpacking the travel gear with a grim air.

"You brought me along to deal with the Healers, Ridge. Please allow me to do my job. Things will go much more smoothly if you don't argue over every little thing. She was only offering to care for the creets out of politeness. There was no need for you to take a stand on the matter. Valica's hardly likely to steal our birds."

Ridge shot her a cool glance as he picked up the bags and started toward the door. "How do you know?"

"Ridge, you're being ridiculous. What's the matter with you, anyway?"

He sighed, opening the door to reveal a room that was furnished with elegant simplicity. A pallet, a low, round table, cushions, two fireside stools, and a graceful, flowering plant were laid out in serene order. "I don't know," he admitted. "If you want to know the truth, I don't like this place. It makes me edgy."

"It doesn't take much to make you edgy, Trade Master," Kalena said with a small grin. "The least little thing will do it sometimes. No wonder they call you Fire Whip." She followed him into the simply furnished room.

"You don't seem to be having any problem," Ridge noted bluntly as he tossed the bags down onto the tapestry carpet. "I get the feeling you're right at home here."

"I think that's exactly how I feel," Kalena said quietly. "At home." She walked through the small sitting area, admiring the simple, uncluttered lines of the furnishings. "How do you think they knew I was coming, Ridge? They say they've been waiting for me. It's strange, isn't it?"

"The High Healers have always seemed strange." As Ridge watched Kalena move about the small cottage, his uneasiness grew. He knew from what other traders had told him that all males tended to feel on edge and vaguely awkward in this beautiful valley. For men there was an unmistakable feeling of being out of their proper element. The valley was female in every sense of the word.

Ridge had been prepared for the out-of-place sensation, but he was quickly coming to realize there was more to his unease than that. The pull the valley exerted on Kalena was obvious. It occurred to him that she had no real home or family to draw her back to Crosspurposes or even to the Interlock valley. Her aunt Olara didn't seem to be much of a reason for Kalena to return. A rough and ready trade marriage to a Houseless bastard probably didn't look like a much better reason for making the trip back out of the mountains. The beautiful valley was a threat to him in a way he hadn't expected. Kalena could be seduced with lures no mere male could match.

Ridge swung around and opened the door. "I'll take care of the creets," he muttered before stepping outside. "The sooner he could take Kalena and the Sand and leave this place, the better as far as he was concerned.

Kalena was well aware of Ridge's wary, brooding mood at dinner that evening. He sat beside her, lounging with a kind of challenging casualness on the embroidered pillows. Kalena made no attempt to serve him in the normal manner. They both knew that in the valley table manners were egalitarian. Everyone helped herself to the platters of beautifully prepared vegetables, bowls of soup and delicate binda egg dishes. Kalena was quite sure Ridge knew how to fill his own plate from the main trays even if he was surrounded by females.

He hesitated for an instant as the food was presented to him, slanting Kalena a speculative glance. But when she made no move to do her wifely duty, he calmly helped himself to what he wanted. Kalena smiled brilliantly and reached for a platter of jellied binda eggs.

"I knew you could do it if you tried," she murmured for his ears alone.

"This place is having a bad influence on your table manners."

"An interesting observation. Might change them forever. Perhaps you'd better get used to serving yourself. I rather like the new style."

"I can tell." He poured himself some wine. "What about the traditions, Kalena? Don't they mean anything to you?"

"I'm more interested in starting new traditions, I think. In any event, you're a fine one to talk of traditions. You weren't exactly born into them." As soon as the words left her lips, Kalena regretted them. She lowered her eyes at once and apologized. "I'm sorry, Ridge. I meant no insult."

"There was no insult," he told her roughly. "You spoke only the truth. What you forget is that some traditions have greater meaning for those of us who had to survive without them."

"Or for those such as my aunt who had only traditions to hold them together," Kalena said with a sigh.

Ridge picked up his fingerspear and lapsed back into silence as the conversation flowed around the six or seven large, round tables that were arranged in the simple room. Kalena ignored them, concentrating on adjusting her normal, kneeling position to something more comfortable. The idea of sprawling like a man at table was novel. It was also rather difficult when one had spent her whole life eating in the kneeling position. Kalena found herself shifting position several times.

"What in the name of the Stones is the matter with you?" Ridge growled at one point just after she wriggled into another new position. "Can't you sit still?"

"I'm trying to get comfortable," she hissed softly.

"Try sitting the way you normally do," Ridge advised sardonically.

"No one else is sitting like that. And after all these years, I'm tired of sitting that way, too. Hand me that platter of cheese, please."

He did so with a sharp movement that spoke volumes concerning his irritation.

"Thank you, Ridge. You did that very well. Perhaps you have a talent in the area of table service." Kalena fingerspeared several slices of cheese and set the platter back down on the table. The woman next to her reached for it with a smile.

"Valica tells me you brought the creets and the man with you through the veil this afternoon."

Kalena nodded. "It was simple enough. I don't understand why it's proven such a barrier to the other women in the trading caravans."

"Ah, that's because it was tuned for one particular woman. You. I'm Arona, by the way. I am in charge of the herb gardens." Arona smiled. She was a handsome woman, her features strong and intelligently formed, her blue eyes warm and inquisitive. A few years older than Kalena, her hair was still a rich, vibrant black without any trace of gray. As was the case with all of the women in the valley, her body was lithe and vigorous from the endless work in the fields.

"Arona, tell me how you knew I would be coming through the mist. I don't understand any of this."

"You will learn more tonight after dinner. It is not my place to explain all of it to you." She quickly glanced at Ridge's implacable profile. "Nor is it a thing that should be discussed in the presence of men."

Kalena noticed that the line of Ridge's jaw tightened, but he said nothing. As the meal continued for a long while, the women asked both Kalena and Ridge many questions concerning matters in the outside world. The women obviously liked to keep themselves informed of what was happening beyond the valley, even though they chose not to participate in those events.

Ridge answered the questions about the new Hall of Balance and the increasingly sophisticated economy of the Northern Continent. Kalena listened to him respond to the women's inquiries, aware of a certain pride in his intelligent, informed answers. Her trade husband might have had humble beginnings, but over the years he had clearly taken steps to make up for his early lack of education.

"We have heard that a ship is being constructed in the port of Countervail," one of the women remarked. "A very special ship that will be used in an attempt to cross the Sea of Clashing Light."

"That's true," Ridge confirmed. "It's being financed by a consortium of wealthy House lords."

"What is the objective? Exploration?"

"Exploration of the lands beyond the sea and the establishment of trade routes," Ridge replied. "Who knows? Perhaps there will be Healers in those other lands who will want to exchange information with you."

"A fascinating thought," Arona murmured.

Ridge hesitated, scowling slightly as he discovered his wine goblet was empty. He was accustomed to having it kept full when he shared a table with Kalena. "There are many who think the ship will never return," he remarked as he reluctantly reached for the wine decanter and helped himself again. "The Polarity Advisors theorize that there may be no other inhabited lands beyond the sea. Some think that the dangers of the voyage will prove so great the ship will be forced to turn back. Whatever happens, it should be interesting."

"Very," Valica agreed. "But all of that lies in the future. Tonight there are more immediate matters that must be dealt with. Would you excuse us, Trade Master? We have a pressing need to discuss business and the future with Kalena."

Ridge took his dismissal with good grace, considering how it must have galled him. He glanced briefly at Kalena's politely composed face, and then got to his feet, maintaining his grip on the wine decanter. He continued to stare down at Kalena.

"I'll be waiting for you," he said very deliberately.

"I understand." She did. Kalena met the fierce gold of his gaze and knew exactly what he was saying. He was the lone male confronting a small world full of women who wanted Kalena in some manner which he didn't fully comprehend. He realized there was a risk here, but he wasn't certain how to combat it. He knew only that he had to try to exert what small authority he retained in an effort to make certain Kalena returned to him. Perhaps he feared that if he lost her, he lost the Sand, Kalena thought, wondering why the realization hurt. This was merely a trade marriage, after all.

"Don't worry, Ridge," she whispered. "I will do my best to see that you get your Sand."

"Damn the Sand. See that you return to the cottage at a decent hour." He turned on his heel and stalked out of the dining chamber. No one asked him to leave the wine decanter behind.

When Ridge had gone, all eyes turned toward Kalena. An odd sense of anticipation suddenly filled the air. Valica smiled reassuringly. "The Sand is yours, Kalena. As much as you can carry. There is a fresh supply in the kiln now. It will be ready by tomorrow morning."

"Thank you," Kalena said quietly. No one knew exactly how the precious Sands of Eurythmia were made. The High Healers' secret has been well guarded for generations. The Sand was not a curative itself; its value lay in the fact that it was a diagnostic tool. When burned, the smoke it produced enabled a Healer with the Talent to somehow "see" inside her patient and determine the exact nature of his illness. Then she prescribed treatment, which usually consisted of concoctions formulated from the plants in her garden. One of the first things a Healer-in-training did was plant her medicinal garden. It was as much a symbol of her profession as the little brazier she used to burn the Sand. The smoke could be used effectively by only a certain number of people, invariably women.

For generations the Healers' Guild had allowed only those women with the Talent to enter training. The test for aptitude was a simple one. The smoke was inhaled by a prospective Healer and she was then told to "look" inside a patient. She was either immediately able to see the source of the illness, even though she might lack the training to identify it, or she was not. Some women had what was generally referred to as a touch of the Talent, which meant they experienced disorienting effects under the influence of the smoke but saw no clear vision of the illness they had been set to diagnose.

"I am not certain how to negotiate for the Sand," Kalena said slowly. "I've never done it before. Please tell me how many grans you want for it and I will see if we have enough to make the purchase."

Valica appeared completely unconcerned. "The usual price of a thousand grans will be sufficient. The Sand is not the crucial matter tonight. It was merely the lure."

"Lure?" Kalena waited, tense with the intuitive knowledge that something very important was about to be demanded of her.

The other women remained silent, allowing Valica to explain. She took her time, choosing her words with obvious care. "You have, perhaps, heard the legend about the Light Key being hidden somewhere in these mountains."

"I've heard the tales."

"They are true, Kalena."

Kalena took a deep breath. "There really is a Light Key?"

"Oh, yes. There is a Light Key." Valica's mouth curved a little sadly. "Do you understand what that implies?"

Kalena acknowledged the obvious truth. She shivered slightly as she responded. "If there truly is a Light Key, then a Dark Key must also exist."

"There is no need to look so horrified, Kalena," Valica said gently. "For all power, there is a focus of opposition. Surely Olara taught you well."

Kalena shook her head wonderingly. "You know of my aunt?"

"Olara was on the verge of becoming one of us a long time ago. She has the Talent in great measure and she chose not to seek an alliance with a male. Her natural inclinations would have led her to this valley eventually if . . . other factors had not intervened."

"The death of the men of my House. My father was her brother," Kalena explained unhappily. "And after their deaths came the death of my mother. It was my fault Olara had no choice but to give up her own desires. She did her duty by me and by the House of the Ice Harvest, instead." Unlike herself, Kalena added silently.

"There is always a choice, Kalena. Remember that. Olara could have brought you here," Valica said quietly. "But she chose the path of vengeance. She raised you to be the instrument of that vengeance instead of the fine Healer you might have become with proper training."

"A Healer? I could have been one? How can you know such a thing? I have never proven myself with Sand." Kalena grappled with that thought. "My aunt never allowed me to learn her secrets. She refused to test me with the Sand. She said such things would only distract me from what I must do."

"She was right. It's impossible for a trained Healer to willingly kill, except, perhaps, in a clear cut case of self-defense or the defense of another. But Olara brought you up with the notion that you must kill coldly and with calculation. The act would have gone against your deepest instincts. So she took steps to conceal those instincts from your awareness."

Kalena remembered the feeling of a barrier being breached in her mind the first time Ridge had made love to her. "How did she hide such knowledge from me for so long?"

"Olara used the techniques Healers learn for dealing with troubled minds. There are ways of making a patient forget things that are so disturbing or painful that they are a hazard to health. Olara used such methods on you. She took a great risk when she negotiated your temporary marriage. She must have known that. Apparently, she could think of no other way to get you close to your quarry."

"She told me that even though I was signing a marriage contract of sorts, she said I must not sleep with my husband or any other man before I carried out my responsibility to my House," Kalena answered. She dropped her eyes. "But I disobeyed her."

"If your aunt had allowed you to breathe smoke, the barrier she had established in your mind would have been shattered. When you chose to form a physical and emotional bond with the man you were to marry, the act had virtually the same effect. It weakened that barrier in your mind to a great extent."

"To such an extent that I failed in my duty."

"You failed your aunt's directive. You did not fail yourself. You were not born to commit cold-blooded murder, Kalena, regardless of the motive." Valica leaned across the table to touch her guest's hand. "Your destiny is far more complex."

Kalena looked at her, aware of the intensity with which the others were watching. "What destiny is this, Valica? I have no other calling except vengeance, and I have had to abandon that."

Valica shook her head. "Vengeance was never your true calling. You see, you are the one who will take the Light Key out of its hiding place."

Kalena went cold. "No," she whispered in a tight voice. "No, that can't be true."

"The Key has not been touched for more generations than any Healer can chart. We believe from all our studies that it has not been touched since it was put into its hiding place."

"If it really exists, it is not meant to be touched," Kalena protested. "It is beyond our comprehension. It must be left where it is forever!"

Valica smiled again, a wary, resigned smile that held infinite sadness and certainty. "It can only stay hidden and untouched as long as the Dark Key is also hidden and untouched."

"What are you saying?"

"We think the Dark Key has been discovered."

Kalena's mouth went dry. "It's said that if the Dark Key and the Light Key are ever brought close together that the Dark will destroy the Light."

"Men say that." Arona spoke for the first time, a derisive amusement in her voice. "Men are fond of believing that in a showdown, they are the stronger and therefore their end of the Spectrum must be the more powerful. But the truth is their beliefs violate the Mathematics of Paradox as well as the Philosophy of the Spectrum. All things must be balanced by equal opposites."

Kalena glanced at her, and then her gaze swung back to Valica. "Do you know for certain that the Dark Key has been discovered?"

"Not for certain, no. But we are deeply suspicious. There have been acts of Darkness near the mountains. Men have died in strange ways. There have been tales told of the hook vipers appearing outside the mountains for the first time in generations . . ."

"Ridge killed one on the trail coming here," Kalena whispered.

"Kalena, the hook vipers are fearsome, but they have always feared humans. If they have begun hunting outside the mountains then it is because something has driven them forth. There are other tales, too. Ones we don't understand but which have gravely alarmed us."

Kalena thought about the dark mist that had tried to envelope her in the caverns. "I don't understand what it is you expect me to do."

"Unfortunately, we cannot completely explain your destiny

to you, because we are not sure of it ourselves," Valica said. "We have had hints over the years. Bits and pieces of information have come to us through Far Seeing. Other clues we have reasoned out on our own. The only thing of which we are certain is that you are the one who can take hold of the Light Key. It would kill anyone else."

"You can't know this for a fact! What would I do with it if I did take it with me—assuming it didn't kill me, too? This makes no sense." Kalena was feeling trapped now, as trapped as she had felt the day Olara told her she must kill Quintel. But at least after the death of Quintel there had been a vague promise of freedom. The legends concerning the Light and Dark Keys claimed that death was the price any human would pay for touching either.

"Calm yourself, Kalena. No one will force you to take the Key. It is not our place to try. The decision must be yours, and only you will know how and when you must act. All we can do is tell you what we have learned over the years through studying the legends and the shreds of ancient manuscripts that have come into our possession."

"You have many such old manuscripts?"

"A few. What do you think we use Quintel's grans for? It costs money to pursue old legends."

"You speak of the days of the Dawn Lords," Kalena said slowly. "Are you telling me that they really existed?"

"We believe so. It was they who discovered the Stones of Contrast and buried them in fire and ice. No one knows where they are hidden. But we believe the Keys to the Stones, both of them, were hidden in these mountains. The Light Key we know for certain is here. The ancient documents hint that the Dark is also."

"Who were the Dawn Lords?" Kalena asked, completely fascinated now. "Another race that inhabited this planet before us?"

Valica answered cautiously. "We don't know for certain, but it is possible the Dawn Lords were as human as we ourselves are. Some students here in the valley," she glanced around at the faces of the other women, "think that the Dawn Lords were our ancestors and that they arrived on this planet from a world that turns about another sun."

"They brought the Stones and the Keys with them?" Kalena asked.

Valica shook her head in denial. "No. At least, we don't think so. We believe they discovered the Stones and the Keys here when they arrived and recognized them as sources of power that were beyond even their comprehension or ability to handle. Such things of power could not be destroyed, so the Dawn Lords hid them, hoping, no doubt, that they would stay buried forever, or at least until we were capable of controlling them."

"What became of the Dawn Lords?" Kalena demanded.

Valica shrugged. "There appear to have been only a few of them, but they fitted themselves to this new world. They seem to have been trapped here, but they were determined that they and their children would survive. They did what was necessary, creating a new society that has proven viable and has flourished. I can tell you little else, Kalena. We simply don't know much more than that. A great deal of what I have told you is speculation and intuition."

"And now your speculation has convinced you that I must take up the Light Key and carry it out of the valley?" Kalena finished warily.

"So we believe."

"You are wrong," Kalena said resolutely. "You have set your lures for the wrong woman. Surely if I were called to such a destiny, I would know it deep inside."

"Who can say?" Valica smiled again. "We are almost as ignorant as you about your fate. Perhaps matters would be clearer now if Olara had brought you here years ago when she found herself in charge of you. Or perhaps it was not meant for you to grow up here at all. In any event, Olara's notions of vengeance and House honor were stronger than the part of her that was drawn to life here in the valley. She tried to twist you to her own ends, and in the process perhaps she succeeded in suppressing your own inner knowledge and instincts too far. Or perhaps it was meant for those things to be temporarily suppressed. Who can say? The ways of fate are often exceedingly complex."

Kalena was feeling desperate. "How long have you known that I was the one you sought?"

"The woman who held my position in the valley before I did first sensed the truth. She was gifted with the ability to slide deep into a Far Seeing trance. That particular gift is very rare, and the results of such trances are often difficult to interpret. My own trances have proven remarkably frustrating at times. Her name was Bestina, and her intuition was astonishing. It was she who named the one who would take up the Light Key. Before she died she summoned Olara and informed her of what she had learned. But by then it was too late. Olara was already started down the path of her choice and she made it clear she was taking you with her. Bestina could do nothing more. But when she told me that I was to take her position here in the valley, she gave me some advice."

"What advice?"

"She said that something stronger than your aunt's training in vengeance was destined to break through the barriers Olara had raised within you. A new bond between you and another would be formed, one that would be stronger than the bond between yourself and your aunt, stronger, perhaps, than even your sense of honor."

"You knew I would form a trade marriage?"

Valica smiled. "Years ago we began insisting on dealing only with married women traders. It was a way of ensuring that the women Quintel used received some legal protection and the right to retain a portion of the profits of the Sand."

"Quintel got around your edict by inventing the institution of trade marriages," Kalena pointed out. "Such marriages are little more than business arrangements. The bonds between men and women in a trade marriage are slight, to say the least. It is a business association."

"True, but marriage agreements serve the purpose of providing the women involved with some legal status. Since we had decided to deal only with such women, it was reasonable to assume that somehow when you came to us it would probably be as a trade wife. We didn't know for certain, of course. Fate could have chosen another way to bring you here, but it was a logical assumption. None but Quintel's traders climb the trail to this valley."

"I understand."

"Several months ago," Valica continued, "when we began to grow anxious about what we sensed was happening with the Dark Key, we decided it would be necessary to give fate a small push. We began informing Quintel's traders that we would deal only with a woman who was truly married, emotionally as well as by contract. We said we wanted a woman with at least a touch of the Talent, although she needn't necessarily be a Healer. Between the information gained from Bestina's trances and my own, we knew that much about you. We could not ask for you directly."

"Why not?"

"For one thing we had lost track of you. We did not know where Olara had taken you to live or under what new House name you were being raised. I was forced to rely on logic and hope to locate you."

"The logical part being that Quintel wouldn't rest until he'd found a way to reopen the Sand trade route. He'd keep searching until he found a woman you would accept through the mist."

"We knew Quintel couldn't get a trained Healer to agree to the kind of contract marriage necessary for a trading venture. He had to come up with a new arrangement a Healer would agree to, which was unlikely, or find an untrained Healer, like you, willing to enter into a trade marriage. There aren't many untrained Healers like you Kalena, so we knew that once we exerted the maximum pressure on Quintel and closed the trail entirely to everyone but you with the mist, we would find you, sooner or later. There was another angle of logic involved, too. Don't forget we were aware that Olara, wherever she might be, was looking for a way to get to Quintel. With Quintel searching for a woman who came from a family of Healers, and Olara waiting for an opportunity to use you against Quintel, the results were inevitable."

"It's all very twisted and complicated, full of what-ifs and had-it-not-been-fors." Kalena shook her head.

"There is a logic to it, however. There is always a hidden logic behind all that happens. We call it fate, but in reality that word means nothing more than the inevitable conclusion of forces that have been set in motion. Once in motion, all such forces must eventually play themselves out." Valica quoted a tenet of the Philosophy of the Spectrum with the certainty of a true believer.

"It was only supposed to be a trade marriage," Kalena said softly. "And it was never meant to last more than a day. You specified a woman who was well and truly married, not just one involved in a business arrangement."

Valica looked at her knowingly. "Would you say that the bond between you and your husband is based only on business?"

Sudden heat burned in Kalena's face. "It's hard to explain my arrangement with Trade Master Ridge. There are times when I'm not certain I understand it, myself. But I am certain it is not my task to take up the Light Key. You have drawn the wrong woman to your valley."

"None of us here tonight can fully explain just why and how you are here, Kalena. Nor will we try more than we already have. It grows late and we are farming women who must rise early. I think it is time we went to bed." Valica's tone of voice announced that the session was at a close.

"Farmers are not the only ones who rise early. So do trade masters," Kalena muttered, getting to her feet along with the others. "Especially when they are anxious to complete a journey. Ridge will want to leave as soon as possible in the morning."

"I will walk with you to your cottage," Arona said, moving close to Kalena as the others filed out of the room.

"That's very kind of you."

"Not at all. My cottage is only a short distance beyond yours." Arona's blue eyes were very deep and intense in the light

of the lamps. She touched Kalena lightly on the arm and turned
to lead the way out of the dining chamber.

Kalena walked beside her new acquaintance in silence, thinking of all that had been said in the dining hall. But soon she grew
uncomfortable, and searched for casual conversation.

"How does the valley floor stay so warm and balmy even
though it's surrounded by snow-covered mountains?"

"There is a source of heat hidden deep in the heart of the
mountains. Perhaps the remains of an old volcano. We don't understand exactly how it works, but the waters that bubble to the
surface nearby are hot and there is always warmth in the air."

"Some of the water flows out of the mountain into the pools
of Hot And Cold, and even beyond, doesn't it?"

"Yes." Arona said nothing more for a while, and when she
spoke her words surprised Kalena. "You are a woman who seeks
her freedom."

"You are perceptive."

Arona's mouth curved faintly. "Not particularly. But I, too,
once went in search of freedom. Perhaps now I simply recognize
the desire in others when I see it."

Now Kalena was curious herself. "You did not find your freedom in the outside world, did you, Arona?"

"I don't think I could ever have found it in a world of men,"
she said simply. "But I am happy here in the valley."

"I understand." They were nearing the cottage. Kalena saw
the glow of the lamps through the windows. Ridge would be
waiting, just as he had said.

Arona halted and turned to face her companion. She put a
hand on Kalena's shoulder. "You, too, could be happy here,
Kalena. Do you understand? There is a freedom to be found here
that does not exist in the kind of relationship you have formed
with your husband."

"I know," Kalena said gently. "There is very little freedom in
marriage."

Ridge stood in the shadows near the cottage and listened to
Kalena's words. His restlessness had made him walk out to check

the creets for the second time that evening. He had seen Kalena and Arona approaching in the moonlight. Something within him had tightened into a cold knot as he sensed all the lures of the valley reaching out to take Kalena from him.

"Here in the valley you are free, Kalena," Arona said softly. "You can make your own choices. There is no need to be guided by the wishes of a man."

Ridge sucked in his breath and stepped out of the shadows. In the moonlight he faced the two women. "Kalena, I've been waiting for you."

"I know, Ridge." She turned to him with an unreadable smile on her lips.

Ridge stood very still, every part of him prepared to fight, but he was unsure of how to go about it. He could easily imagine himself protecting his wife from the attentions of another man. But this sort of situation was totally outside his experience. What did he have to offer that could counter the valley's lures? He sensed that his only hold on Kalena at that moment consisted of the tenuous bonds of a trade marriage. The fact that he could make her respond in his arms might stand as nothing compared to the exotic kind of freedom the valley offered her.

"It's time to go to bed, Kalena." He could think of nothing else to say.

"Yes," she agreed and turned back to Arona. "I wish you good evening, my friend. There is much for me to think about tonight."

"That's very true. Go to bed and dream of freedom."

"I'm not sure any of us are ever completely free," Kalena murmured.

"You are a wise woman. Too bad you were not allowed to become a Healer. I wish you good evening, Kalena." Arona disappeared into the balmy night, her long tunic swirling gracefully around her ankles.

Ridge exhaled slowly, but none of his tension diminished. He moved to stand in front of Kalena and caught her face between his rough palms. Her eyes were wide and luminous as she looked up at him.

"Sometimes you scare me almost to death, lady," he rasped.

"Do I?"

"I won't let you go easily, Kalena," he said thickly as his mouth hovered above hers. "I *can't* let you go. You belong to me. Somehow I must make you understand that." And with that he picked her up and carried her into the cottage.

TWELVE

The lamps cast a warm glow that was pale in comparison to the brilliant glow of Ridge's eyes. Kalena was vividly aware of the leashed strength in him as he carried her across the tapestry rug and lowered her to the narrow pallet in the far corner. The warmth of the fire was nothing compared to the heat she sensed in Ridge.

He came down on one knee beside her and released the band that held her hair. Freed, the wealth of sunset colored curls tumbled over his fingers.

"I want you to find your freedom in my arms, wife." He twisted his hands in the depths of her hair and bent his head to kiss her heavily.

His mouth fastened on hers with an urgency that flowed over Kalena the way a fire flowed over dry kindling. She wasn't sure there was freedom to be found in Ridge's embrace, but there was a heated excitement that was unmatched by anything else she had ever known.

Tonight there was something else, too. Kalena knew. She was

aware of a great sense of readiness on her part. She felt as though she had been waiting for this lovemaking for a long time. Ridge had barely touched her, but already she was warming with the same heat that fired his passion. Her arms went around his neck, pulling him down to her.

"This is where you're supposed to be, Kalena. Whatever fate the Spectrum has decreed for you, you must share it with me."

"I know," she heard herself respond. "I know that tonight." The knowledge was flooding her bloodstream, bringing with it a clear certainty that she could not escape.

Ridge's hands moved impatiently on Kalena's clothing. Her tunic was thrust aside and then the narrow trousers fell to the floor. She writhed naked in his arms and began to fight him for the embrace, driven by an urgency she had never felt before.

"By the Stones," he breathed as he held her still long enough to rid himself of clothing, "tonight you're like the free fire that burns in the mountains. How could you even think of leaving me?"

"I wasn't thinking of leaving you tonight," she told him as her nails sank into his shoulders. "I couldn't leave you tonight." It was the truth and she accepted it unquestioningly. She had to have him inside her, filling her completely. Kalena's breath came quickly and she stifled her soft cries against his skin.

Ridge's face was set in lines of stark passion as he loomed over Kalena. His fingers trembled with the force of his need when he touched her breast.

"Come to me," she whispered achingly. She lifted her hips against his in open invitation. "Come to me, Ridge. I want you tonight."

"Soon," he promised thickly. "Soon."

"No, now." Possessed of an overwhelming need to complete the union, Kalena pressed against his chest with the palms of her hands.

Surprised by the force of her desire, Ridge allowed her to push him onto his back. Instantly, she was climbing astride him. Her hair formed a nimbus of golden red against the glow of the lamp behind her. Ridge's eyes glittered in fierce anticipation as his big hands settled on her flaring thighs.

"Finish it," he grated, lifting her slightly so that she could fit herself to him. "I can feel the liquid fire in you. It's going to consume both of us, *so finish it.*"

Her fingers closed delicately around the hard length of his manhood. Ridge groaned and pushed himself abruptly against the damp core of her body. Kalena gasped and fell forward as he entered her deeply. She braced herself on his shoulders and felt her body tighten around him. Slowly, she levered herself upward again until she sat him almost the way she would a creet.

"Now you're fine, my sweet Kalena," Ridge murmured as he stroked himself into her body. "Go ahead and fly. But you'll have to take me with you."

Kalena's whole body arched with sensual tension. Eyes closed, head thrown back in wild abandon, she rode Ridge with a passion that matched his own. The fire that blazed between Ridge and Kalena threatened to consume them, but neither cared. Kalena flew on a creet that still retained its wings. She soared the skies on a great muscled bird who responded to her slightest whim. Dazzling light and deepest shadow swirled beneath them as Kalena rode Ridge to the heights of the mountains. When at last he folded his wings, enclosing her completely, and plummeted back toward the ground, Kalena called his name in a voice that reached into both the shadow and the light.

Ridge's hoarse shout was as vibrant with life as her own. He seemed to burst inside her, spilling the essence of himself into the deepest part of her body. Then he held her so close she could hardly breathe as the tremors that shook both of them ran their course.

Afterward, there was only dampness and warmth and peace. It was a long time before Kalena finally found the energy to open her eyes. When she did, she found Ridge studying her face in the lamplight. His legs were tangled with hers and one of his hands was resting on her hip. His golden eyes still burned faintly with the lazy aftereffects of passion.

"Tomorrow we leave," he said flatly. "With or without the Sand."

"Yes, Ridge," Kalena agreed with a meekness that must have astonished him. "Don't worry about the Sand. The Healers have promised we can take as much as we can carry." Kalena felt no need to argue. Ridge could not stay here. She knew that. There was no place for him in this valley. And she knew that she would leave with him. She could not stay without him. Tonight she understood at last that she and Ridge were bound together. The bonds might chafe at times, but they were as strong as life itself. She would no longer try to struggle against her destiny with this man.

Ridge exhaled deeply and gathered her close once more. "Thank you, Kalena."

"For what?" she asked in quiet amusement.

"For not fighting me."

"Were you afraid that if I did, you might lose?"

He shook his head gravely. "I was afraid that if you fought me, you would lose, and then, perhaps, you would never forgive me. I don't want that kind of victory, but I can't let you stay here in this damn valley, either."

"Why not?" she asked with calm interest, although she had no intention of staying. "You'll have your Sand."

His mouth hardened. "There is more between us now than a shipment of Sand. You know that as well as I."

Kalena's smile faded with his words. "I know it, Ridge. I just wish I understood what it is that binds us together."

"Why must women question and analyze everything that ties them to men?"

"Perhaps we don't like being at the mercy of things we don't understand," she suggested gently.

His brows came together in a hard line. "You only succeed in making life more difficult for yourself when you fail to accept things as they are."

"I didn't know you were such a philosopher, Ridge. Have you

accepted things as they are, even though you don't understand them?"

He bent to nuzzle the curve of her shoulder, his teeth teasing her skin. "I accepted what the Spectrum brought me the day you handed me that trade marriage contract."

Kalena felt his lower body hardening against her once more, and reached out to touch him wonderingly. "Perhaps your way is best, Ridge."

"I know it is," he told her as he eased himself down on top of her. "I'm your husband, Kalena. You must trust me to know what's best for you."

Kalena wanted to smile at his blatant male arrogance. Ridge was so intently serious about what he said. But he was kissing her again and suddenly her mind was cleared of all things but the sensual demands he was imposing. Everyone seemed to know what was best for her. Olara had forced her to wear the mantle of House vengeance. The women of this valley were convinced she was destined to take hold of the mythical Light Key. Her husband decreed she belonged with him.

Of the three options, Kalena decided as she gave herself up to Ridge's lovemaking, her husband's held the most allure.

They left the valley at dawn the next morning. Ridge had the creets saddled and loaded with the sacks containing the Sands of Eurythmia before Kalena had finished eating the morning meal in the dining chamber. Ridge hadn't been interested in sharing another meal with the valley women. He had helped himself to a wedge of cheese, a piece of fruit and a chunk of bread, then disappeared to see to the loading of the Sand.

Kalena almost wished she could have joined him. She felt awkward sharing the meal with Valica, Arona and the others after having made it clear she did not believe in the destiny they saw for her. But no one seemed to hold her unwillingness to become involved with the Key against her. The morning meal was a cheerful, friendly affair. No one mentioned the previous night until Kalena rose to join Ridge.

Valica came forward to take both her hands, kissed her lightly on each cheek and smiled comfortingly. "Do not worry, Kalena. When the time is right, things will happen as they must. You have not turned your back on us or on the Key."

"But I have," Kalena protested earnestly. "You must understand, Valica, I am not the one you seek. The truth is, I'm not sure I even believe in the Key. But if it does exist, I want nothing to do with it."

"There is no need to talk about it now. The balance has not yet shifted far enough to force you to act."

"What balance?"

"You know as well as I do that all the events of our world and our lives are strung out along an infinite Spectrum. When one thing happens, there must be an opposite action in order to ensure the balance. The balance in our world has begun to shift, Kalena. I can feel it. There have been times lately here in the mountains when there has been more Darkness than Light. Such a situation cannot last long. When matters have fallen too badly out of alignment, there will be a reckoning. When that time comes, you will be obedient to your destiny. Go now and think no more about it until you must."

"Valica, please, listen to me. I am merely the last daughter of a House that ends with me. I have failed in the one responsibility that was left to me. In addition, I have lowered myself to the status of a trade wife. I am not very important, Valica. Great destinies are not carved out for people like me. What's more, we don't particularly want them."

Arona came forward, her eyes gentle with understanding. "You want your freedom, not a preordained destiny. But you told me last night you aren't sure if anything is ever truly free."

"I think I have a chance of building a life for myself," Kalena said steadily. "It may not be memorable to anyone but me, but at least it will be the life I have chosen." She stepped back, bowing her head respectfully. "You have been most generous with the Sand. I will see that it ends up in the hands of honest Healers."

Valica chuckled. "There you go, Kalena, taking on yet another obligation. Olara may have been misguided, but she did manage to instill a sense of duty in you, didn't she? It is that integrity and sense of duty that has brought you this far. I think it will guide you the rest of the way. Go now, and good journey to you."

Kalena glanced around at the faces of the women who had gathered to say good-bye. She felt a curious burning sensation behind her eyes. With a tremulous smile, she turned away and hurried toward Ridge, who waited with the creets.

He gave her a sharp glance as he tossed her up into the saddle. "Are you crying?"

"Of course not." She wiped the sleeve of her tunic across her damp eyes and glared at him challengingly. "I'm ready to leave."

He hesitated, one hand on her saddle. "Kalena, if those women have said or done anything to upset you, tell me about it."

"I'm fine, Ridge."

He appeared unconvinced, but was obviously more than ready to be on his way out of the valley. "The sooner we're out of here, the better," he growled, swinging into his own saddle. "Have you got your cloak within reach? It will be cold again as soon as we start climbing away from the valley floor."

She was mildly amused by his concern as she picked up her reins and urged her animal after his. "I have it within reach."

"We won't be able to move as fast going back as we did coming here. I've got the creets fully loaded with Sand. But they're good, strong birds. We'll still be able to travel a lot faster than a regular caravan of pack creets could."

Kalena glanced over her shoulder at the bags of Sand slung across her creet's rump. Her bird didn't seem overly concerned about the added weight, but she knew the load would slow its pace. "Congratulations, Ridge, there should be more than enough here for you to finance your dreams."

"What about your dreams, Kalena?" he surprised her by asking.

"I'm still working them out," she tried to say lightly.

"We will work them out together," he told her.

Their eyes met for a moment, and then Ridge flicked the reins.

His creet started forward with its usual cheerful willingness. Kalena's fell into step behind its mate. Once, Kalena glanced back over her shoulder and saw the women of the valley watching their departure. There was no greater freedom to be had in this valley than what she would find with Ridge, Kalena thought with sudden certainly. It just took a different shape.

Ridge rode in silence for a while, leading the way across the valley floor and up along the trail that led back through the mountains. Kalena knew he was turning something over in his mind, but she didn't ask what it was. She had her own thoughts to occupy her.

When she turned to reach for her warm cloak, a familiar, small pouch came briefly into view as she scrabbled around inside her bag. It was the packet of crushed selite leaves. Kalena's hand stilled as she remembered she had forgotten to take yesterday's dosage.

"Kalena? Anything wrong?" Ridge glanced back at her as his creet rounded a small bend in the trail.

"No," she called back, and then added under her breath, "at least, I hope not." Desperately, she tried to calculate how long it would be before she knew for certain if she would suffer the consequences of last night's unprotected lovemaking. The memory of her own burning passion was unnerving. But there was nothing she could do about it now. It would be some time before she found out if yet another fate had been bestowed upon her.

Kalena sighed and told herself that the odds were in her favor. Surely she would not have to pay for one day's lapse. She watched Ridge as he rode ahead of her and wondered what he would say if he found out he had fathered a child.

But the answer to that was obvious. Ridge would assume his rights and responsibilities without a second's hesitation. Kalena smiled to herself, wondering at her own deep certainty. For the first time since she had accepted the bonds between herself and Ridge, she began to think of what those ties would mean. She wondered if Ridge had given the matter much thought. It was odd to think of the trade marriage becoming permanent. After all, a real marriage to an aggressive, ruthless, Houseless bastard who was determined to establish himself as a House lord at any cost was not what she had set out to find when she had left the farm.

To be perfectly fair, she probably wasn't the kind of wife Ridge had undoubtedly anticipated being able to buy with proceeds from the Sand trade. He might be a bastard, but when he returned to Crosspurposes he was going to be a rich bastard. Respectable Houses would be forced to take him seriously if he courted their daughters.

But even if she couldn't offer him the economic and political connections that a Great House marriage normally involved, she could bring him all the skills, manners, training, and pride that came with a fine House heritage. Ridge had said that growing up without benefit of the traditions had only made him appreciate them more. She believed him. Ridge would found his Great House with the hard-earned profits of his own sweat, luck and skill. He would provide its economic base. But she could bring him the intangibles, Kalena thought. If he married her, she would make his Great House into a home.

If he married her.

Kalena smiled wryly as she realized where her thoughts had wandered.

"The mist." Ridge reined in his creet as he rounded another bend and found himself confronting the shimmering veil. "It hasn't disappeared."

Kalena shook off her private thoughts and moved forward. "The Healers won't remove it for a while. They're worried."

"About what?"

"They say there have been signs of Darkness in and around the mountains. They believe in the Light Key, Ridge. That means they also believe in the Dark One. They think the Dark Key has been found."

"Is that what they told you last night? I knew I should never have left you alone with those females. A bad influence. Now they've gone and filled your head with nonsense and old legends."

"Stop grumbling. This veil of theirs would make a fairly interesting legend itself. Not exactly the work of silly, story spinning females. Do you want to stand here all day telling me how full of nonsense the Healers are or would you like me to lead you through this mist of theirs that is strong enough to keep any mere male at bay?"

"There are times, wife, when your tongue turns exceedingly sharp." He dismounted. "Lucky for you you've got such a tolerant husband."

"Now that you've got your precious Sand, I expect a great deal of toleration from you. The way I look at it, Fire Whip, you own me."

He grinned wickedly. "I always repay my debts." He held out his hand to clasp Kalena's and stepped into the mist without any hesitation. A moment later, everyone, including the creets, was safe on the other side. Ridge glanced back speculatively.

"I wonder how long they'll leave that there. If no one but you can get through it, Quintel's going to have himself a problem."

"An interesting thought," Kalena said slowly. "The one who holds the secret of getting through that mist could name her own price."

"Don't get any ideas of being too clever with the trade baron," Ridge said as he realized what she was thinking. "He always gets what he wants. I know. I've spent a lot of years making sure of it."

"Then it is you and not Quintel I have to fear, isn't it?"

Ridge gave her an odd glance, but didn't respond to the comment. Instead he asked, "Did the Healers tell you what they plan to do about trading Sand in the future?"

"Not really. We didn't discuss it. They've got other things on their minds at the moment. I think they fully intend to continue the trade, but it may be a while before they feel safe enough to remove the veil."

"If it's safety they want, Quintel can provide them with an armed guard to watch the mountain pass."

"A force of armed men stationed at the entrance of their valley would not be very reassuring to the Healers."

Ridge's mouth twisted. "I guess you're right. They want nothing to do with men, do they?"

"They don't hate men. They simply choose to live without them. It seems to work quite well."

"It's a good thing we didn't stay any longer in that valley. Those women would have played tricks with your mind," Ridge stated gruffly.

For the first time since they had left the valley, Kalena found herself grinning. She was glad Ridge's back was toward her.

The trip back along the mountain trail was slower than the one into the valley, just as Ridge had predicted. Loaded with Sand, the creets simply couldn't make good time.

Dusk began to settle while they were still some distance from the shelter where Ridge intended to camp for the night. Kalena saw the last rays of the sun slip behind a snow-capped peak and realized she was shivering. She would have been warm enough in her fur-lined cloak, she thought. There was no reason to be so aware of the chill in the air.

"The shelter is only a short distance away, Kalena. We'll be there soon." Ridge spoke reassuringly as he glanced back and saw her folding the cloak more closely about her.

She nodded in response and struggled to hide her unease. There was an unpleasant feeling of early darkness. It was true that night fell quickly in the mountains, but surely there should be a reasonable period of twilight. The warmth and light of the day seemed to be disappearing far too rapidly. Huddled in the depths of her cloak, she let the creet pick its way around the next turn in the trail. When it came to an abrupt halt behind Ridge's creet, she lifted her head.

"What's wrong?"

Ridge didn't look back; he was studying something that lay ahead of him on the trail, something Kalena couldn't see. "Nothing."

"Why have your stopped?" She jiggled the reins a little to make her creet move up alongside Ridge's.

"There a stream across the trail." He leaned forward, his elbows folded on the pommel of the saddle.

"We crossed no stream on the trip in to the valley."

"I know."

"Then what—" Kalena stopped short as she caught sight of the foaming black water that emerged from the mountains on one side of the trail, crossed the path and disappeared into the canyon on the far side. Her breath caught in her throat. "Ridge, what is it?"

"Water."

"No, it's more than that. It wasn't here when we came this way the first time."

"It must have rained somewhere back in the mountains during the night. This is just the runoff. It's not deep."

"I don't care how deep it is, we can't cross it," Kalena whispered with absolute conviction. She didn't know how she knew that for certain, but she did.

"Of course we can." Ridge straightened in the saddle and picked up the reins. "Let's go." He walked the creet to the edge of the swiftly moving stream. The bird hesitated, but under Ridge's urging, it stepped into the current.

"Ridge, wait," Kalena called anxiously. "I think we should camp on this side. If it's just runoff from a rain, it should be gone by tomorrow."

"It's too cold to spend the night out in the open when there's no need." Halfway across the stream, Ridge turned in the saddle to regard her impatiently. "Follow me, Kalena."

Realizing he wasn't going to pay any attention to her instinctive dislike of the black water, Kalena tried to make herself approach the stream. The creet lifted its head in a frightened gesture and Kalena knew the poor animal was probably just reacting to her tension. Kalena got herself and the creet to the edge of the water before she became aware of a vague nausea.

The water wasn't that deep where it covered the trail. She knew that. Ridge's creet had only sunk into it up to the tops of its clawed feet. But one ought to be able to see the ground through water that shallow, and Kalena could see nothing but foaming black liquid. She halted the creet.

"I can't cross, Ridge," she said quietly.

"Damn it, Kalena, it's getting late and I want to get to that shelter. What's the matter with you?"

"I don't know. I just know I can't cross it. I know it as surely as you know you couldn't go through the white mist that guarded the valley."

He scowled at her from the other side of the water. "Kalena, this is no Healer's trick. It's just a mountain stream."

"The water's black. I can't even see through it. Water that shallow should be transparent."

"The sun has set and the light is going quickly. That's the only reason the water looks black," Ridge explained with a patience that annoyed Kalena. "Close your eyes if the sight of the water bothers you. The creet won't mind it."

"I can't do it, Ridge." She looked at him pleadingly. "I just can't do it."

"Yes, you can." He sent his own creet back through the stream. "Here, give me your reins," he added more gently. "I'll lead your creet."

"No!" Kalena yanked back on the leather, causing her already confused bird to prance in agitation.

Ridge dropped his arm, making no move to grab the reins again. "Kalena, you have no choice. You have to cross that stream and you must realize it. I don't know what fantasy you're weaving in your head, but whatever it is, I can't allow you to indulge it. There's no reason to make a cold camp on the trail when warmth and shelter are just a short distance ahead."

"Please, Ridge. You must understand. I'm not indulging a fantasy. I simply can't go through that water."

He studied her for a long moment and then the impatience faded from his expression. "All right. I can see you're really upset. Do you want to sleep on the trail tonight?"

She nodded vigorously. "Yes, please. I know it will be cold, but with our cloaks and a fire we won't freeze. Perhaps this water will be gone by tomorrow."

He moved his creet a little closer to hers. "Perhaps. Let's see what we can find in the way of shelter out here."

Kalena finally began to relax. He wasn't going to argue further. "Thank you, Ridge," she said with grateful relief. "I know this seems like so much female nonsense—but—No! Stop! Please, Ridge."

Her sentence ended on a squeak of protest as Ridge leaned forward without any warning and scooped her up out of the saddle. "You're right," he said soothingly as he settled Kalena in front of him. "It does seem like so much female nonsense. But it will all be over before you can count to ten." Holding her firmly with one hand, he grabbed her creet's reins and started into the stream.

"Ridge, no! Please, I beg you . . ."

He folded the edge of his cloak around her, covering her face. "Don't look if it bothers you so much," he said gently.

Kalena knew it was too late to struggle. She buried her face against the warmth of his chest, shivering violently even though she had the covering of two cloaks to shield her from the cold. She squeezed her eyes shut and clung to Ridge's waist.

Kalena waited for the nausea to overwhelm her, but her stomach stayed calm this time as the creets splashed into the stream. She was aware of an intense cold wafting upward from the black water, but that was all. Cradled in Ridge's arms, she made the crossing without further trauma. It was as if the Fire Whip's own heart was protecting her, she thought, half dazed.

When the birds were standing firmly on the far side of the water, Ridge loosened his hold on Kalena. She sat up uncertainly and found him watching her with eyes that were both sympathetic and amused.

"That wasn't so bad, was it? Now you can look forward to a hot meal, a warm fire and a roof over your head."

Kalena still felt a little dizzy. She didn't look back at the black stream. "What do you want me to say, Ridge? Do you want me to thank you for treating me like a witless child?"

The sympathy and rather gentle amusement in his eyes disappeared. "A witless wife, not a witless child," he muttered. "A child would probably have had more sense."

She stiffened and made to jump down from her perch. "I'll ride my own creet the rest of the way."

"Am I going to be treated to a night of the sulks?"

"I'm too tired to spend much time sulking," she informed him as she climbed into her own saddle. "After the evening meal I'm going straight to sleep." She picked up the reins and snapped them briskly against the creet's neck. The bird moved forward obligingly, aware of the promise of shelter and food that lay ahead.

"Kalena . . ." Ridge caught up with her, his face set in its familiar grim lines. "I'm sorry for having to carry you across that stream against your will." His words were stilted. Ridge wasn't accustomed to apologizing. "But I saw no other choice. I couldn't let you spend a night shivering on the trail when shelter was within reach. It would have been stupid and irresponsible on my part. As your husband, I'm supposed to look after you. You must learn to trust me."

"My mood is unpleasant enough as it is," she retorted. "Don't make it any worse by lecturing me on the subject of your husbandly responsibilities and my wifely duties."

"I should never have left you alone with those women last night," Ridge decided gloomily.

Kalena thought about what had been said after dinner the previous evening. "For once, Ridge, you might actually be right."

If Ridge was startled by her unexpected agreement, he didn't show it.

Kalena awoke the next morning and found that Ridge had already vacated the pallet. The cloaks they had used as blankets during the night had been pushed aside and she could feel the bite of dawn in the small room. She yawned and wondered why Ridge hadn't yet lit a fire. Perhaps he didn't want to waste time on a hot meal this morning.

She hadn't exactly sulked the night before, but they had both been unusually quiet. When they had gone to bed Ridge had gathered Kalena close to him but had made no effort to arouse her physically. He had apparently been as exhausted as she.

The creets stirred restlessly in the stalls that adjoined the main room. Kalena ignored them and studied Ridge, who had opened the door and was staring out into the dark gray dawn that hung over the mountains. There was something wrong. She could feel it. Kalena sat up, gathering her cloak around her.

"What is it, Ridge?"

He turned slowly to look back at her. There was a strange expression in his eyes, one Kalena didn't recognize.

"We're lost," he said simply.

She stared at him, appalled. "Lost! But that's impossible. We're in the shelter on the trail. The same shelter that we used the first time we came through the mountains."

"The shelter is here. It's the trail that's gone."

THIRTEEN

Kalena scrambled from the pallet, swinging the cloak around her as she hurried barefoot across the small room. Her feet felt as if they had been immersed in ice before she reached the door. She should have put on her boots, she thought.

But the sight that greeted her when she reached Ridge's side was more than enough to make her forget the cold. An endless swirl of gray confronted her. Nothing was visible through it. It enveloped the shelter and the entire surrounding area.

"Fog?" she suggested hesitantly, knowing the mist was more than that but unwilling to admit it yet.

Ridge shook his head bluntly. "If it's fog, it's unlike any I've ever seen. I tried walking out into it. You can't get more than a few paces before it becomes absolutely impenetrable. The creets won't be able to see any better than we can. They could walk straight off a cliff in that stuff. We're trapped here."

"If it's just fog it will burn off by this afternoon."

"It isn't fog, Kalena."

"What, then?" She glanced at him questioningly.

"I wish I knew. I'd say it was another example of the Healers' tricks, except that we're too far from their valley." His expression grew more shadowed. "At least, I think we are."

"No," Kalena vowed, "this is no Healer's trick. I'd know if it had something to do with them."

"Because you're a woman?"

"Yes, Ridge. Because I'm a woman." She met his unreadable gaze. "What's more, I think it's the fact that you're a man that makes you so sure this isn't normal fog. This is connected to that black water that you forced us to cross last night."

"You're letting your imagination get carried away again, Kalena." He moved past her, striding out into the cold gray atmosphere.

Kalena watched him for a moment, then hurried across the room to slip into her boots. When she returned to the door all she could see of Ridge was the back of his arm and one booted foot. The rest of his body was lost in the fog. Even as she stared, he disappeared completely.

"Ridge! Come back here. I can't see you."

He eased back into view slowly. There was a disorienting moment when all she could see were his golden eyes. They gleamed at her through the fathomless gray, fierce, fiery pools of heat. Kalena stared into that gaze and saw the elemental predator that the philosophers said lay deep inside every male. It sent a jolt of fear through her.

"Ridge," she whispered, unable to move.

And then he was back, coalescing out of the fog. "It's all right, Kalena. I was just trying to see if I can find the mountain wall that lines the trail."

"Did you?" She swallowed heavily, aware of a peculiar dryness in her throat.

"No. It's as if there's nothing out there but this gray fog."

"Surely when the sun has risen this stuff will thin," she said with a touch of desperation.

He shrugged and walked back into the shelter, closing the

door behind him. "I'll build a fire. We're not going anywhere for a while. Might as well eat."

They spent a long day in the small shelter. Ridge kept the fire at full blaze, working his way steadily through the pile of wood that was stored in the creets' stable. The heat was needed to ward off the biting chill. As the day progressed, Kalena felt colder and colder, despite the fire. She kept darting anxious glances out the window, hoping for some indication that the sun was having an effect on the strange grayness that surrounded them. But the fog seemed to grow darker, not lighter as the day passed. During one uneasy moment she had the impression that when darkness fell the mist would convert itself into the same stuff she had encountered in the caverns of Hot And Cold. She sensed that grayness was a temporarily quiescent form of that darker mist.

"A good thing you always carry emergency food in your saddlebags," Kalena tried to say lightly as she prepared the evening meal in front of the fire.

Ridge didn't answer. He had grown increasingly less communicative as the day went by. Kalena felt uncomfortable under his watchful gaze. She kept remembering the hunter's eyes she had seen suspended in the fog that morning. Shaking away the image, Kalena tried again to find some topic of conversation.

"The Healers told me a strange thing about myself, Ridge," she said thoughtfully. "They said I have the Talent but that it was never developed and trained."

"They probably told you that as a way of inducing you to stay behind with them," he responded shortly.

She ignored that. "They said Olara knew about my Talent but kept it a secret from me."

Ridge swung his intent gaze from the fire to her face. "Now that I can believe. Your aunt wanted to use you. If it's true you have the Talent, she would have had a problem, wouldn't she? Healers can't kill. How did she keep such knowledge from you?"

Kalena kept her eyes on the fire, wondering why she felt so little warmth from it. "With the techniques a Healer uses to deal with troubled minds. Or so Valica claims."

"Ha. It makes a certain kind of sense. It would also verify what I told you a few days ago. Your aunt meant you to die in the attempt to kill Quintel."

Kalena threw him a quick glance, then turned back to the fire. "Ridge . . ."

"Hush, Kalena. You know I speak the truth. There are very few recorded cases of a Healer willfully committing murder, but in those rare instances, the Healer herself has died in the process or shortly thereafter. Some sort of deep shock sets in or so I've heard."

Kalena drew a deep breath. "Ridge, if she lied to me about the Talent . . ."

"Yes?"

"She might have lied to me about . . . about other things," Kalena concluded in a sad little rush.

"Such as Quintel being the one responsible for killing the males of your House? Yes, Kalena, she lied."

"But why would she do such a thing? It makes no sense."

Ridge shrugged. "Who knows? If you want my opinion, she sounds as if she's a Healer in need of a good Healer."

Kalena cradled her chin on her arms as she drew her knees up in front of her. "Ridge, I want to ask you something. Something important."

"Ask."

"How would you feel if you discovered that someone who had raised you, educated you, cared for you had also lied to you?"

Ridge let out a deep breath. When he spoke his voice took on that curiously neutral tone that served to emphasize the controlled violence just under the surface of the man. "If I were to discover such a thing about someone I had trusted there would be a reckoning. I would neither forgive nor forget. Do you want me to kill your aunt for you, Kalena? Is that what you're asking?"

She was truly shocked. "By the Stones, no! Never would I ask you to do such a thing. Unlike you, Ridge, all I want to do is forget. How could you ask me a question like that?"

For the first time that day his mouth was briefly edged with a wry smile. "To make you realize that there is nothing you can do except forget your aunt and all her poisonous teachings. It will do you no good to brood on the past. You can do nothing about it. It is beyond you to even exact vengeance for what was done to you."

Kalena shook her head in wonder. "You know a few mind tricks of your own, don't you, Fire Whip? You're absolutely right. There is nothing I can do about Olara now except put her in the past."

"You are not one who can walk the vengeance trail, Kalena, so it's best not even to contemplate it."

"I think you're getting to know me a little too well, Ridge," she said with a rueful laugh.

"I want you to forget your past because your future lies with me." He looked at her, willing her to meet his gaze. "Do you understand that now, Kalena?"

"I understand it, Ridge." As she studied him in the flickering light it seemed to Kalena that the flames on the hearth etched his face in savage lines. The link between them held, but the knowledge of it did nothing to alleviate the wary sensation that was troubling her so deeply tonight. She felt as if there was a third force in the room, sharing the space with her and Ridge. Kalena didn't like the feeling; it chilled her with fear.

They went to bed early that night. Ridge made no move to gather Kalena into his arms, however, and for some strange reason she was just as glad. She felt edgy and restless, poised on the border of an uneasiness that threatened to turn into senseless panic. She had to keep telling herself that she had nothing to fear from Ridge. Nevertheless, it was hours before she fell into a troubled sleep.

Her dreams that night were filled with visions of a bottomless pool of black water, endless gray fog and the golden eyes of a predator who came from the darkest end of the Spectrum. Kalena stirred frequently in her sleep, unconsciously seeking escape, although she couldn't have said what it was she feared.

She awoke with a shudder of alarm, the echo of a scream still on her lips. Her heart was pounding as though she had been fleeing a hook viper. The room was pitch dark. All warmth had died in the fireplace and the lamps were out.

Ridge touched her arm and Kalena jumped. His hand fell away and he made no further move to comfort her. "Are you all right?" His voice was harsh, only remotely concerned. "You screamed."

"A bad dream. Ridge, it's so dark in here."

"I'll rebuild the fire."

She felt him leave the pallet, heard him fumbling with the kindling from the pile of wood near the fireplace. A moment later flames flared into life as Ridge used the tiny tube of firegel he carried to ignite the wood. Kalena lay propped on her side, shivering, and looked at Ridge's harsh profile as he knelt beside the fire. He was wearing only his trousers which he had kept on for warmth.

The firelight gleamed on his shoulders and was reflected in his eyes. There was something strange about him tonight, something she sensed with every fiber of her being. Something had happened. Tonight he was the Other. Everything in him that was opposite to her was suddenly starkly visible to all her senses.

Just as that realization struck her, Ridge got to his feet and came toward her. With his back to the fire his face was in deep shadow. Kalena could see only the gleam of his eyes. She edged back as he came across the room with the lazy stride of a prowling hunter.

Kalena looked up and knew beyond any doubt that a bizarre transformation had taken place. This was not the man to whom she had bound herself, and yet it *was* Ridge. In the shadows he looked at her in a way she half recognized, even though she had never seen such an expression on his face before. He wanted her, but there was no sensuality in this male predator, only a hunger that fed on conquest and violence.

"Ridge, you must stop," she breathed. She sat up and scrambled backward on the pallet until she was against the wall. "Please, stop."

He didn't halt until he was next to the pallet. "Are you afraid of me tonight?"

Her head lifted proudly as she crouched in front of him. "Yes, Ridge, I'm afraid of you tonight."

"Why?" He sounded more amused than curious. But there was no warmth in his amusement. The laughter in him was as cold and ruthless as the hunger in his eyes. All trace of the warm fire that characterized the man was gone.

Whatever drove him tonight, it wasn't passion, Kalena knew. She had witnessed his passion, even when it was laced with his anger, and never had he been like this. She had never seen him so utterly and completely cold. Always before, Ridge had been a man of heat and fire when he reached for Kalena in bed.

"Please don't touch me, Ridge."

"I can do anything I want with you." He said the words thoughtfully, as if the fact had just occurred to him. He put one knee on the pallet and put out his hand to slide his fingers along her throat. "Anything at all. I can take you and use you and when I'm finished . . ."

Wild fear gripped her. Kalena was trapped between him and the wall. He was beyond reason. The gold in his eyes was frozen. Gone was the familiar warmth that characterized everything Ridge said or did. Something was shadowing the fire in him, something that could turn water black and dim a firegel lamp. Something that was a product of the darkening mist that surrounded the shelter.

"No, Ridge!" Kalena caught at his hand. "You're my husband. I wear your lock and key around my throat. You are honor bound to protect me, not hurt me. I'm your wife, Ridge."

She thought she saw some sign of response in his eyes and hope flared within her. He was staring at the amber lock and key with a faintly puzzled expression, as if a part of him sought to comprehend it.

"My wife," he repeated. His hand slowly fell away from her.

"My woman," he added in a harsh whisper. "My responsibility is to care for you . . ."

"You would never hurt me, Ridge."

His eyes lifted back from the lock and key to her strained face. His frown deepened. "No," he agreed, still sounding vaguely puzzled. "I would never hurt you. You belong to me. You're a part of me." He shook his head as if seeking to clear it.

She was reaching him, Kalena thought. In some way she was getting through to him. Whatever it was that had tried to control him was failing.

"Ridge, we must get out of here. Even if it means going through that fog. We must leave this place at once."

And then all hope died in Kalena as the door crashed open, striking the wall with a violent clatter. A blast of cold air shot through the small room. The fire on the hearth dimmed, but it did not die out completely.

Kalena looked over Ridge's shoulder and wanted to scream, but her voice was trapped in her throat. A figure stood in the doorway, a black, hooded cloak swirling around him. In the faint light she couldn't see more than the shadow of a man's face under the wide brim of the hood.

"Go ahead, Fire Whip. Take her if you wish." The hooded man's voice was harsh and brittle. "I'm sure my master would not want to deprive you of one last tumble with the woman."

Ridge turned slowly, as if the small action required a great effort. He confronted the apparition in the doorway, his hand resting on the sintar in his belt. "Who are you?" he rasped.

"One who wears the black glass. There are more of us, Fire Whip, and we have need of you. There is a need for the woman, too, but only for a short while. Soon she will be useless. So take her if that is what you want. Perhaps when you are finished, I will enjoy some sport myself. It has been a long time."

The arrogant, derisive words seemed to free Ridge from whatever force held him partially in thrall. The sintar suddenly appeared in his hand. He moved toward the cloaked figure in the doorway with savage intent. "No one touches her but me. *No one.*"

"I was warned you might make this difficult."

Kalena saw the blade in Ridge's fist begin to glow, and a part of her was violently glad. The fire in him was not yet completely quenched.

The figure on the threshold fell back before Ridge's silent advance. Kalena's flash of relief lasted only a split second. In the next instant a roiling black mist poured through the doorway, swamping the room before Kalena could even shout a warning. The firelight winked out.

Kalena thought she saw a faint glimmer from the sintar before Ridge and everything was lost in the whirling, seething mist. She opened her mouth to cry out as the darkness seized her, and then she was flung into an endless night. All consciousness fled.

The first thing Kalena became aware of was the cold. The sensation was relentless, no matter how much she tried to retreat back into unconsciousness. She had heard somewhere that one fell into a deep sleep before one froze to death. But this chill seemed calculated to keep its victims awake while they suffered.

She opened her eyes to the pale gleam of a lamp hung high above her on a rocky wall. Starkly flaring shadows danced on the stone around her. For a moment she thought she was back in the spa cavern at Hot And Cold. But there was no warmth from the bubbling waters, and this subterranean room was a different shape than the one in which she had been trapped several days earlier. This was a smaller cave, lit by only one lamp. An arched entrance that had been hacked out of the rocky wall was sealed with a barred gate. Beyond the bars she could see an uninviting corridor of stone that vanished into darkness.

Kalena tried to sit up and discovered that she was bound hand and foot. The hard, stony floor on which she had been tossed like a sack was damp and cold. As she struggled to elevate herself slightly she could feel the stiffness in her muscles. There was no way of telling how long she had been lying in the small chamber.

"Ridge? Are you here?" She peered into the thick shadows cast by the single lamp.

"You're awake."

His voice came to her from the depths of a shadow formed by a large boulder on the opposite wall. There was almost no inflection in his words.

"I'm awake," she acknowledged. "Are you all right?"

"I'm not bleeding anywhere and nothing's broken, if that's what you mean. But I'm not all right." He shifted position, emerging slightly from the shadow as he used the surface of the boulder to brace himself in a sitting position. He, too, was tied. Across the short distance of the chamber his golden eyes were brilliant, but as unreadable as his voice. "What about you?"

"I'm not hurt," she murmured. "Just stiff and sore. Ridge, where are we?"

"I don't know. I only woke up a few minutes ago. That black mist that came through the door . . ."

"It was like the mist that trapped me in the pool caves at Hot And Cold."

"I was afraid of that." There was a faint pause. "I should have believed you that night. I thought it was all your imagination."

"Given the circumstances, it was perfectly logical for you to think that way."

"Dammit, Kalena, don't go polite on me now. I know this is my fault. If I'd listened to you back in Hot And Cold, maybe none of this would have happened."

"I don't see what difference you could have made. We still would have gone on to the valley and we still would have been trapped on the way back out of the mountains. You were sent to find out what was happening around here, Ridge. It looks as though you've begun to get the answers to Quintel's questions."

"I'm beginning to wish Quintel had never asked the questions in the first place." Ridge groaned. "I should have known that a cut of the Sand trade was going to cost me more than a quick trip into the mountains and back."

They both heard the scrape of boot leather on the rocky floor of the corridor outside the cave chamber, then saw a flash of lamplight. The barred gate was unlocked and a cloaked and hooded figure stood in the arched opening. When he spoke Kalena knew it was the same man who had entered the shelter during the night.

"Answers are what we all seek," the cloaked man said, holding his lamp so that the light added a bit more illumination to the shadowed room. The reflected glare made a mask of his hooded features. "Final, absolute, powerful answers. You, little whore, are going to help provide them, although you will never have the ability to understand what you have done."

"Only a fool would insult my wife," Ridge said softly. "I will remember every word."

The hooded head turned in Ridge's direction. There was a low chuckle that held no grain of real humor. "I am called Griss, and I am anything but a fool. You deserve that label. You have grown soft because of her, Fire Whip. It is dangerous to consort with women. Their power may be weak, but it is insidious and subtle. An unwary man, blinded by his own lust, too often falls victim to it. Fortunately, the damage is usually not permanent. It can be undone. Soon you will understand what I mean."

"I assumed that all those fancy magician's tricks with that black mist had a purpose," Ridge said bluntly. "You've gone to a lot of trouble to get us here. Those were your men back in Adverse? The ones who wore the black glass pendants?"

"A case of overzealousness, I fear. The fools thought to please their master by delivering you ahead of schedule. You were not meant to be taken until we had proof that the woman was the one who could get through the barrier that guards the Healers' valley. The two in Adverse paid for their disobedience."

"You could say that. They're dead."

The hooded figure nodded somberly. "Of course. Death is the reward for disobedience as well as failure."

"Were they the ones who killed Trantel?" Ridge asked.

"Ah, yes. Trantel was asking too many questions. He was learning too much, you see. He questioned what had driven the hook vipers out of the mountains and he wondered at certain disappearances that have occurred in the neighboring foothills. We needed men, you see. There was work to be done. The Cult of the Eclipse prefers complete secrecy, however. When he began snooping around it became necessary to get rid of him."

"The black mist in the caves at Hot And Cold," Kalena whispered. "You caused it?"

"The caverns at Hot And Cold are linked to these caverns. Over the years we of the cult have explored most of the passages and not long ago we found the ones that lead from the core of the mountains to the pool caverns. We wished to test the black fog. It is a recent creation of our master's, and we were curious to know if it could counter the residual power that flows in the water of those hot springs. It would have been interesting to see its effects against you, too, although we did not intend to take you that night. As I said, it was necessary to see if you could get into the Healers' valley before any move was made."

"You learned that the black mist couldn't overcome even the minor power of the Light Key that is in the water," Kalena observed with satisfaction.

"It is only a matter of time. The mist is being perfected daily. It was finely tuned enough to affect the Fire Whip in the shelter, was it not? You yourself saw that. Of course, it has an affinity for males. Against women it is a weapon. But when used on men it enhances all the power in them that comes from the Dark end of the Spectrum. That power grows daily among those of us in the Cult of the Eclipse. When the Light Key has been destroyed, nothing will stand in our way."

Kalena shivered. "You can't be serious. Nothing can destroy the Light Key."

"So stupid females such as the High Healers would have us all believe. Women know nothing of real power. They exist only because of the indulgence of males, although in their arrogance, women refuse to admit it. Whatever small power a woman possesses derives from the Light end of the Spectrum, the *weak* end. All men know that ultimately the Dark end is stronger than the Light. You will find that out for yourself when the Keys are brought together."

"That can't be done," Kalena stated softly.

"Of course it can be done, little whore. Why do you think the Dawn Lords took such care to separate and hide the Keys if it could not be done?"

Ridge answered. "What makes you and your kind think you have more knowledge than the Dawn Lords? You're fools to play with power you can't possibly comprehend."

"No, Fire Whip. It is you and the other males who have allowed themselves to become tainted with the Light end of the Spectrum who are the fools. You will flock to us soon enough when we have shown you the truth."

"But what will you do if you manage to destroy the Light Key?" Kalena asked desperately. "What's the point of taking such risks?"

"Don't you understand anything, whore? The Cult of the Eclipse will know no boundaries on its power once we have subdued the Light Key. We can then go on to discover the hiding places of the Stones themselves. Without its Key the Light Stone of Contrast will be unable to withstand the power of the Dark."

"You don't know what you're saying," Kalena whispered. "If it's true that the Keys actually exist and if the Stones themselves are real, than you dare not try to destroy any of them. The lines of power that run between them form the Spectrum. If you destroy one end of the Spectrum, the other end becomes meaningless. The instability that would result could destroy our continent, perhaps our world."

"No," the hooded man snapped with cold arrogance, "that is only a story spun by women. The truth is that the destruction of the Light Stone will free the total power of the Dark. The ones who control the Dark Stone's Key ultimately control the Stone itself."

"And who," Ridge asked grimly, "will control the Dark Key? Who the hell are you?"

The man reached inside his cloak and held out the pendant of black glass he wore. Lamplight flickered on the dark glass, producing an odd effect, as if faint sparks danced for a moment on the surface of the pendant. "I am a member of the Cult of the Eclipse, Fire Whip. That is all you need to know. You and the woman have both been brought here to serve the cult."

"How?"

"You have spent too long with the woman, Fire Whip. She has indeed dulled your mind. Don't you understand yet? The Keys can be handled by a very few. According to the ancient books, only a man who can make the steel forged in Countervail glow with fire is capable of holding the Dark Key." The cloaked figure turned to glance disparagingly at Kalena. "And only a special Healer who has never been trained to heal can handle the Light Key, because the power it will draw must be in its raw, unformed state. In addition to their talents, these two people must balance each other on the Spectrum. So say the great books of mystery and the Mathematics of Paradox."

"How long have you known of our existence?" Kalena was stunned by what the man was saying. Her voice was a thin thread of sound that was barely audible in the rocky chamber.

"We knew you were the ones we sought shortly after you came to Crosspurposes to conduct your whore's business, trade wife. When the trade marriage was negotiated we knew that the forces of logic and destiny had finally worked themselves to their ultimate conclusion. It was said the groom was one who could make the steel of Countervail glow and the bride was one who might have been a Healer had she been so trained because the Talent ran in the women of her family. The two of you had formed an alliance and were bound for the Heights of Variance. All the signs were right. We decided to act."

"Are you saying you've got access to the Dark Key?" Ridge asked roughly.

"Oh, yes. It is in our possession, although none of us can

touch it yet. That is for you to do, Fire Whip. Your whore will soon leave for the valley of the Healers to bring back the Light Key. Then the two of you will have the task of bringing the Keys into contact with each other."

"My *wife*," Ridge said with dangerous emphasis, "knows nothing about the location of the Light Key."

"The High Healers will show her." The man seemed unconcerned. "They cannot touch it themselves, but they know its location. It has been their secret for generations. They will give it to her because in their foolishness they will choose to believe that in her hands it will be stronger than the Dark Key."

"If what you say is so," Ridge gritted, "then I will not allow Kalena to bring back the Light Key."

"You will have no choice in the matter, Fire Whip."

The hooded man took a few paces into the room, his cloak swinging around his booted feet. The light reflected upward from the lamp, revealing more of his features. Kalena knew she would never forget that beaked nose, his thin, brutal mouth and dark eyes that reminded her of bottomless pools of black water.

"Listen to me, whore," he rasped, halting a short distance away from Kalena. "You have a task ahead of you. Do you understand it now? You are to return to the valley of the Healers. They will show you the location of the Light Key. You must bring it back down the trail with you. There you will be met and brought here to carry out your destiny."

Ridge's voice was a snarl of anger. "She will not do your bidding, you fool. She is my wife and she will do as I say."

The hooded man chuckled. "It is precisely because she has been in your bed that she will follow my instructions. We soon realized that the physical union between the two of you was a necessary part of all this. You have done your job well, Fire Whip. You have possessed her completely, and in so doing you have bound the woman to you. There is always a danger in such unions because they can weaken a man, but this time I think it will work to our advantage." He turned back to Kalena. "You will go to the valley, won't you whore? You know what will happen to your lover if you don't."

"Damn you," Ridge gritted. "Leave her alone."

Kalena glanced at him and then back at her captor. "You will kill him if I don't return with the Key."

"Ah, I see that you are not entirely brainless after all. Always the chance of that in a woman. Silly, stupid creatures." The hooded man swung back toward the door. "Food will be brought to you and you will be given a short rest. You will need your strength for the trip back to the valley. Then you will be sent on your way." He walked out of the chamber without a backward glance. The barred gate clanged shut behind him.

Silence descended. Kalena looked across at Ridge, who sat with his back against the boulder. "I must go, Ridge. You know that."

"You will let them lead you out of these caves, but they can't follow you into the valley. As soon as you're on the other side of the veil, tell the Healers what's happening. They might be able to get a message to Quintel. He commands enough men who know what they're doing with sintars and crossbows. He should be able to flush out these bastards."

Kalena said nothing, knowing in her heart that such a plan was hopeless against these men in their hidden caverns. She stared at Ridge helplessly.

"Do you hear me, Kalena?"

"I hear you, Ridge."

He closed his eyes in grim despair. "But you're going to try to bring back the Light Key, regardless, aren't you?"

"I will seek another way of freeing you, Ridge, but if there is none, then I will have to try the Key."

Ridge opened his eyes. "Why?"

"You're my husband. I can't abandon you," she said gently. "Would you leave me to my fate if you were the one who had been told to fetch the Key?"

His face was stark. "You know the answer to that."

She nodded, smiling thinly. "Of course. You would return for me."

"You belong to me, Kalena."

"It works both ways."

He leaned his head back against the rock. "You must realize that neither of us is meant to survive the confrontation of the Keys. If the legends are right, they'll destroy us. There is no point in your returning with the Light Key, Kalena. Either way, you can't hope to get me out of here. Leave me to my own devices. I've been in messy situations before this. I've learned a few tricks."

"This is different, Ridge. I know it deep inside. The only way out of this is with the Keys."

"If they exist and if we try to bring them together, we'll only succeed in killing each other."

"I'm not so sure of that, Ridge. It might be true that two people selected at random would have no chance, but I'm beginning to understand there was no real element of chance involved in our marriage. If our coming together has been fated, then perhaps that is because we are the ones who can control the Keys."

"Kalena, no one can control the Keys. That's the whole point of the legends!"

"The Healers believe I can control the Light Key."

He looked at her sharply. "They told you that?"

She nodded. "Right after you were dismissed from dinner."

He sucked in his breath. "You didn't tell me."

"I didn't want to talk about it. They told me I had a duty, you see. An obligation to take the Light Key from its hiding place. But I'd had enough of having everyone lecture me on the subject of my responsibilities. First there was my aunt . . ."

"And then there was your husband," Ridge added wryly.

"Umm, yes." She realized she was slightly amused by the way he had said that. "And then a bunch of strangers in an even stranger valley tell me my obligations. One of these days, Ridge, I'm going to make my own decisions and determine exactly what will bind me. But in the meantime, I don't seem to be able to escape certain responsibilities."

"If you value your duty to obey your husband, you will do as I say and not come back out of the valley until Quintel has cleaned out this cult," Ridge told her roughly.

Kalena wrinkled her nose at him. "The problem is that I value my husband more than I value my obligation to obey him. I will be back, Ridge."

"Stubborn, illogical, irrational female." He swore softly and let his head rest against the stone behind him.

"Look at the positive side, Ridge. Maybe with all those faults you'll be less likely to grow bored with me during the course of our short marriage."

His eyes flared briefly. "This is no joke, Kalena. If you don't realize how dangerous this situation is, then you are more foolish than that man in the cloak said you were."

She sighed. "I'm sorry, Ridge. I assure you I'm taking this all quite seriously. The truth is, I'm scared to death. Maybe that's why I tried such a poor joke."

Ridge was silent for a while, then finally said, "The last thing you could ever do is bore me, Kalena, regardless of how long the marriage lasts."

Something in her unknotted a little at the warmth in his words. "Thank you, trade husband. I can say without any reservation that I return the compliment in full measure. Life has not been dull with you."

He groaned. "Don't remind me."

Kalena fell silent again for a few minutes, then asked the question that had been hovering in the back of her mind. "Ridge?"

"Yes?"

"Do you think of me as a whore because I signed that trade marriage contract with you?"

The gold in his eyes was molten with the controlled fire of his fury. If Ridge had been holding his sintar, Kalena knew the steel would have glowed. But his voice was unnaturally even as he spoke.

"You are my wife, Kalena. I will slit the throat of any man who calls you whore. Before this is over, the one named Griss will learn his lesson in manners the hard way. I will see to it if it's the last thing I do in this world. Unlike you, I'm quite capable of walking the vengeance trail."

Kalena couldn't think of anything to say to that. She swallowed and lapsed back into silence. Perhaps she should try to get some rest. The journey back to the valley would be a long one.

"Kalena?"

"What is it, Ridge?"

"This marriage of ours . . ." he began deliberately.

"What about it?"

"It's going to last as long as we both can draw breath."

Kalena felt warmed by the determination in his words. "I wouldn't dream of arguing with you, husband. A good wife always defers to her husband's superior judgment."

Ridge choked back a rare laugh. "Why is it that you wait until we are in a situation such as this to show me how obedient you can be?"

"I told you, I don't want you to grow bored." Kalena paused. "I've been thinking about the creets, Ridge."

"What a thing to worry about now!" he said brusquely. "I'm sure they're fine. They probably got left behind in the shelter. They'll have plenty of food. And when they get tired of gorging themselves, I wouldn't be surprised if they amused themselves playing a few more of the kind of games that shocked you so much that day by the stream."

"You really think they'll be all right?"

Ridge smiled grimly. "I think they'll be fine. Nice to know some members of this troupe of gallant adventurers are having a good time on the trip, isn't it?"

Griss and another cloaked man came for Kalena after she had slept uneasily for what she estimated was an hour. After giving her a small amount of food, her ankles were silently untied and she was led to the threshold of the dark corridor.

Helplessly, Ridge watched her being taken away from him. "Kalena!"

She glanced back at him over her shoulder, aware that her captors weren't going to let her have any lingering farewells. "Yes, Ridge?"

"Remember what I said."

She smiled mistily, thinking of his impossible orders to hide in the valley with the Healers. "I will remember that I am your wife, Ridge, and not your whore."

He had no chance to respond. Kalena was yanked through the opening and pushed down the bleak underground passage.

FOURTEEN

It was a long walk up the mountain trail without a creet. Kalena had been led back to the surface through an endless series of twisting corridors. She had been blindfolded, but even without the covering over her eyes she was certain she would never have been able to remember the way through the convoluted passages. Eventually, the blindfold had been ripped from her eyes and she had been thrust into the bright sunlight that gleamed on the snowy peaks of the Heights of Variance.

Without a creet.

Parts of the trail looked familiar, and Kalena assumed she had been left within a day's walk of the valley. At least she hoped it was a day's walk. She had been given her cloak and nothing else, not even a small tube of firegel. If she was forced to spend the night on the trail she would be lucky not to freeze to death.

She consoled herself with the thought that her captors did not want her to die just yet. Therefore, she must be close enough to the valley to reach it by sundown.

Thoughts of Ridge waiting in darkness and the insanity she

had seen in Griss' eyes kept her moving steadily throughout the day. The sound of water caught her attention at one point. Surely she had noticed that small waterfall on the first two trips along the trail. If she remembered correctly, it had been fairly close to the section of the pass that had been blocked by the shimmering veil.

But the veil did not come conveniently into sight around the next bend. Kalena kept going. Her feet were tired and her legs ached from the endless climb. She didn't bother to stop for lunch. No one had thought to give her any food to take with her. Presumably, that was another indication that she was reasonably near her destination. She could have used the food, she thought dismally. Her energy sources were failing rapidly. Probably as a result of all the emotional trauma she had been through as much as the actual physical exertion. She was getting very cold. The exercise and the cloak had kept her reasonably warm earlier in the day, but they were both becoming less efficient as she tired.

She had her head down and was leaning into the climb, concentrating on putting one foot in front of the other, when she rounded one last bend shortly before sundown and found herself confronting the shimmering veil of white.

Kalena halted abruptly, swaying a little with exhaustion as she examined the barrier. It looked the same as it had yesterday. Was it only yesterday she and Ridge had left the valley? For the first time she realized she was uncertain of just how much time had passed in the caves of the Cult of the Eclipse.

Frowning a little, she stepped through the gleaming veil, experiencing the now familiar brief, pleasant sensation, and then she was on the other side. The valley stretched below, as green and beautiful as she remembered it. Kalena drew a deep sigh of relief and started down the trail.

Her return to the valley was noticed as soon as she began to walk along one of the paths between the extensive gardens. Women who had been working in the fields dropped their tools and came toward her, converging from all directions. Arona was one of the first to meet her. Her eyes were wide and anxious as she examined Kalena's weary face.

"Valica was right. The time is at hand, isn't it?" the Healer asked worriedly. "You have come for the Key."

"I'll bet Valica is right a great deal of the time, isn't she?" Kalena smiled bleakly. "I should have known."

Valica was already making her way through the throng of women, her aristocratic features set in lines of deep concern. "Are you all right, Kalena?"

"I think so. Just a little tired. I've been walking since dawn. Tell me, how long ago did Ridge and I leave?"

Valica looked startled. "Three days."

"One whole day," Kalena said bemusedly. "We lost one whole day in that cave before we awoke."

"What cave?" Valica took her arm, signalling for the others to step aside. "Where is your husband? Kalena, what has happened?"

"What you said would happen, Valica. I have a need for the Light Key. Ridge will die if I don't take it back with me to the caves."

"What are these caves you keep talking about?" Arona demanded, hurrying alongside as Kalena was guided to a nearby cottage.

"I'm not sure where they are, although one of the entrances to them is within a day's walk of here. They are inhabited by a really nasty crowd of males. Ever heard of a group called the Cult of the Eclipse?"

Valica's breath hissed sharply between her teeth. "They are only a legend!"

"I guess they're as much a legend as the Keys. They seemed very real to me. Too real."

"It is all as bad as we here in the valley had feared. Come," Valica said with authority, "you must eat and rest. We can talk later."

"I haven't got a lot of time, Valica. I must return with the Key as soon as possible."

"We will discuss this after you have eaten."

There was no disagreeing with Valica's tone of voice, and in truth Kalena didn't feel much like arguing, anyway. She was tired and hungry and knew she couldn't walk back down the trail at night. When she was urged into a small cottage and told to sit down she did so with a great deal of gratitude.

Hot, comforting food was brought at once, and for the first time since she was a young child, Kalena found herself being served by someone other than a paid servant. It made her feel a little awkward, but nothing got in the way of her need to fill her empty stomach.

Valica, Arona and a handful of others sat around her, watching anxiously as she consumed the meal. Between bites of food, Kalena told them everything that had happened since she and Ridge had left the valley. When she finished, Valica was silent. Arona spoke first. She was clearly agitated, her expression haunted with concern.

"You would go back to the caves with the Light Key for the sake of this man, Ridge? That's foolish, Kalena. He is a man and he has been captured by men. Let him work out his own destiny. You are safe here in the valley. You must stay here."

Kalena just looked at her, helpless to explain. "He is my husband," she finally said. "His destiny is my destiny. Valica once said there are always choices. I have made mine. I will share my future with Ridge." She knew that probably wasn't sufficient justification in Arona's eyes for what she intended to do. But Kalena was too exhausted to try and explain the often uneasy bonds the marriage had established between her and Ridge, let alone the demands of honor and duty involved. In that moment Kalena wasn't sure she could have explained them to herself, much less anyone else. She only knew she could not hide in the warmth of the valley while Ridge lay awaiting his fate in the cold caverns of the cult. "He is the other half of myself. My opposite on the Spectrum. Together we form a whole, Arona. Do you understand?"

"No," Arona snapped, "I don't understand. He is a male. You don't need him."

Valica raised her hand, quietly demanding attention. "There is no point in argument. Kalena must go back with the Key. She has no choice. We have known this time was coming and now it is upon us. There is no way to avoid the confrontation of the Keys. These events were set in motion eons ago and cannot be halted."

"But all the legends state that the Keys must not be brought together!" one of the other women protested.

Valica shook her head. "No, the legends state that it is very dangerous to bring them together, not that such an event must not happen at all. The ancient manuscripts claim that certain people may control the Keys. Bestina was convinced and I am equally sure that Kalena is a woman who can handle the Light Key. Perhaps this man Ridge is the one meant to handle the Dark Key."

"What will happen if we don't allow Kalena to return to the caves with the Light Key?" Arona challenged.

Valica looked at her sadly. "Then the Darkness that has been growing gradually around us will continue to grow until it begins to reach beyond the mountains. Soon it will touch the small villages and towns of our land. Ultimately, it will have to be stopped. Better to do it now, before it has gained too much strength. Balance must be reestablished or there will be worse to come in the future."

All the women were silent then. Further argument was out of the question and they all knew it. Kalena ran a hand through her thick, windblown curls, sweeping back some of the hair that had fallen forward. She felt obliged to be honest about the whole business that lay before her.

"I think I should tell you, Valica, that I didn't come here to save your mountains, the land beyond or even a village or two. Surely I would know if I had been fated for that kind of destiny. I'm quite sure I'm not the one you've been waiting for all these years. I hate to say it, but I'm afraid there's been some sort of mistake. But if I can handle the Key, I will take it back with me to the caves because that seems to be the only way I can free Ridge."

Valica's expression was wise and gentle. "Your reasons are not important, Kalena. The fact that you are here is all that matters."

She got to her feet. "But right now you need rest. We will leave you for a few hours. Use the time to renew your strength. You will need it."

The other women rose to follow Valica out of the cottage. Kalena watched them go, wanting to argue that she should do whatever had to be done as soon as possible. But she kept quiet, knowing Valica was right. Kalena could feel the exhaustion deep in her bones. Trying to make her way back to the caves in the dark would be too dangerous. She might as well rest until dawn.

It seemed that the cottage door had no sooner closed on the last of the women than Kalena found herself too drowsy even to think about what lay ahead of her. She stretched out on the pallet without bothering to undress. Closing her eyes, she wondered vaguely if there might have been some Healer's sleeping potion in the food. Sleep came quickly, bringing no dreams.

Kalena awoke shortly before dawn, deeply refreshed. She lay still for a moment, gazing at the darkened sky outside the window. For some reason, one of Olara's teachings drifted through her mind.

All darkness, whether that of night or that of the black mist used by the Cult of the Eclipse, belonged to the shadowed end of the Spectrum. Darkness in and of itself was neither good nor bad; it was simply at the opposite end of the Spectrum from that which was light. But extremes at either end of the Spectrum became dangerous. They needed to be balanced. It was the function of light to balance dark, just as it was the role of the feminine to balance the masculine.

Kalena understood that actions, elements or people which originated at the farthest ends of the Spectrum were potentially more dangerous than those that came from some point in the middle because it took more power to balance them. It would take a great deal to counter the black mist, for example. The energy released in doing so could be very dangerous.

Kalena didn't want to contemplate how much energy might be discharged in any attempt to force the Dark Key and the Light Key together.

She sat up on the edge of the pallet just as a knock sounded on the cottage door.

"You are welcome," she called softly.

The door opened to reveal Arona standing on the threshold. She carried a lamp in her right hand. "I wish you good morning, my friend."

Kalena smiled. "Thank you. You didn't by any chance bring some food, did you? I seem to be ravenous this morning."

Arona's beautiful dark eyes were full of regret. She came forward, set down the lamp and seated herself on the pallet beside Kalena. "I'm sorry, Kalena. Valica says you are not to eat until later. There are things that must be done first."

Kalena yawned and stretched her arms high over her head. She felt good this morning, strong and renewed and full of life. "What things?"

"The Key . . ."

"Ah, yes, the Key. When do I get it?"

"You must go into the ice and retrieve it yourself, Kalena. None of us can touch it."

"Ice? So it is hidden in ice just as the legends say. Does that mean that the Dark Key is hidden in fire?"

Arona dismissed Kalena's curiosity. "Probably. The damn legends seem to have been more or less accurate so far. Pay attention, Kalena, please. I don't think you should do this. The Keys are dangerous. Everyone knows that. If you don't feel you are the one to handle the Light Key, then you may be right, in spite of what Valica says. You shouldn't take the risk. No man is worth it."

Kalena thought for a moment, trying to come up with a reason Arona could accept. "There is more to this than a man's life, Arona. There is a matter of honor involved."

"Honor!"

Kalena drew up her knees and rested her chin on folded arms. "I'm afraid so. I am a married woman, Arona. A married woman does not desert her husband unless the alliance between them has been officially ended. I have been somewhat lax in matters of duty lately," Kalena went on with a sigh. "I wonder if Aunt Olara knows yet just how poorly I've done."

"Kalena, you have a right to think of yourself!"

"I know. I've been telling myself that for a long time." She smiled wryly at the other woman. "I know what you're thinking, Arona. I understand what you're trying to say. But you must try to comprehend what it's like to grow up as a member of a Great House. You can never really escape the obligations imposed on you. The honor of the House must always be upheld. From the cradle onward, children are taught that they hold the House honor in their hands. They must protect it. The burden is on the women of the House as well as the men. Under normal circumstances, a woman's obligations are carried out in traditional ways. She is obedient to her father when she is living under his roof and faithful to her husband when she marries. As a wife she respects her House lord's authority, bears his children and is responsible for instructing them in the ways of honor and responsibility. Usually it's all very simple and straightforward, if rather dull."

"Kalena, you are not bound by the traditional obligations. You are the last of your House," Arona argued.

"Yes, well, I'm afraid all that means is that my obligations were a little untraditional. They didn't just fade away into thin air. Since the summer of my twelfth year, Arona, I have known exactly what was required of me. I failed in my duty. Because of that failure I find myself married and surrounded by a whole new set of responsibilities. I'd prefer not to fail my responsibilities a second time. It is hard enough to live with the knowledge that I failed once. I am bound to Ridge. I cannot abandon him."

"Even if what you are going to do will get you killed?"

"If I don't succeed in freeing him, then I myself will never be free. Think about it, Arona, for you are no freer than I. You would die to protect this valley and your friends here, would you not?"

Arona blinked once in abrupt understanding. "Of course."

"You see? There is precious little freedom once the basic choice has been made. I'm beginning to think that freedom isn't the important issue. The crucial thing is that we are all given some degree of choice. After we have made our decisions, we must live with them." Kalena grimaced and decided to change the subject. "Are you sure I can't have something to eat? I really am very hungry."

"Oh, Kalena, I wish I could bring you a meal, but . . ." Arona's anxious voice trailed off as Kalena grinned at her.

"But you can't because you have a sense of honor and duty, too, Arona. You owe yours to the women of this valley and especially the one you have chosen to lead you. Valica says I don't eat this morning so you can't possibly bring me any food. Sometimes life is very simple and straightforward."

Reluctantly Arona smiled. "Sometimes it is. I imagine it gets more complicated when there is no longer a clear-cut knowledge of duty to guide us."

The silence that fell between the two women was broken by another knock on the door. When Kalena called a welcome, Valica appeared on the threshold. She glanced at Arona, her eyes softening slightly in unspoken understanding and then she turned to Kalena.

"You are ready?"

Respectfully, Kalena stood up. "As ready as I will ever be."

Valica came into the room and closed the door behind her. "In a little while we will go to where the Key is hidden, but first we will burn some Sand." She removed the delicate brazier from her belt and held it out to Kalena.

Kalena stared at the object in surprise. "But I am not a Healer."

"Only because you lack training. As I told you, I believe you have the Talent. We will find out soon enough when you burn the Sand."

Confused, Kalena took the small brazier from Valica's hand. "But why? What will this prove?"

The older woman raised an eyebrow in mild amusement and lowered herself to sit cross-legged on a pillow near the small table. She waved Kalena to a seat beside her. "It is not meant to prove anything, only to give you some confidence and understanding."

Kalena sat down slowly, staring at the brazier and remembering all the times she had longed to test herself with the Sand. "My aunt told me she was certain I didn't have the Talent."

"Olara lied to you because she had other goals for you. It is very difficult to turn a young girl with the Talent into an assassin. She could not risk exposing you to the Sand. If you had been allowed to develop your Talent, you would have become a very poor instrument of revenge."

Kalena touched the brazier, captivated by the fine workmanship of the device. "I allowed her to keep me from trying the Sand, but I disobeyed her on another matter. I slept with my husband. Afterward, I knew at once that I had been weakened in some way. I hope that weakness will not affect what I must do now."

"You were not weakened by the act of sharing the pallet with the Fire Whip. The bond you established with Ridge was one involved with life. It countered the bond of death Olara had placed on you. It made you stronger, not weaker. Burn the Sand, Kalena. You will see just how strong this new bond has become."

Kalena hesitated, uncertain for the first time since she had awakened that morning. "I'm afraid," she heard herself whisper.

"There is nothing to fear, Kalena. Not yet, at any rate." Valica took a small, embroidered pouch from her belt, untied the thong that held it closed and handed it to Kalena.

Kalena's fingers shook slightly as she accepted the pouch. In spite of what her aunt had told her, she had always been drawn toward the Sand, had always been very curious about it. She remembered the fierce resentment she had experienced over not knowing exactly what to do the night the woman in the inn had given birth. Now, at last, she was about to find out for certain if she did, indeed, possess some measure of raw Talent.

"Only a pinch," Valica instructed softly. "Too much of the Sand at once can be dangerous. Ignite the firegel in the brazier and then throw just a bit of Sand into it. When the smoke rises, inhale it and look into yourself. I cannot explain the process more clearly. It will explain itself."

Carefully, Kalena set the brazier on the low table, moved the tiny lever that let the catalyst into the gel and waited for the glow of heat. When the tiny pool of firegel flared with light and warmth, Kalena took a pinch of the white Sand and cautiously dropped it into the brazier. At once a tiny plume of white smoke appeared.

"Now," Valica murmured.

Kalena leaned forward and took a deep breath. The smoke stung her nostrils the way hot spices sting the tongue. She closed her eyes and inhaled again.

"Enough." Valica touched Kalena's shoulder and pulled her away from the white smoke. "Only a very little is required. Remember what I said. Too much can be dangerous, not only to you but to those around you." She reached out and snapped the cover over the tiny brazier. The firegel died and the smoke disappeared.

Kalena sat perfectly still, kept her eyes closed and waited. She wished she knew exactly what it was she waited for. Perhaps there would be a light-headed sensation or maybe she would feel unusually alert. The truth was, only a trained Healer knew what to expect. If she had no real Talent after all, Kalena knew she would feel nothing.

"Yourself, Kalena. You are the patient. You must look into yourself."

Valica's voice seemed to come from a great distance. Kalena obeyed, turning her attention inward, trying to focus on the last daughter of the House of the Ice Harvest.

There was a timeless moment during which Kalena felt as though she were standing on one side of a curtain. Mentally she put out a hand to sweep the veil aside. The barrier seemed to disintegrate even as Kalena touched it, and she saw what had been hidden.

Diagnosing this patient was no trick at all. Nor did she need any Healer's training to evaluate what she saw. Kalena of the House of the Ice Harvest, temporary trade wife to a man who could claim no House or respectable heritage, was pregnant.

Pregnant. The raw energy of a new life burned within her. A life she had created with Ridge, the Fire Whip.

The shock of it brought Kalena out of her small trance as

abruptly as if she had been doused with ice water. Her lashes lifted quickly and she found herself gazing directly into Valica's understanding eyes.

"I'm pregnant." The stark words hung in the air.

"I thought it might be so." Valica nodded in quiet satisfaction.

"But how could it have happened? There was only one night when I failed to take the selite powder."

"One night is all that is required, as a great many women have discovered to their everlasting amazement." Amusement tinged Valica's words as she carefully resealed the Sand pouch. "Don't chide yourself. I think it was meant to happen."

Bewildered, Kalcna glanced at the unlit brazier. "But why?"

"Because you are about to take up the Light Key. And even though you are the one born with the heritage and the talent to do so, it will not be an easy task. You must be as strong as it is possible for a woman to be." Valica touched her hand. "Kalena, you must know that right now you are at the height of a woman's power. You hold the future within you. It is a direct counterpoint to the chaos and darkness that marks the opposite end of the Spectrum. It is time to take the Key from its hiding place."

Kalena nodded once, accepting, even welcoming the inevitable. She knew herself ready in a way she couldn't explain. "It is time."

In silence Valica led the way out of the cottage. The first, faint gray of dawn was just beginning to touch the peaks that guarded the valley. Kalena followed the older woman unquestioningly. Arona fell into step behind her, and as the three of them made their way through the gardens and rich, planted fields, other women joined the silent procession.

Valica took a path that climbed out of the valley into the biting chill of the coming dawn. The trail was different than the one Kalena and Ridge had followed in and out of the valley. This path was steep, rising swiftly into snow and ice. The women climbed for over an hour, Valica in the lead. No one spoke.

When Valica at last came to a halt, the gray of dawn was giving way to the first tinge of color. The older woman stood with her cloak wrapped around her and nodded toward an opening in the ice.

"The ancient manuscripts say the Key is hidden in there, Kalena. No one I know has ever been inside the ice cave. I cannot tell you what you will find, only that the time has come to discover it. Go and bring it forth. We will wait for you."

Kalena hesitated, waiting for some last words of wisdom or guidance. None were forthcoming, and she knew that she was on her own. Valica and the others could not help her. Slowly, she turned and walked toward the yawning entrance carved of ice.

The white tunnel was not pitch dark. As the sky overhead continued to lighten, so did the interior of the ice cave. Light filtered dimly through the ice, providing a shadowed path. Kalena followed that path, stepping carefully on the icy floor. As long as she was careful she did not feel in any real danger of slipping. The floor of the cave seemed to have been paved with small blocks of ice. The tiny ridges between the blocks gave her feet a purchase.

A few meters inside the cave the tunnel curved. When Kalena rounded the bend she found herself in a large white cavern. The interior was still shadowed, but it lightened steadily as dawn came to the mountains. The promise of light was everywhere in the ice chamber. It was reflected in the elaborately carved formations of frozen crystals that hung from the ceiling. It danced faintly on the white floor and gleamed from the surface of the high table that stood in the middle of the room. It hinted at a dazzle that could blind. It was energy and power and life waiting to be released.

Waiting for her touch, Kalena thought in sudden realization. She would release it and give it focus. It was her destiny. The knowledge went through her with brilliant clarity, touching all her senses.

Kalena's gaze fell on the table and she went toward it slowly. It was carved out of a single block of opaque ice that had been hewn into a strong, powerful design. It didn't rest on legs, but was solid from the floor to the surface. Kalena came to a halt in front of it and found herself looking down into a pool of clear ice that filled the interior of the structure. At the bottom of the ice rested a case made of silvery white metal.

Kalena knew beyond any doubt that for untold generations nothing had penetrated the clear ice in which the case was imbedded. How long it had lain in this cave was anyone's guess. The Healers had protected it well, although Kalena was not sure the case had ever really needed much protection. There was something forbidding about the simple case frozen in ice. If her need had not been so great, if her inner knowledge had not blossomed forth with such fierce certainty, she could never have brought herself to even attempt to retrieve it.

She examined the surface of the ice, wondering what it would take to melt it. Perhaps she would need to go back outside and ask Valica for a pot of firegel.

Kalena was tentatively considering that action when she lightly put her gloved hand on the ice. It trembled slightly beneath her fingertips, startling her. Hastily she removed her hand. A faint indentation had been left where she had touched the clear, crystal hard surface.

Cautiously, Kalena removed her glove and tensed herself. Then, very slowly, she let her bare hand rest on the ice.

The frozen liquid quivered again, sending a shudder through Kalena as well as the ice. She nearly jerked her hand away as the jolt went through her whole body. But it was too late. The pool of ice trembled, fractured and splintered beneath the touch of her warm palm. She felt nothing more than a slight coolness that was far from the burning cold of solid ice. Even as she stared down into the crystal clear pool, it dissolved completely. Her hand was immersed in transparent water.

"By the Stones!" Kalena's gasp of amazement echoed softly in the cave as she yanked her hand out of the water. The liquid should have been icy cold, but it was only pleasantly cool, just as the ice had been. She wondered if it was not really water at all, but some other clear medium used to shield the silvery case.

Kalena gazed down into the liquid, examining the object at the bottom of the pool. It was only an arm's length away. All she had to do was roll up the sleeves of her cloak and tunic, reach into the water or whatever it was and remove the case. Simple.

Perhaps a little too simple.

Kalena paused to gaze speculatively around the ice chamber, but she saw nothing that would aid her in removing the casket. Reluctantly, she pushed up the sleeve of her cloak and then rolled back the long sleeve of her tunic. Her bare arm felt the cold of the chamber until she immersed it cautiously into the crystal liquid.

A few seconds later her fingers closed around the metal casket. Kalena waited for the world to crumble around her, but nothing happened. She took a deep breath and pulled the case out of the water with a quick movement.

A sweeping sense of power washed over her. It was unlike anything she had ever known. Life, energy, the future was hers to command.

Excitement sang in her blood. *The Key was hers.* She was indeed the one meant to wield it. She no longer felt any doubt. It was part of her, an extension of herself. It belonged to her in a way that was impossible to describe. She was the one meant to command the Light Key.

Dazed with the heady, dazzling thrill, Kalena tried to examine the case she held.

It was obvious the object in her hand was very, very old. As old as the legends of the Dawn Lords. Kalena looked at it wonderingly. The case was about three quarters of a meter long and not particularly heavy. It was thin and chased with an elaborate pattern that might have been the characters of an alphabet. If so, it represented a language as old as the case itself, certainly no modern one. When Kalena looked at the individual marks very carefully she thought one or two seemed oddly similar to the common alphabet of the Northern Continent, but she couldn't really identify any of the curving, angled shapes.

She realized as she stood staring at the casket that she was merely assuming she held the Light Key. Perhaps this wasn't the object of her quest. The only way to know for certain was to open the case.

Kalena wondered just how she would know the Light Key if she saw it. Would it be shaped like the tiny key she wore at her throat? Like a door key? The key to a jewel box? Her fingers fumbled eagerly with the silvery case, seeking a way to open it. What a devastating joke if she had come this far only to discover she couldn't open the box in which the Key was held.

Kalena stood with the casket in one hand, prying at it with questing fingertips. She was quickly becoming impatient. She had come this far, and she would not abandon the task. She had already failed in her duty to her House; she would not fail in this. Ridge was waiting. Her future was waiting.

The casket lid came open as if her thoughts alone had breached some hidden lock.

At least some of her questions were answered immediately. The Light Key was identifiable on sight. It was also unlike any key Kalena had ever seen.

Kalena looked into the case and found herself looking into liquid white fire. The writhing flames were pure white, dazzling to the eye as they burned in an outline that was wedge shaped. Kalena knew instinctively that the Key had been burning inside its case since the Dawn Lords had locked their dangerous treasure in ice.

Now she had to find a way to take the Key of white flames in her bare hand and use it. But Kalena had no real doubt that when the moment arrived she would be able to handle the Key.

She had been born to master it.

FIFTEEN

Ridge stood in a vast chamber of black glass and gazed into a pit of fire that burned in the center of the glass floor. The flames fascinated him. They were the exact color of his sintar when his fury made it glow.

He lifted his gaze and looked into the eyes of the hooded man who stood on the other side of the fire pit. Griss was wearing Ridge's sintar on his belt beneath his cloak. A half circle of deadly silent men dressed in black, hooded cloaks stood behind Griss.

The black glass caught the light of the angry, leaping flames that burned in the center of the chamber and reflected back the fire in a thousand mirrored images. If it had not been for the countless reflections, the chamber would have been almost completely dark. The only other light in the room were the firegel lamps that had been left to mark the entrances. Those passageways were sealed now with the same glass that lined the rest of the room. Without the lamps it would have been impossible to tell where the hidden doorways were. The black glass was everywhere. It lined the cavern ceiling, the curving walls and formed the floor beneath Ridge's feet.

The cloaked men who had brought Ridge to this chamber had unbound him, but his freedom was useless under the circumstances. The ranks of cult members surrounded him, and he would need time to figure out how to open the sealed glass doors. The cowled men would be upon him before he could even begin to work on that problem.

He had not been given anything to eat for what he estimated must be more than a day. He couldn't be sure of the time, but after he had slept for a while, his internal sense of time seemed to indicate that at least a day had passed.

He wondered if Kalena was safe in the valley. He could only hope that the Healers would keep her there when they learned her plan. Ridge didn't try to fool himself too much. He knew Kalena would not obey his last instructions. She would make every effort to return with the Light Key.

Kalena of the House of the Ice Harvest was his wife, bound to him by her own vows as well as the sensual ties Ridge had tried to impose. But there was more involved. Her destiny was entwined with his own. They were each other's future. She would try to return for him or die in the attempt.

Ridge cursed himself for having brought Kalena to the heart of danger, and then, abruptly, he ceased the silent chastisement. The force of his own fury was a potent weapon, not to be wasted on fruitless, self-directed anger. He would channel it against those who held him captive.

Most especially he would focus it on the bastard who had labeled Kalena a whore.

Ridge's unbound hands clenched briefly at his sides, his fingers automatically craving the handle of the sintar. Deliberately, he forced himself to relax. He was unaware of the brutal effects of the firelight on his features. He only knew he was controlling an anger that was threatening to burn higher than it had ever burned in the past. The struggle to leash that fury held him almost immobile.

"What would you have me do?" he demanded in a harsh whisper of the one called Griss.

"Reach into the fire and withdraw the case that holds the Dark Key. It is yours, Fire Whip. You alone can control it."

"But you want to control it, don't you, Griss? You and the others who wear the black glass. Do you think you can do it after I've pulled it out of the fire for you? You're a pack of idiots if you believe that."

"Do as you are told," Griss ordered.

"Why should I bother?"

"Because the woman is already on her way back from the valley of the Healers with the Light Key. The only weapon you will have with which to try to protect her and yourself is the Dark Key." Griss' voice was oily with mockery. "And you do want to protect her, don't you, Fire Whip? At least you think you do. You'll discover that your true feelings are much different when you actually hold the Dark Key in your hand. But in the meantime, your motives for pulling the Key out of the fire are not important to us. You want a weapon, any weapon. You crave a weapon. It is your nature to be armed. Very well, we offer you a weapon unlike any other you have ever held. It's yours if you have the courage to take hold of it."

"I don't see any weapon in the flames."

"Look close, Fire Whip. It's there. It's been there since the Dawn Lords hid it in the pit of fire."

"All these centuries it's been here in the same mountains as the Light Key?" Ridge was stunned by the information.

"It was buried deep, Fire Whip, sealed in fire at the bottom of a crevasse that appeared to have no ending. But our master knew the black opening had to have a floor. It took time to locate it using the old books. And after the so-called bottomless crevasse was found it required years of effort to retrieve the case that held the Key. When it was hauled to the surface here in this cavern it was discovered that the Key was still encased in fire. It sits in the center of those flames and no one can pry it out. The fire which protects it is not natural."

"How many men died retrieving this thing, Griss?"

"The numbers are not important. Recently, when we ran short of men to carry on the task, we took those we needed from the neighboring villages. The goal was achieved."

"Not quite. You still can't figure a way to lift the Key out of the flames, right?"

"We have found a way, Fire Whip. You are the tool that we will use. Once the Dark Key has overcome the Light Key, the power in it will be drained for a time. Perhaps for years. During that time my master will be able to study it. He will learn to control it himself. By the time the Key is fully charged again, he will be its master."

"What happens if I choose to let it stay in the flames?" Ridge asked, knowing the answer already.

"You will die. And as soon as the woman arrives with the Key she will die, too."

"If I manage to hold the Dark Key, what will prevent me from using it on you first?"

"It cannot be wielded like a sintar, fool. It will react to the presence of the Light Key and must be used against it before it can be used for anything else." Griss' eyes glittered in the shadow of his hood. "But when your task is accomplished you will hold a potent weapon, Fire Whip. You are a man who has bought your own life and the lives of others with weapons in the past. You will not turn down the chance to do so again, no matter how great the risk. It is not your nature to do nothing in a critical situation. You will always choose to act, even if the act itself is futile. You will fight. even if there is no hope of winning. *It is your nature.*"

Ridge watched him in savage wonder. "What makes you think you know me so well?"

"We have made a study of you, Fire Whip. Isn't it logical we would study a tool we wished to employ? My master knows your abilities well."

A tool, Ridge thought. Very well. The Cult of the Eclipse would learn this tool had a cutting edge.

He looked deep into the pit of fire that burned at his feet.

There was little heat being generated, considering the violence of the blaze. He was beginning to think that he was the only one in the room who found the warmth from the fire mild, however. The others kept their distance from the fire pit, and Ridge was sure the flames radiated more heat than they could bear.

He took a step closer, the toe of his boot at the very edge of the pit. It looked as though the cult members had managed to drag the circle of fire this far and could get it no farther. The Stones only knew what it had cost them to get it to this point. They had left it alone in the center of the cavern and built the black glass walls around it. The bowl of fire was not deep, perhaps only an arm's length from the peaks of the flames to the molten coals at the bottom. Ridge couldn't begin to guess what had fed the blaze all these centuries, yet some instinct told him it had been burning like this since the Dawn Lords had put it at the bottom of the crevasse.

Deep in the core of the fire lay an object. He could see it now that he was so close. It was a case of some sort made of what looked like black metal. He knew that what he wanted lay inside that case.

A weapon. He needed a blade to defend his woman when she walked back into the hands of the Cult of the Eclipse. The Key was the only weapon he was going to get.

Ridge went down on one knee beside the glowing pit of flame. The heat should have scorched him. He was too close. Yet the warmth was only moderate. It reminded him of the mild heat generated by the sintar when it glowed red in his palm. Even when the sintar was at its hottest, it could still be held in his bare hand. Ridge had long ago decided that the odd effect of his fury on the steel of Countervail was useful only as a psychological weapon. Others saw it and feared it far more than they would a blade of plain steel. Only Ridge seemed to understand that the sintar remained only a blade, albeit a warm one, when it ignited in his hand. It was the fury that drove him at such moments which needed to be feared.

"Take the Key from the flames, Fire Whip. It is your destiny. Your only hope."

Ridge ignored Griss' command. He intended to try for the black case, but he would do so in his own way. Cautiously, he moved his fingers toward the flames. Nothing happened. The strange lack of heat persisted. It was as though he was touched by sunlight; the fire was warm, but not dangerously so.

Ridge edged closer and put his entire hand into the flickering light.

He nearly lost his balance as a wave of pulse pounding fire shot through his blood. A promise of savagely satisfying ecstasy was written in the flames. He could see it, feel it. In a moment he would hold it in his hand.

There was still only a moderate warmth in the flames themselves. They did not burn even though he was on fire inside. Ridge unbuttoned his cuff and rolled up the sleeve of his shirt. Nothing could stop him now. Slowly, he moved his trembling fingers toward the black case. A moment passed as he leaned closer still, and then his hand closed around the black metal box. The excitement that flowed through him in that moment was almost unbearable.

Yet he knew that he had touched the edges of such excitement before. He couldn't seem to think clearly enough in that moment to remember just where or when, but he was certain he had felt this raging longing and satisfaction in some other context. For an instant he tried to focus and remember, but the fleeting thought escaped him.

Ah, well, he decided, it was not important. What was important was another kind of knowledge. This knowledge was not fleeting or vague. It was as strong and fierce and certain as the flames.

The Dark Key was his to control. It was of fire and he was of fire.

As soon as he touched the box, Ridge knew that whatever lay inside was his to master. Ripples of energy washed through him, emphasizing the fact. Never had he felt anything close to this kind of power. He pulled the case from the pit of fire with a strong, steady motion of his arm. The Key was his. He rose to his feet, holding his prize in both hands.

There was a murmur of low voices and the sound of hissing as the room full of cult members saw what he had done. Ridge ignored them. The cult was unimportant now. A stupid, meaningless group of men who had tried to play games with power they couldn't possibly comprehend.

Ridge studied the case in his hands, eager to learn everything he could about it. It was flat and wedge shaped. The black metal had been indented with a series of odd designs. The designs vaguely reminded him of certain figures in the alphabet, but he could make no sense of the similarity.

The fire continued to burn at his feet, but Ridge was no longer aware of it, just as he was unaware of Griss and the others. His full attention was on the casket in his hands. It was his. He alone had pulled it from its hiding place, and he alone could grasp what lay inside. He stared at the metal, looking for a way to open the case.

"Not yet, Fire Whip."

Ridge's head snapped up, his eyes pinning Griss, who had taken a step forward. "Stay away from me."

"We have no wish to harm you," Griss said soothingly. "You and the Key will become one, a formidable weapon for us. The last thing we will do now is cause you injury. But you must rest. Pulling the Key from the fire required more energy than you realize. We will take you back to the chamber you've been using. You will eat and then sleep. When you awaken the woman will have returned. Then it will be time for you to learn the full extent of your power, Fire Whip. And as you learn the truth, so shall we. Come. You must rest."

Ridge considered the situation. He did not feel tired at all. Just the opposite, in fact. There was a strong pulse of energy moving through his body. It was not unlike the sensation he had when he took Kalena in his arms. Even as he made the analogy in his mind, Ridge realized that at least part of his feeling of strength was sexual in origin. If Kalena were here now he would lay her down beside the fire, part her soft thighs and sheath himself in her silky warmth.

It was then he realized where and when he had tasted the kind of longing and satisfaction he felt when he grasped the case that held the Dark Key. It had happened during those moments when he plunged into Kalena and was swept into the vortex of the desire he felt for her.

For a few seconds the image was so strong in his mind that Ridge forgot everything else in the chamber except the black case in his hands. The metal object he held seemed to vibrate in tune with the energy he felt racing through his body. He could subdue Kalena with the force of his lust. She would learn at last that she was his, that she had always been his. The claim he would put on her would be total and her surrender would be complete. She was only a woman, his to use. He could sate himself time after time with her, endlessly. *She was a woman.* Soft, weak, at his mercy. His woman.

"Rest, Fire Whip. Come with us. You need rest."

Ridge shook his head a little, frowning as he tried to clear the lustful images that were clamoring inside his brain. He didn't need rest but he did need solitude. He had to discover the precise nature of what he had pulled from the flames.

"Don't try to touch me," he said quietly to Griss and the others.

"We won't touch you."

Ridge went toward them warily, circling the bowl of fire that continued to burn as strongly as ever in the center of the black glass chamber. None of the cowled men tried to rebind his arms. Instead, they fell into a ragged circle around him, maintaining a respectful distance as they led Ridge from the chamber. When the group reached the room where Ridge had been held, they halted, waiting almost politely for him to willingly step inside.

Ridge hesitated again, but knew he could do nothing yet with the Key. He had to examine it and learn to handle it. He needed time and privacy. Without a backward glance he walked into the rocky cell. The barred gate clanged shut behind him, but he paid no attention. He knew now that the others could not touch him as long as he held the metal case.

Fading footsteps in the corridor outside the gate marked the sound of the retreating cult members. Ridge didn't turn around, but he could still sense Griss' presence.

"It won't be long now, Fire Whip." There was an unnatural anticipation in Griss' voice. "You were found and brought here for only one purpose and soon you will fulfill it."

"What happens after that?" Ridge asked almost idly. He was still staring at the black metal case.

"The Cult of the Eclipse will finally take possession of its rightful heritage. We are the ones who have kept the old knowledge alive. We are the ones who recognize the potential of the powerful tools the Dawn Lords buried so long ago. We are the ones who have studied the past so that we may control the future."

"I wouldn't count on it, Griss. Something tells me you're more of a follower than a leader."

"Fool. You will see. Your control over the Key will be very short-lived. In the end you will understand that you are only a tool."

"Like you, Griss? A tool for someone who thinks he can eventually control the key? Where is this master of yours? The one who uses you to do his bidding? I would meet with him. Let him see if he can take the Key from me. Fetch him for me, Griss. Let me speak with the one who's in charge around here."

"When the power of the Keys claims you and the woman you'll finally understand just who is in control." Griss flung himself away from the grating and disappeared down the corridor.

For a long while after the others were gone Ridge remained where he was, examining the black case in the lamplight. Then the need to know what lay inside overcame him.

Sitting cross-legged on the hard stone floor, Ridge placed the case in front of him and began looking in earnest for a way to open it. His fingers moved lightly over the surface of the black metal, searching for a crack or an unusual indentation. When he found none he restrained his growing impatience and tried again.

He would open the case. It was his by right.

Even as the determined words formed in his head, the lid of the case sprang open. Ridge blinked at the suddenness of it, and then gazed unbelievingly at what lay inside. Somehow he had been expecting fire. He had an affinity for fire.

What he found was ice.

It was the coldest ice he had ever known, and it was deeply, intensely black. The black cold radiated up from the metal case as if it were a living force. The object in the case was shaped like a wedge or the tip of an arrow, but much broader. A narrow portion projected from the wedge and Ridge knew at once it was to be grasped. But how did anyone grasp something so incredibly cold? It would burn like fire. More than that, Ridge decided; it would kill.

But he knew beyond a doubt that he was meant to take hold of the Dark Key. When the time came, he would do so. Ridge realized he was shivering as he carefully closed the case. He didn't know if it was because of the bitter cold thing inside or purely the result of his own inner tension.

He left the case on the stone floor in front of him and sat waiting. Griss was wrong. He didn't need sleep. Ridge knew. Never had he felt so strong, so powerful or so alive. The driving force within him was a relentless source of unending energy. There was a fire in him. He burned like the steel of Countervail.

Before this night was over he would find a way to make the Dark Key burn, too. It was his destiny.

Kalena lost all track of time on her trip down the mountain trail. She moved swiftly, clutching the silvery metal box tightly to her as she made her way. There was a burning urgency in her, a sizzling energy that needed to be released, but which had to be controlled until the time was right to take up the Key.

Thoughts of Ridge alternated with thoughts of his seed that had taken root within her. She couldn't pin down her emotions on either subject, but she was vibrantly aware of the fact that they were connected. Every time she tried to sort out the ramifications of the situation, the sense of urgency took over. She must reach the caves before dark. Sunset was the proper time. Kalena wasn't sure how she knew this or exactly what she must do at sunset, but she was aware of its importance.

Something else had happened to her at sunset, she recalled at one point. That was the time of day she had married Ridge. The traditional time for a wedding ceremony. Her brow furrowed slightly at the memory and she tried to put it out of her mind. How could she have let a man put his lock and key around her throat?

Ridge was only a man, an incomplete creature seeking to control that which he needed in order to re-create himself. His usefulness to her was very limited. The fact that she was pregnant by him meant that she no longer needed him. But she *did* need him. How could that be? Her head spun with the disorienting whirl of thoughts.

He would take away her chance of freedom.

She did not want her freedom without him.

He would seek to control her.

She welcomed the conflict because it reinforced their bond of intimacy. There was a sensual excitement in a battle that could not be completely won or lost.

He had a temper that came from the Dark end of the Spectrum.

She had a talent for soothing the fury that burned in him.

He would use his sensual power over her to master her.

She wielded a similar power over him.

No matter how the argument went in her head it made very little practical difference. The Keys had both been freed. They sought each other now with increasing energy. She knew somehow that the one she held was already vibrating faintly in response to the one Ridge must have found. Kalena could feel the energy flowing from the case into her body. Soon she would be facing the Dark Key and the man who held it.

The black mist caught her by surprise when it swirled angrily around her as she turned a bend in the trail. Kalena halted, aware of the roiling cold that had lain in wait to trap her. Her awareness turned to scorn.

"Foolish men," she called, listening to the echo of her voice. "I have brought the Key with me, just as you ordered. I have no intention of trying to flee. I will be happy to show you the results of your stupid meddling. Call back the mist. It can't touch me now."

There was no response. The black fog continued to swirl around her, but it was clear it could not touch her. It could and did, however, blank out her view of mountains, sky and trail. In a few seconds she was encircled by the mist, although she was safe from its icy tendrils.

Slowly she moved forward. The mist ebbed and flowed around her, seeking to snarl her arms and legs in cold bonds. But Kalena was safe from it and she knew it. She kept walking straight ahead, although she could not see more than a couple paces in front of her.

She knew when she entered the caves. The darkness around her took on a different texture. The mist began to fade and Kalena saw figures moving toward her with lamps. They halted a discreet distance away and she realized that as long as she held the case, they could approach no closer. Kalena smiled the cool, aloof smile of a woman who knew she was safe from the touch of men.

"Idiots," she murmured, "you have no idea of what you have set free. You played with the tools of a power you don't begin to understand, and soon those tools will destroy you."

"Not so, woman." Griss held up his lamp so that she could see his austere face and glittering eyes. "You are the one who lacks intelligence and comprehension. But that is only to be expected. You are merely female. Come. Meet your opposite on the Spectrum. It is almost sunset and your groom awaits. The consummation of this marriage of fire and ice crystal will change the future of the world. Too bad you will not live to see it."

"Your threats are meaningless." Kalena walked forward obediently, amused when the hooded men fell back. "But I will come with you because there is something here that must be done."

There was a shuffling of booted feet along the corridor, and Kalena followed the cloaked figures. She was led through a bewildering array of cavern passages and she realized almost at once there was no need to blindfold her. She was lost by the tenth turning, but somehow, with the Key in her hand, she did not feel lost.

Just when she had begun to wonder if the trip would ever end, Kalena realized that the stone beneath her feet had changed to glass. Black glass.

The Key in her hand vibrated with energy.

She paused, watching as the men ahead of her fanned out into a vast chamber that was completely lined with dark glass. In the center of the room a fire burned, although no one was feeding the flames. Slowly, she moved into the chamber, aware that the case in her hand was pulsing with power.

"Here is where you will meet your fate, woman. Your husband, who is also destined to be your executioner, awaits." Griss waved her farther into the chamber with a mockingly dramatic sweep of his caped arm and then stepped back. "And you, foolish woman that you are, cannot even try to run from him."

Kalena looked across the expanse of the glass room and saw Ridge. He stood with his feet slightly spread apart, as though he were braced for combat. In his hands he held a black metal case.

"So you decided to return," he called softly across the fire.

"I had no choice."

"That much is true." He took a few paces forward so that the firelight glowed on his harshly carved features. The gold in his eyes was the color of the flames and just as dangerous.

Around them the members of the Cult of the Eclipse edged to the farthest walls of the chamber. Kalena sensed them retreat to what they thought was safety and wanted to laugh. There was no safety to be found in this chamber. Not now. A fierce, exultant energy washed through her.

"The Keys have been brought too close together," she told

Ridge. "The power has been loosed and is moving already. Can you feel it?"

"I feel it. Soon you will know just how weak and soft you really are, woman. You will learn the true meaning of surrender. How do you dare to challenge me with the Light Key? I will enfold you in darkness, take you and bind you completely to my will. And when it is done, the Light Key will be destroyed."

"No, Fire Whip, you cannot destroy either me or the Key I hold. You are only a man and that which you wield is darkness. It is the source of your lust and your fury and your pitiful masculine power. It cannot survive a direct confrontation with anything from the Light end of the Spectrum. It can only rage and swagger and try to dominate with no hope of doing so."

"Your female arrogance and pride are as false and foolish as your reasoning. You and all other women exist only to serve men. But you in particular exist to serve me. All that is feminine is meant to bow before all that is male. Just as the Light must ultimately surrender to the Dark, you must finally surrender to me."

"Stupid male. Don't you understand that the Dark exists only because of the Light? The Dark end of the Spectrum is cold and lifeless. Only the Light end can bring forth life out of the Dark."

But the Light is meaningless without the Dark. Each end of the Spectrum is defined in terms of the other end. One cannot exist without the other. To destroy one would be to destroy the other.

The words filtered through the haze of excitement Kalena was feeling. It was a lousy time to remember Olara's teachings in philosophy. Kalena struggled to forget them. She needed to focus the whole of her concentration on winning this confrontation.

"The power of the Dark end of the Spectrum is limitless," Ridge told her in a rough, challenging voice. He faced her from the other side of the fire, his lean, strong body taut with the masculine power that shimmered in the flames in front of him. "All that is female is weak in the face of it, just as you are weak. Don't you recall your own weakness, Kalena? Think about it. Remember the times you have surrendered completely in my arms. When I touch you, you belong to me. You are mine to do with exactly as

I wish. Your Light Key will crumble just as easily when it confronts the Dark. Why don't you try to flee, woman, while you can? I would enjoy the chase. I will come after you, run you down and crush you beneath me. I will take you completely even as I destroy the Key that makes you so foolishly arrogant."

Ridge heard the words he had just spoken and scowled. A part of him really did want her to turn and run to safety. But that made no sense. He was here to conquer her as man had always conquered woman; as the night conquered the day. He didn't want her to escape. He wanted—no *needed*—to subjugate her completely. It was his right, his heritage as a man. She belonged to him and he was free to do what he wanted. But first he must crush her foolish bid for power.

"I would never run from you, Houseless bastard," Kalena taunted. "You are less than dust beneath my feet, an illegitimate bastard who thought he could claim a heritage through me. Why should I run from such as you?"

Ridge felt the fury begin to burn deep in his gut. He took another pace forward, the black case vibrating almost painfully in his hand. "Then stay, Kalena, and learn the full extent of your weakness. Learn the meaning of surrender. You are nothing more than a servant I have chosen to indulge. Before this is over you will call me master."

"And you are nothing more than a tool whose usefulness is over! Before tonight is finished you will kneel at my feet and beg for mercy."

They faced each other in the firelight, neither aware of the heat of the flames or the cowled men who occupied the room with them. No one moved along the glass walls of the cavern. And then, without any warning, both the black case and the silver one sprang open.

Kalena flinched at the shock wave that went through her, but she remained on her feet, staring down at the writhing flames that formed the Light Key.

Ridge, too, felt the jolt of raw energy that coursed through him when his case flew open. Fathomless cold wafted upward from the black object that was exposed in the box. The time had come. He reached eagerly into the case and his fingers closed around ice that was so bitterly cold he thought it would freeze him to his bones. But he held fast. He could do nothing else.

On the other side of the fire Kalena was unable to resist putting her fingers into the white flames of the Light Key even though the heat was so intense she was certain her whole body would ignite. Her hand tightened around a white fire that flowed through her.

The black case and the silvery white case fell to the glass floor unheeded as Kalena and Ridge faced each other with the Keys to the Stones of Contrast.

Kalena knew the Key she held was no longer a tool or an object; it was a part of her. It consumed her, drove her, guided her. With it she was infinitely more powerful than the insolent male with the golden eyes, infinitely more powerful than all he represented. With the Key she could conquer him, make him plead for mercy. She could destroy him if she wished.

But she did not wish to destroy him.

The thought came to her like a cold shock in the midst of hot anger. Ridge was the father of her child. He was the man to whom she had given her heart. He was the other half of herself.

Ridge was aware of the power that was flooding him, urging him to go forward and release the devastating potential of himself and the weapon he held. They were one and the same, he realized. The Key was connected to him in some manner that defied comprehension. With this Key he could master Kalena and all the lightness that surrounded her. If she defied him, he could destroy her.

But he did not want to destroy Kalena.

The realization dazed him. He wanted to subdue her, master her, force her to acknowledge him as her lord, but he did not want to destroy her. He wanted to take her, bury himself in her soft warmth. He wanted to feel that combination of exultation and satisfaction that was his every time he held her in an intimate embrace. She was his and he was sworn to protect her. He was honor bound to protect her. He must protect her. She was his other half. His opposite. She was the Light that balanced the Dark within him.

The Key trembled in his grasp and the icy cold spread deeper into his body. In some distant corner of his mind he understood suddenly that if he didn't control the ice, it would control him. And if the Key held complete power over him he would be unable to stop it from shattering Kalena. Dammit, he would not let himself be used as the instrument of her destruction. He wanted her with a raging desire that was stronger than the Dark Key's drive to destroy the Light.

A deep, hot fury seethed in him, the kind of anger that made the steel of Countervail glow with fire. He would not be used in this way.

He would control the Key.

To do that, Ridge knew, he would need to halt the flow of ice that threatened to ensnare him. He must warm the Key with the force of his own inner fire.

It was the same inner fire he experienced when he enflamed the steel of Countervail and when he sheathed himself in Kalena's soft, sweet, welcoming body. It throbbed in him, pulsed in his veins, ignited his passion and blazed with the promise of the future.

The fire was life.

SIXTEEN

He was her natural opposite. Her mate. The man with whom she had created new life.

The Key trembled in Kalena's grasp as she looked at Ridge across the leaping flames. The promise of fulfillment, ecstasy, power and triumph vibrated within her.

But above all there was the promise of life, the life they had created together.

His eyes blazed at her, hotter than the flames in the pit of fire. *"You are mine."* His face was stark with the lines of his inner battle. He held the Dark Key as if it were both talisman and weapon.

Kalena felt the desire to surrender battling with her equally powerful desire to resist. She felt as if the conflict would rip her apart. "I belong to no man, Fire Whip. I have no need of a man."

"When I take you again I will teach you that you will never be done with me. I have made you mine. I will do so again. If you wandered to the ends of the world you would not be able to rid yourself of me. I am a part of you now."

The babe. Did he know about the babe? Did he sense the life

within her? The Light Key burned more brilliantly than ever. Kalena's mind whirled with the memory of the woman struggling through childbirth alone, her husband downstairs in the tavern. It would never be like that for her, Kalena knew. This man would never abandon his wife and child. He would walk through the fires of the Dark end of the Spectrum for them. He would confront the Light end itself if necessary. She was his, just as he was hers.

On the other side of the fire Ridge stared at her as he stood in the grip of raw wonder.

"*I am a part of you*," he repeated. The dawning realization was there in his eyes, and Kalena was certain he knew about the life they had created together. Somehow he had sensed it.

"Ridge." His name was torn from her, but she could say nothing more. Her mind spun with startling images.

It was as if he had touched her. She could almost feel his hands on her body, stroking her intimately, claiming her passion for his own. Kalena closed her eyes as the exquisite sensations poured over her. Calloused palms grazed her sensitive nipples, urging them into full flower. Strong white teeth nipped the inside of her thigh with a gentle savagery that made her tremble. Golden eyes flared with an exciting hunger that stoked her own desire. The weight of him was a throbbing force that at once subdued and set free the energy of passion that sailed through her blood.

Dizzy with the effects of the sensuality that reached across the fire to embrace her, Kalena struggled to maintain her balance. She couldn't open her eyes. A soft moan escaped her. She could feel him holding her still, capturing her wrists in his large hands, anchoring her writhing legs with his own muscled thighs. His mouth covered hers, his tongue thrusting into her in a way that emulated another kind of possessive thrust. Her blood sang even as she surrendered to the silent embrace.

He was fire and she was ice. The dangerous flames that burned in him could only be quenched by her soft, welcoming femininity, cool and clear as crystal. He would bring her passion and she would bring him peace. Together they could create a future.

Her legs were being parted. The heavy, pulsing weight of him was between her soft thighs, seeking entrance to the hot, damp core of her. She could feel the powerful, blunt force of him pressing into her, demanding admission as if it were his right. She had no choice but to yield. But she longed for no other choice. She was his. She wanted to yield; to take him within her, trap him, chain him, and make him hers. Only in surrender could she win this unique battle. In surrender she would find victory.

In victory, Ridge would learn the meaning of surrender.

It was the way of the Spectrum. The way of male and female.

And then he was there, forging into her, laying claim to the gentle territory he would master. Kalena cried out in the moment of complete possession and dimly heard an answering shout of passion and masculine surrender mingled with triumph. Now they were one. Male and female joined together in a whole that was greater than the sum of its parts. The Paradox of the Spectrum in its most glittering manifestation.

Opposites that could attract. Opposites that could destroy. Opposites that could meld into a union so powerful it could create new life. The wonder of it stopped the world for a timeless instant.

And then Kalena opened her eyes.

Ridge was still standing on the other side of the fire, his whole body taut with triumphant satisfaction, his eyes lit with the wonder of losing himself in his woman.

Kalena knew then that he had shared the strange lovemaking with her in his mind. It was over, yet he still fought a savage battle. She could see it in every inch of his lean, powerful frame.

What battle was he fighting? Kalena wondered silently. Then it came to her with violent impact that he fought to control his Key, just as she must struggle to control hers. If they did not control them, they would destroy each other and the new life they had created. Their survival depended on the battle they must each fight with the Keys.

The reality of what she had come close to doing with the Light Key shook Kalena to her heart, cutting through the intense sense of exultant power. Some of the glittering effects of the trance that gripped her wavered.

A part of her distantly realized what was happening. If she used the Key, she would not merely humble Ridge, she would destroy him completely.

She could not destroy the man she had come here to save. He was the father of her child, her husband, the man to whom she had bound herself. Her destiny.

What was she doing? She had not come here to kill him.

Dazed, she watched as he gripped the Key he held in both hands. She knew the thing was causing him pain and she sensed that he was fighting to control it. The Light Key shimmered with energy, demanding to have that energy released. The heat of the Key was reaching out for her, acting on her, consuming her. Soon it would control her totally.

Unless she controlled it first.

But that was unheard of. No one could control the Keys. That was why they had been locked away for centuries. The wisdom of the ages was useless now. The Keys had been freed, and unless she found a way to handle hers, Kalena knew she would wind up killing Ridge. She fought for breath and put both hands around the flaming handle.

The heat was incredible. It was alive, turning on her, trying to dominate her, consume her. White heat flared along her nerve endings. She had to cool the Key or it would blaze completely out of control. She was an untrained Healer, but she could look inside herself and find the answers she needed.

No Sand burned to light her way, but the Key contained within it all the power of all the Sand that had ever existed. Kalena closed her eyes and breathed in the heat that filled the air around her. The world shuddered. There was a dazzling veil waiting to be lifted. She must find a way to lift it. Inside her mind Kalena reached out to grasp the veil and pull it away. For an instant there was resistance. She didn't think she could manage the feat. And then the veil disappeared.

The answer was evident at once.

The only solution was to cool the white fire of the Light Key the way a Healer cooled a fever, the way she had more than once cooled the raging anger in Ridge. She was the daughter of the House of the Ice Harvest. Deep within her was the power of ice, the power to drain the heat from the fire. It was her heritage to control the Key, not be used by it. Eyes closed, Kalena began to concentrate on the flaming Key.

Raw energy arced between the two Keys and traveled up the arms of those who held them. Lightning flashes of fire and ice flared and flashed around Kalena and Ridge. The glass chamber shook with the sound of a scream, but the anguished protest didn't come from either Ridge or Kalena; they had no strength left to spare for anything but controlling the Keys.

The shriek echoed eerily through the cavern and was quickly followed by another. Kalena opened her eyes to find herself looking directly into Ridge's golden gaze. He had circled the fire and was standing only a short distance from her now. The Key in his hand was changing color. Kalena could see that Ridge was trembling with the force of the energy he sought to contain.

She didn't know who had screamed. Vaguely she realized that the cries must have come from the members of the cult; certainly Ridge had not made a sound. Ridge's mouth was set in a thin, determined line, and his eyes were gleaming with the fire that raged within him. Even as Kalena watched some of that fire seemed to touch the icy black Key in his hand. It began to glow faintly with the same hue as the sintar when it reflected Ridge's temper.

Kalena caught her breath as the Key she held flared for a moment and then began to coalesce. Slowly the white flames congealed, leaving behind a white metallic object that was noticeably cooler.

The screams came again, and this time Kalena knew they were screams of rage. But none of the hooded men dared come forth. Apparently, the power of the Keys was enough to keep them at bay.

"You will not deny us our triumph!" Griss' agonized cry filled the room. "Destroy her, Fire Whip. It is what you are meant to do. It is the only reason you have been spared. Set the Darkness free to consume her and the Key. *Set it free!*"

Ridge was watching Kalena, his eyes fastened on hers as if she were the only important thing in the universe. She could not tear her gaze from his as they both struggled to restrain the power in the Keys.

"I don't know how long I can control it, Ridge." Her husky words came through dry lips.

"Long enough," he said hoarsely. "Just long enough." He forced himself to turn to one side, moving with obvious effort back to where he had dropped the black case. The short walk seemed to have exhausted him. He fell to his knees, the Key held high overhead in his clenched hands. His mouth was set in a grim twist and the fire in his eyes was molten.

"By the Stones!" Ridge cried, his shout drowning out the sounds of rage filling the chamber even as he drove the Key point down into the black glass floor.

A sudden, violent cracking sound exploded in the room.

"No!" Griss screamed as if he had been personally attacked. "Damn you to the end of the Spectrum, *no!*"

Kalena, still struggling with her Key, watched in horror as a long, thin crack appeared in the center of the floor. It began at the point where Ridge still knelt, his shoulders hunched as he gasped for breath. It seemed to pass directly through the bowl of fire and continue on the far side, snaking toward Kalena.

Ridge staggered to his feet, snatching up the black case. With what was obviously one last burst of willpower, he thrust the Key into the case.

Kalena had just time enough to see that the Dark Key was still glowing faintly with the warmth Ridge had infused into it before the lid snapped shut with an awful finality.

Shouts of rage and a curious, truly horrible agony ricocheted around the glass chamber. Hooded figures lurched toward Kalena and Ridge, coming as close as they dared. But it was clear they could still not touch either of them. Kalena clung to her Key, aware that the driving force in it was finally fading. She could and would control it. She sought with her toe along the floor for the silvered box. She found it just as Ridge shoved his Key, case and all, into the bowl of flames that burned in the center of the room.

Instantly, there was another sharp splintering sound and the long jagged line in the floor began to widen as several smaller, spidery lines grew outward from it. There was nothing but endless darkness in the major crack. A deep cold seemed to reach upward from the bottomless pit below.

"Run, Kalena, the room is going to shatter!"

"Not without you, Ridge. I'll be damned if I'll leave without you after having gone through all this!" Her foot collided with the silvered box and she grabbed it, thrusting the now cooling Light Key inside and snapping shut the lid. Almost at once she felt completely in control of herself again. The relief made her dizzy.

Another harsh, fracturing noise filled the room. Kalena looked down to find herself straddling the far end of the deep crack that stretched beneath the fire pit. Cowled figures moved forward, hands outstretched to take hold of her.

"Ridge!"

"Hold on to the Key. They can't touch you as long as you've got the Key." He was racing toward her now as more cracks appeared in the black glass. The firelight seemed to blaze higher, bouncing furiously off the glassy surfaces of the room. The members of the Cult of the Eclipse were screaming uselessly, milling around in a strange panic.

"Which way?" Kalena glanced around helplessly.

"I saw some of them come through the glass over there earlier." He indicated a blank wall of glass that hadn't yet begun to shatter. "They left a lamp on the floor to mark the door. Come on, let's get out of here." Ridge put out a hand to grab Kalena's arm and swore in savage disgust. His hand fell aside and he shook it as if it had been painfully injured. "I can't touch you. Figures. Come on, move! Stay close to me."

He led the way toward the far glass wall. Even as they ran, the black glass ahead of them trembled and began to splinter. Kalena saw the flat, reflective surface shatter, revealing a dark opening behind it. Ridge grabbed up the lamp that had been left on the floor and stood back to make sure that Kalena got through the jagged tunnel entrance.

"Hurry," he snapped. "This glass is going to be down on us any second."

Kalena moved to obey, clinging to her Key case.

"You can't escape!" Griss' voice was a sobbing cry of anguish and fury behind them. "You must not leave. You cannot leave!"

He lunged for Kalena, black robes flying around him. For a moment he looked like some evil bird trying to score her with talons. Kalena glanced back in fear, wondering if the man's blind fury would be enough to get him past the protection the Key case seemed to provide.

But suddenly Ridge was between her and Griss, moving with a lethal swiftness that Kalena knew would end in death for the man who had once made the mistake of calling her whore. A wave of shocked sickness washed through her. She wanted to cry out, to tell Ridge that she was safe enough with the Key in her hands, but there was no chance. Kalena knew she couldn't have stopped him, even if she were able to get the words out of her constricted throat.

He was her other half, her opposite, the dark side of life. Ridge could kill.

There was a blur of motion as Ridge's hand moved. Griss screamed again, his cloak swirling outward to surround both himself and Ridge. For an instant the two men seemed to be trapped together in a violent embrace, and then they both sprawled on the floor. Ridge and Griss rolled twice, Ridge winding up on the bottom. Kalena couldn't see much else because of the enveloping folds of the cloak. Then she heard a keening scream that ended with nerve shattering abruptness.

Both of the thrashing figures went abnormally still. Kalena couldn't move. The lengthening crack in the floor snaked forward another few meters until it ran under the two men.

"Ridge! Get away from there. Hurry, the floor is opening. There is nothing underneath."

Ridge was already kicking himself free of the dead Griss and the tangle of the cloak. He got to his feet, his sintar in one hand. Kalena realized he must have taken it from Griss and used it on the other man. In the fiery light that danced around the room she could see that the blade of the weapon was red. This time the color wasn't from Ridge's fury. The steel was red with Griss' blood.

Ridge rushed toward her, grabbing up the fallen lamp. "I told you to get out of here."

"Yes, Ridge." This was not the time to explain again that she couldn't leave without him. Kalena was already turning back toward the yawning darkness of the waiting tunnel when she saw the central crack in the floor widen abruptly. Griss' body hovered for a moment on an edge of fractured glass and then, with a terrible inevitability, it tumbled into the black chasm.

"The tunnel, Kalena!"

She breathed deeply, trying to quiet her pounding pulse, and moved through the opening in the cracked and shattered glass. Ridge was right behind her. Safe in the corridor, he stopped Kalena for an instant. Unable to help themselves, they both glanced back into the glass chamber. Stunned, they watched as the bowl of searing fire fell from sight and the remainder of the glass floor disintegrated. The fire pit with its hidden secret disappeared into a yawning black chasm. Several shrieking cultists fell with it, their cries echoing horribly.

"Dammit to the Dark end of the Spectrum." Ridge's words were almost inaudible.

"Ridge, what is it?" Kalena glanced at him, more alarmed than ever. He was staring past her into the disintegrating room.

"Someone else found a way out. I saw a lamp disappear into a wall on the other side of the room." He shook off the obvious anger that threatened to consume him and swung around. "Maybe it was just my imagination. It doesn't matter. There is nothing that can be done. We have to get out of here."

Ridge swung around, made another futile effort to grasp Kalena's arm, and swore furiously again when he was unable to touch her. "Now we've got a small problem on our hands." He stared into the blackness of the tunnel.

Kalena turned her back on the destruction of the glass room and followed his gaze. The light from the lamp Ridge was holding didn't penetrate very far.

"I don't think this is the main entrance. The way Griss and the others brought me was well lit," Kalena observed anxiously.

"I know. But some of the cult members came this way. I saw them enter the room. There was a lamp to mark this exit."

Kalena swallowed. "I suppose you realize how lost we could get in these caves?"

"The thought has crossed my mind." He started forward cautiously. "We can't go back into that damn glass chamber, though. We're going to have to try to find our way out using this corridor. And we'd better move quickly. There's no telling how far that chasm will open. It could splinter half this mountain."

"No." Kalena spoke with a conviction that surprised her as much as it did Ridge. "It won't do that. It's gone about as far as it's going to go. We're safe from it now."

Ridge glanced back at her, scowling. "How do you know that?"

She looked down at the case in her hands. "I just know."

He opened his mouth as if to argue, and then appeared to change his mind. He eyed the silvery case. "Maybe you do. Anything else useful you can tell us?"

"Perhaps." She stroked the case in her hand. "This is a thing of light, not darkness."

"I know." He sounded impatient.

She raised her eyes. "It's possible it might lead us to the outside."

"How?"

Kalena shook her head. "I . . . I'm not sure. But now that the Dark Key has vanished, this case no longer feels pulled toward it. It feels free again and I think that it will be drawn toward light. It belongs back in the ice cave above the valley, not here."

"Kalena, are you trying to tell me you're in touch mentally with that damn Key?"

"Not exactly." She hesitated, seeking a way to explain something she didn't understand herself. "But I feel the pull of it. Earlier that pull was toward the Dark Key. There was a drive to destroy it. But now it's a different sensation. It's a weak sensation, though. Perhaps if I took the Key out of the case again—"

"No!" Ridge's refusal to even consider such an action was clear in the single word.

Kalena nodded. "Yes, it would be dangerous. And maybe unnecessary. I can still feel a faint sensation, even through the case." She looked up again. "Do you want to risk having me try to lead us out of here with this?"

Ridge stared at her for a long moment, and abruptly nodded his head. "All right. We haven't got much to lose, have we? Go ahead. Give it a try. I'll count our steps. Whenever we come to a turn in the tunnels, we'll try to leave a marker of some kind. With any luck we might at least be able to find our way back to this point if we decide we're not making any progress. There has to be an exit out of this corridor, but it might take a lot of trial and error to find it."

Kalena closed her eyes and tried to concentrate on the quiet warmth emanating from the silvery casket in her hands. For a long moment she felt nothing beyond a gentle, comfortable heat.

She experimented by deliberately turning to walk back along the corridor toward what remained of the now ominously silent glass chamber. Almost instantly she was aware of a faint resistance. When she swung around and started in the other direction, the resistance faded.

"It feels different when I go in this direction, Ridge. It feels right, somehow."

"Let's get going. Watch your step. There's always the possibility that the cult set a few traps."

"Why should they? These caves are enough of a trap in themselves."

"Mmm." He didn't sound convinced. "Just the same, don't get ahead of the lamplight and let me check the corners before you go around them. The last thing we need to run into tonight is a hook viper."

"I think they've all fled," Kalena murmured. "Probably didn't appreciate the invasion of their caverns."

They walked for what seemed like hours, although Kalena knew it wasn't really that long. Around each bend in the passage she hoped to find lamps that would indicate the new corridor was one of those used frequently by the Cult of the Eclipse. Ridge stayed close, keeping a silent tally of their footsteps and building small pyramids of pebbles every time they started down a new passage.

Whenever a choice of direction was offered Kalena halted, closed her eyes and tried to sense the Key's emanations of warmth. Whenever the warmth dimmed, she opted for a different direction. It was a tedious process, tiring mentally as well as physically. Kalena had a silent fear that she was only imagining the slight changes in temperature that came from the case in her hands. She wondered whether she ought to warn Ridge that she might be working on sheer imagination. No sense bothering him with that bit of useless news, she told herself.

Once during the walk down a particularly long passage, Kalena allowed herself to think about what had happened back in the glass room. Ridge had been moving silently beside her for a long while and she wondered if he was thinking about the same thing.

"How did it feel, Ridge?" Kalena asked quietly. "When you held the Key in your hands. What did it feel like?"

He didn't look at her, but kept his attention on the corridor ahead. "Like I was connected to it. Part of it."

"That's the way it was with the Light Key. But it wanted to take over. It was using me, draining me."

"I know. The Keys would have had us kill each other. Who knows what kind of energy that would have released?"

Kalena chewed on her lower lip. "You think the Keys would have absorbed that energy and used it somehow?"

"I don't know, Kalena. I don't think I want to know."

"The strange part is that I never really got a sense of evil around the Dark Key," she said thoughtfully.

"That makes us even," he muttered. "I never got a sense of sweet, pure goodness around the Light Key."

"I guess that's logical. The Keys are tied to opposite ends of the Spectrum, but not necessarily to any real concept of good or evil. We've been taught that all our lives. They represent different, opposing sources of power."

"Pure power can come from either end of the Spectrum," Ridge agreed slowly. "And according to the Polarity Advisors, so can good or evil. But they're two different sets of concepts. *Balanced* concepts."

"Ah, but you males have always assumed that in a showdown, the Dark end would be stronger, haven't you?"

Ridge shrugged. "Maybe. We think of the Light end of the Spectrum as being the feminine end, and I guess it's fair to say most men think of women as the weaker sex. At least in a physical sense. The Polarity Advisors have always assumed that absolute power wielded by women wouldn't be as strong as absolute power wielded by men."

"Probably because Polarity Advisors are almost always male," Kalena suggested dryly. "Well, at least the cult's stupid experiment proved that notion was a lie," she added, not without some sense of satisfaction.

"Don't sound so smug, Kalena. We both had one hell of a close call back in that glass chamber and we're not out of this yet."

But Kalena's spirits were reviving rapidly as the shock of the experience wore off. "Do you suppose that for the rest of our lives we'll argue about which of us was more powerful?"

"No, we will not."

"Why not?"

"Because as of now I forbid any mention of the subject."

Kalena's mouth curved in the first real amusement she had felt in a long while. "That's what I like about you, Ridge. You don't allow yourself to get mired down in complex philosophical quandaries. Very straightforward in your thinking."

"I'm learning that if he's to stay reasonably sane, a husband doesn't have much choice," he answered, a touch of humor lacing his words.

Neither of them mentioned the uniquely sensual experience that had taken place between them in the chamber. Kalena wanted to ask Ridge if he had felt everything she had felt; she was almost certain he had. But somehow this didn't seem like the appropriate time. She also longed to ask him if he had actually sensed the presence of their babe within her, but that, too, didn't seem like a good topic of conversation at the moment.

Kalena was suddenly aware of a deep coldness invading her. She paused, trying to orient herself.

"What is it, Kalena?" Ridge held the lamp higher so that he could see her face.

"Nothing, I thought I felt a little colder, but I think it was just my imagination. These passages seem endless. I'm not sure we're making any real progress, Ridge. Maybe we should work our way back and start over again from the corridor outside that glass room."

He regarded her quietly for a long moment, his eyes unreadable in the lamplight. "Does the Key case feel any different?"

She glanced down at it. "No, not really."

"Still warm?"

"I think so."

"Then we'll keep going."

"But Ridge, I'm trying to tell you that I'm no longer sure I'm sensing anything at all from it."

"What's wrong, Kalena? You've been fairly certain of yourself ever since we started. Why the sudden loss of nerve?"

"I'm not losing my nerve! I'm just trying to explain that I'm not sure we can trust this case to lead us out of here." Anger flooded back into her bloodstream, driving off some of the cold. The case in her hands seemed warmer again. "Very well, if you don't want to listen to a rational discussion of the matter, let's go on." She stepped past him.

Ridge fell into step beside her. He had been wrong to goad her into continuing, but the truth was, he was certain they couldn't turn back. He didn't know why they had to keep going, he only knew that, in spite of the trail markers he had left, there was no hope for them if they had to turn around.

He had learned to trust his instincts a long time ago on the streets of Countervail. They had kept him alive during the dangerous years of working for Quintel. Deep down, he knew that the senses he had relied on in the past weren't just functioning on instinct. They operated on a subtle process of interpretation and analysis, a matter of filtering through tiny clues and coming to conclusions that would have been impossible to explain in words.

But calling them survival instincts was easier. Ridge was a great believer in choosing the simplest explanation. Kalena was right. He was a straightforward sort of thinker.

He wasn't certain exactly what had happened in the chamber of black glass, but he knew what the results of the confrontation were. He had fought a battle, the most desperate, dangerous battle of his life, but the prize had been worth any price. And he had won. Kalena was his. He would not let her be taken from him by anything, anyone or any power, regardless of which end of the Spectrum that power was from.

Torn between fire and ice, he had learned something else back in the black chamber. Kalena had fought the same savage battle to hold on to him. He was hers. She had confronted the fiercest power of her end of the Spectrum to protect him. Ridge was aware of a violent joy at the knowledge. They were bound together.

Perhaps she didn't think of the bond between them in such simple, straightforward terms. He was sure Kalena's thought processes were far more convoluted and erratic than his own. Far more *feminine*. Polarity Advisors traditionally warned men that it was useless to try to understand how a woman's mind worked, and Ridge was inclined to agree. But it didn't matter as long as she had reached the same conclusion. He frowned suddenly.

"Kalena?"

She glanced at him worriedly. "What is it?"

"I think you may be right."

Her eyes reflected her dismay. "About going in the wrong direction?"

"No, about the cold. It is getting colder. The temperature in these corridors has always seemed the same to me, but now there's definitely a cold draft coming from someplace."

"A draft. Ridge, maybe it's fresh air from outside!"

"How does the case feel?"

She looked down at it. "All right. I mean, it feels the way it has all along. Warm."

He nodded. "Let's keep moving."

Kalena led the way along the passage, her step quickening as she became convinced that she was really feeling cold, fresh air from outside the caves. The floor of the passage began to tilt upward slightly and the corridor narrowed so that there was only room enough to move single file.

Ridge took the lead with the lamp. "Tell me if there's any change in the feel of the case."

"I will."

The passage grew narrower. Ridge was forced to stoop in order to keep from hitting his head on the low ceiling. The closed in feeling began to bother Kalena.

"Ridge, if this corridor gets any narrower, I think we should turn back."

"I can see moonlight, Kalena!"

Her sense of claustrophobia vanished. Kalena hurried forward, rounded a bend behind Ridge, and then she, too, could see moonlight and a handful of stars in the night sky ahead. Fresh, cold air filled her lungs and she wanted to laugh with relief.

"We're free. Ridge, we did it. We're safe!"

"I'm not sure where we are, but any place is better than where we've been." Ridge ducked his head to squeeze his way out of the cave and automatically reached back to grab Kalena's hand. Instantly he yanked his fingers back out of reach.

"Stones! Why do I keep forgetting?" he growled.

"I'm sorry, Ridge."

"Never mind. It's not your fault. It's that damned Key. Just give me a chance to figure out where we are."

They stood on the pebble strewn ledge and gazed around them. The scattered stars shone brilliantly in the night sky overhead. There was snow on the ground around them. Kalena knew they were still somewhere in the mountains, but beyond that she was totally lost.

"With any luck we're just a little west of the trail," Ridge announced.

"How can you tell?"

"Brilliant, masculine logic and luck. Mostly luck." His grin flashed briefly in the light of the lamp. "Plus a lot of years figuring out how to read the night sky. Watch your step."

Kalena followed Ridge down the short incline below the ledge where they had emerged from the cave. The night air was cold, but it was a reassuring, fresh, natural cold that Kalena didn't really mind. Red Symmetra was a shining beacon in the sky.

"If we don't find the trail fairly soon, we'll have to camp out in the open," Ridge said over his shoulder. "Not a major disaster since we've got some firegel, but I'd prefer to find the shelter."

"I'm not sure I want to stay in that shelter again," Kalena muttered.

"We'll be safe enough. We'll have the Key with us."

"You're right. Besides, I don't think very many escaped from that glass chamber." She shuddered. "Griss didn't, that's for sure."

"No," Ridge agreed, his voice hard. "Griss didn't. He was a dead man from the moment he called you whore."

Kalena shivered again but said nothing. Half an hour later they found the main trail. Ridge oriented himself almost immediately. He started upward instead of heading down the path. In a short time they found the shelter. The two creets and their loads of Sand were still safe inside.

The cheerful, welcoming chirps of the birds warmed Kalena as much as the fire Ridge set about building on the hearth.

SEVENTEEN

Kalena sat on the pallet, her knees drawn up so that she could rest her chin on her arms as she watched Ridge feed another log to the flames. The case that held the Light Key lay on the floor near the door. Kalena was certain that its presence was a guarantee against being taken by surprise by more of the cold, black mist. Not that the possibility seemed likely. She had a feeling the destruction in the black glass chamber had been very thorough.

Her thoughts had been running through her head, loose and disorganized ever since she and Ridge had finished the evening meal. In the darkened stables that connected to the main room, the creets stamped contentedly a few times in their stalls as they settled down for the night. There had been plenty of food available to them during the past few days of captivity, and they had made the best of the situation, just as Ridge had predicted. The shelter's stores were going to have to be replenished before another caravan came through the mountains.

Ridge had said very little since he had finished eating. He busied himself with checking the condition of the creets, going through the packs to make certain his supplies and the Sand were still safe, and he kept the fire going strong. Kalena had quietly prepared the meal and cleaned up afterward. They were both tired. Sometimes there was an advantage to accepting the customary division of labor, she decided ruefully.

Now it was time to go to bed, and Kalena was feeling unexpectedly uncertain and nervous. Her anxiety must have shown in her face, because Ridge got slowly to his feet and said without any emotion, "You can stop worrying about it. I'm not going to rape you."

She flinched as if he had struck her. "I know that."

He scowled, unbuttoning his shirt. "You've been sitting there for the past half hour thinking of what almost happened here last time, haven't you?"

"No, Ridge," she said gently, realizing he had misinterpreted her silence.

"Don't lie to me, Kalena." He flung his shirt aside in a gesture of annoyance and self-disgust. "I know exactly what's going through that head of yours, and I'm telling you that you don't have to worry." He sat down on a low stool near the fire and concentrated on tugging off his boots. "I think it was the mist that got to me last time. I know that's not an acceptable excuse, but it's the only one I've got."

"I understand, Ridge."

His head came up abruptly. "Don't be so damn understanding about it! I had no right to frighten you the way I did that night."

"You wouldn't have gone through with it."

"How do you know?"

"Don't you remember how you reacted when I reminded you that I wore your lock and key? Even though you were under the influence of whatever was surrounding this shelter, you stopped. And when Griss came through the door, you wouldn't let him touch me."

"Of course I wouldn't have let him touch you." There was a grim arrogance behind the words. The second boot hit the floor. "You're my wife."

"You would have died trying to defend me," Kalena said in soft wonder.

"I would have *killed* trying to defend you," he corrected her wryly.

"A more useful approach," she admitted, hiding a smile.

He threw her a sharp glance. "Are you laughing at me, woman?"

"Never."

He stood up again, thumbs hooked in his belt, and sauntered slowly toward her. The flames of the fire gleamed on the strong contours of his bare shoulders. There was a wary, speculative look in his eyes, a heated intimacy that slid along Kalena's nerve endings.

"As it happens," he said deliberately, "we wound up saving each other's lives."

"Yes."

Ridge hesitated. "It was a little shaky there for a while, but when the crunch came we worked well together, didn't we?"

Kalena studied the floor in front of her. "Yes," she said again. "We did." Trust a man to phrase it like that. Passion and power, life and death had all been on the line back in that chamber. She and Ridge had survived and he termed it working well together. Well, perhaps that was one way of putting it, she thought in amusement.

He sat down beside her on the pallet, not touching her. "I know you never wanted to be married," he said with a kind of quiet gruffness. "At least, you didn't want anything more than a trade marriage."

Kalena said nothing. She was afraid to open her mouth.

"You've told me often enough about your dreams of being a freewoman."

Kalena tensed inside.

"I can't offer you complete freedom, Kalena," Ridge finally said softly. "I'd be lying if I said I could. The only consolation I can give is to tell you that I don't consider myself free, either. There are things I want to do, things that have to be done. No man who wants to build something lasting for himself and his family is free. I know I haven't any proud House name to offer you. But I swear on my honor that I'll take care of you. Better care than I seem to have taken on this journey, I trust. Someday I'll give you a House name you can be proud of. In the meantime, you won't go cold or hungry, I'll see to that. And I give you my oath that I will not dishonor you by being unfaithful. I want you very badly, Kalena. I need you. I think that we belong together. Will you consider making the marriage permanent?"

Kalena blinked back her tears. She was afraid to meet his eyes. "You honor me with your proposal, Fire Whip."

He was very still. The tension in him was palpable. "Kalena?"

"I accept your offer of a permanent marriage," she stated with gentle formality.

He drew a deep breath. His eyes burned into hers. "Just like that?"

"Do you want me to make it more complicated?"

He groaned and reached for her, pulling her head down to cradle against his shoulder. "No, I do not want you to make it more complicated. I want it to be just like this. Simple. Honest. Real." His hand moved in her hair, twisting in the thick curls. "You're mine, Kalena. I could never let you go now."

"You are as trapped as I am, Fire Whip."

"Don't you think I know that?" He bent his head and found her mouth with his own.

There in the firelight they sealed their vows with a kiss that carried the power of a love that was strong enough to defy both ends of the Spectrum. Without words they acknowledged the bonds that held them fast to each other.

After a long time, Ridge reluctantly lifted his head. A brief, knowing smile edged his mouth.

"What kind of trader's luck brought you to me, Kalena?" he asked whimsically.

She smiled back, touching the hard line of his jaw with a soft fingertip. "It wasn't trader's luck. It was a trade marriage, remember? Not the most auspicious start for a permanent arrangement, I'll wager. I never dreamed my future would take this form."

Ridge put his hands on her shoulders and turned her to face him. His eyes narrowed. "From what I can tell, your path has never been clear to you. You were born with the Talent, but never got a Healer's training. You thought you had to kill a man in order to avenge your House, but found yourself incapable of killing in cold blood. You wanted to be a freewoman, but instead you got yourself chained to a husband and dragged along on a wedding trip that could easily have gotten you killed."

"No wonder I never had a clear vision of my future," Kalena murmured. "I wouldn't have believed it, even if I had been able to envision it."

"The one thing you did see for yourself was freedom. And it's the one thing you don't have," Ridge said carefully, as if suddenly feeling his way over a difficult path.

"I have learned a thing or two about freedom, Ridge. It is a difficult concept. I'm not sure there even is such a thing as freedom. But there are choices. And I have made mine willingly and with a whole heart. I can only be truly happy with you."

He sighed into her hair, holding her to him. "I have learned that I could not have the future I want without you, Kalena. Such a future would be meaningless. I would walk away from it in a minute if I couldn't have you with me. The choice would be easy. I wouldn't even have to think about it. You are life and peace and joy. You're the only really important thing in this world for me."

"And you are the most important thing in this world for me," she whispered.

He groaned and pulled her more tightly against him, his hands tangling in her hair. "You're my wife," he muttered into her hair as if he were having trouble believing it.

"Yes." She heard the sense of wonder and possessiveness in his words and smiled.

"I need you tonight. I have never needed you more than I do right now."

She put her arms around him, nestling close to the reassuring warmth and strength he offered. "I need you, too, Ridge."

"I won't hurt you. I'll take care not to frighten you with memories of the last time we were in this shelter," he promised earnestly. "We'll take it slow and easy this time. Hurting you would be hurting myself." His fingers trembled slightly in her thick hair. He tightened his hands in silent urgency and then forced himself to release her completely.

Kalena lifted her head, eyes wide and trusting. "It's all right, Ridge."

"What nearly happened here that night when the mist surrounded us isn't the only thing I regret, Kalena. I never apologized for the way I took you that night in Adverse," he said heavily. "I had no right to do that. A man shouldn't treat his wife that way."

"You didn't hurt me." Kalena smiled tremulously. "As I recall, you were rather insistent on exercising your marital rights, but you didn't rape me or frighten me, Ridge. As a matter of fact, I was very disappointed when you didn't bother to exercise your rights again until we got to the valley."

"Where it was you who exercised her marital rights, as I remember," he concluded with a husky laugh. He shaped her head between his palms, his thumbs moving on her temples as he stared intently into her eyes. "I haven't always made the right decisions around you, Kalena. I didn't realize being a proper husband was going to be so complicated at times. I thought I would always know my duty to you, but it's not that simple."

"As far as I can tell, nothing is simple."

"There are other complications," Ridge murmured. "Take now, for instance. Right now I want to make love to you so badly it's eating me alive, but I'm afraid of frightening you with the force of my desire."

She put her hands on his shoulders, feeling the hard planes of muscle and bone. The heat in him warmed her palms. "After what we have been through together, do you really believe it would be possible for the power of your desire to frighten me?"

He answered the smile in her eyes with one of his own. "It

would seem my biggest mistake in dealing with you is that of occasionally underestimating you."

"A dangerous error."

"I have a feeling I'm in good company. I think many men
make the mistake of underestimating their women. Or perhaps it's
just a matter of not being able to read their minds."

The humor faded from Kalena's gaze, replaced by the glim-
mering intensity of her emotions. "There was a time during our
meeting in the black chamber when I wondered not only if you
could read my mind but whether you might be sharing it with
me."

"Ah, that." Ridge said nothing more. He just continued to
gaze down into her flame lit face. His own eyes were gleaming
with both reflected fire and the flames that were so much a part of
his nature.

Kalena groaned and sank her nails lightly into his arm. "Don't
you dare tease me, Ridge. Not about this. *I must know.* I'll go crazy
if you don't tell me."

"Perhaps it's only fair for a man to have a few secrets. Women
have so many of their own." Tantalizingly, he drew his palm down
her shoulder until his fingers rested on the tunic just above her
breast.

Kalena felt her nipple blossom under the heat of his palm. Her
eyes widened. She covered his hand with hers. "You know, don't
you?" she whispered half accusingly. "You were there in my mind,
touching me, seducing me. It wasn't some kind of waking dream."

"It seems to me that I am always trying to seduce you. I spend
a great deal of my time plotting ways to do it." He leaned down to
nibble lightly on her earlobe.

"But back in the cavern," she persisted. "Was there something
more than just my imagination at work? Tell me, Ridge! If you
don't tell me the truth, I swear I'll . . ."

"You'll what?"

She drew a deep breath and boldly let her fingers slide down
his leg to the inside of his thigh. "I might do this," she threatened
against his chest. She touched him lightly, stroking the hardening

shaft of his manhood through the fabric of his trousers. Ridge groaned huskily.

"Such torture," he complained encouragingly into her hair. "You are a ruthless woman."

"I've had an excellent teacher."

"I don't break easily," he warned.

"We'll see." With growing exhilaration, Kalena nestled closer and found the fastening of the leather belt that clasped his waist. When she had the buckle undone she let her fingers trail inside. Ridge sucked in air. "Ready to talk?" Kalena asked.

"Talk? I can hardly breathe."

"Why are you being so stubborn about this, Ridge?" She cupped him in her palm and felt his immediate reaction. "I'm only asking for the truth."

"Maybe I happen to enjoy your brand of torture."

"That's what I'm beginning to worry about. I would know exactly what happened back there in the cavern, Fire Whip."

"Would you?" He slipped the tunic from her shoulders, baring her to the waist. He smiled down at her with lazy sensuality as he let his rough palm graze her nipple in exactly the manner it had done during the strange lovemaking in the black chamber.

Exactly the same manner, Kalena thought dizzily. She shivered and curled closer to his heat. She felt him shift his position, rising to his feet with her in his arms. Kalena closed her eyes and the next thing she knew she was lying on the pallet. Ridge's hands were on her thin trousers, sweeping them aside. He pulled briefly away from her, ridding himself of the remainder of his own clothing. Then he was beside her on the pallet.

His teeth nipped at the inside of her thigh, and the sensation was eerily and exactly as it had been in the black glass chamber.

"*Ridge.*" She clutched at him, pulling him to her.

He waited a moment longer, discovering the dampening warmth that was heating her. He stroked her until she began to twist beneath him. When the excitement flared, causing her to tremble with need, he touched her with his tongue. Kalena sank her nails into him, her desire overwhelming her.

Then he caught her wrists, pinning them gently to the pallet on either side of her head. Kalena vividly remembered the way she had been held in her dream. Her wrists had been captured just like this. The weight of him had pressed against her in exactly this manner, exciting her, encouraging her, teasing her until she cried out again and begged for his possession.

"You were there," she breathed. "You were with me somehow, weren't you?"

"Don't you know for certain?" He parted her legs with his own, sliding into the silken warmth between her thighs until the hard, blunt shaft was demanding entrance.

"Yes," Kalena managed, "Oh, yes, Ridge. Come to me. Take me, fill me, I need you so."

He drove into her, a ragged groan on his lips as he possessed her completely.

And that moment, too, was just as it had been in the glass chamber. The moment of possession was also the moment of surrender. It took them both simultaneously.

Ridge began to thrust heavily, deeply into Kalena, following a rhythm as old as the Spectrum. His hands gripped her shoulders as he began to move in a pattern that made the whole world spin.

Kalena cried out again, her nails scoring across his shoulders in ancient, feminine patterns that drew Ridge even more completely into her. He took her with a gentle savagery that freed Kalena completely. She was one with him, bound to him, yet wild and free. He soared with her even though he was forever chained to her. The paradox was as inexplicable as it was unquestionable. It existed. It was real. Kalena didn't try to comprehend it, she simply accepted it, knowing that in that moment Ridge, too, accepted the glittering reality.

"Kalena!"

She heard her name on his lips, felt the deep, shuddering climax that he was no longer able to restrain. Then he moved one last, forceful time within her and she, too, was whispering his name in surrender and triumph.

They clung together, caught in a union that was full and complete. They held each other with the same passionate strength they had used to control the Keys until slowly, inevitably, the room stopped spinning and a languid peace descended.

Kalena eventually lifted her lashes and met Ridge's lazy, sensual gaze. The remnants of passion were fading slowly from his golden eyes, and there was a deeply satisfied curve edging his mouth. He made no move to roll off of her, and she savored the feel of the weight of him down the entire length of her body.

"So," he murmured, "you have learned to find some form of freedom in my arms, haven't you?"

She speared her fingers lightly through his tousled hair. "It's a paradox, but it's true."

"Will it be enough for you, my sweet Kalena?"

"More than enough. And now I have the truth about what happened today in the chamber."

"Do you?" His eyes teased her.

She punished him lightly with her nails and laughed silently up at him. "You seduced me somehow, didn't you? We made love in a way I can't explain. It was no dream, nor was it a thing of imagination. You were with me, touching me, making love to me."

"I will always be with you, touching you and making love to you," he vowed with sudden fierceness.

"You set out to subdue me today," she said thoughtfully.

"You set out to do the same to me," he reminded her. "But there was no difference between surrender and victory for us, was there?"

"No. They are bound together, just as all opposites are linked."

"Just as you and I are linked," Ridge said roughly. Then he smiled wryly. "I think there are going to be times in the future when you and I do battle again, wife. You have learned too much about your own power. I have a hunch I will pay the price."

"You would prefer I went in fear of you?" she asked lightly.

He sighed with exaggerated regret. "I never wanted you in terror of me. But it occurs to me that a little wifely caution might be useful. A wife should have a certain amount of healthy respect for her husband."

Kalena laughed up at him. "Poor Ridge. As a husband you do have to walk a fine line, don't you?"

"I intend to work hard at being a proper husband to you, Kalena. It is not a job for which I have had much training, but I will do my best."

Knowing how completely he meant to honor the promise, Kalena was lost for words. Silently, she pulled his head down to hers and kissed him. "Hold me, Ridge. We've been through a great deal today, you and I. All I want now is to feel safe and warm."

"Do you feel safe and warm when I hold you?"

"More than I can say," she whispered.

He settled himself beside her, gathering her close. His fingers toyed idly with her hair as she fell asleep in his arms. Ridge lay awake for a long while, gazing into the fire and thinking about his future. It would not be exactly as he had once envisioned it. How could he have foreseen Kalena's presence in his world? But the future he saw tonight held more happiness and satisfaction than he had once been capable of imagining.

Kalena opened her eyes to the dawn light streaming through the slatted shutters. For a few moments she lay still, contemplating the twists and turns in her fate. No Healer with the gift of Far Seeing could have guessed the pattern in which her future would unfold, she thought with a smile.

She stretched cautiously so as not to waken Ridge, then thrust one bare foot out from under the pallet covers. Just as she had suspected, the room was quite chilly. A good wife, a *dutiful* wife, would rise briskly, start a fire and brew a pot of yant tea for her husband.

Kalena contemplated the pros and cons of being a good and dutiful wife for a moment and almost crawled back under the covers. Then she remembered one small matter that had not been discussed last night. She opted to be a dutiful wife.

Besides, it hadn't escaped her that on the one occasion when she had made yant tea for Ridge, he had taken a very genuine, very masculine pleasure in the morning ritual. It seemed to put him in a good mood and it made sense to keep Ridge in a good mood whenever possible.

She winced as she slipped out from under the covers and hurried to the small, primitive privacy chamber to dress. She shivered en route. It was more than a little cold in the room. Fall came early to the mountains.

A short while later she was seated on the stool in front of a small blaze heating water for tea. She heard Ridge stir contentedly on the pallet and knew he had opened his eyes to watch her. He had undoubtedly been awake since she had risen, but he was quite content to indulge himself in the role of lazy husband. Actually, Kalena thought with a secret smile, there was a great deal about a husband's life that seemed to appeal to the Fire Whip.

Kalena poured out a mug of tea and rose to carry it across the room. Ridge looked up at her with satisfied appreciation as he levered himself up on one elbow to take the mug.

"It's worth signing a permanent marriage contract with you just to assure myself of hot tea every morning for the rest of my life," he drawled before he took a sip.

Kalena tilted her head to one side, watching him closely. "There may be a few mornings in the future when you will have to get your own tea, you know."

Some of the lazy satisfaction in him was replaced by wariness. "What's that supposed to mean?"

Didn't he realize? Kalena swallowed uncomfortably. This wasn't going quite the way she had planned. "I . . . I understand it's common for women to experience some early morning illness when they are with child."

Ridge nearly choked on a mouthful of tea. He stared up at her in shock. The mug in his hand tipped precariously as he sat up abruptly. "With child! *With child?* My child?" He looked and sounded dumbfounded.

Kalena bit her lip, assailed by a new set of misgivings. "I thought you knew. I thought you realized. Back in the chamber you said you were a part of me. I thought you meant you knew I was pregnant." She rushed into explanations. "I didn't plan it deliberately, Ridge. It must have happened that night we spent in the Healer's valley. I forgot to take the selite powder that day. Do you mind very much? I thought after what happened yesterday that you knew and that it didn't upset you. I know it's rather soon and that you might have preferred to wait, but I don't have much choice."

He didn't seem to be listening to the jumbled explanation. Instead he focused on one tiny fact. "How can you know for sure so soon?"

"The Healers tested me with Sand. They told me to look inside myself as though I were the patient. It was the strangest experience, Ridge. But when I did, I realized at once that I was pregnant." She broke off, eyeing him warily. "Are you very upset about it?"

"Upset? No, of course I'm not upset. I'm just slightly stunned."

"You mean you didn't guess yesterday during our confrontation with the Keys?"

He shook his head slowly. "There was something there I didn't completely understand, something in addition to you. I think I sensed new life, but I wasn't concentrating on it. In any event, it was all tied up with you and I was going to make sure I had you so there was no need to analyze it fully." He grinned at her without any warning. "Besides, I had a lot of other things on my mind at the time."

Kalena cleared her throat. "So you did. Well? How do you feel about it? Are you angry? I have to know, Ridge."

He was still grinning. "Do I look angry?"

"No," she admitted, relief beginning to well up in her. The gleam of pleased satisfaction in his eyes was answer enough, she knew. "No, you don't look angry at all."

He reached out to set down his mug and pulled Kalena gently down across his thighs. "The plain truth, my love, is that I could not be any happier. I don't think it would be possible." He kissed her thoroughly until she was flushed and laughing. Then he lifted his head. "Boy or girl?"

Kalena blinked. "I don't know. I was so startled, I withdrew from myself immediately. Does it matter?"

He shook his head, smiling indulgently. "No, it doesn't matter. Not in the least. Will the babe have my ability with the steel?"

She shrugged. "Probably, if it's a boy. It is not a trait that can be inherited in women, apparently."

Ridge nodded. "If it's a boy, I will teach him to control the fire so that it doesn't get him into trouble," he said decisively. "He'll have a temper."

"A formidable thought." Kalena momentarily pictured a household with two males in it who could both set fire to the steel of Countervail. She would have her hands full.

"But if it's a girl, perhaps she'll have your healing skill and your hair," Ridge went on thoughtfully. "I'd like that, I think. A little girl with hair like yours and eyes the color of Talon Pass crystal."

"I'm glad you're pleased," Kalena said gently.

"Very pleased, wife. Very pleased, indeed." He kissed her soundly again. "Is that the last of the surprises you have for me this morning? Is it safe for me to finish my tea and get dressed so we can get out of here?"

"You don't like surprises?"

"You've thrown enough at me since I met you to make a strong man weak." He gave her a playful slap on her rear and climbed off the pallet.

"Uh, there's just one other thing, Ridge . . ."

He halted halfway to the privacy chamber but didn't turn around. "Let me have it fast. I can't stand it when you string it out."

"It's not a surprise. Just a question," she assured him.

He glanced suspiciously over his shoulder. "Well?"

She hesitated and then asked in a soft little rush, "Do you think I'm too old to enter training as a Healer?"

Ridge looked relieved. "No, I do not think you are too old. I think you would make a very fine Healer, Kalena. I would be very proud of you." He chuckled. "But then, I already am very proud of you."

She smiled brilliantly. "Thank you, my husband. I am very proud of you, too."

His expression became more serious. "We will make a good marriage, Kalena."

"Yes," she said softly, "I think we will." She would give him everything, she decided, love, respect, loyalty, passion and even a certain amount of wifely obedience.

The last thought made her smile again. Not too much of the wifely obedience, she told herself. She didn't want the Fire Whip to grow bored with her.

The creets must surely be getting tired of the trail to the Healers' valley, Kalena decided with a private smile later that day as she led Ridge and the birds through the shimmering white veil. But the creets apparently took the attitude that human ways were too irrational ever to be understood; they seemed to want to ignore the curious events of the past few days. They moved obligingly along the trail into the fertile valley below.

Kalena was aware of Ridge's uneasiness. She knew it would always be this way for him or any other man in this valley. The sooner she got him back out, the better. Glancing at her stony-faced husband, she remarked with a sly smile, "Quintel is always going to need women for this particular trade route, isn't he? Men are never going to be comfortable here."

Ridge shrugged with a deliberate vagueness. "A man feels out of place here. He knows he doesn't belong."

"Exactly," Kalena retorted. "And for that reason, males will always make lousy traders here. Only women will feel at ease enough to strike good bargains with the locals."

Ridge's mouth twitched. "I can see you have learned something of the ways of trading on this venture."

"I've tried to pay attention," Kalena murmured. "It seems to me that since women are so vital to this route, they should be given the largest portion of the trader's commission."

"Uh, Kalena . . ."

"Furthermore, I think it would be a good idea if women were given a wider role in trading ventures in general. If they're useful on this route, they might be useful on others. What's more, I'll bet they could handle some of the clerical tasks involved."

"Now, Kalena, you can't just start making sweeping changes in business."

"The world is changing, Ridge."

"There are times, lady wife, when I get the impression you are out to change it single-handedly," Ridge said with the age-old groan of the long-suffering male.

"From what you've told me, you will be operating this route for Quintel when we return," Kalena went on enthusiastically. "That would put you in a position to make many changes."

Ridge slanted her a very male grin. "It will be interesting to see what position you assume when you try to convince me to make these changes. I shall look forward to the negotiations."

Kalena flushed. "Ridge, I'm talking about business, not sex."

"Sometimes it's hard for a man to tell the difference."

"As I once said, you males are a simpleminded lot."

Valica, Arona and the others came toward them as the cry announcing their arrival went up across the valley floor. By the time Kalena and Ridge reached the first of the cottages, most of the residents of the valley were on hand.

Kalena dismounted, the Key case in her fingers. Ridge made no move to help her. As long as she carried the case he could not touch her. He stayed in his saddle, holding the reins of Kalena's creet while she went forward to meet Valica.

The older woman smiled with a brilliance that held almost as much light as the Key itself. "We knew you had been successful. We were sure of it. Some wanted to dissolve the white mist that guards the trail, but I thought it would be best to leave it in place until you returned. Come. The Key must be taken back to its proper place. You can tell us everything that happened on the way." Without any hesitation, Valica turned, striking out for the path on the other side of the small valley that led to the ice cave.

Kalena glanced at Ridge. "It will take a while. Perhaps a couple of hours."

He nodded brusquely. "I'll wait here."

She turned away to follow the others. Only Arona hung back for a moment. She stood in front of Ridge's creet and examined him with unreadable eyes.

"There is food in the cottage if you wish it."

He inclined his head with a minimum of politeness. "My thanks."

Arona gave him an odd half smile. "You needn't fear, you know. She'll be returning to Crosspurposes with you."

"I know."

Arona hesitated. "She would do better to stay here, but she has a sense of duty and honor that forbid it. She feels her contract demands that she stay with you until the end of the journey."

Ridge answered her coldly. "I am aware of Kalena's sense of duty and honor. But she stays with me for reasons that go beyond our contract."

"And you? Why will you stay with her?"

He did not like this woman, Ridge thought. "I, too, have learned that there are forces that are stronger than even those of honor and duty. Hadn't you better join the others? They're already some distance ahead."

Arona shrugged and turned away without another word. Ridge watched her go, his eyes following the loose cluster of women as they made their way up a mountain path. He kept his eyes on Kalena until she and the others disappeared around a bend in the trail.

His creet stamped one clawed foot with mild impatience and Ridge dropped easily from the saddle. "All right," he murmured soothingly. "I get the point. Let's go find something to eat. Not much else a man can do in this valley."

EIGHTEEN

On the long ride out of the mountains, Ridge allowed himself to examine his memories of the last chaotic scenes in the chamber of black glass.

With deliberate intent he made himself go through the last few minutes in careful detail. He was bothered especially by his clear memory of glancing back just before they fled the chamber and seeing that one of the firegel lamps on the opposite side of the chamber seemed to be carried not in panic and fear, but with calm determination. Ridge was certain a figure in a swirling black cape had retrieved the light and disappeared through an exit with it.

Someone else had escaped the black glass chamber.

Ridge considered that possibility. Even Griss, the master's captain, had been too overcome with the shock of failure and a sick rage to make any effort to save himself. His last goal had been Kalena's throat, not escape. The others had been totally overcome with the consequences of their failed attempt to seize a power they did not understand. But one other man had kept his head.

That man had to be the unknown master of the cult, Ridge

realized. The mysterious leader had to be a man wealthy enough to finance the cost of operating the cult as well as the expense of going after the Dark Key. He had to be a man powerful enough to keep the cult a secret, as well as a man brilliant enough to learn its location from the ancient manuscripts. Such a man had to understand the qualities required to handle the Keys and have the patience to search until he had located a man and a woman who had those unique qualities. He had to be a man clever enough to find a way of putting Ridge and Kalena together so that they could both be used for his ultimate, secret purpose. He had to have access to the kind of inside information required to know Ridge's journey plans. Such a man would have kept his head during the last traumatic moments in the cavern, even though he was seeing his life's work collapse before his eyes.

Without being aware of it, Ridge's hand moved to rest on the handle of his sintar.

"Ridge?" Riding next to him as they left the foothills, Kalena saw the telltale movement of her husband's hand and a small shock of anxiety went through her. "What are you thinking about?"

He glanced at her and then back at the trail in front of them. "I was remembering all that has happened," he told her quietly.

"Ah." Kalena nodded in sudden understanding. "So that you can make a full report to Quintel, hmm?"

"I always make a full report to Quintel."

She didn't understand the distant quality in his voice. It was new, a tone she had never before heard from him. Kalena found it strangely disturbing. She was seeking ways to bring him out of the strange mood when Ridge spoke again.

"Will you miss the Healers' valley, Kalena?"

She thought about it. "No, not really. It is an interesting choice for a woman, but it's not my choice. In any event, it's not lost to me. Surely I can return to visit occasionally."

Ridge's mouth kicked up at one corner. "Only with me along for company."

She smiled. "Afraid I would be lured into staying if I were to return there without you?"

"Let's just say I would prefer to be with you to remind you of the one thing you could never find in the valley."

"And what would that be?" she challenged laughingly.

"You're a woman of strong passions, Kalena. You need a man to satisfy them," he stated bluntly.

"You?"

"Me." He nodded once, unequivocally, then shot her a speculative look. "Going to deny it?"

She shook her head, her eyes glowing. "Not for a moment," she murmured. "You have taught me too well about passion. You are a magnificent lover, Fire Whip. You must know that."

To her astonishment, he hesitated. Instead of gloating, he said with pained honesty, "The truth is, I didn't know it. Not until I had taken you to bed and felt your response to me."

"What are you trying to say?" Kalena asked gently.

She could have sworn she saw a dull red flush of embarrassment on the high bones of his cheeks. Ridge cleared his throat, not looking at her.

"Kalena, I spend a lot of my time on the trade trail. When I get where I'm going, I usually have my hands full doing whatever it is I've been paid to do. Afterward, I spend a lot of time cleaning up whatever mess is left. Then I head back to Crosspurposes. I usually stay there only a short time before heading out on the next assignment. I'm not around long enough to establish any kind of, well, long-term arrangements, if you know what I mean. I'm not saying there haven't been women, but there haven't been that many of them, and the, uh, associations are short-lived." There was a distinct pause before he concluded, "I think I've been a matter of curiosity to some . . ."

His voice trailed off and Kalena stared at him, remembering the jokes Arrisa and some of the other women had made about the steel of Countervail. For an instant she was torn between sympathy for her husband and a wave of glorious feminine amusement. The amusement won out. Kalena started laughing.

Ridge muttered something under his breath and then added, "I'm glad you find it funny."

"I do," Kalena gasped between giggles. The creets cocked their heads inquiringly. "I think it's one of the funniest things I've ever heard in my life. Arrisa and some of the others back in Crosspurposes tried to make me promise to tell them whether the steel of Countervail really glowed when you . . . when you—" She broke off, unable to speak the words. Her laughter bubbled forth again. "You see, Ridge, they have a joke about the real steel of Countervail being that which hangs between . . . uh, never mind. I couldn't possibly explain!"

Ridge drew his creet to a halt and reached out abruptly to stop Kalena's bird. She wiped the tears of laughter from her eyes and tried to assume a more sober expression. It didn't work. Ridge sat scowling at her while Kalena dissolved into another fit of giggles. At last he spoke, his tone weighted with male authority.

"Say one word to Arrisa or anyone else about whether or not the steel glows when I take you to my pallet and I give you my solemn oath I'll make your sweet backside glow hotter than the steel. Understood, wife?"

Kalena tried to nod without giving way to more laughter, but failed. "Yes, my lord husband," she gasped meekly. "I understand. I wouldn't dare discuss such matters outside the privacy of our sleeping chamber. You can rely on my absolute discretion."

"Oh, I do, Kalena." A slow grin revealed his teeth, and Ridge's eyes gleamed. "I have complete faith in your sense of wifely discretion. Just as I assume you have complete faith in my willingness to follow through on my promises."

"You mean threats."

"I mean promises," he reiterated.

"I don't doubt you for a moment, husband."

"Excellent. Now that we've arrived at an understanding on that topic, we will drop it. We have a lot of ground to cover before nightfall." Ridge urged his creet into a brisk pace, leaving Kalena to catch up with him.

"Ridge?"

"What is it, Kalena?"

"Will you still be doing Quintel's trail work after we return to Crosspurposes?" Kalena asked anxiously. "Will you be going away for long periods of time?"

He shook his head with grave certainty. "No, I'm a married man now. I have a family to care for. I'll also be busy enough managing my slice of the Sand trade. There will be no more of Quintel's kind of trail work for me. Ever."

Kalena wondered at the emphasis on that last word.

Much later that evening, when Kalena was seated beside Ridge in front of the trail shelter hearth, he brought up an entirely new subject.

"What happened when you took the Light Key back to its hiding place?" He stared into the flames.

Kalena remembered her trip back into the ice cave. "Not much. I did what you had done with the Dark Key. I put the Key, case and all, back where I had found it. In a pool of ice."

"Ice? How did you get it into hard ice?"

She smiled briefly. "It was liquid until I put the case back into it and then . . ."

"Then what?"

"Then suddenly it wasn't liquid anymore. It's hard to explain. As soon as I withdrew my hand, the pool froze solid again, just as it had been when I first found it."

Ridge studied the flames. "Do you think anyone else could get it out?"

"I'm not sure. I don't know what it takes to melt the ice at a touch the way I did. I don't think it's ordinary frozen water."

"The fire that holds the Dark Key isn't made of ordinary flames, either."

Kalena nodded. "There is something in us that can unlock the Keys. It's possible there are others with the same ability, but I think it's rare. The Healers implied as much."

"It's possible we're the only two people in this generation who could do it," Ridge concluded. He stretched, his muscles moving smoothly beneath his shirt. "But even if someone could handle the Keys themselves, I doubt that it will be easy to locate either of them a second time. Griss told me it took years and a lot of lives to locate the hiding place of the Key and haul the pit of fire out of the bottom of the crevasse in the mountains. Even when the cult got hold of it, no one in the group could even take the case from the flames, let alone handle the Key. The Healers seem to have done a good job of protecting the Light Key for generations."

"They can't touch it, either," Kalena said. "But they guard it well. They said that even the Dawn Lords feared the Keys. They couldn't handle them; they could only try to hide them. There's no knowing what disaster would be caused if the Stones of Contrast were ever unlocked with the Keys."

"If and when that time comes, perhaps there will be others who will know how to control both the Stones and the Keys. In any event, I don't think we'll have to worry about it in our lifetime. Or the lifetime of our child." Ridge cast a meaningful glance at Kalena's slim waist, his eyes glowing with new fire.

Kalena met his gaze. "What are you thinking now, Ridge?"

"That I burn for you, my lady. That I am destined to burn for you all the days of my life." He reached for her and Kalena went joyously into his arms.

Two eightdays after their return to Crosspurposes, Kalena stood beneath the glitter of a magnificent crystal firegel chandelier and watched her husband slip quietly out of the ball full of elegantly dressed people. He had said nothing to her about where he was going, but she knew his destination with a certainty that sent a chill down her spine.

Kalena's second wedding celebration was being provided by the same man who had provided the first: Quintel. This time, however, the crowd was not composed entirely of members of the Traders' Guild. It was true that Arrisa, Virtina and several of Ridge's acquaintances had been invited, but a great many of the guests came from the most powerful Houses of Crosspurposes. When Quintel had issued the invitation to his peers, none had refused.

It was partly curiosity, of course. The fact that the Fire Whip had reopened the vital Sand trade route was no secret. That route supported a good portion of the region's economy, and none present tonight was unaware of that fact. Many had come to meet the man who now owned a slice of the Sand trade. They were also interested in meeting the trade wife with whom Ridge had signed a permanent marriage contract.

The second wedding ceremony was most unusual. Trade marriages occasionally became permanent, but such events were rare. The Polarity Advisor called in this time was the same one who had performed the first ceremony. He was secretly pleased that his assessment of the bride and groom had proven accurate. They were, indeed, excellent counterpoints to each other. He formalized the marriage into a permanent arrangement without a qualm.

This wedding celebration was far more elaborate than the first. The hall was filled with a glittering crowd. The presence of the rich and powerful had a sobering influence on some of the guests whose tendency was to become rowdy in such circumstances. So far, for example, there had been no facetious remarks about the steel of Countervail. Kalena was grateful. She was fairly certain Ridge would have taken exception.

He had worn black to this second, more glittering celebration. Unrelieved black. Not just a cloak of the dark stuff, but also shirt, trousers and boots. Kalena had not questioned his choice, but she sensed it had not been a casual decision. Nor was it based on her own color selection. Not this time.

She herself had chosen to wear a red wedding cloak again. But this time she wore it over a tunic of beautifully embroidered yellow sarsilk, trousers of emerald green and soft velvet slippers. With the profit she had made by selling a portion of her share of the Sand, Kalena had been able to afford to indulge herself in her second set of wedding clothes. She had insisted on paying herself, overriding Ridge's objections with a smile. But she couldn't stop him from buying her the wedding gift he claimed he owed her in exchange for his embroidered shirts.

Ridge's long-delayed wedding gift gleamed on Kalena's left

hand tonight. It was a ring of beautiful, costly Talon Pass crystal. When Ridge had slipped it onto her finger, he had told her the color of the stones matched her eyes.

Fingering the ring with an absent gesture of uneasiness, Kalena glanced around the room, glad of the few moments of peace she was enjoying. She wanted time to think. It was the first time she had been back in Quintel's house since she and Ridge had arrived in Crosspurposes. She had not even seen Quintel until this evening.

As soon as they had ridden into view of the town, Ridge had told her he wanted privacy for both of them. He did not take her to Quintel's house. He had arranged accommodations at an inn that first night back before going to report to his employer. Kalena had made no protest. She didn't particularly wish to see the trade baron. The sight of him would always be a reminder of her personal failure. She had no wish to kill him now, but then, she never had. She just didn't want to spend too much time with him.

That night when he had returned late from his debriefing with Quintel, Ridge had lain awake for a long time staring at the ceiling. Finally, he had announced that they would be staying at the inn until they could find a house of their own.

Kalena had spent the next few days interviewing agents who had properties to sell or lease. Eventually she had settled on a charming little villa overlooking the river. Ridge had taken one look, pronounced himself satisfied, and scrawled his name on the necessary papers. The deal was closed. Kalena had set up housekeeping in the first home of which she was truly mistress.

Several days later, convinced she had her home under control, Kalena began talking to the leaders of the Healers' Guild about the possibility of being taken on as an apprentice. Soon thereafter, she was assigned to three Healers, all experts in various branches of the healing arts, who were willing to undertake instruction.

Tonight Kalena was as proud of the tiny brazier and pouch of Sand that dangled from her belt as she was of the green crystal ring Ridge had given her in honor of the occasion.

As she stood amid the swirling, glittering, laughing crowd

Kalena told herself that everything should have been perfect, but she knew that was not the case.

Quintel had disappeared first from the festivities. Ridge had vanished a short time later. Kalena had watched both of them leave, her intuition sending prickles of alarm through her. The words of her aunt's Far Seeing prophecy suddenly blazed in her mind: *Quintel will die the night of your wedding.*

Kalena was suddenly, coldly, frightened. With blinding clarity, the truth forced its way into her mind; a truth that was based on an intuitive knowledge she had been deliberately suppressing for days. Perhaps she had ignored the inner certainty for Ridge's sake. But now she realized that Ridge was fully aware of the same truth. Being Ridge, he had decided to act on his knowledge. It was not in him to sidestep such a harsh reality. How long had he known? Kalena wondered. Probably since their return to Crosspurposes. He had kept the knowledge to himself while he made his plans. Tonight was the night he had chosen to act.

With an almost silent cry of concern that no one in the hall heard, Kalena set down her goblet and slipped away to follow her husband. She would not let him face this alone. He was her husband. She would be at his side when the inevitable confrontation took place.

Out in the garden, Ridge glanced at the moonlight dancing on the rainstone path. Symmetra was almost full again, her red glow lighting the night. It seemed to him that the color on the rainstones was particularly bright this evening. It reminded him of blood.

The servant carrying Quintel's measure of Encana wine was mildly astonished, but not alarmed when Ridge stepped into the House lord's chambers from the colonnaded walkway. If he thought it strange for the groom to have abandoned the wedding festivities, he was far too well trained to remark on the matter.

"I'll take that in to Quintel." Ridge calmly held out his hand for the tray with its chased goblet. He anticipated no trouble and he had none.

"As you wish, Trade Master." The servant hesitated only slightly before handing over the tray with a small bow. Ridge was a familiar figure in the household. All were aware that Quintel trusted his Fire Whip more than he trusted any other man on the Northern Continent, including his servants. The man turned and disappeared down a corridor.

Ridge glanced down at the wine as the servant vanished. He thought about Kalena's reckless plans the night of the trade marriage ceremony. Ridge flinched, then deliberately pushed the memory from his mind and pulled the cord to ring the bell inside Quintel's sound insulated study.

A moment later the bell on Ridge's side of the door chimed once, and he knew Quintel had approved his entry into the inner sanctum.

Ridge walked into the study and closed the door behind him, but did not lock it. Quintel was seated on a chair in front of a black stone desk, his back to the door. The study looked much as it had the last time Ridge saw it. He had never liked the chamber. He didn't like rooms without windows, and this one had none. Fresh air was provided from the outside by a complicated system of ducts. Quintel insisted on absolute privacy. The hearth in one corner had a small fire in it. The room was lined floor-to-ceiling with books and manuscripts. Some of them, Ridge knew, were very old and handwritten. Others were more recent and had been printed on the new presses that had been invented a few years ago. One locked chest contained Quintel's most precious volumes.

The book collection was extensive, and reflected the tastes and interests of a brilliant, questing, restless mind. The section on mathematics was particularly large, as was that containing the studies of the ancient legends of the Northern Continent and Zantalia itself. Ridge had read some of the books on these shelves. Quintel had seen to it that his Fire Whip did not embarrass himself or his lord for want of a decent education.

"Your wine, Quintel." Ridge stood quietly, holding his burden and waiting for the other man to turn around.

Quintel slowly put down the plumed writing instrument he had been using, but he didn't turn his head. He sat gazing at the swirling motif that had been engraved into the stone of the desk. He was dressed as usual in black, very much as Ridge was dressed. "So, Fire Whip, you have grown bored with weddings? I can't say I blame you. You've been through a number of them lately, haven't you?"

"This second ceremony wasn't meant to happen, was it, Quintel?"

Ridge thought he saw Quintel tense momentarily, and then the older man at last turned around. He studied Ridge for a long while, his near-black eyes unfathomable. Ridge saw a bitter weariness in the lines of Quintel's aristocratic features that he did not remember seeing before he had left on the journey to the Heights of Variance.

"No," Quintel admitted at last. "There should have been no need for tonight's ceremony."

"Because Kalena and I were never meant to return from our journey." Ridge set the tray down on a small table near the door and then straightened again, his hand resting idly on the handle of the sintar. The two men faced each other across the short expanse of the room.

"You know it all?" Quintel's voice was as expressionless as his eyes.

"I figured it out on the way back from the Variance Mountains."

Quintel nodded as if mildly pleased with the show of intelligence. "Does the woman know?"

"Kalena knows nothing. I didn't tell her what I knew had to be the truth."

"Sensible. This is a matter between men. There is no need to involve a mere female."

"You were willing enough to involve her when you wanted the Light Key, Quintel. You were more than willing to see her killed."

Quintel shrugged. "It couldn't be helped. If it comes to that, you must have figured out that I was willing to sacrifice you, too."

"I'm here because of what you tried to do to Kalena, not because you used me. She is my wife, Quintel."

"I was so close to the answers, Fire Whip." One hand clenched briefly into a fist of frustration. "*By the Stones*, I was close. I needed the right female and all the signs indicated she was it. You I had selected years ago and had kept in readiness."

"You needed a man who could control the fire in the steel of Countervail."

Quintel smiled wryly. "The ancient legends were right when they claimed that the Dark Key could only be handled by one who could make the steel of Countervail glow with fire. There are few such men in any generation, Ridge. For years I tracked down every rumor of such a male. I wanted a young man, one I could bind to me with ties of loyalty while I searched for the right female. When I found you on the streets of Countervail, you seemed perfect for my purposes. A tough, intelligent, violent little bastard. No family ties to conflict with the ones I intended to impose. And you rewarded me with such loyalty, Fire Whip. It was amazing, you know. I really did come to trust you completely. I had to take risks with you, of course. Sending you out on the various trade route clean up missions was dangerous. I might have lost you to a bandit's dart or a well aimed sintar, but I needed a man who had been well honed. I needed to make certain you retained the sharp edge I would need when I finally was able to use you. Only real danger can give a man that kind of edge."

"And Kalena?"

"I needed an untrained Healer, or so the old books claimed. One who had the Talent, but who had not had the Talent channeled in specific directions. According to the old manuscripts, the one who wielded the Light Key must have raw and untapped Talent. The Key needs to feed on it and direct it. A trained Healer could not adapt her skills. The conflict between the Key's demands and what the training had done to her would have killed her outright before she could take up the Key. Like your ability with the steel, the Talent is a unique gift. It is a curious product of this world, one the Dawn Lords did not possess because they were newcomers to this land. But they soon began to see occasional signs of it in their children. Somehow they discovered that native born generations to come would continue to produce a few people endowed with certain odd gifts. They knew that somehow the talent for fire and the talent for healing would be needed to handle the Keys. The Healer's Talent is far more common than yours, Fire Whip, but most Healers are discovered early and put into training. It is very rare to find one who has not had the training and a great deal of exposure to Sand smoke. It proved even more difficult to devise a way to get control of her. What decent family would have given up a daughter with the Talent to marriage with a bastard such as you, Fire Whip? It was necessary that both the male and the female be bonded together before they took up the Keys. And then the damn Healers closed the Sand route, making things exceedingly difficult for me with the local Town Council. The right woman was needed, they told my traders. Well, I agreed with them for reasons of my own. I was damn tired of waiting. Then the offer of a trade marriage with her niece arrived from some country Healer in Interlock. It looked as if the forces of fate had finally come together. I knew the moment for which I had planned had finally arrived."

"How did you know Kalena had the Talent?"

"It was a calculated guess based on years of studying the way certain characteristics are passed down through families. By all the rules I have explored and catalogued, the niece of a Healer related by blood should have the skill. Stones only know why Kalena was not trained from an early age, but I was getting desperate. I didn't have time to question my good fortune. Time was running out for me, Fire Whip. The years have been passing more and more swiftly. A lifetime's work and study was being wasted. I had to take a chance."

"The Cult of the Eclipse was operated by you. You were the master that Griss kept referring to who never appeared."

Quintel looked at him. "I was there on the day the two Keys were brought together. I would not have missed the moment I had waited and planned for all these years. I was one of those who stood in the glass chamber."

"You stood there with the others and waited for Kalena and I to kill each other." Ridge was distantly astounded that his temper was so calm. But this was not a time for rage. This was business, the kind of business he had engaged in before in his career with Quintel. He was good at this kind of thing.

"There was another risk I had to take when I brought you and Kalena together. It was that the two of you would form bonds that were stronger than the power of the Keys. It was a delicate balancing act I tried to carry out, you see. The two of you had to be bound together sufficiently to ensure that Kalena would go back to the Healers' valley for the Light Key in order to rescue you. Some bonding between the two of you was also needed to allow both of you to handle the Keys. The mathematics of the situation are formidable, I assure you. The equation was highly complex and involved emotions as well as a balance of power. I worked for years on it."

"But you hoped the tie between us would not be so strong that we could resist the urge to kill each other when the Keys took over, was that it?"

"You are very astute, Fire Whip. If all had gone as planned, the energy that would have been released from the Dark Key would have been enough to destroy the Light Key." Quintel continued speaking, his voice sounding oddly hollow and lifeless. "I was certain the Dark would overcome the Light. For a while all power would have been drained from the Dark Key, and I would have had time to study it, time to learn how to control it myself. I was meant to be the one who could unlock its secrets and the Secrets of the Stones." He glanced at the locked chest of ancient books. "Some of those volumes are in the language of the Dawn Lords. I taught myself to read their tongue to some extent. More importantly, I was able to decipher their mathematics. Absolutely brilliant. Far beyond anything our own mathematicians have yet developed. There are books in that chest that exist nowhere else in the world, Fire Whip. I have the only copies. I have paid dearly for them."

"The price you have paid for some of them was the blood of others, wasn't it, Quintel? I myself helped you obtain some, didn't I? Although I didn't know it at the time. I've killed for you, Quintel. I thought I was protecting your precious trade routes when I did it, but there were times when all I was really doing was paving the way for you to get your hands on another of these dangerous books. I know that now."

Quintel's expression tensed with a violent emotion. Ridge watched him warily. He had never seen the trade baron in a rage. Quintel had always been the most composed, the most coldly, cynically controlled of men. But there was something burning in his dark eyes tonight that Ridge had never seen before. It had nothing to do with composure or control.

"You were born to serve me, Fire Whip, and you have failed me."

"I wasn't born to serve you, Quintel. I realized during the trip back from the Heights of Variance that I was born to kill you."

"Impossible. You can't do it." Quintel's scorn was heavy.

"I'm the only man who can," Ridge countered softly.

"Even if it were possible, it would mean your death, too, have you forgotten? Your new bride will find herself all alone in a world that is very hard on a woman alone. Your anger is legendary, Fire Whip, but you are not equally famous for your brilliant thinking when you are in the grip of that anger, are you?"

"No," Ridge admitted calmly, "but unfortunately for you, I'm not angry tonight. I have thought it all out and I promise you I have no intention of leaving Kalena to fend for herself. I'm about to become a father, Quintel. I must build a House that is suitable for the babe and his mother."

"Fool. How do you propose to kill me without dooming yourself as a murderer?"

"I have planned well. Your death will look like an accident. And there is no one in this town or the whole of the Northern Continent who will call it by any other name. Everyone knows how *loyal* I am to you. No one will dream of accusing me of being your murderer." Ridge's fingers tightened around the sintar. "It's time to go, Quintel. You and I have a trip to make tonight."

"And if I choose not to go with you?" Quintel's quiet rage was laced with a strange amusement.

"Then I'll knock you out and carry you." Ridge was unconcerned with that end of the matter.

"You think I will go tamely with you, Fire Whip?" Quintel scoffed. "I told you once, you were born to serve me. Do you want to know something else? *I should have been the one who had the power to control the steel of Countervail.* Do you hear me, bastard? It should have been me who could make that sintar glow fire red. I was meant to control it just as I was meant to control the Key itself!"

The heavy door to the study suddenly burst opened. Startled, Ridge turned to see a woman he did not know standing on the threshold. Her travel cloak flowed around her as she walked into the chamber and closed the door. When the flames on the hearth illuminated the crystal green of her eyes, Ridge suddenly realized who she must be. No one moved in the chamber.

"Begone, Fire Whip," Olara of the House of the Ice Harvest ordered. "He is not yours to kill. This is Great House business."

NINETEEN

Olara of the House of the Ice Harvest had once been a beautiful woman. Her proud bearing, silvered hair and brilliant eyes would still have been marked as handsome. But years of bitterness and an unfulfilled longing for revenge had taken their toll on her once serene face. Her gaze went briefly to Quintel's impassive features, and then she glanced again at Ridge.

"So you are the bastard who seduced my niece and made her forsake her destiny. I saw the threat in you, Fire Whip, but I was foolish enough to believe I had raised Kalena to be strong enough to resist it."

"It was never Kalena's destiny to kill Quintel," Ridge stated coldly. "Get out, Olara. This is none of your affair."

Quintel lounged back in his chair as if beginning to find a grim pleasure in the confrontation. "There would seem to be no lack of would-be assassins surrounding me tonight."

Olara swung her glittering gaze back to his face. "You were the murderer who began this night's work."

"Of what particular murder are you accusing me, woman?"

"You know well what you have done. I am Olara of the House of the Ice Harvest. Once my clan controlled the trade on the entire Interlock River. But the men of my House stood in your way and you decided to get rid of them. You destroyed my House, and for that you will die."

"The House of the Ice Harvest. I seem to have a vague recollection, but . . ." Quintel shrugged, as if it wasn't worth the effort to try to recall. "I am not easy to kill, Olara of the House of the Ice Harvest. Ask my Fire Whip."

Ridge kept his fingers on the handle of the sintar as he sought for a way to get rid of Kalena's aunt. "This is a matter between men," he told her roughly. "I will deal with it."

"There are no men left in my House," Olara told him. "And this is Ice Harvest business. You are nothing more than a House-less bastard picked up off the streets and dressed in expensive clothing. *Leave us.*"

Ridge set his teeth and took a step forward, intending to grab the old woman and throw her out of the chamber. But before he could touch her, Kalena threw open the door to Quintel's study. Her startled gaze went from Ridge to her aunt and then back. Ridge's growing frustration and fear for Kalena's safety began to eat away at the inner control he needed.

"Kalena! Take your aunt and get out of here. Now!"

"No," she whispered softly, her eyes pleading with him. "I don't want you to kill him. He's not worth it."

Quintel laughed. "All this talk of killing is becoming a bore. None of you can touch me. Do you think I am so vulnerable that I can be killed by an old woman or a street bastard?"

Olara turned on him. "Tonight you will die!"

Quintel's laughter faded abruptly. "No, madam. I think that you will be the one to die tonight. You can take these two with you when you go to the end of the Spectrum. I have no further need of a bastard and his whore."

Kalena saw the flames of fury crackle to life in Ridge's eyes. The sight sent a shock of fear through her, because when she had first entered the chamber, she had seen no emotion at all in

Ridge's golden gaze. He had come here tonight to kill Quintel; she knew that. But there had been no evidence of the red fury that was beginning to consume him now. Kalena suddenly realized that never on the horrific occasions when she had seen him kill had there been any sign of the familiar, flaming anger. The sintar he had used had turned red only with its victims' blood.

With chilling certainty, she understood how Ridge had stayed alive all these years while doing his dangerous work for the trade baron. Ridge was at his most lethal when he was in total control of his fierce emotions. She had cracked that control by entering Quintel's forbidden room.

"Kalena, for the last time, go back to the feasting ball. You shouldn't have come here. Get your aunt out of here."

"She has no duty toward me," Olara said scornfully, not bothering to look at her niece. "She has foresworn her honor to her House. She is no better than you, bastard. She chose to lie on her back sweating beneath you rather than die honorably."

Ridge wasn't looking at either woman any longer. His wary gaze was on Quintel, who still sat at his desk watching his visitors with relentless, predatory hatred.

"I can't leave you alone with him, Ridge," Kalena said softly. "You'll kill him."

"It must be done," Ridge said roughly. "Leave us!"

Quintel flicked a raging, scornful glance at Kalena. "You see how it is with women, Fire Whip? You can never control them. Not as long as you let yourself be weakened by them. And you have done just that, haven't you? The fire in you should have been mine to use, but you tied yourself to this stupid female and the weapon I had forged was ruined. *I should have been the one born with the affinity for fire.* By all the power in the Stones, the gift of the steel should have been mine. Given that talent combined with what I have learned over the years I could have mastered the Dark Key and destroyed the Light. With the power of the Dark Key I could have controlled this whole continent. With it I could have unlocked the Secrets of the Stones. Instead, I was forced to search the streets of Countervail for years to find a flawed tool that failed me when I put it to the test." Quintel's violent eyes swung to Kalena. "Damn you, trade whore. This is all your fault! You should have paid a thousand times over in the caves. You escaped then, but I swear you will pay this night!"

"Shut up, Quintel, or I'll slit your throat here and now." The sintar was in Ridge's hand as if by magic. The tip of the steel blade was already changing color as Ridge's self-control slipped.

"His life is mine to take," Olara proclaimed. She withdrew a large packet from her cloak.

"Ridge! You must stop." Kalena started forward, her arm outstretched to touch him, but she halted as the first wave of cold struck her. She swung around in horror, searching for the cause of the soul-eating chill and saw the first tendrils of black mist swirl forth from the ventilation ducts in the wall behind her. As if attracted to Kalena only, the mist flowed toward her.

"Come any closer, Fire Whip, and she'll die." Quintel hadn't moved from his chair, but his hand rested on a strange device that had been built into his stone desk. "The mist will kill her. I invented it and I can control it."

Ridge started toward Kalena as the mist thickened around her. He reached through the black fog, grasping her arm to pull her free of the heavy darkness. As the light around her began to dim, Kalena saw the flames in his eyes flare higher. She wondered in panic if the black stuff would have the same effect on him as it had in the shelter.

She cried out in relief when she felt his hand close around her arm. As soon as he touched her she knew that the mist was not going to be able to turn him into an enemy.

"I said don't touch her!" Quintel's command echoed through the room and instantly the tendrils of black cold tightened around Kalena.

Helplessly, Ridge released her and stepped back. He whirled to confront Quintel. "Let her go. This is between you and me. It has nothing to do with her."

"It has everything to do with her. She is the reason you were unable to complete the task for which I had prepared you all these years."

"Blame yourself, then. You found her. You signed the trade marriage contract. You brought about your own disaster," Ridge snarled. "It was your fate to be the source of your own destruction."

"I am the source of his destruction," Olara intoned.

Kalena could no longer see the men or her aunt clearly. Even their voices were growing dim. The swirling mist was shrouding her more and more tightly. It coiled around her, imprisoning her in a darkness that was growing colder by the second. She caught a last glimpse of the flames on the hearth, and somehow the sight of the fire got through to her.

Fire. Fire to release the power of the Sand, a power that came from the Light Key.

She fumbled with the small pouch at her belt, almost dropping it. Grasping the tiny brazier in one hand, she moved the little switch that released the catalyst into the firegel. At once she felt a reassuring warmth beneath her fingers.

The mist seemed to writhe with a new, more restless energy as Kalena sprinkled the first pinch of Sand onto the heated firegel. When the white smoke wafted upward she held the brazier aloft. She had no intention of inhaling Sand smoke. She hoped that tonight it would be useful in other ways.

"Kalena!"

Ridge's voice was clearer now. Kalena heard his desperation and tried to respond. "I'm all right, Ridge. I'm burning Sand. The mist is receding. It can't touch me."

For a frantic few seconds she was afraid it was only her imagination that detected the faint withdrawal of the black fog, but soon she realized her senses weren't deceiving her. The mist *was* retreating. She tossed another pinch of Sand on the small brazier and watched the thin plume of white smoke swirl into the thick fog that surrounded it. Everywhere it came in contact with the darkness, the mist thinned. Kalena held the brazier in front of her, and a few seconds later the mist had cleared enough to allow her to see Ridge, Olara and Quintel.

Ridge was holding the sintar as he stood halfway between Kalena and the trade baron. The steel of Countervail was glowing as fiercely as the flames in its owner's eyes. Olara stood poised with the large packet in her hand. She stared at Kalena. Kalena realized it was the first her aunt knew of her niece having discovered the Talent within herself. Olara looked stricken as she took in the significance of Kalena's ability to burn Sand.

"You're all right?" Ridge's voice was as brutal as the blade in his hand.

"I can control the mist with Sand." There was no point mentioning how little Sand there was in the pouch and how short a time it would last.

"Damn you!" Quintel raged, leaping to his feet. The fury in him filled the whole room. "Damn all Healers to the far end of the Spectrum." He stretched out his arms as if he would reach into the thinning mist to grab Kalena. "I will kill you with my own hands, little whore!"

Ridge stepped into his path, the glowing sintar in his fist. He said nothing, merely waited.

Quintel snarled and launched himself at the sintar, instead of Kalena. "It should have been mine! I *can* control the steel. I'll prove I can control it."

Kalena saw the tendrils of mist begin to alter their course as Quintel threw himself toward Ridge. The darkness flickered outward, as if attracted to a new target.

"No!" Olara screamed, hurling the contents of her packet into the flames on the hearth. "Leave him, bastard. He is mine to take."

At once great quantities of white smoke began to billow out into the room. Kalena remembered what the High Healers of the Valley had once said about Sand smoke being dangerous in large amounts. Already there was an acrid taste in her throat and her head was swirling with a sick, dizzy sensation. She knew suddenly that this much of the smoke could kill.

The black fog reacted violently to the white smoke, roiling toward it in great, seething whorls. Dimly, through the gathering black and white haze, Kalena saw the glow of the steel of Countervail. Both smoke and fog were circling toward it as if it were a focus of some sort.

"Ridge, let go of the steel! Let Quintel have it!"

Ridge never did understand why he obeyed Kalena's urgent command. All his instincts and training directed him to stand his ground and use the sintar as it had been designed to be used. Instead, he loosened his grip on the handle just as Quintel's fingers touched the glowing steel.

In that same instant Olara screamed as if in agony and leaped to clutch at the blade.

"The steel is mine!" Quintel shouted, trying to shake off Olara's clinging hands. "I will prove I can hold it when it glows. I am its master. I was born to master it."

"You were born to pay with your life for what you did to my House! You killed my brother." Olara clawed at his wrists even as the smoke and fog whirled toward them in tighter and tighter eddies.

Within seconds both Quintel and Olara were lost inside the tightening vortex. Ridge and Kalena fell back, staring at the writhing energy and listening to the anguished cries from the center of the mingled smoke and fog.

Quintel's scream of agony and rage was enough to make Kalena's blood run cold. But it was her aunt's choked cry that made Kalena start forward. Ridge held her arm, forcing her to stay beside him. She shuddered, the brazier still clutched in her hand as the trade baron and her aunt both fell to the floor. The smoke and fog flowed around them as if seeking to feed. Through a brief break in the mist she could see that Quintel still held the flame-hot weapon in his fists, struggling to control the fire in it.

"Olara, let go of him," Kalena pleaded. There was no response. Olara and Quintel were locked in a death struggle from which there would be no escape.

Ridge stood grimly, holding on to Kalena so that she could not throw herself into the lethal fog in a vain effort to rescue her aunt.

There would be no rescue for either Olara or Quintel. Ridge was
certain of that. He could only imagine the pain Quintel must be
experiencing as the older man continued to clutch the steel of
Countervail. No one but Ridge had ever been able to hold the sintar when it was reflecting its owner's fury. In those brief moments
when he had grasped the glowing steel himself, all Ridge had ever
been aware of was a curious warmth that seemed to match the
heat in his blood. But it was clear the fire Quintel was trying to
contain was unbearable. Ridge didn't understand why the steel
continued to glow. He was no longer holding it. But perhaps it still
held the fire of his fury. Or perhaps the forces alive within the
room tonight kept it on fire.

"The mist and the smoke are both attracted to the sintar,"
Kalena whispered helplessly.

She stared at the horrifying sight in front of them. The white
smoke and the black fog were writhing more tightly than ever
around the two on the floor. And then, without any warning, the
mists slowly began to dissipate. It was as if there was nothing left
for either the smoke or the fog to feed upon.

As the tendrils began to fade, Kalena saw that neither Olara
nor Quintel was moving. The room slowly cleared of smoke and
fog and Kalena saw the frozen rictus of a painful death on Quintel's face. Her aunt lay rigid, her eyes mercifully closed. The sintar
lay on the floor where it had fallen. It no longer glowed red.

Ridge's free hand was on the doorknob behind him. "Come
on, we don't know what the damned stuff is going to do next.
We've got to get out of here."

Kalena shook her head. "No," she said softly. "The mist and
the fog have run out of energy. It will all soon disappear."

Ridge eyed the wispy mist uncertainly. It seemed to be fading
like normal morning mist in the heat of the sun, leaving its unmoving victims behind.

Warily, Ridge went forward. Kalena followed. She didn't need
to inhale any of the last of the brazier smoke to know that Quintel and Olara's stillness was the stillness of death.

"I don't understand exactly how they died." Ridge picked up the sintar.

"Look at Quintel's hands," Kalena said. His palms and fingers where Quintel had clutched the blade were badly burned. She knelt beside the prone figure of her aunt and sniffed delicately at the remnants of smoke that came from her small brazier. Closing her eyes she looked into the bodies of both the victims. "Their hearts," she murmured. "Their hearts failed them. The strain was too great."

"The strain of what? The sintar and the smoke and the fog?"

"Fire and ice," she whispered. "The sintar is a catalyst in some way I don't understand. Quintel thought he could control it, but he was wrong. In the end he was killed by that which he sought to control."

"And your aunt?"

Kalena got slowly to her feet, aware of tears burning behind her eyes. "Healers are not meant to kill," she said simply.

The last of the mist had vanished. Ridge resheathed the sintar and got to his feet. He reached out to touch Kalena in silent comfort. "Call the servants," he ordered quietly.

Without a word, she left the room to do his bidding.

Her new knowledge of the Healing craft told her that when a proper investigation had taken place, the professional Healer's verdict would be death from heart failure. The burns on Quintel's hands would be explained away as having been caused by the fire on the hearth when Quintel pitched forward in his death throes.

In a way, the Healer would be right.

Two eightdays later, Kalena crouched on the narrow rainstone path that wound through her newly planted herb garden and gently patted rich soil over the last of the seeds. She straightened, brushing the dirt from her hands and glancing around the small, elegantly proportioned courtyard with deep pleasure.

The household had settled down well. The villa was easy enough to manage. The two people she had hired to cook, clean and garden were proving to be reliable and well trained. Kalena had ample time to study her books on the Healer's art and tend to her medicinal garden.

Ridge awoke in the mornings to yant tea made by his wife's hand and came home at night to a warm welcome and a smoothly functioning household. He had taken to the domesticated life of a husband and father-to-be with the enthusiasm of a man who knew exactly what he wanted, had found it, and intended to keep it at all costs.

Kalena was pleased with herself and her new life. Occasionally, when she stopped and talked to Arrisa or Vertina in the street, she felt a distant pang of curiosity about what her life would have been like if she had chosen to follow their path. They, on the other hand, were quite pleased with their lives. The fortunes of women involved in trading were on the rise, thanks to certain changes that were being introduced by the Fire Whip. The fact that such changes were being instigated by Ridge's wife was common knowledge.

But Kalena didn't have any regrets. Her work as a talented Healer-in-training was already filling the strange void she had always sensed in herself. She knew instinctively she was at last doing what she had been born to do.

"There you are, Kalena."

She glanced up to see her husband step away from the shaded walk that surrounded the garden and move out into the sunlight. He strode toward her along the path, a small book in his hand. He wasn't smiling as he frequently did when he came across her in the garden. Instead, his golden eyes were serious.

"You're home early, Ridge." Kalena stood and lifted her face for his kiss while keeping her dirt stained hands away from his embroidered shirt. "I thought today was the day you had to attend the meeting of the Town Council."

"It was. That's over and done. I came home to show you this. I found it when I went through a chest of books in Quintel's study this morning."

She took the small, leatherbound volume without glancing at it. "What happened in the council meeting?"

"What I expected would happen. They gave me full control of the Sand trade route."

"Ah," Kalena said with a knowing smile. "The next thing you will get is a seat on the council. Mark my words. After that there will be no stopping you, my lord. You will have the financial resources and the political clout to forge a recognized Great House."

"Possibly." Ridge didn't seem interested in her forecast of their future. "Kalena, this book is a record Quintel kept. It goes back for years. Long before I met him. Everything is in there. It tells how he first became fascinated with the Dawn Lord legends and tales of the Stones and the Keys. I read portions of it this afternoon. He describes how he used the Mathematics of Paradox to discover where the Dark Key was hidden, and he very casually notes all the men who died trying to retrieve it. He felt nothing for those men, Kalena. Whenever one was killed in that crevasse in the caves, he wrote off the death as though he had merely lost another tool."

Kalena nodded sadly, glancing down at the book in her hand. "Everything he did was aimed at unlocking the power of the Keys, and, perhaps, finally the Stones. He cared about nothing and no one else. What have you done with the contents of his library, Ridge?"

Ridge ran a hand through his dark hair. "Many of the books can go to the various libraries maintained by the different guilds. The Healers' Guild will pay a fortune to get possession of some of the volumes. But I'm not sure what to do with the dangerous ones that are in that chest. A few are actually written in the old language of the Dawn Lords. At least I think it's their language. I can't read it, but some of the letters remind me of the letters that were carved into the box that held the Dark Key. There is a vague similarity between the old language and our own. Perhaps that's why we thought the writing on the boxes looked familiar. A part of me says I should destroy the old books, but something else within me resists the idea of destroying such knowledge. There may come a time, Kalena, when this world of ours has need of that knowledge."

Kalena looked at him consideringly. "Every Great House has a few secrets," she told him with a small smile. "And a few very heavy responsibilities. It's possible those dangerous books are meant to be our House's secret burden."

Ridge gave her a sharp glance. "You think we should keep them?"

"We will lock them away. They will be handed down to our children and to our children's children. Who knows how many generations may come and go before the books are needed? When that time comes, we must trust our descendants to do what is right. After all, they will carry within them the power of fire and ice, and they will have something else, something more important."

Ridge watched her closely. "What is that?"

"A sense of honor and duty. I cannot envision any of our descendants lacking either, can you? They will do whatever must be done when the time comes to use the books."

Ridge smiled wearily. "I think you may be right." The smile faded. "But that's not what I came to show you."

"What is it in this little book of Quintel's that you want me to see?"

"The truth about what happened to the men of your House," he said starkly. "Olara was right. Quintel had them killed."

Kalena took a deep breath to steady herself. "Why?"

"Because they were refusing him access to a river route he wanted for his trading ventures. He notes that there were only two males left in the House of the Ice Harvest. The female members of the House, of course, didn't matter to him. He decided it would be simple to get rid of the obstruction the House was causing."

"Of course," Kalena echoed softly. "So he had the men killed. Olara told the truth. I think I already knew that. If she had not been very certain of her facts, she would never have tried to kill. As it was, she felt she had no choice." Her eyes were wide and questioning as she continued to stare at Ridge.

Ridge's mouth tightened as he saw the way she was looking at him. He said with gritty pride, "I wasn't the one Quintel used to kill your father and brother, Kalena. I knew nothing about it. He would have known better than to assign me such a task. I did many things for him, but I never set ambushes designed to make it appear that honorable, innocent men died by accident. I swear it on my honor."

"I know that, Ridge."

He continued to study her carefully for a while, and then he visibly relaxed. "You believe me."

"I have always believed you," she said. "If you had been responsible for the death of my father and brother, you would have told me so long ago."

"Yes."

She held the book out to him. "I think you'd better lock this up with the old books of the Dawn Lords. There is nothing in this diary for either of us now, is there?"

Slowly, he took the small volume from her. "No," Ridge agreed. "There's nothing in it for us." He glanced around the garden. "You've been working hard."

"My first medicinal herb garden," Kalena said with satisfaction. "In a few months this court will be blooming. I just finished putting in the xanthria seeds."

"What's xanthria?" Ridge asked with idle curiosity.

"A very useful herb that is used to treat men who have a particular physical problem." Kalena smiled mischievously.

"What type of physical problem?"

"One that prevents them from properly carrying out their husbandly duties in the sleeping pallet."

He grinned. "You must be sure to keep a good supply on hand for me in case I ever become lax in such duties."

"Somehow," Kalena murmured, stepping into his arms, "I can't envision you ever suffering from such a problem."

"Not as long as I have you in my pallet," he agreed huskily as he pulled her close.

Kalena awoke very early one morning in late spring and knew without lighting the Sand brazier that the time had arrived. She lay quietly beside Ridge, thinking about the past and the future. A serene, secret, womanly smile played about her mouth as she contemplated the richness of her life. And then another contraction warned her that the newest member of the family was eager to enter the world.

Kalena got out of the pallet, moving a little awkwardly because of her temporary roundness, and slipped into the robe that she kept near the hearth. Then she calmly made a mug of hot yant tea and went to wake her husband.

Ridge turned on his side, looking up at her with sleepy eyes as she reached down to hand him his tea.

"It's early," he remarked with a lazy yawn. "Come back to bed." He patted the covers invitingly.

"Not this morning, Ridge." Kalena smiled. "Your son or daughter is on the way."

"What!" He came up out of the sheets and blankets like a sintar being withdrawn from its sheath. The mug of tea went flying. "What in the name of the Stones are you doing running around making yant tea? Get back into the pallet. I'll send for the Healer who's been tending you. Where's that pot of herbs you're supposed to drink?" He dashed across the room, stark naked, and yanked the cord that would summon the servants. "Didn't you hear me, Kalena? I said get back into the pallet."

Kalena's smile broadened. "Yes, Ridge," she said meekly. Then another contraction hit her and her smile grew shaky. She touched her rounded stomach and made her way very carefully to the pallet.

"Dammit, Kalena." Ridge was at her side instantly, easing her down. "You should never have gotten out of bed. You should have awakened me immediately."

"I love you, Ridge," she said serenely.

Ridge's golden eyes blazed down at her. "I love you, too, Kalena. More than my life. You *are* my life. You know that, don't you?"

"I think so," she whispered. "But it's nice to hear it every so often." She gasped as the next wave of contractions struck.

"Maybe we'd better discuss this later. I think you'd better hurry and send for the Healer, my love."

Ridge was already at the door, yelling down the hall to the sleepy servants who were on the run to answer the Fire Whip's summons. Everyone acknowledged that Ridge's temper had undergone a great change for the better since he'd taken a wife, but no one in his right mind took foolish chances by deliberately provoking him.

A few hours later, Ridge and Kalena's son came into the world, making his irritation with the whole event known to everyone within bearing distance. It was obvious from the start that the babe had inherited his father's fiery temper. It was also soon discovered that his mother had the power to soothe the son just as easily as she could the father.

Kalena awoke from the deep sleep into which she had fallen following the birth and found Ridge nearby. He was gazing down into the cradle that stood beside the pallet, examining his son in detail.

Kalena turned her head on the pillow. "Do you approve, my lord?"

Ridge tore his fascinated gaze from the infant and walked quickly over to the pallet. He dropped down beside it, taking Kalena's hand in his. His expression was intense. "You have given me more than I had any right to expect," he said with husky emotion. "Your love and now a son. I swear I will love and care for you as long as I live, Kalena."

"I'm glad you're happy, Ridge," she said softly.

"Happy," he repeated, shaking his head slightly. "I don't have the words to tell you how happy you have made me. I never knew what happiness was until I met you. What about you, Kalena? Any regrets?"

She smiled at the anxiety in his eyes and shook her head. "None," she said truthfully. "We are bound together, you and I. How could I be content without you?"

He leaned forward to kiss her tenderly, and when he lifted his head he was smiling wryly. "I almost forgot." He reached for a leather box that was sitting on a nearby table. "These came from the jeweler's today. I was going to surprise you with them tonight, but you got your surprise in first." He opened the box to reveal three House bands nestled in sarsilk. Two were adult sized. One was for the wrist of an infant.

Kalena reached out wordlessly and picked up the smaller of the two adult bands. Inscribed with exquisite precision on the metal was the emblem of a new Great House. The symbol for fire was interwoven with the symbol for ice. Beneath the symbols were inscribed the words: *House of the Crystal Flame.* After that came the engraved seal of official recognition from the Hall of Balance.

Kalena slipped the House band onto her wrist. Her eyes met Ridge's as she spoke the old, formal words. "I accept the honor of being the Lady of the House of the Crystal Flame, and I accept also the responsibility that goes with it. I will be loyal to the House and its lord. Our children shall be raised knowing that the honor of the House is theirs to keep, protect and defend. I seal this vow with my life."

Ridge took up his own wrist band and slipped it over his arm. "My life, my fortune and my loyalty are bound forever to you, my lady. You are the heart and soul of this House. I will love, keep and defend you as long as I live, and in so doing I will be preserving this House." Then his face broke into a smile.

"There has always been more than honor and duty between us, hasn't there, Fire Whip?" Kalena asked, her gaze as warm as her husband's.

"From the start," he agreed. "We are bound by many things, you and I. But nothing is as strong as the love that holds us together."

He bent his head to take her lips in a kiss that conveyed the full Spectrum of that love. Kalena responded completely, knowing the fires of their passion would warm them the rest of their lives.